Waterst[

OXFORD WORL[

THE ADVEN[
CAPTAIN H[

JULES VERNE was born in Nantes in 1828, the eldest of five children in a prosperous family of French, Breton, and Scottish extraction. His early years were happy apart from an unfulfilled passion for his cousin Caroline. Literature always attracted him and while taking a law degree in Paris he wrote a number of plays. His first two books, entitled *Journey to England and Scotland* and *Paris in the Twentieth Century*, were not published in his lifetime. However, *Five Weeks in a Balloon* was accepted by the publisher Hetzel in 1862, and became an immediate success. It was followed by *Journey to the Centre of the Earth*, *Twenty Thousand Leagues under the Seas*, *Around the World in Eighty Days*, and sixty other novels covering the whole world—and beyond. Verne himself travelled over three continents, before suddenly selling his yacht in 1885. Eight of the books appeared after his death in 1905—although in fact partly written by his son, Michel.

WILLIAM BUTCHER was formerly Head of the Language Centre at the Hong Kong Technical College. He has studied at Warwick, Lancaster, London, and the École Normale Supérieure, and has taught languages and pure mathematics in Asia and Europe. As well as thirty articles on French literature, he has published *Mississippi Madness* (1990), *Verne's Journey to the Centre of the Self* (1990), and translations and critical editions of Verne's *Humbug* (1991), *Backwards to Britain* (1992), *Journey to the Centre of the Earth* (1992), *Around the World in Eighty Days* (1995), and *Twenty Thousand Leagues under the Seas* (1998).

OXFORD WORLD'S CLASSICS

For over 100 years Oxford World's Classics have brought readers closer to the world's great literature. Now with over 700 titles—from the 4,000-year-old myths of Mesopotamia to the twentieth century's greatest novels—the series makes available lesser-known as well as celebrated writing.

The pocket-sized hardbacks of the early years contained introductions by Virginia Woolf, T. S. Eliot, Graham Greene, and other literary figures which enriched the experience of reading. Today the series is recognized for its fine scholarship and reliability in texts that span world literature, drama and poetry, religion, philosophy and politics. Each edition includes perceptive commentary and essential background information to meet the changing needs of readers.

OXFORD WORLD'S CLASSICS

JULES VERNE

The Extraordinary Journeys

The Adventures of Captain Hatteras

Translated with an Introduction and Notes by
WILLIAM BUTCHER

OXFORD
UNIVERSITY PRESS

OXFORD
UNIVERSITY PRESS

Great Clarendon Street, Oxford OX2 6DP

Oxford University Press is a department of the University of Oxford.
It furthers the University's objective of excellence in research, scholarship,
and education by publishing worldwide in

Oxford New York

Auckland Cape Town Dar es Salaam Hong Kong Karachi
Kuala Lumpur Madrid Melbourne Mexico City Nairobi
New Delhi Shanghai Taipei Toronto

With offices in

Argentina Austria Brazil Chile Czech Republic France Greece
Guatemala Hungary Italy Japan Poland Portugal Singapore
South Korea Switzerland Thailand Turkey Ukraine Vietnam

Oxford is a registered trade mark of Oxford University Press
in the UK and in certain other countries

Published in the United States
by Oxford University Press Inc., New York

British Library Cataloguing in Publication Data

Data available

Library of Congress Cataloging in Publication Data
Verne, Jules, 1828–1905.
[Voyages et aventures du capitaine Hatteras. English]
The extraordinary journeys : the adventures of Captain Hatteras /
Jules Verne; translated with an introduction and notes by William Butcher.
p. cm.—(Oxford world's classics)
Includes bibliographical references.
I. Butcher, William, 1951–   II. Title.   III. Oxford world's classics
(Oxford University Press)
PQ2469.V8E5 2005   843'.8—dc22   2004030781
ISBN 0-19-280465-0   978-0-19-280465-5

1

Typeset in Ehrhardt
by RefineCatch Ltd, Bungay, Suffolk
Printed in Great Britain by
Clays Ltd., St. Ives plc., Suffolk

PREFACE

WHY publish a little-known Verne book in Oxford World's Classics, complete with detailed critical apparatus? The answer may be found in the work itself.

The Adventures of Captain Hatteras (1864–5) is a gripping story about a quest for the North Pole. The 140,000-word double-decker was the second book Jules Verne published and, with *Twenty Thousand Leagues under the Seas*, his most personal novel.

Hatteras constitutes the formal beginning of the Extraordinary Journeys, Verne's sixty-four-work, fifty-year series of adventure books. Commentators have been unanimous about this debut novel. Real-life explorers have said that it gives one of the most accurate pictures of Arctic life ever.[1] George Sand described it as 'captivating', Gautier, as 'excellent'; Zola, as embodying 'a great imagination and very keen intelligence'; Julien Gracq, as 'a masterpiece'. Ionesco said 'all my texts were written, directly or allusively, to celebrate [Hatteras's] discovery of the North Pole'. Modern critics have similarly considered it 'masterly' and 'perhaps [Verne's] greatest masterpiece'.[2]

And yet this novel is not well known. Only three or four full-length articles have been written about it, and no attempt has been made to analyse the work as a whole. The changes between the manuscript and the serial and book editions have usually been ignored, as has the novel's intellectual history.

To coincide with the Navy's last North Polar expedition, four different translations appeared in the 1870s, but the book has not been translated since. The paradox is that, although this classic 'British' novel is selling steadily in every major language and is high on the Amazon.fr list, it has long been unavailable in English. The present edition will attempt to fill both gaps by providing a comprehensive critical analysis and the first unabridged translation.

---

[1] e.g. Charcot, cited by Jules-Verne, *Jules Verne* (1973), 101, or Finn Ronne, 'Introduction', in *The Adventures of Captain Hatteras* (New York: Didier, 1951), 5–6.

[2] René Escaich, 'A propos des *Aventures du capitaine Hatteras*', *BSJV* 28 (1973), 88; Dumas, *Jules Verne* (1988), 123. Stevenson is a lone dissenter, accusing Verne of 'torturing us too much upon the way' and the 'sin of . . . a bad end' ('Jules Verne's Stories', in *The Works of Robert Louis Stevenson*, 28. *Essays, Literary and Critical*, 190–3 (192)).

ACKNOWLEDGEMENTS

I WOULD like to record my gratitude to Vicky Chan, Carlo Traverso, Norm Wolcott, Project Gutenberg, and Ian Thompson for their help with the text; to Malcolm Bowie, Art Evans, and Richard Balme for their support; to Jean-Michel Margot for his pioneering work on Verne and his generous provision of materials; to Volker Dehs for his knowledge of all things Vernian, constructive comments, and contribution to the variants studied here; and to Angel Lui for her tremendous help and love and affection over the years. A special acknowledgement of love and gratitude is owed to my mother, Kay Butcher (1917–2004).

CONTENTS

LIST OF ABBREVIATIONS

References to *Hatteras* are of form 'II 19' (i.e. Part II, ch. 19), '*MÉR* IV 33' (i.e. *Magasin d'éducation et de récréation*, volume 4, page 33), or '*MÉR* IV 33 II 19'.

References to other works by Verne are by chapter number (e.g. *JCE* 18) plus volume number if any (e.g. *20T* II 1).

Extracts from letters are from *Correspondance inédite de Jules Verne et de Pierre-Jules Hetzel (1863–1886)*, ed. Olivier Dumas, Piero Gondolo della Riva, and Volker Dehs, vols. 1, 2, and 3 (1999, 2001, and 2002).

References to texts available online at the French National Library (http://gallica.bnf.fr) are indicated simply as 'Gallica'.

All translations from French are my own.

INTRODUCTION

Jules Verne (1828–1905)

JULES-GABRIEL VERNE was born in 1828, on an island in central
Nantes, western France. His father had a successful law practice, and
wrote amateur verses. His mother's maiden name was Allotte de la
Fuÿe, derived from Seigneur N. Allott, a fifteenth-century immigrant
in Louis XI's Scottish Guard of archers.[1]

The family biographer tells us that the boy would often visit
his great-uncle, Jules-Joseph de la Celle de Châteaubourg, Chateaubriand's nephew. Chateaubriand claimed to have originally gone to
America to find the Northwest Passage to Cathay before the British
got there. (We now know that he invented much on the liner back,
probably not even getting as far as the Mississippi.)

In 1847 Jules arrived in Paris to study law. For the next ten years,
he lived in a succession of single rooms, sometimes with barely
enough to eat. Devoting himself to play writing, seven of his thirty
pieces had been performed or published by 1863, one with the help
of Dumas *père*.

Verne also published five short stories, in which many of the
themes and structures of his famous novels are already visible. All
concern the difficulty of getting things going (like Verne's own career) and all are set in foreign parts, are late Romantic in conception,
and finish tragically.

In 1856 the playwright met Honorine de Viane, a widow with two
daughters; they married a few months later, with Verne turning to
stockbroking to support his new family.

Verne's journey to Britain in 1859 (his first outside France) had a
major impact on him, especially Edinburgh and the Highlands. In
just eight days, Verne and his collaborator Aristide Hignard managed to fit in Liverpool docks, open prostitution, scenes from Scott's
novels, Arthur's Seat (his first mountain), ten-storey medieval
houses, flirtation with an Edinburgh lass, nude sea bathing, a 'chateau'

---

[1] Verne's British ancestry was proved with the identification of the chateau built by
Allott, later Allotte, Member of the Royal Household (Butcher, *Jules Verne*
(forthcoming)).

in Fife, Loch Katrine, Ben Lomond, Mme Tussaud's, and the
Great Eastern. *Backwards to Britain* was the first book Verne completed, but lay hidden until 1989, when it was hailed as a fine piece of
travel writing and a vital document for understanding the young
man.

In 1861, Verne visited Norway and Denmark—missing the birth
of his only child, Michel. Travelling with Hignard and a lawyer
friend, he navigated the locks up to Christiana and visited the wild
Telemark region, spending seven weeks away. The sole surviving
chapter of the book describing his travels, 'Joyous Miseries of Three
Travellers in Scandinavia', was published in 2003. Both travel works
point the way to the first novels, especially *Hatteras* and *Journey to
the Centre of the Earth* (1864), which heads into a volcano in Iceland
and down through the layers of the globe's history. All four books,
written in four years, feature small groups of male travellers, borrow
from the same exploration and travel literature, have the same
atmosphere of anguish and mystery, involve labyrinths, electrical
storms, and volcanoes, and employ the same metaphors and writing
strategies. Three of the works pass through (or under) Liverpool,
and three, Hamburg and Denmark.

'Joyous Miseries' proposes a manifesto for the four works:

I was drawn to the hyperborean regions, like the magnetic needle to the
north, without knowing why. . . . I love cold lands by temperament. The
book of M. Énault, *Norvège*,[2] [contains] the following passage: 'As you
head north, you continually get higher; but so uniformly and imperceptibly that you only realize the height you've got to by looking at the rise in
the barometer and the drop in the thermometer.'

Verne equates altitude with latitude and the deliciously cold
temperature—three scales measuring out his obsession for the
north. This three-way equivalence in turn 'over-determines' the
monomaniacal quest for a unique culminating point that generates
and structures *Backwards to Britain*, 'Joyous Miseries', *Hatteras*, and
Journey to the Centre of the Earth, and lies at the very heart of the
Extraordinary Journeys.

---

[2] Louis Énault, *La Norvège: Christiania, les paysans, Trondhjem, chez les Lapons,
Bergen, le Cap Nord* (1857). The first document Verne uses for his British trip is
similarly Énault's *Angleterre, Ecosse, Irlande* (1859). Elsewehere in 'Joyous Miseries', he
cites Cook, Ross, Dumont d'Urville, [Dr John] Richardson, and Dumas, plus the new
periodical *Le Tour du monde*.

From the beginning Verne had visited literary salons, thanks to another uncle; there he befriended Alexandre Dumas *père* and *fils* and photographer and balloonist Nadar. Through them he met Alfred de Bréhat, a boys' writer and fellow Breton, who, in July 1862, introduced him to his new publisher Jules Hetzel (1814–86). This towering figure had brought out Balzac, Stendhal, and Hugo— as well as his own books for boys. A member of Lamartine's government, he had spent eight years in exile after the 1848 Revolution.

Within months of the crucial encounter, *Five Weeks in a Balloon* became a huge success.

The novelist spent 1863–4 in a whirlwind of activity. The family now had five members, one of them a difficult and squalling baby, and moved to a larger flat in suburban Auteuil. Verne was busy writing or publishing four novels as well as several other pieces. He brought out an article praising 'Edgar Allan Poe and his Works' and a historical novella, *The Count of Chanteleine*, and contributed to a second collection of songs with Hignard. He submitted *Paris in the Twentieth Century*, but Hetzel categorically rejected it, calling it 'a painful thing, so dead . . . inadequate on every line' (it became the most successful French novel ever in the United States). Verne also wrote *Hatteras* and *Journey to the Centre of the Earth*,[3] much of the former during an extended stay at his parents' country house, with noisy children all around. All the while, he was slaving at his day-job.

On 16 September 1863 Verne declined to invest 40,000 francs (about £160,000 in modern-day terms) in his publisher's company; he cited financial problems, probably due to the move, his broking commitments, and uncertainty about his future. Hetzel only offered a second one-book contract on 1 January 1864, when *Hatteras* was three-quarters finished, and again took more than five-sixths of the profits and failed to provide any advance for future novels.[4]

And yet Verne was to be pivotal to his new publishing venture, the fortnightly *Magasin d'éducation et de récréation* (March 1864–1906).

---

[3] Although *Journey to the Centre of the Earth* came out in November 1864, the second contract, of 1 January 1864, makes no reference to it, and Verne's letters mention only *Hatteras*, finished by March 1864. *Journey* was probably therefore written after most of *Hatteras* and submitted in about May.

[4] The contract specified payment of 3,000 francs, a print-run of 10,000 plus an indefinite number in the *MER*, an option on two volumes per year, and an advance of 300 francs per month on a history of exploration.

Co-directed by Republican educationalist Jean Macé (and by Verne himself from 1867), the *MÉR* aimed for a young readership, with a pedagogical and moralistic approach. The illustrated magazine was given away with the leading newspaper *Le Temps* for the first eleven months, a 200,000-franc loss-leader that ensured its success. The first issue opened with chapters 1 and 2 of *Hatteras*, which dominated for the next twenty-two months, in conjunction with Hetzel's rewriting and appropriation of *The Swiss Family Robinson*.

Perhaps because of the strain, the novelist suffered an acute attack of facial paralysis in August 1864, with half his face going dead.

In 1866, *Hatteras* appeared in book form, inaugurating Verne's series of Extraordinary Journeys. According to the rather brash Publisher's Announcement, their aim was 'to sum up all the geographical, geological, physical, and astronomical knowledge amassed by modern science and rewrite the story of the universe'.

In 1867 the family moved to the seaside village of Le Crotoy. The same year, Verne sailed to America on the liner the *Great Eastern*. He also bought three boats of successively greater size, visiting the British Isles a total of twelve times and going as far as North Africa. In 1872 the family moved to Amiens. In 1885, Verne sold his yacht for financial reasons and gave up travelling.

Michel tried his hand at many careers, including writing, one story being published under his father's name. After Jules Verne's death in 1905, eight novels and three short stories appeared in the Extraordinary Journeys. Only in 1978 was it realized that Michel had made radical changes. Two-thirds of *The Survivors of the 'Jonathan'*, for instance, are his, including the many philosophico-political passages; and perhaps even more of the masterpiece 'Edom', set 20,000 years in the future.

The Inception of Captain Hatteras

Captain Hatteras can be quickly summarized. Richard Shandon receives a mysterious letter asking him to construct a reinforced ship in Liverpool, purchase six years of supplies, and assemble a highly paid crew for an unknown destination. As the ship heads off for Melville Bay in April 1860, only a 'dog-captain' has appeared. At seventy-eight degrees, the ship is freezing up and the men are unhappy—when a crewman reveals himself as John Hatteras. Despite two previous tragedies, the captain is determined to use his steam-engine to plant the Union Jack at the North Pole. Hatteras hits it off with Dr Clawbonny, who has Dickensian optimism, curiosity, and commonsense, and they set out over the icy wastes to search for fuel. They rescue Altamont, the sole survivor of an American expedition, but when they return, the crew have mutinied and blown up the ship. Hatteras and his companions remain without resources at the coldest point on earth.

The five men build an ice-house 350 miles from the Pole and over the winter months discuss previous expeditions. When Altamont insists on calling the land New America, an argument breaks out, for Hatteras suspects him of designs on the Pole. However, Altamont saves Hatteras from musk oxen and the two are reconciled. Having cannibalized the American ship, the explorers trek north to a warmer zone, with paradisaical frolicking animals. There they discover an open sea, teeming with monsters and birds.

From the beginning, Verne was fascinated by the polar regions, amongst the last virgin areas on the globe. In 1851 he is reported to have visited a maternal uncle in Dunkirk, a major port for Arctic whalers; and consequently to have written 'Wintering in the Ice' (1855), a precursor to *Hatteras*.

The two works share motifs of death, blood, and ice, plus a mutiny, a bear attack, and the immobilization of the brig when forced out of the ice. In the original version, the villains end up eating their faithful huskies, despite the terrible smell—perhaps why the cooking is omitted in a similar episode in *Hatteras*. The story has a note, probably written by the author, describing it as 'in [Fenimore] Cooper's manner' and based on an analysis of 'every traveller's tale'. Verne's attraction to the Arctic consequently predated any interest in science. A decade before meeting Hetzel, he had discovered his path of adventure fiction in remote areas.

Three later novels take place amongst the ice, *The Fur Country* (1873) in northern Canada, *An Antarctic Mystery* (1897), and *The Lighthouse at the End of the World* (1905) at the tip of Patagonia. The 1897 work is a sequel to, or rather continuation of, *The Adventures of Arthur Gordon Pym*, the focus of Verne's 1864 study of Poe. It explains Pym's disappearance with a giant magnet in the shape of a

Sphinx which irresistibly attracts all metals, including the nails holding boats together. *Hatteras, An Antarctic Mystery*, Verne's only literary study, and Poe's lone novel are thus linked. Even the title *The Adventures of Captain Hatteras* echoes *The Adventures of Arthur Gordon Pym*.

Verne's polar obsession is visible in many other works. Captain Nemo dives under the icecap to plant his flag at the South Pole, which is also flown over in *Clipper of the Clouds* (1886). The hero of *The Wreck of the 'Cynthia'* (1885) sails the Northwest Passage and makes the first circumnavigation of the Pole. The title of *The Purchase of the North Pole* (1899) speaks for itself. The Arctic receives one chapter in *Famous Travels and Travellers* (1878) and twenty-one in Verne's unpublished collaboration 'The New World' (1881).

For Mediterranean countries, the north represented barbarian invasion and ill fortune, but Verne was also influenced by classical legends of the warm waters of Hyperborea, the land behind the north wind.

The sources of *Hatteras* have unfortunately not been investigated to date, so only brief indications can be given here. The seventy-five footnotes may be due to the influence of Scott's and Poe's excesses in this regard. Writing at the cusp of Romanticism and Realism, Verne echoes contemporary descriptions of nature, and occasionally pastiches Baudelaire's 'desolations'. The names of his characters are taken from Cooper's *Miles Wallingford* (1844) and Thackeray's *History of Pendennis* (1850); and there are direct borrowings from Sterne's *Tristram Shandy* (1759–67), Chateaubriand's *Travels in America* (1827), and Victor Hugo (see the Explanatory Notes, below, for details).

Above all, *Hatteras* borrows extensively from scores of polar accounts, nearly all British. That nation's dominance of Arctic exploration is often ascribed to Waterloo, for the overmanned post-war Navy was encouraged to channel energy into the Northwest Passage. When Sir John Franklin's 1845 expedition disappeared, more than sixty ships, many financed by his widow, went in search. The Franklin mystery, with its subtext of cannibalism, was much debated,[5] and haunts *Hatteras*.

[5] Dickens, as one example, claimed cannibalism could not have been possible; but was refuted by John Rae (23 Dec. 1854).

But with the discovery of the Northwest Passage (1854), preliminary indications of Franklin's fate (1855), and a document in a cairn (1859), the Franklin question was more or less closed, and attention turned to the Pole.

Closely connected was the idea of an Open Sea, supposedly located beyond the limit of exploration at North Cornwall (see map on pp. xliv–xlv). Following sightings of open water by several explorers in the 1850s, geographers Maury and Petermann defended this thesis, often ascribed to volcanic activity or the Gulf Stream. It lost currency only in the 1890s, when it was found that although the Polar Sea did exist, it was invariably frozen.

Verne put to great effect maps produced by the Admiralty in 1859 and by geographer Malte-Brun. The astonishing number of Arctic expeditions he cites are indicated below in the Selection of Contemporary Documents in the Select Bibliography and in Appendix B: A Chronology of Arctic Exploration.

The expeditions which influenced *Hatteras* the most are those by Scoresby (1806, 1817) who reached about eighty-two degrees, and wrote a definitive *Account of the Arctic Regions* (1820); and by Parry (1819–20 and 1827) who left his ship north of Spitzbergen and continued by boat and sledge, reaching 82° 45′, a record until 1876. The exploration Verne refers to most often is James Ross's (1829–33), when his nephew John Ross discovered the Magnetic Pole. The 1850–4 McClure expedition was the first to cross the Arctic; Verne invariably describes it as having 'sailed' the Passage, a view shared by many modern authorities, although the claim was disputed in the United States. Hatteras's vessel is modelled on McClintock's screw-driven brig (1857–9), and Verne delights in revisiting many of the places of the real-life explorer.

However, it should be borne in mind that Verne could not read English. Furthermore, only about half a dozen of the accounts were translated, principally those by Franklin, Parry, Back, Belcher, McClintock, and John Ross. Verne also used articles from *Le Tour du monde*, *Bulletin de la Société de géographie*, and *Nouvelles annales des voyages*. But three books are by far his most important sources: Hervé and Lanoye, 'Journeys in the Ice ... Extracts from the Reports of Sir John Ross, Parry ... McClure' (1854), Lucien Dubois, 'The Pole and the Equator' (1863), and Lanoye, 'The Polar Sea' (1864).

Verne indeed copies about ten pages of Hervé and Lanoye word for word, including the mistakes, most notably for the Franklin memorial inscription and the extracts from the on-board *North Georgia Gazette*. His borrowings are evident throughout the book.

'The Pole and the Equator', by one of Verne's schoolmates, argues for the existence of 'The Open Sea' (title of chapter 7) and a relatively warm Pole. Both ideas are crucial to Hatteras's wintering and sailing north. Much of Verne's English vocabulary, paraphrased in French, and some of the mistakes are taken from 'The Pole and the Equator'. Where Dubois praises the Creator's remarkable foresight in making snow a good insulator, placing the solution so near the problem, Verne ascribes the foresight to nature. Often, he constructs whole scenes from passing remarks by Dubois.

Verne also cites a French officer,[6] Joseph-René Bellot, author of 'Journal of a Voyage to the Polar Seas' (1853), who volunteered for Kennedy's expedition, but drowned. He was accompanied by a certain Quartermaster Johnson; this same Johnson is ship's bosun in *Hatteras*, and indeed recounts Bellot's loss at great length (I 21).

However, it would be futile to try to explain *Hatteras* in terms of a single source. Verne's reading was voracious and his borrowing from Arctic literature in French very wide.

From first germ to book publication, the novel went through a bewildering number of titles, including: *The Robinsons of the Pole*, *Captain Hatteras*, *The Robinsons in the Ice*, *Journey to the North Pole*, *Surprising Journey of Captain Hatteras to the North Pole*, *(The) British at the North Pole* and *(The) Desert of Ice*, *Adventures of Captain J. Hatteras*, and *Journeys and Adventures of Captain Hatteras*.

Four letters provide precious information about the novel's inception. The first extant communication from Verne to his publisher, dated 26 June 1863, begins:

---

[6] Verne also mentions Émile de Bray (1829–79), who accompanied Belcher. Jean Cornuault claims that de Bray made friends with Verne and gave him his journal, meaning that *Hatteras* contains 'entire pages of de Bray on life in the Arctic' (reported by Escaich, 'A propos des *Aventures du capitaine Hatteras*', *BSJV* 28 (1973), 88). However, Verne's and de Bray's texts contain very few similarities, meaning that Cornuault's claim is not founded.

Other critics have attempted to link *Hatteras* with Hayes's simultaneous search for the open sea via Smith Sound. But Verne does not mention Hayes, whose book was published only in 1867, making influence unlikely.

I have just ploughed forward as sturdily as a Norman-crossed percheron; we'll find out whether I'm right. In any case, I'll give you the first part of *Journey to the North Pole* within a fortnight.

I'm lost in my subject at eighty degrees north and forty degrees below. I'm catching cold just from writing. That's all right in the summer we're having.

We can accordingly date the composition of Part I as late spring 1863.[7] On 4 September, Verne wrote that he was 'working on the second part'. On 16 September, he rejected Hetzel's idea of having a Frenchman on the expedition, but added: 'I strongly support your remark about Hatteras; I will make him very bold and unlucky. His boldness will be frightening.'

The final letter to Hetzel, dated 25 April 1864, is vital for understanding both the meaning of *Hatteras* and the whole author–publisher relationship:

How badly you'd know me if you thought for a moment your letter wasn't welcome . . . It wasn't a director writing to me, but a friend who I totally trust; in any case I repeat that I agree with you. We'll delete the duel at the stroke of a pen; as for the reconciliation, we'll make it happen earlier, but not following *the saving of a life*, which would be diabolically common . . .

From your letter I think you generally approve of the madness and the end of Hatteras. I am very pleased, since that was worrying me the most; I could not see any other way to finish it . . . In any case how to bring Hatteras back to Britain; what would he do there? Clearly the man must die at the Pole. The volcano is the only tomb worthy of him . . .

Have you ever found me recalcitrant as regards cuts or changes? For *Balloon* didn't I follow your advice to suppress the long story of Joe, without hurt?

I will reveal to you exactly what I think, my dear Hetzel; I don't specially want to be an arranger of facts; so I'll always be ready to make changes for the common good. What I'd like to be above all is a *writer* . . .

You said to me some . . . very flattering things about my style which is getting better . . . But I wonder, in some corner of my noddle, as you say, if you didn't want to sweeten the pill slightly. I assure you, my good and dear Director, that there was nothing to sweeten; I swallow very easily and without preparation. So I wonder if you really are as pleased as you say with the writer at the novelist's expense [*sic*] . . .

[7] However, the map is signed 'Jules Verne 1860–1', the action of the novel runs from April 1860 to late 1861, and the author often made the closing scene coincide with the last instalment. It is not clear, therefore, why the novel was not dated 1863–4, unless it was first drafted in 1860–1 or Verne wanted to make it coincide with his own Nordic trip.

All this to tell you how much I'm trying to become a *stylist*, but a serious one; it's the idea of my entire life; and you who are so knowledge-able about such things, when you talk to me like you do at the beginning of your letter, I feel my heart bound.

So, as regards the facts, I'll wait for you to arrive to chat an hour or two, and we'll redo the fifth act.

Verne uses honorifics worthy of the Cultural Revolution, involves the publisher in the authorship ('we'), and emphasizes his willing-ness to cut and change 'for the common good'. He humorously uses the language of love: bounding hearts, 'hurt', 'pleasure', and the obscene 'I swallow very easily and without preparation'.

Verne's literary manifesto is essential. He wishes to be a serious stylist, a writer, even a novelist—qualities the publisher has not rec-ognized in him. Given the decisive influence of Hetzel's publicity, it is interesting to note that from the beginning Verne deconstructed the ascribed pigeon-hole of mere regurgitator-of-facts-for-young-people.

We are fortunately able to judge things for ourselves. In the *MÉR* edition, six chapters of which had already appeared by 25 April, all trace of the duel has disappeared, but the argument between Altamont and Hatteras and subsequent reconciliation take place just before the sailing for the Pole. In the book edition, in contrast, the argument is brought forward (to II 15); and the American's saving of the Briton from the musk oxen leads directly to the reconciliation (II 17)—and to a trite and forced international-friendship scene. Verne had presumably received another letter and, although still consider-ing it 'diabolically common', decided to sacrifice logic and aesthetics for expediency.

The manuscript version of what Verne wanted to publish, namely the duel and the suicide, is extant (quoted in Appendix A, below). Surprisingly, however, it has not been cited to date, apart from a few paragraphs. The survival of the duel episode, covering over a chap-ter, in particular, has never been suspected. And yet this seems to be the longest deleted section in the Extraordinary Journeys.

In 'John Bull and Jonathan' (MS II 21), Hatteras is dreaming on the launch, imagining the Union Jack flying at the Pole, but wakes up to find Altamont has raised the Stars and Stripes. He cuts it down, but Altamont attacks him and angrily reveals that he too had been heading for the Pole, and still wishes to claim it. Although

Clawbonny acts as peacemaker, the captains decide on a duel to the death, to settle the matter once and for all. While everyone else is asleep, Hatteras wakes Altamont up, they land on an ice floe, and start fighting with knives (II 22). The floe gradually sinks, but the battle continues as the water covers their knees, and then their heads. As the men resurface, still grappling, Clawbonny and the sailors seize hold of them. An emotional scene follows, with Clawbonny pouring his heart out in reproaches and humanistic sentiment.

The deletion of this dramatic, albeit slightly comic, episode removes from the book some of the *raison d'être* for Hatteras's dream. More seriously, the excision of the climax of Anglo-American rivalry seriously undermines a central theme of the novel, and with it much of the dramatic tension. Altamont is reduced instead to seeking the Northwest Passage, which in Verne's eyes has already been done, and which is not in any case a worthy pendant to Hatteras's efforts. Altamont's survival in the book indeed becomes almost pointless, since he does little except complain and even the argument is watered down to the point of insipidity. Verne must have deeply regretted agreeing to sacrifice not only the dramatic episodes and the heart of his plot, ones closely reflecting contemporary historical reality, but also virtually the only revelation of Clawbonny's mind.

Sailing on, the expedition reaches eighty-nine degrees, to discover a rugged island at the North Pole, with a volcano in full eruption. Obsessed with reaching the precise point of the Pole, the captain climbs up through the falling ash and flowing lava; and the manuscript closes with a striking commemoration of Hatteras's destiny:

Hatteras was waving [the Union Jack] with one hand, and with the other pointing at the Pole of the celestial globe, directly overhead.

All of a sudden, he disappeared. A terrible cry from his companions must have sounded as far as the mountain peak; a quarter of a minute, a century passed, and then the unfortunate man could be seen launched by the explosion of the volcano to an immense height, his flag distended by the breath from the crater.

Then he fell back down into the volcano, whereupon Duke, faithful to the death, threw himself in so as to share his tomb.

And, of the memories of the Arctic expedition, the most indelible was that of a Mount Hatteras smoking on the horizon, the tomb of a British captain standing at the North Pole of the globe.

In his letter Verne agrees to delete the duel, 'at the stroke of a pen', but feigns to believe that Hatteras can still kill himself. However, in *MÉR*, the suicide of the 'fifth act' has also been removed: just as the captain throws himself in, Altamont implausibly catches him—refinding a minimal function in the global economy of the novel—but the captain is insane. Verne's unhappiness at the forced changes is shown by the captain's implausible swimming to the island, his gravestone on it, and his curious absence from the return journey and the glorious homecoming in the book version.

The manuscript is thus a crucial document. The missing chapters comprise the most significant cut in the works Verne published with Hetzel, and some of the most dramatic episodes of the whole corpus. The original ending is certainly a little abrupt, but is the only one to fit Hatteras's mission and character, and hence the whole novel. In the published version ninety degrees is never actually reached and the return is implausible. Given that duelling had died out, Hetzel's historical sense may be better, but his commercial and literary antennae seem seriously defective in suppressing the episodes of Anglo–American rivalry and especially the duel and suicide. To fully understand the work, then, we are obliged to remember the earliest version.

Following its difficult, sectioned, birth, the novel had a chequered life, for moralistic attacks on *Hatteras* continued and it remained untranslated for a long time. In 1868 Monseigneur Dupanloup, a leading educationalist, criticized the *MÉR* for being insufficiently Christian. In parallel, the influential Catholic journalist Louis Veuillot complained: 'I have not yet read the Extraordinary Journeys of M. Verne. Our friend [Léon] Aubineau tells me they are charming, except for one absence . . . which leaves the marvels of the world an enigma. All is beautiful but inanimate. Someone is missing.'[8] One paradox here is that Verne, vaguely Catholic, was pressurized by the atheist Hetzel to write more pious sentiments so as to sell more copies. Another is that his required insertions may now be read with irony, the final effect being to cast doubt on the existence, or at least detectability, of a benevolent deity.

Most of Verne's novels appeared in English only in the 1870s, well after he had written much of his best work. It must have been galling

---

[8] Cited by Ghislain Diesbach, *Le Tour de Jules Verne en 80 livres* (1969), 199.

for the part-British author of *The British at the North Pole* to see the book unavailable on his frequent visits to that country over the decade following its publication. Fate was perhaps being kind, however, for, when it did come out, the anonymous translations were at best pale and reduced copies of the original.

Hatteras: *Structure and Meaning*

Although Verne scrupulously adheres to contemporary geographical knowledge, he freely indulges his imagination on the white areas of the maps.

Obsessed as he is with the structuring of space, he works in inordinate amounts of research as he follows scores of explorers across the Canadian Arctic. But the second part of the journey, void and virgin, allows full rein to his creativity, which creates a hypnotic mood, an unreal atmosphere of late Romanticism, in the manner of Cooper or Poe. The Pole itself, where the meridians and oceans finally meet, is a miraculous spot for a writer fixated on reaching the ends of the world.

What the author never mentions is the country his novel is set in; he even uses the obsolete French colonial term, 'la Nouvelle-Bretagne'. Verne does also employ the term 'Canada', but only for the traditional settlements around Quebec. Although all the Arctic Islands, and perhaps part of Greenland, belonged to British (North) America, by geography and discovery, Hatteras's only national claims are those relating to his discoveries.

Much early exploration was done from Russian Alaska and Danish Greenland; the French had faded from the area by the nineteenth century. However, since its inception, the United States had exhibited expansionist tendencies, doubling in size in 1803 and gaining Alaska in 1867; popular prophets, including Verne himself, suggested that the whole continent would soon be taken over 'as far as the Pole' (*The Fur Country*, I 12). In the 1850s, Americans began to move north.

Because of the convoluted configuration of the archipelago and the changeability of the ice, heading for the North Pole in 1860 was a complex undertaking. The routes to the Northwest Passage were often the same as to the Pole. Indeed, seekers of the Passage had often had to head east, and polar explorers, south; the same straits

were sometimes navigated in opposite directions by ships heading
for identical goals.

As a result, Hatteras performs a virtuoso exercise in binary choice,
with repeated random searches, dead ends, retreats, loops, and
points revisited. From Baffin Bay, he has to choose between Lancaster
Sound to the west or Smith Sound to the north; from Lancaster,
Prince Regent Inlet south or Barrow Strait west; from Prince
Regent, Fox and Hecla east or Bellot west; from Bellot, Franklin or
Peel; from Franklin, Ross or McClintock; from McClintock, Byam
Martin or Barrow; from Barrow, Lancaster again or Wellington; and
so on.

But both conflicting and blending with the binary labyrinth are
psychological and novelistic structures, making *Hatteras* a brilliant
essay on mapping two-dimensional space. Four particular configur-
ations stand out.

First, *Hatteras* is initially based on previous expeditions, summarized in the names of the twofold maze. However, starting from I 28,
all the geographical features are invented, tying in with Verne's
preference for the unstructured. Not only are the Arctic wastes
devoid of features and the predecessors' distressing nomenclature
but a polar ocean is essential to Hatteras's endeavour. As Verne says:
'The open sea represented freedom for him.'

Second, Verne's timidity in society and literary aims combine to
make him instinctively choose the most roundabout way, the most
complex path, the greatest delay before reaching the desired goal.
Third, however, Hatteras's bold obsession is to thrust forwards.
Only latitude counts for him; parallels are ignored; and so space is
reduced to a straight line culminating at the Pole. The line is irrevoc-
ably ordered: all retreat is impossible, and once at his destination the
captain has nowhere to go. Hatteras is thus merely the first in a
whole succession of linear monomaniacs doomed to disappointment,
from Lidenbrock and the underground depth to Fogg and the
distance covered.

The Pole itself, lastly, represents a supreme point which uniquely
opposes two-dimensional space, casts off the linear straitjacket,
denies the binary maze, and indeed collapses all structure. In Verne's
novel, however, four different Poles exist, geographical, magnetic, of
cold, and stellar, each representing an Ultima Thule, a geographical
limiting point, a magical place to linger a while.

Even the structuring of space, then, is far from simple. In line with the pedagogical pressure, Verne starts off with elementary, demonstrable forms. But he multiplies and combines them, introduces interlocking structures of desire and imagination, and in the end recreates the multi-dimensional space of an imaginary world.

The characters of *Hatteras* are amongst the most successful in Verne. The crew are well drawn, especially the disgruntled then mutinous second-in-command, Richard Shandon.

In his early works Verne shows appreciation for the British, unusual in France at the time. Hatteras and Fogg are often admirable, though frequently incomprehensible and annoying. What distinguishes Verne's Britons is their snobbishness and tendency to derive pride from their very nationality. But nationalism is a refusal to join the human race, and in the later novels, the English, although never the Scots, are often severely criticized.

John Hatteras is depicted with all his faults, making us believe in an authentic historical figure. But he is also presented in supernatural terms, from the way he sends letters and defies the storms to his imperviousness to both shattering cold and volcanic heat.

About 35 years old, this exceptional being has 'an energetic face with lines drawn geometrically on a high forehead . . . eyes . . . beautiful but cold, thin lips on a mouth sparing with words'. His voice is gentle but imperious, persuasive but alarming. He possesses nautical skill, passionate idealism, great intelligence, good mind-reading, iron muscles, manic energy, superhuman courage, and occasional surprising sensibility. He also has violent undercurrents, intolerance of discussion, and hatred for competitors.

Hatteras is invisible when return remains possible. Once in command, he is sombre and withdrawn, signs of his split personality. Psychoanalytic-minded critics have characterized him in terms of melancholy, monomania, manic depression, schizophrenia, catatonia, and autism. The whole novel shows his mounting folly, the fixed idea which freezes speech inside him and makes him sacrifice everything for his overarching goal.

Through it all, Dr Clawbonny provides an invaluable foil. About 40 years old, probably Scottish, he is so full of volubility, familiarity, and obstinacy that he could be a meridional. He has an encyclopedic knowledge of botany, geography, and exploration, universal curiosity, and indestructible optimism, very similar to the Dr Richardson who took part in Franklin's first expedition. He shows the captain loyal friendship and cheerfully undergoes the Arctic winter and deprivations of every sort. His improvisation, humour, sociability, and *joie de vivre* are infectious; the only thing that upsets him is the rivalry between the captains. When Hatteras is absent, it is the good doctor who takes charge, not Altamont. The Dickensian or Sternian Clawbonny is his creator's ideal double.

Because Verne does not belong to any school or movement, his literary devices have often been neglected, or even denied, and yet they are central to understanding his work. Two quintessential tropes of the Arctic can briefly be mentioned. The writer sensualizes the landscape, for the whiteness of the virgin snow inevitably leads him to introduce the physiological into the geographical. The corporeal is emphasized in the protracted detours and the violent penetrations, in the delights of the sinuous straits, and in the joyous explosions; but also in the shock of the bright red snow, whose organic origin and liquidity are repeatedly emphasized. A sustained three-way metaphor is also manifest between the uniform polar landscape, the purity of the white areas on the maps, and the writer's obstinately blank page. In all three it is difficult to progress, to make permanent marks on the pitiless terrain, to avoid following others' tracks, even one's own, to resist the sense of exhaustion and sadness as the saga comes to an end, to overcome the madness haunting those who venture into such domains.

Readers who close *Hatteras* come away with two distinct impressions. First, that they have read a work which captures the very essence of mid-century polar exploration. A documentary impression is created, that the characters really are following, verifying, and on occasion correcting the accounts of their authentic predecessors. Every detail of the lived experience rings uncannily true: the hostile nature, the physical and psychological reality of the terrifying cold, the everlasting white-outs and resultant mental confusion. This extends even to the cultural-linguistic sphere: although possessing barely a few words of English, the author makes us forget we are reading a novel written part-time by a stockbroker in central Paris.

Modern criticism has cast doubt on the existence of representation: that objects from the real world can ever be depicted in artistic form. However, at a naive level, Verne inverts such an argument, by simply copying entire pages of fact recorded by geographical or scientific authorities, and then defying us to argue with McClure or McClintock, Fourier or Victoria.

On another level, however, he concurs, for, insidiously, imperceptibly, he slides the balance towards greater and greater invention. At the beginning the style sometimes oscillates between the noun-laden listing and brief purple passages, all adjectival and near-orgasmic; but as the writing progresses, it comes to transcend the Realist–Romantic division, render irrelevant the factual accuracy, and infiltrate hearts and minds. The chapters of the approach to the Pole and the events on Queen's Island form a sustained climax, through the vibrant rapture in the description, the controlled satisfaction of the hopes and dreams of the characters and the author, and the feeling that the endeavour is the vindication of the tragic efforts that came before. The final effect, then, is of an excitement, a transcendence, a vision of the physical and spiritual world that no other author can give: *Hatteras* is a compulsive page-turner and a disturbing mood-changer.

NOTE ON THE TEXT AND TRANSLATION

The Text

A PROBLEM with *Hatteras* is that the French text was inadequately copy-edited and basic textual checking was not carried out. As a result, all modern editions contain many mistakes in the spelling, internal consistency, and even syntax.[1] In addition, apart from studies of individual paragraphs, the different editions and the manuscript have never been compared.

For the present volume, however, efforts have been made to provide an accurate text, with additional information about its successive revisions. A systematic scrutiny of the manuscript has been carried out, as well as a comparison of the three major editions and extensive research on the historical, geographical, and literary content of the novel.

The first publication of *The Adventures of Captain Hatteras* was in serial form in Hetzel's *Magasin d'éducation et de recréation* (*MÉR*), with the opening two chapters appearing at the beginning of the first issue. They were preceded by a presentation by Hetzel (reproduced in Appendix C, below). Twenty-three fortnightly instalments came out from 20 March 1864 to 20 February 1865 (Part I), and then eighteen more from 5 March to 5 December 1865 (Part II).

The first book publication of *Hatteras* was in 1866 (Hetzel in-18); the first illustrated book edition (Hetzel, large in-octavo), the edition followed here, was dated 1867, but in fact went on sale in November 1866 and had been issued in instalments from 16 July 1866. It contained a 'Publisher's Announcement' (also in Appendix C), inaugurating and defining Verne's series of Extraordinary Journeys in the Known and Unknown Worlds. This much-commented manifesto was signed 'J. Hetzel', but drafted by Verne. From now on nearly all Verne's prose fiction, including the previous three novels, would be part of the series, running until 1919.

At the beginning, the two volumes were published as separate

---

[1] Livre de Poche and Rencontre (both 1966) contain many new mistakes and misguided 'corrections'. The text version available on Gutenberg and the WWW is based on the unillustrated 1881 edition (Part I) and the defective 1966 Rencontre one (Part II).

works. Thus, in both the *MÉR* and 1866 editions, the two parts were
distinct works under separate titles, with *Aventures du capitaine
Hatteras* only as a subtitle. This practice was maintained over all the
unillustrated French editions and most of the English ones. Only
with the '1867' edition does the title page read *Voyages et aventures
du capitaine Hatteras* (translated here as *The Adventures of Captain
Hatteras*), followed by *Les Anglais au pôle nord—Le Désert de glace*
(*The British at the North Pole—The Desert of Ice*) in smaller type.[2] All
single-volume editions from 1867 to the present day read 'Part II'
before 'Le Désert de glace' in the middle, but omit 'Part I' at the
beginning.

Although all subsequent unillustrated editions were apparently
identical to the 1866 one, changes were made both between and
within the reprints of the first illustrated edition. The first copies of
the first printing, of considerable commercial value, are indicated by
some or all of the following features: the bastard title page indicates
the author's name as 'Ver n'; the frontispiece illustration depicts, and
contains the titles of, Verne's first four novels, including '*Aventures
du capitaine J. Hatteras*'; '1867' appears on the title page; illustrations
in I 1 and I 4 show the *Forward* being launched prow first and
Clawbonny and co. enjoying a tenth tot of rum; and the second last
paragraph of the Publisher's Announcement announces the other
three novels already in the series (see Appendix C below). In later
printings, the frontispiece depicts only *Hatteras*, the title in it is
Aventures du capitaine Hatteras, the *Forward* is launched backwards,
and the rum drinkers are removed.

A dialogue between the sailors of about 180 words (I 8) is present
in the 1866 edition, but missing from 1867. Further variants in 1866,
generally less accurate than 1867, are indicated in the Explanatory
Notes.

The 1867 and *MÉR* editions are structurally different (again, full
information is provided in the Explanatory Notes). Thus Part II has
twenty-seven chapters in 1867, but twenty-six in *MÉR*, with the
chapter titles identical up to II 14. Then II 15–16 in 1867 ('The
Northwest Passage' and 'Northern Arcadia') are a single chapter in
MÉR (II 15, 'Northern Arcadia'). II 17–18 ('Altamont's Revenge'
and 'Final Preparations') are also combined in *MÉR* (II 16,

---

[2] However, the vignette at the head of I 1 and the spine read *Aventures du capitaine
Hatteras*.

'Altamont's Revenge'). II 19–20 correspond to II 17–18 in *MÉR*, but II 19 in *MÉR*, 'The Northwest Passage', has no equivalent in 1867. II 21–7 bear the same titles as II 20–6 in *MÉR*. In two cases (I 7 and II 11) the 1867 and *MÉR* titles are identical, but those of 1866 different.

However, the above list conceals many deletions, additions, and transfers of text. In the original version, after Hatteras goes up to thank Altamont for saving him from a musk ox, the American shows that this incident cannot put an end to their rivalry (*MÉR* III 325–6/II 16). There ensues a deathly silence on the march home and over dinner, an early night, a relating of the incident by Clawbonny the following day, and: '"Oh, those Yankees!" replied Johnson, with a gesture of annoyance.' In sum, the two captains remain enemies, with even the narrator criticizing the American, as in 'this time Hatteras could not be faulted!' (*MÉR* III 326). The 1867 edition inserts instead lines where Altamont hesitates for a split-second to save the captain, but decides to sacrifice narrow self-interest (II 17). Two insincere pages are then added, emphasizing the captains' saving of each other's lives, the frank reconciliation, the friendly dinner, the folly of national rivalry, and much weeping and embracing (II 17).

The other major difference in *MÉR* follows the discussion of McClure's discovery of the Northwest Passage. In *MÉR* Hatteras suggests leaving Altamont behind with more resolution, emphasizing his fear that he will try to grab glory; and the argument is more violent, occupies a whole chapter, and takes place just before the navigation to the Pole (*MÉR* IV 33–41/II 19). It contains the phrase '"The launch!" exclaimed Hatteras, who saw an evident intention in these words of Altamont.' Given that the manuscript has '"*To* the launch!"' Altamont apparently wants to sail off alone, making Hatteras take physical possession. In 1867, the argument and reconciliation happen during the wintering (II 15), in line with Hetzel's insistence that Verne bring the scene forward.[3]

Only one manuscript (MS, 1863–4) is known to survive, in the Municipal Library at Nantes (under reference B 141). Part I is in the upright copperplate Verne used for final manuscripts, with dual margins and corrections above the text. Part II is scrawled on one

---

[3] The illustration of Altamont and Hatteras about to fight still shows two tent poles in 1867, out of place in Doctor's House.

half of each sheet, with frequent corrections in red ink on the other half. Although marked up with indications for galley proofs, it is very different from *MÉR*.

At the top of the first sheet, 'Captain Hatteras' is added in Verne's hand, preceded by 'British at the North Pole | Desert of Ice', but with 'Surprising Journey of Captain Hatteras to the North Pole' inserted in another hand. Part II is headed 'The Robinsons of the Pole: Adventures of Captain Hatteras', but also has a note in the same editorial hand. In the first chapter, MS reads 'X . . .' for the name of the captain instead of 'KZ', '6 5 April', and 'shopkeepers' ('boutiquiers') instead of 'merchants', '80' instead of '120 horse-power', 'the *Foreward*' (throughout), and 'Master ~~Harvey~~ Johnson' (up to I 19), plus a few stylistic changes.

Like *MÉR*, Part II of MS has twenty-six chapters, but MS II 20 is entitled 'The Polar Ocean'; II 21, 'John Bull and Jonathan'; II 22, 'The Approach to the North Pole'; II 23, 'The Union Jack'; II 24, 'Lesson in Polar Cosmography'; II 25, 'Mount Hatteras'; and II 26, '276 ~~The Return~~ The Hans Christien'. II 21–2 and 26, partially cut in *MÉR*, are described in the Introduction, above and are cited fully below in Appendix A: The Deleted Duel Episode and the Original Ending.

The present volume benefits from the textual work of the studies in the Select Bibliography; but most of the information is based on original research. Apparent anomalies in 1867 have been checked against at least one other edition. *MÉR* and 1866 have also been compared with 1867 paragraph by paragraph, with deletions, additions, and displacements reported here. The opening, duel, and final chapters of MS have been checked in detail, with Part I also scanned for major variants, especially deletions.

The Translation

Hatteras has been translated into English four times,[4] but all four are of middling quality and cut passages to varying degrees, sometimes apparently because of the difficulty of translating them.

[4] The information in this note was provided by Arthur B. Evans, to whom grateful thanks are recorded. Parts I and II of the four translations open as follows:

The English at the North Pole and *The Field of Ice* (Routledge, 1874): ('To-morrow, at ebb tide, the brig *Forward* will sail from the New Prince's Docks, captain, K.Z.; chief

Hatteras is Verne's most English book, with British measures, terminology, and even language. A few examples of the Anglicisms are 'le parce que et le pourquoi', 'un chien grand danois', 'repousser au moyen de *pôles*', 'les oies boréales', 'la souris arctique', and '[le] gazon nain'. There are also many English words directly in the French text, although some are eccentric, for example 'warfs', 'groose', 'rotches' ('roaches'), 'palch' ('patch'), or even mistranslations, like 'des pastilles de chaux' ('(quick)lime pastils'). In addition, some British ships' names are Gallicized, for example '*l'Intrépide*' or '*le Phénix*'.

Verne places seventy-five mock-learned footnotes in his text (silently deleted in previous translations), with a few repeated in the two parts. A dozen have been retained in the main text; but in most cases they would not make sense. This applies to the nearly forty notes translating into French the mostly English terms in the main text. Since these are impossible to translate, they are cited here, in

officer, Richard Shandon; destination unknown. | Such was the announcement which appeared in the *Liverpool Herald* of April 5, 1860.'; 'It was a bold project of Hatteras to push this way to the North Pole, and gain for his country the honour and glory of its discovery.'

The Adventures of Captain Hatteras (Osgood, 1874–5): 'To-morrow, at the turn of the tide, the brig *Forward*, K.Z., captain, Richard Shandon, mate, will clear from New Prince's Docks; destination unknown. This announcement appeared in the *Liverpool Herald* of April 5, 1860.'; 'The design which Captain Hatteras had formed of exploring the North, and of giving England the honor of discovering the Pole, was certainly a bold one.'

The Adventures of Captain Hatteras (Ward, Lock, and Tyler, 1876): 'To-morrow, at low tide, the brig *Forward*, Captain K.Z—, Richard Shandon mate, will start from New Prince's Docks for an unknown destination. | The foregoing might have been read in the *Liverpool Herald* of April 5th, 1860.'; 'Captain Hatteras's design was a bold one; he had meant that England should have the glory of the discovery of the world's boreal Pole.'

Captain Hatteras: or, the English at the North Pole and *The Frozen Desert—The Desert of Ice* (Goubaud, 1877): 'The brig *Forward*, captain, K.Z., Richard Shandon, mate, will leave New Prince's Dock to-morrow with the first of the ebb. | This was the notice in the *Liverpool Herald*, of the 5th of April, 1866.'; 'Captain Hatteras's design to reach the North, and so to attribute the glory of discovering the North Pole to England, was a bold one.'

Not included in the above are abridgements. At an estimated 120,000 words, an edition published as *At the North Pole* and *The Wilderness of Ice* (1961, Arco/Associated, Fitzroy Edition) cannot be considered a full translation. A number of the texts in the series, purportedly 'translated by I. O. Evans', are in fact the 19th-cent. translations; and the majority cut the text cruelly.

accordance with the aim of integrally presenting Verne's text.[5]
There are a further score providing conversions.[6]

Verne sometimes invents words, like '"printanisaient"' ('"were vernalizing"') or 'ptarmites'. Occasionally he uses Christian names alone, perhaps imitating cases like 'Sir Edward'. His system of quoting temperatures in Fahrenheit, while also providing the centigrade conversion, has been retained here. Verne's fathoms are five (French) feet.

Language errors often necessarily disappear in the translation process, for example 'capes de mouton' for 'caps de mouton' ('dead-eyes'); but factual errors have generally been retained. For example, Verne makes scores of east–west confusions in his works, and here writes 'the closest sea to the west' for 'to the east' and 'the east coast of Greenland' for 'west' (twice!). His spelling of places and names is often shaky, especially English ones, with sometimes different forms on the same page, and is often inconsistent with his own map. All spelling has been checked here, the amendments of proper names being indicated in the endnotes or in the list below. The present edition is thus the first in any language to regularize the text.

---

[5] '*Forward*' ('*Forward*, en avant'), 'lime-juice' ('Jus de citron'), 'blasting-cylinders' ('Sortes de pétards'), 'ice-master' ('Pilote des glaces'), 'groose' ('Sorte de perdrix'), '*drift wood*' ('Bois flotté'), 'ce cap [Farewel] si bien nommé' ('*Farewel* signifie adieu'), 'Islande' ('Île des glaces'), 'ice-fields' ('Champs de glace'), '*crow's-nest*' ('Littéralement *nid de pie*'), 'baie Repulse' ('Baie qu'on ne peut atteindre'), 'la Pointe Turnagain' ('Cap du retour forcé'), 'snow-spectacles' ('Lunettes à neige'), 'eider-ducks' ('Canard-édredon' [*sic*]), 'molly-mokes' ('Oiseaux des mers boréales'), 'rotches' ('Sortes de perdrix de rochers'), '*nipped*' ('Pincé'), '*floes*' ('Glaçons'), 'cairns' ('Petites pyramides de pierres' in 1867, '. . . de pierre' in 1866), 'scrapers' ('Grattoirs'), 'drifts' ('Tourbillons' in 1867, 'Tourbillon' in 1866), 'snow-house' ('Maison de neige'), 'snow-shoes' ('Chaussures à neige'), 'frost-rime' ('Fumée gelée'), 'dog driver' ('Dresseur de chiens'), 'snow-house' ('Maison de neige'), '*teetotalers* [*sic*]' ('Régime qui exclut toute boisson spiritueuse'), 'snow-birds' ('Oiseaux de neige'), 'poker' ('Longue tige de fer destinée à attiser le feu des fourneaux'), 'des snow-blindness' ('Maladie des paupières occasionnée par la réverbération des neiges'), and 'cyclones' ('Tempêtes tournantes').

[6] Both the term and the footnote are translated here: '£16,000 sterling' ('400,000 francs'), '£500' ('12,500 francs'), '£2,000' ('50,000 francs'), '£760,000' ('19 million'), '£40' ('1,000 francs'), '£5,000' ('125,000 francs'), '£1,000' ('25,000 francs'), '£20,000' ('500,000 francs'), '£62. 10s.' ('1,552.50 francs' in 1867, but the correct '1,562.50 francs' in 1866), '£1,125' ('23,125 francs'), '£18,000' ('450,000 francs'), '£375' ('9,375 francs'), 'two hundred yards' ('182 metres'), '1,000 miles' ('more than four hundred leagues'), 'about six hundred miles' ('about two hundred and forty-seven leagues'), 'twenty miles' ('about eight leagues'), 'four hundred miles' ('160 leagues'), '355 miles at most' ('150 leagues'), 'twelve miles' ('five leagues'), '175 miles' ('70⅓ leagues'), and 'three-quarters of a mile' ('1,237 metres').

In the following list, Verne's form appears in brackets: 'Barents' ('Barentz'), 'Cape Acworth' ('... Aworth'), 'Cape Beechey' ('Beecher'), 'Cape Seppings' ('Sepping', but 'Scepings' on Verne's map), 'Cape Warrender' ('Warender', but 'Warrender' on the map), 'Disko' ('Disco' on the map), 'Farewell' ('Farewel', but 'Farewell' on the map), 'Godhavn' ('Godavhn'; map: 'Godhavn'; MS: 'Godavn'), 'Grinnell' ('Grinnel', but 'Grinnell' on the map), 'the *Hans Christian*' ('*Hans Christien*'), 'Haswell' ('Haswelt', taken from HL), 'Holsteinborg' ('Hosteinborg' in I 5 but 'Holsteinborg' in I 7 and 9), 'Horsburgh' ('Horsburg'), 'the *Isabella*' ('*Isabelle*'), 'Kingston Bay' ('Hingston', but 'Higston' on the map), 'Mackenzie' ('Mackensie'), 'Macleod Bay' ('Mac-Leon'), 'Malin Head' ('Malinhead'), 'Mount Rawlinson' ('Mounts . . .' on the map), 'Ommanney' ('Ommaney', but 'Ommanney' on the map), 'Simpson' ('Sompson'), 'Somerset' ('Sommerset', but 'Somerset' on the map), 'Uppernawik' ('Upernavik' on the map), 'Vaughan' ('Vaugham' and 'Waugham'), and 'Wynniatt' ('Wynniat'). In addition, the different editions sometimes exhibit further variants.[7]

[7] 'Ellesmere' is 'Ellesmer' in *MÉR*; 'Camp de Réfuge' in 1867 is 'Camp du Réfuge' in 1866.

SELECT BIBLIOGRAPHY

Verne in General

Hachette, Michel de l'Ormeraie, and Rencontre (reprinted by Edito-Service) represent the only complete editions of the Voyages extraordinaires since the original Hetzel publication, but forty-four of the books have appeared in Livre de Poche.

Although the majority of English translations of Verne hardly merit that name, with up to two-thirds of the text cut and systematic deletion of the real-world information, a number of reliable ones have appeared recently.

Critical editions of Verne have been notable by their absence, especially in French. However, in recent years the following works have appeared in English with introductions, notes, and other critical material: *Humbug* (1991), *Journey to the Centre of the Earth* (1992), *Twenty Thousand Leagues under the Seas* (1993 and 1998), *Around the World in Eighty Days* (1995), *Invasion of the Sea* (2001), *The Mysterious Island* (2002), and *The Mighty Orinoco* (2002).[1]

Scholarly books on Verne in English are Arthur Evans, *Jules Verne Rediscovered: Didacticism and the Scientific Novel* (1988); Andrew Martin, *The Mask of the Prophet: The Extraordinary Fictions of Jules Verne* (1990); and William Butcher, *Verne's Journey to the Centre of the Self: Space and Time in the 'Voyages extraordinaires'* (1990).

In French there exist many stimulating collections of articles, notably P.-A. Touttain (ed.), *L'Herne: Jules Verne* (1974); François Raymond and Simone Vierne (eds.), *Colloque de Cerisy: Jules Verne et les sciences humaines* (1979); Jean Bessière (ed.), *Modernités de Jules Verne* (1988); and the eight volumes of the Minard (Lettres modernes) series, especially *Machines et imaginaire* (1980) and *Texte, image, spectacle* (1983).

Biographies which meet modern standards of scholarship are Volker Dehs, *Jules Verne* [in German] (forthcoming) and William Butcher, *Jules Verne: The Definitive Biography* (forthcoming). The following are of interest for particular aspects: Marguerite Allotte de la Fuÿe, trans. Erik de Mauny, *Jules Verne* (1954); Jean Jules-Verne, trans. and adapted by Roger

---

[1] The first four volumes, trans. and critical material by William Butcher; the 1993 one, trans. with critical material by Walter James Miller and Frederick Paul Walter; 2001, trans. Edward Baxter with critical material by Arthur Evans; *The Mysterious Island*, trans. Sidney Kravitz with critical material by William Butcher; *The Mighty Orinoco*, trans. Stanford Luce with critical material by Walter James Miller and Arthur Evans.

Greaves, *Jules Verne: A Biography* (1976); Charles-Noël Martin, *Jules Verne, sa vie, son œuvre* (1971) and *La Vie et l'œuvre de Jules Verne* (1978); Marc Soriano, *Jules Verne (le cas Verne)* (1978); Volker Dehs, *Jules Verne* (1986); Olivier Dumas, *Jules Verne* (1988), reprinted without the family correspondence as *Voyage à travers Jules Verne* (2000); Jean-Paul Dekiss, *Jules Verne: Le Rêve du progrès* (1991); Herbert Lottman, *Jules Verne: An Exploratory Biography* (1996); Patrick Avrane, *Jules Verne* (1997); Jean-Paul Dekiss, *Jules Verne l'enchanteur* (1999); and Gilles de Robien, *Jules Verne, le rêveur incompris* (2000).

The main secondary bibliographies are Jean-Michel Margot, *Bibliographie documentaire sur Jules Verne* (1989); William Butcher, 'Jules and Michel Verne', in David Baguley (ed.), *Critical Bibliography of French Literature: The Nineteenth Century* (1994); Volker Dehs, *Guide bibliographique à travers la critique vernienne* (2002); and Jean-Michel Margot's labour of love, listing all 10,000 known studies of Verne (forthcoming).

Thinking about Verne has been transformed recently by the revelations of the *Bulletin de la société Jules Verne (BSJV)*; the *Correspondance inédite de Jules Verne et de Pierre-Jules Hetzel (1863–1886)*, volumes 1, 2, and 3, ed. Olivier Dumas, Piero Gondolo della Riva, and Volker Dehs (1999, 2001, and 2002); *Entretiens avec Jules Verne*, trans. Sylvie Malbrancq, ed. Daniel Compère and Jean-Michel Margot (1998); and Jean-Michel Margot (ed.), *Jules Verne en son temps* (2004).

Hatteras

Adler, A., 'Hatteras: Verzweiflung im Namen der Wissenschaft', in *Moeblierte Erziehung* (1970), 82–149.

Anon., 'Centenaire de la découverte du Pôle nord par le capitaine Hatteras', *Viridis Candela: Dossiers acénonètes du Collège de Pataphysique*, 16 (1961), 37–40.

Boichu, Anne, 'De la Création originelle à la création littéraire: Glace et pôles chez Jules Verne', DEA, Paris III (1997–8).

Buisine, Alain, 'Déchirures de la représentation scientifique', *Revue des sciences humaines*, 39/154 (Apr.–June 1974), 301–13.

Butor, Michel, 'Le Point suprême et l'âge d'or à travers quelques œuvres de Jules Verne', *Arts et Lettres*, 4/2 (1949), 3–31.

Chevrier, Alain, 'La "Folie polaire" du capitaine Hatteras', *BSJV* 107 (1993), 9–18.

Compère, Daniel, '*Les Anglais au Pôle nord* selon Jules Verne', *Le Rocambole: Bulletin des amis du roman populaire*, 15 (summer 2001), 23–34.

—— *Approche de l'île chez Jules Verne* (1977).

Constantin, Marc, 'Journal de voyage à bord du *Capitaine Hatteras* de Monsieur Jules Verne' (unpublished).

Dehs, Volker, 'Jules Verne et Théophile Gautier père et fils', *BSJV* 126 (1998), 13–23.

—— 'Quelques témoignages arctiques 1867–1897', *Revue Jules Verne*, 17 (2004) ('Les Pôles'), 61–6.

Dumas, Olivier, 'La Mort d'Hatteras', *BSJV* 73 (1985), 22–4.

Escaich, René, 'A propos des *Aventures du capitaine Hatteras*', *BSJV* 28 (1973), 87–9.

—— *Voyage au monde de Jules Verne* (1955).

Evans, Idrisyn Oliver, 'Introduction', in *At the North Pole, Part One of The Adventures of Captain Hatteras* (1961), 7–9.

Ferry, Jean, 'Erreurs boréales', *Viridis Candela: Dossiers acénonètes du Collège de Pataphysique*, 16 (1961), 19–24.

Gautier, Théophile, 'Les Voyages imaginaires de M. Jules Verne', *Moniteur universel*, 4/197 (16 July 1866).

Gehu, Edmond, 'La Géographie polaire dans l'œuvre de Jules Verne: *Aventures du capitaine Hatteras*', *BSJV* (1st ser.) 2/9 (1937), 181–98.

Giovacchini, D., '*Voyages et aventures du capitaine Hatteras*', in Jean-Pierre de Beaumarchais and Daniel Couty (eds.), *Dictionnaire des œuvres littéraires de langue française* (1994).

Huet, Marie-Hélène, 'Itinéraire du texte', in *Colloque de Cerisy: Jules Verne et les sciences humaines* (1979), 9–35.

—— *L'Histoire des 'Voyages Extraordinaires': Essai sur l'œuvre de Jules Verne* (1973).

Jules-Verne, Jean, *Jules Verne* (1973).

Lutembi, T. S., 'Sur le pôle et la politique', *Viridis Candela: Dossiers acénonètes du Collège de Pataphysique*, 16 (1961), 5–12.

Malte-Brun, Victor-Adolphe, 'Suite du voyage au Pôle du capitaine Hatteras' and two maps, unpublished 1867 manuscripts given to Verne [sold by Drouot in 1980].

Revue Jules Verne, 17 (2004) ('Les Pôles').

Riffenburgh, Beau, 'Jules Verne and the Conquest of the Polar Regions', *Polar Record*, 27 (1991), 237–40.

Robillot, Henri, 'D'un pôle à l'autre', *Viridis Candela: Dossiers acénonètes du Collège de Pataphysique*, 16 (1961), 31–6.

Saint-Martin, Vivien de, '*Les Anglais au pôle nord—Cinq semaines en Ballon*', *MÉR* III (Oct. 1864), 266.

Sigaux, Gilbert, 'Préface', in *Voyages et adventures du Capitaine Hatteras* (Lausanne, Rencontre, 1966), 5–11.

Thines, Raymond, 'Hatteras', *BSJV* (1st ser.) 2/9 (1937), 168–80.

Vierne, Simone, 'Paroles gelées, paroles de feu, ou le double signe de l'écriture de la folie chez Jules Verne', *Europe* 56/595 (Nov.–Dec. 1978), 57–66.

Zola, Émile, untitled piece beginning 'M. Jules Verne est le fantaisiste de la science . . .', *L'Événement*, 12 May 1866.
—— untitled piece beginning 'M. Jules Verne est un autre esprit . . .', *Le Salut public*, 7 (23 July 1866).
Zukowski, Henri, 'Boussoles', in *Modernités de Jules Verne* (1988), 229–45.
—— Henri, 'Boussoles (II)', in *Jules Verne*, 6. *La Science en question* (1992), 155–74.

Contemporary Documents

NB All the expeditions described in these documents are cited by Verne; the most influential being marked with one or two asterisks.

Anon., *Histoire des deux voyages entrepris par . . . le capitaine Franklin, [et] par [le] capitaine Parry* (1824) [trans. of the first part of Parry (1824) and Franklin, *Narrative*].
*Back, George, *Narrative of the Arctic Land Expedition to the Mouth of the Great Fish River, and along the Shores of the Arctic Ocean* (1836; French trans. 1836).
Barrow, John, *A Chronological History of Voyages into the Arctic Regions* (1818; French trans. 1819).
*Beechey, Frederick William, *A Narrative of a Voyage . . . to the Pacific and Behring's Straits* (1831).
—— *A Voyage of Discovery towards the North Pole* (1843).
*Belcher, Edward, *The Last of the Arctic Voyages* (1855; French trans. 1855).
Bellot, Joseph-René, *Journal d'un voyage aux mers polaires* ('Journal of a Voyage to the Polar Seas', 1853).
Bray, Émile de, 'Journal de bord de l'enseigne de vaisseau Émile de Bray 1852–1854' (pub. as *De Bray Pôle Nord* (1998), trans. as *A Frenchman in Search of Franklin: De Bray's Arctic Journal* (1992)).
*Dease, Peter Warren, *From Barrow to Boothia* (2002).
Defauconpret, Auguste-Jean-Baptiste, *Voyage . . . dans la baie de Baffin . . . par l'"Isabelle' et l'"Alexandre', commandés par le capitaine Ross et le lieutenant Parry* (1819).
**Dubois, Lucien, *Le Pôle et l'équateur: Études sur les dernières explorations du globe* (1863).
*Franklin, John, *Narrative of a Journey to the Shores of the Polar Sea* (1823).
*—— *Narrative of a Second Expedition* (1828).
*—— *Thirty Years in the Arctic Regions* [1859].
**Hervé, Amateur, and Lanoye, Ferdinand (eds.), *Voyages dans les glaces du pôle arctique à la recherche du passage Nord-Ouest* (1854) [contains translated extracts, without references, from John Ross, *Voyage*;

Franklin, *Narrative of a Journey*; Parry, *Three Voyages*; Franklin, *Narrative of a Second Expedition*; Beechey, *Narrative*; Parry, *Three Voyages*; John Ross, *Narrative*; Back, *Narrative*; and McClure, *Arctic Dispatches*].

Inglefield, John Nicholson, 'Voyage du capitaine Inglefield ... à la recherche de sir John Franklin', *Bulletin de la Société de géographie* (July–Dec. 1852 and Jan.–Mar. 1853) (translated from 'A Summer Search for John Franklin', *Athenaeum*, 9 July 1853).

Kane, Elisha Kent, *Arctic Explorations: The Second Grinnell Expedition in Search of Sir John Franklin* (1856).

—— 'La Mer polaire', *Le Tour du monde*, 1/1 (1860), 257–72.

*—— *The United States Grinnell Expedition in Search of Sir John Franklin* (1853).

*Kennedy, William, *A Short Narrative of the Second Voyage of the 'Prince Albert'* (1853).

Lanoye, F. (ed.): see Hervé, Amateur, and Lanoye, Ferdinand.

**Lanoye, Ferdinand Tugnot de (ed.), *La Mer polaire: Voyage de l'"Erèbe" et de la 'Terreur' et expéditions à la recherche de Franklin* (1864) [contains short translated extracts from Richardson, James Ross, Austin, Ommanney, McClintock, Kennedy, and de Bray, and chapter-length ones from McClure, *Arctic Dispatches*; Belcher, *Last of Arctic Voyages*; Kane, *Arctic Explorations*; and McClintock, *Voyage of the 'Fox'*].

—— 'Sir John Franklin et ses compagnons, d'après les rapports officiels du capitaine MacClintock [*sic*]', *Tour du monde*, 1/1 (1860), 18–28.

Lebrun, Henri, *Abrégé de tous les voyages au Pôle nord* (1837).

McClintock, Leopold, *The Voyage of the 'Fox' in the Arctic Seas* (1859; French trans. in the *Tour du Monde*, 1/1 (1860).

*McClure, Robert, *The Arctic Dispatches: Containing an Account of the Discovery of the North-West Passage* [1854?].

North Georgia Gazette and Winter Chronicle (1821).

d'Orbigny, Alcide Dessalines, *Voyage pittoresque dans les deux Amériques: Résumé général de tous les voyages de Colomb ... Franklin, Parry, Back, Phipps, etc.* (1836).

**Parry, William Edward, *Three Voyages for the Discovery of a North-West Passage ... and narrative of an attempt to reach the North Pole* (1835; reprinting editions of 1821–4, 1824–5, and 1826; French trans. of first voyage 1822, second voyage 1835).

Penny, William, William Kennedy, and Horatio Austin, *Expédition à la recherche de sir John Franklin et des équipages des navires l'"Erébus" et la 'Terror'* (1851) [reports and letters, ed. P. Daussy].

*Ross, John, *A Voyage of Discovery* (1819; French trans. 1819).

*—— *Narrative of a Second Voyage* (1835; French trans. 1835).

Sabine, Edward, *Remarks on the Account of the Late Voyage of Discovery ... by Captain J. Ross* (1819).

*Scoresby, William, *An Account of the Arctic Regions and Northern Whale Fishery* (1820).

*—— *Journal of a Voyage to the Northern Whale Fishery* (1823).

Further Reading in Oxford World's Classics

Verne, Jules, *Around the World in Eighty Days*, trans. with an introduction and notes by William Butcher.

—— *Journey to the Centre of the Earth*, trans. with an introduction and notes by William Butcher.

—— *Twenty Thousand Leagues under the Seas*, trans. with an introduction and notes by William Butcher.

A CHRONOLOGY OF JULES VERNE

1828   8 February: birth of Jules Verne on Île Feydeau in Nantes, to Pierre Verne, a lawyer and son and grandson of lawyers, and Sophie, née Allotte de la Fuÿe, of distant Scottish descent. Both parents have links with reactionary milieux and the slave trade. The family moves to Quai Jean-Bart, with a magnificent view of the Loire.

1829–30   Birth of brother, Paul, later a naval officer and stockbroker; followed by sisters Anna (1836), Mathilde (1839), and Marie (1842). Jules hears shots from street battles in the July Revolution.

1833–7   Goes to boarding school: the teacher is the widow of a sea-captain, whose return she is still waiting for. The Vernes spend the summers in bucolic countryside with a buccaneer uncle.

1837–41   École Saint-Stanislas. Performs well in geography, translation from Greek and Latin, and singing. During the holidays, the Vernes stay at Chantenay, on the Loire.

1841–6   Petit séminaire de Saint-Donitien, then Collège royal de Nantes. Above average; probably wins a prize in geography. Easily passes *baccalauréat*. Writes short prose pieces.

1847   Studies law in Paris; his cousin, Caroline Tronson, with whom he has long been unhappily in love, marries. Experiences a fruitless passion for Herminie Arnault-Grossetière and writes more than fifty poems, many dedicated to her, plus *Alexandre VI* and *Un Prêtre en 1839* ('A Priest in 1839').

1848   June: revolution in Paris. Verne is present at the July disturbances. Herminie Arnault-Grossetière gets married. Continues his law studies. In the literary salons meets Dumas *père* and *fils*. Writes plays, including *La Conspiration des poudres* ('The Gunpowder Plot').

1849   Passes law degree. Father allows him to stay on in Paris. Writes more plays. Organizes a dining club called The Eleven Bachelors, reciting his love poetry to them.

1850   His one-act comedy *Les Pailles rompues* ('Broken Straws') runs for twelve nights at Dumas's Théâtre historique, and is published.

1851   Meets author Jacques Arago and explorers and scientists and frequents Adrien Talexy's musical salon. Publishes short stories 'Les Premiers navires de la Marine mexicaine' ('A Drama in Mexico') and 'Un Voyage en ballon' ('Drama in the Air'). Has a first attack of facial paralysis.

1852–5   Becomes secretary of the Théâtre lyrique, on little or no pay. Refuses to take over his father's practice: 'Literature above all.' Publishes 'Martin Paz', 'Maître Zacharius' ('Master Zacharius'), 'Un Hivernage dans les glaces' ('Wintering in the Ice'), and the play *Les Châteaux en Californie* ('Castles in California') in collaboration with Pitre-Chevalier. His operetta *Le Colin-maillard* ('Blind Man's Bluff'), with Michel Carré, is performed to music by Aristide Hignard. Visits brothels in the theatre district.

1856   20 May: goes to a wedding in Amiens, and meets a young widow with two children, Honorine de Viane.

1857   10 January: marries Honorine, becomes a stockbroker in Paris, and moves several times.

1859–60   Visits Scotland and England, and is decisively marked by the experience. Writes *Voyage en Angleterre et en Écosse* (*Backwards to Britain*).

1861   15 June–8 August: travels to Norway and Denmark.

          3 August: birth of only child, Michel.

1863   31 January: *Cinq semaines en ballon* (*Five Weeks in a Balloon*) appears, three months after submission to publisher Jules Hetzel, and is an immediate success.

1864   New one-book contract with Hetzel. Publication of 'Edgar Poe et ses œuvres' ('Edgar Allan Poe and his Works'), *Voyages et aventures du capitaine Hatteras* (*Adventures of Captain Hatteras*), and *Voyage au centre de la Terre* (*Journey to the Centre of the Earth*). *Paris au XXᵉ siècle* (*Paris in the Twentieth Century*) is brutally rejected by Hetzel. Moves to Auteuil and begins to give up his unsuccessful stockbroker partnership.

1865   *De la Terre à la Lune* (*From the Earth to the Moon*), *Les Enfants du capitaine Grant* (*Captain Grant's Children*), and 'Les Forceurs de blocus' ('The Blockade Runners'). A new contract specifies 200,000 words a year.

1866   *Géographie de la France et de ses colonies*.

1867   16 March: goes with brother to Liverpool, thence on the *Great Eastern* to the United States. First English translation of any of the novels, *From the Earth to the Moon*.

1868   Buys a boat, the *Saint-Michel*. Visits London.

1869   *Vingt mille lieues sous les mers* (*Twenty Thousand Leagues under the Seas*), *Autour de la Lune* (*Round the Moon*), and *Découverte de la Terre* ('Discovery of the Earth'). Rents a house in Amiens.

1870   Hetzel apparently rejects *L'Oncle Robinson* ('Uncle Robinson'), an early version of *L'Île mystérieuse* (*The Mysterious Island*). Death at 29 of Estelle Duchesnes of Asnières, reportedly Verne's love. During the Franco-Prussian War, Verne is a coastguard at Le Crotoy (Somme).

1871   Verne briefly goes back to the Stock Exchange.

        3 November: father dies.

1872   *Le Tour du monde en quatre-vingts jours* (*Around the World in Eighty Days*) and *The Fur Country*. Becomes member of Académie d'Amiens.

1873–4 *Le Docteur Ox* (*Dr Ox's Experiment, and Other Stories*), *L'Île mystérieuse* (*The Mysterious Island*), and *Le Chancellor* (*The Chancellor*). Begins collaboration with Adolphe d'Ennery on highly successful stage adaptations of novels (*Le Tour du monde en 80 jours* (1874), *Les Enfants du capitaine Grant* (1878), *Michel Strogoff* (1880)). Moves to 44 boulevard Longueville, Amiens.

1876–7 *Michel Strogoff* (*Michael Strogoff, the Courier of the Tsar*), *Hector Servadac*, and *Les Indes noires* (*The Child of the Cavern*). Buys second, then third boat, the *Saint-Michel II* and *III*. Gives huge fancy-dress ball. Wife critically ill, but recovers. Michel rebels, and is sent to a reformatory. René de Pont-Jest sues Verne for plagiarism in *Voyage au centre de la Terre*.

1878   *Un Capitaine de quinze ans* (*The Boy Captain*). Sails to Lisbon and Algiers.

1879–80 *Les Cinq cents millions de la Bégum* (*The Begum's Fortune*), *Les Tribulations d'un Chinois en Chine* (*The Tribulations of a Chinese in China*), and *La Maison à vapeur* (*The Steam House*). Verne sails to Norway, Ireland, the Hebrides, and Edinburgh. Probably has an affair with Luise Teutsch.

1881   *La Jangada* (*The Giant Raft*). Sails to Rotterdam and Copenhagen.

1882   *Le Rayon vert* (*The Green Ray*) and *L'École des Robinsons* (*The School for Robinsons*). Moves to a larger house at 2 rue Charles-Dubois, Amiens.

1883–4 *Kéraban-le-têtu* (*Keraban the Inflexible*). Michel marries, but soon abducts a minor. He will have two children by her within eleven months. Verne leaves with his wife on a grand tour of the Mediterranean, but cuts it short. On the way back, is received in private audience by Pope Leo XIII.

1885   *Mathias Sandorf.* Sells *Saint-Michel III*.

1886   *Robur-le-conquérant* (*The Clipper of the Clouds*).

9 March: his nephew Gaston, mentally ill, reportedly asks for money to travel to Britain. Verne refuses, and Gaston fires twice, laming him for life.

17 March: Hetzel dies.

1887   Mother dies. *Nord contre sud* (*North against South*).

1888   *Deux ans de vacances* (*Two Years Vacation*). Elected local councillor on a Republican list. For next fifteen years attends council meetings, administers theatre and fairs, opens Municipal Circus (1889), and gives public talks.

1889   *Sans dessus dessous* (*The Purchase of the North Pole*) and 'In the Year 2889' (signed Jules Verne but written by Michel).

1890   Stomach problems.

1892   *Le Château des Carpathes* (*Carpathian Castle*). Pays debts for Michel.

1895   *L'Île à hélice* (*Propeller Island*), the first novel in a European language in the present tense and third person.

1896–7 *Face au drapeau* (*For the Flag*) and *Le Sphinx des glaces* (*An Antarctic Mystery*). Sued by chemist Turpin, inventor of melinite, depicted in *Face au drapeau*, but is successfully defended by Raymond Poincaré, later president of France. Health deteriorates. Brother dies.

1899   Dreyfus Affair: Verne is initially anti-Dreyfusard, but approves of the case being reviewed.

1901   *Le Village aérien* (*The Village in the Treetops*). Moves back into 44 boulevard Longueville.

1904   *Maître du monde* (*The Master of the World*).

1905   17 March: falls ill from diabetes.

24 March: dies. The French government is not represented at the funeral.

1905–14 On Verne's death, *L'Invasion de la mer* (*Invasion of the Sea*) and *Le Phare du bout du monde* (*Lighthouse at the End of the World*) are in the course of publication. Michel takes responsibility for the manuscripts, publishing *Le Volcan d'or* (*The Golden*

Volcano—1906), *L'Agence Thompson and C°* (*The Thompson Travel Agency*—1907), *La Chasse au météore* (*The Hunt for the Meteor*—1908), *Le Pilote du Danube* (*The Danube Pilot*—1908), *Les Naufragés du 'Jonathan'* (*The Survivors of the Jonathan*—1909), *Le Secret de Wilhelm Storitz* (*The Secret of Wilhelm Storitz*—1910), *Hier et Demain* (*Yesterday and Tomorrow*—short stories, including 'Le Humbug' (*Humbug*) and 'L'Éternel Adam' ('Édom')—1910), and *L'Étonnante aventure de la mission Barsac* (*The Barsac Mission*—1914). Between 1985 and 1993 the original (i.e. Jules's) versions are published, under the same titles except for *En Magellanie* (*In the Magallanes*), 'Voyage d'études' ('Study Visit'), and *Le Beau Danube jaune* ('The Beautiful Yellow Danube').

1978   For the 150th anniversary of his birth, the novelist undergoes a major re-evaluation in France, with hundreds of editions and thousands of articles, Ph.D.s, and books about them. On a cumulative basis, Verne is the most translated writer of all time.

1989–94   *Backwards to Britain*, 'Uncle Robinson', 'A Priest in 1839', '"San Carlos" and other Stories', and *Paris in the Twentieth Century*, which sets a US record for a French book.

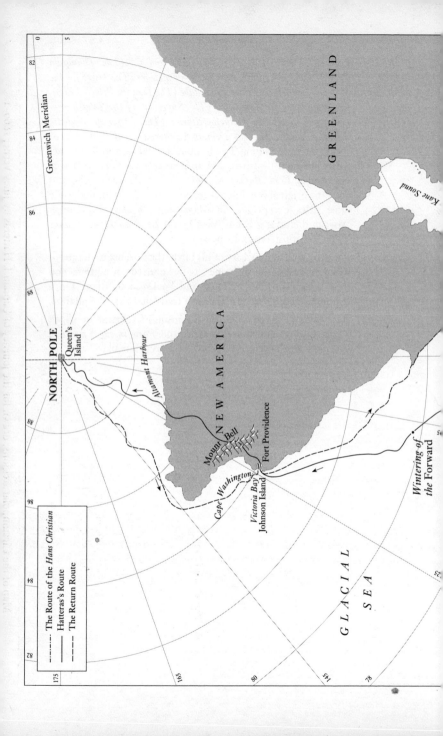

GREENLAND

Kane Sound

NEW AMERICA

Queen's Island

NORTH POLE

Altamont Harbour

Mount Bell

Fort Providence

Cape Washington

Victoria Bay
Johnson Island

Wintering of
the Forward

GLACIAL

SEA

Greenwich Meridian

The Route of the *Hans Christian*
Hatteras's Route
The Return Route

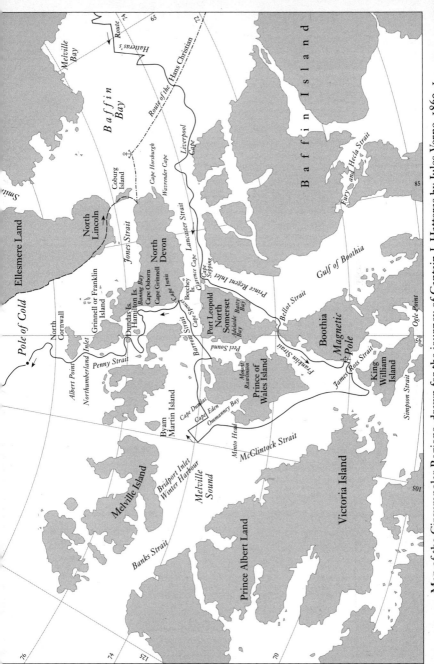

Map of the Circumpolar Regions, drawn for the journey of Captain J. Hatteras by Jules Verne, 1860–1

THE ADVENTURES OF
CAPTAIN HATTERAS

CONTENTS

4 *Contents*

PART TWO — THE DESERT OF ICE

PART ONE

THE BRITISH AT THE NORTH POLE

I

The Forward

'TOMORROW, on the ebb tide, the brig the *Forward*, captain KZ* and second-in-command Richard Shandon, will leave New Prince's Docks; destination unknown.'

Thus read the *Liverpool Herald* of 5 April 1860.*

The sailing of a brig is not an event of any great importance for the busiest port in Britain. Who would notice such an occurrence amongst the ships of every size and nationality* that can hardly fit into the five miles of docks?

Nevertheless, a large crowd covered the quaysides of New Prince's Docks from the early morning of 6 April, as if the city's corporation of naval workers had arranged a meeting there. The dockers from the nearby wharves had abandoned their work, the tradesmen their dark counters, the merchants their deserted stores. Each minute a new cargo of sightseers poured out of the multicoloured omnibuses skirting the dock walls. The city appeared to have but one aim: to watch the *Forward*'s departure.

The *Forward* was a vessel of 170 tons, with a propeller and a boiler producing 120 horsepower. She might easily have been confused with the other brigs in port. But if she did not look at all special to the public, experts noticed several characteristics that were clear to sailors.

On board the *Nautilus*,* at anchor nearby, a group of sailors were deep in a thousand conjectures as to the *Forward*'s destination.

'What d'you make of her masts?' said one. 'It's not normal, I tell you, for steamers to carry so much sail.'

'That ship', answered a quartermaster with a broad ruddy face, 'must use her masts more than her boiler, and if her topsails are so big, the lower ones must often stay furled. So obviously the *Forward*'s heading for Arctic or Antarctic seas, where the icebergs get in the way of the wind more than is healthy for such a fine, solid ship.'

'Dead right, Master Cornhill,'* said a third. 'And did you see how vertical her bow is?'

'Not to mention that she has a steel cutting edge as sharp as a razor, that could split a triple-decker in two by taking her broadside at full speed.'

'Definitely,' answered a Mersey pilot; 'and her screw produces a nice fourteen knots. A sight for sore eyes she was, cutting across the water in the trials. Trust me, a fast ship.'

'Her sails are fine as well; she can sail close to the wind and heed the tiller straightaway. Mark my words, that boat will taste polar seas, or my name isn't Cornhill. And something else. Did you notice the broad trunk holding her rudder head?'

'Aye! But what does that mean?'

'It means, my boys,' retorted the bosun with contemptuous glee, 'that you lot don't use your eyes or heads; it means that the rudder head needed more play, so it could be set or moved easily. Don't you know how often you have to do that sort of trick in ice-packs?'

'Good thinking,' replied the *Nautilus*'s sailors.

'And besides,' one of them ventured, 'the bill of lading confirms Master Cornhill's theory. I got it from Clifton, who's signed on without more ado. The *Forward* has got food for five or six years, and the same amount of coal. Fuel and grub are all she's carrying, with bits of wool and sealskin clothes thrown in as well.'

'Well then,' said Cornhill, 'it's crystal clear. But, since you seem to know Clifton, didn't he say where she was going?'

'He didn't, because he's in the dark as much as anyone; the crew've been taken on just like that. They won't know till they get there.'

'Unless they go to Davy Jones's locker,' chipped in one sceptic, 'as is most likely.'

'But think of the pay,' added Clifton's friend excitedly, 'think of the money! Five times the usual on that sort of trip! Ah, without that, Richard Shandon wouldn't have had many takers. A ship with a strange shape, going the devil knows where, and apparently not planning to come back! That doesn't sound my cup of tea.'

'Whether it does or not, mate,' retorted Master Cornhill, 'the *Forward* wouldn't have had you.'

'And why ever not?'

'Because you don't fit the requirements. It seems that married
men are out. And you fall into the great unwashed majority. So
there's no point in looking down your nose, which would be a major
achievement for you anyway.'

The sailor, trapped in this way, burst out laughing with his
companions, showing the joke was right.

'Even the brig's name', Cornhill continued smugly, 'is pretty bold:
forward to where? Without mentioning that we don't know who the
captain is.'

'But we do,' responded a young sailor with rather a naive face.

'We do?'

'Yes.'

'My lad,' said Cornhill, 'are you so addled you think Shandon is
captain of the *Forward*?'

'But . . .'

'I'm telling you that Shandon is the commander,[1] nothing else;
he's a brave sailor, a tough whaler who's been through it, a solid
fellow fitted for command in every way. But he's not in charge; he's
no more captain than you or me, begging your pardon! And Shandon
doesn't know who's going to be second only to God,* either. In his
own good time and way, the real captain will appear, hailing from
some shore of the Old or New World. And Richard Shandon didn't
say which corner of the globe he'll be pointing his ship at—because
he's not allowed to.'

'All the same,' the young sailor persisted, 'I do assure you
that someone was conducted on board, and announced in the letter
offering Mr Shandon the position of second-in-command.'

'What,' Cornhill replied raising his eyebrows, 'you mean a
captain's already on the *Forward*?'

'I do, Master Cornhill.'

'You're telling me that!'

'Since I got it from Johnson, the bosun.'

'From Master Johnson?'

'Face to face.'

'Johnson told you?'

'Not only that, he showed me the captain.'

'He showed you!' repeated Cornhill in amazement.

---

[1] Second-in-command on a British ship.

'Yes.'

'And you saw him?'

'With my own eyes.'

'And who was it?'

'A dog.'

'A dog with a leg at each corner?'

'Yes!'

General stupefaction amongst the sailors of the *Nautilus*. In any other circumstances they would have been in fits of laughter. A dog, captain of a 170-ton brig! You could gag on less. But the *Forward* was such an extraordinary ship that you needed to think twice before joking or arguing. And Master Cornhill himself was not smiling.

'So it was Johnson who showed you this newfangled sort of captain, this dog?' he asked the young sailor. 'And you saw him?'

'Like I see you, begging pardon!'

'Well, what do you make of it?' asked the sailors.

'I don't make anything of it,' Master Cornhill answered curtly, 'except that the *Forward* is a ship of the devil, or of lunatics fresh out of Bedlam!'

The sailors continued to silently study the *Forward* as her preparations came to an end; and not one dared claim that Bosun Johnson had been making fun of the young sailor.

The dog story had already spread across town, and amongst the crowd of bystanders many hoped to see this dog-captain,* almost believing him to be a supernatural creature.

The *Forward* had in fact been in the public eye for several months; the unusual features of her construction, the veil of secrecy, the incognito of the captain, the way Richard Shandon took up the position as ship's commander, the way the crew were chosen, the mysterious destination hardly guessed at by some—everything contributed to giving this brig an extraordinary aura.

For a thinker, a dreamer, a philosopher, nothing is as moving as a ship about to sail; one's imagination gladly follows her fights against the waves, her struggles with the wind, her perilous course that does not always end up in port. Should an unusual feature emerge, the ship may take on a fantastic form, even to minds resistant to the imagination.

The *Forward* was no exception. And if the common run of

spectators could not produce erudite observations like Master
Cornhill, the rumours built up over the last three months were still
enough to keep Liverpudlian tongues wagging.

The brig had been built in Birkenhead, a veritable suburb on the
left bank of the Mersey, linked to the port by the ceaseless to and fro
of the steamboats.

Scott and Co.,* perhaps the most accomplished manufacturers in
Britain, had received the specifications and blueprints from Richard
Shandon, with the tonnage, dimensions, and floor-plan indicated
down to the last detail. An experienced navigator's knowledge could
be sensed in this project. Since Shandon had considerable means at
his disposal, work had started, and proceeded, quickly, as requested
by the unknown proprietor.

The brig was of a solidity to withstand any force. She had clearly
been designed for enormous pressures, since her frame of teak, a sort
of Indian oak renowned for its exceptional hardness, was in addition
reinforced with thick iron hoops. It was even wondered, in the world
of sailors, why the hull of a ship built according to such specifications of resistance was not made from metal plate, like other steamships. To that it was replied that the mysterious engineer must have
had good reasons for his decision.*

Little by little, the brig had taken shape in the shipyard, with her
qualities of strength and elegance impressing the experts. As noted
by the *Nautilus*'s crew, her stem was at right angles to the keel, and
was not protected by a ram, but a steel cutter cast in the foundries of
R. Hawthorn of Newcastle.* This metal prow, shining in the sun, gave
a particular air to the ship, even if in other ways she did not appear
very military. However, a sixteen-pound cannon had been set up on
the fo'c'sle; mounted on a pivot, it could easily be pointed in any
direction. It should be added that the cannon was like the stem: in
spite of everything it did, it could not manage to look warlike.

On 5 February 1860, this strange ship had been launched in the
midst of an immense crowd of spectators, her first contact with the
water being entirely successful.

But if the brig was not a warship, nor a merchant vessel, nor a
pleasure-yacht—for one does not sally forth on excursions with
six years of provisions in the hold—what was she?

A ship designed to look for the *Erebus* and *Terror* and Sir John
Franklin?* Not that either, for in 1859, the year before, Captain

McClintock had returned from the Arctic Ocean, bringing back incontrovertible proof of the loss of the unhappy expedition.*

So did the *Forward* want to attempt the famous Northwest Passage? What was the point? Captain McClure had found it in 1853, and his second-in-command, Lieutenant Cresswell,* had the honour of being the first to sail round the American continent from the Bering Strait to the Davis Strait.

What seemed clear, however, and even indubitable to people qualified, was that the *Forward* was preparing to take on one of the polar regions. Was she going to push towards the South Pole, further than the whaler Weddell, a greater distance than Captain James Ross* had gone? But why, with what purpose?

It can be seen that, although the field of conjectures was extremely limited, imaginations still found a way of getting lost there.

The day after the brig was launched, her boiler arrived from the workshops of R. Hawthorn of Newcastle.

This engine, of the power of 120 horses and with oscillating pistons, was relatively small; but its force was considerable for a ship of 170 tons, in any case amply equipped with sails and benefiting from a remarkable seaway. Her tests had left no doubt on this subject, and even Bosun Johnson couldn't resist giving his opinion to Clifton's friend:

'If the *Forward* uses her sails and propeller at the same time, it's with the sails that she'll get there fastest.'

Clifton's friend had not understood a single word in this proposition, but believed everything possible for a ship personally commanded by a dog.

After the boiler was fitted, the loading of provisions could start; and this constituted no mean task, for the ship was to carry six years' worth of food. There were dried and salt meats, smoked fish, dried biscuit, and flour; mountains of coffee and tea also poured into the holds in enormous avalanches. Richard Shandon supervised the loading of the precious cargo like a past master; it was all stowed, labelled, and numbered in perfect order; a huge provision of the Indian product called pemmican[1] was also taken on board, for it contains many nourishing constituents within a small volume.

---

[1] A preparation of condensed meat.

The nature of the victuals left no doubt as to the duration of the voyage; an experienced observer would have realized at once that the *Forward* was going to sail for polar seas. He just had to see the barrels of lime juice, the lime pastils, or the packets of mustard and sorrel and Cochlearia seeds*—in a word the profusion of powerful remedies against scurvy so vital in sailing to the furthest south or north. Shandon had clearly been advised to pay particular attention to this part of the cargo, because he took extreme care of it, as he did of the ship's medicine chest.

If there were not many guns on board—reassuring timid spirits— the powder-hold was overflowing—a feature sure to frighten them. The single gun on the fo'c'sle could hardly claim to require such amounts, and this gave food for thought. There were also gigantic saws and powerful tools, such as crowbars, sledgehammers, hand-saws, enormous axes, etc., without counting an impressive array of blasting-cylinders, enough to blow up Liverpool Customs-House. All that was strange, if not alarming, without mentioning the rockets, signals, flares, and lamps of a thousand kinds.

The many spectators on New Prince's Docks stopped to admire a long mahogany whaleboat, a ship's boat of tin-plate covered with gutta-percha, and a number of Halkett boats,* sorts of rubber over-coats that could be transformed into vessels merely by blowing into their linings. Everyone felt more and more intrigued, and even excited, since at ebb-tide the *Forward* was going to set sail for its mysterious destination.

2

An Unexpected Letter

THESE are the contents of the letter received by Richard Shandon
eight months previously:

Aberdeen

2 August 1859*

Mr Richard Shandon
Liverpool

Dear Sir,

Please be informed that a sum of £16,000 sterling has been placed in
the care of Messrs Marcuart and Co., bankers of Liverpool.*
Enclosed is a series of banker's orders signed by myself, which will
allow you to withdraw from the above-mentioned Messrs Marcuart
sums amounting to the £16,000 in question.

You do not know me. This is of no consequence. I know you. That
is what counts.

I offer you the place of second-in-command on board the *Forward*
for a campaign which may be long and dangerous.

If not, everything is cancelled. If you accept, you will be paid
£500 as salary, and at the end of each year during the whole
campaign, your salary will increase by one-tenth.

The brig the *Forward* does not exist. You will have it made so that
it can go to sea at the beginning of April 1860 at the latest. Attached
is a detailed plan with a quotation. You will adhere to it scrupulously.
The ship will be built in the workshops of Messrs Scott and Co.,
with whom you will deal directly.

I recommend that you take special care over the crew of the
Forward; it will be composed of a captain, myself, a second-in-
command, you, a third officer, a bosun, two engineers,* an ice-master,
eight sailors, and two stokers—a total of eighteen men if Dr
Clawbonny* of this city is included, who will present himself to you
at the appropriate time.

Those invited to participate in the campaign of the *Forward* should be British,* free, without family, single, sober—the consumption of spirits or even beer will not be allowed on board—and they must be ready for any endeavour or any hardship. You will preferably choose them with a sanguine constitution and thus carrying within them to the utmost degree the generating principal of animal heat.

You will offer them five times their usual pay, with an increase of a tenth for each year of service. At the end of the campaign, each of them will be guaranteed £500, and £2,000 for you. These funds will be payable at Messrs Marcuart and Co., as mentioned above.

This voyage will be a long and painful one, but honourable. You should not hesitate, therefore, Mr Shandon.

Reply to KZ, Poste Restante, Gothenburg, Sweden.

PS On 15 February next you will receive a great Dane with hanging lips, of blackish-brown colour with black horizontal stripes. You will settle him on board and have him fed with barley bread in suet bread soup.[1] You will send confirmation of receipt of the aforesaid dog to the same initials as above, Livorno (Italy).

The captain of the *Forward* will appear and make himself known in due course. At the departure, you will receive new instructions.

KZ

Captain of the *Forward*

3

Dr Clawbonny

RICHARD SHANDON was a good sailor; for he had commanded whaling ships in the Arctic seas many years, with a solid reputation throughout Lancashire. Such a letter could legitimately surprise him; he felt therefore astonished, but with the self-control of the man who has seen it all before.

He satisfied the conditions: no wife, no child, no relatives—a free man if ever there was one. Having no one to consult, he headed straight for Messrs Marcuart and Co., bankers.

If the money's there, he said to himself, the rest will take care of itself.

---

[1] Suet bread or dog biscuit ideal for feeding dogs.

He was received in the banking house with the respect due a man for whom an account of £16,000 is quietly waiting; this point settled, Shandon asked for a blank sheet of paper and in his large sailor's hand sent his acceptance to the address indicated.

The same day he contacted the shipbuilders in Birkenhead, and twenty-four hours later the keel of the *Forward* was already being laid on the blocks of the workshop.

Richard Shandon was a fellow of about forty—robust, energetic, and brave, three qualities useful in a sailor, for they give confidence, vigour, and self-control. He was known to have a jealous, difficult character, so he was never liked by his sailors, but feared. This reputation was not in any case going to make finding a crew difficult, because he was known to be good at coming out the winner.

Shandon was afraid that the mystery attached to the expedition might reduce his room for manoeuvre.

So, he told himself, it's best to keep it quiet; there are sea dogs who would certainly want to know the why and the wherefore of it all, and as I have no information I wouldn't be able to reply. This KZ is certainly a queer fish; but at the end of the day he knows me, he's counting on me; that's enough. As for his ship, she will be finely turned out, and if she isn't heading for the Glacial Sea* my name is not Richard Shandon. But let's keep that to my officers and myself.

Upon which Shandon set about recruiting the crew, adhering to the captain's conditions concerning family and health.

He knew a very devoted, brave fellow, a good sailor, James Wall by name. Wall was about thirty and had already been to the northern seas. Shandon offered him the place of third officer and James Wall accepted without a moment's hesitation. His only wish was to sail and he loved his profession. Shandon told him everything, as he did a certain Johnson whom he made his bosun.

'Not knowing where you're going,' said James Wall, 'is no harm. If we are to look for the Northwest Passage, some do survive.'

'Not always,' replied Master Johnson, 'but that's not a good reason for not going.'

'Anyway, if we've put two and two together,' responded Shandon, 'then we have to admit that the trip will be well organized. This *Forward* will be a fine ship and you can go far with a good engine. Eighteen crewmen is all we need.'

'Eighteen men,' replied Master Johnson; 'as many as the American Kane had for his famous advance towards the Pole.'*

'It's strange', Wall carried on, 'that someone is still trying to sail from the Davis Strait to the Bering Strait. The expeditions sent in search of Admiral Franklin have already cost Britain more than £760,000, but without producing any practical result! Who the devil can still risk his fortune on such a venture?'

'First of all, James,' replied Shandon, 'we are arguing from a mere hypothesis. Are we really going to the northern or southern seas? I'm not so sure. It's perhaps an attempt to make some new discovery. Anyway, a certain Dr Clawbonny will have to turn up sooner or later, and he will undoubtedly know what is what, having been instructed to tell us. So we'll just have to see.'

'Let's just wait then,' said Master Johnson; 'for my part, commander, I'll come up with some solid fellows; and I can already guarantee their animal heat, as the captain says. You can count on me.'

This Johnson was a good man to have; he was familiar with navigation at extreme latitudes. He was quartermaster on the *Phoenix*, which took part in the 1853 expeditions in search of Franklin; this honest sailor even witnessed the death of Bellot, the French lieutenant,* having gone on his excursion across the ice. Johnson knew the Liverpool sailors, and immediately set about recruiting the men required.

Shandon, Wall, and he managed so well that the crew was complete by early December; but the work had not progressed without difficulty; the lure of high pay had attracted many who were at bottom frightened by the plan of the expedition, and more than one resolutely enlisted, only to later go back on his word and his advance, dissuaded from such a venture by his friends. All tried to solve the mystery, overwhelming Commander Shandon with questions. He passed them all on to Master Johnson.

'What can I say, mate?' the bosun invariably answered. 'I don't know any more than you do. But anyway you'll be in the company of lads who are afraid of nothing; that's something! So not so much thinking: take it or leave it!'

And the majority took.

'You understand', the bosun sometimes added, 'that my only difficulty is in choosing. High pay, higher than any in living memory, and then the guarantee of a fine capital sum when we get back: it's a good offer.'

'The fact is', answered the sailors, 'that it's very tempting! Enough to live on for the rest of our lives!'

'I will not hide from you that the voyage will be long, difficult, and dangerous; that is formally stated in our instructions; so you should be aware what you're signing up for; most likely to try all that is humanly possible, and maybe more! As a result, if you don't feel you have a strong heart, a temperament to withstand anything, if you don't have a screw loose, if you don't tell yourself that you have one chance in twenty-two of coming back, if in sum you prefer to bury your bones in one place rather than another, here rather than there, then show me a clean pair of heels and give your place to a braver man!'

'But at least, Master Johnson,' the sailors would persist, their backs against the wall, 'at least you know the captain?'

'The captain is Richard Shandon, my friend—until another one appears.'

Now, it must be said, this really was what the commander thought; he easily ceded to the idea that at the last moment he would receive detailed instructions concerning the purpose of the voyage, and remain chief of the *Forward*. He even liked to spread this opinion when chatting with his officers or monitoring the building of the brig, whose first struts were rising from the Birkenhead yards like the ribs of an upside-down whale.

Shandon and Johnson had strictly followed the recommendation concerning the health of the crew members; all had a reassuring appearance, as well as a principle of heat capable of fuelling the boiler of the *Forward*; their supple limbs and clear and rosy complexions meant they were suited to resisting the intense cold. They were confident and resolute men, energetic and solidly built; but they did not all share an equal vigour; Shandon had even hesitated about taking on some, such as the sailors Gripper and Garry, or the harpooner Simpson, who seemed a little thin; but at least their bones were good and their hearts warm, so their contracts were duly signed.

All this crew belonged to the same variety of Protestantism; during the long campaigns, collective prayer sessions and the reading of the Bible often have to bring together varied souls, sustaining them at times of discouragement; it is thus essential to avoid disagreements.

Shandon knew from experience how useful these practices are, and how much they influence the morale of a crew; so they are always employed on board ships over-wintering in the polar seas.

The crew chosen, Shandon and his two officers turned to the provisions; they strictly followed the captain's instructions, clear, precise, and detailed ones in which the least items were noted in both quality and quantity. Thanks to the bankers' orders at the commander's disposition, all were settled in cash, at a discount of eight per cent, which Richard carefully added to KZ's credit.

Crew, provisioning, cargo—all were ready by January 1860; the *Forward* was already taking form. Not a day passed that Shandon did not visit Birkenhead.

On the morning of 23 January, he was as usual on one of these broad steamboats which have a helm at each end to avoid tacking and thus ensure rapid service between the banks of the Mersey;* there was at that moment one of those frequent fogs, which oblige the river sailors to navigate by compass, although the journey lasts hardly ten minutes.

However thick the fog, it could not prevent Shandon from spotting a short man, rather fat, with a fine and merry face and a pleasant expression, who advanced towards him, took both his hands, and shook them with a warmth, an exuberance, a familiarity that were completely meridional, as a Frenchman would have said.

But if this character was not from the south, it was by a hair's breadth; he spoke, he gesticulated with volubility; his thought had to emerge at any cost, or run the risk of making him blow his top. His eyes, small like those of witty men, and his mouth, large and mobile, were three safety valves which enabled him to let out this overflow of himself; he talked, so much and so fast admittedly, that Shandon could not understand a single word.

The second of the *Forward* did not take long to recognize this small man he had never seen; he had a brainwave, and when the other paused to breathe, Shandon quickly placed these words:

'Dr Clawbonny?'

'Himself in person, commander! I've been looking for you for almost half a long quarter of an hour, asking everyone everywhere! You can imagine how impatient I feel! Five minutes more, and I'd have lost my head! So it's really you, Commander Richard? You really exist? You're not a myth? Your hand, your hand! So that I can take it in mine again! Yes, it really is Richard Shandon's hand! Now if there is a Commander Shandon, there is a brig called the *Forward* he commands; and if he commands her, she will leave; and if she leaves, she will take Dr Clawbonny on board.'

'Eh well, yes, doctor, I am Richard Shandon, there is a brig the *Forward*, and she will leave!'

'That's logical,' answered the doctor, after taking in a generous provision of air; 'it's logical. So you see me happy, every last wish granted! I've been waiting for such a circumstance for a long time, for I wished to undertake a voyage of this sort. Now with you, commander . . .'

'Allow . . .' said Shandon.

'With you,' Clawbonny carried on, not hearing him, 'we're sure to go far, and not retreat an inch.'

'But . . .' Shandon began again.

'Because you are tried and tested, commander, and I know your service record. Ah, you are a fine sailor, you are a fine sailor!'*

'If you would like to . . .'

'No, I won't have your audacity, your bravery, and your ability doubted one moment, even by you! The captain who chose you for second is a man who knows what he's about, I can tell you!'

'But that is not the point,' said Shandon impatiently.

'And what is the point? Don't keep me hanging on a second longer!'

'You don't give me time to speak, heck! Tell me please, doctor, how you come to participate in the expedition of the *Forward*?'

'But by a letter, a good letter which is here, a letter from a good, honest captain, very laconic, but quite adequate!'

And saying this, the doctor handed Shandon a letter as follows:

Inverness

22 January 1860

Dr Clawbonny
Liverpool

If Dr Clawbonny wishes to embark for a long campaign on the *Forward*, he can present himself to Commander Richard Shandon, who has received instructions concerning him.

KZ
Captain of the *Forward*

'The letter arrived this morning, and here I am ready to go on board the *Forward*.'

'But at least', Shandon tried again, 'you know, doctor, what the purpose of the voyage is?'

'Not at all; but what difference does it make? Provided that I go somewhere! I am said to be learned; that is a mistake, commander: I know nothing, and if I have published a few books that are selling not too badly, I was wrong; the public is very kind to buy them! I do not know anything, I repeat, except that I know nothing. Now someone has offered to add to or rather reconstitute my knowledge of medicine, surgery, history, geography, botany, mineralogy, conchology, geodesy, chemistry, physics, mechanics, and hydrography; well I accept, and I assure you that there's no need to beg!'

'Then,' Shandon disappointedly began again, 'you don't know where the *Forward* is bound?'

'I do, commander; it is bound where there is something to learn, discover, study, compare, where you can find other customs, other regions, other peoples to study in the exercise of their functions;* it is going, in short, where I have never been.'

'But in particular?'

'In particular, I have heard that it is to sail towards the boreal seas. Well, northwards!'

'At least you know the captain?'

'Not in the least! But he's a good man, believe me.'

Once the two had got off at Birkenhead, the commander brought the doctor up to date, and the mystery enflamed his imagination. The sight of the brig caused him transports of joy. From that day on, he did not leave Shandon's side, and came each morning to inspect the hull of the *Forward*.

He was in fact specially charged with supervising the installation of the ship's medical kit. For he was a doctor, and even a good doctor, this Clawbonny, although not practising much. A doctor at 25 like everyone, he was a true scientist at 40; very well known throughout the city, he became an influential member of the Literary and Philosophical Society of Liverpool.* His private means enabled him to distribute some advice which was not any less valuable for being free; liked as an eminently likeable man must be, he never hurt a fly, not even himself; lively and talkative, admittedly, but ready to give the shirt off his back, and stand back to back with everyone.

When the rumour of his installation on board the *Forward* spread across the city, his friends moved heaven and earth to hold him back, which entrenched him even more in his idea; and when the doctor had entrenched himself in something, it took considerable skill to prise him out!

From that day on, the rumours, speculations, and apprehensions grew and grew; but that did not prevent the *Forward* from being launched on 5 February 1860. Two months later, she was ready to go to sea.

On 15 March, as announced in the captain's letter, a Great Dane had been sent by railway from Edinburgh to Richard Shandon's address in Liverpool.* The animal appeared surly, cowardly, even a little sinister, with a singular look in its eyes. The name *Forward* could be read on its copper collar. The same day the commander settled it on board, and confirmed receipt to the initials indicated in Livorno.

The crew of the *Forward* was thus complete, except for the captain. It read as follows:

> KZ, captain
> Richard Shandon, commander
> James Wall, third officer
> Dr Clawbonny
> Johnson, bosun
> Simpson, harpooner
> Bell, carpenter
> Brunton, chief engineer
> Plover, second engineer
> Strong (black), cook
> Foker, ice-master
> Wolsten, armourer
> Bolton, sailor
> Garry, ditto
> Clifton, ditto
> Gripper,* ditto
> Pen, ditto
> Waren, stoker.

4

Dog-Captain

THE day of departure, 5 April, arrived. The inclusion of the doctor slightly reassured people. Where the worthy scientist planned to go, one could follow. However, most of the sailors remained anxious, and Shandon, fearing that some might desert and cause empty places on board, longed with all his heart to be at sea. Once the coast was out of sight, the crew would accept the situation.

Dr Clawbonny's cabin was at the end of the poop deck, and it occupied the whole stern of the ship.

The cabins of the captain and the second, placed slightly back, looked out over the deck. The captain's room remained hermetically closed, after being filled with various instruments, pieces of furniture, travel clothing, replacement garments, books, and utensils, as listed in a detailed note. As the stranger had requested, the key was sent to him at Lubeck; in other words, no one but he could enter his quarters.

This detail upset Shandon, reducing as it did his chances of being overall in command. As for his own cabin, he had perfectly adapted it to the presumed voyage, knowing by heart what was needed for a polar expedition.

The third officer's room was in the orlop deck, which provided a vast room for the sailors; the men were very comfortable, and would have been unlikely to find such accommodation on any other ship. They were looked after like precious cargo; a vast stove stood in the centre of the common room.

Dr Clawbonny was in his element; he had taken possession of his cabin as early as 6 February, the day after the *Forward*'s first launching.

'The happiest animal', he said, 'would be a snail which could grow a shell when it wished, and I will try to be an intelligent snail.'

And, upon my word, his cabin was on track for being a shell he would not leave for a long time; the doctor took a scientist's or child's pleasure in arranging his scientific baggage. His books, his herbaria, his pigeon-holes, his precision instruments, his physics apparatus,

his collection of thermometers, barometers, hygrometers, pluvi-
ometers, telescopes, compasses, sextants, charts, and maps, the
flasks, powders, and bottles of his very complete medical chest—all
this was classified with an organization that would have shamed the
British Museum. This space of six square feet contained incalculable
riches; the doctor had only to stretch out his hand, to instantaneously become a doctor, a mathematician, an astronomer, a
geographer, a botanist, or a conchologist.

He was proud of these arrangements, it must be admitted, and
happy in his floating sanctuary, not able to hold more than three of
his thinnest friends. In the event, his friends indeed rushed there in
numbers which soon became awkward, even for a man as easygoing
as the doctor; and, unlike Socrates, he ended up saying:

'My house is small, but may heaven grant that it is never full of
friends!'*

To complete this description of the *Forward*, suffice it to say that
the Great Dane's kennel was built right under the window of the
mysterious cabin; but her wild occupant preferred to wander around
the ship's 'tween-deck and holds; it seemed impossible to tame, and
nobody was able to get the better of its odd nature; it was heard
making lamentable howls, especially at night, echoing through the
spaces of the ship in a most sinister fashion.

Was it missing its master? Was it instinct on the eve of a perilous
voyage? Was it a presentiment of the dangers to come? The sailors
opted for this last reason; a few joked about it, seriously taking the
dog for a member of a diabolical species.

One day, the brutal Pen ran after it to hit it, and fell so awkwardly
on the edge of the capstan that it split open his skull. As can be
guessed, the accident was ascribed to the fantastic animal.

Clifton, the most superstitious of the crew, pointed out that when
on the poop, this dog always walked on the windward side; and later,
when the brig was tacking on the open sea, the surprising animal
changed position after each putting about, keeping to windward just
as the captain of the *Forward* would have done.

Dr Clawbonny's kindness and caresses would have tamed a tiger,
but he tried in vain to get into the dog's good books; he was wasting
his time and pains.

Moreover, the animal did not answer to any of the names in the
hunting calendar. So the men finished up calling it Captain, because

it appeared perfectly au fait with customs on board. The dog had obviously sailed. It was consequently easy to understand the bosun's pleasant response to Clifton's friend, and why this assumption did not find many disbelievers; several repeated it with a laugh, expecting one fine day to see the dog return in human form and start commanding operations in a resounding voice.

If Richard Shandon did not feel such apprehensions, he was not entirely free from worry, and on the evening of 5 April, the day before departure, he discussed the subject with the doctor, Wall, and Master Johnson, in the wardroom of the poop deck. These four characters were at the time enjoying a tenth tot of rum, undoubtedly their last, because the regulations in the letter from Aberdeen specified that the whole crew, from the captain down to the stoker, had to be teetotal, and would not find wine, or beer, or spirits on board, except in case of illness and on the doctor's orders. Now for an hour the conversation had centred on the departure. If the captain's indications were accurate, Shandon was to receive a letter the following day containing his final instructions.

'If this letter doesn't tell me the name of the captain,' said the commander, 'it must at least say the destination of the ship. Without that, where to sail for?'

'Well in your place, Shandon,' answered the impatient doctor, 'I would leave even without the letter; it will follow us, have no doubt.'

'You don't doubt anything, doctor! But what point of the sphere would you sail for?'

'The North Pole, it's obvious; no doubt is possible.'

'No doubt possible!' Wall retorted. 'And why not the South Pole?'

'The South Pole?' exclaimed the doctor. 'Never! Would the captain have had the idea of exposing a brig to sailing the entire Atlantic! So try to reflect a little, my dear Wall.'

'The doctor has an answer for everything.'

'Go for North,' said Shandon. 'But, tell me, doctor, Spitzbergen? Greenland? Labrador? Or Hudson Bay? If all roads lead to the same place, namely the uncrossable ice-barrier, there are a lot of them, and I would find it very hard to decide on one or the other. Do you have a clear answer you can give me, doctor?'

'No,' he answered, upset to have no reply, 'but to conclude, if you don't get a letter, what will you do?'

'I will not do anything; I will wait.'

'You won't leave!' Clawbonny cried, his glass shaking with his despair.

'Certainly not.'

'That's best,' quietly said Master Johnson, while the doctor paced round the table, unable to stay in one place. 'Yes, best; but waiting too long can have unfortunate consequences: first, the season is good, and if we are to head north, we must profit from the break-up of the ice to get through Davis Strait; besides, the crew are getting more and more worried; their friends and fellow sailors are pushing them to leave the *Forward*, and such opinions could play us a nasty trick.'

'It should be added that if panic set in among our sailors,' said James Wall, 'they'd desert us down to the last man; and I'm not sure, commander, that you'd be able to get a crew together again.'

'But what to do?' exclaimed Shandon.

'What you said,' said the doctor; 'wait, but wait until tomorrow before giving up. The promises of the captain have been kept up to now with a regularity that is a good sign; there is therefore no reason to believe that we won't be informed of our destination in due course; I do not doubt a single moment that tomorrow we'll be sailing through the Irish Sea; so, my friends, I propose a last grog to our happy voyage; it starts in a slightly inexplicable way, but with mariners like you it has a thousand chances of finishing well.'

And all four clinked glasses a last time.

'Now, commander,' added Master Johnson, 'if I have some advice to give you, it is to prepare everything to start; the crew must believe you certain of what you're about. Tomorrow, whether a letter arrives or not, get ready to sail; do not light your boilers; the wind seems to be holding up; nothing will be easier than to go free; have the pilot come on board; when the tide is right, leave the docks; go and anchor beyond the headland of Birkenhead; our men will have no communication with land any more, and if that diabolic letter finally arrives, it will find us there like anywhere.'

'Well spoken, my brave Johnson!' said the doctor holding his hand out to the old sailor.

'So be it!' answered Shandon.

All then headed back to their cabins, and in an agitated sleep waited for sunrise.

The following day, the first delivery of letters had taken place in the town and not one carried the name of Commander Richard Shandon.

Nevertheless, he made his preparations for departure, the rumour spread immediately through Liverpool, and, as we have seen, an extraordinary multitude of spectators rushed on to the wharves of New Prince's Dock.

Many of them came aboard the brig, some to embrace a comrade one last time, some to dissuade a friend, some to look at the strange ship, some to finally know the purpose of the voyage, and people murmured to see the commander more silent and reserved than ever.

He had his reasons for that.

Ten o'clock sounded. Even eleven o'clock. The tide was due to go down at around one in the afternoon. From the poop, Shandon cast an anxious glance at the crowd, seeking to surprise the secrecy of his destiny on an anonymous face. But in vain. The sailors of the *Forward* executed his orders in silence, not taking their eyes off him, still waiting for a message which did not come.

Master Johnson finished the preparations of the equipment. The weather was overcast, and the swell very strong outside the docks; the wind was blowing from the south-east with a certain violence, but it was still easily possible to leave the Mersey.

At midday, still nothing. Dr Clawbonny strode agitatedly, squinting, gesticulating, 'impatient for sea', as he said with a certain Latin elegance. He felt moved, no matter what he did. Shandon bit his lips to blood.

At this moment, Johnson approached and said to him:

'Commander, if we want to profit from the tide, we should not waste time; we will not be out of the docks for a good hour.'

Shandon threw a last glance around him, and consulted his watch. The time for the midday collection had passed.*

'Go!' he said to his bosun.

'Under way, you!' shouted the latter, ordering the spectators to empty the bridge of the *Forward*.

A certain movement occurred then in the crowd, heading for the ship's gangway and thence the quay, while the brig's sailors detached the last mooring ropes.

But the inevitable confusion of these bystanders, pushed back by the sailors without much care, was increased further by the dog's howls. From the forecastle this animal suddenly sprang through the solid mass of visitors. It barked in a dull tone.

The crowd divided before it; it jumped on to the poop deck, and, incredibly, but as observed by a thousand witnesses, this dog-captain held a letter in its teeth.

'A letter!' Shandon cried. 'So is he on board?'

'He was surely here, but is not any more,' answered Johnson, gesturing to the deck completely empty of the inconvenient crowd.

'Captain, Captain! Here!' exclaimed the doctor, trying to take the letter which the dog removed from his hand with violent leaps. He seemed to want to give the message only to Shandon himself.

'Here, Captain!' he said.

The dog approached; Shandon took the letter without difficulty, and Captain then uttered three clear barks in the midst of the deep silence which reigned on board and on the quays. Shandon held the letter without opening it.

'But read it! Read it!' the doctor cried.

Shandon looked. The envelope, without date or indication of place, only read:

> Commander Richard Shandon, on the brig the *Forward*.

Shandon opened the letter, and read:

You will head for Cape Farewell. You will reach it on 20 April. If the captain does not appear on board, you will enter Davis Strait, and cross Baffin Bay to Melville Bay.*
KZ
Captain of the *Forward*

Shandon carefully folded this laconic letter, put it in his pocket, and gave orders for departure. His voice, which rang out alone amongst the whistling of the east wind, had something solemn in it.

Soon the *Forward* was out of the docks, and, directed by a Liverpool pilot, whose small cutter followed at a distance, it found the current of the Mersey. The crowd rushed on to the external wharf which surrounds the Victoria Docks, in order to glimpse this strange ship one last time. The two topsails, the foresail, and the brigantine were quickly hoisted, and, under this sail, the *Forward*, worthy of its name, after rounding the headland of Birkenhead, headed at full speed into the Irish Sea.

5

On the High Seas

THE wind, patchy but favourable, sent down its April squalls with vigour. The *Forward* cut the sea swiftly, with her propeller now hoisted and no obstacle to movement. At about three o'clock she met the steamer plying between Liverpool and the Isle of Man, with the three legs of Sicily quartered on its paddlewheel boxes. Its captain hailed her from his ship, the last goodbye that the crew of the *Forward* were destined to hear.

At five the pilot returned command of the vessel to Richard Shandon and got into his cutter again, which soon tacked into the wind and disappeared south-westwards.

In the evening the brig rounded the Calf of Man, at the southern extremity of the island. The water was very choppy that night; the *Forward* sailed well, leaving the Point of Ayre* to the south-east and heading for the North Channel.

Johnson was right: at sea the sailors' nautical instinct took over; seeing the quality of the vessel they forgot the strangeness of their situation. Life on board settled into a routine.

The doctor intoxicatedly inhaled the marine breeze; he walked vigorously in the gusts and he had quite good sea-legs for a scholar.

'She's a fine thing, is the sea,' he told Master Johnson, going back on deck after lunch. 'I'm making her acquaintance a little late but I want to catch up.'

'You're right, Dr Clawbonny; I would give all the continents of this world for a corner of ocean. Sailors are said to soon tire of their profession; I've been navigating for forty years and I'm as happy as on day one.'

'What perfect bliss to feel a good ship under your feet, for, if my impression is correct, the *Forward* sails lustily!'

'It is correct, doctor,' said Shandon, joining the two: 'she's a fine vessel, and I must admit that never has one designed for ice navigation been better endowed and fitted out. It reminds me that thirty years ago Captain James Ross set out in search of the Northwest Passage . . .'

'On the *Victory*,' the doctor chipped in keenly, 'a brig of about the same tonnage as ours and like her fitted with a steam-engine . . .'*

'What, you knew that?'

'Judge for yourself,' he replied; 'engines were then in their infancy, and the *Victory*'s caused the ship one or two harmful delays; after repairing it piece by piece, Captain James Ross took it apart in the end, but then abandoned it on his first over-wintering.'

'Upon my word,' said Shandon, 'you *are* well informed, I can see.'

'I suppose so; I have looked at Parry, Ross, and Franklin's books and Kennedy, Kane, and McClintock's reports,* and you always retain something. I will even add that McClintock and his *Fox*, a screw-driven brig of the same sort as ours, travelled more easily and directly to the goal than all that went before.'

'Perfectly true; McClintock is a fine sailor, for I've seen him at work. You could add that like him we will be in the Davis Strait by April and if we manage to get through the ice, we will be well on our way.'

'Unless we get trapped the very first year', said the doctor, 'by the floes from the north of Baffin Bay like the *Fox* in 1857 and have to winter amongst the pack ice.'*

'We must hope we'll be more fortunate, Mr Shandon,' replied Master Johnson; 'and if we don't go where we want with a ship like the *Forward*, we should give up once and for all.'

'Anyway,' the doctor carried on, 'if the captain is on board, he'll know better than us what needs doing, since we're completely in the dark, as we can't deduce the purpose of the voyage from his singularly laconic letter.'

'It's already something to know the route to follow,' replied Shandon rather animatedly, 'and now for a good month, I imagine, we can manage without any supernatural intervention from that stranger and his instructions. But anyway, you know what I think of him.'

'Ha ha, like you I thought he'd given up command of the ship, and wouldn't arrive on board. But . . .'

'But what?' said Shandon with annoyance.

'But since his second letter, I've had to change my ideas.'

'And why might that be, doctor?'

'Because although the letter specifies the route to follow, it doesn't tell you the *Forward*'s destination; and we will eventually need to know where we're going. How can a third letter get to us, I ask you, since we're on the open sea! The postal services of Greenland are surely not up to scratch. Look, Shandon, I imagine that fellow is waiting for us at some Danish settlement, Holsteinborg or Uppernawik; he's probably gone there to complete his freight of sealskins and buy his sledges and dogs, in short to get together everything needed for a voyage to the Arctic seas. So I won't be surprised if I see him coming out of his cabin one fine morning, to take command of the ship in the least supernatural way possible.'

'Maybe,' replied Shandon dryly; 'but in the meantime the wind's freshening, and it's not sensible to risk the top gallant sails in such weather.'

He left the doctor and gave orders to brail the topsails.

'He's keen on it,' the doctor said to the bosun.

'More's the shame, as you could easily be right, Dr Clawbonny.'

On the Saturday evening, the *Forward* rounded the Mull[1] of Galloway and bearings were taken of its lighthouse, to the north-east; during the night the Mull of Kintyre was left to the south and, to the west, Fair Head on the Irish coast. At three in the morning the brig passed Rathlin Island to port, disembogued from the North Channel, and was in the Ocean.

It was Sunday, 8 April; this day is very carefully observed by the British, above all by sailors; accordingly, reading from the Bible, which the doctor willingly took on, occupied some of the morning.

The wind was then veering to a hurricane and pushing the brig on to the Irish coast; the waves ran very high and the ship rolled heavily. If the doctor did not suffer from seasickness, it was because he had no desire to, for he had every opportunity. At midday Malin Head was disappearing southwards; it was the last land in Europe that these bold sailors were to see, and some of those endlessly scrutinizing it would undoubtedly never see it again.

The latitude observed was $55°\ 57'$* and the longitude, using the chronometers, $7°\ 40'$.[2]

The hurricane died down at about nine in the evening; the *Forward*, a fine windjammer, maintained her north-westerly route. It had been possible to judge her nautical qualities that day; and as the Liverpool pundits had noted, she was above all a sailing ship.

---

[1] Peninsula.

[2] From the Greenwich meridian.

The following days, the *Forward* continued making good north-westerly progress; the wind became southerly, and the sea took on a large swell. The brig was now using full sail. A few petrels and puffins came and floated above the poop; the doctor dexterously shot one of the latter, which fortunately fell on board.

Simpson the harpooner seized it and brought it to its owner.

'A nasty piece of game, Dr Clawbonny.'

'Which will on the contrary make an excellent meal, my friend!'

'What, are you going to eat that?'

'And you will too, my good man,' laughed the doctor.

'Yerck!' replied Simpson. 'It's oily and rank like all seabirds.'

'Perhaps; but I've got my own way of cooking such game, and if you recognize it as a seabird afterwards, I promise I'll never kill another one in my life.'

'Are you a cook then, Dr Clawbonny?' asked Johnson.

'A scholar has to know a little of everything.'

'Then be careful, Simpson,' replied the bosun; 'the doctor is a clever man and he's going to make this puffin taste like the finest grouse.'

The truth is that the doctor entirely got the better of his fowl; he skilfully took off the fat, situated entirely under the skin, mostly on the thighs, and with it disappeared the rank and fishy smell, which are perfectly legitimate reasons for complaint in a bird. Prepared in this way, the puffin was declared excellent, even by Simpson.

During the hurricane, Richard Shandon had taken account of the qualities of the crew; he had analysed the men one by one as any commander must do, to prepare for future dangers; he knew what to expect.

James Wall, an officer completely devoted to Richard, understood and executed well, but sometimes lacked initiative; as third in command, he was in the right place.

Johnson, accustomed to tussles with the ocean and an old Arctic hand, had nothing to learn in terms of sangfroid and bravery.

Simpson the harpooner and Bell the carpenter were trustworthy men, slaves to duty and discipline. The ice-master Foker, an experienced seaman from the Johnsonian school, would surely provide vital service.

Of the other sailors, Garry and Bolton seemed the best: Bolton was a joker, cheerful and chatty; Garry, a boy of thirty-five with an energetic face, but a bit pale and sad.

The three sailors, Clifton, Gripper, and Pen, seemed less keen and resolute; they often grumbled. Gripper had even wanted to break off his engagement before the *Forward* left; only a sort of shame had kept him on board. If things went well and there were not too many dangers, or manoeuvres to execute, these three men could be relied on; but they required satisfying nourishment, for their hearts were in their bellies. Although forewarned, they adapted poorly to the teetotal regime and missed their mealtime brandy and gin; they made up for it, however, with coffee and tea, freely available on board.

As for the two engineers, Brunton and Plover, plus the stoker Waren, they had been content so far to cross their arms and do nothing.

Shandon knew therefore what to expect from each man.

On 14 April, the *Forward* cut the main current of the Gulf Stream, which, after following the eastern coast of America as far as Newfoundland, heads north-east and up the coast of Norway. They were now at 51° 37′ latitude and 22° 58′ longitude, or 200 miles from the tip of Greenland.* It got colder; the thermometer went down to thirty-two[1] (0°C), or freezing.

The doctor, without yet putting on his Arctic clothing, had donned his sea attire, following the sailors and officers; he was a fine sight in his high boots—into which he lowered himself in one go— his huge oilcloth hat, and his trousers and jacket of the same material; in the heavy rain and broad waves shipped by the brig, he looked like some marine animal, a comparison which invariably flattered his pride.

For two days the sea was extremely rough; the wind veered north- west and slowed the *Forward* down. From 14 to 16 April the swell remained very bad; but on the Monday there came a heavy down- pour, which stilled the sea almost immediately. Shandon mentioned this peculiarity to the doctor.

'Well,' he replied, 'that confirms the curious observations of the whaler Scoresby, who belonged to the Royal Society of Edinburgh,* which I have the honour to be a corresponding member of. You can see that when it rains the waves have less force, even if there is a

---

[1] Fahrenheit.

fierce wind. When the weather is dry, in contrast, the sea would be more troubled by a lesser wind.'

'But how is this phenomenon explained, doctor?'

'It's quite simple; it isn't.'

At that moment the ice-master, on watch on the top gallant cross-trees, reported a floating object to starboard, fifteen miles to leeward.

'An iceberg in these waters!' exclaimed the doctor.

Shandon aimed his glass in the direction indicated, and confirmed the pilot's observation.

'That *is* strange!'

'Are you surprised?' asked the commandant with a laugh. 'What, are we lucky enough to have found something at last?'

'It surprises me without surprising me,' replied the doctor with a smile, 'because in 1813 the brig *Ann of Poole*, coming from Greens-pond, was caught in genuine ice-fields at forty-four degrees north, and because Dyment, its captain, counted hundreds of icebergs!'*

'Well,' said Shandon, 'you're still a mine of information!'

'Oh not really,' modestly replied the agreeable Clawbonny, 'although I must add that ice has in fact been found at even lower latitudes.'

'There you're not telling me anything, my dear doctor, for, having been a cabin boy on the sloop-of-war the *Fly* . . .'*

'In 1818,' added the doctor, 'at the end of March, or virtually in April, when you passed between two huge islands of floating ice, on the forty-second parallel.'

'You're amazing.'

'But it's true; and since we're two degrees further north, there's no reason for me to be surprised at meeting a floating mountain broadside to the *Forward*.'

'You're a well of learning, doctor,' replied the commander, 'and all we need to do is pull up the bucket.'

'Well, I'll dry up quicker than you think; and now if we could observe this curious phenomenon close up, Shandon, I'd be the happiest of doctors.'

'Just so. Johnson,' Shandon called to his bosun, 'the wind, it seems to me, is beginning to freshen.'

'Yes sir,' replied Johnson; 'we're not gaining much, and the currents of the Davis Strait will soon come into play.'

'You're right, Johnson, and if we want to be in sight of Cape

Farewell by 20 April we must use steam, or else be pushed on to the coast of Labrador. Mr Wall, kindly give instructions to light the boilers.'

The captain's orders were carried out, and an hour later the steam had acquired pressure. The sails were furled while the screw, churning the billows with its blades, forcefully pushed the *Forward* into the teeth of the north-west wind.

6

The Great Polar Current

SOON the flocks of birds, more and more numerous, petrels, puffins, and warblers,* inhabitants of these desolate shores, showed they were nearing Greenland. The *Forward* was heading north at speed, leaving to leeward a long trail of black smoke.

At about eleven on Tuesday, 17 April, the ice-master reported the first sight of ice blink.[1] It was at least twenty miles to the north-north-west. Despite the very thick clouds, this strip of dazzling white brightly lit up the whole of the atmosphere near the horizon. Experienced sailors on board could not mistake this phenomenon, recognizing from its whiteness that the blink had to come from a vast field of ice situated about thirty miles beyond the range of vision, being produced by a reflection.

In the evening the wind veered round to the south, or favourable; Shandon was able to haul up a good set of sails and extinguish the boilers as an economy measure. The *Forward* headed for Cape Farewell under its topsails, jib, and foresail.

At three o'clock on the eighteenth an ice stream was spotted: a thin white line, but of dazzling colour, contrasting strongly with the twin lines of sea and sky. It was clearly drifting from the east coast of Greenland rather than Davis Strait, for the ice prefers to stay to the west side of Baffin Bay. An hour later the *Forward* was passing through loose pieces of ice stream; in the densest parts, the ice, although stuck together, followed the movements of the swell.

---

[1] The remarkable, resplendent colour the air becomes when above a great extent of ice.

The following day at dawn the lookout reported a ship. It was the *Valkyrien*, a Danish corvette* sailing on the opposite tack from the *Forward*, heading for the Newfoundland Banks. The current from the strait could be felt and Shandon had to press sail against it.

At that time the commander, the doctor, James Wall, and Johnson were on the poop deck examining the direction and strength of the current. The doctor asked if this current was of uniform strength in Baffin Bay.

'To be sure,' replied Shandon, 'and sailing ships find it difficult to fight.'

'All the more,' added James Wall, 'since it is found on both the east coast of America and the west coast of Greenland.'

'Well, that supports those seeking the Northwest Passage! This current moves at about five knots and it is difficult to imagine that it originates at the end of a bay.'

'All the better reasoned, doctor,' continued Shandon, 'because if this current runs from north to south, an opposing current in Bering Strait, which runs from south to north, must be its source.'

'Hence, gentlemen, it must be agreed that America is completely detached from the polar landmasses and that the waters of the Pacific move round its coasts and into the Atlantic. Anyway the greater height of the waters of the Pacific is another confirmation that they flow towards the seas of Europe.'

'But there must be facts supporting this theory, and if there are,' Shandon added with a certain irony, 'our universal savant will surely know them.'

'Upon my word,' replied the latter with pleasant satisfaction, 'if it interests you, I will say that whales wounded in Davis Strait were captured some time later near Tartary with European harpoons still in their flanks.'*

'So unless they rounded Cape Horn or Cape of Good Hope, they must necessarily have gone round the northern coast of America. That's indisputable, doctor.'

'If, however, you were still not convinced, my good Shandon,' said the doctor smiling, 'I could produce further facts, such as the flotsam Davis Strait is full of, larches, aspens, and other tropical wood species. Now we know that the Gulf Stream would prevent this wood from entering the strait, so when it comes out it can only have got in through Bering Strait.'

'I'm convinced, doctor, and I admit that it would be hard to remain a disbeliever with you around.'

'Upon my word,' said Johnson, 'abreast is a timely illustration of what we're talking about. I can see a piece of wood of fine size; if the commander allows we'll go and fish out this tree-trunk, hoist it on board, and ask it what country it hails from.'

'Good idea,' said the doctor; 'the example after the rule.'

Shandon gave orders; the brig headed for the piece of wood and soon the crew had hauled it on deck, not without difficulty.

It was a mahogany trunk, gnawed by worms to its very heart— otherwise it could not have floated.

'It's perfect!' the doctor enthusiastically exclaimed. 'Since the Atlantic's currents can't have carried it into Davis Strait, since it can't have been sent into the polar basin by the rivers of northern America, and since this tree grows near the equator, it is evident that it has travelled directly from Bering. And notice, gentlemen, the marine worms that have devoured it; they belong to tropical species.'

'This clearly contradicts opponents of the famous Passage,' said Hall.

'It simply kills them,' replied the doctor. 'Look, I'm going to tell you the story of this mahogany. It was carried into the Pacific by some river of the isthmus of Panama or Guatemala; from there the current carried it along the coast of America to Bering Strait, where it had to enter the polar seas willy-nilly. As it's not so old or water-logged, it must have left recently; it must have successfully overcome the obstacles of the long succession of straits culminating in Baffin Bay and, seized by the boreal current, came through Davis Strait to be taken on board the *Forward* for the great joy of Dr Clawbonny, who asks permission to keep a sample.'

'Go ahead,' said Shandon, 'but let me in turn inform you that you won't be the only owner of such a piece. The Danish Governor of the island of Disko . . .'

'. . . on the coast of Greenland, possesses a mahogany table made from a trunk fished out in identical circumstances; I know, my dear Shandon; well, I'm not jealous of his table for, if only I had a bit more space I'd have enough wood to build myself an entire bedroom.'

During the night of Wednesday the wind blew with extreme violence; there was more driftwood visible; the coastal approach would have been dangerous at a season when ice mountains are frequent; the commander therefore had the sails brought down and the *Forward* ran under only the foresail and staysail.

The thermometer fell below freezing. Shandon distributed suitable clothing to the crew: woollen jacket and trousers, flannel shirt, and wadmel stockings like those worn by Norwegian country folk. Each man was also equipped with a pair of watertight sea boots.

As for Captain, its natural fur was enough; it seemed oblivious to the temperature changes; it must have already been through such an experience, and anyway a Dane had no right to complain. It was hardly ever seen, staying hidden in the darkest parts of the ship.

In the evening at 37° 2′ 7″ W the coast of Greenland put in a brief appearance* through a clearing in the fog; through his telescope the doctor glimpsed a succession of peaks furrowed by broad glaciers; but the fog quickly closed again on this vision, like a theatre curtain that falls at the most interesting moment in the play.

On the morning of 20 April the *Forward* was in view of a 150-foot iceberg, stranded at this spot since time immemorial; thaws have no effect on it and respect its strange forms. Snow saw it;* in 1829 James Ross made an exact drawing of it; and in 1851 the French lieutenant Bellot, on board the *Prince Albert*, perfectly observed it.

Of course the doctor wanted to keep an image of this famous mountain and he made a highly successful sketch of it.

It is not surprising that similar masses have run aground and so got permanently attached to the land; for each foot out of the water they have about two under,* giving this one a draft of about eighty fathoms.[1]

At last Cape Farewell was sighted, in a temperature of only twelve (−11°C) at midday and under a snowy sky and fog. The *Forward* had arrived on the day planned; if the unknown captain wished to come and shoot the sun in this diabolical weather, he could not complain.

So, the doctor said to himself, here is the famous cape, with such an appropriate name! Many have sailed past it like us, never to see it again! Is this therefore an eternal adieu said to your friends in Europe? You passed here, Frobisher, Knight, Berley, Vaughan, Scroggs, Barents, Hudson, Blosseville, Franklin, Crozier, and Bellot, never to return home again,* and this was indeed your Cape Farewell!'

----

[1] Four hundred feet.

It was in about 970 that sailors left Iceland and discovered Greenland. In 1498 Sebastian Cabot reached the fifty-sixth parallel; from 1500 to 1502 Gaspar and Miguel Corte Real* reached sixty degrees north, and in 1576 Martin Frobisher reached the bay bearing his name.

To John Davis the honour of discovering his strait in 1585;* on a third voyage two years later, this brave mariner and great whaler reached the seventy-third parallel, or only twenty-seven degrees from the Pole.

Many went more or less through Davis Strait in search of the Northwest Passage, whose discovery would have singularly shortened the distance between the New and Old Worlds: Barents in 1596, Weymouth in 1602, James Hall in 1605 and 1607, Hudson naming this vast bay which eats so deeply into the lands of America, and James Poole in 1611.*

In 1616 Baffin found Lancaster Sound on Baffin Bay; he was followed in 1619 by Jens Munk* and in 1719 by Knight, Berley, Vaughan, and Scroggs, of whom no trace has ever been found.

In 1776 Lieutenant Pickersgill, sent to meet Captain Cook trying to return via Bering Strait, advanced to the sixty-eighth degree; the following year Young reached Woman's Islands* with the same purpose.

Next came James Ross, who travelled round the coast of Baffin Bay in 1818 and corrected the hydrographical errors of his predecessors.

Finally in 1819 and 1820 the celebrated Parry threw himself into Lancaster Sound, reached Melville Island after innumerable difficulties, and won the bonus of £5,000 promised by Act of Parliament to British sailors who first crossed the hundred and seventieth meridian above the seventy-seventh parallel.*

In 1826 Beechey touched Chamisso Island; James Ross wintered from 1829 to 1833 in Prince Regent Inlet* and discovered the Magnetic Pole, amongst other important work.

At this time Franklin was following the land route to explore the northern coast of America from the Mackenzie River to Point Turnagain; Captain Back was following in his footsteps from 1823 to 1835, and these explorations were completed in 1839 by Messrs Dease and Simpson and Dr Rae.*

Finally Sir John Franklin left England in 1845 on the *Erebus* and the *Terror* in search of the Northwest Passage; he entered Baffin Bay but, following his contact with Disko Island, no news of his expedition was ever received.

This disappearance resulted in many searches which led to the discovery of the Passage and the exploration of these profoundly broken-up polar lands; the most intrepid British, French, and American sailors threw themselves into these terrible waters, and thanks to their efforts, the tormented and difficult map of this region was finally able to take its place in the archives of the Royal Geographical Society of London.

The strange history of these lands appeared to the doctor's imagination as, leaning over the rail, he followed the brig's long wake. The names of these brave mariners crowded into his memory, and in the frozen archways of the pack ice he thought he glimpsed the pale ghosts of those who had never come back.

7

*Davis Strait**

THAT day the *Forward* cut an easy route through the half-broken ice; the wind was good, but the temperature very low; as the wind played over the ice-fields, it brought their cold breath with it.

The nights required the most vigilant attention, since the floating mountains were squeezed together in this narrow strait; often the horizon contained a hundred of them; they were breaking off from the high shore under the combined assault of the waves undermining them and the influence of the April weather, to sink or melt into the ocean depths. Long processions of wood were also encountered, and had to be avoided. The crow's nest was accordingly installed at the summit of the foresail; it consisted of a barrel with a movable base from which the ice-master, partly sheltered from the wind, could survey the sea, signal the sight of ice, and even direct operations if necessary.

The nights were short; due to the refraction, the sun had reappeared on 31 January, and was beginning to stay further and further above the horizon. But the snow blocked the view and although not producing darkness, made navigation difficult.

On 21 April Cape Desolation appeared out of the mists; the operations were tiring the crew; since the brig had entered the floes the sailors had not had a moment's rest; it would soon be necessary to use steam to force a way through the piled-up blocks.

The doctor and Master Johnson were chatting together at the rear while Shandon was snatching a few hours' sleep. Clawbonny enjoyed the conversation of the old sailor whose many voyages had provided him with an interesting and practical education. The doctor felt great friendship and the bosun reciprocated.

'You see, Dr Clawbonny, this area is not like others; it's called "green land", but there are not many weeks in the year when it deserves that name.'

'Who knows, friend Johnson, whether this land didn't deserve it in the tenth century? More than one such revolution has affected our globe, and I might astonish you greatly if I told you that, according to the Icelandic chroniclers, two hundred villages flourished on this landmass eight or nine hundred years ago!'

'You wouldn't astonish me so much, Dr Clawbonny, that I wouldn't believe you, for it's a sad country.'

'Well, however sad, it still offers sufficient accommodation for its inhabitants and even for civilized Europeans.'

'Maybe! At Disko and Uppernawik we'll meet people who live in such a climate, but I've always thought they did it through force of circumstance not choice.'

'I can easily believe it; however, people get used to anything, and these Greenlanders don't seem to be as deserving of pity as the workers of our great cities; they can be unhappy, but they most certainly aren't miserable; although I say "unhappy", this word doesn't convey my thought; in fact, if they don't enjoy the comfort of the temperate lands, those used to this tough climate clearly find pleasures in it we can't begin to imagine!'

'That must be true, Dr Clawbonny, since heaven is just; but many voyages have brought me to these coasts and my heart has always sunk on seeing these sad solitudes; the capes, promontories, and bays should have had happier names, since Capes Farewell and Desolation aren't exactly designed to attract navigators!'

'I've also thought that, but these names have an inestimable geographical interest; they describe the adventures of those who invented them; as regards Davis, Baffin, Hudson, Ross, Parry,

Franklin, and Bellot, if I encounter Cape Desolation I soon find Mercy Bay; Cape Providence stands opposite Anxiety Port; Repulse Bay brings me back to Cape Eden,* and on leaving Point Turnagain I go and rest in Refuge Bay; I have before my eyes this unceasing succession of dangers, failures, obstacles, successes, despairs, and triumphs, mixed with my country's great names, and like a series of historic medals this nomenclature traces the entire history of its seas.'

'Well reasoned, Dr Clawbonny, and may we meet more Success Bays than Capes Despair on our journey!'

'I hope so, Johnson, but tell me: are the crew beginning to get over their panic?'

'They're beginning to, but, to tell the truth, since we entered the strait they've been getting obsessed about the fantastic captain; some were expecting him to appear at the tip of Greenland, but we've seen nothing so far. Look, Dr Clawbonny, just between you and me, doesn't that astonish you a little?'

'Yes indeed, Johnson.'

'Do you believe this captain exists?'

'Undoubtedly.'

'But what reasons could have made him act like this?'

'To be frank, Johnson, I believe that this man wants to take the crew so far they can't go back any more. Now if he had appeared on board at the departure, with everyone wanting to know the destination of the ship, he would have been embarrassed.'

'But why?'

'My goodness, if he wants to try some superhuman endeavour, to penetrate where so many have failed, do you think he'd have been able to recruit a crew? Whereas, once under way, you can get so far that going forwards is the only choice.'

'It's possible, Dr Clawbonny; I've known a few intrepid adventurers whose mere name terrified mariners and who wouldn't have found a soul to go on their dangerous expeditions.'

'Except me.'

'Me too, so as to go with you! I think our captain is amongst such adventurers. We'll see in the end; I imagine that on the coast of Uppernawik or Melville Bay this good stranger will quietly move in and tell us just how far his whim plans to take the ship.'

'Presumably, Johnson, but the difficulty will be in getting as far as

Melville Bay. See how the ice surrounds us on every side! It's hardly letting the *Forward* through. Look at that immense plain!'

'In whalers' language, Dr Clawbonny, we call that an ice-field, an unbroken surface whose limits cannot be seen.'

'And over there, that broken field, those long pieces whose edges more or less stick together?'

'It's a pack; if it's round, we call it a patch, and stream when it's stretched out.'

'And, that floating ice there?'

'Drift ice; if it was a bit taller, it would be called icebergs, meaning mountains; they are dangerous for ships, which must take care to avoid them. Look at that one over there, on the ice-field, a protuberance produced by the pressure of the ice; we call that a hummock; if the base of the protuberance was submerged, we'd call it a calf; names had to be given to all that to sort it out.'

'Ah, it's a fantastic sight!' continued the doctor as he contemplated the marvels of the northern seas; 'and your imagination is set afire by all these tableaux.'

'Yes, the ice floes sometimes take on fantastic shapes and the men like to explain them in their own way.'

'Johnson, admire that collection of ice blocks. Doesn't it look exactly like a strange town, an oriental town with its minarets and mosques under the pale light of the moon? And further on are a long succession of Gothic arches just like the Chapel of Henry VII* or the Houses of Parliament.'[1]

'Truly, Dr Clawbonny, all tastes are catered for, but to live in those towns and churches would be dangerous and you mustn't even get too close. The minarets could easily turn upside down and the smallest one would smash a ship like the *Forward*.'

'And people dared come into these seas without steam at their command! How to believe that a sailing ship could have found a way through these moving shoals?'

'They did, all the same, Dr Clawbonny; when the wind was against them, and that has happened to me a few times, me who is talking to you today, they patiently anchored themselves to one of the blocks. They drifted more or less with it and in the end they waited for the best time to carry on. Admittedly, this method of

---

[1] Buildings in London.

travel took months where with a bit of luck we'll only need a few days.'

'It seems to me that the temperature is still falling.'

'That'd be a shame, as we need a thaw for these masses to split up and disappear into the Atlantic. Anyway there are more of them in Davis Strait because the land narrows between Cape Walsingham and Holsteinborg; but in May and June we'll find more navigable seas above the sixty-seventh degree.'

'But we have to get through first.'

'We have to get through, Dr Clawbonny; in June or July we'd have found the route free, as whaling ships do; but the orders were precise: we had to be here in April. So if I'm not mistaken, our captain is an energetic and hardy chap, who has an idea: he only left so early because he wanted to go far. But in the end, time will tell.'

The doctor was right about the falling temperature: at midday the thermometer indicated only six (−14°C) and a north-west wind was blowing, which, while clearing the sky, helped the current push floating ice into the path of the *Forward*. In fact the floes did not behave consistently; it was not rare to encounter some, especially the tallest ones, subject to an underwater current at their bases and drifting in the opposite direction.*

The difficulties of such navigation are therefore easy to understand; the engineers did not have a moment's rest; operating the steam was done from the deck by means of levers which instantaneously opened, closed, or reversed it, according to the orders of the duty officer. Sometimes the ship had to accelerate to reach a gap in the ice-fields or to race an iceberg threatening to close the only way out; or else a block would turn upside down without warning, forcing the brig to suddenly reverse to avoid being destroyed. This mass of ice, dragged, piled-up, amalgamated by the strong north current, rushed into the pass and if a hard frost came down, it would erect a barrier that the *Forward* could not cross.

Uncountable numbers of birds lived in these waters; petrels and warblers fluttered here and there with deafening cries; many seagulls with large heads, short necks, and small beaks could be seen stretching their long wings as they playfully braved the snow whipped up by the storm. The winged creatures' animation enlivened the landscape.

Large amounts of wood were drifting by, colliding noisily; a few sperm whales with enormous swollen heads approached the ship, but there was no question of hunting them, however much Simpson the harpooner wanted to. In the evening several seals were seen swimming amongst the huge blocks, their noses out of the water.

On the twenty-second, the temperature fell further; the *Forward* piled on steam to head for the passes; the wind had decided to stay north-westerly; the sails were furled.

During that Sunday the sailors had little work to do. After the divine office, conducted by Shandon, the crew went hunting guillemots and took a large number. Properly cooked in the Clawbonnian manner, they provided an agreeable addition to the officers' and crew's tables.

At three in the afternoon the *Forward* sighted Kin of Sael east-a-quarter-north-east and the mountain of Sukkertop south-east-a-quarter-east-half-east; the sea was very stormy; from time to time a vast fog suddenly fell from the grey sky. However, an accurate shooting of the sun could be carried out at midday. The ship was at 65° 20′ N, 54° 22′ W. Two degrees still needed to be covered to find a more open sea.

The following three days, 24, 25, and 26 April, were a continual struggle with the ice; managing the boiler became very tiring; each minute the steam had to be suddenly closed down or reversed, and would escape whistling through the valves.

Looming icebergs could only be guessed at through the thick fog by judging the dull explosions of avalanches; the ship then veered immediately; it risked colliding with floating masses of freshwater ice, remarkable for the transparency of their crystal and as hard as rock. Richard Shandon always topped up his provision of water by taking several tons of this ice on board each day.

The doctor could not get used to the optical illusions produced by the refraction in these waters; in effect icebergs often appeared to him as small white shapes close by, whereas they were in reality ten or twelve miles from the brig; he tried to accustom himself to this remarkable phenomenon in order to be able to rapidly correct the error of his eyes in future.

After a while, the crew were broken with fatigue, from hauling the ship over the ice-fields and using long poles to push away the most menacing blocks; and yet on Friday, 27 April the *Forward* was still held up at the uncrossable limit of the Arctic Circle.

8

What the Crew Say

HOWEVER, by slipping adroitly through passes, the *Forward* managed to gain a few minutes northwards; but they would soon have to attack instead of avoiding the enemy: ice-fields several miles long were approaching and as these moving masses often produce a pressure of more than ten million tons they had to be wary of their embraces. Ice saws were therefore set up outside the ship, to be brought into use immediately if necessary.

Some of the crew accepted this hard work philosophically but others complained, although they did not yet refuse to obey. While installing the tools, Garry, Bolton, Pen, and Gripper shared opinions.

'My God,' Bolton said gaily, 'I don't know why I keep thinking that in Water Street there's a fine pub where one tacks nicely between a glass of gin and a bottle of porter. Can you see it from here, Gripper?'

'To tell you the truth,' replied that sailor, who was generally in a bad mood, 'I can't.'

'A manner of speaking, Gripper; obviously, in these snow towns which Dr Clawbonny loves so much there's no trace of a bar where a good sailor can wet his lips with a half-pint or two of brandy.'

'That you can be sure of, Bolton, and you could add that here there's nothing to refresh you properly. A funny idea to take people gallivanting off to northern seas, miles from anything to drink.'

'So, Gripper, have you forgotten what the doctor said? We can't be under the influence if we want to avoid scurvy, stay healthy, and go far.'

'But I don't want to go far, Garry, and if you ask me it's enough to have got this far and forced passes the devil doesn't want us to.'

'Well we'll get stuck!' replied Pen. 'To think that I've already forgotten what gin tastes like.'

'But', said Bolton, 'remember what the doctor told you.'

'Oh,' replied Pen in his big rough voice, 'mere words. And how do you know they're not using our health as an excuse to economize on drink?'

'That bugger Pen is perhaps right,' said Gripper.

'Come on,' replied Bolton, 'his nose is too red for that, so if he loses a bit of colour from sailing like this, he won't have anything to complain about.'

'What's my nose got to do with it?' roughly replied the sailor, attacked at his weak point. 'My nose doesn't need your advice; it doesn't ask for it, so mind your own nose's business!'

'Come on, calm down, Pen. I didn't think your nose was so sensitive. Hey, I like a good glass of whisky as much as the next man, especially in this weather, but at the end of the day if it does more harm than good, I'll willingly give it up.'

'You'll give it up,' said the stoker Waren, joining in; 'well not everybody on board has.'

'What do you mean, Waren?' said Garry, staring at him.

'I mean that for one reason or another, there is drink on board and I imagine they manage quite well at the rear.'

'And how do you know?'

Waren had no reply; he liked to hear the sound of his own voice, as the expression goes.

'You see, Garry,' said Bolton; 'Waren has no idea.'

'Well,' answered Pen, 'we'll ask the commander for a ration of gin; we've earned it and we'll see what he says.'

'I don't think you should do anything like that,' replied Garry.*

'Why not?' cried Pen and Gripper.

'Because the commander will refuse. You knew what the operating conditions were when you came on board; you should have thought of it then.'

'And also,' replied Bolton who often took Garry's side as his character pleased him, 'Richard Shandon is not in charge; he obeys, just like the rest of us.'

'Obeys who?' asked Pen.

'The captain.'

'Always this terrible captain!' exclaimed Pen. 'And can't you see that there are as many captains as pubs in this neighbourhood? It's a way of politely refusing what we've got the right to demand.'

'But there *is* a captain,' replied Bolton, 'and I would bet twice my pay that we'll see him fairly soon.'

'Yes,' said Pen, 'there's one I'd like to have a few words with, face to face.'

'Who was talking about the captain?' said a newcomer at this moment.

It was the sailor Clifton, rather superstitious and envious at the same time.

'Does anyone know anything more about him?' he added.

'No!' came the reply in chorus.

'Well I'm expecting to find he's moved into his cabin one fine morning without anyone knowing how he got there.'

'Come on,' replied Bolton; 'you imagine, Clifton, that that fellow is a sprite, an elf, like those that haunt the Highlands.'

'Laugh as much as you want, Bolton, you won't change my mind. Every day as I pass his cabin, I peer through the keyhole and one of these mornings I'll come and tell you who or what this captain looks like.'

'Eh, confound him,' said Pen, 'he'll look the same as everybody, your captain. And if he's a fellow who wants to take us somewhere we don't want to go, we'll tell him where to get off.'

'Fine,' said Bolton, 'here's Pen who doesn't even know him and who already wants to argue.'

'Who doesn't know him?' said Clifton like someone who knew a great deal. 'We're not sure he doesn't.'

'What the heck do you mean?' asked Gripper.

'I have inside knowledge.'

'But we don't.'

'Well, hasn't Pen already discussed it with him?'

'With the captain?'

'Yes, the dog-captain, for they're one and the same.'

The sailors looked at each other, hardly daring to reply.

'Man or dog,' said Pen through gritted teeth, 'one of these days that animal will get a big surprise, I'm telling you.'

'Come on, Clifton,' Bolton said seriously; 'are you really claiming, as Johnson joked, that the dog really is the captain?'

'Definitely,' replied Clifton with conviction; 'and if you were more observant you'd have noticed his strange behaviour.'

'What? Come on, spit it out.'

'Haven't you seen the way he saunters over the poop with an air of authority, studying the ship's sails as if on watch?'

'True,' said Gripper, 'and one evening I even found him with his paws on the helm.'

'I don't believe it,' said Bolton.

'And now,' Clifton carried on, 'doesn't he leave the ship each night to wander over the ice-fields without worrying about the bears or the cold?'

'Spot on,' said Bolton.

'Can you see that animal seeking out the company of men like an honest dog, prowling near the kitchen, or making eyes at Master Strong when he brings in some fine joint for the commander? Can't you hear him at night when he goes two or three miles from the ship, howling to give you the shivers, which aren't easy to feel in such a temperature? And have you ever seen that dog eating? It takes nothing from no one. It never touches its food and unless someone is secretly feeding it, I'm right to say that he lives without eating. Now if that isn't fantastic, I'm just an animal.'

'Upon my word,' replied Bell the carpenter, who had listened to the whole of Clifton's argument, 'upon my word that might just be the case.'

The other sailors remained silent.*

'Tell me,' asked Bolton, 'where's the ship going?'

'I have no idea; Richard Shandon will receive the rest of his instructions in due course.'

'But from who?'

'From who?'

'Yes, how?' said Bolton, becoming insistent.

'Come on, Bell, say something,' echoed the other sailors.

'I have no idea,' replied the carpenter, embarrassed in turn.

'Eh, from the dog-captain!' exclaimed Clifton. 'He's already written once and can easily do it again.'

'Oh, if only I knew half of what that animal knows, I could be First Lord of the Admiralty.'

'So,' Bolton concluded, 'you're sticking to your idea that the dog is the captain?'

'Yes, like I told you.'

'Well,' said Pen in a dull voice, 'if that animal doesn't want to die as a dog, he'd better hurry up and turn into a man, for I swear I'll fix him.'

'But why?' asked Garry.

'Because I want to,' brutally replied Pen; 'and no one tells me what to do.'

'Enough chatting, boys,' shouted Master Johnson, intervening as

the conversation took a turn for the worse; 'to work. I want the saws
set up at double speed: we need to get through the ice-field.'

'Well, it's a Friday!' replied Clifton shrugging his shoulders.
'You'll see that the Arctic Circle isn't cut so easily!'

For whatever reason, the efforts of the crew were to little avail all
day. Thrown at full steam against the ice-fields, the *Forward* still
failed to split them. She was forced to anchor for the night.

On Saturday the temperature fell again, due to an east wind. The
weather cleared up and one's eyes could range far over these white
plains made dazzling by the reflection of the sun's rays. At seven in
the morning the thermometer read minus eight (−21°C).

The doctor was tempted to remain quietly in his cabin and reread
the Arctic voyages, but, as usual, he asked himself what would be the
least pleasant thing to do at this moment. He replied that going up
on deck and helping the men with the manoeuvres wouldn't be
much fun in this temperature. So, true to his rule of conduct, he left
his well-heated cabin and came to assist with hauling the ship. He
looked wonderful in the green glasses he used to protect his eyes
from the harmful reflections, and on later occasions he was always
careful to use his snow spectacles to avoid opthalmia, very frequent
at this high latitude.

By evening the *Forward* had gained several miles northwards,
thanks to the men's work and Shandon's skill at seizing every
opportunity. At midnight she crossed the sixty-sixth parallel and
when the line reported twenty-three fathoms' depth, Shandon realized that he was on the shallows where HMS *Victory* touched. The
land was thirty miles east and getting closer.

But then the mass of ice, stationary until now, began to break up
and move; the icebergs seemed to spring up from every point of the
horizon; the brig was soon caught up in a succession of moving
shoals of irresistible destructive power; the operations became so
difficult that Garry, the best helmsman, took the wheel; the mountains were starting to close up again behind the brig. It was essential
to get through this icy fleet, and safety as much as duty dictated
moving ahead. The difficulties were increased because Shandon
found it impossible to know the ship's direction amongst these
points, all moving and offering no stable perspective.

The crew were divided into two teams, starboard and port, and
each man took a long pole with an iron tip and pushed back the most

menacing pieces of ice. Soon the *Forward* ventured into a tall pass that was so narrow on both sides that the end of its yards grazed the walls, as hard as rock. Foot by foot she moved into a sinuous valley filled with flurries of snow while the floating ice collided and broke with sinister cracking noises.

However, it soon became clear that there was no way out of this valley; an enormous floating block was moving fast towards the *Forward*; it seemed impossible to avoid it—or to go back, for the channel was already blocked.

Shandon and Johnson stood at the prow and studied the situation. Shandon showed the helmsman the direction to take with his right hand, and with his left gave James Wall, stationed near the engineer, orders for operating the engine.

'How's it all going to end?' the doctor asked Johnson.

'It's in God's hands now.'

The 100-foot block of ice was only a cable from the *Forward* and about to destroy it in its path.

'Fxxx,' exclaimed Pen.

'Silence!' exclaimed a voice, impossible to recognize in the storm.

The ice was hurtling towards the brig and there came an indefinable moment of anguish. The men abandoned their boat-hooks and ran to the stern despite Shandon's orders.

Suddenly a terrible noise was heard; a veritable waterspout, raised by an enormous wave, fell over the ship's deck; the crew uttered a cry of terror, while Garry steered a steady course despite the terrifying yaw of the *Forward*.

When the horrified regards turned to the ice mountain, it had disappeared; the pass was free and behind it a long channel lit by the low rays of the sun provided a route for the brig.

'Well, Dr Clawbonny,' said Johnson, 'will you explain this phenomenon to me?'

'It's quite simple, my friend, and it happens often; when these floating masses split up during thaws, they sail separately and in perfect equilibrium, but little by little they move south, where the water is slightly warmer; their bases, loosened by hitting other pieces, begin to melt and be undermined; so there comes a time when their centres of gravity are displaced and then these masses turn over. But if that iceberg had rolled two minutes later, it would have fallen on the brig and destroyed her as it did so.'

9

*A New Letter**

THE Arctic Circle had finally been crossed; at midday on 30 April the *Forward* passed Holsteinborg; picturesque mountains rose above the eastern horizon. The sea seemed virtually free of ice, or rather its ice could easily be avoided. The wind veered south-east, and under her foresail, spanker, topsails, and top gallant sails, the brig sailed into Baffin Bay.

The day was exceptionally calm and the crew could take a little rest; large numbers of birds swam and swooped around the ship; amongst others the doctor noticed some specimens of alca alle,* very similar to the teal, with white breasts and black necks, wings, and backs; they dived strongly and often stayed underwater for more than forty seconds.

This day would not have been marked by anything new, had the following event not happened, however extraordinary it may seem.

At six in the morning, on returning to his cabin after his watch, Richard Shandon found a letter on his table whose envelope read:

Commander Richard Shandon
On board the *Forward*
Baffin Bay

Shandon could not believe his eyes but before taking cognizance of this strange letter, he called for the doctor, James Wall, and the bosun, and showed it to them.*

'It's strange,' said Johnson.

It's charming, thought the doctor.

'We shall finally know the secret!' exclaimed Shandon.

With a quick hand he tore the envelope, and read the following:

off Cape Walsingham
Monday, 30 April

Commander,

The captain of the *Forward* is pleased with the self-control, skill, and courage that your officers, men, and you have shown in recent circumstances; he requests that you convey his gratitude to the crew.

Please head due north to Melville Bay, and from there you will attempt to enter Smith Sound.*

KZ

Captain of the *Forward*

'And that's all?' cried the doctor.

'That's all.'

The letter fell from Shandon's hands.

'Well,' said Wall, 'this ghost captain no longer talks of coming on board; I deduce he'll never come.'

'But how did this letter arrive?' said Johnson.

Shandon was silent.

'Mr Wall is right,' replied the doctor, who had picked up the letter to study it from every angle; 'the captain won't come on board for a good reason.'

'Which is?' Shandon asked keenly.

'Because he's already here.'

'Already here!' cried Shandon. 'What do you mean?'

'Otherwise how do you explain the arrival of the letter?'

Johnson nodded in agreement.

'It's not possible!' said Shandon energetically. 'I know all the crew; the captain can't have been amongst them since the ship left. It's not possible, I repeat. There's not one of them I haven't seen a hundred times in Liverpool over the past two years. Your reasoning is inadmissible, doctor!'

'Then what do you admit, Shandon?'

'Anything except that. I agree that this captain or one of his men may have been able to use darkness and fog, or anything you want, to slip on board; we are not far from land; there are Eskimo kayaks that can pass unnoticed through the ice; so somebody could have come to the ship and deposited the letter. The fog was thick enough to make this idea feasible.'

'And the brig invisible,' replied the doctor. 'If we didn't spot an intruder slipping on board how could he have found the *Forward* amongst all the fog?'

'He couldn't have,' said Johnson.

'So I come back to my hypothesis. What do you think, Shandon?'

'Anything you want,' replied Shandon with fire, 'except the idea this man could be on board my ship.'

'Perhaps,' added Wall, 'amongst the crew there is one of his men who has received his instructions.'

'Perhaps,' said the doctor.

'But who?'* asked Shandon. 'I know all my men, I repeat, and have done for ages.'

'Anyway,' added Johnson, 'if this captain does show up, whether man or devil, we will greet him; but there is another lesson, or rather piece of news, to be deduced from this letter.'

'Namely?' asked Shandon.

'That we have to head not only for Melville Bay but into Smith Sound.'

'You're right,' replied the doctor.

'Smith Sound,' Richard Shandon repeated mechanically.

'So it's obvious that the destination of the *Forward* is not to look for the Northwest Passage, since we will be leaving on our left the only entrance to it, namely Lancaster Sound. It's a sign that our navigation on the unknown seas will be difficult.'

'Yes, Smith Sound,' replied Shandon; 'that's the route the American Kane took in 1853, at what danger! For a long time he was thought lost at those frightening latitudes. In the end, since we have to head in that direction, we will, but how far? To the Pole?'

'And why ever not?' cried the doctor.

This crazy idea made the bosun shrug his shoulders.

'Anyway,' added James Wall, 'to come back to the captain, if he does exist, on the Greenland coast I can only see the establishments of Disko and Uppernawik where he can be waiting for us. In a few days we'll know what's what.'

'But, aren't you going to let the crew know about the letter?' the doctor asked Shandon.

'Begging the commander's pardon,' said Johnson, 'I would do nothing.'

'And why?'

'Because all this extraordinary stuff, this fantastic aspect, is likely to upset the men; they're already worried how an expedition which has started in this way will end up. Now if we push them into the supernatural, that could have unfortunate effects, and at critical moments we would not be able to rely on them. What do you say, commander?'

'And you, doctor, what do you think?'

'Master Johnson seems to me to be reasoning wisely.'

'And you, James?'

'Without a better alternative, I agree with these gentlemen.'

Shandon thought for a few moments; he reread the letter with care.

'Gentlemen, your opinion is certainly good, but I cannot follow it.'

'And why is that, Shandon?' asked the doctor.

'Because the instructions in this letter are unambiguous; they say I must inform the crew of the captain's congratulations; now I have always blindly obeyed his orders so far, however they were transmitted to me, and I cannot . . .'

'However . . .' said Johnson, who feared how such a communication would affect the sailors.

'My good Johnson,' continued Shandon, 'I understand your insistence; your reasons are excellent, but just read:

'". . . he requests that you communicate his gratitude to the crew."'

'Act accordingly,' said Johnson, who was in fact a strict observer of discipline. 'Should the crew be assembled on deck?'

'Yes.'

The news of a communication from the captain spread immediately through the ship. The sailors quickly took up their stations and the commander read out the mysterious letter.

A heavy silence greeted this reading; the crew broke up, lost in a thousand conjectures; Clifton had plenty of fuel for all the ravings of his superstitious imagination; the role he attributed in this event to Captain-Dog* was considerable and he invariably saluted when by chance he saw him going past.

'I did tell you', he would say to the sailors, 'that this animal knew how to write!'

No reply came to this remark, and even Bell the carpenter would have found it difficult to respond.

It was obvious to everyone that even if the captain was not on board, his shadow or spirit was watching; from that point on, the wisest ones refrained from sharing their assumptions.

At midday on 1 May the position was observed as 68° N, 56° 32′ W. The temperature had risen and the thermometer read twenty-five (−4°C).

The doctor watched with amusement the frolics of a polar bear and her two cubs on the edge of a pack attached to land. Accompanied by Wall and Simpson, he set off to hunt her in the ship's boat; but the animal, not in a belligerent mood, quickly led her young away, and the doctor had to give up following them.

Cape Chidley was rounded during the night in a favourable wind, and soon the high mountains of Disko were looming on the horizon; the Bay of Godhavn,* the residence of the Governor-General of the Danish settlements, was left to starboard. Shandon did not consider it useful to stop, and soon went past the Eskimo canoes trying to reach him.

Disko Island is also called Whale Island; it is from this point that, on 12 July 1845, Sir John Franklin wrote to the Admiralty for the last time. Captain McClintock also put in at the island on 27 August 1859, bringing home the certain proofs of the loss of the Franklin expedition.

The doctor noticed the conjunction of these two facts; this sad parallel produced many memories, but soon the heights of Disko had disappeared from sight.

There were now many icebergs on the coasts, which the strongest thaws fail to remove; this continuous succession of crests took on the strangest forms.

The following day, at about three o'clock, Sanderson's Hope was sighted to north-east; the land was fifteen miles to starboard; the mountains seemed to be reddish-brown. In the evening several whales of the species called finners, due to the fins on their backs, came and played amongst the trains of ice, sending air and water out from their blowholes.

It was during the night of 3 to 4 May that, for the first time, the doctor saw the sun touch the edge of the horizon without sinking its luminous disc behind it; since 31 January its path across the sky had got longer each day and the light was now continuous.

For people not used to it, this persistence of daylight is a continuous reason for astonishment and even tiredness; it is hard to believe how necessary for ocular health night's shades are; the doctor experienced real pain before he got used to this permanent brightness, made more excruciating by the reflection from the icy plains.

On 5 May the *Forward* crossed the seventy-second parallel. Two months later it would have met lots of whaling ships operating at these high latitudes, but the strait was not yet free enough to allow such ships to enter Baffin Bay.

The following day the brig passed Woman's Islands and arrived in view of Uppernawik, the northernmost settlement Denmark possesses on these coasts.

10

Dangerous Navigation

SHANDON, Dr Clawbonny, Johnson, Foker, and Strong the cook got into the whaleboat and headed for shore.

The Governor, his wife, and his five children—all of Eskimo race—politely came to meet the visitors. The doctor, in his capacity as philologist, had a little Danish, which sufficed to establish very friendly relations; in addition Foker, the expedition interpreter as well as ice-master, knew about twenty words of Greenlandic, and with twenty words you can go far if you're not too ambitious.

The Governor was born on Disko Island and had never left his native land; he did the honours of his town, made up of three wooden houses, for him and the Lutheran minister, plus a school and shops, provisioned from shipwrecked vessels. The rest consisted of snow huts into which the Eskimos enter by crawling through a single opening.

A large part of the population had come out to meet the *Forward* and a few natives ventured into the bay in their kayaks, fifteen feet long and at most two wide.

The doctor knew that 'Eskimo' means 'eater of raw fish',* but also that the name is considered an insult in the country; so he made no bones about calling the inhabitants Greenlanders.

And yet from their oily sealskin clothes, their boots of the same material, from all this greasy and repugnant clothing that does not allow men and women to be told apart, it was easy to see what food these people ate. In addition, like all fish-eating peoples, leprosy attacked them in certain parts, but their health was not any the worse for that.

The Lutheran minister and his wife, whom the doctor had hoped to talk to, happened to be visiting Prøven, south of Uppernawik; so he was reduced to talking to the Governor. This government leader did not seem very literate; a little less, he would have been an ass; a little more, he would have been able to read.

Nevertheless, the doctor asked him about the trade, behaviour, and customs of the Eskimos, and he learned, in sign language, that seals were worth about £40 delivered to Copenhagen; a bearskin could be sold for forty Danish dollars, a blue fox skin, four, and a white fox skin, two or three.

To complete his instruction, the doctor also wished to visit an Eskimo hut; it is hard to conceive how far a savant is prepared to go when he wants to become savvier; fortunately the opening of these huts was too narrow, and so the enthusiast could not get in. It was a lucky escape, for nothing is more disgusting than this jumble of dead and living things, seal meat and Eskimo flesh, rotten fish and filthy clothes, that furnishes a Greenland home; not a single window to renew the unbreathable air; only a hole at the top, which lets the smoke out but not the smell.*

Foker gave these details to the doctor, but the worthy savant swore at his corpulence all the more. He would have liked to judge these emanations *sui generis* for himself.

'I am sure that you get used to them in the long run.'

'In the long run' perfectly sums up the good Clawbonny.

During the latter's ethnographic studies, Shandon was busy following instructions and procuring means of transport over the ice; he had to pay £4 for a sledge and six dogs, and still the natives created difficulties before actually handing them over.

Shandon would have liked to engage Hans Christian, a skilful dog driver who took part in Captain McClintock's expedition, but this Hans was at that time in southern Greenland.*

Next came the big question on people's minds: was there in Uppernawik a European waiting for the *Forward*? Did the Governor have any knowledge of a stranger, probably a Briton, settling in the area? When his last contacts with whaling or other ships had been?

To such questions the Governor replied that no stranger had disembarked on this part of the coast for more than ten months.

Shandon asked for the names of the last whalers to arrive; he did not recognize any of them; it was far from encouraging.

'You will admit, doctor, that it's hard to make sense of it all.

Nothing at Cape Farewell, nothing on Disko Island, nothing at Uppernawik!'

'Tell me "nothing in Melville Bay" in a few days' time, dear Shandon, and I will recognize you as the only captain of the *Forward*.'

The whaleboat returned to the brig in the evening, bringing back the visitors; as a change of diet, Strong had got hold of several dozen eider-duck eggs, twice as big as hen eggs and with greenish shells. It was not much, but very refreshing all the same for a crew on a diet of salt meat.

The wind turned favourable the following day but Shandon did not order getting under way; he wanted to wait another day to set his mind at ease, by leaving time for any member of the human race to join the *Forward*. He even had the sixteen-pounder fired every hour, which thundered with a roar between the icebergs; but he only succeeded in frightening the clouds of mollymawks* and roaches. In the night several rockets were launched into the air. But in vain. They had to resolve to leave.

At six in the morning on 8 May, the *Forward*, under topsails, foresail, and main top gallant sail, lost sight of the settlement of Uppernawik and its hideous racks along the shore, from which hang seal intestines and deer stomachs.

The wind was south-easterly and it rose to thirty-two (o°C). As the sun cut through the fog, the ice loosened a little under its dissolving action.

However, the reflections from the white rays had an unfortunate effect on several crewmen's sight. Wolsten the armourer, Gripper, Clifton, and Bell suffered from snow-blindness, a sort of eye problem which is very common in the spring and produces many cases of loss of sight amongst the Eskimos. The doctor advised these four men, and his companions in general, to cover their faces with a veil of green gauze, and he was the first to follow his own advice.

The dogs bought by Shandon at Uppernawik were quite wild; however, they began to get used to the ship and Captain got on reasonably well with his new comrades; he seemed to know their habits. Clifton was not the last to point out that Captain must have already had relations with his Greenland congeners. The latter, always starved or insufficiently fed on land, thought only of building themselves up with the diet on board.

On 9 May the *Forward* passed the westernmost of the Baffin

Islands at a distance of only a few cables. The doctor noticed several
rocks in the bay between the islands and the shore, of the sort called
Crimson Cliffs; they were covered with red snow like fine carmine,
to which Dr Kane ascribes a purely vegetable origin.* Clawbonny
would have liked to study this remarkable phenomenon close up, but
the ice did not allow the coast to be approached; although it was
generally getting warmer, it was easy to see that the icebergs and the
ice streams were building up in the north of Baffin Bay.

Since Uppernawik the land had looked different, and huge glaciers
stood out on the horizon against a greyish sky. On the tenth, the
Forward left Kingston Bay on the right, near the seventy-fourth
parallel; Lancaster Sound debouched to the sea several hundred
miles further west.

But soon the immense expanse of water disappeared under vast
fields, on which rose regular mounds as if a single substance had
turned to crystal. Shandon had the boilers lit and until 11 May the
Forward wove her way through the sinuous passes, her black smoke
tracing against the sky the route she was following over the sea.

New obstacles soon occurred; the passes closed up with the continual movement of the floating masses; at every moment the danger
was that water would disappear under the *Forward*'s prow, and if she
happened to be 'nipped'* it would be difficult to get her out again.
Everyone knew, everyone thought about it.

Accordingly, a few signs of hesitation emerged on board this aimless
ship, with no known destination, madly seeking to head northwards;
amongst these men used to danger, many forgot the financial benefits, and regretted coming so far. A certain demoralization could
already be felt, increased further by Clifton's fears and the remarks
of ringleaders like Pen, Gripper, Waren, and Wolsten.

To the crew's mental worries were soon added exhausting
fatigues, for on 12 May the brig was completely surrounded; its
steam was powerless. A path through the ice-fields had to be opened.
Using saws was very difficult on floes up to six or seven feet thick;
when two parallel cracks ran over the ice for a distance of 100 feet,
the ice between them had to be cut by means of an axe and a handspike; then anchors were dragged along and fixed into holes made
with a large auger. Then working the capstan began, and the ship
was bodily hauled; the biggest difficulty consisted of making the
broken pieces go under the floes, to make passage for the ship, for

they had to be pushed down by means of perches, long poles with iron tips.

In sum, work with the saw, with hauling, at the capstan, with the poles, continuous work, arduous and dangerous in the midst of fog or thick snow, the relatively low temperature, eye problems, mental worries—everything contributed to weakening the crew of the *Forward* and affecting their minds.

When sailors are working with an energetic, audacious, convinced man who knows what he wants, where he is going, what goal he is aiming for, then a confidence buoys them up despite their better judgement. In their hearts they are united with the leader, strong with his strength, and calm with his calm. But on the brig, the commander was felt to be lacking in assurance, to be hesitating in the face of this unknown purpose and destination. Despite the energy of his character, his weakness was betrayed through changes in orders, incomplete manoeuvres, unwise reflections—a thousand details unbeknownst to him but visible to his crew.

But also Shandon was not the captain of the ship, second only to God; a sufficient reason in itself for people to end up discussing his orders; now from discussion to refusal to obey is only a short step.

The malcontents soon rallied the first engineer to their ideas, who until then had been a slave to duty.

On 16 May, six days after the *Forward* reached the ice-field, Shandon had gained less than two miles northwards. The ship was in danger of staying trapped in the ice until the next season. The situation was getting serious.

At about eight in the evening Shandon and the doctor, accompanied by the sailor Garry, set out on a journey of discovery over the immense plains; they were careful not to get too far from the ship, for it was becoming difficult to find landmarks in these white solitudes, whose appearance changed continuously. The refraction produced strange effects; the doctor remained amazed; when he thought he had a jump of only a foot to do, it became five or six feet; or else the opposite occurred, and in both cases the result was a fall, if not dangerous at least highly painful on these shards of ice, as hard and sharp as glass.

Shandon and his two companions set out to find practicable passes; three miles from the ship, they managed, with some difficulty, to climb an iceberg about three hundred feet high.

From there, their view extended over this desolate jumble, like a gigantic town with its obelisks overturned, its spires overturned, its palaces overturned in a trice. Genuine chaos. The sun painfully dragged itself over a spiky horizon to cast long oblique rays of a light without heat, as if athermanous substances had been placed between it and this sad country.

The sea appeared entirely frozen as far as the eye could see.

'How will we get through?' asked the doctor.

'I'm not sure,' replied Shandon, 'but we will pass, even if we have to use gunpowder to blow up these mountains; I certainly won't let myself be trapped until the spring.'

'As happened to the *Fox*, more or less in these waters. Bah,' said the doctor, 'we'll pass with a bit of philosophy! You'll see, that's worth all the machines in the world.'

'Even if this year doesn't look good.'

'It doesn't, Shandon, and I notice that Baffin Bay may be returning to the same state as before 1817.'

'So you think, doctor, that what's happening now hasn't always happened?'

'I do, my dear Shandon, for there occur huge break-ups from time to time that the scientists can hardly explain; thus until 1817 this sea remained constantly blocked, when a huge cataclysm occurred and threw these icebergs into the ocean, where most ended up stranded on the Newfoundland Banks. Starting from then, Baffin Bay was more or less free and became the focus of many whaling ships.'

'So, starting from that date, journeys north were easier?'

'Incomparably; but it has also been noticed that in the last few years, the bay has been closing up again, and perhaps for a long time, to navigators. An extra reason, therefore, to push as far as we can. But we're a bit like people who move into unknown tunnels, whose doors continually close up again after them.'

'So would you advise me to retreat?' asked Shandon, trying to read into the very depths of the doctor's eyes.

'Personally, I have never been able to put one foot behind the other and, even if we were never to come back, I would say that we must proceed. I only consider it important to establish that if we take risks, we are perfectly aware of what we getting into.'

'And you, Garry, what do you think?'

'I would go straight ahead, commander; I share Dr Clawbonny's ideas; in any case you'll do what you want; command and we'll obey.'

'Not everybody talks like you, Garry,' replied Shandon; 'not everybody is in a mood to obey, and what if they do refuse to execute my orders?'

'I've given you my advice, commander, because you asked me,' replied Garry coldly, 'but you're not obliged to follow it.'

Shandon did not reply; he attentively examined the horizon and then with his two companions went back down to the ice-field.

I I

Devil's Thumb

DURING the commander's absence the men had been performing various tasks to reduce the pressure on the ship from the ice-fields. Pen, Clifton, Bolton, Gripper, and Simpson were still busy with this unpleasant work. The stoker and the two engineers even had to come and help their comrades, since as soon as the machine did not require their service, they became sailors again, and so could be employed for any ship's duty.

But this did not happen without great annoyance.

'I declare I've had enough,' said Pen, 'and if the ice hasn't broken up in three days' time, I swear to God I'll cross my arms and do nothing.'

'Cross your arms,' replied Gripper, 'it'd be better to use them to head back! Do you think we're in the mood to winter here?'

'Wintering wouldn't be much fun, admittedly,' said Plover, 'as the ship's sides are unprotected.'

'And who knows', said Brunton, 'whether even come next spring, the sea'll be any freer than today?'

'Next spring is not the problem,' replied Pen; 'today is Thursday; if by Sunday morning the route isn't free, we'll head back south again.'

'Well said!' said Clifton.

'Is that okay?' asked Pen.

'Yes,' replied his comrades.

'And it's only fair,' added Waren, 'since if we have to work like this and bodily haul the ship, I think we should be hauling it back.'

'We'll see on Sunday,' said Wolsten.

'Just give me the order,' said Brunton, 'and my boilers will soon be burning.'

'Eh,' added Clifton, 'we'll light them ourselves.'

'If some officer', said Pen, 'wants to have fun wintering here, he's free to; we'll leave him in peace; he can easily construct a snow hut and live in it like a proper Eskimo.'

'None of that, Pen,' keenly replied Brunton; 'we abandon nobody; did you hear that clearly, you others? Anyway, I don't think the commander will be difficult to win over; he seems already very worried to me, and by putting it gently . . .'

'I'm not so sure,' replied Plover; 'Richard Shandon can sometimes be a tough and stubborn man; we'll have to sound him out carefully.'

'When I think', said Bolton, with a sigh of desire, 'that we could be back in Liverpool within a month! The line of ice to the south could quickly be beaten! The pass into Davis Strait will be open at the beginning of June and we would just have to let ourselves drift into the Atlantic.'

'Not to mention', added the cautious Clifton, 'that by bringing the commander back with us, by acting under his responsibility, our share and our bonuses will be paid; but if we were to head back alone, that side of the business would be much messier.'

'Well reasoned,' said Plover; 'that diabolical Clifton talks like an accountant! Let's try to have nothing to sort out with those Admiralty gentlemen, that's safer, and let's not abandon anyone.'

'But if the officers refuse to go with us?' interjected Pen, who wanted to push his comrades to the limit.

The sailors were unable to answer a question asked so directly.

'We'll see in due course,' replied Bolton; 'anyway, all we have to do is win Richard Shandon over, and I don't imagine that'll be difficult.'

'There's someone I'd like to leave here, all the same,' said Pen with terrible swearwords, 'even if he ate one of my arms.'

'Ah, the dog!' said Plover.

'Yes, the dog, and I'll be fixing him pretty soon.'

'Especially', replied Clifton, coming back to his favourite idea, 'since that dog is the cause of all our problems.'

'He's the one that cast a spell over us,' said Plover.

'He's the one that took us into the ice-field,' replied Gripper.

'He's the one that's picked up more ice along the route than is normal at this period,' added Wolsten.

'He's given us eye problems,' said Brunton.

'He suppressed gin and brandy,' said Pen.

'He's the cause of everything!' everyone exclaimed, their imaginations on fire.

'Without mentioning', added Clifton, 'that he's the captain.'

'Well, unlucky captain,' exclaimed Pen, whose senseless fury increased on hearing his own words, 'since you wanted to come to this place, you can stay here.'

'But how to grab him?' asked Plover.

'Well, now is a good time,' replied Clifton, 'for the commander isn't on board, the lieutenant is sleeping in his cabin, and the fog is too thick for Johnson to see us.'

'But the dog?' exclaimed Pen.

'Captain is asleep near the coal hold,' replied Clifton, 'and if somebody wants to . . .'

'I will,' said Pen with fury.

'Be careful, Pen, his teeth are sharp enough to shatter iron!'

'I'll slit his stomach if he moves,' replied Pen picking up his knife.

And he rushed to the 'tween deck, followed by Waren.

Soon both came back carrying the animal, his muzzle and legs firmly tied; they had surprised him asleep and the unfortunate dog had not been able to get away.

'Hurray for Pen!' exclaimed Plover.

'And what do you want to do with him now?' asked Clifton.

'Drown him, and hope he never comes back,' replied Pen with a terrible smile of satisfaction.

About two hundred paces away from the ship, there was a seal hole, a sort of circular opening made by the teeth of this amphibian, always from the inside out; it is through this hole that the seal comes to breathe on the surface, but it must be careful to prevent the hole icing over, for the shape of its mouth means it cannot open the hole again from the outside, and so if danger arises it cannot escape its enemies.

Pen and Waren headed to the hole and there, despite its energetic struggles, the dog was pitilessly thrown into the sea; an enormous floe was then pushed over the opening, meaning there was no way out for the animal, enclosed in a liquid prison.

'Have a nice trip, Captain!' exclaimed the brutal sailor.

A few seconds later Pen and Waren came back on board. Johnson had seen nothing of the execution; the fog was thickening around the ship and snow beginning to fall heavily.

An hour later, Richard Shandon, the doctor, and Garry came back to the *Forward*.

Shandon had noticed a pass in the north-east which he decided to enter. He gave orders accordingly; the crew obeyed with alacrity; they wanted to make Shandon understand how impossible it was to go any further, and anyway they still had three days' obedience left.

For part of the following day and night the sawing and the hauling were carried out with ardour; the *Forward* gained nearly two miles northwards. On the eighteenth she was in sight of land, being five or six cables away from a remarkable peak whose strange shape has given it the name of Devil's Thumb.

On this same spot, the *Prince Albert* in 1851 and the *Advance* with Kane in 1853 were obstinately held by the ice for several weeks.*

The strange form of Devil's Thumb, the deserted, desolate surroundings, the vast amphitheatres of icebergs, some of them more than three hundred feet high, the cracking of the ice floes, sinisterly repeated by echoes—everything made the *Forward*'s situation desperately unhappy. Shandon understood that she needed to be got out of there and taken further. Twenty-four hours later, he had been able to move about two miles away from this fatal coast, according to his estimate. But it was not enough. Shandon felt himself being gripped by fear, and the false situation he was in paralysed his energy; to obey his instructions and head forwards he had taken the ship into an extremely dangerous situation; the hauling was killing the men; it took more than three hours to cut a channel twenty feet long in ice which was usually four or five feet thick; and the crew's health was already in jeopardy. Shandon was astonished by the silence of his men and their unaccustomed devotion; he feared that this calm might precede some storm.

One can therefore imagine the painful surprise, the disappointment, the despair even, that took hold of him when he noticed that, during the night of the eighteenth to nineteenth, following an imperceptible movement in the ice-field, the *Forward* was losing everything she had gained through so many fatigues. On the Saturday morning she was opposite Devil's Thumb, as menacing as ever, and found herself in an even more critical situation: there were more and more icebergs, passing like phantoms in the fog.

Shandon was completely disheartened; it must be said that fear entered the hearts of both this intrepid man and his crew. The commander had heard about the dog's disappearance; but he dared not punish the guilty parties, for he feared creating a rebellion.

The weather was horrible that day; the snow, plucked up in dense flurries, enveloped the brig in an impenetrable veil; sometimes the storm tore the fog open and in the direction of land frightened eyes would then spot Devil's Thumb erect like a ghost.

With the *Forward* anchored to an immense ice floe, there was nothing else that could be done or attempted; darkness was falling and the helmsman could not have seen James Wall, on duty at the bow.

Shandon returned to his cabin tortured by persistent worries; the doctor sorted out his travel notes; half the crew remained on deck, half in the common room.

At a time when the storm's violence was getting even worse, Devil's Thumb seemed to loom up beyond measure through the torn-open fog.

'Good God!' exclaimed Simpson, retreating in fear.

'What is it?' said Foker.

Immediate exclamations arose from every side.

'It's going to crush us!'

'We're lost!'

'Mr Wall, Mr Wall!'

'We're done for!'

'Commander, commander!'

The men on watch uttered these cries simultaneously.

Wall rushed aft to the fo'c'sle. Followed by the doctor, Shandon rushed on deck and looked.

Through a gap in the fog, Devil's Thumb appeared to have suddenly approached the brig; it seemed to have grown fantastically; on top stood a second cone, upside down and pivoting on its peak; it was threatening to crush the ship under its enormous mass; it was wobbling, it was ready to come crashing down. It constituted a frightening sight. Everyone instinctively drew back, and several sailors jumped hastily down to the ice and abandoned ship.

'Nobody move!' exclaimed the commander, in a severe voice. 'Everyone to his position.'

'Don't be afraid, friends,' said the doctor, 'there's no danger. Look, commander, Mr Wall, it's an illusion—that's all!'

'You're right, Dr Clawbonny,' echoed Master Johnson, 'those ignoramuses got frightened by just a shadow.'

At the doctor's words, most of the sailors had moved forward, switching from fear to admiration at the marvellous phenomenon, which soon disappeared again.

'They call that an illusion,' said Clifton; 'well Satan is behind it, believe me!'

'Definitely,' replied Gripper.

When the fog had opened up, it had shown the commander a huge open pass he had not suspected; the pass headed away from the coast; he resolved to profit from this favourable opportunity without delay; the men were arranged on each side of the channel; they were given hawsers, and began to tow the ship northwards.

For many long hours this operation was executed with ardour, albeit in silence; Shandon had had the boilers lit to profit from this channel, so miraculously discovered.

'It's a providential piece of luck,' he told Johnson, 'and if only we can gain a few miles, we may be at the end of our troubles. Mr Brunton, light the boilers; as soon as there is enough pressure, tell me. This should enhearten the men; so much the better. They're in a hurry to get away from Devil's Thumb. Well, let's profit from their good altitude.'

All of a sudden the brig brutally halted.

'What is it?' asked Shandon. 'Wall, have the tow ropes broken?'

'No, Commander,' replied Wall leaning over the rail. 'Hey, I can see men heading back; they're clambering on to the ship; they seem to be terrified of something!'

'But what is it?' exclaimed Shandon, rushing to the front of the brig.

'To the ship, to the ship!' exclaimed the sailors in tones of the most heartfelt terror.

Shandon looked northwards and could not help shivering.

A strange animal, with alarming movements, and a smoking tongue lolling from an enormous mouth, was leaping a cable away from the ship; it appeared to be more than twenty feet tall;* its hair stood on end; it ran after the sailors, transfixing them, while its formidable tail, ten feet long, swept snow up into thick swirls. The sight of such a monster froze with fear the most intrepid.

'It's an enormous bear,' said one.

'It's the Beast of Gévaudan!'*

'It's the Lion of the Apocalypse!'*

Shandon ran into his cabin to get a rifle, kept loaded; the doctor jumped to his guns, and held himself ready to fire at this animal of a size resembling the antediluvian quadrupeds.

It approached, by means of huge jumps; Shandon and the doctor fired at the same time. The firing of the guns, sending a shock through the atmospheric strata, produced a sudden and unexpected effect.

The doctor looked carefully, and could not help bursting out laughing.

'The refraction!' he said.

'The refraction!' cried Shandon.

But a terrible exclamation from the crew stopped them.

'That dog!' said Clifton.

'The dog-captain!' his comrades repeated.

'Him!' Pen exclaimed. 'Him again!'

It was indeed the dog which, breaking its bonds, had managed to return to the surface of the field through another hole. Through a phenomenon common at these latitudes, the refraction had given it formidable dimensions, which had been dissipated by the shock to the air; but the unfortunate vision was still imprinted on the sailors' minds, unwilling to admit any explanation in purely physical terms.

The adventure of Devil's Thumb and the reappearance of the dog in such fantastic conditions were sufficient to finish off their morale; and murmurs broke out on all sides.

12

Captain Hatteras

THE *Forward* was steaming rapidly ahead between the fields and mountains of ice. Johnson himself was at the helm. Shandon was examining the horizon with his snow spectacles, but his joy was of short duration for he soon recognized that the pass culminated in an amphitheatre of mountains.

However, to the difficulties of retracing the route he preferred the hazards of soldiering on.

The dog was following the brig, running along the plain, although it remained a fair distance away. But if it fell behind, a remarkable whistling would be heard which would immediately call it back.

The first time the whistling happened, the sailors looked around; they were alone on deck, talking all together; no stranger, no unknown people, but the sound was heard again several times.

Clifton was the first to be alarmed.

'Did you hear and did you see how that animal jumps when he hears the whistle?'

'It's unbelievable,' said Gripper.

'It's finished! I'm not going any further.'

'Pen's right,' replied Brunton; 'it'd be tempting God.'

'Tempting Satan, you mean,' retorted Clifton. 'I'd rather lose my whole share of the profits than go an inch further.'

'We won't come back,' said Bolton despondently.

The crew's demoralization could not have been worse.

'Not an inch further!' exclaimed Wolsten. 'Is that what you think?'

'Yes, yes!' replied the sailors.

'Then,' said Bolton, 'let's go and find the commander; I'll take on the job of speaking to him.'

The sailors headed to the poop in a dense group.

The *Forward* was then entering a vast amphitheatre which measured about eight hundred feet across; it was completely closed, with the sole exception of the way the ship had come in.

Shandon understood that he had just imprisoned himself. What could he do? How could he retrace his path? He felt the weight of his responsibility; his hand tightened on the telescope.

The doctor watched, his arms crossed, not saying a word; he contemplated the ice walls, which seemed more than three hundred feet high on average. A dome of fog was suspended above these cliffs.

It was then that Bolton addressed the commander:

'Commander,' he said in an emotional voice, 'we cannot go any further.'

'What did you say?' replied Shandon, as the realization of his unrecognized authority made anger mount to his face.

'We said, commander,' Bolton added, 'that we have done enough for the invisible captain, and we have decided not to go any further.'

'You have decided?' exclaimed Shandon. 'You dare speak in this way, Bolton! Be careful!'

'Your threats make no difference,' brutally retorted Pen; 'we will not go any further!'

Shandon was advancing towards the rebellious sailors, when the bosun came up and said in a low voice:

'Commander, if we want to get out of here, there's not a second to be lost. An iceberg is heading towards the pass; it may block the last exit and imprison us.'

Shandon went to study the situation.

'You will give me an account of your behaviour later, all of you,' he said addressing the mutineers. 'Meanwhile, turn about!'

The sailors rushed to their positions. The *Forward* moved quickly; the boilers were piled with coal; the floating mountain had to be beaten. It was a race between the brig and the iceberg; the former was heading south in order to get through, the latter drifting north, about to close the passage.

'Stoke, stoke!' bellowed Shandon. 'Full steam ahead! Brunton, do you hear me?'

The *Forward* slipped like a bird through the rare ice floes, which its prow cleanly cut; the whole ship was trembling from the impulse of the propeller, as the manometer indicated a prodigious pressure; the steam was whistling out with a deafening din.

'Weigh down the valves!' exclaimed Shandon.

And the engineer obeyed, at the risk of blowing up the ship.

But these desperate efforts were in vain; caught by an underwater current, the iceberg was moving quickly towards the pass; the brig was still three cables away, when the mountain, entering the gap like a wedge, firmly adhered to its neighbours and closed the last way out.

'We're lost,' exclaimed Shandon, unable to hold back this imprudent phrase.

'Lost!' exclaimed the crew.

'Each man for himself!' said some.

'To the boats!' said the others.

'To the storeroom,' exclaimed Pen and a few of his band, 'and if we have to drown, let's drown in gin!'

These unleashed men could not have been rowdier. Shandon felt overwhelmed; he wanted to command; he stuttered, he hesitated; his thought could not emerge in words. The doctor was agitatedly walking up and down. Johnson stoically crossed his arms in silence.

All of a sudden, a strong voice, energetic and imperious, rang out with these words:

'All hands on deck! Ready to tack!'

Johnson trembled, and quickly turned the wheel without realizing.

It was time; launched at full speed, the brig was about to break itself on the walls of the prison.

But while Johnson obeyed instinctively, Shandon, Clawbonny, the whole crew, down to the stoker Waren, who abandoned his firebox, and Strong the black, who left his ovens—everyone found themselves assembled on deck, where they all saw a man emerging from that cabin of which he alone had the key. That man was the sailor Garry.

'Sir!' exclaimed Shandon, going pale. 'Garry you . . . by what right do you command here?'

'Duke,'* said Garry, producing the whistling that had surprised the crew so much.

On hearing its real name, the dog leaped on the poop in a single bound and went to lie quietly at its master's feet.

The crew did not say a word. The key, that only the *Forward*'s captain possessed, the dog sent by him and which confirmed his identity, the accent of command which it was impossible to mistake—all this acted powerfully on the sailors' minds and so was enough to establish Garry's authority.

In any case Garry was unrecognizable; he had cut off the broad sideboards framing his face, which now appeared more impassive, more energetic, more imperious; wearing the costume of his rank, put on in the cabin, he appeared with his insignia of command.

So with natural changeability, the crew of the *Forward*, carried away despite themselves, exclaimed in a single voice:

'Hip, hip, hurray for the captain!'

'Shandon,' he said to his second-in-command, 'have the crew line up; I want to inspect them.'

Shandon obeyed, giving his orders in a new voice. The captain went up to his officers and sailors, telling each individual as he passed down the line what needed to be said and treating him according to his past behaviour.

When he had finished, he went back on the poop and uttered the following words in a calm voice:

'Officers and sailors, I am British like you, and my motto is the same as Admiral Nelson's:

' "England expects every man to do his duty." '*

'As a Briton, I do not wish—we do not wish—others to go where we have not been. As a Briton I will not allow—we will not allow—others to gain the glory of going further north. If ever a human foot is to tread the Pole, it has to be a British foot! That is the flag of our country. I have armed this ship, I have devoted my fortune to this expedition, I will devote my life, and yours, but this flag will float on the North Pole of the world. Trust me. A sum of £1,000 sterling will be paid to you for each degree that we gain northwards starting from today. We are now at the seventy-second degree and there are eighteen left. Count. My name will be my guarantee. It signifies energy and patriotism. I am Captain Hatteras!'*

'Captain Hatteras!' repeated Shandon.

And this name, well known to British sailors, rumbled through the crew.

'Now the brig must be anchored to the ice floes; the boilers must be put out; and everyone must return to his usual work. Shandon, I need to talk to you about ship business. You will join me in my cabin with the doctor, Wall, and the bosun. Johnson, dismiss the men.'

Hatteras, calm and cold, left the poop, while Shandon had the brig secured on its anchors.

Who therefore was this Hatteras and why did his name make such a deep impression on the crew?

John Hatteras, the only son of a London brewer who died six times a millionaire in 1852, embraced a maritime career while still young, despite the magnificent fortune awaiting him. Not that he was impelled by a vocation for trade, but the instinct for geographical discoveries was in his heart; he always dreamed of setting foot where nobody had ever been.

Already at twenty he possessed the vigorous constitution of thin and sanguine men; an energetic face with lines drawn geometrically on a high forehead perpendicular to the plane of his eyes, which were beautiful but cold, thin lips on a mouth sparing with words, average height, and members solidly articulated and moved by iron muscles—all added up to a man endowed with a temperament to resist anything. Seeing him was enough to feel him audacious, hearing him, coldly passionate; he was a type never to retreat, ready to gamble with other people's lives with as much conviction as his own. One needed therefore to think carefully before joining his ventures.*

John Hatteras carried British pride high, and it was he who once made this proud reply to a Frenchman:

The man said in front of him with what he imagined to be politeness and even friendliness:

'If I were not French, I would want to be British.'*

'Personally, if I was not British,' replied Hatteras, 'I would want to be British!'

The man can be judged from his reply.

His desire above all was to make sure all geographical discoveries were made by his compatriots, but to his great despair they had done little in the previous centuries.

America was due to the Genoan Christopher Columbus, the Indies to the Portuguese Vasco de Gama, China to the Portuguese Fernand d'Andrada, Terra del Fuego to the Portuguese Magellan, Canada to the French Jacques Cartier, and the Sunda Islands, Labrador, Brazil, Cape of Good Hope, the Azores, Madeira, Newfoundland, Guinea, the Congo, Mexico, Cap Blanc, Greenland, Iceland, the South Seas, California, Japan, Cambodia, Peru, Kamchatka, the Philippines, Spitzbergen, Cape Horn, Bering Strait, Tasmania, New Zealand, New Britain, New Holland, Louisiana,* and the island of Jan Mayen to the Icelanders, Scandinavians, Russians, Portuguese, Danish, Spanish, Genoans, and Dutch, and not a single Briton was present. Hatteras felt despair at seeing his countrymen excluded from that glorious phalanx of navigators who made the great discoveries of the fifteenth and sixteenth centuries.

Hatteras consoled himself by referring to modern times; the British made up for it with Sturt, McDouall Stuart, Burke, Wills, King, and Gray in Australia, Palliser in America, Cyril Graham, Waddington, and Cunningham in India, and Burton, Speke, Grant, and Livingstone in Africa.*

But that was not enough; for Hatteras, these bold travellers were more perfecters than inventors; better had to be found, and John would willingly have invented a country to have the honour of discovering it.

Now he had noticed that, if the British did not form a majority of

the early discoverers, if one had to go back to Cook to get New
Caledonia, in 1774, and the Hawaian islands, where he perished in
1778, there existed nevertheless a corner of the globe where they
seemed to have concentrated their efforts.

This was precisely the lands and seas of the north of North
America.

Indeed the table of polar discoveries read as follows:

Nova Zembla, discovered by Willoughby in 1553

The island of Waigats	Borough	1556
The west coast of Greenland	Davis	1585
Davis Strait	Davis	1587
Spitzbergen	Willoughby	1596
Hudson Bay	Hudson	1610
Baffin Bay	Baffin	1616*

In more recent years, Hearne, Mackenzie, John Ross, Parry,
Franklin, Richardson, Beechey, James Ross, Back, Dease, Simpson,
Rae, Inglefield, Belcher, Austin, Kellett, Moore, McClure, Kennedy,
and McClintock* ceaselessly searched these unknown lands.

The northern coasts of America had been circumscribed, the
Northwest Passage more or less discovered, but that was not enough;
there was better to be done, and this better, John Hatteras had twice
tried it, by arming ships at his own expense; he wanted to reach the
Pole itself, and thus crown the series of British discoveries with an
endeavour of the highest renown.

Reaching the Pole was the aim of his life.

After wonderful voyages to the Southern Seas, Hatteras tried to
reach the north via Baffin Bay for the first time in 1846; but he could
not get further than the seventy-fourth parallel; he was on the sloop
the *Halifax*;* his crew underwent atrocious suffering, and John
Hatteras pushed his rash adventure so far, that thereafter sailors
were not tempted by other expeditions under such a leader.

However, in 1850, Hatteras managed to enrol about twenty
determined men on the schooner the *Farewell**—determined, above
all, by the high price paid for their bravery. It was on this occasion
that Dr Clawbonny entered into correspondence with John Hatteras,
whom he did not know, and asked to take part in the expedition, but
the place of doctor was already taken, and this was fortunate for him.

Following the route taken by the *Neptune* of Aberdeen in 1817, the *Farewell* sailed north from Spitzbergen, as far as the seventy-sixth parallel.* There it had to winter, but the suffering was so bad and the cold so intense, that not a single man saw Britain again, with the sole exception of Hatteras, brought back by a Danish whaler after a trek of more than two hundred miles across the ice.

The sensation produced by the return of a single man was enormous. But from then on, who would dare follow Hatteras in his mad ventures? All the same, he did not give up the idea of starting again. His father, the brewer, died, and he inherited a nabob's fortune.

Meanwhile, a geographical event took place, which produced the biggest blows for John Hatteras.

A brig, the *Advance*, crewed by seventeen men, armed by the businessman Grinnell,* and commanded by Dr Kane, went in search of Sir John Franklin, and in 1853, via Baffin Bay and Smith Sound, went further than the eighty-second degree of latitude north, nearer the Pole than anyone had gone before.

Now this ship was American, this Grinnell was American, and this Kane was American!

It is easy to understand how the British contempt for the Yankees changed to hate in Hatteras's heart; he vowed to go further than his bold rival at any price, and reach the Pole itself.

For two years, he lived incognito in Liverpool. He passed for a sailor. He recognized in Richard Shandon the man he needed. In anonymous letters he made offers to him and Dr Clawbonny. The *Forward* was constructed, armed, and fitted out. Hatteras was careful not to let his name be known: he would not have found a single man to go with him. He resolved to take command of the brig only when absolutely necessary, when his crew were so far committed that they could not retreat; as we have seen, he had in reserve such riches to offer his men, that not one refused to follow him to the end of the world.

And it was the end of the world he wanted to get to.

Now that the circumstances were critical, John Hatteras had not hesitated to reveal himself.

His dog, the faithful Duke, the companion of his expeditions, had been the first to recognize him,* and fortunately for the brave, unfortunately for the cowardly, it was well and truly established that the captain of the *Forward* was John Hatteras.

13

Hatteras's Projects

THE appearance of this bold character was variously appreciated by the crew; some rallied completely to him, through love of money or bravery; others supported the adventure side, keeping the right to protest later; but in any case resisting such a man seemed difficult for the moment.

All therefore returned to their quarters. The twentieth of May was a Sunday and a day of rest.

An officers' meeting was held in the captain's room, with Hatteras, Shandon, Wall, Johnson, and the doctor.

'Gentlemen,' said the captain in the simultaneously gentle and imperious voice that characterized him, 'you are aware of my project of going to the Pole; I wish to know your opinion. What do you think, Shandon?'

'My role is not to think, captain,' said Shandon coldly, 'but to obey.'

Hatteras was not surprised by this reply.

'Richard Shandon,' he replied no less coldly, 'I ask you to give your opinion yourself on our chances of success.'

'Well, captain, the facts are on my side; all attempts have failed so far; I just hope we are luckier.'

'We shall be. And you, gentlemen, what do you think?'

'As for me,' replied the doctor, 'I find your plan feasible; and since navigators will clearly reach the North Pole one day, I don't see why it shouldn't be us.'

'There are factors in our favour, namely that our plans were made accordingly, and that we shall profit from the experience of those who went before us. And in this connection, Shandon, please accept my thanks for the care you took in fitting out of the ship; there are a few bad apples amongst the crew, whom I will bring to reason; but overall I have nothing save praise for you.'

Shandon nodded coldly. His position on board the *Forward*, which he thought he commanded, was false. Hatteras understood and did not insist.

'As for you, gentlemen,' he said, addressing Wall and Johnson, 'I could not have found better officers thanks to your courage and experience.'

'Upon my word, captain, I'm your man,' replied Johnson, 'and although your endeavour seems a little bold, you can count on me till the bitter end.'

'And on me,' added James Wall.

'As for you, doctor, I know your worth.'

'Well you know more than me,' quickly replied the doctor.

'Now, gentlemen, you should know the incontestable facts on which my claim to get to the Pole rests. In 1817, the *Neptune* from Aberdeen reached the eighty-second degree, north of Spitzbergen. In 1826, following his third voyage to the polar seas, the celebrated Parry also left from the tip of Spitzbergen, and went 150 miles north using sledge-boats. In 1852, Captain Inglefield reached 78° 25′ N through the entrance of Smith.* All these ships were both British and commanded by our compatriots.'

Here Hatteras paused.

'I must add', he continued, embarrassed as if the words would not leave his lips, 'that in 1850 the American Kane, commanding the brig the *Advance*, reached higher still and that his second Morton crossed the ice-fields and raised the flag of the United States beyond the eighty-second degree.* Having said that, I will not come back to it. Now what needs to be known is that the captains of the *Neptune*, *Enterprise*, *Isabella*, and *Advance** had noticed that, starting from these high latitudes, there existed a polar basin entirely free of ice.'

'Free of ice,' exclaimed Shandon, interrupting the captain; 'that's impossible!'

'You will notice, Shandon,' Hatteras calmly carried on, his eyes having shone briefly, 'that I cite facts with names to authenticate them. I will add that during Commander Penny's halt beside Wellington Channel in 1851, his second, Stewart,* also found an open sea, and that this fact was confirmed during Sir Edward Belcher's wintering on Northumberland Inlet in 1853 at 76° 52′ N, 99° 20′ W; the reports are indisputable and one would have to be in bad faith not to accept them.'

'However, captain,' said Shandon, 'these facts are so contradictory . . .'

'Wrong, Shandon, wrong!' exclaimed Dr Clawbonny. 'These facts do not contradict any assertion of science, as the captain will kindly allow me to show.'

'Go on, doctor.'

'Listen to this, Shandon; it follows very clearly from geographical facts and the study of the isothermal lines that the coldest point of the globe is not at the Pole itself; like the earth's magnetic point, it is a few degrees from the Pole. The calculations of Brewster, Bergham,* and other physicists demonstrate that there are two poles of cold in our hemisphere: one seems to be situated in Asia, at 79° 30′ N, 120° E; the other is in America, at 78° N, 97° W. The latter is the one which concerns us here, and notice, Shandon, that it is more than twelve degrees from the Pole. Well, I ask you, why shouldn't the sea be as free of ice at the Pole as it can be in the summer at the sixty-sixth parallel, namely south of Baffin Bay?'

'That is well said,' replied Johnson. 'Dr Clawbonny is a genuine professional.'

'It does seem possible,' added James Wall.

'Pipedreams, assumptions, pure hypotheses!' obstinately replied Shandon.

'Well, Shandon,' continued Hatteras, 'let's consider the two cases: either the sea's free of ice or it isn't, and in either case nothing can stop us reaching the Pole. If it's free, the *Forward* will take us there without problem; if it's ice, we'll try on sledges. You will grant that this is conceivable; once we've reached the eighty-third degree on our brig we'll only have 600 miles to do to get to the Pole.'

'And what is 600 miles,' quickly said the doctor, 'when a Cossack called Alexis Markoff covered a distance of 800 miles in twenty-four hours on the Glacial Sea along the northern coast of the Russian Empire using dog sledges?'*

'You hear, Shandon,' added Hatteras; 'tell me, can Britons do less than a Cossack?'

'Certainly not,' exclaimed the hot-headed doctor.

'Certainly not,' repeated the bosun.

'Well, Shandon?'

'Captain,' he coldly replied, 'I can only repeat my initial words to you: I will obey.'

'Good. Now let's consider our present situation; we're trapped by the ice and it appears impossible to reach Smith Sound this year. So here's what needs doing.'

Hatteras spread over the table one of the excellent maps published in 1859 by order of the Admiralty.

'Please follow me. If Smith Sound is closed to us, this does not apply to Lancaster Sound, on the west coast of Baffin Bay; we should head along the strait as far as Barrow Strait, and from there to Beechey Island; the route has been done a hundred times by sailing ships, so we won't have any problem on a screw-driven one. Once at Beechey Island we'll follow Wellington Channel northwards as far as we can, until this channel debouches and communicates with Queen Channel on the very spot where the open sea was seen. Now it's only 28 May; with luck we'll be there in a month's time, and can head for the Pole. What do you think, gentlemen?'

'It's obviously the only route,' said Johnson.

'We'll take it, starting tomorrow. This Sunday will be devoted to rest; you will make sure, Shandon, that reading the Bible is done regularly. Religious practice has a good influence on men's minds, and sailors must above all have trust in God.'

'Very well, captain,' said Shandon, leaving with the lieutenant and the bosun.

'Doctor,' said John Hatteras, pointing to Shandon, 'that is an offended man who is lost to pride; I can no longer count on him.'

Very early the following day, the captain had the ship's boat launched; he went to reconnoitre the icebergs in the basin, which was less than two hundred yards wide. He even noticed that, with the slow pressure of the ice, the basin was shrinking; it was therefore urgent to make a gap in it, so that the ship would not be crushed by this mountain vice; from the means John Hatteras planned to employ, he was clearly an energetic man.

First of all he had steps cut in the ice wall, and went to the top of an iceberg; from there he calculated that it would be easy to cut a path south-westwards; on his orders a blast-hole was dug nearly to the centre of the ice mountain; this work was carried out quickly and finished on the Monday.

Hatteras could not use the blasting cylinders, containing eight to ten pounds of gunpowder: their action would have been negligible on such masses; they were only suitable for breaking up ice-fields; he had therefore put 1,000 pounds of powder into the hole, whose direction of force had been carefully calculated. This explosive had a long fuse reaching outside, covered with gutta percha. The tube to the hole was filled with snow and sections of ice, which the cold would make as hard as granite during the night. In the east wind it went down to twelve degrees (−11 °C).

At seven the following morning the *Forward* was under steam, ready to take advantage of any way out at all. Johnson had the job of setting off the explosive; the fuse had been calculated to burn half an hour before reaching the powder. Johnson had therefore time to get back on board; in effect, ten minutes after carrying out Hatteras's orders, he was back at his position.

The crew remained on deck, in dry and relatively clear weather; the snow had stopped falling; standing on the poop with Shandon and the doctor, Hatteras calculated the time on his chronometer.

At 8.35 a dull explosion was heard, much less powerful than might have been thought. The outline of the mountains was suddenly changed as if in an earthquake; thick white smoke burst high in the sky and long cracks ran up the flanks of the iceberg, whose upper part, projected to a great height, showered down in pieces around the *Forward*.

But the pass was still not free; enormous portions of ice remained propped up on the adjacent mountains, suspended in the air, and there was a danger that the circle would close up again when they fell.

Hatteras judged the situation at a glance.

'Wolsten!' he shouted.

The armourer ran up.

'Sir.'

'Load the *Forward* cannon with a triple load, and pack it in as much as possible.'

'So we're going to attack the mountain with cannon balls?' asked the doctor.

'No, that would be useless. No cannon ball, Wolsten, just a triple load of powder. Quickly now.'

A few seconds later the gun was ready.

'What can he do without a cannon ball?' asked Shandon between gritted teeth.

'We'll soon see,' said the doctor.

'We're ready, captain,' shouted Wolsten.

'Brunton!' Hatteras cried to the engineer. 'Careful—a few turns forward.'

Brunton opened the slide-valves and the propeller started to move; the *Forward* drifted towards the undermined mountain.

'Aim exactly at the pass!' the captain shouted to the armourer.

When the brig was only half a cable away, Hatteras cried:

'Fire!'

A formidable explosion followed, and the blocks, shaken by the shocks of the air, were suddenly thrown into the sea. Shaking up the atmospheric strata had been enough.

'Full steam ahead, Brunton!' exclaimed Hatteras. 'Straight into the pass, Johnson!'

Johnson held the helm; the brig, thrust forward by the propeller's cutting of the foaming billows, threw itself into the passage, still free. Just in time. The *Forward* had hardly entered the gap, when its prison closed up again behind it.

The moment was a tense one and there was only one strong and peaceful heart on board—the captain's. So the crew, marvelling at the operation, could not hold back a cry:

'Hurray for John Hatteras!'

14

Expeditions in Search of Franklin

ON Wednesday, 23 May the *Forward* continued her adventurous navigation, tacking skilfully through the packs and icebergs, thanks to her steam, that obedient force unavailable to so many navigators of the polar seas. She seemed to be playing with the moving shoals; it was almost as if she recognized an experienced master's hand and, like a horse with a skilful rider, was obeying her captain's thoughts.

The temperature was rising. At six in the morning the thermometer read twenty-six (−3°C), at six in the evening twenty-nine (−2°C), and at midnight twenty-five (−4°C); a slight south-easterly was blowing.

On Thursday, at about three in the morning, the *Forward* arrived in sight of Possession Bay, on the American coast and at the entrance to Lancaster Sound; soon Burney Cape* was glimpsed. A few

Eskimos headed for the ship but Hatteras did not waste time waiting for them.

After the peaks of Byam Martin above Liverpool Cape had disappeared to port in the evening mist, the fog prevented Cape Hay being sighted; in any case its very low point is easily confused with the ice of the coast, a circumstance that often makes hydrographical determination in the polar seas very difficult.

Hundreds of puffins, ducks, and white seagulls appeared. Shooting the sun gave a latitude of 74° 1′; the chronometer, a longitude of 77° 15′. Catherine and Elisabeth Mountains raised their snowy caps above the clouds.*

At ten on Friday, they passed Warrender Cape on the right side of the strait and Admiralty Inlet on the left, a bay still largely unexplored, for navigators generally hurry westwards. The sea became quite strong and often the waves swept over the deck, throwing pieces of ice on to it. The lands of the north coast offered an unusual sight, with their almost horizontal high tables reflecting all the sun's rays.

Hatteras would have liked to follow the northern shores to get to Beechey Island and the entrance to Wellington Channel as fast as possible, but to his great displeasure a continuous ice-field obliged him to skirt the southern passes.

It was for this reason that on 26 May, in the middle of a fog thick with snow, the *Forward* found herself off Cape York, identifiable from the almost vertical mountain of great height; the weather had lifted a little and the sun appeared for a moment at midday, allowing quite a good shooting of the sun: 74° 4′ N, 84° 23′ W.* In other words, the *Forward* was at the end of Lancaster Sound.

On his maps Hatteras showed the doctor the route already followed and the route still to be followed. The brig's position was in fact interesting at this moment.

'I wanted to be further north, but "no one is bound to the impossible". Look, here is our exact position.'

The captain pointed to a spot near Cape York.

'We're in the middle of this crossroads, open to the winds and formed by the mouths of Lancaster Sound, Barrow Strait, Wellington Channel, and Prince Regent Inlet; this is where all navigators on these seas have inevitably ended up.'

'Well, that must have been difficult for them; it's a real crossroads, as you say, where four great routes meet, but I can't see any road signs indicating the true path! So how did the Parrys, Rosses, and Franklins manage?'

'They didn't, doctor, they just let things happen; they had no choice, I assure you; sometimes Barrow Strait was closed for one, but open the next year for another; sometimes their ship was ineluctably dragged into Prince Regent Inlet. People ended up knowing these chaotic seas through the force of events.'

'What a fascinating region!' said the doctor, looking at the map. 'How fragmented everything is, mutilated, torn up, in pieces, without order, without logic! The lands near the North Pole seem broken up only to make the approaches more difficult, whilst in the other hemisphere the lands end in calm, tapered points like Cape Horn, Cape of Good Hope, and the Indian subcontinent! Was it the greater speed of the equator that changed things, while the furthest lands, still fluid in the first days of the world, were not able to coalesce and stick together, because their rotation was too slow?'*

'It must be, for there is a logic to everything on this earth and nothing is done without reason, that God sometimes lets scientists discover; so, doctor, profit from that permission.'

'I'm afraid I won't. But what frightful winds reign in this strait!' added the doctor, pulling his hood up as best he could.

'The northern wind does often rage here, pushing us off course.'

'All the same, it should push the ice south and so free the route.'

'The wind doesn't always do what it should, doctor. Look, this ice-field seems impenetrable. So we'll try and get to Griffith Island, and then work round Cornwallis Island to Queen Channel, avoiding Wellington Channel. But I really need to put in at Beechey Island to fill up on coal.'

'I don't understand?' said the doctor astonished.

'On the Admiralty's orders, generous supplies were deposited on Beechey island, for the use of future expeditions; however much Captain McClintock took in August 1859, I guarantee some will be left for us.'

'In fact, these shores were explored over the past fifteen years and until it became absolutely clear that Franklin was lost, the Admiralty always maintained five or six ships in these seas. Unless I'm mistaken, Griffith Island, that I can see on the map, almost in the middle of the crossroads, has even become the general meeting point for navigators.'

'True, doctor, and one result of Franklin's unfortunate expedition is that we do know these remote areas.'

'Exactly, for there have been many expeditions since 1845. It was only in 1848 that people worried about the disappearance of Franklin's ships, the *Erebus* and *Terror*. The Admiral's old friend, Dr Richardson, aged seventy, rushed to Canada, and followed Coppermine River down to the Polar Sea; for his part James Ross, commanding the *Enterprise* and *Investigator*, sailed from Uppernawik in 1848 to reach Cape York where we are now. Each day he threw a keg into the sea containing documents indicating his position; in fog he fired the cannon; at night he launched rockets and flares, carefully keeping at shortened sail; in the end he wintered in Port Leopold from 1848 to 1849; there he gathered a large number of white foxes, placed copper collars on their necks, engraved with information about the position of the ships and food dumps, and dispersed them in all directions; then in the spring he began to search the coasts of Somerset* on sledges, in dangers and hardship which crippled or sickened nearly all the men, building cairns in which he put copper cylinders with notes to help the return of the lost expedition; during his absence Lieutenant McClure explored the northern coasts of Barrow Strait, but without finding anything. It should be noted, captain, that James Ross had two officers who later became famous: McClure who passed through the Northwest Passage and McClintock who discovered Franklin's remains.'

'Two good and brave captains today, two courageous Britons; but continue the history of these seas, doctor, which you know so well; there is always something to be learned from the tales of those audacious attempts.'

'Well, to finish with James Ross, I'll add that he tried to reach Melville Island, further west; but he nearly lost his ships, and was trapped by the ice and brought back to Baffin Bay against his will.'

'Brought back against his will!' repeated Hatteras with a frown.

'He had discovered nothing; from that year, 1850, British ships began to continuously plough these seas and a bonus of £20,000 was promised to anyone who found the crews of the *Erebus* and *Terror*. Already in 1848, Captains Kellett and Moore, commanding the *Herald* and *Plover*, had tried to enter Bering Strait. I'll add that in 1850 and 1851 Captain Austin wintered on Cornwallis Island, Captain Penny explored Wellington Channel on the *Assistance* and

Resolute,* old John Ross, the hero of the Magnetic Pole, left once
more on his yacht the *Felix* in search of his friend, the brig the *Prince
Albert* made its first journey financed by Lady Franklin, and finally
two American ships sent by Grinnell under Captain Haven* were
pushed out of Wellington Channel and into Lancaster Sound. It was
during that same year that McClintock, then Austin's lieutenant,
reached Melville Island and Cape Dundas, the furthest points Parry
had reached in 1819, and that traces of Franklin's wintering on
Beechey Island were found.'

'Yes, three of his sailors were buried there—luckier than the
others!'

'In 1851–2,' continued the doctor, showing his approval of Hatteras's remark, 'the *Prince Albert* started on a second journey with
the Frenchman Lieutenant Bellot on board; it wintered at Batty Bay
on Prince Regent Inlet, explored south-west Somerset, and reconnoitred the coast as far as Cape Walker. Meanwhile the *Enterprise* and
Investigator, back in Britain, passed under Collinson* and McClure's
command and rejoined Kellett and Moore in Bering Strait; while
Collinson spent the winter in Hong Kong, McClure went ahead and
after three winterings, in 1851–3, he discovered the Northwest
Passage without learning anything about Franklin's fate. In 1852–3 a
new expedition, composed of three sailing ships, the *Assistance,
Resolute*, and *North Star*, and two steamships, the *Pioneer* and
Intrepid, set sail under Sir Edward Belcher, with Captain Kellett as
second-in-command; Sir Edward visited Wellington Channel, wintered in Northumberland Inlet, and worked his way along the coast,
while Kellett, reaching as far as Bridport on Melville Island, unsuc-
cessfully searched this part of the northern lands. But then reports
spread across Britain that two ships abandoned in the ice had been
seen not far from the Nova Scotia coasts. Immediately, Lady Franklin armed the small propeller steamer the *Isabella*, and Captain
Inglefield went up Baffin Bay as far as Victoria Point on the eightieth
parallel, and then came back to Beechey Island, again without finding
anything. At the beginning of 1855* the American Grinnell went to
the trouble of a new expedition, and Dr Kane, seeking to penetrate
as far as the Pole . . .'

'But he didn't,' violently exclaimed Hatteras, 'God be praised!
Where he failed, we shall succeed!'

'I know, captain, and I mention this expedition because it is connected with the search for Franklin. In any case it had no result. I should also tell you that in 1853 the Admiralty, considering Beechey Island the general meeting point for expeditions, instructed Captain Inglefield, on the steamer the *Phoenix*, to transport supplies there; this mariner left with Lieutenant Bellot but lost this brave officer, who had placed himself in the service of Britain for the second time; detailed information about this catastrophe is available to us because Johnson, our bosun, witnessed the tragedy.'

'Lieutenant Bellot was a fine Frenchman, and his memory is honoured in Britain.'*

'Then the ships of the Belcher fleet began to gradually come back; not all, for Sir Edward had to abandon the *Assistance* in 1854, like McClure the *Investigator* in 1853. Meanwhile on 29 July 1854 Dr Rae wrote a letter from Repulse Bay, which he had reached via America, indicating that the Eskimos of King William Island had various objects from the *Erebus* and *Terror*; no doubt was possible now about the expedition's fate; the *Phoenix*, *North Star*, and Collinson's ship came back to Britain; and no more British ships went to the Arctic seas. But if the government seemed to have given up, Lady Franklin continued to hope and, with the remains of her fortune, fitted out the *Fox*, commanded by McClintock; it left in 1857, wintered in the waters where you appeared to us, captain, reached Beechey Island on 11 August 1858, wintered a second time in Bellot Strait, continued its searches in February 1859, on 6 May discovered the document which left no doubt about the fate of the *Erebus* and *Terror*, and came back to Britain at the end of the same year. That is everything that has happened over the past fifteen years in these deadly regions, and since the *Fox*'s return, not a single ship has tried its luck in these dangerous seas.'*

'Well, we'll try ours!' responded Hatteras.

15

The Forward *Pushed back South*

THE weather cleared up in the evening and land could easily be distinguished between Cape Seppings and Cape Clarence, which advances eastwards then southwards and is connected to the west coast by a low strip of land. The sea was free of ice at the entrance to Prince Regent Inlet, but, as if wishing to block the *Forward*'s northerly progress, it formed an impenetrable ice-field beyond Port Leopold.

Very upset but not letting anything show, Hatteras had to use explosive charges to force entry to Port Leopold; he reached it at midday on Sunday, 27 May; the brig was solidly anchored to large icebergs, which were as stable and hard as solid rock.

Immediately the captain, followed by the doctor, Johnson, and his dog, Duke, rushed on to the ice and soon reached land. Duke was leaping with joy; since the captain had revealed himself, he had become very sociable and gentle, reserving his spite for certain crewmen, whom his master did not like any more than he did.

The port was free of the ice generally piled up there by the east wind; the land, cut vertically, displayed gracious waves of snow at its peaks. The house and searchlight constructed by James Ross were still in a reasonable state; but the provisions seemed to have been raided by foxes and even bears, whose recent tracks could be made out; and man was surely involved in the damage, for a few Eskimo huts could be seen at the end of the bay.

The graves containing six of the sailors from the *Enterprise* and *Investigator* could be identified from slight bulges in the ground; they had not been disturbed by any of the whole harmful race of men and animals.

As he set foot on the northern lands for the first time the doctor felt real emotion. It is hard to imagine the feelings flooding one's heart on seeing the remains of houses, tents, huts, and stores, that nature conserves so carefully in the cold regions.

'Here', he said to his companions, 'is the residence that James Ross himself called Camp Refuge! If Franklin's expedition had reached this point, they would have lived. Here is the engine abandoned on this spot and the stove set up on the flat piece of land by the *Prince Albert*'s crew to warm themselves in 1851; things have remained in the same state, and you'd think that Kennedy, its captain, left this hospitable port only yesterday. Here is the launch which sheltered him and his men for a few days, for Kennedy, separated from his ship, was saved by Lieutenant Bellot, who braved the October temperatures to look for him.'

'A courageous and worthy officer, whom I knew,' said Johnson.

While the doctor was searching for the remains of previous winterings with an antique dealer's enthusiasm, Hatteras was busy getting together the provisions and fuel, of which in fact there was only a small quantity. The following day was employed moving them on board. The doctor wandered the countryside, not getting too far from the ship, and sketched the most remarkable views. It was slowly getting warmer and the piled-up snow beginning to melt. The doctor made a relatively complete collection of northern birds, such as seagulls, divers, mollymawks, and eider-ducks. The latter resemble ordinary ducks, with their white breasts and backs, blue stomachs and crests, the rest of the plumage being white with a few green tints; the stomachs of several of them were already stripped of that pretty eiderdown which the male and female use to pad their nest.*
The doctor also noticed some large seals breathing on the surface of the ice, but he could not attract a single one.

In his excursions he discovered a high-water mark, a stone engraved with the symbols

[E I]
1849

commemorating the passage of the *Enterprise* and *Investigator*;* he went as far as Cape Clarence, the spot where in 1833 John and James Ross waited so impatiently for the ice to break up. The land was strewn with animal bones including skulls, and signs of the Eskimos who had lived there could still be made out.

The doctor had had the idea of building a cairn at Port Leopold and depositing a note indicating the passage of the *Forward* and the expedition's purpose. But Hatteras formally opposed this notion: he did not wish to leave any traces a rival could use. In spite of his good reasons, the doctor had to give in to the captain. Shandon was amongst those criticizing such obstinacy, for in case of accident no ship could come to the *Forward*'s aid.

Hatteras refused to give in. His loading was finished on the Monday evening and he again tried to head north by assaulting the ice-field, but after risky attempts he had to resign himself to going back down Prince Regent Inlet; the last thing he wanted was to remain in Port Leopold, as it could close up tomorrow if the ice-fields moved unexpectedly—a very frequent phenomenon in these seas, one that navigators must be particularly careful of.

If Hatteras did not let his worries show on the outside, inside he felt them terribly. He wanted to go north but was forced to head south! Where would he end up? Would he have to retreat as far as Victoria Harbour on the Gulf of Boothia, where Sir John Ross wintered in 1833? Might he find Bellot Strait free and be able to head north by rounding Somerset into Peel Sound? Or would he be captured for several winters like his predecessors and have to waste his strength and provisions?

These fears fermented in his head, but he did have to choose a course of action; he tacked about and plunged southwards.

Prince Regent Inlet is approximately the same width from Port Leopold to Adelaide Bay.* The *Forward* moved quickly through the ice floes, luckier than previous ships, which generally spent at least a month in this channel, even in a higher season; it is true that these ships did not have steam, except for the *Fox*, and so suffered the caprices of an uncertain and often adverse wind.

Most of the crew were visibly delighted to be leaving the northern regions; they did not seem to appreciate the idea of getting to the Pole; they were easily frightened by Hatteras's decisions, whose reputation for boldness was far from reassuring. The captain tried to seize every opportunity to move ahead, whatever the consequences. And yet in these northern seas, to advance is good, but one's position must still be kept and not risked being lost.

The *Forward* was advancing at full steam; her black smoke rose and spiralled around the icebergs' dazzling tips; the weather kept changing, switching from a dry cold to snowy fogs. Thanks to her shallow draught, the brig hugged the west coast; Hatteras did not want to miss the entrance to Bellot Strait, for the Gulf of Boothia has no way out southwards except for little-known Fury and Hecla Strait;* this gulf became therefore a cul-de-sac if Bellot Strait was missed or blocked.

In the evening the *Forward* was in view of Elwin Bay, recognizable from its tall, vertical rocks; on Tuesday morning, Batty Bay was sighted, where, on 10 September 1851, the *Prince Albert* anchored for a long wintering. With his telescope, the doctor studied the coast. From this point spread out the expeditions that established the geographical configuration of Somerset. The weather was clear, revealing the deep valleys surrounding the bay.

Perhaps only the doctor and Master Johnson were interested in these deserted regions. Hatteras, permanently bent over his maps, spoke little; his taciturnity increased with the brig's southerly movement; he often went on the poop deck and there, his arms crossed and his eyes lost in space, he examined the horizon for hours at a stretch. His orders, if any, were concise and abrupt. Shandon maintained a cold silence and gradually retreated into himself, his only relations with Hatteras those for running the ship; James Wall remained devoted to Shandon and modelled his behaviour on his. The rest of the crew awaited events, ready to following their self-interest. No longer was there on board that unity of thought, that communion of ideas necessary for the accomplishment of great things. Hatteras was well aware of it.

During the day two whales were seen moving quickly southwards; a polar bear was also spotted and greeted with several rifle shots, but apparently without success. The captain knew the value of an hour in such circumstances and did not allow pursuit.

On Wednesday morning they passed the end of Prince Regent Inlet; after the tip of the west coast came a deep curve of land. Consulting his map, the doctor recognized Somerset House Point, or Fury Point:

'This is the very spot where the first British ship sent into these seas was lost, on Parry's third polar journey; on its second wintering the ice damaged the *Fury* so badly that the crew had to abandon ship in 1815,* and return to Britain on the sister vessel the *Hecla*.'

'The clear advantage of having a second ship,' replied Johnson; 'it's a precaution that polar navigators should take; but Captain Hatteras wasn't the sort of man to encumber himself with a companion!'

'Do you think him reckless, Johnson?'

'Me? I think nothing, Dr Clawbonny. Look, can you see on the coast those uprights with a few scraps of a half-decayed tent on them?'

'Yes, Johnson, it was there that Parry unloaded all the provisions from his ship, and if my memory serves me well, the roof of the house he made was a topsail from the *Fury*.'

'It must have changed a lot since 1825.'

'Not too much, Johnson. In 1829 John Ross found safety and health for his crew in this fragile abode. In 1851, when Prince Albert sent out an expedition,* the building was still standing; Captain Kennedy had it repaired nine years ago. It'd be interesting to visit it; but Hatteras is in no mood to stop!'

'And he's undoubtedly right, Dr Clawbonny: if time is money in Britain, here it's safety, and with one day's delay, even one hour, you can risk a whole expedition. So let's let him do as he thinks fit.'

On Thursday, 1 June, Cresswell Bay was obliquely crossed by the *Forward*; from Fury Point the coast rose northwards in vertical cliffs, 300 feet high; in the south it tended to become lower; a few snowy summits displayed clean-cut tables, while others projected their strange sharp pyramids into the mist.

That day the weather became milder, but at the price of sight, as the land could no longer be seen; the thermometer rose to thirty-two (0°C); a few grouse fluttered here and there, as flocks of wild geese wheeled north; the crew had to remove some of their clothing; the onset of summer was making itself felt in these Arctic regions.

In the evening the *Forward* doubled Cape Garry, a quarter of a mile from the shore and over a bottom of ten to twelve fathoms, and then hugged the shore as far as Brentford Bay. It was at this latitude that they needed to locate Bellot Strait, not even suspected by Sir John Ross on his 1828 expedition;* his maps show an uninterrupted coast, whose smallest irregularities he carefully noted and named; admittedly, at the time of his exploration, the entrance to the strait, completely blocked by ice, was indistinguishable from the land.

The strait was discovered by Captain Kennedy on a trip of April 1852; he gave it Bellot's name, 'a justified acknowledgement', he said, 'of the great service the French officer rendered our expedition'.

16

The Magnetic Pole

As he approached this strait, Hatteras felt his anxiety increasing; in effect the fate of his voyage was going to be decided; until now he had done better than his predecessors, of whom the luckiest, McClintock, took fifteen months to reach this part of the polar seas; but it was little, or nothing, if he failed to get through Bellot Strait; unable to retrace his steps, he would be blocked till the following year.

So he trusted no one with the task of examining the coast; he climbed up to the crow's nest and spent several hours of Saturday morning there.

The crew perfectly realized the situation the ship was in; complete silence reigned on board; the engine slowed down; the *Forward* stayed as near land as possible; the coast was bristling with ice that the warmest summers failed to dissolve; it needed a sharp eye to make out an entrance amongst it.

Hatteras compared his maps with the land. When the sun came out for a moment at noon he asked Shandon and Wall to make an exact shooting of the sun, which was communicated to him orally.

Everybody had had half a day of anxiety. But suddenly at about two o'clock these resounding words fell from the top of the foresail mast:

'Turn west, and full steam ahead.'

The brig obeyed instantaneously; she turned her prow to the point indicated; the sea foamed under the pales of her propeller, and the *Forward* rushed at top speed between two chaotic ice streams.

The route had been found; Hatteras came back down on deck and the ice-master returned to his position.

'So, captain,' said the doctor, 'we're finally in this famous strait?'

'Yes,' Hatteras replied lowering his voice, 'but getting in isn't the difficult part; you need to get out as well.'

And he went back into his cabin.

'He's right,' the doctor said to himself; 'it's as if we're in a mouse-trap, without room to manoeuvre, and we had to winter in this strait!

Oh well, we wouldn't be the first to have such an adventure and where others have got out of fixes, we'll be able to get away with it as well!'

The doctor was right. It was on this very spot, a sheltered little port named Port Kennedy by McClintock himself, that the *Fox* wintered in 1858. At this moment the tall granite chains and steep cliffs of the two shores could be identified.

Bellot Strait, a mile wide by seventeen long, with a current of six to seven knots, is enclosed between mountains of a height estimated to be 1,600 feet. It separates Somerset from Boothia; ships do not have much elbow room here. The *Forward* proceeded carefully, but at least she was proceeding; storms are frequent in this narrow space and the brig did not escape their customary violence; on Hatteras's orders, the yards of the top gallant sheets and main topsails were lowered, the masts unreeved; but the ship still laboured enormously; during the cloudbursts breakers arrived together with heavy seas; the smoke fled eastwards at astonishing speed; the ship was sailing rather at random amongst the moving ice. The barometer fell to twenty-nine inches, and it was difficult to stay on deck, so most of the men stayed in the crew room in order not to suffer needlessly.

Hatteras, Johnson, and Shandon remained on the poop, despite the flurries of snow and rain; after wondering what was the most disagreeable thing to do at this moment, the doctor immediately went up on deck; speaking and even seeing were barely possible; so he kept his thoughts to himself.

Hatteras was trying to penetrate the curtains of fog, since he estimated he would be at the end of the strait at about six in the evening; but in the event every way out seemed closed; Hatteras was therefore forced to stop and anchor himself solidly to an iceberg; but he remained under pressure all night.

The weather was dire. At any moment the *Forward* was about to break her chains; it could be feared that, torn from its base by the violence of the west winds, the mountain would drift away with the brig. The officers were constantly on the lookout and in extreme apprehension; to the heavy snow was added a genuine hail swept up by the storm from the melted surface of the ice-fields; it was like so many sharp arrows spiking the atmosphere.

It got considerably warmer during that terrible night; the thermo-meter read fifty-seven (14°C) and to his great surprise the doctor thought he saw a few bolts of lightning in the south followed by very distant thunder. This seemed to corroborate what the whaler Scoresby said, for he observed a similar phenomenon beyond the sixty-fifth parallel. Captain Parry also witnessed such a meteorological singularity in 1821.

At about five in the morning the weather changed with surprising speed; it suddenly fell to freezing; the wind veered north and dropped. The western opening of the strait could be made out, although entirely closed. Hatteras greedily surveyed the coast, wondering if the passage really existed.

Meanwhile the brig got under way and slid slowly between the ice streams while ice broke noisily over its sheathing; at this season the packs were still six to seven feet thick; it was essential to avoid their pressure, for even if the ship had resisted, she would have been in danger of being lifted up and thrown on her side.

At noon and for the first time, a magnificent solar phenomenon could be admired: a halo with two parhelia; from observation the doctor discovered its exact dimensions; the external arc was visible over only thirty degrees on each side of the horizontal diameter; the two images of the sun were remarkably clear; the colours in the rainbows were, starting from the inside: red, yellow, green, a very pale blue, and finally white light without clear external limit.

The doctor remembered Thomas Young's ingenious theory about meteors;* this physicist reasons that the air contains clouds made of ice prisms; the sunlight reaching these prisms is decomposed at angles of sixty and ninety degrees. The haloes can therefore only be formed in clear skies.

The doctor found this explanation highly ingenious.

Sailors, accustomed as they are to northern seas, consider the phenomenon a sign of abundant snow. In such an eventuality, the *Forward* would be in a difficult situation. Hatteras accordingly resolved to move on; for the rest of that day and night he did not take a moment's rest, scrutinizing the horizon, rushing into the ratlines, not losing an opportunity to get close to the strait's exit.

But in the morning he had to stop in the face of impenetrable pack ice. The doctor joined him on the poop. Hatteras took him full astern to talk without being overheard.

'We're trapped,' said Hatteras, 'and it's impossible to go any further.'

'Impossible?'

94   *The British at the North Pole*

'Yes, all the powder in the *Forward* would not gain us quarter of a mile!'

'What to do then?'

'Who knows? Damn this disastrous year which is beginning so badly!'

'Well, captain, if we have to winter, then we'll winter! This place is as good as any!'

'Perhaps,' said Hatteras quietly; 'but we mustn't winter, especially in June. Wintering is full of physical and moral dangers. The crew's spirits are quickly lowered by the long rest amidst genuine suffering. So I was counting on stopping only at a latitude closer to the Pole!'

'Yes, but fate has decreed that Baffin Bay is closed.'

'The bay was open for another,' angrily exclaimed Hatteras, 'for that American, that . . .'

'Look, Hatteras,' said the doctor, interrupting him on purpose, 'it's still only 5 June; we should not give up; a passage may suddenly open up in front of us; you know that the ice tends to split into blocks, even in calm weather, as if a repulsive force acted on the parts composing it; we may therefore find the sea open in an hour's time.'

'Well, if it does we'll take it. After Bellot Strait we can quite possibly head north through Peel Sound or McClintock Channel and then . . .'

'Captain,' James Wall came to say, 'we're in danger of losing our rudder to the ice.'

'Well, we'll risk it! I refuse to have it removed; I want to be ready at any time of day or night. Please take steps, Mr Wall, for it to be protected as much as possible by pushing away the ice floes; but it must stay in place, do you hear me?'

'All the same . . .' said Wall.

'I do not want to hear your comments,' Hatteras said sharply; 'now go.'

Wall returned to his post.

'Ah,' said Hatteras with an angry gesture, 'I'd give five years of my life to be further north! I don't know a more dangerous passage. To cap it all, the compass is asleep so close to the Magnetic Pole: the needle goes lazy or crazy, jumping about.'

'I'll admit that it's dangerous sailing; but those who signed on must have expected danger and nothing here should surprise them.'

'My crew have changed a great deal and as you've just seen, the officers are already making comments. The financial benefits the sailors get made them sign on; but they have their bad side, because once they've left they long all the more to return! Doctor, I am not supported in my endeavour and if I fail it will not be such and such a sailor's fault, who can be won over, but the ill will of certain officers . . . Ah, they'll pay for it!'

'You're exaggerating, Hatteras.'

'I'm not exaggerating one bit! Do you think the crew are bothered by the obstacles I meet on the way? Quite the opposite! They hope that I'll abandon my ideas! So they're not complaining and as long as the *Forward* heads south they won't. The fools! They think they're getting closer to Britain! But if I can turn north you'll see things changing! I swear that no living creature can make me deviate from my route! A passage, an opening, enough to slip my brig in, even if I have to leave behind her copper sheath, and I'll win.'

Some of the captain's desires were to be satisfied. As the doctor foresaw, a sudden change came about in the evening; whether due to wind, current, or temperature, the ice-fields opened up; the *Forward* headed boldly on, breaking the floes with her steel prow; she sailed all night and disembogued from Bellot Strait at about six on Tuesday morning.

But what was Hatteras's secret annoyance at finding the way north obstinately blocked! Nevertheless he had enough strength of character to hide his despondency, and behaving as though the only route open was his first choice, he let the *Forward* go down Franklin Strait; not able to go up Peel Sound, he resolved to reach McClintock Channel by going round Prince of Wales Island. But he could sense that Shandon and Wall were not fooled and were aware of his disappointment.

No particular incident occurred on 6 June; the sky was snowy in line with the halo's forecasts.

For thirty-six hours the *Forward* followed the sinuosities of the coast of Boothia Peninsula without managing to get near Prince of Wales Island; Hatteras forced steam, prodigally burning his coal; he still counted on replacing his provisions on Beechey Island; on Thursday he reached the mouth of Franklin Strait and found the path north impassable once more.

It was enough to make him give up; he couldn't even retrace his steps; the ice was pushing him forward and he constantly saw the route closing up behind him, as if the open sea crossed an hour before had never existed.

Thus not only was the *Forward* unable to gain ground northwards, but she was unable to stop for a moment, for she would have been trapped; so she fled before the ice like a ship before the storm.

On Friday, 8 June she was near the coast of Boothia, at the entrance to James Ross Strait, which had to be avoided at all costs, as it has no way out westwards* and leads directly to the lands of America.

Shooting of the sun made here at noon gave 70° 5′ 17″ for the latitude and 96° 46′ 45″ for the longitude;* when the doctor learned these figures he referred to his map and saw that he was finally at the Magnetic Pole—the very spot where James Ross, the nephew of Sir John, came to determine this curious phenomenon.

The land was low, rising to a height of only sixty feet a mile away inland the sea.

Since the boiler of the *Forward* needed to be cleaned, the captain had the ship anchored to an ice-field and allowed the doctor to land with the mate. Oblivious of anything not to do with his projects, he shut himself into his cabin, devouring the map of the Pole with his eyes.

Accompanied by his usual companion, the doctor easily landed, taking a compass for his experiments: he wanted to check James Ross's work; he easily discovered the small pile of limestone Ross built; he ran up to it; through a gap could be seen the tin box in which he deposited the signed record of his discovery. Not a single living being seemed to have visited this deserted coast in thirty years.

At this spot a magnetic needle, suspended as delicately as possible, immediately adopted an approximately vertical position under the magnetic influence; the centre of attraction was therefore very near or immediately below the needle.

The doctor performed his experiment with care.

But if James Ross could only find an inclination of 89° 59′ for his needle, it must have been because of the imperfection of his instruments or because the true magnetic point was a minute away.* Dr Clawbonny was luckier, and a short distance away he had the huge satisfaction of seeing his inclination at ninety degrees.

'This is the exact Magnetic Pole of the earth!' he exclaimed, kicking the ground.

'It's really here?' asked Master Johnson.

'On this very spot, my friend.'

'Then we have to give up any idea of a magnetic mountain or magnetized body?'

'Yes, my good Johnson,' replied the doctor with a laugh; 'ideas for the gullible! As you can see, there is not the slightest mountain capable of attracting vessels, tearing off their iron, anchor by anchor, nail by nail,* and even your shoes are as free as on any point of the globe.'

'But then how to explain it all?'

'We don't, Johnson; we don't know enough. But what is certain, true, mathematical is that the Magnetic Pole is here!'

'Ah, Dr Clawbonny, how happy the captain would be to say the same for the North Pole!'

'He shall, Johnson, he shall say it.'

'May it be God's will.'

The doctor and his companion built a cairn on the exact spot of the experiment; on receiving the signal to return, they went back on board at five in the afternoon.

17

Sir John Franklin's Tragic Fate

THE *Forward* managed to cut directly across James Ross Strait, but not without difficulty; they had to use the saw and the charges; the crew experienced extreme fatigue. The temperature was fortunately very bearable, thirty degrees higher than James Ross had at the same season. The thermometer read thirty-four (2°C).

On Saturday Cape Felix was doubled, at the northern tip of King William Island, one of the medium-sized islands of these northern seas.

The crew then felt strong and painful emotions; they cast curious but sad looks at the coast they were following.

They were in the presence of King William Island, the scene of the worst tragedy of modern times! A few miles west the *Erebus* and *Terror* had been lost for ever.

The sailors of the *Forward* knew the efforts made to find Admiral Franklin, and their failure, but they were unaware of the distressing details of the tragedy itself. Now while the doctor was plotting the ship's progress on the map, several of them, Bell, Bolton, and Simpson, came up and engaged him in conversation. Soon their comrades followed, drawn by unusual curiosity; meanwhile the brig was sailing extremely fast, and the bays, capes, and points of the coast passed before their eyes like a huge panoramic picture.

Hatteras was rapidly pacing up and down the poop. The doctor, on the deck, was soon surrounded by most of the crewmen; he understood the interest of the situation and the power of a tale told in such circumstances; so he carried on the conversation begun with Johnson:

'You know Franklin's beginnings, my friends; he was a cabin boy like Cook and Nelson; after his youth on great maritime expeditions, he resolved in 1845 to set off in search of the Northwest Passage; he commanded the *Erebus* and *Terror*, two tough ships which, in 1840, had made an expedition towards the Antarctic Pole with James Ross. The *Erebus*, under Franklin, had a crew of seventy, including officers and sailors, with Fitzjames as commander, Gore and Le Vesconte as lieutenants, Des Voeux, Sargent, and Couch as mates, and Stanley as surgeon.* The *Terror* had sixty-eight: Captain Crozier, lieutenants Little, Hodgson, and Irving, mates Hornby and Thomas, surgeon Peddie.* You can read in the bays, capes, straits, points, channels, and islands of these waters the names of most of these wretches: not a single one saw his country again! In all 138 men! We know that Franklin's last letters were addressed from Disko Island, dated 12 July 1845.

' "I hope to set sail tonight for Lancaster Sound," he said. What happened after his departure from Disko Bay? The captains of the whalers the *Prince of Wales* and the *Enterprise* saw the two ships for the last time in Melville Bay; and the vessels were never heard of again. However, we can follow Franklin as he sailed westwards; he entered Lancaster Sound and Barrow Strait and reached Beechey Island, where he spent the winter of 1845–6.'

'But how do we know?' asked Bell the carpenter.

'From three graves on the island that the Austin expedition discovered in 1850, containing three of Franklin's sailors; and from a document dated 25 April 1848, found by Lieutenant Hobson of the *Fox*.* So we know that after their wintering the *Erebus* and *Terror* went up Wellington Channel as far as the seventy-seventh degree; but instead of continuing northwards, which was undoubtedly impossible, they came back south again.'

'And that was their fatal mistake!' said a solemn voice. 'Salvation was northwards.'

All turned round. Leaning over the poop rail, Hatteras had hurled this terrible remark at his crew.

'Franklin's intention was probably to return to the coast of America; but storms beset him on the fatal route, and on 12 September 1846 the two ships were held by the ice, a few miles from here, north-west of Cape Felix; they were dragged to a spot north-north-west of Point Victory: just there,' said the doctor pointing at a spot on the sea. 'Now the ships were only abandoned on 22 April 1848. What happened during those nineteen months? What did those wretches do? Undoubtedly they explored the surrounding lands, tried everything to save themselves, for the admiral was an energetic man! And if he didn't succeed . . .'

'It was because his crews betrayed him,' Hatteras said in a hollow voice.

The sailors dared not look up; these words weighed heavily on them.

'In sum, the fatal document tells us that Sir John Franklin succumbed to his fatigues on 11 June 1847. Let us remember him with honour!' said the doctor baring his head.

His listeners silently imitated him.

'What became of the wretches, deprived of their leader for ten months? They remained on board and only decided to abandon the ships in April 1848; 105 men still remained out of 138. Thirty-three were dead! Then Captains Crozier and Fitzjames built a cairn on Point Victory and deposited their last document in it.

'Look, my friends, we're passing that very headland! You can still see the remains of the cairn, at virtually the furthest point John Ross reached in 1831. That's Cape Jane Franklin! That's Franklin Point! That's Point Le Vesconte! And that's Erebus Bay, where the launch was found, built from the remains of one of the ships and placed on a sledge! There were discovered silver spoons, abundant provisions, chocolate, tea, religious volumes! For the 105 survivors, under the command of Captain Crozier, set off for Great Fish River! How far did they get? Did they manage to reach Hudson Bay? Are any of them still alive? What happened to them after leaving that last time?'

'What happened to them, I will tell you!' John Hatteras said loudly. 'Yes, they tried to reach Hudson Bay, and broke up into several groups! Yes, they headed south! Yes, a letter by Dr Rae in 1854 stated that in 1850 the Eskimos had encountered a detachment of forty men on this King William Island:* hunting seals, travelling over the ice and pulling a boat, thin, hollow, utterly exhausted from work and suffering. And later the Eskimos discovered thirty bodies on the main island and five on a neighbouring island, some half-buried, the others abandoned without ceremony, some under an upside-down boat, others in the remains of a tent, here an officer with his telescope at his shoulder and loaded gun near him, further on cooking pots with the remains of a horrible meal! At this news the Admiralty asked the Hudson Bay Company to send its best agents to the scene of the events. They went down Back River to its mouth. They visited Montreal and Maconochie Islands and Ogle Point. But nothing! All these wretches had died of misery, of suffering, of hunger, trying to prolong their existence with the appalling resource of cannibalism! That's what happened to them on that southward route, strewn with their mutilated bodies! Well, do you still want to follow in their footsteps?'

Hatteras's vibrant voice, passionate gestures, and ardent face had an indescribable effect. Over-excited and emotional in the presence of these fatal lands, the crew exclaimed with one accord: 'The north, the north!'

'Yes, the north, where survival and glory are! Northwards! Heaven is on our side! The wind is changing! The pass has freed! Prepare to tack!'

The sailors rushed to their operations; the ice streams slowly broke up; the *Forward* headed quickly for McClintock Channel, at full steam.

Hatteras was right to count on a freer sea; he was following the presumed route of Franklin but in the opposite direction; he was working his way along the east coast of Prince of Wales Island, by then adequately charted, while the opposite shore is still unknown.* Clearly the break-up of the ice southwards was due to the eastern sound, for this strait seemed entirely free; as a result the *Forward* was able to regain lost time; it forced steam, and on 14 June passed

Osborne Bay and the furthest points reached by the 1851 expeditions. The ice was still dense in the strait, but there was now no danger of the sea freezing under the *Forward*'s keel.

18

Northwards Ho!

THE crew seemed to have resumed to their habits of discipline and obedience. The infrequent and untiring operations left them a great deal of free time. It stayed above freezing, and this thaw was now removing the main obstacles to navigation.

Duke, become friendly and sociable, had formed a sincere friendship with Dr Clawbonny. Perfect harmony. But since one friend is always sacrificed to the other in friendship, it must be admitted that the doctor was not the other. Duke could twist him round his little finger. The doctor obeyed like a dog does his master. Duke was friendly in fact with most of the officers and sailors; he fled Shandon's company only by instinct, undoubtedly; he also bore a grudge, but what a grudge, against Pen and Waren; his hatred surfaced in half-muffled growls whenever they came near. But, these two men hardly dared attack the captain's dog, his guardian spirit, as Clifton called him.

In sum the crew had got its confidence back and felt good.

'Our men seem to have taken the captain's speech seriously,' said James Wall one day to Richard Shandon; 'they don't appear to doubt any longer that we'll succeed.'

'They're wrong; if they thought, if they examined the situation, they'd realize that we're moving from one folly to another.'

'But here we are in a freer sea; we're returning to routes that have already been reconnoitred; aren't you exaggerating a little, Shandon?'

'I'm not exaggerating at all, Wall; the hate, the jealousy if you want, that Hatteras inspires in me doesn't make me blind. Answer me: have you visited the coal hold?'

'No.'

'Well, go down and you'll see how quickly our supplies are going down. Normally we ought to have navigated mostly by sail; the propeller should have been used only against opposing currents or winds; the fuel should have been used with the utmost economy, for who can say where and for how many years we will be held up in these seas? But Hatteras is driven by his frenzy to get to the unreachable Pole, and doesn't bother with such details. Whether or not the wind is against us, he applies full steam and if that carries on just a bit longer, we may be in danger, or perhaps done for.'

'Is that the situation, Shandon? It's serious then!'

'Yes, Wall, not only for the engine, which at critical moments would be of no use to us without fuel, but also our wintering, sooner or later. We need to take into consideration the cold in a place where the mercury often freezes in the thermometer!'[1]

'But isn't the captain counting on finding new provisions at Beechey Island? He'll find plenty of coal there.'

'Do you always go where you want in these seas, Wall? Can you count on finding a particular strait ice-free? And if he does fail to find or reach Beechey Island, what'll happen to us?'

'You've convinced me. Hatteras does seem reckless, but why don't you raise this subject with him?'

'No,' replied Shandon with ill-concealed bitterness, 'I've decided not to say anything; I don't have responsibility for the ship any more; I'll wait and see what happens; I'm commanded, I obey, and I don't give my opinion.'

'Let me say you're wrong, since the common good is in question and the captain's recklessness may cost us all dear.'

'And if I spoke to him, would he listen?'

Wall did not dare reply in the affirmative.

'He might listen to the crew's views.'

'The crew!' replied Shandon, shrugging his shoulders. 'But, my poor Wall, don't you realize anything? They're governed by emotions which have precious little to do with their safety! They know they're heading for the seventy-second parallel and a sum of £1,000 for each degree after that.'

'Yes, and the captain's using the best leverage over his men.'

'Probably—for the time being at least.'

'What do you mean?'

---

[1] Mercury freezes at minus forty-two degrees centigrade.

'That things will go smoothly on the open sea and when the men are not exhausted or in danger; Hatteras has got to them using money; but what you do for money you do badly. When problems happen, like danger, misfortune, illness, discouragement, or cold, which we're rushing towards like madmen, you'll soon find out whether they're still thinking about their bonus!'

'Then, according to you, Shandon, Hatteras won't succeed?'

'No, Wall, he won't; in such an endeavour, you need a perfect sympathy and harmony of ideas between the leaders, which isn't the case here. Anyway, Hatteras is insane; his whole past proves it! We'll see what happens. It may be that circumstances arise where the ship's command has to be given to a safer captain.'

'However,' said Wall shaking his head doubtfully, 'Hatteras will always have on his side . . .'

'He'll have Dr Clawbonny, a scientist who thinks only of research, Johnson, a slave to duty who doesn't bother to reason, perhaps one or two others like Bell the carpenter—four at most; and there are eighteen of us on board! No, Wall, the crew don't trust Hatteras; he's aware that money is his lure; he skilfully used Franklin's catastrophe to win over the undecided; but that won't continue, I tell you, and if he doesn't manage to land on Beechey Island, he's done for!'

'If the crew had the slightest inkling . . .'

'You must promise', Shandon replied sharply, 'not to tell them about these ideas; they'll find out for themselves soon enough. Anyway, it's a good idea to head north for the moment. But what Hatteras thinks is a route to the Pole may easily be the way home. At the end of McClintock Channel is Melville Sound,* plus all those straits leading back to Baffin Bay. Hatteras should be careful. Heading east is easier than north.'

Shandon's attitude can be seen from these words, and the captain was right to suspect a traitor in him. His reasoning was indeed correct when he said the crew were happy because they hoped they would soon reach the seventy-second degree. This desire for money took hold of even the most cowardly on board. Clifton had calculated how much each wanted with great accuracy.

Apart from the captain and the doctor, excluded from the bonus, there were sixteen men on board. The amount was £1,000, which gave £62. 10s. per man and per degree. If ever the Pole was reached, the eighteen degrees covered would give each man £1,125—a fortune.

This dream would cost £18,000, but the captain was rich enough to treat himself to such a trip to the Pole.

As can be imagined, these calculations excited the crew's greed, and quite a few, who had been rejoicing at heading south again a fortnight before, now longed to reach that golden latitude.

On 16 June the *Forward* rounded Cape Acworth. Mount Rawlinson thrust its white peaks heavenwards; by exaggerating the distance, the snow and mist made it seem colossal; the temperature stayed a few degrees above that of ice; waterfalls and improvised cascades proliferated on the mountainside; avalanches rushed down, sounding like the continuous rumbling of heavy artillery. Glaciers, spread out in long white sheets, produced glaring reflections.

Northern nature in the grip of a thaw was a wonderful sight. The brig hugged the coast; on a few sheltered rocks occasional heather was spotted, with pink flowers timidly emerging through the snow, together with thin reddish lichens and shoots of a species of dwarf willow crawling along the ground.

Finally on 19 June, at the much-discussed seventy-second parallel, the brig doubled Minto Head, which forms one side of Ommanney Bay, and entered Melville Bay, nicknamed 'the silver sea'* by Bolton; this cheerful sailor cracked a thousand jokes on the subject, which good Clawbonny heartily laughed at.

Despite a strong north-east wind, the navigation of the *Forward* was straightforward and on 23 June she reached the seventy-fourth degree. She was now in the middle of Melville Bay, one of the largest seas of these regions. It was crossed for the first time by Captain Parry on his great 1819 expedition, and there his crew got the bonus of £5,000 promised by government decree.

Clifton merely remarked that from the seventy-second to seventy-fourth degree made two degrees, which added £125 to his account. But he was told that a fortune was worth little in these waters, that you couldn't consider yourself rich unless you could drink your wealth; celebrations and gleeful rubbing of hands should be saved for when they could roll under the tables of a Liverpool pub.

19

A Whale in Sight

MELVILLE Bay was not ice-free, although easily navigable; huge ice-fields could be seen stretching to the horizon; here and there rose icebergs, but fixed as if moored to the frozen fields. The *Forward* was heading at full steam, following broad passes where she could easily manoeuvre. The wind changed frequently, briskly jumping from one point of the compass to the other.

The variability of the wind in the Arctic seas is a known phenomenon and often a dead calm turns into a raging storm within a few minutes. This is what happened to Hatteras on 23 June, in the centre of the immense sea.

The prevailing winds generally blow from the ice-field out to the open sea and are very cold. That day the thermometer went down a few degrees; the wind veered south and huge storms, passing over the ice-fields, dropped their moisture as thick snow. Hatteras immediately furled the sails, which were helping the propeller, but not quickly enough, for his fore-top-gallant-sail was carried away in the twinkling of an eye.

Hatteras commanded his manoeuvres with the greatest self-discipline and left deck not once; he had to flee before the storm and head west. The wind whipped up enormous waves, containing floating ice of all shapes, torn from the surrounding fields; the brig was shaken like a child's toy and debris from the packs showered over its hull; at times she rose perpendicularly at the summit of a liquid mountain; her steel prow, picking up the diffuse light, sparkled like an ingot being smelted; then she would descend into a great hole, shooting down through her spiralling smoke, until her re-emerging propeller ran free with strange noises as it hit the air with its pales. Rain fell torrentially, mixed with sleet.

The doctor could not miss out on such an occasion to get drenched to the bone; he remained on deck, full of the exhilarating admiration that a scientist can extract from such a spectacle. His closest neighbour would not have heard his voice; so he remained silent and looked; but while looking, he witnessed a bizarre phenomenon particular to the hyperboreal regions.

The storm covered a limited area, not more than three or four miles; in effect, winds that pass over ice-fields lose much of their strength and cannot take their disastrous violence very far; from time to time the doctor noticed a calm sky through some clearer sections and a peaceful sea beyond the ice-fields; the *Forward* only needed to head through the passes to find calm navigation; but if she did, she would risk being thrown on to the ice-fields which moved with the waves. However, after a few hours Hatteras managed to bring his ship to a calmer sea while the violence of the storm, raging in the distance, came to die a few cables away from the *Forward*.

Melville Bay now looked different; because of the waves and winds a large number of mountains had detached from the coasts and were drifting north, coming together and colliding everywhere. Several hundred could be counted; but the bay is very large and the brig easily avoided them. The spectacle was magnificent: floating masses moving at different speeds, vying with each other on this vast racecourse.

The doctor was still at this stage of his enthusiasm, when Simpson the harpooner came up and pointed out a change in the colour of the sea; it varied from intense blue to olive-green; long strips stretched from north to south with lines of demarcation so sharp they remained visible to the horizon. Sometimes also, transparent parts contrasted with others, entirely opaque.

'Well, Dr Clawbonny, what you think of this unusual phenomenon?' asked Simpson.

'My friend, the same as Scoresby the whaler thought of these diversely coloured waters: it's because the green water is full of billions of animalcules and jellyfish but the blue water isn't; he did quite a few experiments on the subject and I can easily believe him.'

'There's another lesson to be drawn from the sea colour, sir.'

'Really?'

'Yes, Dr Clawbonny, and take a harpooner's word for it, if only the *Forward* was a whaler, I think we'd have us a fine time.'

'But I can't see a single whale.'

'It won't be long, I promise. It's amazing luck for whalers to meet green bands at this latitude.'

'And why?'

The doctor was fascinated by these remarks from a man who knew what he was talking about.

'Because it's in these green waters that the most whales are caught.'

'And the reason, Simpson?'

Because they find most food here.'

'Are you certain?'

'I've experienced it a hundred times in Baffin Bay; I don't see why it should be any different in Melville Bay.'

'That does make sense.'

'And look,' replied Simpson, leaning over the rail.

'It looks like a ship's wake.'

'It's a greasy substance the whale leaves after it. Believe me, the animal which produced it can't be very far!'

The atmosphere was indeed full of a strong odour of fresh fish. The doctor began to study the surface of the sea, and the harpooner's prediction did not take long to come true. Foker's voice was heard from the top of the mast.

'A whale!' he cried. 'Downwind.'

All eyes turned in that direction; a small waterspout visible a mile away.

'There it is, there it is!' exclaimed Simpson, drawing on his experience.

'It's disappeared,' said the doctor.

'It'd be easy enough to find it again if we wanted,' said Simpson in a regretful tone.

But, to his astonishment and although nobody would have dared ask, Hatteras gave orders to arm the whaleboat; it was an opportunity for his crew to get some distraction and even a few barrels of oil. This permission was warmly welcomed.

Four sailors got into the whaleboat; Johnson, at the rear, was responsible for the rudder; Simpson stood at the front, his harpoon at the ready. The doctor could not be prevented from joining the expedition. The sea was quite calm. The whaleboat headed off quickly and ten minutes later was a mile from the brig.

The whale, with a new supply of air, had dived again, but it soon came back to the surface and its blowholes sent a mixture of steam and mucus up to a height of fifteen feet.

'There!' said Simpson, indicating a spot eight hundred yards from the launch.

The boat headed quickly towards the animal, and the brig, having also spotted it, approached at easy steam.

The enormous whale was disappearing and reappearing with the waves, showing its blackish back, like a shoal stranded on the open sea; a whale does not swim quickly when not pursued and this one was lazily moving up and down. The launch moved in silently, following the green water whose opacity prevented the creature seeing its enemy. It is always a stirring sight to see a fragile skiff attacking these monsters; this one measured about a hundred and thirty feet, and between the seventy-second and seventy-fourth degrees it is not rare to encounter whales of more than one hundred and eighty feet;* classical writers even spoke of animals 700 feet long; but these must be classified amongst species of the imagination.

Soon the launch was near the whale. On a sign from Simpson, the oars stopped and the skilful sailor balanced his harpoon, then threw it hard; the gun, armed with barbed points, sank into the thick layer of fat. The wounded whale thrust its tail and dived. Immediately the four oars were placed vertically; the rope, attached to the harpoon and ready at the front, unrolled very quickly and the launch was dragged along while Johnson steered it expertly.

In its flight the whale moved away from the brig and headed for the moving icebergs; for half an hour it ran; the harpoon rope had to be drenched so the friction would not set it on fire. When the creature appeared to be slowing down, the rope was gradually pulled in and carefully coiled up; the whale soon reappeared on the surface which it was beating with its formidable tail; the waterspouts it sent up fell back down on the launch like fierce rain. The boat moved in quickly; Simpson had picked up a long lance and was preparing to fight the animal hand to hand.

But the whale headed at full speed into a pass between two ice mountains. The pursuit had now become extremely dangerous.

'Jesus!' said Johnson.

'Forward, forward! Pull, my friends,' exclaimed Simpson, caught up in the thrill of the chase; 'we've got it!'

'But we can't follow it between the two icebergs,' replied Johnson, maintaining the launch.

'We can!' cried Simpson.

'No, no!' shouted some of the sailors.

'Yes!' exclaimed the others.

During the discussion the whale had headed between two floating mountains that the waves and wind were pushing together.

The launch was in danger of being pulled into that dangerous pass and so trapped, when Johnson rushed forward hatchet in hand and cut the rope.

It was time; the two mountains came together with irresistible force, crushing the unfortunate animal between them.

'Lost!' exclaimed Simpson.

'Saved!' replied Johnson.

'Well,' said the doctor, who had not batted an eyelid, 'that was worth seeing!'

The pressure from these mountains is enormous. The whale had just had an accident often witnessed in these seas. Scoresby recounts that during a single summer thirty whaling ships perished in Baffin Bay in this way; he saw a three-master flattened in a minute between two huge walls of ice which came together with frightening speed and sank it with all hands. Two other ships were pierced right through as if by lance attacks before his very eyes: sharp pieces of ice more than one hundred feet long went straight through the wood.*

A few moments later the launch came alongside the brig and was put back in its usual place on deck.

'It's a lesson', said Shandon out loud, 'for people who rashly venture into passes!'

20

Beechey Island

ON 25 June the *Forward* arrived in sight of Cape Dundas, at the north-western tip of Prince of Wales Island. There the difficulties increased along with the number of floes. The sea narrows at this point and the line of Crozier, Young, Day, Lowther, and Garret Islands, in a row like forts before a haven, causes the ice streams to build up in the strait. What in any other circumstance would have taken the brig a day, took her from 25 to 30 June; she stopped, came back, and then waited for the best time to reach Beechey Island, using a great deal of coal, lowering her fire during halts but without ever putting it out, in order to be under pressure at any hour of day or night.

Hatteras knew the level of supplies as well as Shandon; but certain to find fuel on Beechey Island, he was reluctant to waste a minute on economies; he had been much delayed by his detour south and, although he had taken the precaution of leaving England as early as April, he was now no further on than previous expeditions at a similar season.

On the thirtieth, they sighted Cape Walker, at the north-eastern tip of Prince of Wales Island; this was the furthest Kennedy and Bellot reached, on 3 May 1852, after an excursion over the whole of Somerset. Already in 1851 Captain Ommanney* of the Austin expedition had been fortunate enough to replenish his supplies here.

This tall cape has a distinctive reddish-brown colour; when the weather is clear, the view from it can extend to the entrance to Wellington Channel. In the evening (Bellot) Point was seen, on the opposite side of Macleod Bay from Cape Walker. (Bellot) Point* was named in the presence of the young French officer, greeted by the British expedition with three hurrays. In this area the coast is made of yellowish limestone of a very rough appearance; it is protected by enormous ice floes magnificently piled up by the north winds. The *Forward* soon lost sight of land as it continued across Barrow Strait, through loosely adhering ice floes, heading for Beechey Island.*

Hatteras was determined to follow a straight line so as not to miss the island, and hardly left his post the following days; he often climbed to the cross-trees of the top gallant sails to choose the most promising passes. During that crossing of the strait he did everything that could be done with skill, self-control, boldness, and even sailor's genius. Luck, admittedly, did not favour him, for he should have found the sea more or less free at this season. But eventually, by sparing neither his steam, nor his crew, nor himself, he reached his goal.

At 11 a.m. on 3 July the ice-master reported land to north; by determining the position, Hatteras confirmed Beechey Island, the general meeting-point of Arctic navigators. Almost all the ships venturing into these seas put in at this island. Franklin wintered there for the first time, before forcing his way into Wellington Channel. There Cresswell, McClure's lieutenant, having covered 470 miles over the ice, re-embarked on the *Phoenix* and went back to Britain.* The last ship before the *Forward* to anchor on Beechey Island was the *Fox*; McClintock replenished his supplies there on 11 August 1855* and repaired the huts and stores; that was less than two years ago; Hatteras was up to date with recent events.

The mate's heart beat strongly at the sight of the island; when he had last been here, he had been quartermaster on the *Phoenix*; Hatteras questioned him about the shape of the coasts, the anchoring facilities, how to land; the weather turned very fine; it stayed at fifty-seven degrees (14°C).

'Well, Johnson,' asked the captain, 'do you know where you are?'

'Yes, captain, it's definitely Beechey Island. But we need to head slightly north; it's easier to land there.'

'But the houses, the stores?'

'Oh, you can only see them after you land; they're hidden behind those mounds over there.'

'And did you carry large amounts of provisions?'

'Yes, sir. It was here that the Admiralty sent us under Captain Inglefield in 1853, with the steamer, the *Phoenix*, and a transport ship laden down, the *Breadalbane*; we brought enough to supply an entire expedition.'

'But the commander of the *Fox* took a lot of these provisions in 1855.'

'Don't worry, captain, there'll be some left; the cold preserves things amazingly and we'll find it all as fresh and shipshape as when we left it.'

'The food doesn't worry me; I have enough for several years. What I need is coal.'

'Well, captain, we left more than a thousand tons, so there's no reason for concern.'

'Let's move in,' said Hatteras, ceaselessly observing the coast with his telescope.

'Can you see that point?' said Johnson. 'When we've rounded it, we'll be near the landing point. We left from there for Britain with Lieutenant Cresswell and the twelve sick men from the *Investigator*. But if we were lucky to bring back Captain McClure's second-in-command, officer Bellot, who was also with us on the *Phoenix*, never saw his country again! Ah that is a sad memory. Captain, I think we should anchor here.'

'Very well.'

And Hatteras gave orders accordingly.

The *Forward* was in a little bay, sheltered from the north, east, and south winds, lying about a cable from the coast.

'Mr Wall, prepare the launch and send six men to bring the coal on board.'

'Yes, sir.'

'I am going to land in the boat with the doctor and mate. Mr Shandon, would you like to come with us?'

'At your orders.'

A few moments later, with all his hunting and scientific equipment, the doctor sat down with his companions in the boat. Ten minutes later they landed on a low, rocky coast.

'Lead on, Johnson,' said Hatteras. 'Do you know where you are?'

'Perfectly, captain; but there's a monument I didn't expect!'

'I know what it is!' exclaimed the doctor. 'Let's have a look; the stone itself will tell us what it's doing here.'

The four men went up, and the doctor, taking off his cap, solemnly said:

'This, my friends, is a monument to the memory of Franklin and his companions.'

In effect Lady Franklin gave one tablet of black marble to Dr Kane in 1855 and entrusted another one to McClintock in 1858, to be installed on Beechey Island.* McClintock religiously fulfilled his duty, placing the tablet near a funeral stele already erected in Bellot's memory, thanks to Sir John Barrow.*

This tablet had the following inscription:

TO THE MEMORY OF

FRANKLIN, CROZIER, FITZJAMES,

AND ALL THEIR GALLANT VALIANT BROTHER

Officers and faithful companions who suffered, perished for the
cause of science and the glory of the nation.

This stone is erected near the place where they spent their first
Arctic winter and whence they departed to overcome obstacles or else
to perish.

It perpetuates the memory of their compatriots and comrades who held them in respect, and the memory of fear overcome by the faith of the person who lost, in the leader of the expedition, the most devoted and affectionate of husbands.

———

So He brings them into the deserved haven

1855*

This stone on a coast lost in faraway regions was painfully touching; in the presence of these moving regrets, the doctor felt tears coming to his eyes. On the spot where Franklin and his companions arrived, full of energy and hope, there now remained nothing to remember them but a slab of marble! And despite this sombre warning of destiny, the *Forward* was to follow the same path as the *Erebus* and *Terror*.

Hatteras was the first to tear himself away from this dangerous contemplation, and quickly climbed a highish mound, almost devoid of snow.

'From there,' Johnson said, following him, 'we'll be able to see the stores.'

Shandon and the doctor caught up as they reached the top.

But, they could see no shelters on the vast plains, or any other trace of buildings.

'That's strange!' said the mate.

'But the stores?' Hatteras said sharply.

'I'm not sure . . . I can't see . . .' spluttered Johnson.

'Perhaps you're not in the right place?' suggested the doctor.

'But I thought that on this same spot . . .' said Johnson, still thinking.

'Come on, man,' Hatteras said impatiently; 'which way should we go?'

'Down, for I may have made a mistake; in seven years I could have forgotten what these places look like.'

'Especially when the countryside is so monotonous and uniform,' added the doctor.

'But . . .' muttered Johnson.

Shandon had not said a single word.

Johnson stopped after a few minutes.

'But no, no, I was right!'

'Well?' said Hatteras, looking round.

'Why do you say that, Johnson?'

'Can you see those bulges in the ground?' said the mate, pointing to a sort of extumescence near him, in which three swellings could clearly be seen.

'And what do you think it is, Johnson?' asked the doctor.

'That's the graves of Franklin's three sailors! I'm sure it is, and the buildings should be a hundred paces away, and if they're not, it's because . . .'

He did not dare finish his idea; Hatteras rushed ahead, a strong feeling of despair taking hold of him. The desired storehouses should have been there, with the supplies of all sorts he was counting on; but ruin, pillage, upheaval, and destruction had intervened where civilized hands had provided immense resources for exhausted navigators. Who had done the damage? The animals of these regions— wolves, foxes, bears? No, for they would only have destroyed the food; and not a shred of tent remained, not a plank of wood, not a sliver of iron, not a shard of any sort of metal, and, still worse in the present situation, not a scrap of fuel!

Clearly the Eskimos' contacts with European ships had eventually made them realize the value of such objects, which they are completely deprived of; since the *Fox*'s visit, they had often come to this place of plenty, taking and destroying each time, with the logical idea of not leaving any trace of what had been there; and now nothing but a broad blanket of snow covered the ground.

Hatteras was dumbfounded. The doctor looked and shook his head. Shandon remained silent and an attentive observer might have noticed an unpleasant smile on his lips.

At this moment, the men sent by Lieutenant Wall arrived. They understood everything. Shandon went up to the captain and said:

'Mr Hatteras, it seems to me pointless to despair; fortunately we're at the entrance to Barrow Strait – which will take us back to Baffin Bay!'

'Mr Shandon, we are fortunately at the entrance to Wellington Channel, which will take us north!'

'And how will we proceed, captain?'

'Using sail! We still have two months' fuel, more than enough for our next wintering.'

'You will allow me to say . . .' started Shandon.

'I will allow you to follow me back on board.'

And turning his back on his second-in-command, he returned to the brig and shut his cabin door.

For two days the wind was unfavourable; the captain did not appear on deck. The doctor used this enforced stay to explore Beechey Island; he picked up a few sparse plants, which benefited from the relatively high temperature on the snowless rocks: a few heathers, uniform lichens, a species of yellow buttercup, a sort of plant like sorrel with leaves a fraction of an inch across, and vigorous saxifrage.

In this region there appeared more fauna than such limited flora; the doctor noticed long flocks of geese and cranes flying north; the order of birds was fully represented by the partridges, the blue-black eider-ducks, the sandpipers, a sort of surfbird of the class of woodcocks, the northern divers with very long bodies, the many ptarmites, a sort of grouse, very good to eat,* the dovekies with black bodies, white spots on their wings, and feet and beaks as red as coral, the loud bands of kittywakes and the big loons with their white stomachs. The doctor was lucky enough to kill a few grey hares that had not yet put on their white winter fur, plus a blue fox which Duke ran down with remarkable skill. A few bears, clearly accustomed to man's presence, kept their distance, and the seals were extremely shy, undoubtedly for the same reason as their enemies, the bears. The Bay abounded with a sort of whelk, very agreeable to the taste. The class of articulates, order of Diptera, family of *Culicidae*, division of *Nemocera*, was represented by a mere mosquito, a single one, which the doctor had the joy of catching after suffering its bites. He was less lucky in his capacity as conchologist, and had to be content with picking up a sort of mussel and a few bivalve shells.

21

Death of Bellot

ON 3 and 4 July it stayed at fifty-seven (14°C); this was the highest observed during the whole campaign. But on Thursday the fifth, the wind swung round to the south-east, accompanied by heavy flurries of snow. The thermometer had fallen twenty degrees the night before. Without worrying about the crew's bad mood, Hatteras gave orders to cast off. For the last thirteen days, since Cape Dundas, the *Forward* had been unable to gain a single degree northwards, upsetting the party represented by Clifton. His desires, it is true, coincided for the moment with the captain's decision to head up into Wellington Channel, and so he did not make any difficulties with operations.

The brig took sail with difficulty. But having hoisted the foresail, topsails, and top gallant sails during the night, Hatteras advanced boldly through the trains of ice carried south by the current. The crew grew very tired during this sinuous navigation, which often obliged them to counterbrace.

Wellington Channel* is not very broad; it is squeezed between North Devon to the east and Cornwallis Island to the west, considered a peninsula for a long time. It was Sir John Franklin who sailed round it in 1846, following its west coast and then coming back to the channel from the north.

Wellington Channel was explored in 1851 by Captain Penny on the whalers *Lady Franklin* and *Sophia*; one of his lieutenants, Stewart, reached Cape Beechey at 76° 20′ N, and there discovered the open sea. The open sea, that Hatteras was longing for!

'What Stewart found, I will find,' he told the doctor, 'and then I'll be able to use sail to head for the Pole.'

'But aren't you afraid your crew . . .'

'My crew!' Hatteras said harshly.

Then he murmured in a soft voice, to the doctor's astonishment: 'Poor men.'

This was the first sentiment of such a nature he had detected in the captain's heart.

'But no,' the captain continued forcefully, 'they have to follow me. They *will* follow me.'

However, if the *Forward* had no reason to fear collision with the ice streams, still spaced out, it was not gaining much northwards, for the adverse winds often brought it to a halt. With great effort, it passed Capes Spencer and Innis* and then finally on the tenth, a Tuesday, the seventy-fifth parallel, to Clifton's great joy.

The *Forward* was at the very spot where the American vessels, the *Rescue* and *Advance*, commanded by Captain De Haven, experienced such terrible dangers. Dr Kane was on that expedition; at the end of September 1850, surrounded by ice floes, the ships were irresistibly forced back into Lancaster Sound.

It was Shandon who narrated this disaster to James Wall in front of some of the men:

'The *Advance* and *Rescue* were so badly shaken, lifted up, and tossed about by the ice that they had to extinguish fire on board, although it fell to minus eighteen. For the whole winter, the unfortunate crew were kept prisoners by the ice-field, constantly ready to abandon ship, and they did not even take off their clothes for three weeks. It was such a terrible situation that, after drifting 1,000 miles, they were driven back into the middle of Baffin Bay!'

The effect these tales had on the morale of the already unhappy crew can be guessed.

While this discussion was going on, Johnson was conversing with the doctor about an event that had happened in these waters; he had asked the doctor to tell him when the brig was at exactly 75° 30′ N.

'It's there, on that very spot!' exclaimed Johnson. 'That dreaded land!

And tears came to the worthy mate's eyes.

'You mean Lieutenant Bellot's death?'

'Yes, Dr Clawbonny, that heroic officer who was so generous and brave!'

'And it's here the catastrophe happened, you say?'

'On this very spot, this point of the North Devon coast! Oh, fate was very much at work, and the tragedy wouldn't have happened if Captain Pullen* had come back on board sooner!'

'What do you mean?'

'Listen, Dr Clawbonny, and you will see what survival often depends on. Did you know that Lieutenant Bellot first went in search of Franklin in 1850?'*

'Yes, on the *Prince Albert*.'

'Well, back in France in 1853, he got permission to sail on the *Phoenix*, which I was a sailor on, under Captain Inglefield. Using the *Breadalbane*, we had just transported the supplies to Beechey Island.'

'The supplies we so unfortunately couldn't find!'

'The same, Dr Clawbonny. We reached Beechey Island at the beginning of August; on the tenth, Captain Inglefield left the *Phoenix* to join Captain Pullen, who had been separated from his ship the *North Star* for a month. On his return he planned to give the dispatches from the Admiralty to Sir Edward Belcher, wintering in Wellington Channel. Now soon after the departure of our captain, Commander Pullen came back on board. Why couldn't he have got there before Captain Inglefield left! Lieutenant Bellot was afraid our captain might be away for a long time, and knowing the Admiralty dispatches were urgent, offered to take them himself. He entrusted the command of the two ships to Captain Pullen and left on 12 August, with a sledge and a rubber boat. He took with him Harvey, the quartermaster of the *North Star*, and three sailors, Madden, David Hook,* and me. We thought Sir Edward Belcher had to be near Cape Beechey, north of the channel; so we headed in that direction on our sledge, hugging the eastern shore. On the first day we camped three miles from Cape Innis; the next day we halted on an ice floe about three miles from Cape Bowden. During the night, as clear as day, Lieutenant Bellot decided to go and camp on the land, since it was only three miles away; he tried to reach it in the rubber boat; twice a strong south-easterly pushed him back; Harvey and Madden tried in turn and were luckier; they had a rope with them and used it to link the sledge to the coast; we transported three objects with the rope; but during a fourth attempt, we felt our floe beginning to move; Mr Bellot shouted to his companions to let go of the rope, and we were carried away, the lieutenant, David Hook, and me, far from the coast. The wind was blowing strongly from the south-east and it was snowing. But we weren't in great danger yet, and he could easily come back, since we came back!'

Johnson broke off for a moment while examining the fatal coast, then continued:

'After losing sight of our companions, we first tried to take shelter in the tent from our sledge, but in vain; then with our knives we began to cut ourselves a house in the ice. Mr Bellot sat down for half an hour and talked with us about the danger of our situation; I told them I wasn't afraid. "With God's protection," he replied, "we won't lose a single hair from our heads." I then asked him what time it was; he replied about quarter past six. It was 6.15 in the morning on Thursday, 18 August. Then Mr Bellot tied on his books and said he wanted to go and see how the ice was floating; he had only been gone four minutes, when I went to look for him everywhere on the floe we were on; but I couldn't see him and when I returned to our shelter I noticed his stick on the other side of a crevasse, about thirty feet wide and where the ice was all broken up. I called out but got no reply. At that moment the wind was blowing very strongly. I again searched the floe, but could find no trace of the poor lieutenant.'

'And what do you think happened?' asked the doctor, moved by this tale.

'I think that when Mr Bellot came out of the shelter, the wind swept him into the crevasse, and as his coat was buttoned, he couldn't swim back to the surface! Oh, Dr Clawbonny, I've never felt so unhappy in my life! I couldn't believe it! That brave officer had fallen victim to his own devotion, for he wanted to follow Captain Pullen's orders by getting back to land before the ice broke up. A fine young man, popular with all on board, helpful and courageous! He was mourned by everybody in Britain; and when the Eskimos learned that the good lieutenant was dead, from Captain Inglefield on his return from Pound Cove, they themselves wept and exclaimed like me: "Poor Bellot, poor Bellot."'

'But how did you and your companion get back to land?' asked the doctor, touched by this affecting narration.

'For us, it was not difficult; we stayed on the floe without food or fire for another twenty-four hours; but in the end we ran into an ice-field that was stranded on shallows; we jumped on to it and with the help of an oar that we still had, we pulled in a floe that could carry us and manoeuvre like a raft. That was how we reached shore, but alone and without our brave officer!'*

By the time this tale was over, the *Forward* had gone past that fatal coast and Johnson had lost sight of the place of the terrible catastrophe. The next day Griffin Bay was left to port, then two days later, Capes Grinnell and Helpman;* finally on 14 July, Cape Osborn was doubled, and on the fifteenth, the brig moored at the end of the channel, in Baring Bay. The navigation had not been very difficult; Hatteras encountered a sea almost as free as Belcher, when he wintered with the *Pioneer* and *Assistance* at nearly the seventy-seventh degree. It was from 1852 to 1853, during his first wintering, for he spent the winter of 1853–4 on this Baring Bay where the *Forward* was now moored.

Following the most frightening experiences, trials, and dangers, Belcher had to abandon his ship the *Assistance* amongst the eternal ice.

Shandon narrated this catastrophe in front of the demoralized sailors. Did Hatteras know of this betrayal by his first officer? It was impossible to say, for he remained silent on the subject.

Opposite Baring Bay is a narrow strait which connects Wellington Channel with Queen Channel.* There the trains of ice were packed close together. Hatteras made vain efforts to traverse the passes north of Hamilton Island; the wind was adverse; he had therefore to slip between Hamilton and Cornwallis Islands; five days were lost in useless efforts. The temperature was generally dropping, and even fell to twenty-six (−4°C) on 19 July; it went up the following day; but this early threat of the Arctic winter meant Hatteras should not wait any longer. The wind was tending to be westerly, opposing the progress of his ship. And yet he was in a hurry to reach the point where Stewart found the open sea. On the nineteenth he resolved to advance into the channel at all costs; the wind was blowing against the brig, which could have used its screw to fight these violent snow-laden squalls; but Hatteras absolutely had to save his fuel; also, the pass was too broad to allow the brig to be hauled. Without taking into account the crew's tiredness, Hatteras resorted to a method sometimes employed by whalers in similar circumstances. He had the boats placed on the surface, while at the same time maintaining them suspended in their tackle at the sides of the ship; these boats were made fast fore and aft; the oars were outfitted to starboard or port; in rotation the men sat on the rowing benches and had to pull* vigorously in order to push the brig against the wind.

The *Forward* advanced slowly into the channel; one can understand the fatigue produced by this sort of work; muttering could be heard. Navigation continued in this way for four days, until 23 June,* when they managed to reach Baring Island in Queen Channel.

The wind was still unfavourable. The crew couldn't put one foot in front of another. The doctor thought that the men's health was weakened, and that he could see the first signs of scurvy in some of them; he neglected nothing to fight that terrible scourge, having abundant supplies of lime juice and pastils at his disposal.

Hatteras understood that he could no longer count on the crew; gentleness and persuasion would have had no effect; so he decided to be ruthless and on occasion pitiless; he distrusted Richard Shandon especially, and even James Wall, who did not dare speak up. Hatteras had the doctor, Johnson, Bell, and Simpson on his side, men devoted to him body and soul; amongst those floating he noted Foker, Bolton, Wolsten the armourer, and Brunton the first engineer, who could turn against him at any time; as for the others, Pen, Gripper, Clifton, and Waren, they were openly discussing plans to mutiny; they wanted to win over their comrades and force the *Forward* back to Britain.

Hatteras could see that he could no longer get this crew, ill-disposed and above all exhausted, to continue the manoeuvres. For twenty-four hours he remained in sight of Baring Island without moving an inch. Meanwhile, the temperature was falling and the influence of winter is already felt in July at these high latitudes. On the twenty-fourth it went down to twenty-two (−6°C). Young ice formed each night, to a thickness of six- to eight-tenths of an inch; if it snowed on top it would soon be strong enough to bear the weight of a man. The sea was already turning the dirty colour that precedes the formation of the first crystals.

Hatteras did not misread these alarming symptoms; if the passes did close up, he would be forced to winter here, far from the purpose of his voyage, and without even glimpsing the open sea that had to be so close, according to his predecessors' reports. He decided therefore to head forward, whatever the cost, so as to gain a few degrees north; with the crew at the end of their tether, he knew he could not use the oars, or the sails in a permanently adverse wind, so he gave the order to light the boilers.

22

First Signs of Mutiny

ON this unexpected command, there was considerable surprise on board the *Forward*.

'Light the boilers!' said some.

'With what?' said others.

'When we've got less than two months' coal in our bellies!' exclaimed Pen.

'And how will we heat in the winter?' asked Clifton.

'Will we have to burn the ship down to its flotation line?' asked Gripper.

'And put the masts in the stove,' replied Waren, 'from the fore top gallant to the bowsprit jib-boom?'

Shandon stared at Wall. The stupefied engineers were unsure whether to descend to the machine room.

'Did you hear me!' exclaimed the captain irritatedly.

Brunton headed for the hatch, but stopped before going down.

'Don't go, Brunton.'

'Who spoke?' exclaimed Hatteras.

'Me,' said Pen, advancing towards the captain.

'And you said?'

'I . . . said,' Pen replied with swear words, 'I said that we've had enough, that we won't go any further, that we don't want to die from cold and exhaustion this winter, and that we won't light the boilers!'

'Mr Shandon,' Hatteras said coldly, 'clap this man in irons.'

'But, captain,' answered Shandon, 'what this man said . . .'

'If you repeat what this man said, I will have you placed in your cabin under lock and key! Have this man arrested, do you hear?'

Johnson, Bell, and Simpson headed towards Pen, beside himself with anger.

'The first to touch me . . . !' he exclaimed, picking up a handspike and brandishing it above his head.

Hatteras went up to him.

'One move, Pen, and I'll blow your brains out!'

Calmly saying this, he cocked his revolver and pointed it at the sailor.

Muttering could be heard.

'Not a word, you others, or this man is dead!'

At the same time, Johnson and Bell disarmed Pen, who no longer resisted and allowed himself to be led to the bottom of the hold.

'Go, Brunton.'

The engineer went back down to his post, followed by Plover and Waren. Hatteras came back to the poop.

'That Pen is a wretch,' the doctor said.

'Never has a man been closer to death,' was all the captain replied.

Soon the steam had gained sufficient pressure; the anchors of the *Forward* were hauled in; cutting east, the ship set sail for Cape Becher,* using its stem to slice through the new ice.

Between Baring Island and Cape Becher, there are a fair number of islands, stranded so to speak amongst the ice-fields; the many ice streams had to crowd together into the many narrow straits; they were beginning to stick together as it was fairly cold; hummocks were forming here and there, and it was clear that as the ice floes were already getting more compact, packed, and dense, they would soon form an impenetrable mass, with the help of the first hard frost.

The *Forward* was sailing into this channel, with great difficulty and through the whirlwinds of snow. However, with the changeability that characterizes the weather of these regions, the sun appeared from time to time; the temperature would rise a few degrees; the obstacles melted as if by enchantment; and a fine expanse of water, charming to contemplate, would extend where previously ice floes studded every pass. The horizon took on magnificent orange hues, pleasantly soothing to the eye after the eternal whiteness of the snows.

On Thursday, 26 July the *Forward* hugged Dundas Island, and then veered north; but she soon found herself facing an ice shelf, eight or nine feet high, made up of small icebergs torn from the coast; so for a long time she was obliged to continue curving westwards. The continuous cracking of the ice added to the groans of the ship, to produce a sad sound, resembling sighs and complaints. Finally the brig found a pass and struggled into it; often an enormous ice floe would paralyse her route for long hours; the fog restricted the pilot's view; provided he could see a mile ahead, obstacles could easily be avoided; but in the midst of the flurries, vision was often limited to less than a cable. The strong swell was tiring.

Sometimes the smooth, polished clouds had a remarkable sheen, as if reflecting the ice-fields; but there were days when the yellowish sunlight was unable to penetrate the unrelenting fog.

Birds were still very numerous, their cries deafening; seals, lazily stretched out on drifting ice floes, raised their unfrightened heads and twisted their long necks as the ship passed; as she cut past their floating dwellings, she occasionally left torn-off sheets of her cladding.

Finally, after six days of slow navigation, Cape Becher was sighted to the north on 1 August; Hatteras spent his last hours in the top gallant sail cross-trees; the open sea that Stewart glimpsed at about 76° 20′ N on 30 May 1851 could not be far; and yet, however far Hatteras looked, he could see no sign of an ice-free polar basin. He climbed down again without a word.

'Do you believe in this open sea?' Shandon asked the lieutenant.

'I'm beginning to wonder.'

'Wasn't I right to dub that so-called discovery a pipedream and guesswork? Nobody believed me, Wall, and even you didn't support me!'

'We'll believe you in future.'

'When it's too late.'

And Shandon returned to his cabin, where he had spent most of the time since his discussion with the captain.

The wind veered south again in the evening. Hatteras had the sails unfurled and the boiler put out; for a few days, the crew executed the most difficult manoeuvres; at each moment, they had to luff, fall off, or back the sails to slow down the brig; the braces of the yards, already stiffened by the cold, ran poorly through the distorted pulleys and added further to the fatigue; it took more than a week to reach Barrow Point. In ten days the *Forward* had gained less than thirty miles.

There the wind veered north again, and the propeller was started up once more. Hatteras still hoped to find a sea free of obstacles beyond the seventy-seventh degree, like Edward Belcher.

And yet, according to Penny's stories, the part of the sea he was now on should have been free, for Penny reached the limit of the ice and used a small boat to reconnoitre the shore of Queen Channel as far as the seventy-seventh degree.

Was he therefore to consider these narrations as fictional? Or had a precocious winter descended on these northern regions?

On 15 August Mount Percy thrust its peaks up through the mist, covered with eternal snows; a vicious wind noisily fired a grapeshot of fine hail. The next day the sun set for the first time, finally ending the long series of twenty-four-hour days. The men had in the end got used to this permanent light; but the animals had not been much affected; the Greenland dogs went to sleep at the usual time, and Duke himself went to bed regularly each evening, as though darkness covered the horizon.

However, it never got completely dark on the following nights; although below the horizon, the sun still gave sufficient light by refraction.

On 19 August, after a goodish shooting of the sun, Cape Franklin was sighted on the east coast, and Cape Lady Franklin, on the west; at probably the furthest point reached by that bold navigator, the name of his devoted wife stands opposite his own, a sign of his compatriots' gratitude—and of the love still uniting the couple!

The doctor was moved by this rapprochement, this moral union between two pieces of land at the heart of these isolated regions.

On Johnson's advice, the doctor was already getting used to the low temperatures; he was invariably on deck, braving the cold, wind, and snow. Although a little thinner, his health was not affected by the cruel climate. In any case he expected further dangers, and even observed the impending signs of winter with high spirits.

'Look,' he said one day to Johnson, 'look at those flocks of birds emigrating south! They're escaping with regular wing-beats, crying farewell!'

'Something's told them to go and so they're off.'

'Quite a few of our men might be tempted to do the same!'

'Weak hearts, I'll be hanged! The animals haven't stocked up on food like us, so they need to live their lives in other places! But sailors with a good ship under their feet can go to the ends of the world.'

'So you think Hatteras'll win?'

'He will win, Dr Clawbonny.'

'Even if he kept only one faithful companion!'

'There'd be two of us!'

'Yes!' said the doctor, shaking the good sailor's hand.

The *Forward* was now working its way along Prince Albert Land, also known as Grinnell Land,* in fact the normal name—although Hatteras would never have seen it like that, with his hatred for the Yankees. It has two names because, at the same time as the Briton Penny was baptizing it Prince Albert, the commander of the *Rescue*, Lieutenant De Haven, was calling it Grinnell, in honour of the New York businessman who had financed his expedition.

Following the coast's ins and outs, the brig experienced terrible problems, now using sail, now steam. On 18 August Mount Britannia was sighted, barely visible through the mist, and the following day the *Forward* cast anchor in Northumberland Inlet. It was completely surrounded.

23

The Assault of the Ice Floes

AFTER supervising the anchoring, Hatteras returned to his cabin and carefully plotted the position on the map: he was at 76° 57′ N, 99° 20′ W, only three minutes from the seventy-seventh parallel. It was on this very spot that Sir Edward Belcher spent his first winter on board the *Pioneer* and *Assistance*. It was from here that he organized sledge and boat excursions, discovering Table Island, North Cornwall, the Victoria Archipelago, and Belcher Channel. Having crossed the seventy-eighth degree, he saw the coast getting lower south-eastwards. The shore seemed to connect with Jones Strait, whose entrance is on Baffin Bay. But to the north-west, in contrast, an open sea stretched as far as the eye could see, according to his report.

Hatteras avidly studied the marine charts where an extended white section indicated unknown regions, and his eye returned to the ice-free polar basin over and over again.

With so much evidence, he said to himself, with the accounts of Stewart, Penny, and Belcher, it must exist! There can't be any mistake! Those brave sailors saw it with their own eyes! Can one doubt their reports? But if this sea, free at that time, was, after a precocious winter . . . but no, the observations were made over several years; this basin exists; I'll find it; I shall see it!

Hatteras went back to the poop. A thick fog enveloped the *Forward*; the tip of the mast was barely visible from the deck. All the same, Hatteras had the ice-master come down from his crow's nest, and took his place; he wanted to seize the slightest clearing of the weather to examine the north-west skyline.

Shandon had taken the opportunity to ask the lieutenant:

'Well, Wall, and the open sea?'

'You're right, and we've only got six weeks' coal left in our holds.'

'The doctor will find some scientific process to warm us without fuel. I've heard that you can make ice with fire; perhaps we can make fire with ice?'

Shandon went back to his cabin, shrugging his shoulders.

The following day, 20 August, the fog opened for a few seconds. Hatteras was seen looking quickly at the horizon from his high position; then he came down again without a word, and gave orders to proceed; but it was easy to see that his hopes had been dashed one last time.

The *Forward* hauled in her anchor and set off uncertainly northwards. As she was making heavy weather, the topsails and top gallant sails were brought down, together with their yards; the masts were unreeved; the ship could no longer use the wind, too variable because of the winding passes; big whitish patches were forming here and there on the sea like oil slicks; they were the first sign of an impending general frost; as soon as the wind fell, the sea would freeze almost instantaneously; but when the wind came back, the young ice broke up again and disappeared. In the evening the thermometer went down to seventeen ($-7°$C).

When the brig reached the end of a closed pass, she would change into a ram and throw herself at the obstacle at full steam, and so force it open. Sometimes she seemed to be trapped once and for all; but an unexpected movement of the streams would open up a new passage and she would head boldly on; during these pauses the steam from her valves condensed in the cold air and fell as snow on deck. Something else made the brig halt: every now and then the ice floes got caught up in the pales of the propeller, so hard that all the machine's exertions could not break them off; the steam then had to be reversed, the ship come back, and men sent to free the propeller using levers and handspikes; hence difficulties, exhaustion, and delays.

For thirteen days it was like that; the *Forward* dragged herself painfully along Penny Strait. The crew were muttering, but they did obey; they realized that going back was now impossible. Heading north was less dangerous than fleeing south; the wintering needed to be considered.

The sailors talked amongst themselves about this new situation and one day they even mentioned it to Richard Shandon, whom they knew to be on their side. In neglect of his duties, the officer was not afraid to let them discuss the captain's authority in his presence.

'So you say, Mr Shandon,' Gripper asked, 'that we can't retrace our steps?'

'It's too late now.'

'So,' added another sailor, 'wintering is the only thing to think about?'

'It's all we can do! People didn't want to believe me . . .'

'Next time we will,' answered Pen who had returned to his usual work.

'Since I won't be in charge,' retorted Shandon.

'Who knows?' said Pen. 'John Hatteras is free to travel as far as he thinks fit, but we don't have to go with him.'

'You just need to look', added Gripper, 'at his first visit to Baffin Bay and how it all turned out!'

'Plus his command of the *Farewell*,' said Clifton, 'which got lost in the seas around Spitzbergen!'

'And when he came back on his own,' added Gripper.

'With his dog,' replied Clifton.

'We don't want to be sacrificed just to please this man,' added Pen.

'We don't want to lose the bonus we've worked so hard for!'

Clifton could be recognized in this self-interested remark.

'When we've passed the seventy-eighth degree,' he added, 'and we're not far from it, that'll make £375 each—six times eight degrees!'*

'But,' replied Gripper, 'wouldn't we lose it if we went back without the captain?'

'No,' replied Clifton; 'provided there was evidence that heading back was the only choice.'

'But the captain . . . all the same . . .'

'Don't worry, Gripper,' said Pen; 'we'll have a captain, and a good one, who Mr Shandon knows. When commanders go mad, they're impeached and others appointed. Aren't they, Mr Shandon?'

'My friends,' Shandon replied evasively, 'you will always find me a devoted soul, but let's see what happens.'

A storm was clearly building up over Hatteras's head. Firm, energetic, always confident, unshakeable, the captain was boldly advancing. Although he had not been in control of where his ship had gone, she had performed valiantly; in five months she had done as much as other navigators had done in two or three years! Hatteras now found himself forced to winter; but the situation could not frighten strong, firm hearts, tried and tested souls, intrepid and steely minds! Did Sir John Ross and McClure not spend three successive winters in the Arctic? It had been done once, so why not again?

'Definitely, and more if we have to! Ah,' Hatteras would say wistfully to the doctor, 'why didn't I force the entrance to Smith at the north of Baffin Bay; I'd be at the Pole now!'

'Right!' invariably replied the doctor, who would have feigned confidence if need be. 'We'll get there, captain, along the ninety-ninth meridian instead of the seventy-fifth, it's true, but what difference does it make? If all roads lead to Rome, it's even truer that all meridians lead to the Pole!'

On 31 August the thermometer read thirteen (−10°C). The end of the sailing season was near; the *Forward* left Exmouth Island to starboard, and three days later went past Table Island, in the centre of Belcher Channel. At a less advanced season, she would perhaps have been able to get back to Baffin Bay by this route, but that could not now be contemplated, as the channel was entirely blocked by ice and would not have offered an inch of water to the *Forward*'s keel; the view consisted of endless ice-fields, motionless for another eight months.

Fortunately, a few minutes northward could still be gained, but on condition the new ice was broken with big rollers or explosives. What was to be feared at these low temperatures was a calm atmosphere, for the passes froze quickly; and so even adverse winds were greeted with joy. One calm night and everything would be frozen.

The *Forward* could not winter in its present position, exposed to the winds and icebergs drifting through the channel; a safe shelter was the first thing to find; Hatteras hoped to reach the coast of New Cornwall and find a sufficiently protected bay beyond Albert Point. So he doggedly continued north.

But on 8 September, a massive ice floe, impenetrable and uncrossable, moved between him and the north; it went down to ten (−12°C). A worried Hatteras could not find a way through, despite risking his ship a hundred times, getting out of dangerous situations through prodigious skill. He could be accused of rashness, lack of planning, madness, blindness; but a good sailor he certainly was, amongst the best!

The situation of the *Forward* had become truly dangerous; the sea was closing up behind her, and within a few hours the ice became so hard that the men could walk on it and pull the ship without danger.

Hatteras was unable to go round the obstacle, so he decided to attack it face on; he employed his strongest blasting cylinders, with eight to ten pounds of powder; first the ice was bored right through; next a cylinder was carefully placed in a horizontal position, to maximize the amount of ice affected by the explosion, and the hole filled with snow; then the fuse, protected by a gutta percha tube, was ignited.

In this way the men worked to break the ice-pack, for it could not be sawn, as the cuts immediately joined up again. Hatteras could hope to get through the following day.

But the wind raged during the night; the sea rose under its icy crust as if shaken by some submarine commotion; and the pilot uttered these terrified words:

'Danger to stern!'

Hatteras looked; what he saw through the dawn light was frightening.

A tall ice floe was being pushed northwards and was heading towards the ship as fast as an avalanche.

'All hands on deck,' he cried.

The mountain was now less than half a mile away; the ice floes were jumping over each other, turning each other over, like enormous grains of sand swept before a formidable storm; a terrifying din shook the air.

'This is one of the worst dangers we've met,' said Johnson.

'Yes,' calmly replied the doctor, 'it is rather frightening.'

'A genuine attack that we need to ward off.'

'It's like an enormous herd of antediluvian animals, the ones that are meant to have lived at the Pole! They're speeding up! They're racing to see who can get here first.'

'And some are armed with sharp lances which I challenge you to withstand, Dr Clawbonny.'

'It's a genuine siege! Well, let's man the ramparts.'

And he rushed to the stern, where the crew, armed with perches, iron bars, and handspikes, were getting ready to resist this alarming assault.

The avalanche was getting closer and gaining height, growing with the surrounding ice that it carried along in its swirling progress; on Hatteras's orders, the for'ard cannon was fired, to try to break this menacing line. But it arrived and threw itself over the brig; there was a cracking noise, and as the starboard quarter was rammed into, part of the bulwark broke.

'Nobody move!' exclaimed Hatteras. 'Watch out for the ice!'

The ice was mounting irresistibly; ice floes weighing many hundredweight were climbing up the sides of the ship; smaller ones, thrown up to the tops, fell down like sharp arrows, breaking the shrouds, cutting the rigging. The crew could not cope with these enemies without number, whose weight would have crushed a hundred ships like the *Forward*. They were all trying to push back the invading rocks, and quite a few were wounded by their sharp edges, including Bolton, whose left shoulder was badly cut. The noise was reaching a frightening level. Duke was barking angrily at this new sort of adversary. The shades of night soon added to the horror of the situation, but without hiding the irritable blocks whose whiteness reflected the last gleams in the air.

Hatteras's commands still rang out during this strange, impossible, supernatural battle between men and ice floes. Because of the enormous pressure, the ship was listing to port and the end of her main yard was already bending against the ice-field, at the risk of breaking the mast.

Hatteras understood the danger; it was a terrible moment; the brig was threatening to turn upside down, the masts to be lost.

One enormous block, as big as the ship itself, now seemed to rise up the hull; it was climbing with irresistible force; it got higher, and soon went past the poop; if it fell on the *Forward*, everything was finished; soon it stood straight up, higher than the yard of the top gallant sail, and it moved back and forth.

A cry of terror escaped from every breast. All fled to starboard.

But suddenly the ship was totally eased.* She was carried away and floated in the air for an imperceptible moment, then leaned over, fell on the ice floes, and there she underwent a rolling motion which made her rails crack. What was happening?

Lifted by the rising tide, pushed on by the blocks attacking her from behind, she was crossing the uncrossable ice-pack. After a minute—a century—of this strange navigation, she had traversed the obstacle and fell back down on an ice-field; her weight made her pass through, and soon she was back in her element.

'We're past the ice-pack!' exclaimed Johnson, rushing to the front of the brig.

'Thank God,' replied Hatteras.

In effect, the brig was in a basin; ice surrounded her on all sides and, although her keel was in water, she could not move; but although she remained motionless, the field was moving for her.

'We're drifting, captain,' cried Johnson.

'Let it happen.'

And how could this force possibly have been resisted?

Day broke, and it was observed that the ice-field was floating north, in a strong submarine current. This floating mass transported the *Forward*, nailed to the heart of the field, without visible limit; foreseeing catastrophe if the brig was dashed on the coast or crushed by the ice, a large quantity of provisions, camping equipment, and blankets for the crew were brought on deck; like Captain McClure in similar circumstances, Hatteras had the ship protected with a ring of hammocks inflated with air, to prevent the worst damage; with soon a temperature of seven (−14°C) and a build-up of ice, the ship was surrounded by a high wall, only its mast emerging.

For a week it navigated like this; Albert Point, which forms the western tip of New Cornwall, was glimpsed on 10 September, but soon lost; the ice-field headed east from that moment on. Where was it going? Where would it end up? Who could say?

The crew waited, arms crossed. Finally, at about 3 p.m. on 15 September, the ice-field suddenly halted, having presumably collided with another field; the ship received a violent shock; Hatteras had taken his bearings that day and now consulted his map; he was in the north with no land in view, at 78° 15′ N, 95° 35′ W, at the centre of that region, that unknown sea, where geographers have placed the pole of cold!*

24

Preparations for Wintering

THE southern hemisphere is colder than the northern at the same latitude; but the temperature of the New Lands is still fifteen degrees below that of other parts of the world; and these regions of America, known as the pole of cold, are the most redoubtable.

The average temperature over the year is only minus two (−19°C). Dr Clawbonny shared the opinion of scientists, as follows.

They have explained that the prevailing winds of the northern regions of America are the south-westerlies; they leave the Pacific at a constant and tolerable temperature; but to reach the Arctic seas, they have to cross the immense snow-covered territory of America; the contact cools them down and they spread their glacial bitterness over the northern regions.

Hatteras was at the pole of cold, past the regions glimpsed by his predecessors; he was therefore expecting to spend a terrible winter on this ship lost in the midst of the ice and with a semi-mutinous crew. He resolved to fight the various dangers with his usual energy. He regarded the situation squarely, without blinking.

He began by taking every step needed for the wintering, helped by Johnson's experience. According to his calculations, the *Forward* had been carried 250 miles from the last known land, New Cornwall; she was held in an ice-field as if in a granite bed, and no human power could get her out again.

There was no longer a drop of free water in these vast seas, struck by the Arctic winter. The ice-fields stretched as far as the eye could see, although not offering a uniform surface. Far from it. Numerous icebergs impaled the icy plain, and the *Forward* was sheltered by the tallest ones at three points of the compass; only the south-east wind blew at her. If one imagines rocks instead of ice floes, greenery instead of snow, and the sea liquid once more, the brig could have been quietly mooring in a pretty bay sheltered from the worst of the wind. But what desolation at this latitude, what saddening nature, what lamentable contemplations!*

However motionless the ship seemed, she still had to be firmly fixed using her anchors; a break-up of the ice or underwater pressure was a real danger. On learning that the *Forward* was at the pole of cold, Johnson monitored the wintering measures even more severely.

'We're going to see hard times!' he said to the doctor. 'Just our captain's luck! To go and get nipped at the worst point on the globe! But we'll get out of it, just you see.'

As for the doctor, deep down he was quite simply delighted by the situation. He would not have changed it for any other. To winter at the pole of cold: what luck!

Outside works occupied the crew first; the sails remained bent instead of being put at the bottom of the hold, as the first winterers did. They were merely folded into their covers and soon the ice made an impermeable envelope for them; the top gallant masts were not even unreeved, and the crow's nest remained in place. It was a natural observatory. Only the running rigging was taken down.

The surrounding field had to be cut to reduce the pressure on the ship. The ice floes built up on her sides weighed a lot; she was not at her usual flotation line. Excruciating work. After a few days the hull was free from its prison, and the opportunity was taken to examine it; it had not suffered thanks to the strength of construction; only the outer layer of copper had almost entirely been stripped away. When the ship was free again, she had risen nearly nine inches; the men then bevelled the ice to follow the shape of the hull; in this way the ice under the keel of the brig was in one piece and itself resisted any change in pressure.

The doctor participated in these works; he skilfully wielded the snow knife; he buoyed up the sailors with his good mood. He instructed and was instructed. He warmly approved the arrangement of ice under the ship.

'That's a sensible precaution.'

'Without it,' replied Johnson, 'we couldn't resist. Now we can safely build a wall of snow to the top of the gunnel, making it ten feet thick if we want, as there's plenty of material.'

'Excellent idea; snow is a poor conductor of heat; it reflects instead of absorbing; and so the warmth will be kept in.'

'Exactly; we'll increase the protection against the cold—and the animals, if they get it in their heads to pay us a visit; once the work's finished, it'll look good, you'll see; we'll use a knife to cut two stair-cases in that mound of snow, creating access at both the front and rear of the ship; once the steps are cut, we can pour water on them; the water will turn to ice, as hard as rock, and we'll have us a right royal staircase.'

'Perfect,' answered the doctor; 'it's lucky that cold produces snow and ice, material to protect us against it. Without that, we'd be in a right pickle.'

In effect, the ship would soon disappear under a thick layer of ice, which would conserve her internal heat; a roof made of thick oiled canvas was built the whole length of the deck and then covered with snow; the material came far enough down to cover the sides of the ship. As the deck was protected from any outside effect, it provided a perfect place for strolling; two and a half feet of snow were placed on it; the snow was compressed and beaten so as to become hard; it thus provided another obstacle to the release of the internal heat; a layer of sand was added which became a tough macadamization as it worked itself in.

'With a few trees,' said the doctor, 'I'd almost believe I was in Hyde Park or the Hanging Gardens of Babylon.'*

A circular hole was made in the field not far from the brig; it was a real well, to be kept permanently open; each morning the ice on top was broken; it was to provide water in case of fire and for the crewmen's frequent baths, ordered as a hygiene measure; care was even taken to save fuel by drawing the water from the deeper parts where it was less cold; this result was achieved by means of an apparatus noted by a French scientist;* lowered to a certain depth, it gave access to the surrounding water by means of a cylinder with an adjustable double bottom.

To gain room, the objects cluttering up ships are usually removed for the winter months and deposited in stores on land. But what can be done on a coast is impossible for a ship moored to an ice-field.

Everything was arranged inside to combat the two great enemies at these latitudes: cold and humidity; the first produced the second, still more redoubtable; cold can be resisted, but humidity kills; so it needed to be prevented.

The *Forward* was designed for navigation in Arctic seas, and so had an ideal layout for wintering; the main crew room was wisely planned; corners, where humidity gathers first, had been eliminated; in effect when the temperature drops, a deposit of ice forms in the corners of the open spaces, and when it melts it produces constant humidity. A circular crew room would have been even better; but, heated by a huge stove and suitably ventilated, the room would surely be perfectly liveable; the walls were covered with buckskin,* and not woollen material, for wool traps the water vapour as condensation, which then fills the air.

The partitions were taken down in the poop, and the officers gained a bigger common room, with better aeration and heat from the stove. This room and the crew's each had a sort of antechamber, so that there was no direct communication with the outside. The heat could not escape; and one went progressively from one temperature to another. Clothes with snow on them were left in the antechambers; feet were cleaned on scrapers* outside, to avoid introducing unhealthy elements.

Canvas tubes served to let in the air for the drawing of the stoves; other tubes allowed the water vapour to escape. Condensers were also set up in the two rooms and collected the water vapour and so reduced the total amount of humidity; they were emptied twice a week and sometimes held several bushels of ice, a considerable victory over the enemy.

The fires were perfectly easily regulated by means of air tubes; it was realized that a small quantity of coal was sufficient to maintain a temperature of fifty degrees (10°C). However, after inspecting his holds, Hatteras conceded that even with the greatest economy, he had less than two months' fuel left.

A drying area was set up for the clothes, which had to be often washed; they could not be dried in the open air, for they would have become hard and fragile.

The fragile parts of the engine were carefully taken apart; and the engine room was hermetically sealed.

Life on board became the subject of serious consideration; Hatteras regulated it with the greatest attention, the guidelines being posted in the common room. The men got up at six; the hammocks were aired three times a week; the floors of both rooms were scrubbed with hot sand each morning; boiling tea accompanied each meal; the food changed as much as possible, depending on the day of the week: sugar, cocoa, tea, rice, lemon juice, preserved meat, beef, salt pork, cabbage, and pickled vegetables; plus puddings made from bread, flour, beef suet, and raisins; the kitchen was situated outside the common rooms; its heat was lost, but cooking is a constant source of evaporation and hence humidity.

Health depends a great deal on the sort of food eaten; at these high latitudes as much animal produce as possible must be eaten. The doctor had been in charge of planning the diet.

'We need to imitate the Eskimos; they received lessons from nature and are past masters; if Arabs and Africans can thrive on a few dates and handfuls of rice, here it is important to eat a great deal. The Eskimos ingest up to ten or fifteen pounds of oil a day. If you don't like this diet, we'll have to employ substances rich in sugar and fat.* In a word, we need carbohydrates; let's have carbohydrates! It's good to put coal in the stove, but let's not forget to fill the precious stoves we have inside us!'

As well as this diet, strict cleanliness was imposed on the crew;

every other day, each man had to bathe in the icy water provided by the fire hole—an excellent way of maintaining natural heat. The doctor set an example; he did it first of all as a surely unpleasant thing; but this pretext soon disappeared, for he ended up really enjoying this ultra-hygienic immersion.

When the work, hunting, or reconnaissance took men outside in the extreme cold, they had to take special care not to get frostbitten; if some part of their body did get frozen, then snow had to be rubbed on it quickly to restore blood circulation. For this reason, the men were carefully dressed in wool over their whole bodies, and wore buckskin caps and sealskin trousers, perfectly impervious to the wind.

Getting things organized on the ship and settling in on board took about three weeks; and thus 10 October passed without further incident.

25

An Old Fox from James Ross's Time

THAT day it went down to minus three (−16°C). It was quite calm; the cold could easily be borne when there was no wind. Hatteras took advantage of the clear weather to reconnoitre the surrounding plains; he climbed one of the highest icebergs northwards, but with the eyepiece of his telescope discovered only a succession of ice mountains and fields. No land in view, just a vision of chaos in its bleakest form. He came back on board trying to estimate how long his captivity would last.

The hunters, especially the doctor, James Wall, Simpson, Johnson, and Bell, were nearly always able to provide fresh meat for the ship. Most of the birds had disappeared, seeking gentler climes to the south. Only the ptarmigans—rock partridges particular to this latitude—had not fled with the winter; they were easy to kill and because there were so many of them, they offered abundant game reserves.

Hares, foxes, wolves, ermines, and bears abounded; a French, British, or Norwegian huntsman would have had no reason to complain; but these shy animals nearly always ran away; also, it was difficult to make out the white animals against the white plains, for they change colour and put on their winter fur before the great colds. Contrary to what certain naturalists believe, the doctor observed that this change was not due to the fall in temperature, for it happened before October; so it was not physical reasons, but providential fore-thought, which enabled these Arctic animals to face the rigours of a northern winter.

The hunters often encountered harbour seals, sometimes known as 'sea dogs', included in the general category of seals; hunting them was very useful, for both their skins and their fat, perfect fuel. In addition their livers provided excellent food, if need be; there were hundreds of these enormous amphibians, and the ice-field two or three miles north of the ship was punctuated by the holes they had made; but they had a remarkable ability to scent hunters and, even when wounded, many escaped by diving under the ice.

However, on the nineteenth, Simpson managed to catch one 400 yards away from the ship; as he had blocked its escape hole, the animal was at his mercy. It fought for a long time but was finally overcome after several shots; it was nine feet long; with its bulldog head, its sixteen teeth, its large pectoral fins, and its small tail equipped with another pair of fins, it formed a magnificent specimen of the family of harbour seals. The doctor wanted to preserve its head for his natural history collection and its skin for future use; he prepared both using a quick and cheap method. He dropped the body into the fire hole, whereupon thousands of small shrimps removed every fragment of flesh; half a day later the work was finished, and the most skilful member of the Honourable Guild of Tanners of Liverpool could not have done better.

As soon as the sun had passed the autumn equinox, on 23 September, the Arctic winter had effectively begun. This precious heavenly body descended below the horizon and disappeared on 23 October, after grazing the crests of the icy mountains with its oblique rays. The doctor said a scientist and traveller's farewell. He would not see it again until February.

But it should not be thought that darkness is complete during the sun's long absence.

Each month the moon comes to replace it as best she can; there is also the very clear scintillation from the stars, the light from the planets, the frequent Northern Lights, and the peculiar luminescence of landscapes white with snow; but in any case, at the moment of the sun's greatest southerly declination, 21 December, it is still only thirteen degrees below the polar horizon; so a half-light reigned for a few hours each day. But the fog and snow swirls often plunged this cold land into uttermost darkness.

All the same, the weather had been quite favourable until now; only the partridges and hares could complain, for the hunters gave them not a moment's rest; a number of fox traps had been set, but these suspicious animals did not fall into them; several times they cleared the snow off the traps and took the bait without danger; the doctor sent them to the blazes, miserable at giving them such free gifts.

On 25 October the thermometer read minus four (−20°C). A vicious storm blew up; thick snow filled the air, stopping a single speck of light reaching the *Forward*. For a long time those on board were worried about Bell and Simpson, hunting too far away; they only came back the following day, having spent an entire day lying in their deerskins while the storm swept over and buried them under five feet of snow. They were virtually frozen and the doctor found it very difficult to restore their blood flow.

The storm blew continuously for a whole week. No one was able to put a foot outside. In a single day it could vary fifteen to twenty degrees.

Everyone lived separately during this enforced leisure, some sleeping, some smoking, others talking quietly, but stopping when Johnson or the doctor approached; there was no moral bond in this crew; the only times they gathered together was for evening prayers and Sunday Bible reading and divine office.

Clifton had soon realized that, with the seventy-eighth degree reached, his share of the bonus was now £375; he found it a tidy sum and his ambition went no further. Most of the men were the same, dreaming of enjoying all the money earned by so much hard work.

Hatteras remained almost invisible. He did not take part in the hunting or excursions. He was not interested in the meteorological phenomena the doctor admired so much. He lived with a single idea, which could be summed up in just three words: the North Pole. He thought only of the time when the *Forward*, finally free, could resume her daring navigation.

In sum, the general mood was gloomy. Nothing could be as disheartening as the sight of this ship, captive, no longer in her element, unrecognizable under the thick coats of ice; she had no shape; made for movement, she could not move; designed to brave the wind and storms, she had metamorphosed into a store, a wooden residence, a sedentary dwelling. This anomalous, false situation produced an ineffable feeling of worry and regret in every man's heart.

During the vacant hours the doctor organized his travel notes—of which this narrative is the faithful reproduction;* he was never idle and his mood did not change. But he looked forward to the end of the storm and to when he could go hunting once more.

At six in the morning on 3 November, in a temperature of minus five ($-21\,°$C), Clawbonny went out with Johnson and Bell; there was not a single crack in the ice plains; the snow, spread copiously the last few days and hardened by the frost, was perfect for walking; a dry, bristly cold had slipped into the air; the moon shone with incomparable purity, casting an astonishing light on the slightest irregularities in the field; the edges of footprints were lit up, and the hunters left a luminous trail, their long shadows stretching out over the ice with startling clarity.

The doctor had brought his friend Duke with him; he preferred him to the other dogs for hunting game; the Greenland ones are not much use in such a situation, not displaying the sacred fire of the race from the temperate zones. Duke sniffed as he ran, often stopping dead at fresh bear tracks. However, in spite of his skill, the hunters did not sight a single hare in two hours' march.

'Has all the game headed south?' said the doctor, halting in the shelter of a mound.

'You'd think so,' replied the carpenter.

'I'm not sure if I agree,' answered Johnson; 'the hares, foxes, and bears are used to this climate; I imagine they've just disappeared because of the storm; but the southern winds will soon be back. Ah, if you'd said reindeer or musk oxen, that'd be different!'

'But there are large herds on Melville Island,' said the doctor, 'further south admittedly; Parry always had as much magnificent game as he wanted while wintering.'

'We're not so lucky,' replied Bell; 'but if only we could get our hands on some bear meat, we'd be in clover.'

'That's just the problem,' replied the doctor; 'the bears seem very rare and wild; they're not civilized enough to come and get shot.'

'Bell's talking about the meat, but we need its fat more than its flesh or fur.'

'You're right, Johnson, you always think of fuel.'

'We need to. Even using as little as possible, we've only got three weeks left!'

'Yes, that's the problem, for it's only the beginning of November, and February is the cruellest month in the glacial zone; but if we don't get any bears, we'll still be able to get seal fat.'

'Not for long,' said Johnson, 'since they'll soon leave us; through cold or fear, they'll soon vanish from the surface of the ice.'

'Then we really need to fall back on bears, and I must admit they're the most useful animals in the Arctic, for they're the only ones to provide food, clothing, light, and heat. Do you hear, Duke,' the doctor said, patting the animal; 'we want bears, my friend; find, go and find!'

Duke was sniffing at the ice but, stimulated by the doctor's voice and stroking, immediately ran off like an arrow. He barked vigorously and his voice easily reached the hunters, despite the distance.

This range of sound at low temperatures is an astonishing feature; it is equalled only by the clearness of the stars in the northern sky; especially in the dry cold of the boreal nights, light and sound travel considerable distances.

Guided by the distant barks, the huntsmen hurried after Duke; he was a mile away and they arrived out of breath, for lungs quickly choke in this atmosphere. Duke was standing stock still, fifty paces from an enormous mass moving on top of a mound.

'Second helpings!' exclaimed the doctor, loading.

'A bear, goodness, a fine one.'

'A remarkable one,' said Johnson, waiting to fire after the other two.

Duke was barking furiously. Bell advanced twenty feet and fired, but the animal had apparently not been hit, for it continued heavily moving its head.

Johnson approached, aimed carefully, and squeezed the trigger.

'Unlucky!' exclaimed the doctor. 'Oh, cursed refraction, we're still out of range—we'll never get used to it! It's over a mile away!'

'After it,' said Bell.

The three rushed towards the bear, not troubled by the shots; it seemed to be huge, and, forgetting the dangers of the attack, the hunters were already celebrating their victory. Once at reasonable range, they fired again; undoubtedly mortally wounded, the bear made an enormous leap and fell at the foot of the hill.

Duke rushed forward.

'That bear was not difficult to kill.'

'Only three shots,' replied Bell suspiciously, 'and it's a goner!'

'Strange.'

'Unless we arrived just when it was dying from old age,' added the doctor with a laugh.

'Well, old or young,' said Bell, 'it'll still be a fine kill.'

Chatting, the huntsmen reached the mound, and to their stupefaction found Duke savaging the body of a white fox!

'Oh my God,' exclaimed Bell, 'that's a bit much!'

'We shoot a bear and it's a fox that falls down dead!'

Johnson did not know what to say.

'The refraction again,' exclaimed the doctor, with a burst of laughter mixed with disappointment, 'always the same refraction!'

'How do you mean?' asked the carpenter.

'My friend, it made us misjudge the size and distance! We saw a bear in fox's clothing! This is not the first time such errors have happened to hunters. But we've paid the price for our imagination.'

'Well,' said Johnson, 'bear or not, we'll still eat it. Let's take it back.'

But just as the mate was putting the fox over his shoulders:

'That's incredible!'

'What is?'

'Look, this animal has a collar!'

'A collar?' repeated the doctor, leaning over.

A worn-out copper collar was indeed visible in the fox's white fur; the doctor thought he could see engraved letters; in no time at all, he had taken it off; it seemed to have been round its neck for a long time.

'What does it all mean?' asked Johnson.

'It means, my friends, that we've just killed a fox more than twelve years old, a fox caught by James Ross in 1848.'*

'I don't believe it!' said Bell.

'There can't be any doubt; I regret killing this poor animal! While wintering, James Ross had the idea of trapping a large number of white foxes; he put copper collars on their necks, with engravings of where his ships were, the *Enterprise* and *Investigator*, plus the food stores. These animals often cover huge distances in search of food, and James Ross hoped that one might fall into the hands of men from Franklin's expedition. This explains everything, and our guns uselessly killed that poor animal, which once might have saved the lives of two crews.'

'Goodness, we won't eat it,' said Johnson; 'in any case a twelve-year-old fox! But we'll keep its skin, to remember this strange encounter by.'

He draped the animal around his shoulders. The huntsmen headed for the ship, navigating by the stars. Their excursion was not completely fruitless, for they were able to shoot several brace of ptarmigans.

An hour away from the *Forward*, something else astonished the doctor. Shooting stars were raining down; there were thousands, like rockets at the climax of a fireworks display. The moonlight was pale. One's eye could never tire of looking at such a show, which lasted several hours. A few Moravian Brothers observed a similar occurrence in Greenland in 1799.* It was like a carnival the heavens were putting on for the land at these desolate latitudes. Back on board, the doctor spent the whole night watching the phenomenon, which stopped at about seven in the morning, with a deep silence in the atmosphere.

26

The Last Piece of Coal

THE bears seemed decidedly uncatchable; several seals were killed on 4, 5, and 6 November; then, with a change of wind, it went up several degrees; but the drifting snow came back in great strength. It was now impossible to leave the ship and the humidity began to win. At the end of the week the condensers held several bushels of ice.

The weather changed again on 15 November, and with it the thermometer went down to minus twenty-four ($-31\,°C$). This was the lowest observed till now. This cold would have been bearable in a still atmosphere; but the wind was blowing, and felt like sharp blades cutting the air.

The doctor regretted his imprisonment, for the snow was flattened by the wind and so provided good support for walking, meaning that he could have done a long excursion.

However, it must be said that any demanding exercise in such cold quickly makes you out of breath. A man can produce only a quarter his usual work; metal tools are impossible to use; hands that touch them without taking precautions feel pain similar to a burn, and pieces of skin remain stuck to carelessly picked-up objects.

The crew were confined to ship, and reduced to walking on the covered deck for two hours, where they had permission to smoke, unlike the common room.

There, as soon as the fire went down a little, ice invaded the walls and the gaps in the floor; there was not a peg, nail, or metal plate that did not immediately acquire a layer of ice.

The instantaneity of the phenomenon fascinated the doctor. The men's breath condensed in the air and, switching from fluid to solid, fell as snow around them. Only a few feet from the stoves, the cold took on full force, and so the men stayed in tight groups close to the fire.

However, the doctor advised them to harden themselves, to get used to the cold, which certainly had forces in reserve; he advised them to gradually get their skin used to its intense burning, and he practised what he preached; but laziness or torpor tied most to the quarters; they did not want to move and preferred to doze in the deleterious heat.

The doctor insisted there was no danger in leaving a heated room and exposing oneself to great cold; these sudden changes are only harmful for people who are wet; the doctor quoted examples to support his view, but his lessons were more or less wasted.

As for John Hatteras, he did not seem to feel the temperature. He walked in silence at the same even speed. Did the cold have no effect on his energetic constitution? Did he possess to the utmost degree that principle of natural heat he had sought in his sailors? Was he so armour-plated in his fixed idea as to escape all external sensation? His men were always astonished to see him braving minus twenty-four degrees; he left the ship for hours on end, and came back without any signs of cold on his face.

'That man's strange,' the doctor told Johnson; 'he astonishes me! He carries a fiery furnace within him. He's one of the most powerful natures I've ever studied.'

'The fact is he comes and goes, and strolls in the open air without putting more clothes on than in June.'

'Oh, clothing doesn't matter; what's the point of someone wearing warm clothes if he can't produce heat himself? It's like trying to melt ice by wrapping it in a wool blanket. Hatteras has no such need; he's made like that; and I wouldn't be surprised if he radiated warmth like glowing coals.'

Johnson, responsible for freeing the fire hole each morning, noticed that the ice was more than ten feet thick.

Almost every night the doctor could observe a magnificent Aurora (Borealis); between four and eight o'clock the sky slightly to the north changed colour; then the coloured part formed a pale yellow trellis, whose ends seemed to be supported by the ice-field. Little by little the bright area rose in the sky as it followed the magnetic meridian, until it was covered with blackish bands; flashes of luminous matter darted out, then got longer, diminishing or increasing in brightness; at its highest point the phenomenon was often composed of several arcs bathing in red, yellow, or green waves of light. It was dazzling, it was an incomparable sight. Soon the various curves would meet in a single point and form boreal coronas of celestial magnificence. Finally the arcs would crowd together, the splendid Aurora grow pale, the intense beams melt into gleams, pallid, vague, indeterminate, and unclear, and the marvellous display, reduced, almost extinguished, would slowly vanish into the darkened clouds lying to the south.

It is difficult to comprehend the beauty of such a sight at high latitudes, less than eight degrees from the Pole; the Northern Lights glimpsed in temperate zones do not give the slightest impression;* it is as though Providence wanted to reserve its most astonishing wonders for these climes.

Numerous paraselenes also appeared when the moon was out, with several images together in the sky, increasing the brightness; often too, mere lunar haloes surrounded the queen of the night, shining with wonderful intensity at the centre of a luminous circle.

On 26 November a high tide occurred and the water rushed violently up through the fire hole;* the thick ice was shaken by the upheaval of the sea, with sinister cracking noises betraying the submarine battle; fortunately the ship held firm in its bed and only its chains clanked noisily, although Hatteras had had them fixed, foreseeing such an event.

The following days were still colder; the sky was covered with a penetrating fog; the wind carried off the piled-up snow; it became difficult to see whether the flurries were born in the sky or on the ice-fields; indescribable confusion reigned.

The crew worked on various tasks inside, the main one being to prepare the fat and oil produced by the seals; it formed blocks of ice which had to be split with axes; the pieces produced were as hard as marble; the equivalent of ten barrels was thus produced. As can be imagined, no container was needed; in any case the liquid would have broken them as it absorbed the cold.

On the twenty-eighth the thermometer went down to minus thirty-two (−36°C); there was only ten days' coal left and everyone fearfully calculated the date when the fuel would run out.

As an economy measure Hatteras had the poop stoves put out; and Shandon, the doctor, and he had to share the crew's common room. As a result Hatteras was more often in contact with the men, who sent him numb, wild glances. He heard their complaints, their reproaches, even their threats, and could not punish them. In actual fact he seemed deaf to remarks. He did not lay claim to the place nearest the fire. He remained in a corner, arms crossed, not saying a word.

Despite the doctor's advice, Pen and his friends refused to take the slightest exercise; since they spent entire days leaning on the stove or under the blankets of their hammocks, their health soon worsened; they could not resist the harmful effect of the climate, and terrible scurvy appeared on board.

Nevertheless, for a long time the doctor had been distributing lemon juice and lime pastils each morning; but these precautions, usually so effective, had no visible effect on the sick men and as it followed its course the illness soon showed its most horrifying symptoms.

What a sight these wretches were, with their nerves and muscles contracted by pain! Their legs swelled extraordinarily and were soon covered with large blackish-blue areas; their bleeding gums and swollen lips uttered only inarticulate sounds; their blood, completely altered, defibrinated,* no longer transmitted life to their extremities.

Clifton was the first to contract this terrible infirmity; soon Gripper, Brunton, and Strong were unable to leave their hammocks. Those spared the illness could not escape the sight of suffering; the only shelter was the common room; staying put was the only choice; soon it became a hospital, for thirteen of the *Forward*'s eighteen sailors got scurvy within a matter of days. Pen seemed to escape the outbreak; his vigorous nature preserved him; Shandon felt the first symptoms; but it went no further and exercise managed to keep him reasonably healthy.

The doctor looked after the sick with complete devotion, although his heart sank at an illness he could not alleviate. However, he spread as much gaiety as possible amongst this desolate crew; his words, his consolation, his philosophical reflections, his happy inventions broke the monotony of the long days of pain; he read out loud; his astonishing memory provided him with amusing tales, while the healthy men clustered round the stove in a tight circle; but groans from the patients, complaints, and cries of despair sometimes interrupted him and, postponing his story, he became an attentive and dedicated doctor.

His own health resisted; he did not lose weight; his corpulence was better than the warmest clothing; and he said he felt pleased he was clad like a seal or a whale, which, thanks to their thick layers of fat, easily withstand the attacks of the Arctic atmosphere.

As for Hatteras, he experienced nothing, physically or mentally. Even the suffering of his crew did not seem to affect him. Perhaps he did not allow emotions to show on his face; but an attentive observer would have sometimes surprised a man's heart beating in his iron exterior.

The doctor analysed him, studied him, but could not classify this strange organism, this supernatural temperament.

The thermometer went down again; the deck walking area remained deserted; the Eskimo dogs paced up and down alone, producing lamentable barks.

There was always someone on duty near the stove to make sure it was fed; it was important not to let it die down; as soon as the fire dropped, cold slipped into the room, ice encrusted the walls, and condensed humidity fell as snow on the brig's unfortunate inhabitants.

It was in the midst of these inexpressible torments that they got to

8 December; that morning the doctor went as usual to consult the thermometer outside. He found the mercury frozen in the bulb.

'Forty-four degrees!' he said in fright.

That day the last piece of coal was thrown into the stove.

27

The Great Colds of Christmas

A moment of despair was felt. The thought of death, and by cold, was present in all its horror; the last piece of coal was burning with a sinister spitting noise; the fire was already dropping; the room got noticeably colder. Johnson went to get a few pieces of the new combustible from the seals, and put them in the stove; he added oakum soaked in frozen oil and soon made sufficient heat. The smell of the fat was unbearable; but there was no way to avoid it. It needed to be got used to. Johnson himself agreed that his solution was not perfect and would have been declined in the middle-class households of Liverpool.

'But this awful stench may easily have a good side-effect.'

'Namely?' said the carpenter.

'It may attract bears, for they like the smell.'

'But what's the point of attracting bears?'

'Friend Bell, we've run out of seals; they moved off ages ago; if bears don't supply fuel instead, I'm not sure what'll happen to us.'

'You're right, our future is far from assured; it's a frightening situation we're in. If this new heating runs out, I can't see any solution.'

'There is one.'

'There is?'

'Yes, a last resort . . . but the captain will never . . . although we may need to.'

Old Johnson shook his head sadly as he cogitated in silence, and Bell was reluctant to interrupt him. He knew that these pieces of fat, acquired with such effort, would not last a week, even used sparingly.

The mate was right. Drawn by the foul emanations, several bears were seen downwind from the *Forward*; men who were well enough went out to hunt them; but these animals can move surprisingly fast and possess an ingenuity that defeats all stratagems; it was impossible to get near them; and the best-aimed bullets missed.

The crew were in serious danger of dying from cold; they would be unable to resist forty-eight hours of a similar temperature in the common room. All thought with terror of the end of the last piece of fuel.

That end happened at 3 p.m. on 20 December; the fire went out; grouped round the stove, the sailors looked haggardly at each other. Hatteras remained motionless in his corner; as usual the doctor was agitatedly pacing up and down; he did not know what to apply his ingenuity to.

In the room it quickly fell to minus seven (−22°C).

But if the doctor had no imagination left, if he no longer knew what to do, others knew for him. A cold and determined Shandon, a Pen with anger in his eyes, and two or three comrades who could still crawl went up to Hatteras.

'Captain.'

Absorbed in his thoughts, Hatteras did not hear.

'Captain,' repeated Shandon, touching him.

Hatteras stood up.

'Yes?'

'The fire has gone out, sir.'

'Well?'

'If you intend us to die of cold,' said Shandon with terrible irony, 'we request that you inform us.'

'My intention', replied Hatteras gravely, 'is for each man to do his duty to the end.'

'There is something above duty, captain: the right to life and limb. There is no fire, I say, and if that continues not one of us will be alive the day after tomorrow!'

'I have no wood,' Hatteras dully replied.

'Well, when you don't have any,' fiercely exclaimed Pen, 'you go out and cut some where it grows!'

Hatteras turned pale with anger.

'And where would that be?'

'On board,' came the insolent reply.

'On board?' repeated the captain, his fists clenched, his eyes shining.

'Yes; when the ship can't carry her crew, the ship is burned!'

At the beginning of this sentence Hatteras picked up a hatchet; at the end it was raised above Pen's head.

'Scoundrel!'

The doctor threw himself in front of Pen, pushing at him; the hatchet fell and deeply cut into the floor. Johnson, Bell, and Simpson stood round Hatteras, as if to protect him. But distressing voices, pitiful complaints, emerged from the berths acting as deathbeds.

'It's cold, it's freezing!' desperately cried the sick, feeling the chill inside their blankets.

Hatteras exercised self-control and, after a few seconds' silence, calmly said:

'If we destroyed our ship, how would we get back to Britain?'

'Captain,' suggested Johnson, 'perhaps we could burn the least useful parts, the gunnels and the rails?'*

'We'll always have the launches,' added Shandon; 'and can't we always build a smaller ship from the remains of the old?'

'Never!'

'But . . .' said several sailors, raising their voices.

'We have plenty of spirits of wine; let's burn every last drop!' said Hatteras.

'Yes, let's burn the spirits of wine,' repeated Johnson, feigning confidence.

And with the help of thick wicks soaked in spirits, whose pale flames licked the sides of the stove, the room became a few degrees warmer.

In the days following this tragic scene, the wind veered south and the thermometer went up again; the snow swirled through a warmer air. Some of the men could leave the ship in the driest part of the day; but snow-blindness and scurvy kept most on board; in any case neither hunting nor fishing was possible.

The respite from the atrocious violence of the cold, however, proved of short duration, and on the twenty-fifth, after an unexpected change of wind, the mercury again froze in the bulb; they had to use the spirits of wine thermometer again, which never freezes.

The doctor was horrified to find it at minus sixty-six (−52°C). Man has virtually never had to bear such a temperature.

The ice stretched over the floor in long dull mirrors; a thick fog invaded the room; the humidity fell as thick snow; they could no longer see each other; the heat withdrew from the extremities of their bodies; feet and hands became blue; an iron band circled their heads, and their thoughts, confused, slowed down, frozen, tended towards delirium. A frightening symptom: tongues could no longer articulate words.

From the day the men threatened to burn his ship, Hatteras prowled on deck for hours at a time. He surveyed, he kept watch. This wood was his flesh! Cutting a spar was removing one of his limbs! While maintaining security, he was armed, impervious to the cold, snow, and ice which stiffened clothing and wrapped him in a granite coat. Duke, understanding the situation, barked behind Hatteras and went with him, howling.

However, on 25 December, the captain came back down to the common room. Using a last reserve of energy, the doctor went straight up to him.

'We'll die if we don't light a fire!'

'Never!' said Hatteras, understanding the implication.

'We need to,' the doctor said gently.

'Never!' the captain repeated with more force. 'I will not give consent. Disobey me if you want!'*

He was in fact granting freedom to act. Johnson and Bell rushed on to deck. Hatteras heard the wood of his brig cracking under the axe. He wept.

That day was Christmas Day, the family celebration in Britain, the party for children! What bitter memories of happy infants around the ribbon-festooned tree! Who could forget those long pieces of roast meat from the specially fattened ox? And those pastries, those mince pies, where ingredients of all sorts are mixed for that day so dear to British hearts? But here, absolute pain, despair, and penury, and as Yule logs wood cut from a ship lost in the midst of the Arctic!

However, with the fire, feeling and strength came back to the sailors' hearts; boiling tea and coffee produced instant well-being; and hope is so tenacious in people's minds that they began to hope again. It was in these fluctuating moods that that fateful 1860 ended, whose premature winter had undone Hatteras's bold plans.

Now it happened that a startling discovery was made on 1 January 1861. It was a little less cold; the doctor had taken up his customary studies once more; he was reading Sir Edward Belcher's relation of his expedition to the polar seas. Suddenly a passage he had not noticed till then bewildered him; he read it again, and could not have misunderstood it.

Sir Edward Belcher recounts that when he reached the end of Queen Channel he discovered various signs that men had visited and indeed stayed there:

These were the remains of houses much superior to what can be attributed to the crude customs of the wandering Eskimo tribes. Their walls were solidly and deeply built into the ground; the interior, covered with a thick layer of excellent gravel, was fashioned of stone. Large quantities of reindeer, walrus, and seal bone could be seen. *We found coal there.**

At these last words, an idea came to the doctor's mind; taking his book, he went to speak to Hatteras.

'Coal!'

'Yes, Hatteras, coal: meaning we could find a solution.'

'Coal on this deserted coast! Not possible!'

'Why doubt it? Belcher wouldn't have said such a thing if he hadn't been certain, seen it with his own eyes.'

'Well, doctor?'

'We're only 100 miles from the coast where Belcher saw this coal. What is an excursion of 100 miles? Nothing. Longer searches across the ice and in similar cold have often been done. So let's leave!'

'Yes, let's leave!' exclaimed Hatteras, who had quickly made up his mind and, with his fluid imagination, glimpsed a chance of survival.

Johnson was straightaway told about the decision; he completely supported it; he told his comrades; some were in favour, others greeted it apathetically.

'Coal on these coasts!' said Wall, buried in his sick-bed.

'Let them do what they want,' Shandon darkly replied.

But even before preparations had begun, Hatteras wanted to measure the position of the *Forward* with the greatest precision. It is easy to understand why this calculation was important, why the position had to be known mathematically. Once out of sight, the ship could only be found again with rock-solid figures.

Hatteras went on deck; he measured several lunar distances and the meridian heights of the main stars several times.

These uses of the sextant presented serious difficulties, for at this low temperature, the glass and mirrors were covered with a layer of ice from Hatteras's breath; a few times his eyelids were entirely burned touching the copper of his telescopes.

However, he obtained very precise figures for his calculations before going back to his room to calculate them. When his work was done, he lifted his head in stupefaction, took his map, plotted it, and looked at the doctor.

'Well?'

'What latitude were we at when we began wintering?'

'At 78° 15′ N and 95° 35′ W—at the very pole of cold.'

'Well,' said Hatteras in a low voice, 'the ice-field is drifting! We're two degrees further north and two west, at least three hundred miles from your coal dump!'

'And those poor men don't realize!' exclaimed the doctor.

'Silence,' said Hatteras, finger on lips.

28

Preparations for Departure

HATTERAS was reluctant to inform his crew of the new situation. He was right. These wretches, knowing themselves dragged northwards with irresistible force, would perhaps have gone mad with despair. The doctor understood and approved the captain's silence.

Hatteras had hidden in his heart the impressions caused by the discovery. It was his first moment of happiness in the long months of unceasing fight against the elements. He found himself 150 miles further north*—hardly eight degrees from the Pole! But he hid his joy so deeply that the doctor did not suspect it. Clawbonny did wonder why Hatteras's eyes shone with unusual brightness; but that was all, and the obvious reason did not enter his mind.

As she approached the Pole, the *Forward* had moved away from the coal deposits Sir Edward Belcher observed; to get there meant going 250 miles south, instead of 100. However, after a short discussion on this subject between Hatteras and Clawbonny, the journey was maintained.

If Belcher was correct—and his truthfulness could not be doubted—things had to be as he left them. No new expedition had come to these extreme lands since 1853.* Few Eskimos, if any, were encountered at this latitude. The disappointment of Beechey Island could not be repeated on the shores of New Cornwall. The low temperature indefinitely preserved objects left here. The chances were therefore very much in favour of this excursion across the ice.

The journey was calculated to last at least forty days and preparations were made by Johnson accordingly.

He started with the sledge; it was the typical Greenland shape, thirty-five inches across by twenty-four feet long. Some of those constructed by the Eskimos are more than fifty feet in length. This one was made of long pieces of wood bent at the front and rear and held taut by two strong ropes, like a bow. This gave it some flexibility, making collisions less dangerous. The sledge ran easily over ice; but when it snowed and the white sheets were still soft, two adjacent vertical frames were added, raising it and enabling it to move without increased effort. Also, by rubbing it with a mixture of sulphur and snow, following the Eskimo method, it slid with remarkable ease.

The team was composed of six dogs; hardy in spite of their thinness, these animals did not seem to be suffering too much from the hard winter; their buckskin harness was in good condition; this crew could be counted upon, as they had been scrupulously sold by the Greenlanders of Uppernawik. These six alone could pull a weight of nearly a ton without getting especially tired.

The camping equipment comprised a tent, for when building a snow-house was not feasible, a large mackintosh sheet, to prevent the snow melting from body contact, and several blankets of wool and buffalo-skin. The Halkett boat would also be taken.

The provisions consisted of five boxes of pemmican, weighing about four hundredweight; one pound of pemmican was allocated per man and dog; there were seven dogs, including Duke, plus four men. They were also taking twelve gallons of spirits of wine, weighing about one hundred and fifty pounds, tea, sufficient quantities of biscuit, a small portable stove with generous supplies of wicks and oakum, powder, ammunition, and four double-barrelled guns. The four were to use Captain Parry's invention of wearing rubber belts in which body heat and movement maintained coffee, tea, or water liquid.

Johnson used special care to make the snow shoes, wooden frameworks with leather straps; they could serve as ice skates; on very hard and icy terrains, the buckskin moccasins were more useful; each traveller would have two pairs of both.

These preparations required four whole days; they were important since a single neglected detail can easily lose an expedition. Hatteras carefully plotted the position of his ship at noon each day; she was no longer drifting and this guarantee was needed to be able to return.

Hatteras thought about the men to go with him. It was a serious decision to make; some were not fit to be taken, but leaving them on board also had to be weighed up. All the same, everyone's survival depended on the journey; the captain thought it best to select reliable and experienced companions.

Shandon was therefore excluded; in any case he showed no regret. James Wall, ill, could not take part.

The sick were not getting any worse; their treatment consisted of repeated rubbing and strong doses of lemon juice; this was not difficult to do and did not require the doctor's presence. Clawbonny was the first to join the travellers, and his departure did not produce any objection.

Johnson longed to go on the perilous expedition with the captain; but Hatteras took him aside and said affectionately, almost emotionally:

'I have confidence in you alone. You are the only officer I can leave my ship to. You need to be here to keep an eye on Shandon and the others. They can't move because of the winter conditions; but who knows what catastrophic decisions their evil ways may lead them to? You will be given my formal instructions which will put command in your hands if necessary. You will be another me. Our absence will be for four or five weeks at most, and I won't worry having you where I can't be. I'm aware you need wood. But spare my poor ship as much as possible. Do you hear me, Johnson?'

'I hear you, and I'll stay since that's what you want.'

'Thank you!' said Hatteras shaking the mate's hand, before adding:

'If we don't come back, wait for the next break-up of the ice and try to reconnoitre towards the Pole. If the others object, forget about us, and sail the *Forward* back to Britain.'

'Is that what you want, captain?'

'Absolutely.'

'Your orders will be carried out.'

Once the decision was taken, the doctor regretted his worthy friend, but he recognized that Hatteras was right to act like this.

The other two companions would be Bell the carpenter and

Simpson. Bell was in good health, brave and devoted, and would render great service while camping on snow; although less determined, Simpson still agreed to take part and might be very useful as huntsman for land and marine animals.

So the party was composed of Hatteras, Clawbonny, Bell, Simpson, and the faithful Duke: four men and seven dogs to feed. Supplies had been calculated accordingly.

At the beginning of January, it was normally minus thirty-three (−37°C). Hatteras watched impatiently for a change in the weather; several times he checked the barometer, but it could not be trusted; the instrument seems to lose its usual accuracy at high latitudes; in these climes nature causes notable exceptions to its general laws; thus a clear sky was not always accompanied by cold, and snow did not always raise the temperature; the barometer was unreliable, as many polar navigators have remarked; it often went down with north and east winds; low, it forecast fine weather; high, snow or rain. Its indications could not be counted on.

Finally, on 5 January, an east wind brought a rise of fifteen degrees; the thermometer went up to minus eighteen (−28°C). Hatteras decided to leave the following day; he could not bear seeing his ship broken up before him; the whole of the poop had already disappeared into the stove.

So orders to leave were given on 6 January, amongst squalls of snow. The doctor gave his final advice to the sick; Bell and Simpson shook hands with their companions without a word. Hatteras wanted to make his farewells out loud, but he was surrounded by unfriendly expressions. He thought he saw an ironic smile on Shandon's lips. He remained silent. Perhaps he even hesitated for a moment to leave, as he gazed at the *Forward*.

But he could not go back on his decision; the sledge was waiting on the ice-field, loaded and harnessed; Bell went ahead; the others followed; Johnson accompanied the travellers for quarter of a mile; then Hatteras asked him to go back on board, and the old sailor made a long sign of farewell.

As he moved off, Hatteras turned round one last time and saw the tips of the brig's masts disappearing into the dark snow filling the sky.

29

Across the Fields of Ice

THE little group headed south-east. Simpson was in charge of the sledge team. Duke helped him energetically, not too surprised at the work of his brothers. Hatteras and the doctor walked behind, while Bell, responsible for determining the route, walked at the head, sounding the ice with his iron-tipped stick.

The rise in the thermometer implied snow; it soon arrived and fell in thick flakes. These opaque swirls added to the problems of the journey; it was difficult to maintain a straight line; they did not move fast; however, they could plan on an average of three miles an hour.

The ice-field, tortured by the pressure of the freezing, had a very uneven surface; the sledge often hit obstacles and, depending on the slope, sometimes leaned at worrying angles; but they always got through in the end.

Hatteras and his companions covered themselves up carefully in their fur clothes, of Greenland design; the cut was not very distinguished, but appropriate to the climate; the travellers' faces were wrapped in a tightly drawn hood, impermeable to the wind and snow; only the mouth, noses, and eyes were exposed, which is strongly recommended; nothing is worse than fur neckpieces or mufflers, soon stiffened by the ice; in the evening they could only have been removed with a hatchet, not a convenient way to get undressed, even in the Arctic. Breath, which would have frozen on meeting an obstacle, had to be unobstructed.

The interminable plain continued with tiring monotony; there were piled-up ice floes of uniform appearance, hummocks whose irregularity ended up seeming regular, blocks cast from the same mould, and icebergs enclosing tortuous valleys; they marched compass in hand; the travellers did not say much. Opening their mouths was painful in this cold air; sharp fragments of ice suddenly formed on their lips and their breath could not melt them. They trekked on in silence, each using his stick to test the new ground. Bell's feet marked the soft snow; they followed carefully, for, where he had passed, the rest of the team could follow.

Numerous bear and fox tracks crossed in all directions, but on this first day they did not spot a single animal; in any case hunting would have been dangerous and useless; already heavily laden, the sledge could not be further weighed down.

In excursions of this sort, travellers normally leave dumps of food along their route; they hide them with snow to stop animals getting them, and pick them up in stages on the way back, saving the effort of carrying them.

Hatteras could not resort to this method on an ice-field that was perhaps moving; on dry land these dumps would have been practicable, but not here, for the uncertainties of the route meant they might easily not return the same way.

At midday Hatteras stopped the little team in the shelter of an ice wall; lunch was pemmican and boiling tea; the restorative qualities of this drink produced real well-being, and the travellers made full use of it.

They carried on after an hour's rest; about twenty miles were covered during this first day of marching; in the evening men and dogs were all exhausted.

However, in spite of the fatigue, a snow-house had to be built for the night; the tent would not have sufficed. It took an hour and a half. Bell was a past master; the blocks of ice, cut with a knife, rose rapidly, curved over into a dome, and a last section formed a keystone to ensure the building was solid; soft snow served as cement and filled the gaps; hardening quickly, the whole construction became a single block.

A small entrance gave access to this improvised grotto; the doctor crawled in, not without difficulty, and the others followed him.

Dinner was quickly prepared on the spirits of wine stove. The temperature inside the snow-house was very bearable: the wind raging outside could not get in.

'To table!' soon exclaimed the doctor in his warmest voice.

This meal, always the same but comforting, was taken in common. When it was over, sleep was the only thing on their minds; stretched-out mackintosh sheets protected them from the humidity produced by the snow. Their socks and shoes were dried with the portable stove; then three of the travellers went to sleep wrapped in their woollen blankets, while the fourth kept guard; he ensured the safety of all and prevented the house's opening from getting blocked, for otherwise they risked being buried alive.

Duke shared the common room; the dog team stayed outside and after sharing the supper, curled up under the snow, which soon made an impermeable cover for them.

The fatigue of the journey brought prompt oblivion. The doctor stood watch from three in the morning; a storm broke out during the night. A strange situation, isolated people lost in the snow, buried in this grave whose walls grew with the flakes!

At six the following day, the monotonous march started again; always the same valleys, the same icebergs, a uniformity with few reference points. Nevertheless, it went down a few degrees and the layers of snow froze, helping the travellers' progress. Often they encountered little mounds resembling cairns or Eskimo caches; the doctor demolished one just to be sure, but found nothing inside except ice.

'What are you hoping for, Clawbonny?' Hatteras said. 'Aren't we the first to reach this part of the globe?'

'Probably; but who knows?'

'Let's not waste time in useless searches; I'm in a hurry to get back to my ship, even if we don't bring back any fuel.'

'I have high hopes.'

'I was wrong to leave the *Forward*,' Hatteras often said, 'it was a mistake; the captain's place is on board, nowhere else.'

'Johnson's there.'

'Yes, but let's hurry, hurry.'

The team moved quickly; Simpson's cries to the dogs rang out; due to a strange case of phosphorescence, the dogs were running over a burning ground and the sledge's runners produced showers of sparks. The doctor had moved ahead to examine the nature of the snow; while trying to jump over a hummock, he suddenly disappeared. Bell, near him, immediately ran up.

'Dr Clawbonny,' he cried anxiously, as Hatteras and Simpson joined him, 'where are you?'

'Doctor?' said the captain.

'Here, in a hole,' came a reassuring voice; 'a piece of rope and I'll soon be back on the surface of the globe.'

A rope was dropped to the doctor, crouched at the bottom of a tapering hollow about ten feet deep; he tied it round his waist and his three companions hauled him up, not without difficulty.

'Are you hurt?' asked Hatteras.

'Not on your life! There's no danger of that with me,' replied the doctor, shaking his good, snow-covered face.

'But how did it happen?'

'It's all the fault of the refraction,' he replied laughing, 'always the refraction. I thought I was crossing a gap of a foot and I fell into a hole ten feet deep! Optical illusions are the only illusions left to me, my friends, but it won't be easy to lose them! May that teach you not to take a single step without sounding the terrain, for you can't count on your senses here! Your ears and eyes can't be trusted; it's a wonderful country.'

'Can we get on!'

'Let's get on, Hatteras, let's get on. This tiny fall did me more good than harm.'

The travellers set off south-east again, and stopped in the evening, having covered a distance of twenty-five miles; they were utterly exhausted, which did not prevent the doctor from climbing an ice mountain while the snow-house was being built.

The moon was still almost full and shining with extraordinary brightness in the clear sky; the stars produced light of surprising intensity; from the top of the iceberg, the view extended over the immense plains bristling with mounds and strange shapes; seeing them spread out, one would have said a vast cemetery, treeless, sad, silent, eternal, in which twenty generations of the whole world could easily have lain down for eternal slumber.*

In spite of his cold and exhaustion, the doctor remained contemplating a long time, and his companions found it very difficult to tear him away; but he needed to think about resting; the snow hut was ready; the four travellers huddled in it like moles and fell asleep.

The following days went by without any particular incident; the journey was carried out with either ease or difficulty, quickly or slowly, depending on the whims of the temperature, now harsh and glacial, now wet and penetrating; and depending on the nature of the ground, they had to wear moccasins or snow shoes.

They reached 15 January; the moon, in its last quarter, did not remain visible for long; from six in the morning, although still hidden below the horizon, the sun gave out a sort of half-light, not enough to illuminate the route; so the way needed to be marked out, following the compass direction. Bell took the lead; Hatteras marched in a straight line behind him. Then Simpson and the doctor relieved each other in such a way that they could only see Hatteras, trying to stay in a straight line. But in spite of their efforts, they sometimes wandered thirty or forty degrees off course; they needed then to start their work of marking out again.

On 15 February, a Sunday,* Hatteras estimated they had done about a hundred miles south; that morning was devoted to repairing various camping and washing utensils; divine service was not forgotten.

They set off again at midday; it was cold; the thermometer read as low as minus thirty-two (−36°C), in a very clear atmosphere.

Suddenly, without anything announcing the surprising change, completely frozen water vapour rose from the ground; it reached a height of about ninety feet and remained motionless; they could not see more than a single pace ahead; the water vapour stuck to their clothes, which it filled with long, sharp prisms.

The travellers, surprised by this phenomenon of rime, had one immediate thought: to find each other.

Immediately shouts could be heard:

'Hey, Simpson!'

'Bell here.'

'Dr Clawbonny?'

'Doctor!'

'Captain, where are you?'

The four travelling companions, their arms outstretched, were seeking each other through this thick fog, where nothing could be seen. But what surely troubled them most was that no replies reached them; this vapour seemed to block sounds.

Each then had the idea of discharging his gun to send a message to assemble. But if their voices were not loud enough, the noise of their firearms was too loud, producing echoes which rebounded in all directions, causing a confused rumbling so that the direction could not be guessed.

Each then acted according to his instincts. Hatteras stopped and waited with crossed arms. Simpson merely held back the sledge—not without difficulty. Bell turned round and went back, carefully feeling for his footprints with his hand. The doctor went in all directions, hitting blocks of ice, falling down and getting up, crossing his own tracks, getting more and more lost.

After five minutes he said to himself:

It can't go on like this. Strange climate: too many surprises! You don't know what to expect, without mentioning these sharp fragments that cut your face. 'Ahoy, ahoy, captain!'

But he got no reply; just in case, he reloaded his rifle and, despite his thick gloves, the cold of the barrel burned his hands. While so doing, he thought he saw a confused shape moving a few feet away.

'At last! Hatteras, Bell, Simpson, are you there? Come on, say something.'

A dull groan was heard.

Oh no! thought the good doctor. What can it be?

The shape approached; while one dimension got smaller, its silhouette grew bigger. A terrifying thought came into the doctor's mind:

A bear!

In actual fact, it was a huge bear; lost in the fog, it was wandering back and forth, turning round and going back, at the risk of bumping into the travellers, whose presence it did not suspect.

Getting complicated, thought the doctor, not moving.

Sometimes he felt the breath of the animal, which emerged from the rime soon after; sometimes he glimpsed the monster's enormous paws beating the air, passing so near him that more than once his clothes were torn by the sharp claws; he jumped back, upon which the shape vanished like a phantasmagorical ghost.

But as the doctor moved backwards, he felt the ground rising under his feet; using his hands to grip the icy ridges, he climbed on to one block, then another; then he felt with his outstretched stick.

'An iceberg! If I can get to the top, I'm saved.'

With surprising agility he climbed about eighty feet; his head emerged from the frozen fog, clearly visible from above.

'So!'

And looking round, he spotted his three companions coming out of the dense fluid.

'Hatteras!'

'Clawbonny!'

'Bell!'

'Simpson!'

These four shouts were heard at almost the same time; the sky, lit up by a magnificent halo, cast pale rays which coloured the rime as if it were clouds, and the tops of the icebergs seemed to be emerging from a mass of mercury. The travellers were less than one hundred feet away from each other. Thanks to the clearness of the upper reaches of air at the very cold temperature, their words were audible, and they could talk from the summits of their icebergs. After the first rifle shots, not hearing a reply, each had found nothing better to do than climb above the fog.

'The sledge!' shouted the captain.

'Eighty feet below us,' replied Simpson.

'Safe and sound?'

'Safe and sound.'

'And the bear?'

'What bear?' replied Bell.

'The one I met which nearly split my head.'

'A bear!' said Hatteras. 'Let's get back down then.'

'But,' said the doctor, 'we'd get lost and have to start again.'

'And if the beast attacks our dogs!' said Hatteras.

Duke started barking; his voice emerged from the fog and easily reached the travellers' ears.

'It's Duke!' exclaimed Hatteras. 'Something's wrong. I'm going down.'

Different howls were coming out of the fog like a frightening concert; Duke and the other dogs were enraged. All this noise resembled a formidable but dull buzzing, like sounds in a padded cell. Some invisible battle was taking place in that thick fog, and the water vapour sometimes shook like the billows when sea-monsters fight.

'Duke, Duke!' shouted the captain, getting ready to head into the rime.

'Wait, Hatteras, wait; the fog seems to be lifting.'

It was not in fact lifting, but descending like water from a slowly emptying pond; it appeared to go into the ground whence it had come; the shining peaks of the iceberg grew; others, submerged until then, came out like new islands; through an optical illusion, easy to imagine, the travellers, holding on to their icy cones, felt they were rising into the air, while in fact the fog was dropping below them.

Soon the top of the sledge appeared, then the dog team, then about thirty other animals, then large masses thrashing round, and

Duke jumping, whose head was emerging from the icy layer before plunging back in.

'Foxes!' exclaimed Bell.

'Bears!' replied the doctor. 'One, three, five.'

'Our dogs, our provisions!' shouted Simpson.

A large pack of foxes and bears were around the sledge, making large inroads into the provisions. Their instinct for pillage united them in perfect harmony; the dogs were barking furiously, but the group paid no attention, and the scene of destruction continued relentlessly.

'Fire!' said the captain, discharging his gun.

His companions did likewise. At this fourfold shot, the bears raised their heads and, producing comic groans, got ready to leave; they adopted a little trot, faster than a horse's gallop,* and, followed by the fox pack, disappeared amongst the ice floes northwards.

30

The Cairn

THIS phenomenon, particular to the polar climate, had lasted three-quarters of an hour; the bears and foxes had had time to take as much as they wished; these provisions arrived at an ideal juncture in the hard winter to revive the starving animals. The sledge tarpaulin torn by powerful claws, the boxes of pemmican opened and smashed, the bags of biscuit pillaged, supplies of tea spread over the snow, a keg of spirits of wine with broken staves and its precious contents spilled, the camping equipment spread everywhere and ransacked— everything showed the single-mindedness of these wild animals, their half-starved greed, their insatiable hunger.

'It's a catastrophe,' said Bell, looking at the scene of destruction.

'And we probably can't do anything about it,' replied Simpson.

'Let's assess the damage,' replied the doctor, 'and then we can discuss it.'

Without a word, Hatteras was already assembling the scattered boxes and bags. The pemmican and biscuit that were still edible were picked up next. The loss of much of the spirits of wine was annoying; without it, no more hot drinks, no more tea, no more coffee. While drawing up the inventory of the surviving provisions, the doctor realized that 200 pounds of pemmican had disappeared and 150 pounds of biscuit; if the journey was to continue, the travellers would have to go on half-rations.

So they discussed what to do in such circumstances. Should they go back to the ship and then start off again? But how to give up the 150 miles already covered? Going back without fuel would inevitably have a disastrous effect on the morale of the crew! Would they still be prepared to continue over the ice?

Clearly it was best to keep on moving, even at the price of the worst hardships.

The doctor, Hatteras, and Bell were in favour of this plan. Simpson wanted to return; the fatigues of the journey had affected his health; he was visibly weakening; but in the end, seeing that no one shared his opinion, he went back to his place ahead of the sledge and the little caravan resumed its southward route.

For the next three days, from 15 to 17 January, the monotonous journey continued. They advanced more slowly; they were growing tired; lassitude took hold of their legs; the dog team pulled with difficulty. The inadequate food was not enough to support the animals and people. The weather changed with its usual unpredictability, going from intense cold to damp penetrating fogs.

On 18 January the ice-fields suddenly changed appearance. A large number of peaks, like sharp-pointed pyramids of great height, stood up on the horizon. The ground, in certain places, could be seen through the snow; it seemed to be made of gneiss, schist, and quartz with some samples of limestone rocks. The travellers were finally treading terra firma, and this land, according to their estimate, had to be the one called New Cornwall.* The doctor could not prevent himself from kicking this solid ground with satisfaction; they had only 100 miles left to get to Cape Belcher; but their exhaustion increased greatly on this tormented ground, strewn with sharp rocks and dangerous overhangs, crevasses, and precipices; they had to move inland and climb on to high coastal cliffs, through narrow gorges where the snow was piled up thirty or forty feet deep.

The travellers soon regretted the more or less even path of the ice-fields, suited to the sliding of the sledge and so almost easy. Now it had to be forcefully pulled. The exhausted dogs were no longer strong enough; the men, forced to buckle up alongside, used up all their strength helping them. Several times they had to unload all the provisions to cross steep hills whose icy surfaces allowed no foothold. A distance of ten feet could take several hours; as a result, they barely covered five miles on this first day on Cornwall, assuredly well named, for it presented the ruggedness, the sharp headlands, the convulsed rocks of the south-western extremity of England.

The sledge reached the top of the cliffs the following day; the travellers, utterly exhausted, were unable to construct a snow-house, and had to spend the night in the tent, wrapped in buffalo skins and warming their wet socks on their chests. The inevitable consequences of such hygiene can be understood; and during the night the thermometer went below forty-four (−42°C) as the mercury froze.

Simpson's health deteriorated worryingly; a stubborn cold, aggressive rheumatism, and unbearable aches and pains forced him to lie down on the sledge, which he could not steer any more. Bell replaced him; he was ill, but not enough not to walk. The doctor also felt the effect of this excursion through a terrible winter; however, he allowed no complaints to emerge; he walked on, leaning on his stick; he reconnoitred the route, he helped with everything. Hatteras, impassive, impenetrable, insensible, as fit as the first day, with his iron temperament, silently followed behind.

On 20 January it was so cold that the slightest effort immediately brought utter exhaustion. Meanwhile, the ground became so difficult that the doctor, Hatteras, and Bell teamed up with the dogs again; unforeseen impacts broke the front of the sledge, meaning it had to be mended. These delays were in fact happening several times a day.

The travellers were following a deep valley, in the snow up to their waists, sweating despite the extreme cold. They walked on in silence. Suddenly Bell looked at the doctor with fright; then without a word, he took a handful of snow and energetically rubbed his companion's face.

'Bell!' said the doctor, struggling.

But Bell just rubbed harder.

'Come on, Bell,' said the doctor, his mouth, nose, and eyes full of snow. 'Have you gone mad? What's up?'

'What's up is that if you've still got a nose, it's thanks to me.'

'A nose?' replied the doctor, feeling his face.

'Yes, Clawbonny, you were completely frostbitten; your nose was entirely white when I saw you, and without my vigorous treatment you would have lost that ornament, inconvenient while travelling, but necessary to existence.'

In effect, the doctor's nose would soon have been frozen; with the circulation restored just in time, thanks to Bell's forceful rubbing, all danger disappeared.

'Accept my gratitude, Bell, on condition I do the same for you.'*

'I hope so! And may heaven grant that we never have greater problems to face!'

'Alas, Bell, you're referring to Simpson. The poor boy is suffering terribly.'

'Do you fear for his life?' Hatteras asked keenly.

'Yes, captain.'

'And the cause?'

'A serious attack of scurvy. His legs are already swelling and his gums are deteriorating; the poor man is lying half frozen under his blankets, and the jolts of the sledge just adding to his suffering. I pity him, Hatteras, and can do nothing to relieve him.'

'Poor Simpson,' murmured Bell.

'Perhaps we should stop for a day or two?'

'Stop,' exclaimed Hatteras, 'when the lives of eighteen men depend on our return!'

'However . . .'

'Clawbonny and Bell, listen to me. We have less than twenty days' food left! We can't waste a single moment!'

Neither the doctor nor Bell said a word, and the sledge started off once more.

In the evening they stopped at the foot of an ice hill, in which Bell quickly cut a cave; the trekkers took refuge in it; the doctor spent the night looking after Simpson; the scurvy was already making its awful ravages on the poor man, and because of his suffering continuous moans came from his swollen lips.

'Ah, Dr Clawbonny!'

'Hang on, my boy.'

'I won't survive, I can feel it, I can't carry on. I prefer to die!'

To these despairing words, the doctor replied with unceasing care; although himself exhausted by the fatigues of the day, he spent the night preparing calming potions for the patient; but already the lime juice was having no effect, and rubbing did not prevent the scurvy from slowly spreading.

The following day, the unfortunate man had to be put back on the sledge, although he asked to be left alone to die in peace; then this awful march was resumed, in the face of increasing difficulties.

The icy mists penetrated the three men's very bones; the snow and fine hail whipped their faces; although performing the tasks of beasts of burden, they did not even have enough food.

Like his master, Duke moved to and fro, braving the fatigue, always alert, instinctively finding the best route to follow; they trusted to his marvellous shrewdness.

On 23 January, Duke had taken the lead, in almost complete darkness, since the moon was new; for several hours he was out of sight; Hatteras was worried, especially since many bear tracks could be seen; he was still wondering what he could do, when loud barking was heard.

Hatteras speeded up the sledge, and soon reached the faithful animal, at the end of a valley.

Duke was absolutely motionless, as if turned to stone, barking before a rough cairn made of pieces of limestone reinforced with a layer of ice.

'This time,' said the doctor, removing his harness, 'it's a cairn; there's no doubt about it.'

'What's it got to do with us?'

'Hatteras, if it's a cairn, it may hold a document useful to us; it may contain food, so it's worth taking a look.'

'And what Europeans could have reached here?' said Hatteras, shrugging his shoulders.

'But even without Europeans, couldn't Eskimos have put a cache, to store the results of their hunting? It's what they usually do, remember.'

'Well, go and have a look, Clawbonny. But I'm afraid you're wasting your time.'

Carrying pickaxes, Clawbonny and Bell headed for the cairn. Duke continued to bark furiously. The limestone was firmly cemented with ice; but a few blows had soon strewn pieces over the ground.

'There's clearly something.'

'Yes.'

They quickly demolished the rest of the cairn. Soon a cache was discovered; in it was a soaking piece of paper. The doctor picked it up, his heart beating. Hatteras ran up, took the document, and read:

'Altam. . . . *Porpoise*, 13 Dec. . . . 1860, 12 . . . ° long. . . . 8 . . . ° 35′ lat. . . .'*

'The *Porpoise*!'*

'The *Porpoise*,' repeated Hatteras. 'I don't know any such name of a ship frequenting these seas.'

'Evidently sailors, perhaps shipwrecked, passed here less than two months ago.'

'That's clear,' said Bell.

'But what should we do?'

'Continue,' coldly replied Hatteras. 'I don't know what ship this *Porpoise* is, but I do know that the brig the *Forward* is waiting for our return.'

31

Death of Simpson

THE journey was resumed; everybody's minds were full of new and unexpected ideas, for an encounter is the most serious event that can happen in these northern lands. Hatteras was furrowing his brow with worry.

The *Porpoise*, he wondered, what sort of ship can it be? And what can it be doing so near the Pole?

At this thought, a shiver took hold of him, despite the temperature. As for the doctor and Bell, they were thinking only of the two outcomes possible following the discovery of the document: to save fellow humans or be saved by them.

But their difficulties, obstacles, and fatigues soon came back and they had to concentrate on their own situation, now desperate.

Simpson's condition was getting worse; Clawbonny could not mistake the signs of approaching death. The doctor could do nothing; he was suffering cruelly himself from a painful snow-blindness which might lead to loss of sight if he was not careful. At that time the half-light was sufficient, and this light, reflected by the snow, burned his eyes; it was difficult to protect himself from the reflection, for the lenses of his glasses often got covered with ice and so became opaque, stopping him seeing. But they had to avoid the slightest accidents on the journey, preventing them as much as possible; they were therefore obliged to run the risk of snow-blindness; the doctor and Bell took turns leading the sledge and covering their eyes.

The sledge was sliding poorly on its worn-out runners; pulling it became more and more difficult; the terrain was not getting any easier; they were faced with a landmass of volcanic origin, covered with bare crests and ridges; the travellers had had to slowly climb to a height of 1,500 feet to cross the mountains. The cold was worse here; gusts and flurries broke with unparalleled violence; and these wretches dragging themselves over the desolate peaks constituted a sad sight.

They also suffered from white sickness;* this uniform glare made them ill; it intoxicated, it made them dizzy; the ground seemed to disappear and the immense sheet have no fixed point; the feeling was the same as pitching and rolling, the deck missing under the sailor's foot; the travellers could not get used to it and the constant sensation went to their heads. Torpor seized their limbs, somnolence their minds, and often they walked while half-asleep; then a jolt, an unforeseen collision, even a fall, would shake them out of their inertia, which resumed a few seconds later.

On 25 January they began to descend steep slopes; their exhaustion increased still more on these icy slopes; one false step, fatally easy to take, could cast them into deep ravines; and there they would be lost without hope.

In the evening an extremely strong storm swept the snowy peaks; they could not resist it; they had to lie down; it was very cold and they ran the risk of freezing on the spot.

Helped by Hatteras, Bell painfully built a snow-house in which the wretches sought shelter.

There they had a few shreds of pemmican and a little hot tea. Just four gallons of spirits of wine remained; it had to be used now to help satisfy their thirst for it should not be thought that snow can be absorbed in its natural form; it needs to be melted first. In temperate lands, where the cold does not go much below freezing, snow is not harmful; but the situation above the Arctic Circle is quite different; the snow reaches such a low temperature that it is as difficult to pick up as a piece of red-hot iron, although it conducts heat very badly; there is consequently such a difference of temperature between the snow and the stomach that swallowing it literally produces suffocation. The Eskimos prefer to endure long tortures than drink this snow, which can in no circumstances replace water and increases one's thirst instead of satisfying it. The travellers could therefore quench theirs only by first melting the snow using the spirits of wine.

At three in the morning, at the height of the storm, the doctor took over the watch; he was sitting in a corner of the hut when a pitiful groan from Simpson drew his attention; he got up to help him, but when he stood up, he hit his head hard on the ice roof; without worrying about it, he bent over Simpson and began rubbing his swollen, bluish legs; after quarter of an hour of this treatment he tried to stand up and again hit his head even though he was now kneeling.

'That's strange,' he said.

He raised his arm; the roof was lowering appreciably.

'Good God,' he exclaimed; 'we have a problem, my friends!'

At his cries, Hatteras and Bell quickly got up and hit their heads in turn; they were in complete darkness.

'We're being buried alive!' said the doctor. 'Outside, outside!'

And all three, dragging Simpson through the opening, left the dangerous shelter; just in time, for the blocks of ice, insufficiently supported, then collapsed with a crash.

The unfortunate men were now in the midst of the storm, without shelter, assailed by extreme cold. Hatteras hurried to put up the tent; they were not able to maintain it against the violence of the weather, and had to shelter under the unsupported canvas, which a thick layer of snow soon covered; but at least this snow prevented heat loss, and so protected the travellers from being frozen as they lay.

The squalls only stopped until the next day; while harnessing the insufficiently fed dogs, Bell noticed that three of them had begun to gnaw at their leather straps; two were very ill and could not go far.

However, the caravan set off again as best it could; the destination was still sixty miles away.

On the twenty-sixth, Bell, walking ahead, suddenly called to his companions. They ran up, and with a stunned expression he pointed at a gun leaning against an ice floe.

'A rifle!' the doctor said.

Hatteras picked it up; it was in good condition, and was loaded.

'The men of the *Porpoise* can't be far away,' said Clawbonny.

Examining the gun, Hatteras noticed that it was an American one; his hands clenched the ice-cold barrel.

'Let's go, come on!' he said dully.

They continued down the mountain slopes. Simpson was insensible; he did not complain any more; he was not strong enough.

The storm continued; the sledge got slower and slower; they hardly covered a few miles each twenty-four hours and, in spite of the strictest economy, their food was reducing significantly; but, as long as there was enough to get back, Hatteras moved forward. On the twenty-seventh, they found a sextant almost buried in the snow, then a flask; it contained brandy, or rather a piece of ice with a ball of spirits hidden in the centre; it was no longer usable.

It was clear that Hatteras was inadvertently following the signs of a major disaster; he was advancing along the only practicable route, collecting the remains from some horrible shipwreck. The doctor looked carefully in case new cairns appeared; but in vain.

Sad thoughts came into his mind: if he discovered these unfortunate men, how could he help them? He and his companions were out of nearly everything; their clothes were almost in shreds, their food exhausted. If there were many castaways, they would all die of starvation. Hatteras looked as though he wanted not to find them! Was he not right, since the safety of his crew rested on his shoulders? Could he bring strangers on board, and so compromise the survival of all? But these strangers were human beings, their fellow men, maybe compatriots! However small their chance of survival, could they remove it? The doctor wanted to know what Bell thought on this question. Bell did not answer. His own suffering had hardened his heart. Clawbonny did not dare question Hatteras; so he trusted in Providence.

On 17 January,* in the evening, Simpson appeared to be nearing the end; his limbs already stiff and frozen, his breath panting and forming a mist around his head, his convulsive starts—all indicated that his final hour was near. The expression on his face was terrible, desperate, with looks of powerless anger at the captain. They contained a pure accusation, a whole series of dumb but significant reproaches, perhaps merited!

Hatteras did not approach the dying man. He avoided him, he fled him, more taciturn, more concentrated, more turned into himself than ever.

The following night was dreadful; the storm redoubled its violence; the tent was torn away three times, meaning the snow drifted over these wretches each time, blinding them, freezing them, piercing them with pointed darts torn from the surrounding ice floes. The dogs howled pitifully; Simpson was exposed to this cruel temperature. Bell managed each time to restore the miserable canvas shelter, which protected them from the snow, if not the cold. But then a stronger gust removed it a fourth time, and carried it off in its turning with awful whistlings.

'Ah, it's all too much!' Bell exclaimed.

'Courage, courage!' answered the doctor, hanging on to him so as not to roll into the ravine.

Simpson produced a death rattle. Suddenly, in a last effort, he half sat up, thrust his clenched fist at Hatteras, who stared back at him, uttered a heart-rending cry—and fell back, his threat unfinished.

'Dead!' the doctor exclaimed.

'Dead,' repeated Bell.

Hatteras approached the body, but was driven back by the strength of the wind.

Simpson was thus the first of the crew to fall to this murderous climate, the first not to return to port, the first to pay with his life for the captain's inexorable stubbornness, after incalculable sufferings. The dead man had called him a murderer, but Hatteras had not lowered his head at the charge. However, a tear, slipping from his eye, fell on his pale cheek and froze there.

The doctor and Bell looked at him almost in terror. Leaning on his long stick, he seemed to be the guardian spirit of these hyperboreal regions, straight amidst the hyperactive squalls and ominous in his terrible immobility.

He remained upright, not moving, until the first gleams of dawn: fearless, firm, indomitable, and apparently challenging the storm howling all around him.

32

Back to the Forward

THE wind fell at six in the morning, and, veering suddenly northerly, chased the clouds from the sky; the thermometer read minus thirty-three (−37 °C). The first gleams of twilight silvered the horizon that they would emblazon a few days later.

Hatteras went up to his two dejected companions, and said in a sweet, sad voice:

'My friends, we are still more than sixty miles from the spot Sir Edward Belcher indicated. We have only the barest minimum of food needed to get back to our vessel. To go further would be to court certain death, which would benefit no one. We have to turn round and go back.'

'A wise decision, Hatteras,' said the doctor; 'I'd have followed you wherever you wanted to go, but our health is weakening with each passing day; we can hardly set one foot in front of the other; so I'm in complete agreement with the idea of returning.'

'Is that your opinion too, Bell?'

'Yes, sir.'

'Fine; we'll take two days' rest. It's not too much. The sledge needs major repairs. It seems to me we'd best build a snow-house, where we can recover.'

This point settled, the three men set to work with new vigour; Bell took precautions to ensure his construction was solidly built, and soon an adequate shelter rose at the bottom of the valley where they had made their halt.

Hatteras had doubtless done himself terrible violence to interrupt his journey in such a way. So much wasted effort and fatigue! A useless excursion, paid for by the death of a man! To return on board without a single piece of coal! What would happen to the crew? What might they not attempt under Richard Shandon's inspiration? But Hatteras was unable to fight any more.

All his efforts now turned to preparations for the return. The sledge was repaired: its load had in any case decreased and was now less than two hundred pounds. The men patched up their clothes, worn-out, torn, covered with snow, hardened by ice; fresh moccasins and snow shoes replaced the old ones, no longer serviceable. These activities took up the whole of the twenty-ninth and the morning of the thirtieth; in addition, the three travellers rested as best they could and prepared for the future.

During these thirty-six hours spent in the snow hut on the ice in the valley, the doctor had observed Duke, whose behaviour seemed strange, even unnatural; the animal prowled endlessly about, making a thousand unexpected circles which appeared to have a common centre, a sort of rise, a swelling in the ground composed of many superimposed layers of ice. Duke turned round this point, barking quietly, wagging his tail impatiently, looking at his owner, seeming to interrogate him.

Having thought about it, the doctor attributed this state of anxiety to Simpson's body, which his companions had not yet had time to bury.

He resolved to proceed to this sad ceremony, since they had to leave the following day at dawn.

Equipped with pickaxes, Bell and Clawbonny returned to the bottom of the valley; the mound indicated by Duke offered a suitable place for the cadaver; it needed to be buried deep to be safe from bears' claws.

The carpenter and the doctor began by removing the top layer of soft snow, and then attacked the hardened ice; at the third pick blow, the doctor struck a hard body which broke; he removed some of the pieces, and recognized a glass bottle.

Bell himself brought up a shrivelled bag containing crumbs of perfectly preserved ship's biscuit.

'H'm?'

'What does it all mean?' replied Bell, stopping work.

The doctor called to Hatteras, who immediately came over.

Duke was barking loudly, and trying to scrabble with his paws at the thick layer of ice.

'Is it a provisions cache?'

'It would seem so,' replied Bell.

'Carry on!' said Hatteras.

A few pieces of food were removed, then a box quarter-full of pemmican.

'If it's a cache,' observed Hatteras, 'the bears must have got here before us. Look, these provisions aren't intact.'

'I fear so,' answered the doctor, 'because . . .'

He did not finish his sentence, interrupted by a shout from Bell: having pushed aside a heavy block, the carpenter was pointing at a stiff frozen leg emerging from the ice blocks.

'A body!' cried the doctor.

'It's not a cache,' countered Hatteras, 'it's a grave.'

The body, once brought out, was a sailor of around thirty, in perfect conservation. He had the clothing of Arctic navigators; the doctor was not able to say how long he had been dead.

But after this corpse, Bell discovered another, a fifty-year-old man, with the signs of the suffering that had killed him still on his face.

'These aren't bodies that have been buried; these unfortunates were caught by death exactly as we find them.'

'You're right, Dr Clawbonny.'

'Carry on, carry on!' said Hatteras.

Bell hardly dared. Who could say how many bodies lay in that ice mound!

'These people were victims of the misfortune that almost befell us,' said the doctor; 'their house of snow collapsed. Let's see if by any chance some are still breathing!'

The spot was speedily excavated and Bell brought up a third body, a forty-year-old man; he did not have the deathly appearance of the others; the doctor bent over, and thought he could detect signs of life.

'He's still alive, alive!' he cried.

With Bell he transported the body into the snow hut, while Hatteras, motionless, contemplated the collapsed abode.

The doctor completely stripped the dug-up wretch; he found no trace of wounds; helped by Bell, he rubbed him vigorously with brandy-drenched cotton, and he felt life coming back to him little by little. However, the poor man was in a state of absolute prostration, completely unable to talk; his tongue, perhaps frozen, was stuck to the roof of his mouth.

The doctor went through his pockets; they were empty. No documents. He let Bell carry on rubbing and returned to Hatteras.

The captain, who had dug down into the cavities of the snow

hut and carefully searched the ground, came back up holding a half-burned fragment from an envelope. On it could be read:

> . . . tamont,
> *. . . orpoise*
> w York.

'Altamont.* On the vessel *Porpoise*! From New York!'

'An American!' replied Hatteras with a shudder.

'I will save him,' said the doctor. 'I can vouch for it, and we shall know the solution to this dreadful enigma.'

He turned back to Altamont's body, while Hatteras remained pensive. By dint of care, the doctor managed to bring the unlucky man back to life, but not consciousness; he could not see, hear, understand, or speak, but at least he was alive!

The following morning, Hatteras said to the doctor:

'We must leave, all the same.'

'Let's, Hatteras! The sledge isn't full, so we can transport this wretch to the vessel.'

'Carry on. But first let's bury the bodies.'

Both unknown sailors were once more placed under the remains of the snow hut; and Simpson's corpse replaced Altamont's.

The three travellers said a prayer, as a last remembrance for their companion; and resumed their march towards the vessel at 7 a.m. Two of the harness dogs having died, Duke came of his own accord to pull the sledge, and performed with the conscience and resolution of a Greenlander.

For twenty days, from 31 January to 19 February, the return was similar to the outward journey. The only difference was that in February, the coldest month, the ice now offered a uniformly hard surface; the travellers suffered terribly from the temperature, but not from swirls or gusts of wind.

The sun had appeared for the first time on 31 January; every day it climbed further above the horizon. Bell and the doctor were at the end of their strength, nearly blind and half-lame; the carpenter could not walk without crutches.

Altamont was still alive, but totally inanimate; sometimes they gave up hope, but intelligent care returned him to life each time! And yet the good doctor needed to look after himself, because his health was deteriorating with his increasing weariness.

Hatteras thought of the *Forward*, his brig! What state would he find her in? What might have happened on board? Would Johnson have been able to stand up to Shandon and his men? The cold had been terrible! Had the unfortunate vessel been burned? Had her masts and hull at least been spared?

While thinking all this, Hatteras marched ahead, as though wanting to see the *Forward* from afar.

On the morning of 24 February, he stopped suddenly. Three hundred paces ahead shone a reddish light, above which floated a huge black column of smoke disappearing into the grey clouds of the sky!

'Smoke!'

His heart beat as though about to break.

'Look there! Smoke!' he cried to his two companions joining him. 'My vessel is burning!'

'But we're more than three miles away,' said Bell. 'It can't be the *Forward*!'

'It is,' answered the doctor; 'a mirage makes it seem closer.'

'Let's run!' Hatteras cried, dashing ahead.

The two others, leaving the sledge to Duke's care, rushed after the captain.

An hour later, they arrived in view of the vessel. What a terrible sight! The brig was burning in the middle of the ice melting around her; flames covered her hull, as the southerly breeze carried the bizarre crackles to Hatteras's ears. Five hundred paces away, a man had raised his arms in despair; he stood there, powerless before the fire twisting the *Forward* in its flames.

This man was alone, and this man was old Johnson.

Hatteras ran up to him.

'My vessel, my vessel!' he demanded in a broken voice.

'You, captain!' answered Johnson. 'Stop, not a step further!'

'Well?' said Hatteras in a terrible, menacing tone.

'The wretches!' answered Johnson. 'They left forty-eight hours ago, after setting fire to the vessel.'

'Hell!' said Hatteras.

A formidable explosion happened; the earth trembled; icebergs lay down on the frozen field; a column of smoke rose to unfurl through the clouds; and with the conflagration of her powder magazine, the *Forward* exploded and disappeared into the fiery depths.

At that moment the doctor and Bell caught up with Hatteras. The captain, absorbed in his despair, suddenly rose up.

'My friends,' he said energetically, 'the cowards have fled! The strong will succeed! Johnson and Bell, you have the courage; doctor, the knowledge; I, the faith! The North Pole is yonder! To work, to work!'

Hatteras's companions felt their strength return as they listened to the invigorating words. And yet the situation was terrible for these four people, in the company of a dying man. They were without resources, lost and alone at the eightieth degree, in the heart of the Arctic!*

PART TWO

THE DESERT OF ICE

I

The Doctor's Inventory

IT was a bold plan that Captain Hatteras had had to head north, and reserve for Britain, his country, the glory of discovering the North Pole of the world. This bold sailor had done everything human strength could do. After struggling for nine months against the currents and storms, breaking ice mountains and fields, fighting against the cold of an unprecedented winter in the hyperboreal regions, summing up in his expedition the efforts of his predecessors—verifying and repeating, so to speak, the history of polar discoveries—after pushing his brig the *Forward* beyond the known seas, in sum, after accomplishing half of his task, he had seen his great project suddenly reduced to nothing! The betrayal, or rather the discouragement, of his crew, worn out by their trials, and the criminal madness of a few ringleaders, now left him in a terrifying situation: of the eighteen men who had sailed, only four remained, and they were abandoned without resources, without a ship, more than two thousand five hundred miles from their homeland!

The explosion of the *Forward*, which had just happened before their eyes, had removed their last means of survival.

However, Hatteras's courage did not weaken with this terrible catastrophe. His remaining companions were the best of his crew—all heroic men. By appealing to Dr Clawbonny's energy and knowledge, Johnson and Bell's devotion, and his own faith in the endeavour, he dared to speak of hope in this situation beyond hope. His valiant companions hearkened to him, and the past record of these resolute men meant their courage could be counted on.

After the captain's energetic words, the doctor wanted to gain detailed knowledge of the situation and, leaving his companions waiting 500 paces from the ship, headed for the scene of the catastrophe.

Of the *Forward*, that ship built with so much care, that dear brig, nothing remained. The only signs of the violent explosion were twisted pieces of ice, shapeless, blackened, burned debris, contorted metal rods, pieces of cable still burning like artillery blasters, and, in the distance, spirals of smoke crawling here and there over the ice-field. The fo'c'sle cannon, thrown to a distance of several fathoms, was lying on an ice floe like a gun carriage. The ground was strewn with fragments of every sort over a distance of 500 feet; the keel of the brig lay under a pile of ice; the icebergs, partly melted by the heat of the fire, had already become as hard as granite again.

The doctor began to think about his obliterated cabin—his collections lost, his precious instruments in pieces, his books lacerated and burned to ashes. So many treasures destroyed! With a damp eye he contemplated the terrible disaster, thinking, not of the future, but of this irreversible ill fortune which had struck him so directly.

He was soon joined by Johnson. The old sailor's face bore the marks of his recent suffering, acquired while fighting his rebellious companions to defend the ship under his guard.

The doctor held out his hand, and the mate sadly took it.

'What's to become of us, my friend?'

'Who knows?'

'Above all, let's not give in to despair. We must be men!'

'You're right, Dr Clawbonny. Major disasters need major decisions. We're in an awkward situation. We need to figure out how to get out of it.'

'Poor ship,' said the doctor with a sigh; 'I had grown attached to her. I loved her like you love your home—the house where you've spent your entire life—but not a single recognizable piece is left!'

'Who could believe that that collection of beams and planks could be so dear to us!'

'And was even the launch destroyed?' said the doctor, looking all around.

'It wasn't, but Shandon and his men took it with them when they abandoned us!'

'And the ship's boat?'

'In a thousand pieces! See those few fragments of still-warm tin-plate? That's all that's left.'

'So we've just got the Halkett boat?'[1]

'Lucky you had the idea of taking it on your sledge.'

'It's not very much.'

'Those wretched traitors who ran away! May heaven punish them as they deserve!'

'Johnson,' gently replied the doctor, 'don't forget that their suffering severely tested them! Only the best can remain good in such difficulties, while the weak falter. We should pity our companions of ill fortune, not curse them!'

Following these words, the doctor fell silent for a while, worriedly examining the landscape.

'What happened to the sledge?' asked Johnson.

'It's a mile back.'

'Guarded by Simpson?'

'No, my friend. Simpson—poor Simpson!—succumbed to fatigue.'

'Dead?' exclaimed the mate.

'Dead!'

'The poor man! Though, all the same, we should perhaps envy his fate.'

'But in place of the dead man we left, we've brought back a dying man.'

'A dying man?'

'One Captain Altamont.'

The doctor briefly told the mate about their meeting.

'An American,' said Johnson thoughtfully.

'Yes, everything leads us to believe he's a citizen of the Union. But what sort of ship was this *Porpoise*, obviously shipwrecked, and what was it doing here in the first place?'

'It was coming here to die; it was dragging its crew down to oblivion with it, like all who seek these skies! But, Dr Clawbonny, did you at least do what you hoped?'

'The coal deposits?'

'Yes.'

The doctor sadly shook his head.

'Nothing?'

---

[1] A rubber dinghy in the form of a piece of clothing, which can expand as much as wished.

'We didn't have enough food, and exhaustion shattered us en route! We didn't even reach the coast described by Edward Belcher!'

'So no fuel?'

'No!'

'No food?'

'No!'

'And no ship to get us back to Britain!'

The doctor and Johnson fell silent. It took remarkable courage to face up to this situation.

'Well at least our position is clear; we know what we're up against! But first things first; it's freezing—we need to build a snow-house.'

'It'll be easy with Bell's help; then we'll go and fetch the sledge, bring back the American, and hold a meeting with Hatteras.'

'Poor captain,' said Johnson, finding a way not to think about his own problems, 'he must really be suffering!'

The doctor and the mate rejoined their companions.

Hatteras was standing, mute and motionless, his arms crossed as usual, gazing at the future in space. His face had resumed its usual firmness. What was this extraordinary man thinking? Was he worried by his desperate situation or by the failure of all his efforts? Was he at last thinking of turning back, since men, the elements—everything—were conspiring against his endeavour?

Nobody could read his thoughts. Nothing revealed them on the outside. His faithful Duke stayed close, braving the temperature which had fallen to minus thirty-two (−36°C).

Stretched out on the ice, Bell was not moving at all; he appeared inanimate; but unconsciousness could cost his life; he was in danger of freezing into a single block.

Johnson shook him vigorously, rubbed him with snow, and, not without difficulty, managed to draw him from his torpor.

'Come on, Bell, buck up,' he said; 'don't get discouraged. Get up; we have to talk about our situation and we need shelter! You can't have forgotten how to make a snow-house? Come on, help me, Bell! There's an iceberg over there just waiting to be dug into! Let's get to work! Let's bring back what we need now, namely courage and brave hearts!'

A little restored by these words, Bell let the old sailor guide him.

'Now,' the latter added, 'Dr Clawbonny will be so good as to go to the sledge, and bring it back with the dogs.'

'I'm ready,' replied the doctor; 'I'll be back in an hour.'

'Are you going with him, captain?' said Johnson.

Although preoccupied with his own thoughts, Hatteras heard the mate's question, for he gently replied:

'No, my friend, if the doctor can manage . . . A hard decision has to be made today, and I must be alone to think. Go, do what you think is needed for the present. I'll be considering the future.'

Johnson went back to the doctor.

'It's strange, the captain seems to have forgotten all anger; never has he spoken to me so kindly.'

'His self-control has returned. Believe me, Johnson, that man is capable of saving us!'

With these words, the doctor wrapped himself up as best he could and, metal-tipped stick in hand, headed back to the sledge through a mist made almost luminous by the moonlight.

Johnson and Bell immediately set to work. The old sailor encouraged the carpenter, who worked in silence. No construction was necessary—only digging into the ice beneath; a task made more difficult because they had only knives and the ice was stone-hard. The only compensation for their toil was the knowledge that such hardness would mean a solid shelter. Soon Johnson and Bell were protected as they worked in their hollow, throwing everything out they excavated from the hard material.

Sometimes Hatteras moved off, but then he would stop short. He was obviously reluctant to approach the site of his poor brig.

As he had promised, the doctor soon returned. He brought back Altamont, lying on the sledge and wrapped in the material of the tent. The Greenland dogs, thin, exhausted, starving, could hardly pull, and were gnawing at their harnesses and straps. It was high time that the entire troop, animals and men, took food and rest.

While the house was being dug out, the doctor rummaged here and there, and was lucky enough to find a small stove that the explosion had mostly spared, with a twisted flue that could easily be bent straight. The doctor brought it in with a triumphant expression. After three hours the ice-house was habitable: the stove had been set up, pieces of wood inserted, and soon it was roaring and giving out a heat that did them a great deal of good.

The American was brought inside and laid to rest at the end, on the blankets; the four Britons gathered round the fire. The last food from the sledge—a little biscuit and boiling tea—did much to revive their spirits. Hatteras said nothing, and each respected his silence.

The meal finished, the doctor made a sign to Johnson to come outside.

'Now,' he said, 'we need to prepare an inventory of what's left. We must know exactly the state of our riches. They're strewn here and there; we need to bring them together. Snow may fall at any moment, and then it'll be impossible to find anything from the ship.'

'Let's not lose any time; food and wood are the most important.'

'Yes, let's each search a different part, so as to cover the whole area of the explosion; starting with the centre, we can move towards the circumference.'

The two companions immediately headed for the bed of ice bearing the remains of the *Forward*. In the dim moonlight, each carefully examined the debris. It was a genuine hunt; the doctor put into it the passion—not to mention the pleasure—of the Hunter, and his heart beat wildly when he found a box more or less in one piece. But most were empty, their contents strewn over the whole ice-field.

The force of the explosion had been considerable. Many items were mere dust or ashes. The main parts of the boiler lay here and there, twisted and shattered; the propeller's broken blades had been thrown 120 feet from the ship, and sunk deep into the hardened snow; the twisted pistons had been torn from their pivots; and the chimney, split end to end, was half-crushed beneath an enormous floe, the remains of chains still hanging from it. Nails, hooks, and deadeyes—all the metal from the brig—were spread far and wide, like grapeshot.

This metal, which would have enriched a whole tribe of Eskimos, was useless in the present circumstances; what was needed, above all, was food, and the doctor found very little.

'This isn't going at all well,' he said to himself; 'the storeroom, situated near the powder-hold, must have been destroyed by the explosion; what didn't burn must have been blown to smithereens. It's a problem, and if Johnson doesn't have better hunting, I can't imagine what will become of us.'

However, by increasing the circle of his search, the doctor was able to gather a few pieces of pemmican[1]—about fifteen pounds'

---

[1] A product made from condensed meat.

worth—and four stoneware bottles, thrown into a faraway bank of still-soft snow and so intact. The bottles contained a total of five or six pints of spirits of wine.

Further on, he picked up two packets of Cochlearia seeds; this compensated for the loss of lime juice,* so vital in fighting scurvy.

Two hours later, the doctor and Johnson came and shared their discoveries. In terms of food, there was not much: a few scarce pieces of salt meat, about fifty pounds of pemmican, three bags of biscuits, a small supply of chocolate, the spirits of wine, and about two pounds of coffee, gleaned grain by grain from the ice.

Neither blankets, nor hammocks, nor clothing could be found; the fire had clearly consumed them.

In sum, the doctor and the mate had gathered food for three weeks, provided they carefully rationed it—not much to restore exhausted men. It seemed that, in a run of bad luck, Hatteras had run out of coal, and almost out of food too.

The wooden debris from the ship's masts and hull could serve as fuel; but that could only last three weeks. Before they began using it to heat the ice-house, the doctor asked Johnson if there was any way to use the pieces to build a smaller vessel, or at least a launch.

'No chance,' replied the good mate; 'Dr Clawbonny, there's not a single whole piece of wood we could use; all this is only useful for heating us for a few days, and after that . . .'

'After that?'

'God's mercy!'

Having finished the inventory, the doctor and Johnson went to fetch the sledge. They harnessed the poor, tired dogs as best they could; returning to the scene of the explosion, they loaded the rare but precious remains of the cargo, and brought them back to the ice-house; then, half-frozen, they rejoined their companions in misfortune.

2

Altamont's First Words

AT about eight in the evening, the sky was, for a few moments, clear of its snowy mists, and the constellations shone brilliantly in the night, now colder.

Hatteras took the opportunity to go outside and measure the height of a few stars. He went out without a word, taking his instruments. He wanted to establish the position, to see if the ice-field had drifted any further.

Half an hour later, he came back and lay down in a corner of the ice-house, remaining plunged in a deep immobility which was clearly not sleep.

The following day, the snow began to fall very heavily again. The doctor congratulated himself on undertaking the searches the day before, for an enormous white curtain soon fell over the ice-field and any trace of the explosion disappeared under a shroud three feet deep.

It was impossible to go outside that day; fortunately the shelter was comfortable, or at least it seemed so to the long-suffering travellers. The small stove worked well, except sometimes when strong gusts of wind pushed the smoke back down. It provided boiling drinks of tea or coffee—so marvellous at such low temperatures.

The shipwrecked men, for so they can be called, felt well-being they had not experienced for a long time; they concentrated on the present, on the comforts of warmth and temporary rest; forgetting and defying the future, which threatened them with impending death.

The American was suffering less now and gradually coming back to life; he opened his eyes, but did not yet speak; his lips showed signs of scurvy, and could not produce any sound; however, he could listen and was informed of the situation. He moved his head as a sign of thanks; he knew that he had been saved from his entombment under the snow, and the doctor was wise enough not to tell him how little his death had been delayed, for in a fortnight, three weeks at most, there would be no food left at all.

At noon, Hatteras emerged from his immobility, and went over to Johnson, Bell, and the doctor.

'My friends,' he said, 'we must come to a final decision on what needs to be done. But before that I will ask you, Johnson, to tell me the circumstances of the act of betrayal that brought about our downfall.'

'What is the point of knowing?' said the doctor. 'It's happened, and we shouldn't think about it any more.'

'And yet I do think about it,' responded Hatteras. 'After Johnson's tale, I won't any more.'

'This is what happened. I did everything to prevent that crime . . .'

'I'm certain you did, Johnson. I will add that the ringleaders had been planning something of the sort for a long time.'

'That's what I think too,' said the doctor.

'Agreed,' added Johnson, 'for almost immediately after you left— the very next day—Shandon went bad and, with the support of the others, took command of the ship; I tried to stop them, but couldn't. After that everybody acted more or less as they liked; Shandon allowed them; he wanted to show the crew that the period of toil and deprivation had passed. So no more economies of any sort; the stove burned mightily; fires were even made on the deck. The men could have as much to eat as they wanted, alcohol too, and for people deprived of spirits for so long, you can imagine how much they drank! This continued from 7 to 15 January.'

'So,' said Hatteras gravely, 'it was Shandon who incited the crew to mutiny?'

'Yes, captain.'

'The subject of that man is now closed. Continue, Johnson.'

'It was on about 24 or 25 January that they decided to abandon ship. They planned to reach the west coast of Baffin Bay; from there they would sail in the launch, looking for whalers, or even try for the settlements on the east coast of Greenland.* There were plenty of provisions; even the sick men recovered a little, excited at the hope of returning. So they began preparing to leave; a sledge was built to carry the food, fuel, and launch; the men were to pull it. That took until 15 February. I still hoped you would return, captain; and yet at the same time I feared your presence. You wouldn't have got anything out of the crew—they would have preferred to murder you rather than remain on the ship. It was as though they were drunk with freedom. I took aside all my companions in small groups; I spoke to them, I begged them, I emphasized the dangers of such an expedition and the cowardice of abandoning you! I got nowhere, even from the best! Departure was set for 22 February. Shandon felt impatient. They piled up on the sledge and in the launch as much food and alcohol as they could take; then they loaded large amounts of wood on top; the starboard side of the brig was already dismantled down to the waterline. The last day was one of orgy; they pillaged, they destroyed, and it was in their drunkenness that Pen and two or three others set fire to the ship. I fought with them; they knocked me down and beat me; finally those wretches left, led eastwards by Shandon, and vanished from my sight! I was alone; what could I do against the fire, spreading by then to the whole ship? The fire hole was covered with ice, and I didn't have a drop of water. For two days the *Forward* twisted in the flames, and the rest you know.'

This tale over, a long silence hung over the ice-house; the gloomy scene of the burning ship and the loss of the precious brig appeared more vividly in the minds of the shipwrecked men; they felt themselves up against the impossible; and the impossible consisted of getting back to Britain. They dared not look at each other, for fear of seeing absolute despair on their faces. The only sound was the American's hurried breathing.

Finally Hatteras spoke.

'Thank you, Johnson; you did everything you could to save my ship; but alone you could not resist. I thank you once again, and let's not speak of the catastrophe any more. Let's unite our efforts for the common good. We are four companions here, four friends, and the life of one is worth the life of another. We should each give our opinion as to what should be done.'

'Ask us questions, Hatteras,' replied the doctor; 'we are entirely devoted to you—our hearts will answer. First of all, do you have any ideas yourself?'

'On my own it would be difficult to have an opinion,' said Hatteras sadly. 'My views might seem self-interested. So I want above all to hear yours.'

'Captain,' said Johnson, 'before deciding in such serious circumstances, I have an important question to ask you.'

'Speak, Johnson.'

'You went yesterday to measure our position; well, has the ice-field drifted further, or are we still in the same place?'

'It hasn't moved. I found 80° 15′ N and 97° 35′ W, the same as before our departure.'

'So what distance are we from the closest sea to the west?'

'About six hundred miles,' replied Hatteras.

'And its name?'

'Smith Sound.'

'The same as the one we tried to go through last April?'

'The same.'

'Well, captain, now we know our situation, and can make a decision accordingly.'

'Speak then,' replied Hatteras, dropping his head into his hands.

In this way he could listen to his companions without looking at them.

'Come on, Bell,' said the doctor, 'what do you think the best plan of action is?'

'We don't need to think for too long: we need to head back, without losing a day or an hour, southwards or westwards, and get to the nearest coast . . . even if our journey takes two months!'

'We've only got three weeks' food left,' replied Hatteras, not raising his head.

'Well then,' continued Johnson, 'we need to do the journey in three weeks—it's our only chance of survival; even if we are crawling on our hands and knees when we reach the coast, we must leave and arrive within twenty-five days.'

'This part of the polar landmass is unknown,' replied Hatteras. 'We might meet obstacles—mountains, glaciers—that would completely block the way.'

'I don't think that that is sufficient reason not to try the journey,' said the doctor; 'we will suffer a great deal, that is clear; we will have to restrict the food to the absolute minimum, unless the luck of the hunt . . .'

'There's only half a pound of powder left.'

'Come now, Hatteras, all your objections are valid; I don't harbour any false hopes. But I think I can guess your idea; do you have a viable alternative?'

'No,' replied the captain, after hesitating.

'You can't doubt our courage,' added the doctor; 'we'll follow you to the end, you know; but shouldn't we give up all hope now of reaching the Pole? The betrayal scuppered your plans; you could have fought the obstacles of nature and even overcome them, but not man's perfidy and fallibility. You did everything humanly possible, and you would have succeeded, I'm sure; but in the present situation, aren't you forced to postpone your plans, and to try and get back to Britain in order to be able to resume them one day?'

'Well, captain?' asked Johnson.

Hatteras did not reply for a long time. Finally, he raised his head and said, in an uneasy voice:

'Do you think you'd be sure to reach the strait, tired as you are and almost without food?'

'No,' replied the doctor; 'but surely the coast will not come to us—we need to go and find it. Perhaps we'll find tribes of Eskimos further south, who we can easily make contact with.'

'In any case,' said Johnson, 'mightn't we meet some ship forced to winter in the strait?'

'And if necessary,' said the doctor, 'since the strait is frozen, cross it and reach the west coast of Greenland, and from there either Prudhoe Land or Cape York, and hence maybe a Danish settlement? If you think about it, Hatteras, the ice-field here has nothing at all like that! The road to Britain is over there, southwards, and not here, northwards!'

'Yes,' added Bell, 'Dr Clawbonny is right; we need to leave, without delay. Up till now we've forgotten what is truly precious to us—our home and dear ones!'

'Is that your opinion, Johnson?' Hatteras asked once again.

'Yes, captain.'

'And yours, doctor?'

'It is.'

Hatteras was silent again; but he could not stop his face revealing his interior agitation. The choice he was about to make would decide the destiny of his whole life. If he turned round and went back, his bold plans would be finished for ever; he couldn't hope to make a fourth expedition like this.

Seeing that the captain was not going to speak, the doctor said:

'I will add, Hatteras, that we must not waste a moment: we need to load the sledge with all our food, and carry as much wood as possible.

A 600-mile journey, in these conditions, is a long one, but not, I think, impossible; we can, or rather must, do twenty miles a day to reach the coast in a month—for by about 26 March . . .'

'But', said Hatteras, 'can't we wait a few days?'

'What do you hope will happen?' asked Johnson.

'I don't know. Who can foresee the future? A few days more! In any case, a few days is hardly enough for you to recover! Without a snow-house to shelter in, you won't do two marches without collapsing from exhaustion!'

'But a horrible death is waiting for us here!' exclaimed Bell.

'My friends,' said Hatteras in a pleading voice, 'you're giving in too soon! Even if I suggested trying to find safety in the north, you would refuse to follow me! And yet, do not tribes of Eskimos live near the Pole, like on Smith Sound? The open sea, whose existence is certain, must be surrounded by land. Nature is logical in everything she does. Well, it is highly probable that vegetation starts growing again where the great cold stops. Is a promised land not waiting for us in the north, which you want to give up once and for all?'

Hatteras became excited as he spoke, his inflamed mind conjuring up entrancing tableaux of those lands whose very existence was so controversial.

'One more day,' he said, 'one more hour!'

Dr Clawbonny, with his adventurous character and burning imagination, was gradually feeling moved; he was going to give in; but Johnson, wiser and cooler, brought him back to reason and duty.

'Bell,' he said, 'let's go to the sledge!'

'All right.'

The two sailors headed for the exit of the snow-house.

'Johnson,' exclaimed Hatteras, 'well then, go! I'm staying. I'm staying!'

'Captain . . .' said Johnson, stopping against his will.

'I'm staying, I tell you! Go and leave me like the others! Come on, Duke, we're staying, just the two of us.'

The good dog stood near his master, barking. Johnson looked at the doctor. Clawbonny did not know what to do; it was best to calm Hatteras down, and sacrifice one day to his ideas. The doctor was going to resign himself to that, when he felt something touch his arm.

He turned around. The American had left his blankets and was crawling over the ground. Finally he got to his knees and, through his damaged lips, produced inarticulate sounds.

The doctor looked at him in silent astonishment, a little frightened. As for Hatteras, he went up to the American and examined him carefully. He tried to understand the words that the poor man could not pronounce. At last, after five minutes of effort, he made out one word, 'Porpoise.'

'The *Porpoise?*' exclaimed the captain.

The American nodded.

'In these seas?' asked Hatteras, his heart beating wildly.

Same reaction from the sick man.

'Northwards?'

'Yes,' from the wretch.

'And you know its position?'

'Yes!'

'Precisely?'

'Yes!'

There was a moment of silence. Those watching this surprising scene were on tenterhooks.

'Listen carefully,' Hatteras said at last to the sick man; 'we need to know the position of that ship! I'm going to count the degrees out loud . . . Stop me with a sign.'

The American nodded in agreement.

'Let's see,' began Hatteras; 'we'll start with longitude. A hundred and five? No. Hundred and six? Hundred and seven? Hundred and eight? It is westwards?'

'Yes,' replied the American.

'Let's continue—a hundred and nine? Hundred and ten? Hundred and twelve? Hundred and fourteen? Hundred and sixteen? Hundred and eighteen? Hundred and nineteen? Hundred and twenty?'

'Yes.'

'Hundred and twenty degrees west? And how many minutes? I'll count . . .'

Hatteras began with one. At fifteen, Altamont made him stop.

'Good,' said Hatteras. 'Now the latitude. Can you hear me? Eighty? Eighty-one? Eighty-two? Eighty-three?'

The American stopped him with his hand.

'Fine! And the minutes? Five? Ten? Fifteen? Twenty? Twenty-five? Thirty? Thirty-five?'

A new sign from Altamont, smiling weakly.

'So,' said Hatteras gravely, 'the *Porpoise* is at 120° 15′ W, 83° 35′ N?'

'Yes!' indicated the American one last time, before falling unconscious in the doctor's arms.

The effort had made him collapse.

'My friends,' exclaimed Hatteras, 'you can see that survival is northwards, ever northwards! We're saved!'

But after his first words of joy, Hatteras suddenly appeared to be struck by a terrible idea. His face changed, and he felt his heart smitten by the serpent of envy.

Somebody else, an American,* had gone three degrees further than him towards the Pole! Why? And heading where?

3

Seventeen Days' March

THIS unprecedented event, this first utterance by Altamont, completely changed the situation of the shipwrecked men. Previously, they had been beyond any possible help, without serious hope of reaching Baffin Bay, in danger of running out of food on a journey that was too long for their tired bodies; and now, less than four hundred miles from their snow-house, there was a ship offering them plentiful resources and perhaps a way to continue their bold march to the Pole. Hatteras, the doctor, Johnson, and Bell started hoping again, after being so close to despair—a joyous hope, almost delirium.

But the information from Altamont was still incomplete, and after a few minutes' rest, the doctor continued the previous conversation; asking him questions in a form where he only had to move his head or eyes to answer.

Soon he discovered that the *Porpoise* was an American three-master from New York, stranded in the middle of the ice with great quantities of food and fuel; although leaning on her side, she must have resisted the pressure, and it would be possible to save her cargo.

Altamont and his crew had abandoned her two months before,

carrying the launch on the sledge; they wanted to reach Smith
Sound, find a whaler, and return to America; but little by little,
fatigue and illness struck these wretches, and one by one they had
fallen by the wayside.

Finally only the captain and two sailors remained from a crew of
thirty men, and though he, Altamont, had survived, it was only
through a miracle of Providence.

Hatteras wanted to know from the American why the *Porpoise* had
gone so far north.

Altamont informed them that it had been carried by the ice
without being able to resist it.

Hatteras then anxiously asked him what the purpose of his
journey had been.

Altamont claimed to have been trying to sail the Northwest
Passage.

Hatteras did not persist, and asked no more questions of this sort.

Then the doctor spoke:

'Now,' he said, 'all our efforts must be directed towards finding
the *Porpoise*; instead of trying for Baffin Bay, we can take a route only
two-thirds as long, and find a ship that will provide all the resources
we need for wintering.'

'It's the only thing to do,' said Bell.

'I will add', said the mate, 'that we must not waste a moment; we
need to calculate the amount of time for our journey according to the
time our food will last, the opposite of what is usually done; and we
need to set off as soon as possible.'

'You're right, Johnson,' said the doctor; 'if we left tomorrow,
Tuesday, 26 February, we'd arrive at the *Porpoise* on 15 March, or
else die of starvation. What do you think, Hatteras?'

'Let's make our preparations straightaway, and then leave. The
journey may take longer than we imagine.'

'Why do you say that? Altamont seems to be sure where
the ship is.'

'But what if the *Porpoise* has drifted on its ice-field, like the
Forward?'

'Yes, that may easily have happened!'

Johnson and Bell did not respond to the idea of a possible drift like
the one they had undergone.

But Altamont, attentive to this conversation, indicated to the doctor that he wanted to speak. Clawbonny acquiesced, and after a long quarter of an hour of circumlocutions and hesitations, acquired the certainty that the *Porpoise* was stranded near a coast, and could not have moved from its rock bed.

This piece of news reassured the four Britons; however, it took away any hope of getting back to Europe, unless Bell could somehow build a vessel with the remains of the *Porpoise*. But in any case, their greatest priority was simply to get to the site of the wreck.

The doctor asked the American one last question: had he found an open sea at eighty-three degrees north?

'No,' replied Altamont.

The conversation stopped there. They all got ready to leave straightaway. First Bell and Johnson prepared the sledge; it needed a complete overhaul; since there was no lack of wood, its uprights were strengthened; they used the experience acquired in the excursion to the south; they knew the weak points of this method of transport, and as they could expect thick and abundant snow, the runners were raised.

Inside, Bell arranged a sort of couchette covered with the canvas of the tent, designed for the American; the food, unfortunately in small quantities, did not increase the weight of the sled very much; but to compensate, the load was completed with all the wood they could carry.

While dealing with the food, the doctor made a scrupulously accurate inventory; he calculated that each traveller had to go on three-quarters rations over the three-week journey. The four dogs in harness would get a full ration. If Duke pulled with them, he would have the same right.

The preparations were interrupted by a need for rest and sleep, which made itself imperiously felt at seven in the evening; but before going to bed, the shipwrecked men gathered round the stove, not sparing the fuel; the poor men gave themselves the luxury of heat which they had been without for such a long time. Pemmican and biscuit and several cups of coffee soon restored their good humour, jointly shared,* together with the hope that was coming back to them so quickly and from so far.

At seven in the morning they started work again, and had entirely finished at about 3 p.m.

It was already dark—the sun had first appeared above the horizon on 31 January, but it still gave only a weak, short light; fortunately the moon was to rise at half-past six, and in this clear sky its light would be enough to illuminate the route. The temperature, which had gone down considerably over the last few days, finally reached minus thirty-three (−37°C).

The time to leave came. Altamont welcomed the idea of setting off, although the jolts would surely add to his suffering; he informed the doctor that he would find the anti-scurvy items needed for his recovery on board the *Porpoise*.

He was moved to the sledge, and installed on it as comfortably as possible; the dogs, including Duke, were harnessed to it; the travellers looked one last time at the bed of ice where the *Forward* had lain. For a moment, a flash of undiluted anger crossed Hatteras's face; but he regained his self-control, and the small troop soon penetrated the dry-weather mist, heading north-north-west.

Each went back to his usual place: Bell at the head; the doctor and the mate beside the sledge, keeping lookout and pushing when necessary; Hatteras behind, correcting the route so as to make sure the team followed Bell's line.

Progress was relatively quick; at this very low temperature the ice was hard and polished, making it suitable for gliding; the five dogs easily pulled the load, less than nine hundred pounds. However, men and beasts soon lost their breath, and often had to stop to catch it again.

At about seven in the evening, the moon freed its reddish circle from the mists of the horizon. Its calm light cut through the atmosphere, its beams clearly reflected from the ice. To the north-west, the ice-fields formed an enormous, perfectly flat, white plain. Not a single icepack, not a single hummock. This part of the sea seemed to have frozen calmly, like a peaceful lake.

It was a huge desert, smooth and monotonous.

Such was the impression this sight produced on the doctor, and he communicated it to his companion.

'You're right, Dr Clawbonny, it's a desert—but one where there's no danger of dying of thirst!'

'A clear advantage. However, this immensity proves one thing to me: we must be a long way from any land. Generally speaking, near the coast there are lots of ice mountains, but we can't see a single iceberg.'

'But we can't see nearly as far as usual because of the mist.'

'Yes, but all the same, we've found nothing but this flat and apparently endless ice-field since we left.'

'Did you realize that our march is a dangerous one? You get used to it, and don't think about it any more; but below this icy surface are bottomless chasms.'

'You're right, my friend, but there's no danger of drowning; the strength of this white crust is considerable at minus thirty-three degrees. Indeed, it's getting stronger every day, for at these latitudes the snow falls nine days out of ten, even in April, May, and June; and so I estimate that the crust must be nearly thirty or forty feet thick.'

'Reassuring.'

'We're not like those skaters on the Serpentine River[1] who are constantly afraid the fragile support will disappear under them: there's no such danger for us.'

'Is the strength of resistance of ice known?' asked the old sailor, always keen to learn from the doctor's store of knowledge.

'Perfectly!' replied the doctor. 'We now know most things that can be measured in this world, except the bounds of human ambition! Indeed, is it not ambition that drives us towards the North Pole, which man wants finally to discover? But to come back to your question: ice two inches thick can support a man; three and a half inches, a horse with its rider; five inches an eight-pounder; eight inches, a full artillery carriage with its team of horses; and finally at ten inches an army—a numberless crowd! Where we are walking now you could build the Liverpool Customs House or the Houses of Parliament in London.'

'It's hard to imagine such strength; but a moment ago you said that on average the snow falls nine days out of ten in these regions; that is obviously true, so I won't discuss it; but where does all that snow come from? With the seas frozen, I can't see how they can provide the huge quantity of water vapour needed to form the clouds.'

'Your question is a good one, Johnson. In my view, most of the snow or rain that we receive in the polar regions is made of water from the seas of the temperate zones; any given flake might have come from a drop from a river in Europe, absorbed into the air as water vapour to form a cloud, and finally coming to condense here. It

[1] A small river in Hyde Park, in London.

is possible, therefore, that by drinking this snow we are quenching our thirst with the rivers of our own country.'

'Small mercies.'

At that moment, Hatteras's voice could be heard correcting the mistakes of the route, interrupting the conversation. The fog was getting thicker, making it difficult to maintain a straight line.

Finally the little troop stopped at about eight, having covered fifteen miles; the tent was put up; the stove lit; supper eaten; and the night was spent peacefully.

Hatteras and his companions were greatly favoured by the weather. Their journey continued without difficulty the following days, although the cold became exceptionally bitter and the mercury was still frozen in the thermometer. If the wind had joined in, not one of the travellers could have borne such a temperature. The doctor was able to confirm Parry's observations during his excursion to Melville Island. That celebrated sailor declares that suitably dressed men can walk without problem in the open air in the harshest cold, provided that the atmosphere is still; but as soon as the slightest wind starts blowing, a biting pain is felt in their faces, and they develop a headache of extreme violence, soon followed by death. Because of this, the doctor felt worried, fearing that the merest gust of wind would freeze them to the very marrow.

On 5 March, he witnessed a phenomenon particular to this latitude; the sky was perfectly clear and shining with stars; thick snow fell without trace of a cloud; the constellations shone through the flakes as they fell on the ice-field with elegant regularity. This snow lasted about two hours, and stopped without the doctor being able to find a good explanation for it.

The last quarter of the moon had vanished; there was now complete darkness for seventeen out of twenty-four hours; the travellers had to tie themselves together with a long rope in order not to be separated; a straight route became almost impossible to maintain.

However, and despite their iron will, these courageous men began to tire; their rests became more frequent, and yet not a single hour could be wasted, for the food was diminishing appreciably.

Hatteras often measured the position, using observation of the moon and the stars. Seeing the days go past and the purpose of the journey recede indefinitely, he sometimes wondered if the *Porpoise* really did exist, if the American's mind hadn't been disturbed by his suffering, or even if—seeing himself lost beyond hope—hatred of the British had made him wish to take them down to death with him.

He related these suspicions to the doctor; Clawbonny absolutely rejected them, but realized that an unpleasant rivalry existed between the British and American captains.

It'll be hard to maintain good relations between these two, he said to himself.

On 14 March, after sixteen days' march, the travellers were still only at the eighty-second degree; their strength was exhausted and they were still 100 miles from the ship; though it increased their own suffering, the men had to go on quarter rations to keep whole rations for the dogs.

The result of hunting could unfortunately not help much, for only seven charges of powder and six bullets were left; they had shot at a few polar hares and some very rare foxes, hitting nothing.

However, on Friday the fifteenth, the doctor was lucky enough to surprise a seal stretched out on the ice, and wounded it by using several bullets. Since it could not escape through its already closed hole, the animal was soon caught and knocked out; it was a big one; Johnson cut it up skilfully, but the amphibian was so thin that it offered little of use to men who could not bear to drink its oil like Eskimos.

However, the doctor did bravely try to imbibe the viscous liquid; in spite of his best efforts, he could not. He kept the animal's skin, not knowing why, perhaps through some hunting instinct, and loaded it on the sledge.

The following day, the sixteenth, they spotted a few icebergs and ice hills on the horizon. Was this the sign of a nearby coast, or only a break in the ice-field? It was difficult to be sure.

On reaching one of these hummocks, the travellers used a snow knife[1] to hollow out a more comfortable shelter than the tent, and after three hours' stubborn work they were finally able to stretch out around the lighted stove.

---

[1] Broadbladed knife for cutting blocks of ice.

4

The Last Charge of Powder

JOHNSON had to let the utterly exhausted dogs into the ice-house; when the snow falls abundantly, it serves as cover for the animals, conserving their natural heat. But in the open air, in dry colds of forty degrees, the poor animals would have quickly frozen to death.

Johnson, who made an excellent dog driver, tried to feed the dogs with the blackish meat of the seal, which the travellers could not eat; and to his astonishment the team made a real feast of it; bowled over, the old sailor informed the doctor.

Clawbonny was not surprised; he knew that in the north of America horses mostly eat fish, and what was enough for a herbivorous horse could easily suffice for an omnivorous animal.

Although sleep had become an absolute necessity after dragging themselves over fifteen miles of ice, before going to bed the doctor wanted to discuss the present situation, without understanding its seriousness.

'We're still only at eighty-two degrees,' he said, 'and we're almost out of food!'

'All the more reason not to waste a moment!' replied Hatteras. 'We need to move! The strong will pull the weak.'

'But will we find the ship at the place indicated?' asked Bell, dejected against his will by the rigours of the journey.

'Why not?' replied Johnson. 'The American's survival depends on ours.'

The doctor wanted to ask Altamont again, just to be sure. The American could now speak quite easily, although in a weak voice; he confirmed all the details previously given; he repeated that the ship was wrecked on granite rocks, and thus could not have moved, and that it was at 120° 15′ W, 83° 35′ N.

'We can be sure of this information,' added the doctor; 'the problem is not finding the *Porpoise*, but getting there at all.'

'How much food do we have left?' asked Hatteras.

'Three days at most.'

'Well, we need to get there within three days!'

'Yes, and if we do we've no reason to complain, since we've had exceptional weather. The snow has spared us for a fortnight, and the sledge has slid easily over the hardened ice. Ah, how I wish it were carrying two hundredweight of food! Our good dogs could easily have managed such a load! But since it isn't, there's not much we can do about it.'

'With a bit of luck and skill,' said Johnson, 'couldn't we use the few charges of powder we've got left? If we could get near a bear, we'd have plenty of food for the rest of the journey.'

'Probably, but such animals are rare, and shy; also just thinking about how important the last remaining rifle shots are often makes your eye go out of focus and your hand shake.'

'But you're a fine shot,' said Bell.

'When four people's dinners don't depend on it; but if it comes to it I'll do my best. In the mean time, my friends, let's manage with this meagre supper of pemmican crumbs, then try and sleep, and we'll carry on in the morning.'

A few moments later, the excess of fatigue cancelled all other thoughts, and everyone fell into a deep sleep.

Early on Saturday, Johnson woke his companions; the dogs were harnessed to the sledge, and they started off north again.

The sky was magnificent, the atmosphere perfectly clear, the temperature very low; when the sun appeared above the horizon, it had become a long ellipse, its horizontal diameter twice its vertical, due to the refraction. It projected rays of clear, but cold, beams on to the enormous ice plain. The return of light, if not heat, made the travellers feel happier.

The doctor, rifle in hand, headed off a mile or two, braving the cold and solitude; before doing so, he had counted his ammunition; he had four charges of powder left, and three bullets, that was all. It was not much, especially when one considers that a strong and lively animal like a polar bear is often felled only with the tenth or twelfth shot.

So the good doctor's ambition did not go as far as finding such formidable game; a few hares or a brace of foxes would have been enough for him, providing plenty of new provisions.

But that day, each time he spotted one of those animals, either he could not get near enough to shoot or, misled on one occasion by the refraction, he wasted his rifle shot. That day cost him one powder charge and one bullet.

His companions, after trembling with hope at the sound of the gun, saw him coming back with lowered head. They said nothing. In the evening, they retired to bed as usual, setting aside the two quarter rations for the following two days.

The next day, their journey became more and more difficult. They were no longer walking—they were dragging themselves along; the dogs had devoured even the entrails from the seal, and were beginning to gnaw at their straps.

A few foxes passed near the sledge, and the doctor, having wasted another rifle shot in hot pursuit, no longer dared risk his last bullet and his second-to-last powder charge.

In the evening they stopped early; the travellers could no longer put one foot in front of the other, and although the route was lit by a magnificent Aurora (Borealis), they still had to halt.

This last meal, eaten that Sunday evening in the icy tent, was depressing. If heaven did not come to the aid of these wretches, they were surely lost.

Hatteras said nothing, Bell was no longer thinking, and Johnson reflected in silence; but the doctor had not yet given up hope.

Johnson had the idea of building a few traps for the night; without any bait to put in them, he was not optimistic; and he was right, for when he checked his inventions in the morning he saw many fox tracks, but not a single animal in the traps.

So he was returning in disappointment when he noticed a bear of colossal size sniffing at the tracks of the sledge less than three hundred feet away. The old sailor believed that Providence was sending him this unexpected animal to be killed; and so, without waking his companions, he grabbed the doctor's rifle and headed towards the bear.

Once he got close enough, he aimed; but just as he was about to press the trigger he felt his arm shaking; and his thick skin gloves were in the way. He quickly took them off, and grasped the rifle with a firmer hand.

Suddenly, he gave a cry of pain. The skin of his fingers was burned by the cold of the gun, and stuck to the gun when he let it fall to the ground. It went off as it hit the ground, sending its last bullet into the air.

At the sound of the shot, the doctor ran up; he immediately understood everything. He watched as the animal calmly moved away; Johnson was in despair, no longer thinking of his pain.

'I'm such a weakling,' he exclaimed, 'a child unable to bear pain! Me, at my age!'

'Come on, let's head back, Johnson—you're going to freeze; look, your hands have already turned white; come on!'

'I'm not worth treating, Dr Clawbonny. Leave me!'

'Oh come on, you stubborn old man! Come on! It'll soon be too late.'

And the doctor, dragging the sailor into the tent, made him put his hands into a jar of water that the heat from the stove was keeping liquid, although still cold. Hardly had Johnson's hands gone in than it froze immediately.

'You see, it was urgent to come back in; otherwise I would have been forced to amputate.'

Thanks to his care, all danger had disappeared an hour later, but not without difficulty; repeated rubbing was needed to bring the circulation back to the old sailor's fingers. The doctor told him to be careful and to keep his hands away from the stove's heat, which would have caused serious complications.

That morning they had no breakfast; there was no pemmican or salt meat left. Not a crumb of biscuit; and hardly half a pound of coffee; they made do with just the piping-hot drink, and set off again.

'Nothing left,' Bell said to Johnson, in inexpressible tones of despair.

'Trust in God; he is omnipotent, and will surely save us.'

'Ah, that madman Captain Hatteras came back from his first two expeditions! But he'll never get back from this one; and we'll never see our country again.'

'Courage, Bell! I must admit that the captain is a bit bold, but he has a man with him good at solving problems.'

'Dr Clawbonny?'

'Himself!'

'But what can he do in such a situation?' retorted Bell, shrugging his shoulders. 'Can he turn ice into meat? Is he a god, can he perform miracles?'

'Who knows. But I have confidence in him.'

Bell shook his head, and returned to his total silence, not thinking about anything at all.

That day, they covered hardly three miles; in the evening they didn't eat; the dogs were threatening to devour each other; and the men as well felt the gnawing torment of hunger.

They did not see a single animal. In any case, what was the use? They couldn't hunt them with knives. But Johnson thought he glimpsed the huge bear, a mile downwind, seeming to follow the unfortunate troop.

He's watching us, he thought; *he thinks he's found sure prey.*

But Johnson said nothing to his companions; in the evening they made their usual halt, and supper was just coffee. The wretches felt their eyes becoming haggard, and their brains freezing; tortured by hunger, they were unable to sleep a single hour; strange dreams of the most unpleasant sort invaded their brains.

When Tuesday morning arrived, the wretches had not eaten for thirty-six hours, at a latitude where the body demands nourishment. However, driven by superhuman courage and iron will, they set off once more, pushing the sledge that the dogs could no longer pull.

After two hours they fell down exhausted.

Hatteras wanted to keep going. Energetic as always, he employed supplications and prayers to convince his companions to get up again: he was demanding the impossible!

Then, aided by Johnson, he cut an ice-house in an iceberg. As they worked, these two men looked as though they were digging their graves.

'I don't mind dying of hunger,' said Hatteras, 'but cold is different.'

After cruelly exhausting work, the house was ready, and the troop huddled together in it.

In this way the day passed. In the evening, while his companions remained motionless, Johnson had a sort of hallucination—he dreamed of an enormous bear.

His repetition of that word caught the doctor's attention and woke him from his torpor; he asked the old sailor why he kept talking about a bear, and what bear it was.

'The bear that's following us.'

'Following us?'

'Yes, for two days now.'

'Two days? You saw it?'

'Yes, it's a mile downwind.'

'And you didn't tell me, Johnson?'

'What good would it have done?'

'It's true we don't have a single bullet left.'

'Not even an ingot, piece of iron, or nail!'

The doctor said nothing, but began to think. Suddenly he said to the mate:

'Are you sure the animal's following us?'

'He's counting on a feast of human flesh! He knows we can't escape!'

'Johnson!' said the doctor, moved by his companion's despairing tones.

'He's sure of getting food,' continued the delirious wretch; 'he must be hungry; why do we keep him waiting?'

'Johnson, that's enough!'

'Since it's inevitable, why prolong the animal's suffering? He's hungry like us; he's got no seal to eat! If heaven has sent him, then so much the better for him!'

The old man was going mad, and trying to leave the ice-house. The doctor found it very difficult to restrain him and if he succeeded, it was less through strength than because he uttered the following words in a tone of absolute conviction:

'Tomorrow I'll kill that bear!'

'Tomorrow!' repeated Johnson, as if coming out of a nightmare.

'Tomorrow!'

'You haven't got any bullets!'

'I'll make one.'

'You haven't got any lead!'

'No, but I've got some mercury!'

Saying that, the doctor took the thermometer, which indicated fifty inside the ice-house (10°C). He went out, placed the instrument on a piece of ice, and came back in. The external temperature was minus fifty (−47°C).

'See you tomorrow; let's go to sleep now, and wait for sunrise.'

The night passed in the agony of hunger, assuaged only by the faint hope of the doctor and mate.

The following day, at the first rays of the sun, the doctor rushed out to the thermometer, followed by Johnson; all the mercury had dropped into the bulb, forming a small cylinder. The doctor broke the instrument, and with his fingers carefully gloved, extracted a very hard piece of metal. It was a true slug.

'Ah, that's wonderful! You're a real genius!'

'No, my friend; I'm only a man who's read a lot and has a good memory.'

'What do you mean?'

'I remembered a story related by Captain Ross; in his description of his journey, he said he pierced a plank an inch thick using a gun loaded with a bullet of frozen mercury. If we had any oil it would be almost the same thing, for he also recounts that a bullet of almond oil, fired at a post, split it, and landed on the ground without breaking.'

'But that's incredible!'

'It's simply true; so here is a piece of metal which might save our lives; let's leave it in the open air until we use it, and see if the bear is still following us.'

At that moment Hatteras came out of the hut; the doctor showed him the metal, and explained his plan; the captain shook his hand, and the three hunters began to explore the horizon.

The weather was very clear. Having gone ahead of his companions, Hatteras discovered the bear less than two-thirds of a mile away.

The animal was sitting on its behind, calmly moving its head back and forth, breathing in the smell of these unusual guests.

'There he is!' exclaimed the captain.

'Silence!' said the doctor.

But the enormous quadruped did not move when he saw the hunters. He gazed at them without fear or anger. All the same, it looked as though it would not be easy to get close.

'My friends,' said Hatteras, 'this is not idle pleasure, our lives are at stake in this hunt. We must be careful.'

'I agree,' replied the doctor, 'we've just got one shot. We mustn't miss; if he runs away, he'll be no use to us; he can run faster than a greyhound.'

'Well then, we need to head straight for him,' replied Johnson. 'So what if it is risky? I want to go!'

'I'll do it!' exclaimed the doctor.

'Me!' responded Hatteras firmly.

'But aren't you more useful for everyone's survival than a fellow of my age?' exclaimed Johnson.

'No, Johnson, let me do it; I won't risk my life needlessly; in any case, I may have to call you to help me.'

'Hatteras,' said the doctor, 'are you just going to walk straight up to him?'

'If I were sure of killing him, I'd do so, even if he tried to split my head open; but he might simply run away. Bears are full of tricks; we must be trickier than him.'

'What do you plan to do?'

'Get to ten paces away, without him suspecting.'

'How?'

'My method is dangerous but simple. Did you keep the skin of that seal you killed?'

'It's on the sledge.'

'Good! Let's go back to our ice-house, while Johnson stays here to keep watch.'

The mate slid behind a hummock that hid him entirely from the bear.

The animal remained in the same place, continuing its strange rocking and sniffing of the air.

5

The Seal and the Bear

HATTERAS and the doctor returned to the ice-house.

'Did you know', said the captain, 'that polar bears hunt seals as their main source of food? They watch for them beside cracks for days on end, and smother them with their paws as soon as they appear on the ice. A bear won't be frightened of a seal. Just the contrary.'

'I think I understand your plan; it's very dangerous.'

'But it offers some chance of success; so we must try. I'm going to put that sealskin on and crawl over the ice-field. Let's not waste time! Load your gun and give it to me.'

The doctor had no objection to the plan; he would himself have done what the captain was attempting; he left the house carrying two axes, for Johnson and for him; then, with Hatteras, he headed to the sledge.

There, Hatteras put the sealskin clothing on; it covered him almost completely.

Meanwhile the doctor was loading his gun with the last powder charge, and sliding into the barrel the piece of mercury, now as hard as steel and as heavy as lead. Then he handed the gun to Hatteras, who hid it, and himself, under the sealskin.

'Go back to Johnson; I'm going to wait a while to confuse the enemy.'

'Good luck, Hatteras!'

'Don't worry! And above all, hide until you hear my shot.'

The doctor ran to the hummock where Johnson was hiding.

'Well?'

'Well, we just have to wait! Hatteras is risking his life to save us.'

The doctor felt agitated; he observed the bear, which himself showed signs of increasing agitation, as if realizing the impending danger.

Quarter of an hour later, the seal was crawling over the ice; it had made a detour past the shelter of some large blocks, so as to better fool the bear; at that point it was only 300 feet away. The bear saw it and curled up, trying to conceal himself from the seal.

Hatteras imitated the movement of seals perfectly; if he had not known, the doctor would have been taken in.

'Yes, spot on!' said Johnson quietly.

Even as it moved nearer, the amphibian gave the impression of not noticing the bear—as if only looking for a hole in the ice so as to dive back into its element.

As for the bear, he was working his way around the pieces of ice, closing in with extreme care; his burning eyes displayed the most ardent greed; he had not eaten for a month, perhaps two, and chance was sending him a sure meal.

Soon the seal was only ten paces from its adversary. Suddenly, the bear reared up, made a gigantic bound, and then stopped, stupefied, terrified, only three paces from Hatteras, who had thrown off his sealskin and, one knee on the ground, was aiming at his heart.

The shot went off, and the bear rolled on the ice.*

'Come on, come on!' exclaimed the doctor.

And, followed by Johnson, he rushed to the scene of the battle.

The huge creature had got up again, striking the air with one claw, while with the other he picked up a piece of snow and blocked the wound.

Hatteras did not waver; he stood there waiting, knife in hand. But he had aimed well, and struck the bear with a good bullet, with a hand that had not trembled; before his companions could get there, he plunged his knife into the animal's throat, and he fell, and did not get up again.

'Victory!' exclaimed Johnson.

'Well done, Hatteras, well done!' shouted the doctor.

Hatteras looked at the gigantic body without emotion, crossing his arms.

'My turn,' said Johnson; 'congratulations on getting this game, but we mustn't wait for the cold to make it as hard as stone; our teeth and knives would be no use then.'

Johnson began by skinning the monstrous creature, nearly as big as an ox; it was nine feet long and six around; two enormous fangs, three inches long, emerged from its gums.

He opened it up, and found only water in its stomach; the bear had clearly not eaten for a long time; however it was very fat, and weighed more than fifteen hundred pounds. They divided it into four quarters, each of two hundred pounds, and the hunters dragged all this flesh to the snow-house, not forgetting the animal's heart which, three hours later, was still beating strongly.

The doctor's companions would have willingly thrown themselves on the raw meat, but he restrained them, asking for time to roast it.

As he entered the house, Clawbonny was struck by the cold inside; he went up to the stove, and found it completely out; the challenges and emotions of the morning had made Johnson forget his usual duty.

The doctor tried to revive the fire, but could not find a single spark amongst the already cold cinders.

Come on, a bit of patience! he said to himself.

He went back to the sledge to look for tinder, and asked Johnson for his tinder box.

'The stove has gone out,' he explained.

'It's all my fault.'

Searching in the pocket where he usually kept his lighter, Johnson found to his surprise that it was not there.

He tried his other pockets, without success. Going back into the snow-house, he searched the blanket on which he had spent the night, but was no luckier.

'Well?' cried the doctor.

Johnson came back, and looked at his companions.

'You don't have the lighter, Dr Clawbonny?'

'No.'

'Nor you, Captain?'

'No.'

'You always kept it,' said the doctor.

'Well, I don't have it any more . . .' muttered the old sailor, going pale.

'You don't!' exclaimed the doctor, who couldn't help trembling.

It was the only lighter they had, and this loss could have terrible consequences.

'Look again, Johnson,' said the doctor.

He returned to the ice floe where he had observed the bear, then to the spot where the fight and slaughter had occurred; but found nothing. He came back in despair. Hatteras looked at him but did not utter any reproach.

'It's serious,' he said to the doctor.

'Yes.'

'We don't have even an instrument, a telescope whose lens we could take out to make fire.'

'I know, and it's a shame,' replied the doctor, 'for the sun's rays would have been strong enough to light tinder.'

'Well,' answered Hatteras, 'we need to ease our hunger with this raw meat; then we'll continue our march, to try and reach the ship.'

'Yes,' said the doctor, plunged into thought, 'yes, that would be doable if need be. Why not? We could try . . .'

'What are you thinking?' demanded Hatteras.

'I've had an idea . . .'

'An idea?' exclaimed Johnson. 'One of your ideas? Then we're saved!'

'But will it work?' said the doctor. 'That is the question . . .'

'What is your idea?' asked Hatteras.

'If we haven't got a lens, we'll make one.'

'How?' asked Johnson.

'By cutting a piece of ice.'

'What, you think that'll work?'

'Why not? We just need to make the sunlight focus at a single point, and ice can work as well as the best crystal.'

'Is it possible?' said Johnson.

'Yes, but I would prefer freshwater ice to saltwater; it's clearer and harder.'

'But if I'm not mistaken,' said Johnson, pointing to a hummock 100 paces away, 'that block has an almost blackish surface and a green colour indicating . . .'

'You're right; come on, my friends; bring your axe, Johnson.'

The three men headed for the block in question, which was indeed freshwater ice.

The doctor had a piece cut off about a foot wide, and then he began to roughly shape it with his hatchet; next he made the surface smoother with his knife; then he polished it gradually with his hand, and he had soon obtained a transparent lens as clear as if made of the finest crystal.

Then he returned to the entrance of the snow-house, took some tinder, and began his experiment.

The sun was shining quite brightly; the doctor put his ice lens in its rays, focusing them on the tinder.

It caught fire a few seconds later.*

'Hurray, hurray!' exclaimed Johnson, unable to believe his eyes. 'Dr Clawbonny, Dr Clawbonny!'

The old sailor was overjoyed; he marched up and down like a madman.

The doctor had gone back inside; a few minutes later, the stove was roaring, and soon the savoury smell of roasting drew Bell from his torpor.

One can guess how well this meal was celebrated; however, the doctor advised moderation to his companions; he preached by setting an example, speaking while he ate.

'Today is a day of happiness; we have enough food for the rest of our journey. However, we should not fall asleep in the delights of Capua,* and we would do well to set off again.'

'We can't be more than forty-eight hours from the *Porpoise*,' said Altamont, whose voice had come back almost completely.

'I hope', said the doctor with a laugh, 'that we'll find some way to make fire there?'

'Indeed,' replied the American.

'My ice lens may work now, but will be less than perfect on days without sun, which are frequent less than four degrees from the Pole!'

'Yes,' replied Altamont with a sigh, 'less than four degrees! My ship went where no ship has ever gone!'

'Off we go,' curtly commanded Hatteras.

'Off we go,' repeated the doctor, glancing anxiously at the two captains.

The travellers' strength had quickly come back; the dogs had had their fill of the remains of the bear, and all quickly set off north again.

While travelling, the doctor tried to get Altamont to clarify why his ship had gone so far, but the American replied evasively.

'Two we need to watch,' the doctor said in the ear of the old mate.

'Absolutely!' replied Johnson.

'Hatteras never talks to the American, and Altamont doesn't seem willing to show gratitude! Luckily, I'm here.'

'Dr Clawbonny,' replied Johnson, 'ever since that Yankee came back to life, I haven't liked the look on his face.'

'If I'm not mistaken, he suspects Hatteras's plans.'

'So you think that this foreigner had the same purpose?'

'Who knows, Johnson? The Americans are bold and audacious; what a Briton wants to do, an American might also try.'

'So you think that Altamont . . .'

'I don't think anything, but the position of his ship on the way to the Pole does make you think.'

'However, Altamont says he was carried off against his will.'

'That's what he says, but I thought I could see a strange smile on his lips.'

'Hell, it would be a shame to have rivalry between two men of that stamp!'

'I hope to God I'm wrong, Johnson; such a situation could have serious, perhaps disastrous, consequences.'

'I hope that Altamont will remember we saved his life.'

'Isn't he going to save ours in turn? I admit that without us he wouldn't be alive; but without him, his ship, and the supplies it contains, where would we be? What would happen to us?'

'In the end you're here, Dr Clawbonny; and I hope that with your help everything will be all right.'

'I hope so too, Johnson.'

The journey continued without incident; there was no lack of meat, and they ate copious meals of it; there was even a certain good humour in the small troop, thanks to the doctor's jokes and his amiable outlook on life; this good man always found in his savant's knapsack some lesson to be learned from events and phenomena. His health remained good; he hadn't lost too much weight, in spite of the exhaustion and deprivation; his friends in Liverpool would easily have recognized him, especially from his good mood, apparently indestructible.

On the Saturday morning, the immense ice-plain changed notice-ably; the distorted ice and piled-up hummocks showed that there was great pressure on the ice-field; clearly some unknown landmass, some new island, had squeezed the passes to produce these upheavals. Blocks of freshwater ice became commoner and larger, indicating that a coast was near.

So, not far away was a new land, and the doctor burned with the desire to add it to the maps of the northern hemisphere. It is difficult to imagine the pleasure of surveying unknown coasts, and tracing their outlines with a sharp pencil; this was the doctor's aim, just as Hatteras's was to tread the very Pole, and he was jubilantly anticipat-ing the thought of the names to baptize the seas with, the straits, the bays—every last sinuosity of these new lands. Certainly, in the glories of nomenclature, he would not forget his companions, or his friends, or Her Gracious Majesty, or the Royal Family;* nor would he forget himself, and so he dreamed of a 'Clawbonny Point' with legitimate satisfaction.

These thoughts took up the whole day. They set up camp as usual in the evening, and each took turn on watch during that night spent near an unknown land.

The following day, a Sunday, after a large breakfast of bear paws, which was excellent, the travellers headed northwards and slightly westwards; the route became harder, but they walked quickly.

From his position on the sledge, Altamont gazed at the horizon with feverish concentration; his companions felt involuntary anxiety. The last solar shootings had given their latitude as exactly 83° 35′ N, 120° 15′ W; this was the position ascribed to the American ship; the life or death question was going to be resolved that very day.

Finally, at about two in the afternoon, Altamont stood right up, stopped the little troop with a resounding cry, and, pointing at a massive white shape that any other eye would have taken for an iceberg, exclaimed loudly:

'The *Porpoise*!'

6

The Porpoise

THE twenty-fourth of March was that great festival, Palm Sunday,* when the streets of the villages and towns of Europe are covered with flowers and branches; bells ring out in the air, and the atmosphere is full of powerful aromas.

But here, in this desolate region, what sadness, what silence! A rough and biting wind and not a single leaf, not a blade of grass!

And yet this Sunday was still a day of joy for the travellers, for at last they were within reach of resources, without which they were destined for an early death.

They began to move faster; the dogs pulled with more energy, Duke barked with happiness, and soon the troop arrived at the American ship.

The *Porpoise* lay entirely buried under the snow; it had lost its mast, its yard, its cordage; all its rigging had broken in the wreck. The ship was lodged on an invisible rock bed. Lying on its side after the collision, its hull yawning cavernously, the *Porpoise* seemed uninhabitable.

This is what the two captains, the doctor, and Johnson admitted after getting inside the ship, not without difficulty. They had to remove more than fifteen feet of ice to reach the main hatch; but to everybody's joy, they saw that the animals whose tracks covered the field had not reached the precious provisions.

'Though there's plenty of fuel and food,' said Johnson, 'this hull doesn't seem inhabitable to me.'

'Well, we'll just have to build a snow-house,' said Hatteras, 'and settle as best we can on dry land.'

'Yes,' said the doctor, 'but let's not hurry—let's do things properly. If necessary, we can stay in the ship for the moment; during that time we can build a solid house, capable of protecting us from both cold and animals. I'll take on being the architect, and you'll see me doing things!'

'I don't doubt your talent, Dr Clawbonny,' said Johnson; 'let's settle here as best we can, and draw up an inventory of what the ship contains; unfortunately I can't see any launch or boat, and these pieces are in too bad a condition to build a new boat.'

'Who knows?' said the doctor. 'With time and thought, one can do a good job; what we're doing now isn't sailing, but creating a fixed dwelling; so I suggest we don't make other plans—each thing in its time.'

'That's sensible,' said Hatteras; 'let's start with the most urgent.'

The three companions left the ship, returned to the sledge, and shared their ideas with Bell and the American. Bell declared himself ready to work; the American shook his head on learning that nothing could be done with his ship; but as further discussion on that point seemed pointless, they talked about taking refuge on board the *Porpoise* at first, and then building a large habitation on the coast.

At four in the afternoon, the five travellers were settled, more or less, in the orlop deck; using spars and the remains of the masts, Bell had built a more or less horizontal floor; they placed on it the bedding, hardened by the frost and cold, which the heat from the stove soon returned to its normal condition. If he leaned on the doctor, Altamont could walk without too much difficulty to the corner reserved for him. Setting foot on his ship, he produced a sigh of satisfaction, which did not seem a good omen to the mate.

He feels at home, thought the old sailor, you'd almost say he was inviting us in!

The remainder of the day was devoted to rest. The weather seemed about to change, with squalls blowing in from the west; the outside thermometer read minus twenty-six (−32°C).

In sum, the *Porpoise* was situated beyond the pole of cold and at a relatively less glacial latitude, although further north.

That day, they finished eating the remains of the bear, accompanied by biscuit found in the ship's hold and a few cups of tea; then exhaustion overcame them, and each fell into a deep sleep.

In the morning, Hatteras and his companions woke up somewhat late. Their minds followed new lines of thought; the uncertainties of the future no longer troubled them; instead they thought only of arranging things comfortably. These shipwrecked men now considered themselves settlers who had reached their destination and, forgetting the suffering of the journey, thought only of creating a bearable future.

'Phew!' exclaimed the doctor, stretching. 'It's good not to have to wonder where you'll sleep tonight, and what you'll eat tomorrow.'

'We should begin with the inventory of the ship,' replied Johnson.

The *Porpoise* had been well fitted out and provisioned for a distant campaign.

The inventory gave the following quantities: 6,150 pounds of flour, fat, and raisins for puddings; 2,000 pounds of beef and salt pork; 1,500 pounds of pemmican; 700 pounds of sugar and the same quantity of chocolate; one and a half chests of tea, weighing 96 pounds; 500 pounds of rice; several barrels of preserved fruit and vegetables; lime juice in abundance, as well as Cochlearia, sorrel, and watercress seeds; and 300 gallons of rum and brandy. The hold contained large quantities of powder, bullets, and shot; coal and wood were plentiful. The doctor carefully collected the physical and navigational instruments, plus even a large Bunsen battery,* which had apparently been brought along for electrical experiments.

In sum, there were sufficient provisions of all sorts for five men for two years, on full rations. Any fear of dying of hunger or cold had vanished.

'Well, we won't die,' the doctor told the captain, 'and now nothing can stop us reaching the Pole.'

'The Pole!' answered Hatteras with a start.

'What will prevent us sending out a reconnaissance across the land in the summer?'

'Across land, yes! But across the sea?'

'Couldn't we build a launch with the wood from the *Porpoise*?'

'Wouldn't that be an American vessel?' replied Hatteras, disdainfully. 'And one commanded by that American?'

The doctor understood the captain's reluctance, and did not consider it useful to pursue the question. So he changed the subject.

'Now that we know where we are with regards to provisions, we need to build stores for them and a house for us. As there are plenty of materials, we can settle very comfortably. Bell, my friend, I hope you're going to perform well; I can give you some good advice.'

'I'm ready; if need be, I would have no problem building an entire town, complete with streets and houses, out of blocks of ice . . .'

'We don't need so much; let's imitate the agents of the Hudson Bay Company; they build forts to protect themselves from animals and Indians; that's all we need; let's dig ourselves in as best we can;

the house on one side, the stores on the other, with a sort of curtain wall and two bastions to protect us. I only hope I can remember what I used to know about castrametation.'

'Goodness, doctor!' said Johnson. 'I'm sure we'll build something close to perfection under your direction.'

'Well, my friends, first of all we need to choose the spot; a good engineer must above all survey the land. Would you like to come, Hatteras?'

'Please take charge, doctor. Carry on while I head up the coast.'

Still too weak to take part in the work, Altamont was left on board the ship, and the Britons disembarked.

The weather was cloudy and heavy; at noon, the thermometer read minus eleven (−20°C); but it remained bearable without wind.

Judging from the shape of the coast, a considerable sea, entirely frozen, stretched westwards as far as the eye could see; to its east was a rounded coast, cut with deep estuaries and abruptly rising 200 yards from the shore; it formed a huge bay, with sharp, dangerous rocks on which the *Porpoise* had come to grief; inland stood a far mountain estimated by the doctor to be about 3,000 feet high. Northwards, a promontory sank into the sea after forming one side of the bay. An island of modest size, or rather an islet, emerged from the ice-field three miles from the coast, so that, had it not been for the difficulty of entering the inlet, it offered a safe and sheltered anchorage. There was even a gap in the coast, forming a little harbour that would be very accessible to ships—if a thaw ever freed this part of the Arctic Ocean. According to Belcher and Penny's tales, the whole of this sea did indeed melt in the summer months.

Halfway along the coast, the doctor noticed a sort of circular plateau, about two hundred feet across; three of its sides looked out on to the bay, and the fourth consisted of a vertical wall 120 feet high; the plateau could not be reached unless steps were cut into the ice. This spot seemed ideal for placing a solid construction, and could easily be fortified; nature had done the basic work; all that needed to be done was to utilize the shape of the place.

The doctor, Bell, and Johnson reached the plateau by cutting into the ice with an axe; the plateau was smooth and horizontal. Realizing that the spot was suitable, the doctor decided to remove the ten feet of hardened snow on top; the house and stores needed to rest on a solid base.

That Monday, Tuesday, and Wednesday they worked without rest; finally the floor was finished; it was made of a very durable, fine-grained granite; it also contained garnets and large crystals of feldspar, on which the pick made sparks.

The doctor then indicated the dimensions and floor plan of the snow-house; it would be forty feet long by twenty wide by ten high; it would be divided into three rooms, a living room, a bedroom, and a kitchen; more were not needed. The kitchen was on the left, the bedroom on the right, and the living room in the middle.

For five days they worked hard. There was no lack of material; the ice walls had to be strong enough to resist thaws, as they could not run the risk of being without shelter, even in summer.

As the house rose, it took a turn for the better; its front had four windows, two for the living room, one for the kitchen, and one for the bedroom; the windows were made of magnificent sheets of ice, following the Eskimo custom, and admitted a soft light, like unpolished glass.

Leading to the living room, between its two windows, stretched a passage* like a covered walkway, giving access to the house; a solid door, taken from one of the *Porpoise*'s cabins, completely sealed it off. Once the house was finished, the doctor was delighted with his handicraft. However, it would have been difficult to say what style of architecture the ice-house belonged to, even though the architect had admitted his preference for the Saxon Gothic* so common in Britain; but solidity was the most important; so the doctor restrained himself, and merely covered the front with strong buttresses, as squat as Roman columns; above them, a steep roof rested on the granite wall. The wall also held up the pipes from the stoves, channelling their smoke outside.

When the main structure had been finished, they proceeded to the internal arrangements. The berths from the *Porpoise* were carried into the bedroom, and arranged in a circle around a huge stove. Benches, chairs, easy-chairs, tables, and cupboards were set up in the living room, which also served as a dining-room; finally, the ovens from the ship were put in the kitchen, along with the various uten-sils. Sails laid on the ground provided carpets, and also served as dividing-curtains for the internal doorways without doors.

The typical thickness of the walls was five feet, and the openings of the windows were like cannon gun-ports.

Everything was very solid; what more could be needed? Ah, if only they had heeded the doctor, they could have done almost anything with just ice and snow, which allow all possible combinations! All day long, he dreamed of a thousand wonderful projects which he hardly thought of realizing, but his fertile imagination entertained his companions during their work.

As a bibliophile, he had read a relatively rare book by Mr Krafft, entitled *A Description and Exact Representation of the House of Ice, Constructed in St. Petersburg in the Month of January 1740.** And this memory served to overheat his inventive mind. One evening he even told his companions about the wonders of that ice palace.

'Can't we do here what was done in St Petersburg? What are we lacking? Nothing, not even imagination!'

'So was it good?' asked Johnson.

'It was magic, my friend! The house built by order of the Empress Anne*—where she held the wedding of one of her jesters in 1740—was about the same size as ours; but along its front were six ice-cannons, lined up on their carriages; they were fired several times with balls and powder, and did not break up; there were also mortars, sculpted for explosives of sixty pounds; if need be, we could build up a formidable artillery; there is bronze nearby, for it falls to us from the sky. But taste and art triumphed, especially in the pediment of the palace, adorned with ice statues of great beauty; the front flight of steps displayed flower and orange-tree pots, also of ice; on the right stood an enormous elephant, which squirted water in the daytime and burning naphtha at night. We could make a complete menagerie if we wanted!'

'We'll meet plenty of animals,' answered Johnson, 'and though not made of ice, they'll be just as interesting!'

'Oh,' replied the bellicose doctor, 'we can defend ourselves against their attacks; but to come back to my house in St Petersburg, I will add that inside were tables, dressing rooms, mirrors, candelabras, candles, beds, mattresses, pillows, curtains, clocks, chairs, playing cards, cupboards with complete sets of kitchen tools and utensils, everything of chiselled, cut, and sculpted ice—in sum every conceivable piece of furniture and item.'

'So was it a real palace?' asked Bell.

'A wonderful palace, worthy of a queen. Ah, ice! What a good thing Providence invented it, since it serves for so many wonders, and can provide comfort for shipwrecked men!'

Arranging the ice-house took until 31 March; that day was Easter Sunday, and devoted to rest; they spent the whole day in the living room, where divine office was performed, and each could appreciate how well built the snow-house was.

The following day, they busied themselves building the food stores and powder store; this took about a week, including the time for unloading the *Porpoise*, which was not easy since the extreme temperature meant they could not work for long. Finally, on 8 April, the food, fuel, and ammunition were on dry land and in shelter; the food stores were at the north end of the plateau, the powder store at the south, about sixty feet from the end of the house; a sort of kennel was built near the stores; it was for the Greenland team, so the doctor baptized it 'Dog Palace'. As for Duke, he lived in the snow-house.

Next, the doctor turned to the defence. Under his direction, the plateau was enclosed in a wall of ice, which protected it from any invasion; being so high up, it formed a natural scarp, and as it had neither recess nor projection, was equally strong in every direction. While organizing this system of defence, the doctor inevitably resembled Sterne's good Uncle Toby,* whose gentle goodness and equanimity he shared. He had to be seen calculating the angle of the inside slope, the inclination of the lawn, and the size of the overhang; but this work was so easy with the obliging snow that it was a genuine pleasure, and the amiable engineer could make his ice fortifications seven feet thick; in any case, the plateau looked out on to the bay, and thus he didn't have to build a counter-escarpment, external slope, or ramp; the two ends of the snow parapet followed the shape of the plateau as they left the rock wall and came to join the two sides of the house.* These works of castrametation were finished on about 15 April. The fort was complete, and the doctor appeared very proud of his work.

In truth, the fortified enclosure could have held a long time against an Eskimo tribe, if such enemies could be found at this latitude; but there was no trace of human beings on this coast; while charting the shape of the bay, Hatteras had not seen a single trace of those huts usually found on the coasts frequented by Greenland tribes; the shipwrecked men of the *Forward* and *Porpoise* seemed to be the first to tread this unknown ground.

But if men were not to be feared, the animals could be redoubtable;

defended appropriately, the fort could easily protect its little garrison
against their attacks.

7

A Cartological Discussion

DURING these wintering preparations, Altamont had completely
regained his health and strength; he even helped unload the ship. His
robust constitution had finally won the day, and his paleness could
not long resist the vigour of his blood.

His robust and sanguine United States nature was seen reasserting itself—the energetic and intelligent man, endowed with a resolute character, the enterprising American, audacious and ready for
everything; he was a native of New York and had been sailing since
childhood; his ship, the *Porpoise*, had been fitted out and sent to sea
by a company of rich Unionist businessmen, headed by the famous
Grinnell.*

There were certain affinities between Hatteras and him—affinities
of character, not affection. This resemblance was not of the kind to
make friends of the two men; on the contrary. In any case, an observer would have been able to detect important differences between
them; although he seemed to display more frankness than Hatteras,
Altamont was surely in actual fact less frank than the captain; though
he was less formal, he was less loyal; his open character did not
inspire as much confidence as the captain's sombre temperament.
Hatteras would carefully express his idea one good time, and then
enclose himself in it. Though the other spoke a great deal, he often
said nothing.

The doctor gradually began to understand the American's character, and he correctly detected signs of animosity, if not hatred,
between the captains of the *Porpoise* and *Forward*.

And yet, of the two commanders, only one was needed for command. Certainly Hatteras had every right to obedience from the
American, rights of precedence and of force. But if one of them was
at the head of his own men, the other was on board his own ship.
That could be felt.

By design or instinct, Altamont was immediately drawn to the doctor; he owed him his life, but he was impelled less by gratitude than by sympathy for the good man. Such was the invariable effect of the worthy Clawbonny's character; friends grew around him like wheat in the sun. Some people are reputed to get up at five in the morning to make enemies; the doctor could have got up at four without making any.

He resolved to get the most out of Altamont's friendship, and discover his real reason for being in the polar seas. But the American, with all his verbosity, replied without replying and repeated his usual story of the Northwest Passage.

The doctor suspected another motive for the expedition, the very one feared by Hatteras. So he decided never to set the two adversaries against each other on the matter; but he was not always successful. Despite his best efforts, the simplest conversations threatened to change subject, and words become sparks because of the collision of interests.

In fact, this soon happened. When the house was finished, the doctor decided to celebrate the occasion with a splendid meal; a good idea, for Clawbonny wished to bring the habits and pleasures of European life to this land. Bell had just killed a few ptarmigans and an Arctic hare, the first harbingers of spring.

They had their feast on 14 April, the second Low Sunday,* in beautiful, perfectly dry weather; but the cold did not take the risk of coming into the ice-house; the roaring stoves would have eaten it alive.

They dined well; the fresh meat made a pleasant change after the pemmican and salt meat; a marvellous pudding made by the doctor produced the obligatory call for second helpings; then for thirds; the learned master chef, apron around waist and knife in belt, would not have dishonoured the kitchens˙ of the Lord Chancellor of Great Britain.

Spirits were produced with the dessert; the American was not following the Britons' teetotal rule; so there was no reason for him not to have a glass of gin or brandy; the other guests, normally sober men, could allow themselves to break the rule without harm; so, on doctor's orders, each drank a toast at the end of this happy meal. But during the toast to the Union, Hatteras remained silent.

It was then that the doctor raised an interesting question.

'My friends,' he said, 'though we have accomplished much in

getting through straits, ice floes, and ice-fields, our duties are not finished; something still needs to be done. I propose we give names to this hospitable land, where we have found safety and rest; this is the custom followed by every navigator in the world, and not one of them would have neglected it in such a circumstance; when we return, we need to bring back not only the hydrographical configuration of the coasts, but also the names of the capes, bays, points, and promontories identifying them. We have no choice.'

'Well said!' exclaimed Johnson. 'If we give these lands special names, that'll lend them all an air of importance; and then we can't consider ourselves abandoned on an unknown land.'

'Not to mention', answered Bell, 'that it simplifies explanations when travelling, and helps with carrying out orders; we might need to split up on an excursion, or while hunting, and nothing beats knowing the name of your path for finding it again.'

'Well, since we're in agreement on the subject, let's decide the names to give now, and let's not forget either our country or our friends in the nomenclature. As for me, when I look at a map, nothing gives me greater pleasure than finding a compatriot's name at the tip of a cape, beside an island, or in the middle of a sea. It's friendship charmingly invading geography.'

'You're right, doctor,' replied the American, 'and the way you say such things makes them more valuable.'

'Let's see, then, we need to begin at the beginning.'

Hatteras had not yet taken part in the conversation; he was thinking. However, since his companions' eyes were on him, he got up and said:

'I think it would be a good idea, and nobody will object, I hope (here Hatteras looked at Altamont), if I name our house after the skilful architect who designed it, the best of us; and thus call it Doctor's House.'

'Spot on,' said Bell.

'Great!' exclaimed Johnson. 'The House of the Doctor.'

'That's perfect,' responded Altamont; 'congratulations to Dr Clawbonny!'

A triple hurray sounded out in response, with Duke adding barks of approval.

'Then', added Hatteras, 'let this house be so named—until some new land can have our friend's name too.'

'Ah,' said old Johnson, 'if earthly paradise still needed to be named, Clawbonny's name would be perfect!'

The doctor, though touched by the thought, wanted to modestly refuse; he had no choice in the matter; there was no way to do so. Accordingly it was duly promulgated that this happy meal had just taken place in the living room of Doctor's House, after being cooked in the kitchen of Doctor's House, and that they would joyfully go to sleep in the bedroom of Doctor's House.

'Now,' said the doctor, 'let's turn to the more important question of our discoveries.'

'There is the huge sea surrounding us, and whose waves have never been sailed by a ship.'

'Never sailed! It seems to me, all the same,' replied Altamont, 'that the *Porpoise* should not be forgotten—unless it came overland,' he added sarcastically.

'That could be believed,' replied Hatteras, 'looking at the rocks it's floating on now.'

'Really, Hatteras,' said Altamont with a piqued expression; 'but all things considered, isn't that better than being blown sky-high like the *Forward*?'

Hatteras was about to make a sharp reply, when the doctor intervened.

'My friends,' he said, 'the point here is not ships, but a new sea.'

'It's not a new sea,' replied Altamont. 'It already has a name on all the maps of the Pole. It's called the Northern Ocean, and I don't think it's appropriate to change its name for the moment; if we later discover that it's only a strait or gulf, we can see what needs doing.'

'So be it,' said Hatteras.

'Well that's agreed,' said the doctor, almost regretting raising a subject so full of national rivalry.

'Let's now consider the land we're standing on,' said Hatteras. 'As far as I'm aware, it doesn't have a name, even on the most recent maps.'

Saying this, he stared at Altamont, who did not lower his eyes but replied:

'Perhaps you're mistaken again, Hatteras.'

'Mistaken? What! This unknown land, this new ground . . .'

'Already has a name,' calmly replied the American.

Hatteras remained silent. His lips were trembling.

'And what is this name?' asked the doctor, surprised at the American's assertion.

'My dear Clawbonny, it is the custom, if not the right, of every navigator to name the landmass he is the first to reach. So it seems to me that in the present juncture I could, indeed I had to, exercise this incontestable right.'

'However . . .' said Johnson, who did not like Altamont's curt self-control.

'It seems to me difficult to claim that the *Porpoise* did not land on this coast; and even if one thought that it got there overland,' he added, looking at Hatteras, 'that would make no difference.'

'It is a claim that I cannot seriously accept,' replied Hatteras, holding himself back. 'In order to name, one needs to at least discover, and that is not what you did, I imagine. In any case, where would you be without us, sir; you who wish to impose conditions? Twenty feet under the snow!'

'And without me, sir,' riposted the American, 'without my ship, what would you be now? Dead of hunger and cold!'

'My friends,' said the doctor, intervening as best he could, 'calm down, everything can be settled; listen to me.'

'This gentleman,' continued Altamont, pointing at the captain, 'can name all the other lands he discovers, if any; but this land belongs to me! I cannot even accept the proposition that it carry two names, in the same way that Grinnell Land is also called Prince Albert Land, because a Briton and an American found it at almost the same time. Here it is different; my rights of precedence are incontestable. No ship before mine touched this coast with its side deck. Not a human being before me set foot on this land; I have given it a name, and it will keep it.'

'And what is the name?' asked the doctor.

'New America.'*

Hatteras's fists clenched on the table. But he controlled himself with a superhuman effort.

'Can you prove to me', said Altamont, 'that a Briton ever stood on this ground before an American?'

Johnson and Bell stayed silent, although they were no less irritated than the captain by the imperious aplomb of their opponent. But there was nothing that could be replied.

The doctor spoke again after a few moments of awkward silence.

'My friends, the first human law is the law of justice; it contains all the others. So let's be equitable, and not give in to bad thoughts. Altamont's priority seems incontestable to me. No discussion is possible; we'll get our own back later, and Britain will have a fine share of future discoveries. Let this land keep the name of New America. But in naming it such, I imagine that Altamont did not dispose of the bays, capes, points, and promontories it contains, and I can see nothing to prevent us calling this Bay Victoria Bay!'

'None,' replied Altamont, 'if the cape which stretches into the sea over there receives the name Washington Cape.'

'You could have chosen a less disagreeable name for a British ear,' exclaimed Hatteras, beside himself.

'But not dearer to an American one,' replied Altamont proudly.

'Come on, come on!' said the doctor, finding it difficult to maintain peace in the little group. 'No more discussion on this point! An American should be allowed to be proud of his great men! Let us honour genius everywhere it occurs, and since Altamont has made his choice, let us speak now for ourselves and those close to us. Our captain should . . .'

'Doctor, since this land is American I don't want my name on it.'

'Is your decision irrevocable?' asked the doctor.

'Absolutely.'

The doctor did not insist.

'Well then,' he said, addressing the old sailor and carpenter, 'let's leave some trace of our passage. I propose we call the island we can see three miles out Johnson Island,* in honour of our mate.'

'Oh,' he said, a little embarrassed, 'Dr Clawbonny!'

'And as for that mountain we identified to the west, we'll give it the name Mount Bell, if our carpenter agrees!'

'That's too much honour.'

'It's entirely deserved,' replied the doctor.

'Perfect,' added Altamont.

'There only remains the need to baptize our fort,' said the doctor; 'on that we will have no discussion; it is not to Her Gracious Majesty Queen Victoria, nor to Washington* that we owe our present shelter, but to God, who by uniting us, saved us all. So let's give it the name Fort Providence.'*

'Well chosen,' replied Altamont.

'Fort Providence', said Johnson, 'sounds great. So when we get back from our northwards excursions, we'll go past Washington Cape, arrive at Victoria Bay, and finally see Fort Providence, where we know we'll find shelter and food in Doctor's House.'

'Agreed,' replied the doctor; 'later, as we make further discoveries, we'll have other names to give which will not produce debate, I hope; for, my friends, we should support and love each other; we represent the whole of humanity on this piece of coast; so let's not give in to those detestable passions which so often mar society; let's unite to stay strong and unshakeable in the face of adversity. Who knows what dangers heaven reserves for us, what suffering we must endure before seeing our countries again? Let's therefore be five-for-one and abandon rivalry, which is never justified—here even less than elsewhere. Do you hear me, Altamont? And you, Hatteras?'

The two did not reply, but the doctor continued as if they had.

Then they spoke of other things. They discussed hunts to organize so as to replenish and vary the meat supplies; with the spring, hares, partridges, and even foxes and bears would return; they decided not to let a suitable day go by without sending a reconnaissance out into the land of New America.

8

Excursion to the North of Victoria Bay

THE following day, at the first rays from the sun, Clawbonny climbed the steep slope of the rock wall Doctor's House leaned against; it suddenly ended at a sort of truncated cone. The doctor reached this top, not without difficulty, and from there his eyes extended over a huge area of deformed land, apparently the result of some volcanic upheaval; an immense white curtain covered the land and sea, making it impossible to tell the difference.

Realizing that this point was the highest of the surrounding plains, the doctor had an idea which would not astonish those who knew him.

He matured his idea, he refined it, he elaborated it, and he was entirely its master when he got back to the snow-house and communicated it to his companions.

'I've had the idea of building a beacon on top of the cone above our heads.'

'A beacon?'

'Yes. It'll have two advantages: guiding us at night when we come back from our distant excursions, and illuminating the plateau during our eight winter months.'

'Certainly such apparatus will be useful,' replied Altamont; 'but how will you make it?'

'Using one of the lanterns from the *Porpoise*.'

'Agreed; but what fuel will you use for the lamp? Seal oil?'

'No, light produced by that oil is not very powerful, and can hardly cut the fog.'

'Are you claiming then that you can extract hydrogen from our coal and make lighting gas from it?'

'Hardly! That light would still not be strong enough, and it would be silly to use up part of our fuel.'

'Then,' replied Altamont, 'I can't see . . .'

'As far as I'm concerned,' said Johnson, 'after the mercury bullet, the ice lens, and the building of Fort Providence, I consider Dr Clawbonny capable of anything.'

'So are you going to tell us what sort of beacon you're going to build?'

'It's simple. An electric one.'

'An electric beacon!'

'Yes; didn't you have a Bunsen battery in perfect condition on board the *Porpoise*?'

'Yes.'

'Clearly, when you brought it you planned some experiment, for everything is there: the perfectly insulated conducting wires and the acid needed to put the elements to work. So it's easy for us to obtain electric light. We'll see better, and it won't cost us a penny.'

'Perfect,' replied the mate, 'and the less time we lose . . .'

'Well, the materials are here,' replied the doctor, 'and in less than an hour we can build an ice column ten feet high, which will be enough.'

The doctor went out; his companions followed him to the top of the cone; the column promptly appeared, and was soon crowned with one of the lanterns from the *Porpoise*.

Then the doctor fitted conducting wires, which were connected to the battery; as it was placed in the living room of the ice-house, it was protected from the frost by the heat from the stoves. From there, the wires ran all the way up to the lantern.

All of this was set up quickly, and then they waited for sunset to enjoy the effect. When night fell, the two carbon rods, until then kept at a suitable distance from each other in the lantern, were brought together and gleams of intense light* that the wind could not moderate or extinguish sprang from it. It was a wonderful sight; those trembling beams, whose light competed with the whiteness of the plains, produced a sharp shadow behind all the surrounding shapes. Johnson couldn't help clapping his hands.

'Dr Clawbonny is producing sunlight now!'

'One needs to try a little of everything,' modestly replied the doctor.

The cold put an end to the general admiration, and everyone returned to huddle under their blankets.

Life now got properly organized. The following days, from 15 to 20 April, the weather was very uncertain; it would suddenly jump twenty degrees and the atmosphere change without warning, sometimes loaded with snow and stirred up by strong winds, sometimes so cold and dry that they could not go outside for a moment without precautions.

However, the wind fell that Saturday; this event made an excursion possible; they decided to devote a day to hunting, in order to replenish the provisions.

Early in the morning, Altamont, the doctor, and Bell left in overcast weather, each with a double-barrelled rifle, sufficient ammunition, a hatchet, and a snow knife, in case it was necessary to build a shelter.

While they were away, Hatteras was to reconnoitre the coast and make measurements. The doctor was careful to switch on the beacon; its beams successfully fought the sun's rays; in effect, electric light, equivalent to 3,000 candles or 300 gas lamps, is the only kind that can be compared with sunlight.

The cold was sharp, dry, and still. The hunters headed for Washington Cape, the hard snow aiding their walking. In half an hour they covered the three miles between the cape and Fort Providence. Duke gambolled around them.

As the coast bent round eastwards, the high peaks of Victoria Bay to the north became lower. This implied that New America could easily be just an island; but determining its configuration was not on the agenda for the moment.

The huntsmen followed the sea coast as they strode on. There were no traces of habitation, no remains of huts; they were treading on ground untouched by human foot.

They covered about fifteen miles in the first three hours, eating as they walked; but their hunt looked as though it would be fruitless. In effect, they hardly saw any hare, fox, or wolf tracks. However, a few snow birds fluttered here and there, announcing the return of spring and the Arctic animals.

The three companions had to head inland to get around the deep valleys and steep rocks that abutted Mount Bell; but after a few problems, they managed to get back to the shore. The ice had not yet broken up; far from it; the sea was still frozen; however, marks left by seals when they surfaced through the ice-field to breathe revealed the presence of these amphibians. It was even clear, from the large marks and fresh breaks in the ice, that several had ventured on to land very recently.

These animals love sunlight, and often stretch out on the shore to soak up its health-giving warmth.

The doctor pointed these details out to his companions.

'Note this place carefully; it's quite possible that in the summer we'll find hundreds of seals here; they are easy to approach in areas rarely visited by man, and are thus caught without difficulty. But you have to be careful not to frighten them, for then they disappear as if by magic and don't come back; inexperienced hunters have often attacked them en masse instead of killing them one by one, and the resultant noise and vociferations have meant they lost much or all of their catch.'

'Are they hunted only for the skin and oil?' asked Bell.

'By Europeans, yes; but goodness, the Eskimos eat them; they live on them, taking pieces of seal and mixing them with blood and fat— not at all appetizing! But I suppose it depends how you go about it, and I promise to produce fine chops you cannot turn your noses up at, once you get used to the blackish colour.'

'We'll watch you work,' replied Bell; 'I promise, without fear, to eat seal flesh as long as you want me to. Do you hear me, Dr Clawbonny?'

'My good Bell, you mean as long as you want to. But whatever you do, you'll never equal the voracity of the Greenlanders, who eat up to ten or fifteen pounds of this meat per day.'

'Fifteen pounds, what stomachs!'

'Polar stomachs are prodigious stomachs, which expand at will, and, I will add, contract, suitable for dealing with starvation or abundance. At the beginning of his dinner, an Eskimo is thin; at the end, fat, and you can't recognize him! It's true that his dinner often lasts all day.'

'Clearly', said Altamont, 'this voracity is particular to the inhabitants of the cold lands?'

'Probably; in the Arctic you need to eat a great deal; it's one of the preconditions not only for strength but continued existence. So the Hudson Bay Company gives each man eight pounds of meat, twelve pounds of fish, or two pounds of pemmican a day.'

'A comforting diet,' said the carpenter.

'But not as much as you assume, my friend, and an Indian, stuffed like that, does not provide any more work than a Briton fed on his pounds of beef and pint of beer.'

'So, Dr Clawbonny, everything is for the best.'

'Yes, but an Eskimo meal can still astonish us. On Boothia Peninsula, during his wintering, Sir John Ross was always surprised at the voracity of his guides; somewhere he narrates how two men— only two—devoured a whole quarter of a musk ox in one morning; they cut the meat into long strips, which they crammed down their throats; then each cut under his nose what his mouth could not contain, and passed it to his companion; well, these gluttons, trailing ribbons of flesh down to the ground, swallowed them little by little, like a boa digesting an ox, although they were stretched out over the ground!'

'Ugh,' said Bell, 'disgusting brutes!'

'Each to his own dining habits,' replied the American philosophically.

'Fortunately,' said the doctor.

'Well,' said Altamont, 'since eating is so important at these latitudes, I'm not surprised that in the narratives of Arctic travellers, meals are always discussed.'

'You're right,' said the doctor, 'and I've noticed it too; it comes from needing lots of food, but also from food being very difficult to get hold of. So you think of it all the time, and so speak about it as well.'

'However,' said Altamont, 'if my memory serves me well, in Norway, in the coldest regions, the peasants don't need such substantial food: a little dairy produce, eggs, bread made from birchskin,* sometimes salmon, never meat; and that produces fellows who are just as solidly built.'

'It's a question of constitution,' replied the doctor, 'and that, I can't explain. However, I think a second or third generation of Norwegians transplanted to Greenland would end up eating in the Greenland manner. And as for ourselves, my friends, if we stayed in this blessed country, we would end up living like Eskimos, in other words as awful gluttons.'

'Dr Clawbonny', said Bell, 'is making me hungry.'

'Goodness no,' said Altamont, 'that would disgust me, and make me hate seal meat. But I think we're about to find out. If I'm not mistaken I can see over there, stretched out on the ice, a mass which seems alive.'

'It's a walrus!' exclaimed the doctor. 'Silence now. And off we go.'

In fact, a huge amphibian was taking its pleasure 200 yards away; it was voluptuously stretching out and rolling over in the sun's pale rays.

The three huntsmen split up so as to surround the animal and cut off its retreat; in this way they got to within a few fathoms, hid behind hummocks, and fired.

The walrus turned over, still full of life; it crashed over the floes, trying to escape; but Altamont attacked it with his axe, and managed to cut off its fins. The walrus tried a desperate defence; more shots finished it off, and soon it lay lifeless on the ice-field, red with blood.

It was a fine animal; it measured nearly fifteen feet from tip to tail; it would certainly have provided several barrels of oil.

The doctor took all the best cuts, and left the rest to the mercy of a few crows, already hovering at this season.

Night was already falling. They decided to head back to Fort Providence; the sky was totally clear and, lit up with magnificent starlight until the moon came out.

'Come on, off we go,' said the doctor; 'it's late; our hunt wasn't very successful, all in all; but provided he brings back his dinner, a huntsman has no right to complain. Let's take the shortest route and try not to get lost; the stars are there to show us the way.'

However, in lands where the North Star shines directly over the traveller's head, it is difficult to use it as a guide; in fact, when north is exactly at the summit of the celestial vault, the other cardinal points are difficult to determine; fortunately, the moon and main constellations came to help the doctor determine his route.

To shorten the distance, he decided to avoid the ins and outs of the shore and to cut across the land; it was more direct, but risky; so after a few hours' march, the little troop was completely lost.

They discussed spending the night in an ice-hut, sleeping where they were; or waiting for daylight to find their direction, even if that meant returning to the shore to follow the ice-field; but the doctor, afraid of causing Hatteras and Johnson worry, insisted on continuing the journey.

'Duke is leading us, and he can't be wrong; he has an instinct which doesn't need a compass or stars. Let's just follow him.'

The dog was already moving off, so they trusted to his intelligence. They were right, for soon a light appeared on the far horizon; it could not be a star, which would not have penetrated such low mists.

'There's our beacon!' exclaimed the doctor.

'You think so, Dr Clawbonny?' asked the carpenter.

'I'm certain of it. Forward march!'

As the travellers approached, the light became stronger, and soon they were surrounded by a trail of luminous dust; they were walking through an immense ray of light, and behind them their gigantic shadows, sharply delineated, stretched out exaggeratedly over the snow carpet.

They walked faster, and half an hour later were climbing the slope up to Fort Providence.

9

Cold and Warm

HATTERAS and Johnson had waited anxiously for the three hunts-men. The trio were delighted to find a warm and comfortable shelter again. With nightfall it had got much colder, and the thermometer outside read minus seventy-three (−31°C).*

The men who had just arrived, exhausted and frozen, could not

have taken a step more; luckily the stoves were working well; the
oven just needed the results of the hunt; the doctor changed into a
cook, and grilled a few walrus chops. At 9 p.m., the five men sat
down to a restorative supper.

'Goodness!' said Bell. 'At the risk of being taken for Eskimos, let's
admit that meals are the high point of wintering; when you manage
to catch one you shouldn't turn up your nose!'

All had mouths full, and so could not reply; but the doctor nodded
in agreement.

The walrus was declared excellent, not actually in so many
words, but devoured down to the last chop, which was worth all the
declarations in the world.

For the last course, the doctor prepared coffee as usual; he would
let nobody else distil this excellent brew; he brewed it on the table in
a coffee-maker heated with spirits of wine, and served it piping hot.
It had to burn his tongue or else he found it unworthy to wet his
whistle. That evening he imbibed it at a temperature his companions
could not imitate.

'But you're going to set yourself on fire, doctor,' protested
Altamont.

'Never.'

'Is your mouth copper-bottomed?' asked Johnson.

'Hardly, my friends; you should do the same. There are some
people, including me, who can drink coffee at a hundred and thirty-
one (55°C).'

'A hundred and thirty-one,' exclaimed Altamont; 'but your hand
can't stand such a heat!'

'Obviously, Altamont, since your hand can't stand more than a
hundred and twenty-two (50°C) in water; but your palate and tongue
are less sensitive than your hand, and they resist where it can't.'*

'You surprise me.'

'Well, I'll show you.'

And taking the thermometer from the living room, the doctor put
its bulb in his scalding cup of coffee; he waited for the instrument to
read more than hundred and thirty-one degrees, and then swallowed
the beneficial liquid with obvious pleasure.

Bell bravely tried to imitate him, but scalded himself and
exclaimed loudly.

'Lack of practice,' said the doctor.

'Clawbonny,' said Altamont, 'can you tell us the highest temperatures the human body can tolerate?'

'Easily; experiments have been done, producing some interesting facts. One or two spring to mind, which prove that you can get used to anything, even temperatures to cook a steak. Thus it is said that the serving girls at the communal oven in the town of La Rochefoucauld, in France, could remain in the oven for ten minutes at a temperature of three hundred (132°C)—eighty-nine above boiling point—whilst around them potatoes and meat were roasting away.'

'What girls!' exclaimed Altamont.

'Look, here is another example that cannot be disputed. In 1774 nine of our compatriots—Fordyce, Banks, Solander, Blagden, Home, Nooth, Lord Seaforth, and Captain Phillips—stood a temperature of two hundred and ninety-five (128°C) while eggs and roast beef cooked beside them.'*

'And they were British,' said Bell proudly.

'Absolutely,' said the doctor.

'Oh, Americans would have done better,' said Altamont.

'They would have roasted,' said the doctor with a laugh.

'And why not?'

'In any case, they didn't try; so I can only speak about my countrymen. I will add one last fact, incredible if one could doubt the veracity of the witnesses. The Duke of Raguse and Dr Jung, a Frenchman and an Austrian,* saw a Turk enter a bath measuring a hundred and seventy degrees (78°C).'

'But', began Johnson, 'that doesn't seem as good as the girls in the communal oven or our compatriots.'

'Begging your pardon; there is a huge difference between entering air and water; hot air brings on sweating, which protects your flesh, whereas you don't sweat in boiling water and consequently you're scalded. So the upper limit assigned to baths is, in general, only one hundred and seven (42°C). Therefore that Turk must have been an exceptional man to bear such a heat.'

'Dr Clawbonny,' asked Johnson, 'what is the normal temperature of living beings?'

'It varies; birds have the highest temperature, and amongst them the duck and chicken are the most remarkable; the temperature of their bodies is more than a hundred and ten (43°C), whilst the tawny owl, for example, is only a hundred and four (40°C); then, in second position, come the mammals and men; the temperature of the British is normally a hundred and one (37°C).'*

'I'm sure Mr Altamont will claim a better result for the Americans,' said Johnson with a laugh.

'Goodness,' said Altamont, 'some are very hot men; but as I have never inserted a thermometer into their thoraxes or under their tongues, it is impossible to be sure of that observation.'

'Right, the difference is imperceptible between people of different races, in identical circumstances and eating the same kinds of food; I will even say that human temperature is more or less the same at the equator as at the Pole.'

'So,' said Altamont, 'our internal heat is the same here as in Britain?'

'Very much the same,' responded the doctor; 'as for other mammals, their temperature is generally slightly higher than humans'. Horses are very similar to us, as are hares, elephants, porpoises, and tigers; but cats, squirrels, rats, panthers, sheep, oxen, dogs, monkeys, goats, and billy-goats reach one hundred and three degrees; and finally the luckiest of all, the pig, attains more than one hundred and four (40°C).'

'Humiliating,' said Altamont.

'Next are the amphibians and fish, whose temperatures vary considerably with the water. Snakes are only eighty-six (30°C), frogs seventy (25°C), and sharks the same temperature in an environment one and a half degrees colder; finally, insects seem to have the same temperature as the water or air.'

'All that is fine,' said Hatteras, who had not yet spoken, 'and I thank the doctor for putting his knowledge at our disposal; but we're talking as if we were in danger of great heat. Wouldn't it be better to speak of cold, to know what humans are exposed to and the lowest temperatures observed to date?'

'That's fair,' said Johnson.

'Nothing easier,' said the doctor.

'I can believe it, you seem to know everything.'

'My friends, I only know what others have taught me, and after I've finished, you'll know as much as me. So here's what I can say about low temperatures in Europe. Many memorable winters have been recorded, and it seems that extremes come back periodically, about every forty-one years, a period which coincides with the most frequent appearance of sunspots.* I should mention the winter of 1364, when the Rhone froze as far as Arles; the 1408 one, when the whole length of the Danube froze and wolves crossed the Kattegat without getting their feet wet; the 1509 one, when the Adriatic and Mediterranean were frozen solid at Venice, Sète, and Marseilles, as was the Baltic until 10 April; the 1608 one, when all the livestock in Britain died; 1789, when the Thames was frozen as far as Gravesend, six leagues below London; 1813, which the French have retained such terrible memories of; and the winter of 1829, the longest of the nineteenth century and the one that hit earliest. That covers Europe.'

'But here, above the Arctic Circle, what temperature can it go down to?' asked Altamont.

'My goodness, I do believe we have had the worst colds ever observed, since the alcohol thermometer read minus seventy-two (−58°C) one day, and if my memory serves me well, the lowest temperatures observed until then by Arctic travellers were only sixty-one degrees on Melville Island, sixty-five at Felix Port, and seventy at Fort Reliance* (−56.7°C).'

'Yes,' said Hatteras, 'a severe winter stopped us, very unluckily.'

'Stopped you?' repeated Altamont, staring at the captain.

'As we headed west,' said the doctor, quickly.

'So,' added Altamont, going back to the original subject, 'the difference between the highest and lowest temperatures borne by man is about two hundred degrees?'

'Yes; a thermometer in the open air, protected from light, never goes above a hundred and thirty-five (57°C); in the same way, in the coldest weather it never goes below minus seventy-two (−58°C). So you can see we don't need to worry, my friends.'

'However,' said Johnson, 'if the sun suddenly went out, wouldn't the earth become much colder?'

'The sun won't go out; but if it did, the temperature would probably not go below the temperature I mentioned.'

'That's strange.'

'Oh, I know that in the past they thought that space beyond the atmosphere could vary thousands of degrees; but following experiments by a French scientist, Fourier, a hasty retreat was beaten; he proved that if the earth was placed in an environment without heat, the cold we observe at the Pole would be much more intense, and that huge differences of temperature between night and day would exist; so, my friends, it is not significantly colder a few million leagues away than on this spot.'*

'Tell us, doctor,' asked Altamont, 'isn't the temperature in America lower than in other countries?'

'Yes, but it's nothing to boast about,' replied the doctor with a laugh.

'And how is this phenomenon accounted for?'

'People haven't really explained it very convincingly; it occurred to Halley* that a comet, obliquely hitting the earth in the past, changed its axis of rotation, that is its Poles. According to him, the North Pole, previously at Hudson Bay, was thereby shifted eastwards, but because the land of the former Pole had been frozen for so long, it remained colder, and long centuries of sunlight haven't been able to warm it up again yet.'

'So you don't agree?'

'Not for a moment, because what applies to the east coast of America doesn't to the west coast, where it is warmer. No, we have to simply observe that there are isotherms which are not the same as the globe's parallels, and that's all we can say.'

'Did you know', said Johnson, 'that it's great fun to chat about the cold in our present conditions?'

'Exactly; we're able to contribute to theory by means of practice. This area is a vast laboratory, where you could do interesting experiments on low temperatures; but always keep your eyes and ears open; if some part of your body is frozen, rub it immediately with snow to restore the circulation, and if you come back near the fire, be careful because you might burn your hands or feet without realizing; that would necessitate amputation, and we must try not to leave any part of ourselves behind in the northern regions. Upon which, my friends, I think we'd be best to get a few hours' rest.'

'Willingly,' replied his companions.

'Who's on watch for the stove?'

'Me,' said Bell.

'Well, my friend, do make sure the fire doesn't go down—it's diabolically cold tonight.'

'Don't worry, Dr Clawbonny, the cold may be biting, but look, the sky is alight!'

'Yes,' said the doctor, going to the window, 'a fine Aurora (Borealis)! What a wonderful sight! I'll never get tired of looking at it.'

In truth, the doctor always admired these cosmic phenomena, which his companions no longer paid much attention to; he had noticed that their appearance was always preceded by perturbations in the compass needle, and he was preparing observations on this subject for *The Weather Book*.*

While Bell watched over the stove, each man, stretched out on his bunk, soon fell into a peaceful sleep.

10

The Pleasures of Wintering

LIFE at the Pole is sadly uniform. People are entirely subject to the atmosphere's caprices, which brings storms and intense cold with depressing regularity. Most of the time it is impossible to set foot outside, and you have to stay cooped up in ice-huts. Long months pass this way, meaning that winterers lead a mole's life.

The next day, the temperature fell a few degrees, and swirls of snow filled the air and blocked all the daylight. The doctor was stuck in the house and so crossed his arms; there was nothing to do except clear the entrance corridor, which sometimes got obstructed, and repolish the ice walls dampened by the heat from the stoves; but the snow-house was built very solidly, and the snow drifts only added to its resistance by making the walls thicker.

The storehouses were also resisting well. All the things unloaded from the ship had been arranged in perfect order in the 'merchandise docks', as the doctor called them. Now although these stores were hardly sixty paces from the house, on certain days the drifts made it very difficult to get there; so a certain quantity of food always had to be kept in the kitchen, for daily needs.

The precaution of unloading the *Porpoise* had been a good one. The ship was subject to a slow and imperceptible but irresistible pressure, gradually crushing it; it seemed clear that nothing could be done with what was left of it. However, the doctor still hoped to build a launch of some sort out of the hull, to head back to Britain in; but the time was not ripe for such a construction.

So most of the time the five winterers remained totally idle. Hatteras was thoughtful, stretched out on his bed; Altamont drank or slept; the doctor was careful not to disturb them, for he was always afraid of some dangerous quarrel. The two men rarely spoke to each other.

At meals, Clawbonny was always careful to guide the conversation away from patriotic sentiments; but it was not easy to divert over-excited sensibilities. He tried, as much as he could, to instruct, to entertain, and to interest his companions; when he was not organizing his travel notes, he spoke of history, geography, or meteorology—subjects arising from their situation; he presented things pleasantly and philosophically, drawing a useful lesson from the slightest incident; his inexhaustible memory never failed him; he applied his doctrines to the details of his companions' lives; he told them about similar incidents in similar circumstances, and he completed his theories with the force of personal arguments.*

The worthy man could be considered the soul of this little world, a soul radiating feelings of frankness and justice. His companions had absolute confidence in him; he even won Captain Hatteras over, who had come to like him; he made such good use of his words, methods, and habits that this life of five men, abandoned six degrees from the Pole, seemed entirely ordinary; when the doctor spoke, it was as if he were in his Liverpool surgery.

And yet, how different the situation was from men shipwrecked on the Pacific islands, those Robinsons whose attractive stories invariably made readers wish they were there! There, a prodigal earth, an opulent nature, offered a thousand varied resources; in those fine lands all you needed for material happiness were a little imagination and work; nature anticipated man's desires; hunting and fishing satisfied all his needs; trees grew for him, caves opened up to shelter him, brooks flowed to quench his thirst; magnificent shade protected him from the heat of the sun, and in the gentle winters of the Pacific, terrible cold never came to threaten him; a seed, casually thrown on this fertile ground, produced abundance a few months later. It was complete happiness outside society. And then those enchanted islands, those generous lands, were on shipping routes;

the castaway could always hope to be picked up, and so wait patiently to be torn from his happy life.

But here, on this coast of New America, how different it all was! The doctor sometimes pondered the comparison, but he kept his thoughts to himself, and above all cursed having nothing to do.

He longed with all his heart for a thaw that would allow new excursions, and yet he feared it as well, for he foresaw serious arguments between Hatteras and Altamont. If ever they headed for the Pole, what would these two men's rivalry produce?

So all incidents had to be avoided, the rivals gradually brought to a sincere harmony, a frank communion of ideas; but to reconcile an American and a Briton—two men whose common origin made them still greater enemies, the one full of all the insular arrogance, the other with his nation's speculative, audacious, and brutal mind*— what a heavy task!

When the doctor thought of the implacable competition between the men, the rivalry of their nationalities, he couldn't help shrugging his shoulders over the whole matter—which didn't usually happen to him, but in this case he just couldn't help giving in to human weakness.

He often spoke with Johnson; they both agreed on this subject; they wondered what to do, and how to reach their goal by degrees; and they foresaw many problems in the future.

Meanwhile the poor weather continued; they couldn't consider leaving Fort Providence even for an hour. They had to stay in the snow-house day and night. They were all bored, except for the doctor, who always found something to do.

'So isn't there any entertainment available at all?' Altamont said one evening. 'Living like this is not living; we're like reptiles, buried for a whole winter.'

'Indeed,' replied the doctor; 'unfortunately there aren't enough of us to organize a system of entertainment.'

'In other words,' said the American, 'you think it'd be easier to remain active if there were more of us?'

'Without a doubt. When complete crews spent the winter in the boreal regions, they easily found ways of avoiding boredom.'

'Really?' said Altamont. 'I'd like to know how; they must've been really clever to get any fun out of such a situation. I don't suppose they played charades!'

'You're warm; they introduced two great entertainments into these hyperboreal regions: newspapers and the theatre.'

'What? They had newspapers?' replied the American.

'And they acted?' exclaimed Bell.

'Yes, and got tremendous pleasure out of it. During his winter on Melville Island, Commander Parry suggested these two pleasures to his crews, and the idea was hugely successful.'

'Well frankly,' replied Johnson, 'I wish I'd been there; it must've been interesting.'

'Interesting and entertaining, my good Johnson; Lieutenant Beechey became the theatre manager, and Captain Sabine, the editor of the *North Georgia Gazette and Winter Chronicle*.'*

'Fine titles,' said Altamont.

'This newspaper appeared every Monday from 1 November 1819 to 20 March 1820. It covered everything that happened that winter, the hunts, the short news items, the incidents of the weather, the temperature; it included more or less funny columns; certainly you wouldn't have expected the wit of Sterne or the wonderful pieces of the *Daily Telegraph*; but they made do, and so entertained themselves; the readers were not difficult or blasé, and never, I believe, was the journalist's job more fun.'

'Goodness,' said Altamont, 'I'd be interested to see pieces from that *Gazette*, my dear doctor; its articles must have been frozen solid from beginning to end.'

'Not really; in any case, what might have seemed slightly naive to the Philosophical Society of Liverpool or the Literary Institution of London* was good enough for crews buried under the snow. Do you want to judge for yourselves?'

'What! You can remember . . . ?'

'No, but you had Parry's journeys on the *Porpoise*, and I can read you his own account.'*

'Yes!' exclaimed his companions.

'Nothing easier.'

The doctor went to the living room cupboard to get the book, and had no difficulty finding the passage in question.

'Listen,' he said, 'here are a few extracts from the *North Georgia Gazette*.* First a letter to the editor:

It was with real pleasure I saw in circulation among us, your proposals for a weekly newspaper ... I am confident that such a paper will, under your censorship, be productive of much amusement, and serve to relieve the *tedium* of our hundred days of darkness.

The interest which I take in your present plan has, however, enabled me to do more than speculate upon the probable support which your publication will receive at your hands ... I have now much pleasure in assuring you, in the language of our London journals "that they have produced a great sensation in the public mind".

The very day after your Prospectus appeared, as my reporters inform me, there was a greater demand for ink than has been known during the whole voyage; the green baize of our mess tables has been ever since covered with innumerable pen-parings, to the great detriment, by-the-by, of one of our servants, whose finger has been terribly festered by a prick he received in sweeping them off; and I have it from authority, on which you may rely, that Serjeant Martin* has, within the last week, sharpened no less than nine penknives.

It has been remarked that our tables absolutely groan under the weight of writing desks, which for months past have not seen 'the blessed light'; and it is well known that the holds have been more than once opened of late, for the express, though not professed, purpose of getting up fresh packages of paper, originally intended for next year's consumption, but which is now destined to grace your file.

I forgot to mention to you, that I have some reason to suspect an attempt will occasionally be made to slide into your box communications which are not *quite* original, and therefore not quite corresponding with your plan; for a gentleman was seen at his desk late the other night, with a volume of the *Spectator* before him, while he was thawing his ink over a lamp. With all due deference to your extensive reading, I think it right to put you on your guard against such attempts; for I have no idea, Mr Editor, of being obliged to read in the *Winter Chronicle* what our great grandfathers conned over at their breakfast tables more than a century ago.'

'Well, well,' said Altamont when the doctor had finished reading. 'It's funny, the letter's author must have been a bright boy.'

'Bright is the word,' replied the doctor; 'listen, here is an amusing notice:

Wanted, a middle-aged Woman, not above 30, of good character, to assist in DRESSING the LADIES at the THEATRE. Her salary will be handsome; and she will be allowed tea and small beer into the bargain. None need apply but such as are perfectly acquainted with the business, and can produce undeniable references.—A line addressed to the committee will be duly attended to.—NB A widow will be preferred.'

'Goodness, our countrymen didn't do things by halves,' said Johnson.

'And did they find a widow?' asked Bell.

'Presumably, for here is a reply to the theatre committee:

GENTLEMEN—I am a widow, twenty-six years of age,* and can produce undeniable testimonials of my character and qualifications; but before I undertake the business of dressing the ladies at the theatre, I wish to be informed whether it is customary for them to keep on their breeches; also, if I may be allowed two or three of the stoutest able-seamen or marines, to lace their stays. So no more at present from,

Gentleman, yours as may be,

ABIGAIL HANDICRAFT

PS Could you allow hollands* instead of beer? As for tea, that is no object.'

'Brilliant!' exclaimed Altamont. 'I can just visualize those chambermaids lashing you to the capstan. Captain Parry's companions had great fun.'

'Like all those who reach their goal,' said Hatteras.

The captain threw this remark into the conversation, then went back to his usual silence. Not wanting to discuss the subject very much, the doctor quickly carried on reading.

'Now here is a tableau of Arctic tribulations; it could be varied indefinitely; but some of the observations hit the nail on the head. Judge for yourselves:

Going out in the winter morning for the purpose of taking a walk, and before you have preceded 10 yards from the ship, getting a cold bath in the cook's steep hole.*

When on a hunting excursion, and being close to a fine deer, after several attempts to fire, discovering that your piece is neither primed nor loaded, while the animals [*sic*] four legs are employed in carrying away the body.

Setting out with a piece of new bread in your pocket on a shooting party, and when you feel inclined to eat it, having occasion to observe that it is so frozen your teeth will not penetrate it.

Being called from table by intelligence the wolf is approaching the vessels, which, on closer inspection, proves to be a dog; on going again below, detecting the cat in running off with your dinner.

Returning on board your ship after an evening visit in a contemplative humour, and being roused from a pleasing revelry by the close embrace of a bear.'

'You see, my friends, it wouldn't be difficult to find a few more polar problems; but given that they had to undergo these miseries, it became a pleasure to relate them.'

'Goodness!' replied Altamont. 'That *Winter Chronicle* is a fun newspaper—a shame we can't take out a subscription.'

'Why not try to do one ourselves?' asked Johnson.

'The five of us?' said Clawbonny. 'We'd only just about manage the writing, and wouldn't have enough readers.'

'Or spectators, if we did some acting,' replied Altamont.

'In fact, Dr Clawbonny,' said Johnson, 'did they put on any new plays in Captain Parry's theatre?'

'Most definitely; two volumes on board the *Hecla* were meant to be used, with plays performed every fortnight; but soon the repertoire was as threadbare as could be; so amateur authors set to work and Parry himself wrote a wonderfully apt comedy for the Christmas holidays; it was hugely successful, and was called *The North-West Passage; or, The Voyage Finished*.'*

'A fine title,' replied Altamont, 'but if I had to deal with such a subject, the closing scene might cause problems.'

'You're right,' said Bell, 'who can say how it'll all end?'

'All right!' exclaimed the doctor. 'Why worry about the last act when the first few have gone so well? Let's leave that to Providence, my friends; let's play our part as best we can, and since the final scene is to be decided by the author of all things, let's trust to his ability; I'm sure he'll know how to get us out of it.'

'So let's go and dream of that,' replied Johnson; 'it's late, and since it's the time to sleep, let's do just that.'

'You're in such a hurry, my old friend,' said the doctor.

'What do you expect, Dr Clawbonny; I'm so comfortable in my bunk! And I usually have good dreams; I dream of hot countries, so that to tell the truth half my life is spent on the equator and half at the Pole.'

'Heavens!' said Altamont. 'You're lucky to have such a temperament!'

'I suppose so.'

'Well,' concluded the doctor, 'it would be cruel to make good Johnson wait any longer. His tropical sun is waiting for him. And so to bed.'

I I

*Worrying Tracks**

DURING the night of 26 to 27 April, the weather changed; the temperature went down, the inhabitants of Doctor's House noticing it from the cold slipping under their blankets; Altamont, on guard near the stove, was careful not to let the fire die down, and had to feed it generously to keep the internal temperature at fifty (10°C).

The cold snap indicated that the storm was coming to an end, pleasing the doctor; they would soon be able to go back to their usual occupations, hunting, going on excursions, and reconnoitring the land; their idle solitude, a condition in which even the best of men become embittered,* would finally end.

The following morning, the doctor got up early, and forced a path through the piled-up ice to the cone of the beacon.

The wind had veered north; the air was clear; long white sheets offered his feet a firm and resistant carpet.

Soon the five wintering companions had left Doctor's House; their first task was to free the house of the icy mass weighing it down; on the plateau, everything was different; it would have been impossible to find traces of a habitation; by filling in the irregularities of the terrain, the storm had levelled everything; the ground had risen at least fifteen feet.

First the snow had to be removed, then the architectural form of the edifice restored—reviving its entombed outlines and re-establishing its balance. This task was easily accomplished; once the ice had been removed, a few attacks with the snow knife brought the walls back to their normal thickness.

After two hours of hard work, the granite base reappeared; access to the supply stores and the powder magazine became possible again.

But since in those uncertain climes a similar state of affairs could occur again at any time, new supplies of food were transferred to the kitchen. The need for fresh meat was felt in these stomachs, over-stimulated by salt food; so the huntsmen took on the task of making a change from the 'heating' diet, and got ready to leave.

However, the end of April did not bring the polar spring; the time for new life had not yet come; at least six more weeks were needed; still too weak, the sunlight was unable to burrow into the snowy plains and persuade the meagre population of boreal flora to thrust up from the ground. It was to be feared that living creatures would be scarce, whether birds or four-footed. All the same, if they could only catch a hare, a few brace of ptarmigan, or even a young fox, it would honour the table of Doctor's House, and so the huntsmen resolved to try to hunt down anything coming within range of their rifles.

The doctor, Altamont, and Bell volunteered to explore the countryside. Altamont, to judge from his habits, had to be a skilful and determined huntsman, a fine shot although a little boastful. So he joined the party, as did Duke, who was just as good, but less boastful.

The three companions in adventure climbed up the east cone, and headed across the immense white plains; but they didn't need to go far, as numerous tracks could be seen less than two miles from the fort. They led down to the shore of Victoria Bay, and seemed to surround Fort Providence with their concentric circles.

After following these tracks with curiosity, the huntsmen looked at each other.

'Well,' said the doctor, 'it seems clear.'

'Too clear,' replied Bell; 'they're bear tracks.'

'Fine game,' replied Altamont, 'but with one undesirable quality today.'

'Which?'

'Abundance.'

'What do you mean?' said Bell.

'I mean that there are tracks of five separate bears, and five bears is a lot for five men!'

'Are you sure of that?' said the doctor.

'Look and judge for yourself: the footprint over here is not like the one over there; the claws of these ones are more spread out than those. Here are the tracks of a smaller bear. Study the differences and you'll see the tracks of five animals within a small area.'

'Definitely,' said Bell, after careful examination.

'Well then,' said the doctor, 'we mustn't run useless risks, but remain on our guard; those animals are starving at the end of a severe winter; they can be extremely dangerous; and since their number can no longer be doubted . . .'

'Or their intentions,' added the American.

'Do you think', said Bell, 'they have realized we're here on this coast?'

'Yes, unless we just happen to have chanced on bear tracks; but then why do the tracks run in circles rather than stretching off to the horizon? See, the animals came from the south-east, and then they stopped and began reconnoitring the area here.'

'You're right,' said the doctor, 'it's even clear that they came last night.'

'And probably the other nights,' replied the American, 'but the snow hid their tracks.'

'No, more probably the bears waited for the end of the storm; then, driven by need, they headed for the coast, perhaps planning to catch a few seals—and got wind of us there.'

'That must be it; in any case, it'll be easy to find out if they come back tonight.'

'How?' asked Bell.

'By hiding the tracks on part of their path; if tomorrow we find new tracks, it will be obvious that Fort Providence is their goal.'

'All right,' said the doctor; 'then we'll know what we're up against.'

The three huntsmen set to work, and by scraping up snow they had soon hidden the footprints over a distance of about six hundred feet.

'All the same,' said Bell, 'it's strange that the beasts smelled us at such a range; we didn't burn any greasy substance to attract them.'

'Oh, bears have tremendous eyesight, and a very good sense of smell; they are also very intelligent, if not the most intelligent of all animals,* and they smelled something unusual here.'

'In any case,' said Bell, 'how do we know they didn't get as far as the plateau during the storm?'

'If so,' said the American, 'why would they have stopped there?'

'There's no reply,' said the doctor, 'we have to believe they're gradually reducing the distance of their search round Fort Providence.'

'We'll see.'

'Now let's continue, but keeping our eyes open.'

The huntsmen watched carefully; they feared that some bear was lying in wait behind the ice mounds; sometimes they even mistook the giant blocks of ice for animals, for they had the same size and whiteness. But in the end their fears proved ill-founded, to their great relief.

Finally, they went halfway up the cone again, and from that spot their eyes examined the entire area from Cape Washington to Johnson Island, but did not find anything.

Everything was motionless and white; there was no noise, not a single crunching noise.

They went back to the snow-house.

Hatteras and Johnson were told about the situation, and it was decided to keep watch as carefully as possible. Night fell; nothing troubled the splendid calm and nothing was heard to indicate impending danger.

At dawn the following day, Hatteras and his companions took their guns and went to look at the snow; they found tracks identical to the day before, but closer in. Clearly, the enemies were making plans to besiege Fort Providence.

'They've dug a second parallel trench so to speak,' said the doctor.

'They've even made an advance,' replied Altamont; 'look at these tracks heading for the plateau; it's a powerful animal.'

'Yes, the bears are moving in gradually,' said Johnson; 'they're obviously planning to attack us.'

'That's clear,' replied the doctor; 'let's not show ourselves. We're not strong enough to fight.'

'But where can these damn bears be?' exclaimed Bell.

'Behind the ice floes to the east, where they're spying on us; let's not go too far.'

'And our hunting?' said Altamont.

'Let's leave it for a few days; let's hide the closest tracks again, and see if there are any fresh ones tomorrow morning. Then we'll know about our enemies' manoeuvres.'

They followed the doctor's advice, and came back to their fortified barracks; the presence of these terrible beasts prevented any excursion. They carefully surveyed the area around Victoria Bay. The beacon was switched off; it had no use at present, and could draw the attention of the animals; the lamp and electric wires were stored in the house; then each in turn began observations from the upper platform.

They had to suffer the problems of isolation again; but how could they do otherwise? They couldn't take risks in such an unequal fight, and each of their lives was too precious to risk carelessly. If the bears saw nothing, they might be thrown off the scent, and if the men came across them individually on their excursions, they could attack them with a reasonable chance of success.

However, this inaction was broken up by a new interest: they had to keep watch, and no one completely regretted doing so.

The whole of 28 April passed without the enemy giving any sign they were still there. The following day, they went to look at the tracks with curiosity, and exclamations of astonishment were heard.

There were no tracks at all, and the snow stretched out into the distance in an untouched carpet.

'Well,' exclaimed Altamont, 'the bears have been thrown off the scent! They weren't patient enough! They got tired of waiting, and left. I hope they have a nice trip, and now let's hunt!'

'But who knows?' exclaimed the doctor. 'Just to be safe, my friends, I'm asking you for one extra day of surveillance. Clearly the enemy didn't come back last night, or at least not near here.'

'Let's go around the plateau,' said Altamont, 'and we'll find out the extent of the problem.'

'Good idea.'

They carefully checked the whole area, over a distance of two miles; but couldn't find the slightest trace.

'Well, can we hunt now?'

'Let's wait till tomorrow.'

'All right,' said Altamont, who found it difficult to restrain himself.

They went back to the fort. All the same, like the day before, they each had to take two turns as lookout.

When Altamont's turn came, he went to relieve Bell at the top of the cone.

As soon as he had gone out, Hatteras called his companions around him. The doctor left his notebook, and Johnson his oven.

One might think that Hatteras was going to talk of the dangers of the situation; the thought didn't even cross his mind.

'My friends, let's profit from the absence of that American to talk business; there are certain things that don't concern him, and which I don't want him poking his nose into.'

The captain's interlocutors looked at each other, not knowing quite where he was getting to.

'I wish to discuss our future plans.'

'All right,' said the doctor, 'let's talk, since we're now alone.'

'In a month's time, six weeks at the most, the time for long journeys will come again. Have you any suggestions as to what should be done this summer?'

'And you, captain?' enquired Johnson.

'As for me, I can say that not an hour of my life goes by without coming back to my idea. Would I be correct to say that not one of you wants to go home?'

This suggestion did not receive a reply for the moment.

'As far as I'm concerned, I will go to the North Pole, even if I have to go alone; we're at most three hundred and sixty miles from it. Never have men got so close to this longed-for goal, and I will not let such an opportunity pass without trying everything, even the impossible. What are your ideas on this?'

'The same as yours,' keenly replied the doctor.

'And yours, Johnson?'

'The same as the doctor's.'

'Your turn, Bell.'

'Captain, we have no family waiting for us back home, I'll admit, but your country is your country after all! Have you never thought about heading back?'

'We can head back just as well after the discovery of the Pole. Better in fact. The difficulties won't have got any greater, for as we head north we'll leave the coldest areas of the globe. We have fuel and food for a long time still. So nothing can stop us, and we'd be wrong not to go to the end.'

'Yes,' said Bell, 'we all share your opinion, captain.'

'Good. I never doubted it for a moment. We shall succeed, my friends, and all the glory of our success will go to Britain.'

'But there's an American with us,' said Johnson.*

At this remark Hatteras could not prevent a trace of anger crossing his face.

'I know,' he said gravely.

'We can't leave him here,' said the doctor.

'No, we can't,' repeated Hatteras mechanically.

'And he'll certainly have to come with us.'

'Yes, he'll have to come with us! But who'll be in charge?'

'You, captain.'

'And if you obey me, will that Yankee refuse to?'

'I don't think so,' said Johnson; 'but what if he did refuse your orders?'

'It would then be a matter between him and me.'

The three Britons looked at Hatteras in silence. The doctor spoke again.

'How will we get there?'

'By following the coast as much as possible.'

'But what happens if we reach the open sea, as we probably will?'

'Well then, we'll cross it.'

'How? We haven't got a boat.'

Hatteras didn't reply; he was clearly thinking.

'Perhaps we could build a launch from the remains of the *Porpoise*?' said Bell.

'Never!' exclaimed Hatteras loudly.

'Never!' said Johnson.

The doctor shook his head, although he understood the captain's repugnance.

'Never!' repeated Hatteras. 'A launch made of wood from an American ship would be an American one.'

'But, captain . . .' said Johnson.*

The doctor made a sign that the old mate should put off the question. It was better to keep it for a more suitable moment; while understanding Hatteras's attitude, the doctor did not share it, and he decided he would try at a later stage to persuade his friend to change his mind about such an absolute decision.

So he spoke of other things, of the possibility of simply following the coast north, and of that unknown point called the North Pole.

In short, he changed the dangerous subject of conversation, until it suddenly stopped, when the American came in.

Altamont had nothing to report.

The day ended, and the night was spent peacefully. The bears had obviously disappeared.

12

Prison of Ice

THE next day they discussed organizing a hunt, with Hatteras, Altamont, and the carpenter; the worrying tracks had not reappeared and the bears had apparently given up their attack, either through fear of these unknown enemies or because nothing had revealed the presence of living creatures under the snow mountain.

While the three huntsmen were away, the doctor headed for Johnson Island, to study the state of the ice and make hydrographical measurements. The cold was very severe, but the winterers had little problem bearing it; their epidermis had got used to the exaggerated temperatures.

The mate was to stay in Doctor's House, and keep house.

The three huntsmen got ready to leave; they each took a double shotgun, with rifled barrel and conical bullets; they took a small supply of pemmican, in case night fell before the end of their excursion; in addition, each carried the vital snow knives—the most indispensable tool of these regions—plus a hatchet in the belt of his deerskin jacket.

Thus equipped, clothed, and armed, they could go far, and with enough skill and courage, could hope for a good result from their hunt.

They were ready at eight o'clock, and set off. Duke ran gambolling in front; they climbed the east hill, worked their way round the beacon cone, and headed into the southern plains near Mount Bell.

As for the doctor, after agreeing on an alarm signal with Johnson in case of danger, he went down to the shore, so as to reach the variegated ice blocks on Victoria Bay.

The mate remained alone at Fort Providence, although not idle. First, he freed the Greenland dogs who were getting excited in the Dog Palace; delighted, they ran and rolled in the snow. Then Johnson busied himself with the complicated household chores. He had to replenish the fuel and food, organize the stores, mend many broken utensils, darn the worn blankets, and mend the shoes for the long summer excursions. There was no lack of work, and the mate laboured with all the skill of a sailor who knows many trades.

While working, he considered the conversation of the day before; he thought about the captain, especially his obstinate, very heroic, and honourable refusal to let an American, or even an American launch, reach the Pole before him or at the same time.

All the same, he said to himself, it seems difficult to cross the ocean without a boat, and if we have an open sea in front of us, we'll have to agree to navigate it. You can't swim 300 miles, even if you're the best Briton on earth. Even patriotism has its limits. We'll see in the end. We still have time; Dr Clawbonny hasn't said his final word; he's clever; he might be able to change the captain's mind. I even bet that when he's near the island, he'll take a look at the remains of the *Porpoise*, and decide what can be done with them.

Johnson had reached this stage in his thoughts, and the hunters had been away from the fort for an hour, when a shot, loud and clear, went off two or three miles downwind.

Good! They've found something without having to go too far, since I can hear them distinctly. Also the air is so clear.

A second shot came, then a third, without much gap.

So, said Johnson, they've found the right place for a hunt.

Three more shots, even closer together.

'Six! Their guns are now discharged. There must be problems. Has by any chance . . .'

Johnson paled at the idea; he ran out of the snow-house, and climbed to the top of the cone in a few seconds.

What he saw made him tremble.

'The bears!'

The three huntsmen, followed by Duke, were running back at top speed, chased by five gigantic animals; their six bullets had been unable to stop them; the bears were gaining on them; Hatteras was the last, and only managed to stay ahead of the animals by throwing down first his hat, then his axe, even his gun. The bears stopped, as was their habit, to smell the object dropped for their curiosity;* and lost a little ground, despite being fast enough on such terrain to overtake the quickest horse.

Hatteras, Altamont, and Bell, out of breath, rushed up to Johnson, and from the top of the slope they all slid down to the snow-house.

The five bears were almost touching them, and the captain had to fend off a violent attack with his knife.

In the twinkling of an eye, Hatteras and his companions were inside the house. The animals had stopped on the upper plateau of the truncated cone.

'At last we can defend ourselves properly,' exclaimed Hatteras, 'five against five!'

'Four against five!' exclaimed Johnson in terror.

'What?'

'The doctor!' he answered, indicating the empty living-room.

'Well?'

'He's gone to the island!'

'The poor man!' exclaimed Bell.

'We can't just abandon him,' said Altamont.

'Let's run!' said Hatteras.

He quickly opened the door, but he barely had the time to close it again before a bear almost broke his head with its claws.

'They're out there!'

'All of them?' asked Bell.

'All!'

Altamont rushed to the windows, and blocked them with ice taken from the walls of the house. His companions did likewise in silence; the only sound was Duke's suppressed yapping.

To tell the truth, these men had but a single thought; they forgot their own danger, thinking only of the doctor. Of him, not themselves. Poor Clawbonny, so good, so devoted, the soul of the little colony! For the first time, he wasn't there; extreme danger, perhaps a horrifying death, awaited him, for once he had finished his excursion he would come calmly back to Fort Providence, and would find himself confronted with these ferocious beasts.

And there was no way to warn him!

'However,' said Johnson, 'if I'm not seriously mistaken, he'll be on the lookout; your repeated shots must have alerted him, and he'll surely think that some extraordinary event has happened.'

'But what if he was already a long way away,' said Altamont, 'or didn't understand? All in all, he must have an eighty per cent chance of coming back without thinking of any danger. The bears are hidden behind the hill the fort is on, and he can't see them!'

'So we need to get rid of these dangerous animals before he comes back,' said Hatteras.

'But how?' asked Bell.

The question was a difficult one. Attempting a sortie did not seem possible. They had carefully barricaded the passage, but the bears might remove these obstacles if the idea came to them; they knew their adversaries' number and strength, and would find it easy to reach them.

The prisoners had positioned themselves in all of the rooms of Doctor's House, so as to detect any invasion attempt; straining their ears, they could hear the bears coming and going, groaning dully and scratching at the snow walls with their enormous paws.

Meanwhile something needed to be done; time was moving on. Altamont decided to make a loophole, to fire at the assailants; in minutes he had dug a sort of hole through the ice wall; he put his gun through it; but hardly had the gun reached the outside than it was torn from his hands with irresistible force, without him being able to fire.

'Hell,' he exclaimed, 'we aren't strong enough!'

And he quickly closed the loophole again.

The situation had continued for an hour already, and there was no end in sight. The chances of a sortie were again discussed; they were poor, since the bears could not be fought separately. Nevertheless, Hatteras and his companions wanted to get it over with, for, it must be admitted, they were embarrassed at being imprisoned by animals; they were about to attempt a direct attack when the captain came up with a new means of defence.

He picked up the poker Johnson used for the oven, and placed it in the burning stove; then he made an opening in the snow wall, but without going all the way through, keeping a thin layer of ice outside.

His companions watched him. When the poker was white-hot, Hatteras said:

'This glowing piece of metal will help me repulse the bears, as they can't grab hold of it, and so it will be much easier to shoot them through the hole without them taking our guns away.'

'Great idea!' exclaimed Bell, taking up position beside Altamont.

Then Hatteras took the poker from the stove and quickly thrust it into the wall. The snow vaporized on contact, hissing deafeningly. Two bears ran up, grabbed the red-hot iron, and produced terrible howling noises, while four shots went off one after the other.

'Hit!' exclaimed the American.

'Hit!' added Bell.

'Let's try again,' said Hatteras, temporarily filling in the hole.

The poker was placed in the stove; after a few minutes it was red-hot once more.

Altamont and Bell reloaded their guns and went back to their position; Hatteras opened up the loophole, and thrust the glowing poker through again.

But this time an impenetrable obstacle stopped him.

'Curses!' exclaimed the American.

'What's the problem?' said Johnson.

'The problem is that these cursed animals are piling up blocks, shutting us into our house and burying us alive!'

'Impossible!'

'Look, the poker can't get through; this is getting ridiculous!'

Worse than ridiculous, it was getting worrying; and was getting worse. Highly intelligent, the bears were using this method to suffocate their prey. They were piling up the pieces of ice to prevent any escape.

'It's not easy!' said old Johnson with a hurt air. 'Men doing this to you is one thing, but bears!'

After this, two hours went by without any change in the prisoners' situation; the idea of a sortie had become impracticable; the thicker walls stopped all noise from outside. Altamont was agitatedly walking up and down, an audacious man exasperated to find a danger greater than his courage. Hatteras was thinking with fright about the doctor, and about the serious danger he would be in when he came back.

'Ah,' exclaimed Johnson, 'if only Dr Clawbonny was here!'

'Well, what would he do?'

'Oh, he'd know how to save us.'

'But how?' the American asked pointedly.

'If I knew, I wouldn't need him. But I can guess what advice he'd give us now.'

'What?'

'Eat something! It can't do any harm. On the contrary. What do you think, Captain Altamont?'

'Let's eat if you want, although this situation is crazy and even humiliating.'

'I bet that after lunch we'll find a way out.'

No one replied, but they did sit down to eat.

Johnson, trained in the doctor's school, tried to be philosophical in danger, but did not succeed; his jokes stuck in his throat. In addition, the prisoners were beginning to feel uncomfortable; the air was thickening in this perfectly airtight dwelling; the atmosphere could not be renewed through the pipes of the stove, which was not drawing properly, and it was easy to see that very soon the fire would go out; the oxygen absorbed by the lungs and the fire would soon be replaced by carbon monoxide, whose fatal effect is well known.

Hatteras was the first to notice this new danger; he did not think of hiding it from his companions.

'We need to get out at any cost,' said Altamont.

'But let's wait for night,' said Hatteras; 'we'll make a hole in the roof to replenish our air; then one of us will take up position and fire at the bears.'

'We've got no choice,' said the American.

This agreed upon, they waited for the best moment, and in the following hours Altamont did not spare his curses at their situation, saying, 'between bears and men, the latter weren't getting the best parts to play'.

13

Explosives

NIGHT fell, and the lamp in the living room was already beginning to dim in the poorly oxygenated atmosphere.

At eight o'clock, the last preparations had been made. The guns were carefully loaded, and the men made an opening in the roof of the snow-house.

The work had already been going on for a few minutes, and Bell was making good progress, when Johnson rushed out of the bedroom, where he was on watch.

He looked worried.

'What's the matter?' the captain asked.

'The matter? Nothing,' answered the old sailor hesitantly; 'and yet . . .'

'What is it?' said Altamont.

'Quiet, can't you hear that strange noise?'

'Where's it coming from?'

'Over there! Something is happening in the bedroom wall!'

Bell stopped work; all listened.

A faraway noise could be heard, apparently coming from the side wall; clearly, a hole in the ice was being made.

'There's scratching,' said Johnson.

'Definitely,' answered Altamont.

'The bears?' said Bell.

'The same.'

'They've changed tactics,' said the old sailor, 'they've given up suffocating us.'

'Or they think we've already suffocated!' said the American, in the throes of anger.

'They're going to attack us.'

'Well, we'll fight hand-to-hand,' said Hatteras.

'Heavens,' exclaimed Altamont, 'I prefer that! I've had enough of these invisible enemies! We'll see them and we'll fight them!'

'Yes,' said Johnson, 'but not with guns; it's impossible in such a small space.'

'All right, with hatchets and knives then!'

The noise was increasing; they could distinctly hear the scratching of the claws; the bears* had attacked the wall at the very place where it joined the snow slope that leaned upon the rock.

'The animal that's digging is less than six feet away.'

'You're right, Johnson,' replied the American, 'but we've time to get ready to say hello to it!'

The American took his hatchet in one hand, his knife in the other; his weight on his right foot, body leaning back, he adopted an attacking position. Hatteras and Bell did the same. Johnson got his gun ready, in case the firearm was needed after all.

The sound got louder and louder; the torn away ice was cracking under the violent incisions of claws of steel.

Finally, only a thin crust separated the assailant from his adversaries; suddenly, this crust broke like a hoop of paper when a clown jumps through, and an enormous black body appeared in the dark room.

Altamont quickly brought back his hand to strike.

'Stop, for heaven's sake!' said a familiar voice.

'The doctor!' exclaimed Johnson.

It was indeed Clawbonny, who, carried forward by his weight, came rolling into the middle of the room.

'Hello, my good friends,' he said, nimbly getting up.

His companions were stupefied; but their astonishment soon turned to joy; each wanted to take the worthy man in his arms; Hatteras was very moved, and held him to his breast for a long time. The doctor responded with a warm handshake.

'Can it be you, Dr Clawbonny?' said the mate.

'In person, my old Johnson, and I was more worried about what had happened to you than you could have been about me.'

'But how did you know we'd been attacked by the bears?' asked Altamont. 'Our biggest worry was that you might calmly come back to Fort Providence, not knowing about the danger.'

'Oh, I saw everything; your gunshots alerted me; at that moment I was near the remains of the *Porpoise*; I climbed a hummock, and saw the five bears in hot pursuit; ah, how afraid I was for you then! But in the end, your tumble down the hill and the animals' hesitation reassured me for the moment; I realized that you'd had time to barricade yourselves in the house. Then gradually I approached, sometimes crawling, sometimes slipping between the ice; I got near the fort, and I saw the enormous animals working like huge beavers; they were hitting the snow, and piling up blocks; in sum they were burying you alive. It's lucky they didn't have the idea of sending blocks of ice down from the top of the cone, for you would have been totally crushed.'

'But you weren't safe, Dr Clawbonny,' said Bell. 'Couldn't they have given up and come after you instead?'

'They hardly thought of it; the Greenland dogs that Johnson let out came several times to prowl close by, and the bears didn't think of chasing them; they thought they were sure of tastier game.'

'Thanks for the compliment,' said Altamont with a laugh.

'Oh there's nothing to be proud of. When I realized what the bears were up to, I decided to join you. To be safe I had to wait for night; at the first shades of dusk, I moved silently towards the part of the slope near the powder magazine. I had a reason to choose that point; I wanted to make a tunnel. So I started work; I attacked the ice with my snow knife, a wonderful tool, thank goodness! For three hours I burrowed, I dug, and here I am, starving, exhausted, but here . . .'

'To share our fate?' said Altamont.

'To save us all; but give me some biscuit and meat; I'm weak with hunger.'

Soon the doctor's white teeth were biting into a fine piece of salt beef. While eating, he did not mind replying to the many questions.

'To save us!' Bell repeated.

'Yes,' replied the doctor, making room for his reply with a vigorous movement of his staphyline muscles.

'In fact,' added Bell, 'now Dr Clawbonny's here, we can leave by the same route.'

'Why didn't I think of that—and let that evil bunch do what they want, including finding our stores and pillaging them!'

'We must stay here,' said Hatteras.

'Yes, but all the same, we need to get rid of the animals.'

'Is there a way to do so?' asked Bell.

'A good way.'

'I told you!' said Johnson, rubbing his hands. 'With Dr Clawbonny, nothing is ever hopeless; he's always got some invention in his scientist's bag.'

'Oh, oh! My poor bag is getting rather depleted, but by going deep . . .'

'Doctor,' said Altamont, 'can't the bears come in through the tunnel you dug?'

'No, I blocked up the hole again carefully and solidly; and now we can go from here to the powder magazine without them knowing.'

'Great! Well, now tell us how you plan to get rid of these ridiculous visitors!'

'A very simple method, since some of the work's already been done.'

'It has?'

'You'll see. But I forgot to tell you I didn't come here on my own.'

'What do you mean?' asked Johnson.

'I have a companion to introduce to you.'

And so saying, the doctor pulled out of the tunnel the body of a freshly killed fox.

'A fox!' exclaimed Bell.

'This morning's hunt,' replied the doctor, modestly, 'and you'll see that no fox has ever been killed more opportunely.'

'But what's your plan?' asked Altamont.

'I hope to be able to blow up the bears all together, using 100 pounds of powder.'

Everybody looked at the doctor in surprise.

'But the powder?'

'In the magazine.'

'And the magazine?'

'This passage goes there. I had a good reason for digging my tunnel sixty feet long; I could have attacked the parapet nearer the house, but I had an idea.'

'But this explosive . . . where are you planning to put it?' asked the American.

'Opposite our slope, that is at the furthest point from the house, the powder magazine, and the stores.'

'But how to make sure the bears all come at the same time?'

'I have a plan; enough talking, let's act. We've got 100 feet of tunnel to dig tonight; it's tiring work; but with five of us taking turns, we can do it. Bell will begin, and during that time we can take some rest.'

'Good Lord!' exclaimed Johnson. 'The more I think about it, the better I find Dr Clawbonny's idea.'

'It should work.'

'Oh, as soon as you say so, the bears are dead, and I can already feel their fur on my back.'

'To work then.'

The doctor crawled into the dark tunnel, with Bell coming after; if the doctor could get through, his companions were sure to have plenty of room. The two reached the powder magazine, and came out among the neatly arranged barrels. The doctor gave Bell the necessary indications; the carpenter attacked the opposite wall adjoining the slope, and Clawbonny went back into the house.

Bell worked for an hour, digging a passage about ten feet long through which it was possible to crawl. Then Altamont came to replace him, doing about the same work in the same time; the snow taken out of the tunnel was carried to the kitchen, where the doctor melted it on the fire to save room.

After the American came the captain, then Johnson. In ten hours, or by about eight in the morning, the tunnel was entirely finished.

At the first gleams of dawn, the doctor studied the bears through a hole he made in the wall of the powder store.

The patient animals had not left. They were still coming and going, groaning, but in reality maintaining the siege with exemplary perseverance; they were prowling around the house, hidden behind piled up blocks. But then the time came when their patience was finally exhausted, for the doctor saw them suddenly pushing away the pieces of ice they had piled up.

'Good!' he said to the captain, near him.

'What are they doing?'

'They seem to want to demolish their work and get at us. But just wait, they'll be demolished themselves before that. There's no time to waste.'

The doctor crept to the place where the explosive was to be put; then he enlarged the room to the entire width and height of the slope; soon, nothing of the upper part remained, except a crust of ice a foot thick at most; and even that had to be reinforced to stop it collapsing.

A post, solidly placed on the granite ground, served as support; the fox's body was attached to its top part, and a long rope tied to its lower part ran through the tunnel to the powder magazine.

The doctor's companions followed his instructions without understanding them very much.

'Here's the bait,' he said, pointing at the fox.

Beside the foot of the post, he rolled a keg containing about a hundred pounds of powder.

'And here's the explosive.'

'But won't we blow ourselves up with the bears?' asked Hatteras.

'No, we'll be far enough away from the scene of the explosion; in any case, our house is solid; if it's loosened a bit, we'll just have to repair it.'

'Fine,' said Altamont, 'but how are you planning to set it off?'

'By pulling this rope we'll remove the post that holds up the crust of ice above the explosive; the fox's body will suddenly appear on the slope, and you'll agree that animals starving after a long fast won't think twice about grabbing this unexpected prey.'

'All right.'

'Well, at that moment I will set off the explosive, and make it blow up the guests and the meal in one go.'

'Wonderful!' exclaimed Johnson, listening with great interest.

Having full confidence in his friend, Hatteras did not ask for more explanation. He waited. But Altamont wanted to know everything.

'Doctor, how will you calculate your fuse precisely enough for the explosion to go off at the right time?'

'It's very simple: I won't.'

'So you've got a fuse 100 feet long?'

'No.'

'Then . . . you'll simply use a trail of powder?'

'Not at all; it might not work.'

'So someone needs to sacrifice himself and set off the explosive?'

'If a man is needed,' said Johnson eagerly, 'I'd be glad to volunteer.'

'No need, my worthy friend,' said the doctor, stretching his hand out to the old mate; 'our five lives are precious, and will not be sacrificed, thank God!'

'Then I give up.'

'Look,' replied the doctor with a smile, 'if we can't get out of this situation, what's the point of studying physics?'

'Ah,' said Johnson, glowing with happiness, 'physics!'

'Haven't we got an electric battery and long enough wires, the ones we used for our beacon?'

'Well?'

'Well, we can set off the explosive whenever we want, instantaneously and without danger.'

'Hurray!' exclaimed Johnson.

'Hurray!' repeated his companions, not worrying if their enemies heard them.

Straightaway the two electric wires were unrolled through the tunnel, from the house to the explosive chamber. One of the four ends was still wound around the battery, and two ends were placed in the middle of the keg, a short distance apart.

By nine everything was finished. It was time; the bears were furiously demolishing the ice.

The doctor judged the moment ripe. Johnson was placed in the powder store, with responsibility for pulling the rope tied to the post. He took up position.

'Now,' said the doctor to his companions, 'get your guns ready, in case our besiegers aren't killed the first time around, and stand near Johnson; rush out immediately after the explosion.'

'Agreed,' replied the American.

'And now we have done everything that men can! We've tried everything to help ourselves; so may God help us now!'

Hatteras, Altamont, and Bell went into the powder magazine. The doctor remained alone beside the battery.

Soon, he heard the faraway voice of Johnson shouting:

'Ready!'

'Everything's set!' he replied.

Johnson pulled the rope hard; it moved towards him, pulling the post; then he rushed to the hole and looked out.

The surface of the slope had collapsed. The fox's body was visible above the pieces of ice. The bears, at first surprised, soon rushed in a tight group towards this new prey.

'Now!' cried Johnson.

The doctor immediately established the electric current between the wires; there was a massive explosion; the house shook as if an earthquake was happening; cracks ran along the walls. Hatteras, Altamont, and Bell rushed out of the powder magazine ready to fire.

But their guns were not needed; after the explosion, four bears out of five were falling here and there in unrecognizable pieces, mutilated and burned, while the last one, half-cooked, was running away as fast as his legs could take him.

'Hip, hip, hurray!' exclaimed Clawbonny's companions, whilst the smiling doctor rushed to hug them.

14

Polar Spring

THE prisoners had been set free; their joy showed in the warm displays and eager thanks to the doctor. All Johnson regretted was that the bears' skins were burned and useless; but this disappointment did not really affect his mood.

The remainder of the day was spent repairing the snow-house, which had greatly suffered from the explosion. The blocks piled up by the animals were removed, and the walls repointed. The work was done quickly, to the voice of the mate, whose fine songs were a joy to hear.

The next day, the temperature rose considerably, and with a sudden change of wind the thermometer went up to fifteen (−9°C). Such a big difference was felt by everyone and everything. The southerly wind brought with it the first signs of the polar spring.

This relative warmth lasted several days; the thermometer, sheltered from the wind, even read thirty-one (−1°C), and signs of a thaw could be seen.

The ice began to crack, sending up spurts of salt water here and there, like fountains in a British park; a few days later, rain fell in great abundance.

Thick steam rose from the snow; it was a good omen, as the huge masses seemed about to melt. The pale circle of the sun was taking on more colour and making longer spirals above the horizon; the nights lasted hardly three hours.

Another sign, just as significant, was the ptarmigans, snow geese, plovers, and hazel grouse coming back in flocks; the air gradually filled with their deafening cries, which the navigators remembered from the previous spring. Hares, which they successfully hunted, began to appear on the shore during the day, as well as Arctic mice, whose small burrows formed a system of regular alveoli.

The doctor pointed out to his companions that nearly all these animals were beginning to lose their white fur or feathers, and to put on their summer clothing; they were 'vernalizing' visibly, while nature allowed their food, in the form of mosses, poppies, saxifrage, and dwarf grass, to peep up through the snow.

But with the harmless animals, came their starving enemies; foxes and wolves arrived in search of prey; lugubrious howls echoed through the short darkness.

The wolf of these lands is a very close relative of the dog; like him, he barks, but in such a way as to deceive the most experienced ears, those of the canine race itself; they are even said to employ the ruse to lure dogs and eat them. This was observed in the area around Hudson Bay, and the doctor could see that it was true in New America as well; Johnson was careful not to let his dog team run free, for they could have easily fled.

As for Duke, he had seen plenty of water pass under the bridge and was too clever to go and put his head in the lion's den.

For a fortnight they did a great deal of hunting; supplies of fresh meat were abundant; they killed partridges, ptarmigans, and snow ortolans, which provided delicious food. The hunters did not have to go far from Fort Providence. The small game came almost of its own accord to greet gunshot; by its presence it gave tremendous life to these silent beaches, and for once Victoria Bay became a sight for sore eyes.

The fortnight that followed the great bear adventure was full of activity. The thaw made clear progress; the thermometer went up to thirty-two (0°C); rivulets began to tinkle in the valleys and thousands of waterfalls were born on the slopes of the hills.

After clearing an acre of land, the doctor sowed watercress seeds, sorrel, and Cochlearia, ideal against scurvy; small green leaves were already emerging from the ground, when, suddenly and with inconceivable speed, the cold returned to its empire.

With a single night, in a strong north wind, the thermometer fell nearly forty degrees; it went down to minus eight (−22°C). Everything was frozen; birds, quadrupeds, and amphibians disappeared as by magic; the seal holes closed up, the cracks vanished, the ice became hard as granite again, and the waterfalls froze in their flow, becoming long crystal pendicles.*

It was a real change before their eyes; it happened in the night of 11 to 12 May. And when Bell put his nose outside in the morning, he almost left it there in the severe frost.*

'Oh, nature is cruel in the north!' exclaimed the doctor, a little disappointed. 'But the only harm done is needing to replant my seedlings.'

Hatteras took it less philosophically, so much in a hurry was he to continue his search. But he had to accept it.

'Will this cold last long?' asked Johnson.

'No, my friend,' replied Clawbonny, 'it's the cold's dying blow. You have to understand that he's at home here, and if you try and drive him out, he'll fight.'

'He fights well,' replied Bell, rubbing his face.

'I ought to have expected it and not wasted my seeds like an ignoramus, especially as I could perhaps have grown them beside the kitchen oven.'

'What,' said Altamont, 'you should have foreseen this change in temperature?'

'Yes, and without being a magician! I should have put my seed-lings under the direct protection of Saints Mamertus, Pancras, and

Servatius, whose feast days fall on the 11th, 12th, and 13th of this month.'*

'You're amazing, doctor,' exclaimed Altamont; 'what difference can those saints possibly make to the temperature?'

'A tremendous one if gardeners are to be believed, for they call them "the three ice saints".'

'And why, if I may ask?'

'Because generally a periodic cold occurs in May, and the greatest drop in temperature takes place from the 11th to 13th of that month. It's a fact, that's all.'

'Most curious, but can it be explained?' asked the American.

'Yes, in two ways: either by the presence of a great number of asteroids[1] between the earth and the sun at that time of year, or simply by the melting of the snow, which necessarily absorbs much heat. Both causes are plausible; but are both accepted as fact? I don't know; but though I'm not certain why it occurs, I shouldn't have forgotten that it does occur, and so risked my planting efforts.'

The doctor was correct. For whatever reason, the cold was very severe for the rest of May; hunting had to be interrupted, not only because of the temperature, but the complete absence of game; for-tunately, the reserves of fresh meat were not yet exhausted, far from it.

The winterers found themselves condemned to a new idleness. For a fortnight, from 11 to 25 May, their monotonous existence was interrupted only by a single incident, a serious illness, diphtheria, which struck the carpenter out of the blue; from his swollen tonsils and the false membrane covering them, the doctor could not mistake the nature of the terrible disease; but he was in his element, and the illness, which had undoubtedly not expected to meet him, was quickly headed off. The treatment Bell underwent was very simple, and did not involve a distant pharmacy; the doctor merely put a few small pieces of ice into the patient's mouth; within a few hours the swelling was going down and the false membrane disappeared. Twenty-four hours later, Bell was back on his feet.

When his companions expressed wonder at the doctor's medica-tion, he said:

'This is the country of sore throats; the remedy needs to be near the illness.'

[1] Shooting stars, probably the remains of a large planet.

'The remedy, and above all the physician,' added Johnson, the doctor growing in his estimation, and now nearly as big as the Pyramids.

During his new leisure time, Clawbonny decided to engage an important conversation with the captain; he needed to change Hatteras's mind about continuing the route north without a launch or small boat, a piece of wood, anything whatsoever to cross estuaries or straits. The captain, so absolute in his ideas, had emphatically vowed not to use a boat made from the remains of the American ship.

The doctor didn't quite know how to broach the subject, and yet the point needed to be settled quickly, for with the month of June would come the season for long journeys. Finally, after reflecting for a long time, he took Hatteras aside one day and said, with his air of gentle goodness:

'Hatteras, do you think of me as your friend?'

'Certainly,' replied the captain keenly, 'my best, and even only one.'

'If I give a piece of advice, one you're not asking for, will you consider it as disinterested?'

'Yes, for I know that personal interest has never guided you; but what are you driving at?'

'Wait, Hatteras, I've got one more question to ask. Do you consider me a good Briton like you, keen on glory for my country?'

Hatteras stared at the doctor in surprise.

'Yes, I do,' he answered, scanning the doctor's face for the reason for the questions.

'You want to reach the North Pole; I understand your ambition, and share it; but to reach that goal, certain things have to be done.'

'Well, up till now, haven't I sacrificed everything to succeed?'

'No, Hatteras, you haven't sacrificed your own prejudices, and at this very moment I see you about to reject the way to reach the Pole.'

'Ah,' replied Hatteras, 'you mean that launch, that man . . .'

'Come on, Hatteras, let's reason without passion, and examine this question from every angle. The coast we've just wintered on may not be uninterrupted; there's no evidence it carries on for six degrees; if the information which brought you here is true, then during the summer we'll find a vast expanse of open sea. Now if we are faced with an Arctic Ocean free of ice and suitable for easy navigation, what will we do if we don't have any way to cross it?'

Hatteras did not reply.

'So do you want to find yourself a few miles from the North Pole, without being able to get there?'

Hatteras had dropped his head in his hands.

'And now,' continued the doctor, 'let's examine the question from the moral point of view. I understand that a Briton can sacrifice his fortune and life to give Britain one more reason for glory. But does the honour of the discovery diminish if the boat we use to cross the unknown ocean is made of a few pieces of wood torn from a worthless, shipwrecked American ship? If you had found the hull of an abandoned ship on this beach, would you have hesitated to use it? Isn't it the leader of the expedition who deserves all the credit? And I ask you, if that launch is built by four Britons, won't it be British from the keel to the gunnels?'

Hatteras still remained silent.

'Now, let's speak frankly,' said Clawbonny, 'it's not the launch that upsets you; it's the man.'

'Yes, that American; I hate him with a very British hatred, that man whom fate placed on my route . . .'

'To save you!'

'To beat me! He seems to be taunting me when he speaks as if a master here, when he imagines that he holds my destiny in his hands and that he has guessed my plans. Didn't he give his game away when we named these New Lands? Has he ever admitted what he came to do at these latitudes? You can't remove from my mind the idea that's killing me: that this man is the leader of an expedition of discovery sent by the government of the Union.'

'And even if he was, Hatteras, what proves the expedition was trying to reach the Pole? Can't America seek the Northwest Passage like Britain? In any case, Altamont has no knowledge whatsoever of your plans; for neither Johnson, Bell, yourself, nor I have ever said a single word in front of him.'

'Well may he never know of them, then!'

'He'll have to find out at some stage, for we can't leave him here alone.'

'Why not?' harshly asked the captain. 'Couldn't he stay at Fort Providence?'

'He wouldn't agree, Hatteras; and also, to abandon this man, whom we wouldn't even be sure of finding again on the way back, would be worse than negligent, it would be inhuman; Altamont will come, he has to come! But as it won't help to give him ideas he's not had, let's say nothing to him, and build a launch apparently designed for exploring these new shores.'

Hatteras could not decide whether to give in to his friend's ideas; Clawbonny waited for a reply which did not come.

'And if that man refuses to let his ship be broken up?' said the captain finally.

'In that case, you have right on your side; you would build that launch against his will, and his claim would be worth nothing.'

'May heaven grant that he refuses!'

'Before a refusal, we need an offer; I'll take on that duty.'

That very evening at supper, Clawbonny brought the subject round to their plans for excursions during the summer, in order to chart the coasts hydrographically.

'I imagine, Altamont,' he said, 'you'll be coming with us?'

'Certainly; we need to know how far New America stretches.'

Hatteras stared at his rival as he made this reply.

'And to do that,' he continued, 'we need to make the best possible use of the remains of the *Porpoise*; so let's build a solid launch that can take us a long way.'

'You hear, Bell?' said the doctor keenly. 'We'll start work tomorrow.'

15

The Northwest Passage

THE following day, Bell, Altamont, and the doctor headed for the *Porpoise*; there was no lack for wood; though broken by the impact of the ice, the launch from the three-master could still provide the main parts for a new one. Accordingly the carpenter set to work; they needed a boat that was seagoing and yet light enough to be carried on the sledge.

During the last few days of May the temperature rose; the thermometer went up to freezing point; spring came back for good this time, and the winterers had to abandon their winter clothing.

Rain was frequent; the snow soon began to take advantage of the slightest slope to move off in falls and cascades.

Hatteras could not hide* his satisfaction on seeing the ice-fields showing the first signs of thaw. The open sea represented freedom for him.

Whether his predecessors were right on this great question of the polar basin was what he hoped to know before long. On that depended the entire success of his endeavour.

One evening, after a warm day when the signs of the ice breaking up became all the more evident, he turned the conversation to this fascinating subject of the open sea.

He repeated the series of arguments so familiar to him; and, as always, found in the doctor a warm supporter of his doctrine. In any case, his conclusions were largely founded.

'It is obvious', he said, 'that if the ocean gets rid of its ice off Victoria Bay, its southern part will also be free as far as New Cornwall and Queen Channel. Penny and Belcher saw it in that state, and they saw it clearly.'

'I think as you do, Hatteras,' said the doctor, 'and we can't question the good faith of those illustrious sailors; people have tried to explain their discovery in terms of a mirage; but the two were so categorical that the fact must be certain.'

'I have always thought so,' said Altamont, speaking in turn; 'the polar basin stretches not only westwards, but eastwards.'

'That can indeed be assumed,' said Hatteras.

'That must be assumed,' said the American, 'for the same open sea captains Penny and Belcher saw near Grinnell Land was sighted by Morton, Kane's lieutenant, in the strait bearing that bold scientist's name!'*

'We are not on "Kane Sea",'* dryly replied Hatteras, 'and consequently we cannot confirm that fact.'

'It is supposable at least.'

'Certainly,' replied the doctor, who wanted to avoid a useless discussion. 'What Altamont thinks must be the case; unless the surrounding lands behave differently, the same effects are produced at the same latitudes. So I believe in the open sea eastwards as well as westwards.'

'In any case, what do we care!'

'I don't agree, Hatteras,' said the American, beginning to be upset at the captain's feigned indifference; 'it might be important for us.'

'And when, I beg you?'

'When we think about returning.'

'Returning! Who said anything about that?'

'Nobody,' replied Altamont, 'but in the end, we will have to stop somewhere, I imagine.'

'Where?'

For the first time the American was asked this question directly. The doctor would have given his right arm to halt the discussion at this point.

Altamont did not reply, so the captain repeated the question.

'*Where?*'

'Where we're going!' calmly replied the American.

'And who knows?' said the conciliatory doctor.

'So I think that if we want to take advantage of the polar basin to return, we can and should attempt to reach Kane Sea; it will lead us more directly to Baffin Bay.'

'You think so?' the captain said sarcastically.

'I think so, as I think that if ever these northern seas do become practicable, that route would be the most direct. Oh, Dr Kane's discovery was indeed a great one!'

'Really?' said Hatteras, biting his lip until it bled.

'Yes,' said the doctor, 'that cannot be denied; to each his due.'

'Without mentioning that before that celebrated sailor,' added the American obstinately, 'nobody had gone as far north.'

'I like to believe that the British are now one step ahead.'

'And the Americans?'

'The Americans?'

'So what am I?'

'You are,' replied Hatteras in a barely controlled voice, 'you are a man who claims to give the same share of glory to chance and science. Your American captain did get far north, but only by luck . . .'

'Luck! You dare to say that Kane's great discovery was not due to his energy and knowledge?'

'I say that Kane's name is not one to pronounce in a region made famous by the Parrys, the Franklins, the Rosses, the Belchers, the Pennys, in these seas which opened the Northwest Passage to the Briton McClure . . .'

'McClure,' sharply riposted the American, 'you cite that man, but you criticize the role of luck? Was it not luck alone that helped him?'

'No,' replied Hatteras, getting excited, 'no! It was his courage, his obstinacy at spending four winters in the midst of the ice.'

'He was trapped and couldn't go back, and in the end he abandoned his ship, the *Investigator*, to return to Britain!'

'My friends . . .'

'In any case, let's leave the man and look at the result. You speak of the Northwest Passage: well, that passage still has to be found!'

Hatteras jumped at this phrase; never had a more vexatious question emerged between two rival nationalities!

The doctor again tried to intervene.

'You're wrong, Altamont,' he said.

'No! In my opinion,' added the obstinate fellow, 'the Northwest Passage still has to be discovered, or sailed, if you prefer. McClure didn't sail it, and never, till this day, has a ship left the Bering Strait and arrived at Baffin Bay!'

The fact was true, in the absolute. How then could they reply to the American?

In the event, Hatteras stood up and said:

'I will not allow the glory of a British captain to be attacked in my presence!'

'You won't allow it!' replied the American, also getting up. 'But the facts are there, and your power cannot change them!'

'Sir!' said Hatteras, pale with anger.

'My friends,' said the doctor, 'a little calm when discussing a scientific point.'

The good Clawbonny did not want to engage a geographic discussion involving the hatred of an American and a Briton.

'I'll tell you the facts,' Hatteras said threateningly, no longer listening.

'And I will speak!' said the American.

Johnson and Bell did not know what attitude to take.

'Gentlemen!' said the doctor forcefully. 'You will allow me to speak! I must; the facts are known to me as well as to you, indeed better; and you will grant that I can speak of them impartially.'*

'Yes, yes!' said Bell and Johnson, worried where the discussion was going and creating a majority in the doctor's favour.

'Go on, Dr Clawbonny,' said Johnson, 'these gentlemen will listen to you, and that will instruct us all.'

'Speak then,' said the American.

Hatteras sat down again, making a sign of acquiescence and crossing his arms.

'I will tell you the whole truth, and you can correct me if I omit or change any facts.'

'We know you, Dr Clawbonny,' replied Bell; 'you can narrate without fear.'

'Here is the map of the polar seas,' said the doctor, who had got up to fetch the legal evidence; 'it'll be easy to follow McClure's navigation, and you can judge from all the facts.'

The doctor spread out on the table one of those excellent maps published by order of the Admiralty, which contained the most recent discoveries made in the Arctic regions; then he continued as follows:

'In 1848, as you know, two ships, the *Herald*, under Captain Kellett, and the *Plover*, under Captain Moore, were sent to the Bering Strait to try and find traces of Franklin; their searches were unsuccessful. In 1850 they were joined by McClure, commanding the *Investigator*, a ship on which he had just completed the campaign of 1849 under James Ross. He was followed by Captain Collinson, his superior, commanding the *Enterprise*; he went ahead and, upon reaching Bering Strait, declared that he would not wait any longer, that he would depart alone on his own responsibility; and—listen to me, Altamont—that he would find Franklin or the Passage.'*

Altamont showed neither agreement nor disagreement.

'On 5 August 1850, after communicating one last time with the *Plover*, McClure headed into the eastern seas, following a more or less unknown route; look, very few lands are indicated on this map. On 30 August, the young officer sighted Cape Bathurst; on 6 September, he discovered Baring Land, which he realized afterwards was part of Banks Land, then Prince Albert Land; next, he moved resolutely through the long strait separating these two large islands, which he named Prince of Wales Strait. Go through it in your imagination with the bold navigator! He hoped to come out in Melville Basin, which we crossed, and he was right to hope; but the ice at the end of the strait was an uncrossable barrier for him. So, prevented from advancing, McClure wintered from 1850 to 1851, and during that time he crossed the ice-field to see whether the strait connected with Melville Basin.'

'Yes,' said Altamont, 'but he didn't sail it.'

'Wait. During this wintering, McClure's officers searched the neighbouring coasts. Cresswell took Baring Land; Haswell, Prince Albert Land to the south; and Wynniatt,* Cape Walker to the north. In July, at the first thaws, McClure tried a second time to haul the *Investigator* into Melville Basin; he got within twenty miles—a mere twenty miles!—but the winds pushed him irresistibly south, without him being able to force the obstacle. Then he decided to go back down Prince of Wales Strait, around Banks Land, and try via the west what he could not via the east; so he tacked about; on the eighteenth he observed Cape Kellett, and on the nineteenth Prince Alfred Cape, two degrees higher; then, after a terrible battle with the icebergs, he got stuck in Banks Passage, at the entrance to that succession of straits which brings you back to Baffin Bay.'

'But he wasn't able to get through.'

'Again wait, and have McClure's patience. On 26 September, he prepared for wintering in Mercy Bay, north of Banks Land, and stayed there until 1852; April arrived; McClure only had supplies for eighteen months. Nevertheless, he decided not to head back; he crossed Banks Strait by sledge, and reached Melville Island. Let's follow him. He hoped to find on these coasts the ships that Captain Austin sent to meet him via Baffin Bay and Lancaster Sound; on 28 April, he reached the same Winter Harbour where Parry had wintered thirty-three years before. There were no ships; but in a cairn he discovered a document from which he learned that McClintock, Austin's lieutenant, had spent the previous year there, but had left again. Where another would have given up hope, McClure did not. He placed a new document in the cairn, just in case, where he announced his intention to go back to Britain via the Northwest Passage, which he found, reaching Lancaster Sound and Baffin Bay. If no more news was heard of him, this was probably because he was dragged north or west of Melville Island; then he came back, undiscouraged, for a third wintering in Mercy Bay, from 1852 to 1853.'

'I never doubted his courage, just his success.'

'Let's follow him further. In March, they were reduced to two-thirds rations, after a very hard winter in which game was absent. McClure decided to send half his crew back to Britain, either via Baffin Bay or the Mackenzie River and Hudson Bay; the other half were to take the *Investigator* back to Europe. He chose the weakest men, for whom a fourth wintering would have been fatal; everything was ready for departure, planned for 15 April, when on the sixth, walking on the ice with his lieutenant, Cresswell, McClure saw a man running from the north and waving his arms; this man was Lieutenant Pim from the *Herald*, the lieutenant of the same Captain Kellett whom he had left two years before on Bering Strait, as I mentioned at the beginning. Kellett had reached Winter Harbour, and found the document McClure left just in case; having learned in this way his position in Mercy Bay, he sent Lieutenant Pim* to meet the daring captain. The lieutenant was accompanied by a detachment of sailors from the *Herald*, amongst them a sub-lieutenant from a French vessel, M. de Bray,* serving as a volunteer on Captain Kellett's staff. You don't dispute this meeting between our compatriots?'

'Not at all.'

'Well, let's see what happens after that, and if the Northwest Passage was really done. Notice that if you connect Parry's discoveries with McClure's, you find that the northern coast of America has been gone around.'

'Not by a single ship.'

'No, but by a single man. Let's continue; McClure went to visit Captain Kellett on Melville Island; in twelve days he covered the 170 miles from Mercy Bay to Winter Harbour; he agreed with the commander of the *Herald* to transfer his sick to him, and came back on board; you might have thought that in McClure's situation he had done enough, but the intrepid young man wanted to tempt fate again. Then—and it is here that I request your attention—his Lieutenant Cresswell, accompanying the sick and wounded of the *Investigator*, left Mercy Bay, reached Winter Harbour, and, after a journey of 470 miles across the ice, arrived at Beechey Island on 2 June; a few days later, with twelve of his men, he went on board the *Phoenix*.'*

'Where I was serving, with Captain Inglefield,' said Johnson; 'then we went back to Britain.'

'And on 7 October 1853, Cresswell arrived in London, having covered the whole distance between Bering Strait and Cape Farewell.'

'Well,' said Hatteras, 'to have left from one coast and come out at the other, can that be called a "passage"?'

'But covering 470 miles over the ice.'

'What's the difference?'

'Everything. Did McClure's ship itself do the Passage?'

'No,' replied the doctor; 'after a fourth wintering, McClure had to abandon it in the ice.'

'Well, in a marine voyage it is the vessel and not the man that must pass. If ever the Northwest Passage is to be practicable, it must be by ship and not by sledge. In other words, the ship must accomplish the journey, or if not the ship, the launch.'

'The launch!' said Hatteras, who saw the evident intention in the American's words.

'Altamont,' the doctor said quickly, 'you're making a puerile distinction, and in this respect we must find you in the wrong.'*

'It's easy for you to say that: there are four of you against one. But that will not prevent me from keeping my opinion.'

'Keep it then,' exclaimed Hatteras, 'and keep it well, so we don't hear it any more!'

'And by what right do you speak to me in that manner?' said the American furiously.

'By my right as captain,' replied Hatteras angrily.

'Am I therefore under your orders?'

'Yes! And woe to you if . . .'

The doctor, Johnson, and Bell intervened. It was time; the two enemies were measuring each other up. The doctor felt heavy-hearted.

However, after a few conciliatory words, Altamont went to bed whistling the national anthem, 'Yankee Doodle',* and, asleep or not, said not a single word more.

Hatteras left the tent and strode about outside; he only came back an hour later, and went to bed without opening his mouth.

16

Northern Arcadia

ON 29 May, for the first time, the sun did not set; its disc skimmed the edge of the horizon, hardly grazing it, before rising; the period of twenty-four-hour days was beginning. The next day, the radiant body appeared surrounded by a magnificent halo, a luminous circle shining with all the colours of the rainbow; these frequent phenomena always caught the doctor's attention; he never forgot to note the date, the dimensions, and the appearance; the behaviour of the one he observed that day is still poorly understood, because of its elliptical form.

Soon the whole shrill race of birds reappeared; groups of bustards and flocks of Canada geese, coming from the far regions of Florida or Arkansas, were winging north at amazing speed, bringing the spring under their wings. The doctor was able to shoot a few, plus three or four early cranes and even a solitary stork.*

Meanwhile, the snow was melting everywhere because of the sun; salt water, spread over the ice-fields by crevasses and seal holes, speeded up the thaw; when mixed with sea-water, the ice formed a sort of dirty mixture called slush by the Arctic navigators. Broad ponds formed on the land near the bay, and the cleared ground seemed to be sprouting as if it were itself growing in the northern spring.

The doctor began his planting again; he had plenty of seeds; in addition, he was surprised to see a sort of sorrel pushing up naturally between the dry stones, and he admired this creative force of nature, which requires so little to show itself. He sowed some watercress, whose young shoots were already almost half an inch long three weeks later.

The heather was also beginning to timidly reveal its tiny flowers, of a faint pink bordering on the colourless, a pink in which a clumsy hand had put too much water.* All told, the flora of New America was not entirely satisfactory; however, this rare and timorous vegetation was a pleasure to behold; it was all that the weak rays of the sun could provide, a last memory of Providence, which had not completely forgotten these faraway lands.

Finally, it began to get really warm; on 15 June, the doctor noticed that the thermometer read fifty-seven (14°C); he didn't want to believe his eyes, but he had to accept the evidence; the landscape was being transformed; innumerable noisy waterfalls fell from every sun-caressed summit; the ice was breaking up, and the great question of the open sea was finally going to be settled. The air was filled with the sound of avalanches, tumbling down from the tops of the hills to the bottoms of the valleys, and the cracking of the ice-field added a deafening din.

They made an excursion as far as Johnson Island; it was really only an islet without importance, arid and deserted; but the old mate was no less delighted to have his name attached to a few rocks lost in the sea. He even wanted to engrave it on an elevated rock, and almost broke his neck doing so.

During these sorties, Hatteras had carefully surveyed the land past Cape Washington; the melting of the snow noticeably changed the landscape; valleys and hillsides appeared where the immense white carpet of winter had implied uniform plains.

The house and storehouses were in danger of melting, and often needed repair; fortunately, temperatures of fifty-seven degrees are rare at those latitudes, and the average is hardly above freezing point.

On 15 June, the launch was already well advanced and was shaping up well. While Bell and Johnson worked on it, a few big hunts were attempted, with some success. They managed to kill some reindeer; these animals are very difficult to approach; however, Altamont used the method of the Indians of his country; he crawled over the ground, with his gun and his arms arranged like the horns of one of those timid quadrupeds, and in this way, got within range and was able to hit them.

But the game par excellence—musk ox, of which Parry found numerous herds on Melville Island*—did not seem to dwell on the shores of Victoria Bay. So they decided to make a long excursion, both to hunt this precious animal and to reconnoitre the eastern lands. Hatteras was not proposing to head for the Pole via this part of the landmass, but the doctor was pleased to discover the general lay of the land. They accordingly decided to advance eastwards from Fort Providence. Altamont planned to hunt. Duke was naturally in the party.

So on Monday, 17 June, in fine weather, with the thermometer reading forty-one (5°C) and in a calm and clear air, Duke and the three huntsmen, each armed with a double-barrelled gun, a hatchet, and a snow knife, left Doctor's House at six in the morning; they were equipped for an excursion that might last two or three days, and thus carried a corresponding amount of food.

At eight, Hatteras and his two companions had covered about seven miles. Not a living being had come to seek gunshot from them, and their hunt was threatening to turn into a mere pleasure outing.

This new land revealed vast plains, stretching further than the eye could see; streams born yesterday crisscrossed it and many huge, motionless ponds and pools shimmered in the oblique sunshine. The melting of the ice layers meant their feet were walking directly on rock belonging to the great division of sedimentary terrains, produced by the action of water, a kind of rock that is widespread on the surface of the globe.

However, they saw a few erratic blocks of a very different nature from the ground beneath, whose presence was difficult to explain; and they also encountered slate-coloured shales, various products of limestone, and above all different sorts of transparent, colourless crystal, with a refraction similar to Icelandic spar.

Although they were not actively hunting, the doctor still did not have time to act as a geologist; he could only behave scientifically at a canter, for his companions walked quickly. Nevertheless, he did study the terrain all the while, and he spoke as much as possible, for without him an absolute silence would have sunk over the little group. Altamont had no wish to speak to the captain, who did not want to answer him.

At about ten, the huntsmen had gone about ten miles east; the sea was hidden below the horizon; the doctor proposed a halt for lunch. They ate quickly, and started off again after half an hour.

The ground was descending in gentle slopes; certain areas of snow, sheltered from the sun by the slope or the rocks, remained intact; they looked like white horses breaking on the open sea in a strong wind.

The land before them still had no vegetation at all, and it seemed that no living creature had ever lived there.

'Our hunts are not lucky,' Altamont said to the doctor; 'I admit this region has few resources for animals; but the game here in the north hasn't got the right to be difficult, and it should be more cooperative.'

'Let's not give up; summer has hardly begun, and if Parry found various animals on Melville Island there is no reason not to find some here.'

'Except that we're further north,' observed Hatteras.

'Yes, but north doesn't have much relevance here; it's the pole of cold we need to consider, that glacial immensity where we wintered on the *Forward*; as we continue, we're getting further away from the coldest part of the globe; so on this side we should find what Parry, Ross, and other navigators encountered on the other side.'

'Yes,' said Altamont with a sigh, 'but until then we're more like travellers than huntsmen!'

'Patience, the country around here is beginning to change, and I'll eat my hat if there's no game in valleys where vegetation has found some way to grow.'

'We should simply admit we're in a country that's completely uninhabited and completely uninhabitable.'

'Oh, completely uninhabitable is saying a great deal; I don't believe in uninhabitable lands; with sacrifice, after exhausting a few generations and using all the resources of agricultural science, man could fertilize such a country.'

'Do you think so?' said Altamont.

'Definitely! If you went to the celebrated first lands of the dawn of history, to the sites of Thebes and Nineveh and Babylon, to the fertile valleys of our forefathers, you would find it impossible to believe anyone could have lived there, for even the atmosphere has deteriorated since the humans disappeared. It's a general law of nature which renders unhealthy and sterile the lands where we have never lived or no longer live. So you must understand that it is man who makes the country habitable, by his presence, his habits, his industry, and even, I will say, by his breath. He gradually changes the exhalations of the ground and the atmospheric conditions, and he purifies things by the very act of breathing! So to say that there are uninhabited places is evident, but uninhabitable, never.'

While chatting, the huntsmen, now converted to naturalists, continued on their way, and reached a sort of vale, without surrounding hills, at the bottom of which snaked a more or less unfrozen river; because of its southerly exposure there grew some vegetation on the banks and a certain way up the slopes. The ground displayed a veritable desire to be fertilized; with a few inches of topsoil, it would have asked for nothing better than to produce. The doctor pointed out these manifest tendencies.

'Look, couldn't a few enterprising settlers settle this valley, if they had to? With hard work and perseverance, they would transform it; not to a temperate countryside—I wouldn't go so far—but at least a presentable patch of land. If I'm not mistaken, over there are even a few four-legged inhabitants! Such fellows know all the best places.'

'Goodness, they're polar hares!' exclaimed Altamont, loading his gun.

'Wait,' cried the doctor, 'wait, you crazy huntsman! The poor animals aren't about to flee. Come on, leave them be; let them come to us!'

In fact three or four young hares, gambolling in the thin heather and new moss, were approaching the three men, whose presence they did not fear; they ran up with beautiful naive airs, which hardly managed to disarm Altamont.

Soon they were between the doctor's legs, who stroked them saying:

'Why use shots for those who seek caresses? The death of these small creatures wouldn't serve us.'

'You're right,' replied Hatteras, 'their lives should be spared.'

'Like those of the ptarmigans flying towards us,' exclaimed Altamont, 'and the sandpipers advancing gravely on their long stilts.'

A whole feathered race was approaching the huntsmen, not suspecting the danger the doctor had averted. Even Duke, holding himself back, watched in admiration.

It was a curious and touching sight to see the pretty animals running, jumping, and leaping trustingly; they landed on the good Clawbonny's shoulders; they lay down at his feet; they spontaneously offered themselves to the unaccustomed caresses; they did their utmost to welcome the unknown guests; the many birds, joyously chirping, called to each other and came from all points of the valley; the doctor resembled a veritable charmer. The huntsmen continued their journey by climbing up the soggy banks of the stream, followed by this friendly group; and at a bend in the valley they spotted a herd of eight or ten reindeer, grazing on some lichen half-buried under the snow, charming animals to look upon, gracious and calm, the females bearing antlers as proudly as the males. Their woolly hides were already exchanging wintry whiteness for the brown and dull grey of summer; they appeared no more frightened and no less tame than the hares or birds of this peaceful country. Such must have been the relationship between the first man and the first animals when the world was young.*

The huntsmen arrived in the middle of the troop, without them having taken a single step to flee; this time, the doctor found it difficult to hold back Altamont's instincts; the American could not calmly contemplate this magnificent game without an intoxicating rush of blood to the brain. Moved, Hatteras gazed at these gentle creatures rubbing their nostrils on the doctor's clothes, the friend of all living creatures.

'But at the end of the day,' said Altamont, 'didn't we come to hunt?'

'Musk oxen, and nothing else!' retorted Clawbonny. 'We wouldn't know what to do with this game; we have enough supplies; let's just enjoy this touching sight of man mixing with the frolics of peaceful animals, and not causing them any fear.'

'This proves they have never seen us,' said Hatteras.

'Clearly,' replied the doctor, 'and it follows that these animals are not of American origin.'

'Why is that?' asked Altamont.

'Because if they were born in northern America, they would know what to think of that two-legged and two-handed mammal, and they would surely have fled when they saw us!

'They probably came from the north instead; they must originally be from those unknown lands of Asia humans have never reached, and have crossed the area around the Pole. It seems, Altamont, that you don't have the right to claim them as your countrymen.'

'Oh, a huntsman doesn't look twice at his prize, and game is always from the country of the person who kills it.'

'Come on, calm down, my good Nimrod!* For my part, I would rather give up shooting for the rest of my life than frighten these charming denizens. Look how Duke himself is fraternizing with these fine creatures. Believe me, let's be good while we can. Goodness is a strength!'

'Fine, fine!' said Altamont, who could hardly understand such sensitivity. 'But I would like to see you in a pack of bears and wolves with that goodness as your only weapon!'

'Oh, I do not claim to be a charmer of wild animals; I don't believe in the enchantments of Orpheus;* in any case, bears and wolves wouldn't come to us like the hares, partridges, and reindeer.'

'Why not, if they have never seen men?'

'Because such animals are naturally fierce, and fierceness—like nastiness—creates suspicion; it's an observation which people have made concerning men as well as animals. Nastiness leads to mistrust, and fear is easy for those who provoke it.'

And with this little lesson in natural philosophy, the discussion was closed.

The whole day was spent in this valley, that the doctor wanted to call Northern Arcadia, to which his companions agreed. In the evening, after a meal which had not cost the inhabitants of this country a single life, the three huntsmen fell asleep in a cavity of a rock, whose shape was custom built to offer them comfortable shelter.

17

Altamont's Revenge

THE following day, the doctor and his two companions woke after a night spent in the most perfect calm. The cold, without being keen, had stung them a little as morning rose; but, well covered, they slept deeply under the watch of the peaceful animals.

The weather remained fine, and so they decided to spend another day reconnoitring the land and searching for musk oxen. They had to give Altamont some chance of hunting, and it was decided that even if these oxen were the most naive animals in the world, he would have the right to shoot them. In any case, their flesh, although tasting strongly of musk, is good to eat, and the huntsmen wanted to take a few pieces of fresh meat back to Fort Providence.

The journey offered little in the early hours of the morning; the countryside to the north-east began to change; a few rises in the ground, the first undulations of hilly country, seemed to be the forerunners of a different kind of terrain. If New America was not a continent, it had at least to be a large island; but they were not there to check this geographical point.

Duke was running in the far distance, but stood stock still upon discovering the tracks of a herd of musk oxen; then he shot ahead very quickly, and soon disappeared from view.

The men followed his clear and distinct barks, whose excitement told them the faithful dog had finally found the object of their desire.

They rushed forward, and after an hour and a half, found themselves in the presence of two animals, bigger than expected and of frightening appearance; these remarkable quadrupeds appeared astonished by Duke's attacks, but did not seem fearful; they were grazing on a sort of pink moss which carpeted the snow-free ground. The doctor identified them easily from their modest height, broad horns joined at the base, curious lack of muzzle, Roman nose like that of sheep, and very short tail: all these features have led natural- ists to call them 'ovibos',* a compound word from the two sorts of animals they look like. They had coarse long hair and a hide of fine brown silk. The two animals ran away on seeing the huntsmen, who pursued them as fast as their legs could take them.

But getting close was difficult for people completely out of breath after a sustained run of half an hour.* Hatteras and his companions stopped.

'Hell!' said Altamont.

'Hell is right,' replied the doctor as soon as he had caught his breath. 'I'd bet those ruminants are American, and have a poor opinion of your countrymen.'

'Which proves we're good hunters.'

However, the musk oxen, seeing they were no longer pursued, stopped in an astonished posture. It was clear that they could not be caught by running; they needed therefore to be surrounded; the plateau they were on suited this manoeuvre. The huntsmen, leaving Duke to harry the prey, descended into the neighbouring valleys so as to get to the far side of the plateau. Altamont and the doctor hid near one of its sides, behind some jutting rocks, while Hatteras, moving to surprise them from the opposite direction, was to drive the pair towards them.

After half an hour, each was at his post.

'You have no objection this time to greeting these quadrupeds with gunfire?' enquired Altamont.

'All's fair in love and war,' replied the doctor, who despite his natural gentleness was a huntsman to the depths of his soul.

They were still chatting when they saw the musk oxen starting to move off, Duke at their heels; further on, Hatteras was shouting loudly, driving them towards the doctor and the American, who soon rushed to meet this magnificent prey.

The oxen immediately stopped and, less frightened by the sight of a single enemy, went back towards Hatteras; the captain waited for them without flinching; he aimed at the closer one and fired, but, although the bullet hit it in the middle of the forehead, it did not slow down. Hatteras's second shot had no other effect than to enrage the animals; they galloped at the disarmed huntsman and knocked him down.

'He's done for!' exclaimed the doctor.

While Clawbonny was pronouncing these words in a despairing tone, Altamont took a first step forward to go and help Hatteras; then he stopped, fighting himself and his prejudices.

No, he exclaimed, that would be cowardice!

And he rushed to the scene of the combat with Clawbonny.

His hesitation had lasted less than half a second.

The doctor perhaps saw what was happening in the American's soul; but Hatteras understood it all too well, although he would have preferred to die rather than beg his rival to intervene. Nevertheless, he barely had time to realize before Altamont arrived.

The captain was lying on the ground, trying to fend off the attacks from the horns and feet* of the two animals; but he could not continue such a battle for long.

He was inevitably going to be cut to pieces, when two shots rang out; Hatteras felt the shots skim past his head.

'Hold on!' exclaimed Altamont, throwing away his empty gun, and charging the enraged animals.

One of the oxen was struck to the heart, and fell down dead; the other, at the height of fury, was about to disembowel the unfortunate captain, when Altamont stood in front and plunged his hand and snow knife through its open jaws; with his other, he split open its head with a terrible axe blow.*

This all happened with marvellous swiftness, and a lightning bolt would have lasted long enough to illuminate the whole scene.

The second ox bent its knees, and fell down dead.

'Hurray, hurray!' shouted Clawbonny.

Hatteras was saved.

So he owed his life to the man he detested the most in the world! What passed through his mind at that moment? What human emotion, beyond his control, transpired?

That is one of the secrets of the heart which escape all analysis.

Be that as it may, Hatteras went up to his rival without hesitation and gravely said to him:

'You saved my life, Altamont.'

'You saved mine.'

There was a moment's silence, then Altamont added:

'We're quits, Hatteras.'

'No, Altamont; when the doctor rescued you from your ice grave, I did not know who you were, but you risked your life to save me, knowing who I am.'

'You're my fellow human being, and whatever his feelings, an American is not a coward!'

'No, certainly!' exclaimed the doctor. 'He's a man like you, Hatteras.'

'And, like me, he will share the glory we're going to achieve.'

'The glory of going to the North Pole!' said Altamont.

'Yes!' said the captain proudly.

'I'd guessed! So you dared to plan such an expedition! You dared to head for that inaccessible point! Ah, that's good! It's sublime, I tell you!'

'But what about you?' asked Hatteras keenly. 'You weren't heading for the Pole, like us?'

Altamont seemed to hesitate.

'Well?' asked the doctor.

'Well, no! The truth before self-interest! I did not have that glorious idea which brought you here. I was trying to sail the Northwest Passage, that's all.'

'Altamont,' said Hatteras, stretching his hand out to the American, 'be our companion in glory, and come with us to the North Pole!'

The two men warmly shook each other's frank and loyal hand.

When they turned back to the doctor, Clawbonny was weeping.

'Ah, my friends!' he murmured, wiping his eyes. 'How can my heart hold the joy you fill it with! My dear companions! You've sacrificed that miserable question of nationality to join together for common success! You've shown that Britain and America are irrelevant in all this, and that the dangers of our expedition will bring us together! If the North Pole is reached, it doesn't matter who discovers it. Why lower oneself to taking pride from being American or British, when you can boast of being men!'

The good doctor clasped the two former enemies to his heart; he could not calm his joy; the two new friends felt themselves still closer because of the friendship the worthy man bore them. Unable to restrain himself, Clawbonny was speaking of the vanity of competition, the folly of rivalry, the concord so necessary for men abandoned far from their countries. His words, his tears, his embraces—everything came from the bottom of his heart.

However, he did calm down after embracing Hatteras and Altamont for the twentieth time.

'And now,' he said, 'to work! To work! Since I was useless* as a huntsman, let's employ my other talents.'

And he began to cut up the animal, which he called 'the ox of reconciliation', so skilfully that he resembled a surgeon practising a delicate autopsy.*

His two companions watched him, smiling.* After a few minutes, the dextrous practitioner had taken a hundred-odd pounds of appetizing flesh from the animals; he divided it into three, each man took one, and they set off back for Fort Providence.*

At ten o'clock, walking in the oblique rays of the sun, the hunters reached Doctor's House, where Johnson and Bell had prepared a good meal.

But before sitting down, the doctor exclaimed triumphantly while indicating his two hunting companions:

'My old Johnson, I took with me a Briton and an American, didn't I?'

'You certainly did, Dr Clawbonny.'

'Well I've brought back two brothers!'*

The two sailors joyously stretched their hands out to Altamont; the doctor told them what the American captain had done for the British captain, and that night the snow-house held five perfectly happy men.*

18

Final Preparations

THE following day, the weather changed; the cold came back; snow, rain, and wind alternated for several days.

Bell had finished his launch; it perfectly suited its purpose; partly decked over, with a high board, it could fight the sea in rough weather with its foresail and jib; its lightness allowed it to be carried on the sledge without adding too much to the dogs' burden.

Finally, a change of momentous importance came to the polar basin. The ice was beginning to move in the middle of the bay; the tallest parts, constantly undermined by collisions, merely required a strong enough storm to tear themselves from the shore and form icebergs. However, Hatteras did not want to wait for the break-up of the ice-field to begin his journey. Since it was to be over land, he did not care whether the sea was free; so he fixed the departure for 25 June; before then, all preparations had to be finished. Johnson and Bell busied themselves making sure the sledge was in perfect condition; the chassis was reinforced and the runners replaced. The travellers planned to profit from the few weeks of fine weather nature grants to the hyperboreal regions. Enduring the suffering would be less cruel, overcoming the obstacles, easier.*

On 20 June, a few days before the departure, the ice contained a few free passes, which they used to try out the launch on a trip to Cape Washington. The sea was not entirely free, far from it; but at least it no longer presented a solid surface; and it would have been impossible to cross the broken ice-fields on foot.

This half-day of navigation allowed them to appreciate the launch's excellent nautical qualities.*

As they returned, the navigators witnessed a curious incident. A gigantic bear was hunting a seal; the bear was fortunately too busy to see the launch, for it would surely have pursued it; it remained on the lookout beside a gap in the ice-field, through which the seal had clearly dived. The bear was watching for it to reappear with a huntsman's patience, or rather a fisherman's—for it really was fishing. It lay in wait in silence; it did not move; it gave no sign of life.

But suddenly the surface of the water moved; the amphibian was coming up to breathe; the bear lay down flat on the icy field, and stretched its two arms around the hole.

A moment later, the seal's head popped out; but it had no time to dive back down again; the bear's paws, as if uncoiled by a spring, snapped together, embraced the animal with irresistible strength, and lifted it out of its natural element.

It was a quick battle; the seal struggled for a few seconds, but was suffocated by the breast of its gigantic adversary; the bear carried it without difficulty, despite its size; and jumping lightly from one floe to another, it reached dry land, and disappeared with its prey.

'*Bon voyage!*' Johnson shouted after it. 'That bear has too many paws for my liking.'

The launch soon returned to the little cove Bell had built in the ice.

There were still four more days before Hatteras and his companions were due to leave.

Hatteras speeded up the final preparations; he was in a hurry to quit this New America, this land he hadn't named; he didn't feel at home.

On 22 June, they began to put the tent, the camping equipment, and the provisions on the sledge. The travellers were taking 200 pounds of salted meat, three boxes of vegetables and preserved meat, fifty pounds of brine and lime juice, five quarters* of flour, and packs of watercress and Cochlearia from the doctor's seedbeds; adding to that 200 pounds of powder, the instruments, the guns, and miscellaneous items, plus the launch, the Halkett boat, and the sledge itself, it was a total weight of nearly fifteen hundred pounds to pull—a great deal for four dogs, especially since, unlike the Eskimos who do not usually make them work more than four days running, these ones would have to pull every day, not having any replacements; but the travellers promised to help when necessary, and planned to march only short days; the distance from Victoria Bay to the Pole was 355 miles at most, and at twelve miles a day, a month was needed; also if there was no land, the launch would enable the journey to be continued without fatigue for the dogs or the men.

All five were well; their health was excellent; the winter, although hard, was ending in conditions suitable for well-being; with advice from the doctor, all had avoided the illnesses endemic in these hard climates. Admittedly they had lost a little weight, which delighted the good Clawbonny; but in body and soul they had got used to this rough existence, and now these acclimatized men could face the most brutal tests of fatigue and cold without giving in.

Finally they were going to march towards the aim of their journey, the unreachable Pole, after which they only had the question of the return to deal with. The friendship which now united the expedition would surely help them to succeed in their audacious journey, and no one doubted the success of their endeavour.

In preparation for a long expedition, the doctor had recommended that his companions prepare themselves long before, and train with the greatest care.

'My friends,' he said, 'I'm not asking you to imitate the British runners who lost eighteen pounds in two days' training and twenty-five in five days'; but we do need to do something to get us in the best possible condition for a long journey. Now the first principle of training is to get rid of fat, rather like jockeys do, by means of purgative sweating and hard exercise; those gentlemen know how much medicine will make them lose, and they get incredibly accurate results; thus one man, who before the training could not run a single mile without getting out of breath, easily did twenty-five after! A certain man named Townsend did 100 miles in twelve hours without stopping.'

'A fine result, and although we're not very fat, if we still need to lose weight . . .'

'Unnecessary, Johnson; but without exaggeration, it is clear that training has good effects; it gives stronger, more elastic muscles, better hearing, and clearer sight; so let's remember.'

In the end, whether trained or not, the travellers were ready by 23 June; it was a Sunday and so completely devoted to rest.

The time arrived for leaving the hospitable beach where they had spent the last few months of the wintering, and the inhabitants of Fort Providence felt a certain emotion. They were upset to be leaving the snow-house which had lodged them so well, Victoria Bay. Would they find the buildings still there when they got back? Would the sunlight complete its destruction of these fragile walls?

In sum, the time spent there had been good. At dinner, the doctor reminded his companions of these touching memories, and he did not forget to thank Heaven for its visible protection.

Finally it was time to sleep. All went to bed early, so as to be up even earlier. Thus passed the last night spent in Fort Providence.

19

Northwards March

THE following day, at dawn, Hatteras gave the signal to leave. The dogs were harnessed to the sledge; well fed and rested after a winter spent in very comfortable conditions, they had no reason not to give fine service during the summer. So they did not need to be asked twice to put on their travelling harness.

The Greenland dogs were fine animals, after all; their savage nature had slowly been educated; they were losing their resemblance to wolves, and approaching Duke, the accomplished model of the canine race; in a word, they were becoming civilized.

Duke could certainly ask to help with their education; he had given them lessons in good society, and preached by example; in his capacity as a Briton, attaching great importance to the question of cant,* he took a long time to familiarize himself with these dogs 'who had not been introduced to him', and did not speak to them on principle; but, by sharing the same dangers, shortages, and destiny, these animals of different races gradually came to intermix. Duke had a good heart, and made the first steps, and the whole four-legged race soon became a band of brothers.

The doctor patted the Greenlanders, and Duke watched the pats given to his congeners without jealousy.

The men's condition was as good as the animals'; if the dogs were going to pull strongly, their companions would march correspondingly.

They left at six, in fine weather; after following the edge of the bay and passing Cape Washington, Hatteras set a course due north; at seven, the travellers lost sight of the cone of the beacon and Fort Providence in the south.

The journey was just starting, and conditions were much better than those for the midwinter expedition to fetch coal! That time, Hatteras had to leave mutiny and despair on his ship, without being certain of the purpose he was aiming for; he had abandoned a crew half-dead with cold, companions weakened by the miseries of an Arctic winter; he, the man of the north, had headed south! Now in contrast, he was surrounded by vigorous friends in good health, and thus supported and encouraged, he was heading for the Pole—the aim of his entire life! Never had a man been nearer to acquiring tremendous glory for his country and himself.

Did he think about all these questions, so naturally generated by the present situation? The doctor liked to think so, and could hardly doubt it on seeing him so ardent. The good Clawbonny took pleasure from what surely pleased his friend, and after the reconciliation of the two captains—of his two friends—he found himself the happiest

of men, to whom ideas of hate or rivalry were foreign, he the best of
creatures! What would happen? What would come from this journey? He did not know; but at least it was beginning well. That was
already a great deal.

The coast of New America stretched westwards, and consisted of
a succession of bays beyond Cape Washington; the travellers decided
to head north after crossing the first slopes of Mount Bell, following
the other plateau, so as to avoid a huge curve. This saved them
considerable distance; unless unforeseen obstacles of strait or mountain stopped him, Hatteras wanted to describe a straight line
350 miles long from Fort Providence to the Pole.

The journey was easy; the high plains offered immense white
carpets on which the sledge slid easily on its sulphured runners; and
with their snow shoes the men found a sure and quick footing.

The thermometer read thirty-seven (3°C). The weather seemed a
little changeable, sometimes clear and sometimes cloudy; but neither
the cold nor the wind could have stopped travellers so determined to
press ahead.

The route could easily be determined with the compass; the
needle was getting less lazy as it moved away from the Magnetic
Pole; it no longer hesitated; it was true that having gone past the
magnetic point, it pointed back at it, and indicated south to men who
were walking northwards; but this inverted indication did not necessitate any awkward calculations.

In any case the doctor invented a very simple marker method,
which meant that constant recourse to the compass was no longer
necessary; once the position had been established, the travellers
would identify in clear weather an object situated due north, two or
three miles ahead; then they walked towards it until they reached it;
upon which they chose another reference point in the same direction, and so on. In this way, they deviated little from the correct
path.

The first two days of the journey, they walked at a speed of twenty
miles in twelve hours; the rest of the time was devoted to meals and
rest; the tent was enough to protect them from the cold during their
hours of sleep.

The temperature was rising; the snow was melting entirely in
places, following the vagaries of the ground, while other parts kept
their immaculate whiteness; large ponds of water formed here and

there, often real pools that might have been taken for lakes, with a little imagination; sometimes the travellers stepped knee-deep into them; this amused them greatly; the doctor was happy at these unexpected bathes.

'Water isn't allowed to wet us in this country,' he said; 'this element only has the right to be solid or gas; its liquid state is an abuse! Ice or water vapour is all right, but water—never!'

Hunting was not forgotten during the march, for it would provide fresh food; so Altamont and Bell, without going too far, hunted in the neighbouring valleys; they forced out ptarmigans, guillemot geese, and a few grey hares; these animals were slowly changing from confidence to fear; they were becoming very shy, and very difficult to approach. Without Duke, the hunters would often have wasted their powder.

Hatteras advised them not to go more than a mile away, for he had not a day or an hour to waste, being able to count on only three months of good weather.

In any case, each needed to be at his position near the sledge when it reached a difficult part, like some narrow gorge or inclined plateau; each then harnessed himself, or leaned against the vehicle, pulling, pushing, or lifting; more than once they had to entirely unload it, and that still did not prevent crashes and consequently damage, which Bell repaired as best he could.

On the third day, Wednesday, 26 June, the travellers found a lake several acres in extent and still completely covered by ice, due to its shape and lade of exposure to the sun; the ice was even strong enough to bear the weight of the travellers and the sledge. This ice seemed to date from a far-off winter, for the lake's position meant it had probably never thawed; it was a small mirror on which the Arctic summers had no effect; what seemed to confirm this idea was that dry snow was built up around it, the lower layers of which certainly belonged to previous years.

From that moment on, the countryside began to drop perceptibly, from which the doctor concluded that it could not stretch very far northwards; in any case, it was probable that New America was only an island, and did not continue as far as the Pole. The ground gradually grew flatter; to the west, a few hills, flattened by distance, bathed in a bluish mist.

Until then, the expedition had not caused any fatigue; the travellers only suffered from the reflection of the sunlight; this intense reflection could give them snow-blindness, and was impossible to avoid. At any other time they would have travelled at night to avoid the problem; but there was now no night. Fortunately, the snow was melting, and lost a great deal of its brilliance when about to turn into water.

On 28 June it went up to forty-five (7°C); this rise was accompanied by abundant rain, which the travellers accepted philosophically, even with pleasure; it speeded up the melting of the snow; but they had to put their deerskin moccasins back on, and change the method of the sledge's sliding. Progress was undoubtedly slower; but given that there were no serious obstacles, they still moved ahead.

Sometimes the doctor picked up round or flat stones on his path, like pebbles smoothed by the sea, and then he thought he was near the polar basin; however the plain stretched forward endlessly, as far as the eye could see.

There was no sign of habitation; no cairns, no Eskimo caches; the travellers were clearly the first to tread this new land; the Greenland tribes that haunt Arctic lands had never got this far, and yet hunting here would have been profitable for those perpetually starving wretches; they sometimes saw bears, following the little troop downwind without showing signs of attacking; in the distance, numerous herds of musk oxen and reindeer appeared; the doctor would very much have liked to catch some of the latter to add to his team; but they were very shy and impossible to take alive.

On the twenty-ninth, Bell killed a fox and Altamont was lucky enough to shoot a musk ox of average size, showing his companions how much self-control and skill he had; he was really a marvellous huntsman, and the doctor, who was an expert, greatly admired him. The ox was cut into pieces, and provided abundant fresh food.

Such opportunities for good and succulent meals were always well received; the least greedy could not help glancing satisfiedly at the slices of naked flesh. Even the doctor himself laughed when he caught himself in ecstasy at the sight of such rich meat.

'Let's not be afraid to eat our fill,' he said; 'meals are important on polar expeditions.'

'Especially', replied Johnson, 'when they depend on skill with a gun!'

'Definitely,' said the doctor. 'You think much less about eating when you know there's a stew simmering on the kitchen range.'

On the thirtieth, the countryside, contrary to their expectations, became very uneven, as if it lifted up by some volcanic upheaval; cones and sharp peaks multiplied indefinitely, reaching great heights.

A south-east wind began to blow strongly, and soon turned into a real storm; it plunged between the crowned snow-capped rocks and through the ice mountains, which on dry land became hummocks and icebergs; their presence on these high plateaux remained inexplicable, even to the doctor, who nevertheless explained everything.

After the storm came warm wet weather; it was a real thaw; the cracking of ice sounded from all sides, mixing with the more imposing noise of avalanches.

The travellers carefully avoided following the bases of the hills, or even speaking loudly; the sound of a voice could produce catastrophes, merely by shaking the air; they often witnessed terrible falls that they would not have had the time to avoid; in fact, the principal characteristic of polar avalanches is a frightening instantaneity; in that they are different from those of Switzerland and Norway; in those countries a ball forms, at first small, which picks up snow and rocks on its way, descends with increasing speed, destroys forests and flattens villages, but at least requires some time to come crashing down; in the lands of the Arctic cold, things happen differently; the movement of a block of ice is without warning and dazzlingly quick; its arrival is simultaneous with its departure, and anyone in its line of fall who sees it wobbling will inevitably be crushed by it; a cannon ball is not quicker, nor lightning more prompt; the movement, the detaching, and the crushing impact are simultaneous for an avalanche of the northern lands, and all that with a frightening rumbling noise like thunder and strange reverberation and echoes more plaintive than they are loud.

So sometimes real changes in the view happened before the very eyes of the stupefied watchers; the land metamorphosed; a mountain became a plain due to a sudden thaw; when water from the sky got into cracks between great blocks and froze in the cold of a single night, its irresistible expansion could break any obstacle, water becoming a more powerful force when it turns into ice than into water vapour, and this phenomenon happened with frightening instantaneity.

Fortunately, no accident beset the sledge and its drivers; by taking precautions, they avoided all danger. In any case, though it bristled with crests, foothills, rumps, and icebergs, this land did not stretch very far; and three days later, on 3 July, the travellers found easier going, on plains.

But then they were surprised by a new phenomenon, one which for a long time stimulated the patient research of scientists in Europe and America; the little troop was following a chain of hills which seemed to stretch for several miles, each fifty feet high at the most; their eastern slopes were covered with snow, but a snow that was entirely red.

Imagine the group's surprise, their gasps, and even the first stirrings of fear as they confronted this crimson snow bank. Dr Clawbonny hastened to reassure and instruct his companions. He had heard of this strange red snow, and of the chemical analyses done upon it by Wollaston, de Candolle, and Bauer. He explained that this snow was found not only in the Arctic, but in Switzerland, in the middle of the Alps. De Saussure had collected a sizeable quantity of it on Le Breven in 1760, and since that time Captains Ross* and Sabine and other navigators have reported it on their northern expeditions.

Altamont asked the doctor what this extraordinary substance was. The latter explained that the coloration was due to the presence of organic corpuscles. For a long time, scientists wondered if these corpuscles were animal or vegetable. But they finally decided that they belonged to a species of microscopic mushrooms, of the genus *Uredo*, which Bauer called *Uredo nivalis*.

Then the doctor, testing this snow with his eye and his stick, showed his companions that the scarlet layer was nine feet thick, and he asked them to calculate how many mushrooms there could be in an area of several miles, given that scientists have counted as many as 43,000 in a square centimetre.

Its coloration, given the shape of the slope, had to have been there for an extremely long time, for these mushrooms do not decompose, either in evaporation or during the snowmelt, and their colour does not change.

The phenomenon, although explained, was no less strange; red is not common in large stretches in nature; the reflection of the sunlight on this purple carpet produced strange effects; it gave the surrounding objects, the rocks, the men, and the animals, an inflamed colour, as if they had been lit by a blaze within, and when this snow melted, it seemed that rivers of blood were flowing under the travellers' feet.

The doctor, who had been unable to examine the substance when he saw it at the crimson cliffs in Baffin Bay, now took as much as he wanted, gathering several precious bottles' worth.

This red ground, this field of blood as he called it, carried on for three hours' march, and only then did the countryside return to its usual appearance.

20

Footprints in the Snow

THERE was thick fog throughout 4 July. The route north could only be maintained with the greatest difficulty; the compass had continually to be corrected. Fortunately no accident happened in the gloom; but Bell did lose his snow shoes when they broke on a projecting rock.

'Goodness,' said Johnson, 'I thought that after the Mersey and the Thames we knew all about fog, but I guess I was wrong!'

'So then,' replied Bell, 'we should light our torches, like in London or Liverpool.'

'Why not,' said the doctor; 'it's an idea; we wouldn't light our route very much, but at least we'd see the man in front, and could find our way more easily.'

'But where are we going to get torches?' asked Bell.

'Using oakum soaked in spirits of wine and nailed to the ends of our sticks.'

'Good idea,' replied Johnson, 'and it won't take too long.'

A quarter of an hour later, the little troop started off again, torches held aloft in the damp darkness.

But though they now moved straighter, they went no quicker, and the impenetrable fog did not dissipate until 6 July; then the ground cooled, and a gust of wind from the north carried it off like the shreds of a piece of clothing.

Straightaway the doctor calculated the position, and deduced that they had covered less than eight miles a day in the mist.

So on the sixth, the travellers made up for lost time, by starting earlier in the morning. Altamont and Bell again took up position at the head, testing the terrain and getting wind of game; Duke accompanied them; the weather, with its astonishing changeability, had become very clear and dry again, and although the pair were two miles from the sledge, the doctor could see their every movement.

He was accordingly amazed to see them stop all of a sudden, in positions of stupefaction; they seemed to be carefully studying the distance, like people interrogating the horizon.

Then, leaning over, they examined the ground with great concentration and stood up in surprise. Bell even seemed to want to move ahead; but Altamont held him back.

'Aha! What can they be doing?' the doctor asked Johnson.

'I'm looking at them like you, Dr Clawbonny, but I can't understand anything from their gestures.'

'They've found animal tracks,' said Hatteras.

'That's not possible,' said the doctor.

'Why?'

'Because Duke would be barking.'

'And yet they're looking at footprints.'

'Let's continue,' said Hatteras, 'we'll soon know what's happening.'

Johnson spurred the dog team on.

Twenty minutes later, the five travellers were together again, with Hatteras, the doctor, and Johnson sharing Bell and Altamont's surprise.

Tracks of men, visible, unmistakable, and fresh as if made the day before, stretched out over the snow.

'Eskimos,' said Hatteras.

'Yes,' replied the doctor, 'they're the marks of their snow shoes.'

'Do you think so?' said Altamont.

'I'm positive.'

'Well then, what about these?' said Altamont, pointing to another set of footprints.

'What about them?'

'Do you still say it's an Eskimo's?'

The doctor looked more carefully, and was flabbergasted; the outline of a European shoe, with its nails, sole, and heel, was deeply marked on the snow; there could be no doubt about it; a man, a foreigner, had passed this way.

'Europeans here!' said Hatteras.

'Clearly,' said Johnson.

'And yet', said the doctor, 'it's so unlikely that we need to look again before deciding.'

So the doctor examined the footprints twice, even three times, and was obliged to admit their extraordinary nature.

Daniel Defoe's hero could not have been more surprised when he found a footprint on the shore of his island;* but what he felt was fear, whereas Hatteras felt disappointment. A European so near the Pole!

They moved off further to study the tracks, which continued for a quarter of a mile, mixed with other tracks of snow shoes and moccasins, and then turned west.

Having reached this point, the travellers wondered if they should follow them any further.

'No,' replied Hatteras, 'let's go . . .'

He was interrupted by an exclamation from the doctor, who had just picked up from the snow a still more convincing object, whose origin was absolutely clear. It was a lens from a pocket telescope.

'This time,' he said, 'there can be no doubt whatsoever that a foreigner is present on this land!'

'Forward!' exclaimed Hatteras.

And he said this word so energetically that all followed him; the sledge started off again.

Everyone was studying the horizon, except Hatteras, who was full of a dull anger and blind to everything. All the same, as they ran the risk of meeting a team of travellers, they had to take some precautions; it was terrible luck to find they were not the first to tread this unknown land! The doctor, without experiencing Hatteras's anger, could not help feeling disappointed, in spite of his natural philosophy. Altamont seemed equally annoyed; Johnson and Bell grumbled threatening words through clenched teeth.

'Come on,' said the doctor, 'let's show what sort of stuff we're made of.'

'It must be admitted', added Johnson without Altamont being able to hear him, 'that if we found sitting tenants it'd make us want to give up on the Pole!'

'And yet', said Bell, 'the thing is absolutely clear.'

'Yes,' replied the doctor; 'I've tried everything—looking at the adventure from all angles, telling myself it's improbable, or impossible—but we do need to accept it; the prints in the snow did not get there without being on the ends of legs, nor without those legs being attached to a human body. Eskimos I would forgive, but a European!'

'The fact is', said Johnson, 'that if we were to find the beds full at the inn of the end of the world, it would be most annoying.'

'Extremely,' said Altamont.

'We'll see in the end,' said the doctor.

And they headed off again.*

That day finished without anything new to confirm the presence of foreigners on this part of New America, and so they set up evening camp.

The wind had swung north, and become stronger; so they had to look for a valley for protection for the tent; the sky was turning threatening. Elongated clouds were racing through the air; they skimmed quite close to the ground, and were difficult to follow in their mad course; sometimes shreds of the vapours trailed to the ground, and the tent held against the storm only with the greatest of difficulty.

'A nasty night we're in for,' said Johnson after supper.

'It won't be cold, but it'll be noisy,' said the doctor; 'let's be careful and weigh the tent down with large stones.'

'You're right; if we lost our canvas to the storm, God knows where we'd find it again.'

So the tired travellers took every precaution against the danger, and then they tried to sleep.

But that was impossible; the storm had broken, and was rushing northwards with incomparable force; the clouds spread out like steam from a boiler which had just exploded; the last avalanches caused by the storm were falling into the ravines, and their echoes rang out continuously; the atmosphere resembled the scene of a tremendous battle between air and water, two formidable elements when they are angry, with only fire absent from the fight.

The travellers' over-excited ears perceived particular noises amongst the general roar, not the hubbub which marks the fall of heavy bodies, but the clear cracking of bodies breaking; plus a distinct and unmistakable sound, like that of steel snapping, in the midst of the longer rolling of the storm.

The latter could be explained easily by the avalanches, twisted by the whirlwinds, but the doctor did not know what to attribute the former to.

Taking advantage of the moments of anxious silence, during which the storm seemed to catch its breath before becoming stronger still, the travellers discussed what it could be.

'It must be things hitting,' said the doctor, 'like icebergs or ice-fields coming together.'

'Yes,' said Altamont, 'it's as if the earth's crust was disintegrating. Did you hear that one?'

'If we were near the sea, I would really think it was ice breaking up.'

'Agreed,' said Johnson; 'those noises cannot be explained any other way.'

'Have we finally got to the coast then?' said Hatteras.

'Quite possibly,' said the doctor.

'Look,' he added, after a deafening cracking noise, 'wouldn't you say that was an ice floe breaking up? We might easily be very close to the ocean.'

'If we are, I shall not hesitate to head over the ice-fields.'

'But they're surely in pieces after such a storm,' said the doctor. 'We'll just have to see tomorrow; but if some troop of men is really travelling on such a night, I pity them from the bottom of my heart.'

The storm lasted nearly ten hours, with none of the occupants of the tent sleeping a single wink; the night was spent amidst great anxiety.

In such circumstances, any new incident—a storm or an avalanche—might produce serious delays. The doctor would have liked to go out to check on things; but how to venture out in these unleashed winds?

Fortunately, the storm died down in the early morning; they were finally able to leave the tent, which had valiantly resisted; the doctor, Hatteras, and Johnson headed for a hill of about three hundred feet; they climbed it quite easily.

Their eyes ranged over a changed landscape, made of rocks and ridges entirely free of ice. It was as if summer had suddenly replaced winter blown away by the wind; the snow, cut like a sharp blade by the storm, had not had time to change into water, and the ground appeared with all its original harshness.

But Hatteras's eyes quickly turned north. The distant horizon seemed to be covered in dark mist.

'That could easily be the ocean,' said the doctor.

'You're right, the sea must be there.'

'That colour is what we call the "blink" of the open sea,' said Johnson.

'Exactly.'

'To the sledge!' cried Hatteras. 'And let's head for the new ocean!'

'It's brought joy to your heart,' Clawbonny said to the captain.

'Certainly!' he replied enthusiastically. 'Soon we will be at the Pole! And, my good doctor, doesn't that idea make you happy as well?'

'I'm always happy, especially at the happiness of others!'*

The three Britons returned to the valley, and once the sledge was ready, they struck camp. They set off, fearing to find tracks like the day before; but for the rest of the way, not a trace of foreign or indigenous feet was seen on the ground. Three hours later they reached the coast.

'The sea! The sea!' they said in unison.

'The open sea!' exclaimed the captain.

It was ten in the morning.

The storm had in effect removed everything from the polar basin; the ice, cracked and broken up, was moving off in all directions; the largest pieces, forming icebergs, had just raised anchor, as the maritime expression has it, and were sailing over the open sea. The field had suffered from the attack of the wind; a hail of thin blades, barbs, and ice dust covered the rocks nearby. The little which remained of the ice-field, on the shoulder of the shore, was crumbling; on the rocks, where the waves were breaking, were stretched out large pieces of seaweed and clumps of a pale varec.

The ocean stretched further than the eye could see, without any island or other landmass cutting the horizon.

The coast formed twin capes eastwards and westwards, whose gentle slopes disappeared into the waves; the sea broke over their tips, and on the wings of the wind a light spray flew off in white sheets; New America came thus to die in the Polar Ocean, quietly and without convulsion; the two gently sloping promontories formed a broad, open bay, an open roadstead. Halfway along the bay, a transversal piece of rock produced a sheltered little natural harbour at three points of the compass; the harbour worked its way into the land along the broad bed of a brook, the normal route of snow melting after winter and torrential at this moment.

After surveying the shape of the coast, Hatteras decided to make immediate preparations for leaving by launching the boat, dismantling the sledge, and putting it in the launch for excursions to come.

That would take the rest of the day. So they put the tent up, and after a comforting meal, the work began; during this time, the doctor took his instruments to go and shoot the sun, and determine the hydrographical outline of part of the bay.

At five o'clock, Johnson and Bell could sit and cross their arms. The launch was bobbing gracefully on the little haven, its mast erected, its jib down-hauled; the supplies and dismantled sledge had been embarked; all that remained was the tent and a few items of camping equipment to put on the following day.

On his return, the doctor found these preparations completed. Seeing the launch calmly sheltered from the wind, he had the idea of giving this little port a name, and suggested Altamont's.

No objection was raised, and everyone found this suggestion perfectly appropriate.*

As a consequence, the port was called 'Altamont Harbour'.

According to the doctor's calculations, it was situated at 87° 5′ N, 118° 35′ W of Greenwich, that is less than three degrees from the Pole.

The travellers had covered a distance of 200 miles from Victoria Bay to Altamont Harbour.

21

The Open Sea

THE next day, Johnson and Bell proceeded to loading the camping equipment. At eight, the preparations were finished. Just before sailing, the doctor began to think again about the travellers whose tracks they had found, which continued to preoccupy him.

Did those men plan to head north? Did they have some way of crossing the Polar Ocean? Would they meet them again on this new route?*

For the last three days there had been no sign of the travellers, and, whoever they were, they could certainly not have reached Altamont Harbour. The place was still unsullied by any human foot.

Pursued by his thoughts, the doctor wanted to examine the countryside one last time, and so he climbed a hill about a hundred feet high at most; from there his regard could range over the whole southern horizon.

Having reached the top, he put his telescope to his eye. He was very surprised not to see anything, either over the plains in the distance or at a few paces away! It seemed strange; he looked again, and finally studied his telescope. The lens was missing.

'The lens!'

The sudden flash in his mind can easily be understood; he uttered a shout loud enough for his companions to hear, and they felt worried to see him rushing down the hill as fast as his legs could take him.

'Well, what is happening now?' asked Johnson.

Out of breath, the doctor could not utter a word; finally he said:

'The footprints . . . the troop!'

'Well?' said Hatteras. 'Are they here?'

'No . . . no . . .' said the doctor. 'The lens . . . My lens . . . Mine . . .'

And he showed them his incomplete instrument.

'You lost it?' cried the American.

'Yes!'

'Then those footprints . . .'

'Ours, my friends, ours!' cried the doctor. 'We got lost in the fog! We walked in a circle, and we came across our own tracks!'

'But the imprint of a shoe . . . ?' said Hatteras.

'Bell's! Bell broke his snow shoes, and had to use his boots for a whole day.'

'Perfectly true.'

The mistake was so obvious that all burst out laughing, all except Hatteras, who was nevertheless one of the happiest at the discovery.

'How ridiculous!' said the doctor, when the laughter had died down. 'The wonderful assumptions we made! Strangers on this coast! What an idea! We should have thought before opening our mouths. But in the end, since no harm was done but our worry, all we have to do now is leave.'

'Let's go!' said Hatteras.

A quarter of an hour later, all were in the launch, which was moving quickly out of Altamont Harbour, its foresail unfurled and jib hoisted.

This marine voyage began on Wednesday, 10 July; the sailors were very close to the Pole, exactly 175 miles; if any sort of land was situated at that point of the globe, the navigation would be very short.

There was a slight breeze, but a favourable one. The thermometer read fifty (10°C); it was warm.

The launch had not been damaged by the journey on the sledge; it was in perfect condition, and manoeuvred well. Johnson held the tiller; the doctor, Bell, and the American had squeezed themselves as best they could amidst the travelling equipment, some of it arranged on the deck, some below.

At the prow, Hatteras stared at that mysterious point towards which he was drawn with irresistible power, like the magnetized needle to the magnetic Pole. If some shore existed, he wanted to be the first to sight it. That honour was his.

He noticed, in any case, that the Polar Ocean was covered with short waves, like those produced by interior seas. He saw there a sign that land was not far, and the doctor shared his opinion.

It is easy to understand why Hatteras longed to find land at the North Pole. What disappointment he would feel if he saw the sea, uncertain and elusive, stretching out where a portion of ground, however small, was needed for his plans! In effect, how could you give a specific name to an indeterminate area of ocean? How could you plant the flag of your country in the middle of the waves? How could you take possession of part of the liquid element in the name of Her Gracious Majesty?

So, his eyes staring, compass in hand, Hatteras devoured the north.

However, nothing limited the polar basin; the horizon disappeared into the distance, melting into the pure sky of these regions. The ice mountains, running out to sea, seemed to yield passage to these bold navigators.

This area had an unusual appearance. Was the impression due to the travellers' frames of mind, very moved and hyper-nervous? It is

difficult to say. Be that as it may, the doctor depicts the odd aspect of
the ocean in his daily notes; he speaks of it like Penny, for whom
these regions 'offer the most striking contrast of a sea inhabited by
millions of living creatures'.

This liquid prairie, in vague shades of ultramarine, was simultaneously transparent and endowed with an incredible dispersive
power, as if made of sulphur carbide. This transparency allowed one
to look down into the immeasurable depths; it seemed that the polar
basin was lit from below, like an immense aquarium; some electric
phenomenon, produced at the bottom of the sea, must have illuminated the furthest reaches. The launch seemed suspended over a
bottomless chasm.

On the surface of these astonishing waters, the birds flew in flocks,
in thick clouds. Birds of passage, birds of the shore, fluttering birds,
every specimen of the great aquatic family was present, from the
albatross of the southern lands to the penguin of the Arctic seas,* but
in gigantic numbers. Their cries formed a deafening continuous
noise. Looking at them, the doctor forgot to be a naturalist; the
names of these prodigious species escaped him, and he was surprised
to find himself lowering his head as their wings beat the air with
indescribable power.

The wingspan of some of these aerial monsters was as much as
twenty feet; they entirely covered the launch as they flew over, and
there were legions of them, whose nomenclature has never appeared
in the *Index Ornithologicus* of London.*

The doctor was flabbergasted, stupefied, to find his science
powerless.

Then, when his eyes left the marvels of the sky, and glided to the
surface of the peaceful ocean, he encountered other citizens of the
animal kingdom, no less astonishing; amongst them were jellyfish up
to thirty feet across; they served as general nourishment for the aerial
race, floating like veritable islets amongst algae and gigantic seaweed.
How astonishing they were! What a difference from those microscopic jellyfish observed by Scoresby in the seas off Greenland,
whose number the navigator calculated as 23,888,000,000,000,000 in
an area of two square miles!*

Finally, when one's eye plunged from the liquid surface down into
the transparent waters, the sight was no less supernatural; that element was crisscrossed by thousands of fish of every species; sometimes

these creatures dived rapidly to the bottom, and the eye could see them gradually disappearing, like phantasmagorical ghosts; sometimes they emerged from the depths, getting bigger all the while. The sea-monsters did not seem frightened by the presence of the launch; they rubbed against it with their enormous fins; where professional whalers would legitimately have been terrified, the navigators were not even aware of the danger they were in, and yet some of the seas' inhabitants attained formidable proportions.

The young seals played together; the narwhale, as fantastic as the unicorn, armed with its long narrow conical tusk, a marvellous tool which it uses to saw ice-fields, pursued the more apprehensive cetaceans; uncountable whales vented columns of water from their blowholes, and mucilage filled the air with a particular whistling; with its slender tail, and its broad tailfins cutting the water with incomparable speed, the north caper fed as it pounced on animals as quick as it, gadoids and scombrids, while the white whale more lazily and peacefully swallowed molluscs as calm and indolent as it.

Further down, rorquals with pointed muzzles, Greenland anarnaks, longer and blackish giant cachalots, of a species visible in every sea, swam through shoals of ambergris, or indulged in Homeric battles which reddened the ocean over an area of several miles; the cylindrical physales, the large tegusik of Labrador, the dolphins with dorsal fins like sword blades, all the members of the seal and walrus family—sea dogs, sea-horses, fur-seals, sea-lions, and sea-elephants—seemed to be browsing on the liquid pastures of the ocean, and the doctor could admire these countless animals as easily as he would have done the crustaceans and fish in the crystal basins of the Zoological Gardens.*

What beauty, what variety, what power in nature! How strange and prodigious everything seemed at the heart of these circumpolar regions!

The atmosphere took on a supernatural purity; it might have been over-laden with oxygen; the navigators breathed this air with bliss, which poured burning life into them; without realizing, they were subject to veritable combustion, of which no idea, even incomplete, can be given; their passionate, digestive, and respiratory functions were exercised with superhuman energy; their ideas, over-excited in their brains, turned grandiose; in an hour they lived an entire day.

In the midst of these astonishments and marvels, the launch sailed peacefully in a breath of moderate wind, which the huge albatrosses sometimes disturbed with their vast wings.

In the evening, Hatteras and his companions lost sight of the coast of New America. Far away from them, the hours of the night chimed for the temperate and equinoxial zones; but here the orbit of the sun was flat, and traced a circle uniformly parallel to that of the ocean. Bathed in its oblique rays, the launch could not leave the luminous centre, for the two moved in unison.

The living creatures of the hyperboreal regions nevertheless felt evening coming, as if the radiant body had hidden below the horizon. The birds, the fish, and the cetaceans disappeared. Where to? The top of the sky? The bottom of the sea? No one could say. But after the cries, the whistling, and the waves rippling from the breathing of the sea-monsters, there came silent immobility; the deep went to sleep in an imperceptible undulation, and night exerted its peaceful influence once more under the sparkling regard of the sun.

Since leaving Altamont Harbour, the launch had gained one degree north; the next day, nothing still appeared on the horizon, neither those high peaks which indicate faraway land, nor those special signs from which a sailor guesses that islands or landmasses are near.

The wind held firm without being strong; the sea was not very rough; the procession of birds and fish returned, as numerous as the day before; leaning over the water, the doctor could see the cetaceans leaving their deep retreats and climbing slow to the surface; a few icebergs, and here and there a solitary floe, alone broke the immense monotony of the ocean.

In sum, ice was rare, and could not have slowed a ship. It should be noted that the launch was now ten degrees above the pole of cold, and as regards the temperature parallels, it was as if they were ten degrees below. Not surprisingly, the sea was free at this season, as surely as Disko Bay and Baffin Bay were. So a vessel would have been able to sail freely in the summer months.

This observation is of great practical importance; in effect, if ever whalers can reach the polar basin, from the seas of the north of America or the north of Asia, they are sure to quickly complete their cargo, for this part of the ocean seems to be a universal breeding ground—the general reserve for whales, seals, and all marine animals.

At midday, the line of the water was still indistinguishable from the line of the sky; the doctor began to doubt that land could exist at these elevated latitudes.

However, upon reflection, he was necessarily led to believe in the existence of a northern landmass; he reasoned that in the first days of the world, after the cooling of the terrestrial crust, the waters, formed by the condensation of the atmospheric water vapour, had to obey centrifugal force and move towards the equatorial zones, abandoning the immobile extremities of the globe. Hence the parts near the Pole had to emerge from the water. The doctor found this reasoning convincing.

The captain kept trying to penetrate the mists on the horizon. His telescope did not leave his eye. It searched for signs of nearby land in the colour of the water, the shape of the waves, and the breath of the wind. His head leaned ever forwards, and someone who did not know his thoughts would nevertheless have admired him for the energy with which he pursued his plans and his anxious interrogations.

22

The Approach to the Pole

TIME went by amongst all this uncertainty. Nothing appeared on the distinctly drawn circular horizon. Not a point that was neither sky nor sea. Not even a blade of that terrestrial grass on the billows that made Christopher Columbus's heart beat on the way to finding America.

Hatteras still looked.

Finally, at about six in the evening, a mist of indistinct form appeared, slightly above sea-level; it looked like smoke; the sky was perfectly clear; so this water vapour could not be explained as a cloud; it disappeared at times, and then reappeared, as if not stationary.

Hatteras was the first to notice this phenomenon, this indecisive point, this inexplicable mist; he fixed his telescope on it and examined it continuously for an hour.

Suddenly some certain sign must have reached his eye, for he stretched his arm out to the horizon and in a thundering voice cried:

'Land, land!'

At these words, each rose as if from an electric shock.

The indefinable smoke rose perceptibly above the sea.

'I can see, I can see it!' exclaimed the doctor.

'Definitely . . . yes!' said Johnson.

'It's a cloud,' said Altamont.

'Land, land!' repeated Hatteras with unshakeable conviction.

The five navigators looked again with utmost concentration.

But as so often happens with objects made indistinct by distance, the point seemed to have disappeared. Finally, their eyes picked it up again, and the doctor even thought he could see a rapid gleam twenty or twenty-five miles north of the launch.

'It's a volcano!' he cried.

'A volcano?' Altamont repeated.

'Yes.'

'At such a high latitude?'

'And why ever not? Isn't Iceland a volcanic land, one made of volcanoes so to speak?'

'Iceland, but so near the Pole!'

'Well, didn't our illustrious countryman Commodore James Ross observe Erebus and Terror, two fire-breathing mountains on the southern continent, fully active at a hundred and seventy degrees north, seventy-eight degrees west? So why couldn't a volcano exist at the North Pole?'

'It's possible, I suppose,' said Altamont.

'Ah!' exclaimed the doctor. 'I can see it distinctly now—it *is* a volcano!'

'Let's head straight for it then,' said Hatteras.

'We're head to wind,' said Johnson.

'Trim the foresail, and tack into the wind.'

But this operation merely resulted in the launch moving away from the observed point, and they could not find it again, despite their most careful search.

All the same, no doubt was now possible that the coast was near. The purpose of their journey had been glimpsed, if not realized; and within twenty-four hours a human would probably be setting foot on this new land. After allowing these bold sailors to get so near, Providence would surely not prevent them landing.

But in the present circumstances nobody showed the joy that such a discovery ought to have produced; each withdrew into himself, wondering what this land at the Pole could be. The animals seemed to flee it; in the evening the birds, rather than seeking refuge, flew south as fast as their wings could fly! Was it therefore so inhospitable that a seagull or a ptarmigan could not take shelter? In the transparent water, the very fishes, even the great cetaceans, were rapidly fleeing that coast. What caused such a feeling of revulsion, perhaps terror, shared by every creature that dwelled in that part of the globe?

The navigators shared the general mood; they gave in to the feelings produced by the situation and little by little could feel slumber making their eyelids droop.

Hatteras was on watch. He took the helm; the doctor, Altamont, Johnson, and Bell stretched out on the seats and fell asleep one after the other, each plunging quickly into the world of dreams.

Hatteras tried to resist; he didn't want to waste any precious time; but the slow movement of the launch imperceptibly rocked him, and despite all his efforts, he succumbed to irresistible somnolence.

Meanwhile the boat was hardly moving; the wind was unable to fill its flaccid sail. In the westerly distance, a few motionless floes reflected the rays of light, producing incandescent patches in the middle of the ocean.

Hatteras began to dream. His rapid thought wandered over his whole existence; he went back through the itinerary of his life with the speed peculiar to dreams, that no scientist has ever been able to calculate; he returned to days gone by; he saw his wintering again in Victoria Bay, Fort Providence, Doctor's House, the encounter with the American under the ice.

Then he went further back into the past; he dreamed of his ship, of the blazing *Forward*, of his companions, the traitors who had abandoned him. What had become of them? He thought of Shandon, Wall, and the brutal Pen. Where were they now? Had they managed to reach Baffin Bay across the ice?

Then his imagination soared higher still, and he went back to his departure from Britain, his previous journeys, his failures, his ill fortune. Then he forgot his present situation, his impending success, his half-realized hopes. His joy forgotten, his dream cast him into anguish.

This continued for two hours; then his thoughts took a new

course; they took him towards the Pole; he saw himself finally setting foot on this new British territory and unfurling the Union
Jack.*

While he slept thus, an enormous olive cloud rose from the
horizon and darkened the ocean.

It is difficult to imagine the meteoric speed storms move at on the
Arctic seas. The water vapour generated in the equatorial regions
comes and condenses above the immense glaciers of the north, and
sucks in masses of air to replace it with irresistible violence. This is
what helps explain the energy of northern tempests.

On the first impact of the wind, the captain and his companions
tore themselves from sleep, ready to trim the sail.

The sea was surging in high waves with small bases; the launch,
buffeted by a violent swell, was diving into its deep chasms, or oscillating uneasily on the cusps of sharp waves, leaning at angles of more
than forty-five degrees.

Hatteras took the helm with a firm hand, as it moved noisily in the
rudder head; the tiller, violently seized in a yaw, threw him back and
forth against his will. Johnson and Bell were busy baling out the
water that poured in with every plunge of the launch.

'A storm we weren't expecting,' said Altamont, holding firm to his
seat.

'We should expect anything up here,' answered the doctor.

These words were exchanged through the whistling of the air
and the crashing of the waves, turned to impalpable liquid dust
by the force of the wind; it became almost impossible to hear
anything.

It was difficult to keep a northerly course; the thick spray limited
visibility to a few fathoms; all reference points had disappeared.

This sudden tempest, at the moment when their goal was about to
be reached, seemed to contain stern warnings; it appeared to their
frenzied minds to be an interdiction to go any further. Did nature
wish to forbid access to the Pole? Was this point of the globe surrounded by a fortification of tempests and storms, which prevented
it ever being reached?

However, on seeing these men's energetic faces, it could be understood that they were not about to yield to either the wind or the
waves, that they would carry on to the bitter end.

They struggled in this way for the whole day; braving death every second; getting no further north, but not giving any ground either; they were soaked in a tepid rain, and drenched in buckets of sea-water that the storm threw in their faces; the whistlings of the air were sometimes mixed with the sinister cries of birds.

But in the very midst of a resurgence in the wrath of the swell, at about six in the evening, there came a sudden calm. The wind fell miraculously silent. The sea became calm and smooth, as if the swell had not been rising for twelve hours. The storm seemed to be sparing this part of the polar ocean.

What was happening? All around them was an extraordinary and inexplicable phenomenon, one which Captain Sabine witnessed during his voyages to the Greenland seas.

The fog, without rising, had turned strangely luminous.

The launch was sailing through a region of electric light, an immense St Elmo's fire that radiates without heat. The mast, the sails, and the tackle were outlined in black with incomparable clarity against the phosphorescence of the sky; the navigators were plunged into a bath of transparent rays, and their faces were coloured with inflamed reflections.

The sudden calming of this portion of the ocean came undoubtedly from the upward movement of columns of air, while the storm, belonging to the category of cyclones, was turning rapidly around this peaceful centre.

But this fiery atmosphere brought an idea to Hatteras's mind.

'The volcano!' he cried.

'Is it possible?' said Bell.

'No, no!' the doctor answered. 'We would have been suffocated if its flames had reached us.'

'Perhaps it's the volcano's reflections in the fog,' said Altamont.

'Hardly. We would have to be close to land, and so would be able to hear the roar of the eruption.'

'But then . . . ?' asked the captain.

'It's a cosmic phenomenon,' answered the doctor, 'a phenomenon rarely observed till now! If we carry on, we will soon leave this luminous sphere, and find the darkness and the storm again.'

'In any case, forward!' Hatteras answered.

'Forward!' his companions repeated, not even thinking of catching their breath in this peaceful hollow.

The sail, with folds of fire, hung down the sparkling mast; the oars plunged into the burning waves, and appeared to be raising showers of sparks as they lifted the brightly lit drops.

Compass in hand, Hatteras turned north again; little by little, the fog lost its luminosity, then its transparency; the wind produced howlings a few fathoms away, and soon the launch, flattened by a violent gust, returned to the domain of the storm.

But the hurricane had fortunately turned one point southwards, and the boat could run before the storm, heading straight for the Pole; it was most likely to sink, but they could move at crazy speed; shoals or ice floes could emerge from the billows at any time, and would inevitably break it into pieces.

However, not one of these men raised a single objection; not one spoke with the voice of prudence. They were caught up in the madness of danger. The thirst of the unknown overwhelmed them. They went on, not blind but blinded, finding the appalling speed of this race too slow for their impatience. Hatteras maintained the helm in its imperturbable direction, amongst the miasma of waves foaming from the whipping of the storm.

All the same, they sensed the approach of the coast; there were strange signs in the air.

Suddenly the fog was split like a curtain torn apart by the wind and for a moment as brief as lightning they could see an immense plume of flames standing up on the horizon and heading into the sky.

'The volcano, the volcano!'

The words escaped from every mouth; but the fantastic vision had disappeared; the wind, veering south-east, hit the boat broadside and forced it to flee the unreachable land once more.

'Damn!' said Hatteras, furling the foresail. 'We were three miles from the coast!'

Hatteras could not resist the violence of the storm; instead, he tacked into the wind, which was unleashing itself with indescribable energy. At times, the launch lay on its side, raising fears that its keel might totally emerge; however it ended up righting itself, obeying the rudder, like a racehorse whose knees buckle but whose rider picks it up again with the bridle and the spur.

Hatteras, dishevelled, his hand welded to the tiller, seemed to be the soul of the boat, to be one with it, just as man and horse were at the time of the centaurs.

Suddenly, a horrifying sight appeared before their eyes.

Less than sixty feet away an ice floe was oscillating on the stormy peaks of the waves; it descended and rose like the launch; it threatened them if it fell, for it had only to touch to crush them.

But with this danger of being cast into the abyss, came another, no less terrible, for the ice floe was covered with polar bears, crushed against each other and mad with terror.

'Bears, bears!' cried Bell in a strangled voice.

And each saw, terrified, what he saw.

The ice floe was making alarming yaws; sometimes it leaned at such acute angles that the animals rolled pell-mell into each other. Then they pushed and growled, partly covering the clamour of the storm as a formidable concert rose from this floating menagerie.

If this ice raft happened to turn over, the bears, rushing towards the boat, would inevitably try to climb aboard.

For fifteen minutes, a century, the launch and the ice floe sailed in tandem; now 120 feet apart, now about to collide; sometimes the floe hung over, and all the monsters had to do was drop down. The Greenland dogs trembled with fright. Duke was motionless.

Hatteras and his companions stayed silent; it did not occur to them to turn the tiller and thus escape that redoubtable proximity, and they maintained their route with inflexible rigour. A vague sentiment, closer to astonishment than terror, took hold of their brains; they remained in admiration as this terrifying sight added to the battle of the elements.

Finally, the floe moved slowly away, pushed by the wind which the launch resisted with its foresail flat aft, and disappeared in the fog, revealing from time to time its presence by the faraway growls of its monstrous crew.

At that moment the storm redoubled its force and there came an unleashing without name of the aerial waves; the boat lifted out of the water, and began to spin at vertiginous speed; its foresail was torn away, and fluttered off into the darkness like a great white bird; a circular hole, a new Maelstrom,* formed in the swirls of the waves. The navigators, enlaced in this whirlpool, moved so fast that the lines of the water seemed motionless, in spite of their incalculable speed. The men were sinking little by little. At the bottom of the pit, a powerful aspiration was operating, an irresistible suction, which was pulling them down and swallowing them alive.

All five had stood up. They looked around with terrified eyes.

Then giddiness took hold of them. They had within the ineffable feeling of the abyss!

All of a sudden, the launch stood straight up. Its bow rose above the lines of swirling water, whose speed was transferred to the boat, projecting it away from the centre of attraction; escaping along the tangents from the circumference, which was performing more than a thousand turns a second,* the five were launched with the speed of a cannon ball.

Altamont, the doctor, Johnson, and Bell were thrown back on to the benches.

When they got up, Hatteras had disappeared.

It was two in the morning.

23

The Union Jack

CRIES from four breasts followed the first moment of stupor.

'Hatteras?' said the doctor.

'Disappeared!' replied Johnson and Bell.

'Lost!'

They looked round. Nothing was visible on the rough seas. Duke was barking in a despairing tone; he wanted to dive into the water, and Bell was barely able to hold him back.

'Take the helm, Altamont!' said the doctor. 'Let's try everything we can to find our unfortunate captain!'

Johnson and Bell sat down again. Altamont gripped the tiller, and the wandering launch turned into the wind once more.

Johnson and Bell began to row vigorously; for an hour they did not leave the area of the catastrophe. They searched, but in vain! The unfortunate Hatteras had been carried off by the storm and lost.

Lost, so near the Pole! So close to the goal he had merely glimpsed!*

The doctor called, shouted, and fired his guns; Duke added his lamentable barking to the doctor's voice; but no reply reached the captain's two friends. Then a terrible sadness took hold of Clawbonny; his head fell into his hands, and his companions heard him sobbing.

In effect, at this distance from the land, without an oar or piece of wood to hold on to, Hatteras could not have reached the coast alive; and if a part of him finally touched that wished-for land, it would be his bruised and swollen body.

After an hour of searching, they had to continue their route northwards and fight the dying fury of the storm.

At five in the morning on 11 July, the wind fell; the swell gradually subsided; the sky took on its polar clarity and, less than three miles away, the land offered itself in all its splendour.

This new land was only an island, or rather a volcano, standing up like a beacon at the Northern Pole of the world.

The mountain, in full eruption, was vomiting a mass of burning boulders and slabs of glowing rock; it seemed to be repeatedly trembling, like a giant's breathing; the ejected matter rose to a great height in the air amidst jets of intense flames, and lava flows wound down its flanks in impetuous torrents;* here inflamed serpents twisted their way past the smoking rocks; there burning waterfalls fell through a purple mist; further on a river of fire, formed of a thousand igneous streams, threw itself into the sea as a boiling outfall.

The volcano seemed to have but a single crater, from which a column of fire escaped, crisscrossed with diagonal flashes of lightning; perhaps electricity played some part in this magnificent phenomenon.

Above the panting flames shimmered an immense plume of smoke, red at the bottom, black at the top. It rose with incomparable majesty before unwinding in broad, thick spirals.

At a great height the sky took on the colour of cinder; the darkness they had experienced during the storm, which the doctor had been unable to understand, evidently came from the columns of ash blocking the sun like an impenetrable curtain. He remembered then a similar occurrence in 1812 on the island of Barbados, which at high noon was plunged into total darkness by the masses of ash thrown out of the crater of the island of St Vincent.*

This enormous fire-breathing rock emerging from the middle of the ocean was 5,000 feet high, approximately the same as Hekla.*

The line from its summit to its base formed an angle of about eleven degrees to the horizon.*

As the launch approached, the rock seemed to grow gradually out of the heart of the waves; it displayed no trace of vegetation. It did not even have a shore and its flanks fell steeply to the sea.

'Can we land?' asked the doctor.

'The wind is taking us there,' replied Altamont.

'But I can't see a scrap of beach to walk on!'

'It may seem so at this distance,' said Johnson, 'but we'll surely find enough to land our boat on; that's all we need.'

'Let's go,' Clawbonny replied sadly.

The doctor no longer had eyes for that strange land looming up before him. The land of the Pole was there, but not the man who had discovered it!

Five hundred paces from the rocks, the sea boiled where it came into contact with underground fires. The circumference of the island it surrounded was about eight or ten miles, and could be estimated to be very close to the Pole, if the axis of the globe did not pass exactly through it.

As they approached the isle, the navigators noticed a little fiord, enough to shelter their vessel; they immediately headed for it, at the same time fearing they would find the captain's body thrown on the coast by the storm!

However, it did not seem likely that a body could be lying there; there was no beach, and the sea broke abruptly on the rocks; thick ash, untouched by humans, covered them where the waves could not reach.

Finally the launch slipped into a narrow opening between two breakers, where it was perfectly protected from the undertow.

Then Duke's lamentable howling got louder; the poor creature cried out for the captain in his moving language, he demanded that the pitiless sea and the echo-less rocks give him up. He barked in vain, and though the doctor caressed him, he was unable to calm him down; the faithful dog, as if wishing to act in his master's place, made a prodigious leap and rushed over the rocks, in the midst of the dust and ash rising in clouds around him.

'Duke! Here, Duke!' cried the doctor.

But Duke did not hear and disappeared. Clawbonny and his three companions disembarked; they set foot on the land, and the launch was firmly tied up.

Altamont was just about to climb up an enormous pile of rocks, when Duke's barking sounded out at some distance with unusual energy; it expressed not anger, but unhappiness.

'Listen,' said the doctor.

'Smelled some animal?' said the mate.

'No, no!' replied the doctor, trembling. 'He's moaning, sobbing; it's Hatteras's body.'

At these words, the four rushed after Duke over the ash, getting blinded; they reached the end of the ten-foot-wide fiord, where the waves came imperceptibly to die.

Duke was barking beside a body wrapped in a Union Jack.*

'Hatteras! Hatteras!' shouted the doctor, throwing himself on his friend.

But immediately he made an exclamation impossible to describe.

The bloodied body, seemingly inanimate, had moved as he touched it.

'Alive! Alive!' he exclaimed.

'Yes,' came a weak voice, 'alive on the land of the Pole, where the storm cast me, alive on Queen's Island!'

'Hurray for Britain!' exclaimed the five men with a common accord.

'And for America!' added the doctor, stretching out one hand to Hatteras and the other to the American.

Duke too was crying hurray in his own fashion, which was as good as any.

At first these good men had no thought except their happiness at finding the captain again; they felt their eyes flooding with tears.

The doctor checked Hatteras's condition. He was not badly hurt. The wind had pushed him on to the coast, where landing was very dangerous; the hardy sailor, thrown back several times into the sea, had finally managed to hang on to a piece of rock by brute force, and then he had managed to hoist himself out of the water.

There he lost consciousness, after rolling himself up in his flag, and he only came to life with Duke's caresses and the sound of his barking.

After some first aid, Hatteras was able to get up and, supported by the doctor, make his way back to the launch.

'The Pole! The North Pole!' he kept repeating as he walked.

'You're happy!' the doctor said to him.

'Yes, happy! And you, my friend, can't you feel the happiness, the pure joy of being here? This land we're on is the land of the Pole! This sea we crossed is the sea of the Pole! This air we're breathing is the air of the Pole! Oh the North Pole! The North Pole!'

Speaking thus, Hatteras was prey to violent exultation, a sort of fever, and in vain did the doctor try to calm him down. His eyes shone with extraordinary brightness and thoughts boiled in his mind. Clawbonny attributed this state of over-excitement to the terrifying dangers the captain had passed through.

Hatteras clearly needed rest, and so they started looking for a place to camp.

Altamont soon found a grotto, built from rocks falling and forming a cavern; Johnson and Bell put the supplies inside, and freed the Greenland dogs.

At about eleven, everything was ready for a meal; the canvas of the tent served as tablecloth; lunch, composed of pemmican, salt meat, and tea and coffee, was laid out on the ground, just asking to be eaten.

But beforehand, Hatteras insisted on knowing the island's position; he wanted to be sure exactly where he was.

The doctor and Altamont picked up the instruments, and after observation measured the precise position of the grotto as 89° 59′ 15″ N. The longitude this far north no longer had any importance, for the meridians all came together a few hundred feet away.

In sum, the island was situated at the North Pole, and the ninetieth degree was only forty-five seconds away, or exactly three-quarters of a mile, at the summit of the volcano.*

When Hatteras learned of this conclusion, he asked for it to be recorded in a formal statement, and for copies to be deposited in a cairn on the coast.

On the spot, the doctor took out his pen and composed the following document, of which one copy now resides in the archives of the Royal Geographical Society of London.

On this 11 July 1861, at 89° 59′ 15″ of latitude north, Queen's Island was discovered at the North Pole by Captain Hatteras, commanding the brig the *Forward* of Liverpool, who signed, together with his four companions.

Whosoever finds this document is requested to convey it to the Admiralty.

Signed: John Hatteras, commander of the *Forward*; Dr Clawbonny; Altamont, commander of the *Porpoise*; Johnson, boatswain; Bell, carpenter.

'And now, my friends, let's eat,' happily said the doctor.

24

Lesson in Polar Cosmography

I T goes without saying that they sat on the ground to eat.

'But', said Clawbonny, 'who wouldn't give all the tables and dining-rooms in the world to eat at 89° 59′ 15″ N!'

Everyone's thoughts were about the present situation; their minds were full of the sole idea of the North Pole. In this unique victory, they forgot the dangers braved reaching it and the perils still to overcome to get back. What neither the ancients nor the moderns, what neither the Europeans nor the Americans nor the Asians had yet been able to do, had just been accomplished.

So the doctor's companions listened carefully when he told them everything that his knowledge and inexhaustible memory were able to provide him with concerning their present situation.

It was with great enthusiasm that he made the first toast to the captain.

'To John Hatteras!'

'To John Hatteras!' replied his companions in a single cry.

'To the North Pole!' responded the captain in a strange tone: a voice until then so cold, so controlled, and now tinged with an imperious over-excitement.

The cups were clinked, and the toasts were followed by warm handshakes.

'So this is the most important geographical event of our time! Who could have imagined that this discovery would come before those of the centres of Africa and Australia!* Truly, Hatteras, you are above the Sturts, the Livingstones, the Burtons, and the Barths! Congratulations!'

'You're right, doctor,' said Altamont; 'because of the difficulties involved, the North Pole should have been the last point on earth discovered. As soon as the government absolutely wanted to know the centre of Africa, it could easily have done so, by sacrificing enough men and money; but here success was never certain, and there could have been totally impossible obstacles.'

' "Impossible!" ' vehemently exclaimed Hatteras. 'There are no impossible obstacles; there are just stronger and weaker wills, that's all!'

'At the end of the day,' said Johnson, 'we're here, and that's what's important. But at least can you tell me once and for all, Dr Clawbonny, why the Pole's so special?'

'It's so special, my good Johnson, because it's the only point of the globe that is motionless, while every other point turns at great speed.'

'But I can't see that we're moving any slower here than in Liverpool!'

'You won't notice our movement any more than in Liverpool, because in both cases you yourself are moving along with the rest! But the fact is no less true. The earth undergoes a complete movement of rotation every twenty-four hours, and this movement is centred on an axis passing through the North and South Poles. We're at one end of the axis, and thus necessarily motionless.'

'So whilst our countrymen are turning quickly, we're stationary?' said Bell.

'Approximately, as we're not quite at the Pole!'

'You're right, doctor,' said Hatteras in a grave tone, shaking his head; 'we still have forty-five seconds to do to that precise point!'

'It's not much,' said Altamont, 'and so we can consider ourselves not moving.'

'Yes,' said the doctor, 'while the inhabitants of every point on the equator are doing 396 leagues an hour!'

'Without getting tired!' said Bell.

'Precisely.'

'But, independent of this movement of rotation,' said Johnson, 'isn't the earth undergoing another movement around the sun?'

'Yes, a movement of translation, which it takes a year to do.'

'Is it faster than the other one?'' asked Bell.

'Infinitely, and I must say that although we're at the Pole, it is carrying us along like all the other inhabitants of the earth. Consequently, our so-called immobility is just a figment of the imagination: motionless with respect to the other points of the globe, yes; but not with respect to the sun.'

'Well,' said Bell, with an accent of comical regret, 'I thought I was so tranquil! I need to give up that illusion! There is decidedly no rest to be had in this world.'

'As you say, Bell,' said Johnson, 'and will you tell us, Dr Clawbonny, the speed of this movement of translation?'

'It is considerable; the earth moves around the sun seventy-six times as fast as a twenty-four-pound ball, which does 1,170 feet a second. Its speed of translation is therefore 7.6 leagues a second; as you can see, it's in a different class from the movement of the points on the equator.'

'Whew!' said Bell. 'It's almost unbelievable, Dr Clawbonny. More than seven leagues a second, when it would have been so easy to stay at the same spot if God had wanted!'

'Well,' said Altamont, 'think about it, Bell! No days or nights and no spring, autumn, summer, or winter!'

'Without considering a quite simply terrifying consequence,' said the doctor.

'Yes?' said Johnson.

'We would have fallen into the sun.'

'Into the sun!' repeated Bell in surprise.

'If this translation movement happened to stop, then the earth would be precipitated into the sun within sixty-four and a half days.'

'A fall of sixty-four and a half days!' said Johnson.

'No more and no less; for there's a distance of thirty-eight million leagues to cover.'

'What is the weight of the terrestrial globe?' asked Altamont.

'5,881,000,000,000,000,000,000 tons.'*

'There's a number that's not gentle on the ear, or easy to understand!'

'So, my good Johnson, I'm going to give you two terms of comparison which will remain in your mind: remember that you'd need seventy-five moons to make the weight of the earth, and 350,000 earths for the weight of the sun.'*

'That's a crushingly huge amount!' said Altamont.

'Crushing is the right word; but let's come back to the Pole, since never has a lesson of cosmography about this part of the globe been more appropriate, if, that is, it doesn't bore you.'

'Do go on, doctor,' said Altamont.

'I told you that the Pole was motionless with respect to the other points of the earth,' said Clawbonny, who took as much pleasure in teaching as his companions did in learning. 'Well, it's not completely true.'

'What, we need to give ground again!'

'Yes, Bell, the Pole doesn't always occupy exactly the same position; the Pole Star used to be further from the celestial Pole than now. Our Pole is subject to a particular movement; it describes a circle in about 26,000 years. That comes from the precession of the equinoxes I was telling you about before.'

'But', said Altamont, 'might the Pole move even more one day?'

'Eh, my dear Altamont, you have touched on a great question, that the scientists debated for ages following a remarkable discovery.'

'What was that?'

'As follows. In 1771, the body of a rhinoceros was discovered on the edge of the Glacial Sea, and in 1799, an elephant's on the coast of Siberia.* How did quadrupeds from warm countries come to be at such latitudes? Hence, a strange rumour ran amongst the geologists, who were not as knowledgeable as a Frenchman, M. Élie de Beaumont, who later demonstrated that these animals lived at already high latitudes,* and that the streams and rivers had quite simply brought their bodies to the points they had been found at. But since this explanation was not yet produced, guess what the imaginations of those scientists invented?'

'Scientists are capable of anything,' said Altamont with a laugh.

'Yes, anything to explain a fact; well, they assumed that the earth's Pole was formerly at the equator, and the equator at the Pole.'

'Heck!'

'Seriously; now if that had been the case, since the earth is more than five leagues flatter at the Pole, the seas transported to the new equator by centrifugal force would have covered mountains twice as high as the Himalayas; all the lands close to the Arctic Circle—Sweden, Norway, Russia, Siberia, Greenland, and British America*—would also have been covered by five leagues of water, while the equatorial regions thrown out towards the Pole would, contrariwise, have formed plateaux of five leagues.'

'Oh, what a difference!' said Johnson.

'That hardly frightened the scientists.'

'And how did they explain this upheaval?' asked Altamont.

'A collision with a comet. Comets are the *deus ex machina*; every time you're embarrassed in cosmography, you bring in a comet. It is the most helpful heavenly body I know, for at the slightest sign from scientists it does its level best to fix everything!'

'So, you think, Dr Clawbonny, that such an upheaval can't have happened?' said Johnson.

'Yes!'

'And if it happened now?'

'If it did, the equator'd be frozen solid within twenty-four hours!'

'Well, if it happened now,' said Bell, 'people might easily say we hadn't been to the Pole.'

'Don't worry, Bell. To return to the immobility of the terrestrial axis, there is one interesting consequence: if we were here during the winter, we'd see the stars describing a perfect circle around us. At the spring equinox, on 23 March, the sun would appear to us exactly cut in two by the horizon (I ignore the refraction), and would then climb gradually, following very long curves; here it has the remarkable characteristic that, as soon as it has risen, it no longer sets; it remains visible for six months; then its disc comes and skims the horizon again at the autumn equinox of 22 September and, as soon as it has set, disappears for the whole winter.'

'You were speaking just now of the flattening of the earth at the Poles; could you please explain, Dr Clawbonny?'

'Here goes, Johnson. Since the earth was not solid in the first days of the world, you will understand that its rotation made part of its mobile mass swell at the equator, where the centrifugal force was greater. If the earth had been motionless, it would have remained a perfect sphere; but because of the phenomenon I have just mentioned, it has an ellipsoid form, and the Poles are closer than the equator to the centre, by approximately five and a third leagues.'

'So,' said Johnson, 'if one day our captain wanted to take us to the centre of the earth, we'd have to do five leagues less to get there?'

'As you say, my friend.'

'Well, captain, so much the better! It's an opportunity we should take . . .'

Hatteras did not reply. He was evidently not following the conversation, or listening without hearing.

'Heavens!' replied the doctor. 'According to some experts, it would be worth trying such an expedition.'

'Really?' said Johnson.

'But let me finish; first things first; I'd like to inform you that the flattening of the Poles is the reason for the precession of the equinoxes, in other words the reason the spring equinox always arrives one day earlier than if the earth were perfectly round. That comes quite simply from the attraction of the sun operating differentially on the inflated parts of the globe at the equator, which thus undergo a retrograde movement. This is what displaces the Pole a little, as I said before. But independent of such an effect, the flattening has another curious, more personal consequence, which we'd notice if we had a mathematical sensitivity.'

'What do you mean?' asked Bell.

'I mean that we're heavier here than in Liverpool.'

'Heavier?'

'Us, our dogs, our guns, and our instruments.'

'Are you sure?'

'Yes, for two reasons; the first is we're closer to the centre of the globe, which consequently attracts us more: now this attractive force just means the weight. The second is that the force from the rotation is zero at the Pole, and very strong at the equator; the objects there have a tendency to move away from the earth; they are therefore lighter.'

'Seriously? We don't weigh the same at both places?'

'No, Johnson; according to Newton's laws, bodies attract each other in direct proportion to their masses, and in inverse proportion to the square of their distances. Here, I weigh more because I am closer to the centre of attraction, and on another planet I would weigh more or less depending on the mass of the planet.'

'What about the moon?' asked Bell.

'On the moon my weight, which is sixteen stone in Liverpool, would only be two.'

'And on the sun?'

'Oh, on the sun I'd weigh two and a half tons!'

'Good God!' said Bell. 'You'd need a jack to lift your legs!'

'Presumably,' replied the doctor, laughing at Bell's shock; 'but here the difference is negligible, and with an equal effort from his knee muscles, Bell could jump as high as on the banks of the Mersey.'

'And on the sun?' repeated Bell, who couldn't get over it.

'My friend, the consequence of all this is that we're fine where we are, and that it's foolish to rush to other places.'

'You were saying just now', added Altamont, 'that it would perhaps be worth trying to reach the centre of the earth! Has anyone ever thought of undertaking such a journey?'*

'Yes, and this finishes my remarks on the Pole. There is no point on the globe which has produced more hypotheses and chimeras. The ancients, highly ignorant of cosmography, placed the Garden of Hesperides* here. In the Middle Ages, it was supposed that the earth was supported by towers at the Poles, on which it turned; but when they saw comets moving freely in the circumpolar regions, they had to give up the idea of a support. Later, there was a French astronomer, Bailly, who maintained that the Atlanteans, that civilized lost race of which Plato speaks, lived on this very spot.* Finally, in our day, it has been claimed that immense openings exist at the Poles, from which emerges the light of the Aurora (Borealis), and through which one could go to the interior of the globe; then, in the hollow sphere, it has been suggested that there are two planets, Pluto and Proserpina, and air that is luminous, because of the high pressure it is at.'*

'All that has really been said?' asked Altamont.

'And written, and taken very seriously. Captain Symmes, one of our compatriots, even suggested to Humphry Davy, Humboldt, and Arago* that they attempt the journey! But those scientists refused.'

'And they were right.'

'I think so. Whatever the truth of the matter, you can see, my friends, that people's imagination has enjoyed free play vis-à-vis the Pole, and that sooner or later it will have to return to the naked truth.'

'In any case, we shall see,' said Johnson, who had not given up on his idea.

'We'll see on our excursion tomorrow,' said the doctor, smiling to see the old sailor unconvinced; 'and if there is a special opening for going to the centre of the earth, we'll travel together!'

25

Mount Hatteras

AFTER this substantial conversation, all settled down in the grotto as best they could, and dropped off.

All except for Hatteras. Why did this extraordinary man not sleep?

Had the aim of his life not been accomplished? Had he not accomplished the bold project he held dearest? Why did calm not succeed agitation in that burning soul? Was it not natural that, his projects accomplished, Hatteras would fall into a sort of despondency, that his relaxed nerves would need rest? After his success, it would have even been normal to feel that sadness which always follows satisfied desires.*

But no. He still appeared over-excited, more so than ever. However, it was not the idea of returning which made him agitated. Did he want to go even further? Did his travel ambition not have any limit, and did he find the world too small because he had been everywhere on it?*

Whatever the reason, he could not sleep. And yet, that first night spent at the Pole of the globe was clear and calm. The island was completely uninhabited. Not a single bird in the burning air, not an animal on the cindery ground, not a fish in the boiling waters. Only the dull and distant rumbling of the mountain, with its head producing dishevelled plumes of incandescent smoke.

When Bell, Johnson, Altamont, and the doctor awoke, Hatteras was no longer with them. Worried, they left the grotto, and found the captain standing on a rock. His eyes remained immutably fixed on the summit of the volcano. He had his instruments in his hand; he had clearly just measured the mountain's position.

The doctor went up to him and spoke several times before he could interrupt his contemplation. Finally, the captain seemed to understand.

'Off we go!' said the doctor, examining him attentively. 'Let's explore everywhere on our island; we're ready for our last excursion.'

'The last,' said Hatteras with the intonation of people dreaming out loud, 'yes, the last. But also', he added very keenly, 'the most wonderful!'

While he spoke, he rubbed his hands over his forehead as if to calm the boiling inside.

Altamont, Johnson, and Bell joined them; Hatteras now seemed to emerge from his hallucinatory state.

'My friends,' he said emotionally, 'thank you for your courage; thank you for your perseverance; thank you for your superhuman efforts, which have enabled us to set foot on this land!'

'Captain,' said Johnson, 'we only followed orders, and the honour belongs to you.'

'No, no,' replied Hatteras in a violent outpouring; 'to all of you as much as to me! To Altamont and all of us and the doctor as well! Oh, may my heart blow its top in your hands!* It can no longer contain its joy and gratitude!'

Hatteras seized the hands of his good companions around him. He came, he went, he was no longer in control of himself.

'We only did our duty as Britons,' said Bell.

'And friends,' added the doctor.

'Yes, but not everyone was able to do his duty. Some failed! However, those who betrayed should be forgiven, like those who let themselves be dragged into betrayal! Poor men! I pardon them, do you hear, doctor?'

'I do,' replied Clawbonny, who was seriously worried at Hatteras's exultation.

'So I don't want them to lose the riches they came so far to earn. No, nothing in my arrangements has changed, and they will be wealthy . . . if ever they get back to Britain!'

It would have been difficult to remain unmoved by the tone Hatteras said these words in.

'But, captain,' said Johnson, trying to joke, 'you'd think you were making your last will and testament.'

'Perhaps I am,' replied Hatteras gravely.

'But you still have a good long life of fame before you,' continued the old sailor.

'Who knows?' said the captain, followed by a long silence.

The doctor did not dare interpret the meaning of these last words.

But Hatteras needed to ensure he was understood, for he added, in a hurried voice he could hardly control:

'My friends, listen to me. We have done a great deal so far, and yet there remains much to do.'

The captain's companions looked at each other with astonishment.

'Remember, we're at the land of the Pole, but not the Pole itself!'

'What do you mean?' said Altamont.

'Could you please explain?' exclaimed the doctor, afraid to guess.

'Yes,' said Hatteras forcefully; 'I said that a Briton would set foot on the Pole of the globe; I said it, and it shall come to pass.'

'What . . . ?' said the doctor.

'We are still forty-five seconds away from that mysterious point,' said Hatteras with growing emotion, 'and to it I shall go!'

'But it's on top of that volcano!' said the doctor.

'I shall go.'

'You can't get there!'

'I shall go.'

'It's a wide open flaming crater!'

'I shall go.'

The energy and conviction with which Hatteras said these last words cannot be conveyed. His friends were stupefied; they looked in terror at the mountain, which was waving its plume of flames in the air.

The doctor then spoke; he insisted; he pressed Hatteras to renounce his projects; he said everything his heart could conjure up, from humble prayers to friendly threats; but he obtained nothing from the unquiet soul of the captain, caught up in an insanity that could be called 'polar madness'.

There remained only violent means to prevent this madman, who was heading for a fatal fall. But foreseeing that such means would produce serious disorders, the doctor decided to employ them only as a last resort.

In any case, he hoped that physical impossibilities and impenetrable obstacles would prevent Hatteras from executing his project.

'Since such is the case,' he said, 'we will go with you.'

'Good, but only halfway up the mountain! No further! You need to take back to Britain the copy of the affidavit attesting to our discovery if . . .'

'Nevertheless . . .'

'It's decided!' replied Hatteras in an unshakeable tone. Since the prayers of his friends had not changed matters, the captain remained in command.

The doctor did not try to insist further, and a few moments later the little troop had equipped themselves to face difficulties and, led by Duke, had set off.

The sky was shining brightly. The thermometer read fifty-two (11°C). The air was dramatically imbued with the clarity particular to that high latitude. It was eight in the morning.

Hatteras took the lead with his good dog; Bell, Altamont, the doctor, and Johnson followed close behind.

'I'm afraid,' said Johnson.

'There's nothing to fear,' replied the doctor. 'We're right beside you.'

What a remarkable island, and how to depict its special physiognomy, which had the unexpected newness of youth! This volcano did not seem to be very old, and geologists would have concluded that it had been formed at a recent date.

The rocks clung to each other, maintaining themselves only through a miracle of equilibrium. The mountain was, so to speak, merely an agglomeration of stones thrown there. No earth, no moss, not the thinnest lichen, no trace of vegetation. The carbonic acid vomited by the crater had not yet had time to join up with hydrogen from the water or ammonia from the clouds, to form organized matter under the effect of the light.

This island, lost in the open sea, was due only to the accumulation of the successive volcanic ejections; several other mountains of the globe were formed in a similar way; what they threw out from their breast was sufficient to build them, like Etna, which has already vomited a volume of lava larger than its own mass, and Mount Nuovo, near Naples, generated by scoria in the short space of forty-eight hours.*

The pile of rocks composing Queen's Island had clearly come out of the entrails of the earth; it was plutonian to the utmost degree. Where it now stood, the endless sea had once stretched, formed in the first days by the condensation of water vapour over the cooling earth; but, as the volcanoes of the old and new worlds went out, or more precisely became dormant, they had to be replaced by new fire-breathing craters.

In effect, the earth can be compared to a vast spherical boiler. Because of the central fire, immense quantities of vapours are generated, stored at a pressure of thousands of atmospheres, and they would blow up the earth if there were no safety valves.

These valves are the volcanoes; when one closes, another opens; and at the Pole, where the terrestrial crust is thinner because of the flattening, it is not surprising that a volcano should have formed, and become visible as its massif rose above the water.

The doctor, while following Hatteras, noticed the strange features; his foot found volcanic tuff, as well as pumiceous slag deposits, ash, and eruptive rocks similar to the syenites and granites of Iceland.

But if he concluded that the islet was of recent formation, this was because the sedimentary terrain had not yet had time to form.

Water was also absent. If Queen's Island had had the advantage of being several centuries old, springs would have been spurting from its breast, as in the neighbourhood of volcanoes. Now, not only was it devoid of liquid molecules, but the steam which rose from the lava streams seemed to be absolutely anhydrous.

This island was thus of recent formation, and just as it had one day appeared, it could easily disappear on another and sink back to the depths of the ocean.

As the men climbed, the going became more and more difficult; the flanks of the mountain were approaching the vertical, and careful precautions had to be taken to avoid landslides. Often tall clouds of ash twisted around the travellers, threatening to suffocate them, and torrents of lava blocked their path. On the few horizontal parts, streams of lava, cooled and solid on the surface, allowed lava to flow bubbling under their hard crusts. Each man therefore had to carefully test the ground in front of him so as not to be suddenly plunged into the rivers of fire.

From time to time the crater vomited out blocks of rock, red hot from the inflamed gases; some of these masses exploded in the air like bombs, and the debris flew enormous distances in all directions.

It can be imagined what countless dangers this ascent of the mountain involved, and how insane one had to be to attempt it.

However, Hatteras climbed with surprising agility and, disdaining the help of his iron-tipped stick, moved up the steepest slopes without hesitation.

Soon he arrived at a circular rock, a sort of plateau about ten feet wide; an incandescent river divided at a ridge of rock higher up, then surrounded it, leaving only a narrow pathway, along which Hatteras boldly moved.

There he stopped, and his companions were able to join him. He seemed to be visually estimating the distance still to be covered; horizontally, he was less than 600 feet from the crater and the mathematical point of the Pole; but vertically, 1,500 feet still remained to be climbed.

The climb had already lasted three hours; Hatteras did not appear tired; his companions were exhausted.

The summit of the volcano could apparently not be reached. The doctor resolved to prevent Hatteras from climbing any more, at any price. He tried first with gentle means, but the captain's exultation had reached the point of delirium; during the march he had shown every sign of increasing insanity, but anyone who knew him, who had followed him through the various stages of life, could hardly be surprised. As Hatteras rose higher above the ocean, his excitement grew; he no longer lived in the realm of men; he was becoming greater than the mountain itself.

'Hatteras,' the doctor said to him, 'enough! We can't take a single step more.'

'Stay then,' replied the captain in a strange voice. 'I am going higher!'

'No, what you're doing is useless! You're at the Pole of the world!'

'No, no! Higher!'

'My friend, it's me talking to you, Dr Clawbonny. Do you recognize me?'

'Higher, higher!' repeated the madman.

'No! We will not let . . .'

The doctor had not finished before Hatteras made a superhuman effort, jumped across the lava flow, and was out of the reach of his companions.

They uttered a cry; they thought Hatteras had fallen into the torrents of fire; but the captain had landed on the other side, together with his dog Duke, who refused to leave him.

He was hidden behind a curtain of smoke, and his voice could be heard diminishing with the distance.

'Northwards, northwards!' he was crying. 'To the top of Mount Hatteras! Remember Mount Hatteras!'

They could not consider joining the captain; they had only a slim chance of repeating his feat, imbued as he was with the strength and skill particular to madmen; it was impossible to cross that stream of fire, impossible also to go around it. Altamont tried in vain to get over; he nearly perished trying to jump the lava; his companions had to restrain him bodily.

'Hatteras, Hatteras!' the doctor shouted.

But the captain did not reply, and only the barely perceptible barking of Duke echoed over the mountain.

Nevertheless, Hatteras could occasionally be glimpsed through the columns of smoke and ash raining down. Sometimes his arms, sometimes his head emerged from the swirling shapes. Then he would vanish only to reappear higher up, clinging on to rocks. He got smaller at that fantastic speed of objects rising in the air. Half an hour later, he already seemed to be only half his real height.

The air was full of the dull sounds of the volcano; the mountain was vibrating and groaning like an overheated boiler; its flanks could be felt shivering. Hatteras was still climbing. Duke still followed.

Occasionally landslides occurred behind them and enormous boulders, accelerating as they rebounded on the crests, rushed down to drown at the bottom of the polar basin.

Hatteras did not even turn round. He had used his stick as a shaft to hoist the Union Jack.* His terrified companions hung on to his every move. He gradually became microscopic, and Duke had shrunk to the size of a large rat.

There came a time when the wind pushed a vast curtain of flame over them. The doctor shouted in anguish; but Hatteras reappeared, still standing, waving his flag.

The vision of this frightening ascent lasted more than an hour. An hour of battle with the loose rocks and the holes full of ash, into which this hero of the impossible often disappeared up to his waist. Sometimes he performed acrobatics, buttressing himself with his knees and back against the projections of the mountain; sometimes he hung by his hands from some ridge, blown in the wind like a dried tuft of dry vegetation.

Finally he reached the top of the volcano, the very mouth of the crater. The hope then came to the doctor that the wretch, having reached his goal, would come back down again, and would only have the dangers of the return to face.

He shouted one last time:

'Hatteras! Hatteras!'

The doctor's appeal was heart-rending and moved the American to the depths of his soul.

'I'll save him!' exclaimed Altamont.

With a single leap across the torrents of fire, almost falling into them, he disappeared amongst the rocks.

Clawbonny had not had time to stop him.

Meanwhile, having reached the peak, Hatteras was advancing over the abyss on an overhanging rock below which there was nothing. Boulders rained down all around. Duke was still with him. The poor animal was apparently already caught up in the vertiginous attraction of the abyss. Hatteras was waving his flag, which was lit up with incandescent reflections, as the red muslin stood out in long folds in the breath from the crater.

Hatteras was shaking the standard with one hand.* With the other, he was pointing at the Pole of the celestial globe, directly above him. However, he still seemed to be hesitating. He was still seeking the mathematical point where all the lines of meridian meet, and where, in his sublime obstinacy, he wanted to set foot. All of a sudden, the rock gave way under his feet. He disappeared. A terrible cry from his companions sounded as far as the mountain peak. A second, a century passed! But Altamont was there,* and Duke too. The man and the dog had seized the unfortunate creature just as he fell into the chasm.

Hatteras was saved, saved against his will,* and half an hour later, the captain of the *Forward* was lying senseless, reposing in the arms of his despairing companions. When he came to again, the doctor examined his eyes in silent distress. But this unconscious regard, like a blind man who looks without seeing, did not respond.

'Good God,' said Johnson, 'he's blind!'

'No, he isn't. My poor friends, we have saved only Hatteras's body. His soul has remained at the summit of the volcano! His reason is dead!'

'Insane!' cried Johnson and Altamont in dismay.

'Insane,' the doctor replied. And large tears ran from his eyes.

26

South Again

THREE hours after this sad ending of the adventures of Captain Hatteras, Clawbonny, Altamont, and the two sailors were assembled again in the grotto at the foot of the volcano.

There the doctor was asked for his opinion as to what should be done.

'My friends,' he said, 'we cannot stay on Queen's Island any longer; but the sea is free before us; we don't have enough supplies;

we need to leave and get back to Fort Providence as soon as possible, where we can winter until next year.'

'That is what I think too,' said Altamont; 'the wind's favourable, and tomorrow we can set sail again.'

The day was spent in deep gloom. The captain's madness was a terrible blow, and when Johnson, Bell, and Altamont thought about their return, they were frightened by their abandonment, they were terrified of the distance. They missed Hatteras's intrepid soul.

Nevertheless, as they were energetic souls, they got ready to fight the elements once more, and fight themselves if ever they felt their resolve weakening.

The following day, Saturday, 13 July, the camping equipment was loaded, and soon everything was ready for departure.

But before leaving this rock, never to see it again, the doctor did what Hatteras had intended, and built a cairn at the precise point where the captain had landed on the island; this cairn was made of large stones, built up in such a way as to form a perfectly visible seamark, provided of course the volcano spared it.

On the face of one of the stones, Bell engraved this simple inscription with a chisel:

JOHN HATTERAS

1861*

A copy of the affidavit was placed inside the cairn, in a cylinder of totally airtight tin-plate, and the account of the great discovery was in this way abandoned on those deserted rocks.

Then the four men and the captain, a poor body without a soul, together with his faithful Duke, sad and pitiful, embarked for the journey home. It was ten in the morning. A new sail was rigged with canvas from the tent. The launch, with the wind behind, left Queen's Island; and in the evening, standing on his seat, the doctor said a last farewell to Mount Hatteras, still blazing on the horizon.

Their voyage was quick; the sea, now completely ice-free, offered easy navigation, and it truly seemed that the Pole was easier to flee than approach.

But Hatteras was not in a state to understand what was happening around him; he remained stretched out in the launch, mouth closed, eyes dead, arms crossed on his chest, Duke lying at his feet. In vain did the doctor talk to him. Hatteras could not hear.

For forty-eight hours the wind stayed favourable and the sea calm. Clawbonny and his companions gave a free hand to the northerly.

On 15 July, they sighted Altamont Harbour to the south; but as the Polar Ocean was free along the whole coast, rather than cross New America by sledge, they decided to go round it and sail to Victoria Bay.

Such a journey was quicker and easier. In effect, the distance that the travellers had taken a fortnight to do with the sledge, took hardly a week by boat; and after following the sinuosities of a coast fringed with numerous fiords, whose configuration they determined, they arrived at Victoria Bay on the evening of Monday, 23 July.*

The launch was firmly lashed to the shore, and all rushed to Fort Providence. But what devastation! Doctor's House, the stores, the powder magazine, the fortifications—all had been turned to water by the warmth of the sunbeams, and the supplies had been raided by carnivorous animals.

What a sad and disheartening sight!

The mariners had almost reached the end of their supplies, planning to find more at Fort Providence. It was clear that spending the winter there was impossible. Used to making quick decisions, they resolved to head for Baffin Bay by the shortest route.

'There's nothing else we can do,' said the doctor. 'Baffin Bay is less than six hundred miles away; we can keep going as long as there's water under our launch and so reach Jones Strait, and from there the Danish settlements.'

'Agreed,' said Altamont; 'let's get together what's left of our supplies, and go.'

By searching carefully, they found a few boxes of pemmican strewn here and there, plus two surviving barrels of preserved meat. In sum, supplies for six weeks and sufficient quantities of powder. It was quickly gathered; they spent the day caulking and repairing the launch, and the following day, 24 July, they set off once more.

At about the eighty-third degree, the landmass bent eastwards. It was possible that it connected with those lands, known as Grinnell, Ellesmere, and North Lincoln, which form the coast of Baffin Bay. It was certain therefore that Jones Strait opened into the interior seas, exactly like Lancaster Sound.

The launch sailed on without great difficulties; it easily avoided the floating ice. The doctor, anticipating possible delays, put his companions on half-rations; but in sum, they did not tire themselves excessively, and remained in good health.

In addition, they were able to fire their rifles a few times; they shot ducks, geese, and guillemots, providing fresh and healthy food. As for drinking, they could easily replenish their supplies with ice floes or fresh water encountered en route; for they were always careful not to leave the coasts, the poor state of the launch not allowing them to face the open sea.

At this season, the thermometer remained constantly below freezing; having often been rainy, the weather turned to snow and darkness; the sun was already beginning to skim along the horizon, and its disc was getting smaller each day. On 30 July, the travellers lost sight of it for the first time; in other words they had a night of a few minutes.

However, the launch sailed well, and sometimes covered a distance of sixty or sixty-five miles in twenty-four hours; they did not stop a single moment; they knew what fatigues were to be borne and what obstacles overcome if the land route became their only option, and indeed these narrow seas were sure to freeze again soon; here and there small ice floes were forming. Winter succeeds summer without warning at high latitudes; there is neither spring nor autumn; the intermediate seasons are absent. So they needed to hurry.

On 31 July, the sky was clear at sunset, and they noticed the first stars in the constellations of the zenith. But from that day on, there hung constant fog, which made the navigation difficult.

Seeing the signs of winter, the doctor felt very worried; he knew what difficulties Sir John Ross encountered before reaching Baffin Bay and abandoning ship; having tried to cross the ice a first time, that bold sailor was forced to return to the vessel, and winter for a fourth year; but at least he had shelter for the bad season, as well as supplies and fuel.

If such ill fortune happened to the survivors of the *Forward*, if they needed to stop or turn round, they were lost; the doctor said nothing of his worries to his companions, but he pushed them to head as far east as possible.

Finally, on 15 August, after thirty days of relatively fast sailing, after forty-eight hours spent fighting against the ice building up in the passes, after risking their fragile launch a hundred times, the sailors found themselves absolutely stuck and unable to go any further; the sea was frozen in all directions, and the thermometer read only fifteen (9°C) on average.

In addition, it was clear that to the north and east the coast was near, from the flat round pebbles that the water wears out on the shore; they also met freshwater ice more often.

Altamont measured the position with scrupulous precision, and obtained 77° 15′ N, 85° 2′ W.

'So,' said the doctor, 'this is our exact position; we've reached North Lincoln, exactly at Cape Eden; we're entering Jones Strait; with a bit more luck we'd have found it free of ice as far as Baffin Bay. But we can't complain. If poor Hatteras had encountered such an easy sea at the beginning, he'd have arrived quickly at the Pole. His companions would not have abandoned him, and perhaps his mind would not have gone due to his terrible anguish!'

'Then there's only one thing to do, abandon the launch, and head for the east coast of Lincoln with the sledge.'

'Abandon the launch and use the sledge again, agreed,' replied the doctor. 'But instead of crossing Lincoln, I suggest going through Jones Strait over the ice, and reaching North Devon.'

'Why?' said Altamont.

'Because the closer we get to Lancaster Sound, the more chance we will have of meeting whalers.'

'You're right, doctor; but I'm afraid the ice may not be solid enough yet to offer a practicable route.'

'We can but try.'

The launch was unloaded; Bell and Johnson rebuilt the sledge; all the components were in good condition; the next day the dogs were harnessed to it, and the troop began following the coast to get to the ice-field.

Then began that journey, so often described, tiring and slow; Altamont had been right not to have confidence in the state of the ice; they were unable to cross Jones Strait, and had to follow the coast of Lincoln.

On 21 August, the travellers cut across the bay, and reached the entrance to Glacier Strait; there they ventured on to the ice-field, and the following day reached Coburg Island, which they crossed in less than two days, amid squalls of snow.

They were now able to take an easier route across the ice-fields and finally, on 24 August, they set foot on North Devon.

'Now,' said the doctor, 'all we have to do is cross this land, and reach Cape Warrender, at the entrance to Lancaster Sound.'

But the weather became very poor and very cold; the swirls of snow, the whirlwinds returned to their winter violence; the travellers had no strength left. Their supplies were nearly finished, and each man had to go on to one-third rations so as to give the dogs food proportional to their work.

The nature of the ground added to the fatigue of the journey: the terrain of North Devon was extremely uneven; they had to cross the Trauter Mountains* and pass through valleys, fighting against the unleashed elements. The sledge, the men, and the dogs were virtually unable to get out, and more than once, despair took hold of the little troop, although they were hardened and used to the exhaustion of a polar expedition. Without realizing, these poor men had worn themselves out, morally and physically; eighteen months of unceasing fatigues and an enervating succession of hope and despair are not borne without effect. In addition, it should be pointed out, outward journeys are done with energy and conviction, which are lacking for the return. Accordingly, the poor wretches dragged themselves along with much difficulty; it can be said that they walked through habit, through the remnants of their animal energy, almost independently of their will.

It was only on 30 August that they finally emerged from this chaos of mountains—of which the orography of low-lying areas can give no idea—but they did emerge, albeit half-dead and frozen. The doctor, on the point of collapse, was no longer strong enough to support his companions.

The Trauter Mountains terminated in plains, not flat because of the original lifting of the mountains.

There the travellers had no choice but to take a few days' rest; they could no longer put one foot in front of another; two of the dogs had died of exhaustion.

So they sheltered behind a block of ice, at a temperature of minus two degrees (−19°C); nobody had the energy to put up the tent.

Their supplies had gone down a great deal and, in spite of the extreme parsimony of the rations, could only last one week more; game was getting rare, heading back down south for a milder winter. Death from starvation rose in front of these exhausted victims, taunting them.

Altamont, who showed great devotion and self-sacrifice, used his little remaining strength and decided to hunt for food for his companions.

He picked up his gun, called Duke, and headed north to the plains; the doctor, Johnson, and Bell watched him go almost with indifference. For an hour they did not hear his gun, and saw him coming back without a single shot having been fired; but the American was running up in terror.

'What's the matter?' asked the doctor.

'Over there, under the snow!' replied Altamont with fear, pointing to the horizon.

'What?'

'A whole troop of men!'

'Living?'

'Frozen, dead, and even . . .'

The American dared not complete his thought, but his face expressed the most inexpressible horror.

Brought back to life by this incident, the doctor, Johnson, and Bell found the energy to get up, and dragged themselves along Altamont's tracks to the area of plain he had pointed at.

They soon reached a narrow gully at the end of a deep valley, but what a sight appeared before their eyes!

Bodies, already stiff, half-buried under the white shroud, emerged in places from the covering of snow; here an arm, there a leg, further on clenched fists or heads still expressing threats or despair!

The doctor went up, but then retreated, his features pale and broken up, while Duke barked in sinister terror.

'Horror! Horror!' he said.

'Well?' asked the mate.

'Don't you recognize them?' said the doctor in a faltering voice.

'What do you mean?'

'Look!'

Not long previously, this valley had been the scene of a last battle against time, against despair, against hunger; and from certain horrible remains, it could be understood that the wretches had fed on human bodies, perhaps living bodies; and amongst them, the doctor recognized Shandon, Pen, and the whole miserable crew of the *Forward*; strength had been lacking in these unfortunate men, as well as food; their launch had probably been buried in an avalanche or fallen into a chasm, and they had been unable to profit from the open sea; they had presumably also got lost in these unknown lands. In any case, people caught up in the excitement of mutiny could not maintain for long that union which allows great things to be accomplished. A ringleader of mutineers never has anything but an uncertain power in his hands. And without doubt, Shandon had soon lost control.

Whatever the truth, the crew had clearly experienced a thousand tortures and a thousand despairs, before encountering this terrifying catastrophe; but the secret of their misery is buried with them under the snows of the Pole for ever.*

'Let's leave! Let's leave now!' shouted the doctor.

And he took his companions far away from that place of disaster. The horror gave them energy for a while. They set off once more.

27

Conclusion

WHAT would be the point of relating all the problems the survivors of the expedition encountered? They themselves were later unable to retrieve from their memories the details of the week following the discovery of the horrible remains of the crew.

On 9 September, through a miracle of energy, they found themselves at Cape Horsburgh, on the tip of North Devon.

They were dying of starvation; they hadn't eaten for forty-eight hours; their last meal had been the flesh of the final Eskimo dog. Bell could not go on any more, and old Johnson felt he was dying.*

They were on the shores of Baffin Bay, partly frozen, that is on the way to Europe. Three miles from the coast, waves broke noisily over the sharp edge of the ice-field.

They had now to wait for a whaler to come past, and how long would that take?

But heaven had pity on these wretches, for Altamont spotted a sail on the horizon the following day.

It is well known what anguish accompanies such appearances of ships, what fears of dashed hopes! The vessel seems to alternately get closer and move away. There exist horrible examples of hope and despair, and only too often, at the moment the shipwrecked men believe they are saved, the glimpsed sail moves off and disappears below the horizon.

The doctor and his companions went through all these trials; they had reached the western end of the ice-field, carrying each other, pushing each other, and they saw the ship disappear little by little without realizing they were there. They shouted, but to no avail!

It was then that one last inspiration came to the doctor from his hard-working mind of genius, which had served him so well.

An ice floe, caught by the current, came and struck the ice-field.

'This ice floe!' he said, pointing at it.

They did not understand.

'Let's get on! Get on!' he exclaimed.

It was a bolt of lightning in everybody's minds.

'Ah, Dr Clawbonny, Dr Clawbonny!' repeated Johnson, kissing the doctor's hands.

Helped by Altamont, Bell ran to the sledge; he brought back one of the runners, planted it as a mast in the ice, and secured it with ropes; the tent was torn up for a makeshift sail. The wind was favourable; the poor abandoned men rushed on to this fragile raft,* and headed for the open sea.

Two hours later, after incredible efforts, the last men from the *Forward* were taken on board the *Hans Christian*, a Danish whaler heading back to Davis Strait.

The captain, a generous man, welcomed these spectres who no longer had human appearance; at the sight of their suffering, he understood their story; he gave them the most attentive care, and he succeeded in keeping them alive.

Ten days later, Clawbonny, Johnson, Bell, Altamont, and Captain Hatteras disembarked at Korsoeur, in Zeeland, Denmark; a steamer took them on to Kiel; from there, via Altona and Hamburg, they reached London, where they arrived on the thirteenth of the same month,* having hardly recovered from their long suffering.

The doctor's first task was to ask the Royal Geographical Society of London for consent to make a presentation; he was invited to the session of 15 July.

The astonishment of this scientific assembly can easily be

imagined, as well as the enthusiastic hurrays that followed the reading of Hatteras's document.

This unique journey, without precedent in the annals of history, summed up all the previous discoveries done in the circumpolar regions; it united the expeditions of Parry, Ross, Franklin, and McClure; it completed the map of the hyperboreal lands between the hundredth and hundred-and-fifteenth meridians; and it culminated at that point of the globe inaccessible until then: at the very Pole.

Never, no, never did such an unexpected piece of news explode across a stupefied Britain!

The British are excited by great geographic accomplishments; they felt moved and proud, from the Lord to the Cockney, from the merchant prince to the dockworker.

The news of the great discovery ran down all the telegraphic wires of the United Kingdom at the speed of lightning; the newspapers inscribed the name of Hatteras in their titles, like that of a martyr, and Britain trembled with pride.

The doctor and his companions were fêted, and formally presented to Her Gracious Majesty by the Lord Chancellor.

The government confirmed the name of Queen's Island for the rock at the North Pole, Mount Hatteras for the volcano, and Altamont Harbour for the port of New America.

Altamont remained with his companions in misery and glory, and became their friend; he went with the doctor, Bell, and Johnson* to Liverpool, which acclaimed them on their return, after believing them long dead and buried in the eternal ice.

But Dr Clawbonny always gave the glory to the man who deserved it above all others. In his account of the journey, entitled *The British at the North Pole* and published the following year by the Royal Geographical Society, he presented John Hatteras as the equal of the great travellers, the successor of those daring men who indefatigably sacrificed themselves for the advancement of science.

Meanwhile, this sad victim of his sublime passion was living peacefully in Sten Cottage Nursing Home,* close to Liverpool, where his friend the doctor had personally placed him. His madness was of the gentle sort, but he did not speak, he no longer understood, for power of speech had apparently departed at the same time as his reason. Only one emotion linked him to the external world, his friendship for Duke, from whom it had not been thought wise to separate him. This disease, this 'polar madness', thus quietly followed its course, not presenting any special symptoms. But while visiting his poor patient one day, Dr Clawbonny was struck by his gait.

For some time, Captain Hatteras had been walking several hours each day, followed by his faithful dog, who gazed at him with soft, sad eyes; but it was invariably in a particular direction along a certain avenue at Sten Cottage. Once the captain reached the end of the avenue, he would retrace his route, walking backwards. If somebody stopped him, he would point to a fixed spot in the sky. If someone tried to make him turn round, he would flare up, and Duke, sharing his anger, would bark furiously.

The doctor attentively observed such a strange mania, and soon understood the reason for such a singular obstinacy; he guessed why the walk followed a fixed direction, under the influence, as it were, of a magnetic force.*

Captain John Hatteras marched constantly north.

THE END

APPENDIX A

THE DELETED DUEL EPISODE AND THE ORIGINAL ENDING

THE manuscript version of *Hatteras* is very different, but Hetzel made Verne radically rewrite it (see the Introduction and the Note on the Text and Translation, above). While several articles have been written about the paragraphs of the suicide and the closing lines, the rest of the manuscript has never been studied. Extracts are provided here from the duel scene and the closing pages, by kind permission of the Municipal Library of Nantes, the owner of the manuscript.

The Deleted Duel Episode

In MS (II 21, 'John Bull and Jonathan'), it is Altamont at the helm, rather than Hatteras, as they sail for the Pole. As in 1867, the British captain dreams first of the past, then of the future, in particular the Pole and the Union Jack:

> His impression was then so strong, that he thought he heard it floating above his head; it seemed to him that the wind was playing in its folds; he woke and opened his eyes.
>
> He was not mistaken: a flag was waving at the tip of the launch's mast, a red flag with twenty-two stars on a sky-blue background, an American flag!
>
> Hatteras uttered a terrible cry. His companions awoke.
>
> 'Wretch!' exclaimed the captain, addressing the American. And he quickly severed the halyard, bringing the flag down.
>
> Altamont wanted to rush at him; but Johnson and Bell held him back.

Altamont says the launch is his, but Clawbonny says Hatteras is in charge, and reminds Altamont they had saved his life. The American angrily ripostes that he has guessed their aim of conquering the Pole, and says that that is also his aim.

Hatteras agrees, saying even the floes are American; that Altamont is safe while he remains on the launch; and the idea of a duel suddenly arises, although Clawbonny repeatedly tries to calm the two down. The two captains decide to fight the duel on neutral terrain, that is when they reach land.

Much later, they see what may be a volcano, leading to a discussion as to whether it is possible so close to the Pole—and as, Hatteras says, whether they need 'the permission of the President of the United States' to visit.

While everyone sleeps, Hatteras takes the helm, and eventually wakes Altamont up. He says only one of them can land first, and apologizes twice to Altamont for calling him a 'coward', but is rebuffed. A duel is inevitable, but cannot be fought on land, since it first needs to be decided who has precedence for setting foot on it. They decide to fight it out on a floating ice floe.

Chapter 22 reads:

Half an hour later the launch drew alongside the scene for the combat. The wind had completely fallen; not a breath, not a whisper in the atmosphere, just one of those sinister silences, the silences which in less elevated regions herald storms.

The flaccid sail hung on the mast; useless to brail it; the launch was undulating on the last ripples of the waves.

Hatteras manoeuvred near the floe without touching it, for the impact might have woken his companions; Altamont leapt on to the slippery surface, holding the launch while his foe disembarked in turn. Then the captain gently pushed it away with his foot . . .

The floe Hatteras had chosen was twenty feet long by eight wide, approximately oval. The two men headed for the middle part. Each held his snow knife with its broad sharpened blade.

A terrible duel was about to happen, in strange surroundings and without witnesses.

'Altamont,' said Hatteras, '. . . no cries should be made during the fight; we will allow ourselves to be killed without complaint . . . this duel must not be stopped before one of us is dead.'

'Hurray for America,' quietly replied Altamont.

'Hurray for Britain,' added Hatteras.

The two men squared up, and attacked each other with great fury.

What a sight, this soundless battle on the fragile floe, while the boat moved away on a slow current.

The Briton and the American, of equal strength and bravery, rained terrible blows down on each other, successfully parried. Their greatest difficulty was keeping their footing on the slippery surface; one false step could bring death . . .

How this fight would have finished without an unforeseen event, nobody will ever be able to say.

From the moment the two fighters had set foot on the floe, an attentive observer would have noticed it gradually sinking under their weight; because of the relative warmth of the sea, it . . . was slowly disappearing; Hatteras and Altamont did not realize, but soon the seawater was over their ankles; two minutes later it was up to their knees; their battle continued although they could feel little under their feet; no less did they make furious assaults at each other; neither man wanted to stop.

They were soon in the water . . . as far as their chests . . . their heads remained above water, then they disappeared without uttering a single cry; from the disturbance of the waves above them, it was clear they were still fighting.

Meanwhile the launch, abandoned to its own devices . . . had collided, in a providential piece of luck, with one of the rare ice floes on the Polar Sea.

Woken by the collision, Johnson opened his eyes.

His first cry was:

'The captain! Altamont!'

At these words the doctor understood everything . . .

'Over there,' he said.

Quickly in position, the oars made the launch fly towards the spot indicated. At the precise moment when the Briton and American, in a tight embrace, came back to the surface almost drowned, their companions took firm hold of them and pulled them on to the boat.

'Oh, wretches!' exclaimed the doctor.

And tears came to his eyes, while Hatteras and Altamont, now separated, measured each other up with looks of hate. The doctor treated their hands with his tears; his heart was overflowing. With passion he produced everything his perfect soul could inspire from him in the form of bitter words and reproaches . . . caresses, supplications, everything came from the heart.

'You too! My poor friends! To fight, to kill each other, for a miserable question of nationality! And what have Britain and America got to do with it! If the North Pole is reached, what does it matter who discovered it! Why . . . call yourself American or British when you can call yourself a man!'

The doctor spoke thus for a long time . . . with no effect whatsoever! [Were] . . . these tough beings, savages so to speak . . . [moved by] the tears which they drew from that best of men? It could be doubted given the hate-filled daggers the captains' eyes threw at each other.

The night was spent keeping watch over them.

From this point, with the blowing up of a storm, the text is similar to 1867.

The Original Ending

In the manuscript the climax of the novel and the following events (II 25–6) read as follows:

'Hatteras! Hatteras!'

But then he saw the wretch advancing along a section overhanging the abyss, in the midst of the flames, oblivious of the slabs of rock raining down around him. Duke was following two paces behind: the faithful animal seemed able to resist the vertigo threatening to engulf him. The captain was waving his flag, illuminated with strange reflections as the reddened muslin folds stood out in the incandescent light.

Hatteras was shaking the standard with one hand, and with the other indicating the zenith, that Pole of the celestial globe.

All of a sudden, he vanished from view. A terrible cry from his companions must have sounded as far as the mountain peak; a quarter of minute, a century passed, and then the unfortunate man could be seen once more launched ~~into the air~~ by the explosion of the volcano to an immense height, his flag distended by the exhalations of the crater.

Then he fell back down into the volcano, whereupon Duke, faithful to the death, threw himself in so as to share his grave.

Chapter 2~~7~~6
~~The Return~~ The Hans Christien

It is xx to depict the despair which took hold of the doctor and his companions xx captain, their friend, victim of his attempt, and of the companions of the unfortunate Hatteras who had just perished before their eyes at the price of xx.

In the hope of finding the remains of the poor man, they went down the mountain again and reached, after xx difficulties, the southern face. The opposing volcanic slopes.

But it was soon realized that nothing of Hatteras could be found, and that he had found death in the xx of the volcano. The grave was worthy of him. The doctor xx to go down again and after three hours' march the four survivors of this great ~~endeavour~~ expedition were back in the grotto.

There, the doctor was asked for his opinion . . .

Hatteras's death is in many ways more logical, more in line with his character, and better prepared by the previous chapters. Furthermore, his death represents the only way of reaching the absolute Pole, the meaning of his life and of the novel; in the published version his madness presumably stems from his failure to reach the point where the meridians finally meet.

The closing lines are also quite different, and equally striking:

A few days later, after hearty hugs from his companions in glory and suffering, Altamont left for America. The doctor, Bell, and Johnson returned to Liverpool and great acclaim, after being given up for dead for so long.

But the doctor always bestowed the glory on the man who deserved it above all others. In his account of the journey, entitled The British at the North Pole and published the following year by the Royal Geographical Society, he presented John Hatteras as the equal of John Franklin, for both were fearless victims of science. And, of the memories of his Arctic expedition, the most indelible was that of a Mount Hatteras smoking on the horizon, the grave of a British captain standing at the North Pole of the globe.

THE END

APPENDIX B

A CHRONOLOGY OF ARCTIC EXPEDITIONS[1]

Expedition Dates	Ships	Leader and Accomplishments
983		Eric the Red discovers Greenland.
c. 1000		Leif Eriksson to Newfoundland.
1594–7		Willem Barents discovers Spitzbergen.
1607–10	*Hopewell*	Henry Hudson to Greenland, Spitzbergen, Jan Mayen, Hudson River, and Hudson Bay.
1615–16	*Discovery*	William Baffin and Robert Bylot to Baffin Bay.
1733–43	*St Peter*	Vitus Bering to the Bering Sea and Arctic Siberia.
1769–72	overland	Samuel Hearne to the Canadian Arctic coast.
1773	*Racehorse*	Constantine John Phipps, with Horatio Nelson, to Svalbard.
1776–8	*Resolution*	James Cook to North-East Siberia and Alaska.
1789–93	overland	Alexander Mackenzie down the Mackenzie River to the Arctic.
1806		William Scoresby senior, a whaler, with William Scoresby junior, discovers the Polar Sea east of Svalbard, reaching 81° 30'.
1817		Scoresby junior to Jan Mayen, reaching 82° 30' and finding the coast free of ice.
1818	*Isabella* and *Alexander*	John Ross, with William Edward Parry and James Ross, explores Baffin Bay, looking for a Northwest Passage; make the first contacts with polar Eskimos.
1819–20	*Hecla* and *Griper*	Parry, with Frederick Beechey and James Ross, in search of the Northwest Passage, reaches Melville Island, the first European to visit the Arctic archipelago and the first to winter there.

---

[1] With acknowledgements to the chronology in Pierre Berton, *The Arctic Grail* (2001). Dates in italics are those of the expeditions most cited in *Hatteras*.

1819–22	overland	John Franklin, with John Richardson and George Back, down the Coppermine River and east to Point Turnagain (in conjunction with Parry), ending catastrophically with cannibalism and eleven men dead.
1821–3	*Fury* and *Hecla*	Parry to Fury and Hecla Strait.
1824–5	*Hecla* and *Fury*	Parry, with Francis Crozier, to Somerset Island.
1825–7	overland	Franklin, with Richardson, Back, and Peter Dease, explores the coastline from Coronation Gulf to Alaska.
1825–8	*Blossom*	Frederick William Beechey, with Sir Edward Belcher, to Chamisso Island and Icy Cape.
1827	*Hecla*	Parry via Spitzbergen, reaching 82° 45′ N, a record for fifty years.
1829–33	*Victory*	John Ross to Prince Regent Inlet; James Ross discovers the North Magnetic Pole.
1833–4	*La Lilloise*	Jules Poret de Blosseville to Greenland.
1833–5	overland	Back down the Great Fish River.
1836–7	*Terror*	Back to Hudson Bay.
1837–9	overland	Dease and Thomas Simpson survey the Arctic coast.
1839–40	*Bon Accord*	William Penny to Cumberland Sound.
1845–8	*Erebus* and *Terror*	Franklin, with Crozier and James Fitzjames, in search of the Northwest Passage.
1846–7	overland	John Rae to Boothia Peninsula.
1848–9	*Investigator* and *Enterprise*	James Ross, with Robert McClure and Leopold McClintock, in search of Franklin, as are all the expeditions below, except Rae (1853–4) and Hayes (1860–1).
1848–9	*Plover*	Thomas Moore tries to enter Bering Strait.
1848–51	*Herald* and *North Star*	Henry Kellett, with William John Samuel Pullen, Bedford Pim, and Émile de Bray, to Bering Strait to wait for Franklin.
1848–51	overland	Richardson, with Rae, to Mackenzie River and Victoria Island.
1850–1	*Resolute, Assistance, Pioneer,* and *Intrepid*	Horatio Austin, with Erasmus Ommanney and McClintock, to Cornwallis Island.
1850–1	*Felix*	John Ross on a privately financed expedition.

1850–1	*Advance* and *Rescue*	Edwin De Haven, with Elisha Kent Kane, on first US Arctic expedition.
1850–1	*Lady Franklin* and *Sophia*	Penny, with Alexander Stewart, finds traces of Franklin's wintering on Beechey Island.
1850–3	*Prince Albert*	William Kennedy, with Charles Codrington Forsyth, W. Parker Snow, and Joseph-René Bellot, on Lady Franklin's expedition.
1850–4	*Investigator*	McClure, with S. Gurney Cresswell, William Haswell, and Robert Wynniatt, via Bering Strait. Although abandoning his ship, he finds the last link in the Northwest Passage and receives the official reward for its discovery.
1851–4	*Enterprise*	Richard Collinson through Bering Strait to McClintock Strait.
1852	*Isabella*	Edward Inglefield to Smith Sound and Jones Strait.
1852–4	*Assistance, Resolute, North Star, Pioneer,* and *Intrepid*	Edward Belcher, with Kellett, de Bray, and Pullen, rescues McClure and his crew.
1853–4	*Breadalbane* and *Phoenix*	Inglefield, with Johnson and Bellot; the *Breadalbane* takes supplies to Beechey Island, but sinks. Inglefield leaves the *Phoenix*, which then takes Cresswell back early from McClure's *Investigator*.
1853–4	*North Pole* and *Magnet*	Rae, surveying King William Land and Boothia, finds remnants from the Franklin expedition in Eskimos' hands.
1853–5	*Advance*	Kane, with William Morton, Isaac Hayes, and Hans Hendrik, to 80° 35′ N. Morton claims he has reached 81° 22′.
1857–9	*Fox*	McClintock, with William Robert Hobson, paid for by Lady Franklin, confirms Franklin's crew's fate on King William Island.
1860–1	*United States*	Hayes searches for open Polar Sea.

APPENDIX C

PUBLISHER'S ANNOUNCEMENTS AND EARLY REVIEWS

Publisher's Announcements

PAGE 18 of the opening issue of the *MÉR* (I 1864) contains a significant presentation by 'J.H.' (Hetzel), as follows:

> Under this double title, *The British at the North Pole* and *The Desert of Ice*, the author of *Five Weeks in a Balloon* today gives us the account of a curious and absorbing journey, in which discoveries in the Arctic seas up to our time are summed up with the scientific precision, the expert geographical knowledge, and the persuasive storytelling talent which made his first book a work unique in its kind to date.
>
> Every clear fact that has transpired in those seas so rich in dramas and of the most gripping interest is collected again before the eyes of our readers. Transported with *Captain Hatteras* into those unknown lands, they will observe all the cosmic phenomena of the northern seas, and reach the Pole itself.
>
> Agreements passed with M. Jules Verne guarantee our collection a *New Journey around the World* and a *General History of Geographical Voyages and Discoveries*, carried out according to an entirely new plan by the scholarly writer [*savant écrivain*].

Vol. II of the *MÉR* closed with Hetzel's 'To Our Subscribers' (375–6), announcing plans for 1865–6, notably:

> In *The Desert of Ice*, M. Jules Verne will give us the sequel and conclusion of *The British at the North Pole*, which so greatly interested our readers of all ages. He will show what man, buoyed up by an energetic will and scientific knowledge, can do even when abandoned to his own resources, in the most difficult conditions. This second and final part, whose title could have been *The Robinsons of the Ice*, will perhaps be more interesting than the first. [*sic*]

The illustrated single-volume edition of July to November 1866 contained an illuminating 'Publisher's Announcement' (1–2):

> The excellent books of M. Jules Verne are amongst the few that can be offered with confidence to the younger generations. Amongst con-

temporary creations there are none that respond better to the generous impulse of modern society, finally familiarizing it with the marvels of the universe where its destiny is unfolding. There are none who better justified the rapid success they encountered when they first came out.

If the public's fancy can be distracted for a while by showy and unwholesome volumes, in the longer term taste has only remained with what is fundamentally wholesome and good. What has especially helped the reaction to M. Jules Verne's charming books is that they have both the qualities of substantial nourishment and the savour of the tastiest dishes.

The most qualified critics[1] have acclaimed M. Jules Verne as a writer of an exceptional nature, to whom it was only fair to assign a new place in French literature straightaway. A storyteller full of imagination and fire, a pure and original writer, a sharp and lively mind, the equal of any in the art of building up and resolving astonishing dramas, which give such great interest to his bold conceptions, and, on top of that, profoundly learned, he has created a new genre. What is so often promised but so rarely delivered, education that entertains and entertainment that educates, is prodigally provided by M. Verne on each page of his exciting stories.

The Novels of M. Jules Verne arrive at just the right time. When one sees people rushing to the lectures at a thousand places in France, when one sees that beside art and theatre criticism, space in our newspapers has had to go to the proceedings of the Academy of Sciences, people really need to tell themselves that in our age Art for Art's Sake is no longer enough, that the time has come for science to take its place in the realm of literature.

M. Jules Verne's merit is to have placed his thought on this new land first, as a master; it is to have deserved what one illustrious scientist could say, without flattery, of the books we publish: 'These novels, which will entertain you like Alexander Dumas's best, will instruct you like François Arago's works.'

Young and old, rich and poor, uneducated and learned—all will find pleasure and profit in making M. Verne's excellent books family friends and giving them pride of place on their bookshelves.

The edition illustrated by M. Riou [*sic*] which we offer today at an unusually low price and in a format of true luxury demonstrates the confidence we have in both the work's value, which we have the honour

---

[1] Presumably de Saint-Martin and Zola (see their reviews below), Gustave Landrol, *Bibliothèque d'éducation et de récréation* (catalogue d'étrennes) (1864), 25–8, and Landrol, *Le Constitutionnel*, 11 Dec. 1864.

of popularizing, and the good taste of the public of every class and age, to whom we offer it.

After the *Adventures of Captain Hatteras*, composed of two parts, *The British at the North Pole* and *The Desert of Ice*, we shall publish successively *Journey to the Centre of the Earth*—revised, with several new chapters composed by the author—*From the Earth to the Moon*, and *Five Weeks in a Balloon*.

M. Verne's new volumes will be successively added to this edition, which we shall take care to keep up to date. Both the works already published and those yet to appear will in this way follow the programme the author resolved upon, when he gave his collected works the subtitle of Journeys in the Known and Unknown Worlds. His aim is to sum up all the *geographic, geological, physical, and astronomical* knowledge accumulated by modern science, and hence to rewrite, in the attractive and picturesque form which is his speciality, the history of the universe.

    J. Hetzel

While Hetzel's version is illuminating for the ideological straitjacket Verne is placed in, equally important is its draft, in Verne's handwriting, also written in mid-1866:[2]

Amongst the books which it is the duty of the press to bring to the public's notice, there are few which make the critic's task easier than the excellent works of M. Jules Verne. From their first appearance their double success as books of science and books of the imagination has brought them support from what had seemed incompatible voices. The truth is that M. Jules Verne is the creator of a new genre and he deserves a place apart in contemporary literature. A storyteller full of fire, the equal of the best novelists, he is also one of the most scientific intelligences of the time. Nobody has given fiction a more immediate reality, and, while reading his books, one really comes to wonder if such works are the product of imagination. The reader is carried away against his will with the audacious characters that the author puts on stage.

    Public favour sometimes attaches itself to loud and unhealthy works; but it only ever settles in durable fashion on works with solid contents and truly literary form . . . Vivian de Saint-Martin rightly said that 'if Arago had written such works he would not have written them differently'.

Both texts are thinner on substance than on self-publicity—and the

[2] In the French National Library (Archives Hetzel, Naf 17008, fos. 30–2); the draft is reproduced and commented by Volker Dehs, 'Où Jules Verne annonce ses "œuvres completes" ', *Cahiers du Centre d'études verniennes*, 7 (1987), 48–50.

variation in the 'quotations' from de Saint-Martin implies they are probably invented. Hetzel emphasizes science, exhaustive knowledge, and education, whereas Verne writes better, and underlines the 'place apart' which
he deserves in 'contemporary literature', as 'the equal of the best novelists', and his vision, shared with Flaubert and Hugo, of fiction being
exposed to the marketplace. It is unfortunate that Hetzel's interpretation
of the nature of Verne's writing was the one that prevailed.

Early Reviews

The first review of *Hatteras*, by Vivien de Saint-Martin, came out while
the book was still being published. It is in the *MÉR* (III 266 (October
1864)/II 14), on the same page as Verne's text itself. It is preceded by the
following presentation, signed 'D.G.' [Ferdinand, Comte de Gramont, a
friend of Verne's]:

> We borrow from the *Annuaire géographique*,[3] by M. Vivien de Saint-
> Martin, the following page on the geographical studies [*travaux*] of
> M. Jules Verne, published both in the *Magasin* and in the Bibliothèque
> d'éducation et de recréation. We are happy in every respect to see a
> scholar as eminent as M. Vivien de Saint-Martin, the most qualified
> geographer of our time, rendering such brilliant justice to our
> collaborator.

Although clearly prompted by Hetzel, with even the language identical
to his Announcement ('qualified', 'a new place', 'solid', 'instructive', as
well as the denial of terms like 'novel' or 'literary'), the review itself would
help determine Verne's reputation for the next century and a half. It
reads:

THE BRITISH AT THE NORTH POLE – FIVE WEEKS IN A BALLOON

There is one expedition whose characters and adventures belong to
fiction, but which one would be tempted to classify amongst true journeys, so much truth do the details contain. This is the tale that M. Jules
Verne is publishing in an excellent educational series, *The British at the
North Pole: The Story of Captain Hatteras*. We already had occasion last
year to mention a similar publication by the same author, devoted to
Africa and no less remarkable by the solidity of its contents and the
welcome originality of its form. Certainly, the genre where the authors
of *Robinson* and *Gulliver* distinguished themselves, without mentioning
the tedious numbers of what are called *Imaginary Journeys*, is not new

---

[3] In fact the *Année géographique* (3 (1864 [for 1865]), 270, 'Régions arctiques'), under
the title 'Histoire du capitaine Hatteras'. Verne returns the compliment by referring to
de Saint-Martin in both his fictional and non-fictional works.

in geographical literature; but at his first attempt M. Verne has been able to carve out a new place and make his mark as an innovator, thanks to the special flavour he has given his composition. It is neither satire, nor allegory, nor a novel in the normal sense; it is a serious and deep study of places, things, and characters, placed most skilfully within a tale which becomes true through being so natural! Each speaks his own idiom, whether a sailor or a scientist; geography and polar phenomena are presented with a master's hand; the slightest details of the ship and its operations often give the impression that the author has spent his life on the deck of an Arctic boat. It is very difficult for science and fiction to come into contact, without one of them being weighed down or the other lowered; here the two work in a happy union, which reinforces the instructive side of the relationship while retaining the instructive attractiveness of the adventure side. The most expert will discover things to be learned, and, almost without realizing, the great mass of readers will find irreproachable notions that very few would have sought in books of a severer aspect. I will add—and for me this is the greatest merit of M. Verne's compositions—that far from dissuading us from more serious readings, they rather draw us to them, and, by pointing the way, show how much attractiveness and varied gain can be found in the tales of a scholarly traveller who is at the same time a witty storyteller.

Two further accounts of the illustrated edition, again derived from Hetzel's Announcement, appeared in December 1866.[4] The first one mentions:

the books, so curious, so interesting, so instructive, by M. Verne . . . *The Adventures of Captain Hatteras* sums up, in an attractive and dramatic form, all the voyages of exploration in the glacial seas and towards the North Pole.

The second reads:

The Adventures of Captain Hatteras, journey to the North Pole, sums up everything which has been written on the subject, from the remotest times to the expeditions of Sir John Franklin and his successors. The same procedure, the same style, the same science, and the same talent are put to work each time. But in this case even the verisimilitude no longer has anything that needs changing, and every moment one believes one is dealing with a true account, so much do the adventures

---

[4] Respectively in 'Bibliographie', *Musée des familles* (Dec. 1866), and reproduced in G. Vapereau, *L'Année littéraire* (1869), 503–6 (506).

and problems of Captain Hatteras touch and move us. This is the triumph of what M. Jules Verne's intelligent publisher rightly calls instruction which entertains and entertainment which instructs. The new popularizer shows the merit of the generation coming after us, and one can, without flattery, repeat what one illustrious scientist said of his books: 'These novels, which will entertain you like Alexander Dumas's best, will instruct you like François Arago's works.'

However, more perceptive reviews of the unillustrated book edition appeared, the first two written by an obscure critic called Émile Zola and the last by the famous writer Théophile Gautier. These three pieces are of great importance, since no substantive reviews[5] of Verne appeared before the 1870s:

M. Jules Verne is the fantasist of science. He puts all his imagination at the service of mathematical deductions, he takes theories and draws plausible, if not practical, facts from them.

It is not Edgar Allan Poe's nightmare, it is a pleasant and instructive fantasy; these are tales written for children and people who have seen life, full of dramatic interest and useful lessons . . .

What Franklin and Bellot could not do, Hatteras accomplishes. He reaches the promised land of navigators, the island containing the geographical point of the Pole.

But the captain and his crew only get there at the end of the second part, that is after passing through the greatest dangers and the most terrible emotions. All along the route these men suffer and study; the dramatic and scientific elements work together here, and nothing could equal the strangeness of the adventures, apart from the strangeness of the discoveries.

It was an excellent idea to dramatize science to make it accessible to the profane. I do not believe that one can become a great scientist by reading such books, but at least they do produce the curiosity for knowledge; in addition they interest, they have the great merit of being healthy and could free your soul.

M. Jules Verne is different. He has given himself the task of accomplishing certain actions which science describes as theoretically possible, but which nobody has been able to complete to date in practice.

. . . today in *The Adventures of Captain Hatteras* . . . the author takes

[5] Respectively in *L'Evenement* (12 May 1866), *Le Salut public* (23 July 1866), and *Le Moniteur universel*, 197 ('Les Voyages imaginaires de M. Jules Verne' (16 July 1866)—repr. in *L'Herne: Jules Verne*, ed. P. A. Touttain (1974), 85–7).

man further than man has ever gone, to the geographical point of the Pole.

The great interest of such books is easy to understand. They instruct while arousing curiosity to the utmost degree. You hold in your hands the very naturally composed solution to problems considered insoluble. These are tales, or lies, which, if I can put it in this way, facilitate truth to children and society people.

I find there a great imagination and very keen intelligence. Since our children are meant to have become well behaved and serious, since they no longer want those beautiful golden tales, *Donkey Skin*, *Tom Thumb*, *The Sleeping Beauty*, and *Bluebeard*, since tots of eight are in a hurry to turn grey and to know that two and two make four, I prefer the scientific fantasies of M. Jules Verne to certain indigestible compilations that I know. Here the human element appears; in these books is found a model of the great battle which man has always fought with nature.

M. Verne is not a writer to march on the charming nonsense of childhood. He would not throw Perrault in the fire, I can feel that from some of his emotional and smiling pages. Take it as read that if science has its deep and imperious charms, ignorance is a gentle mother who rocks her children in the blue sky of fine peaceful dreams.

Gautier's review reads:

When the alcohol in the thermometer . . . pushes its red thread [to the maximum] . . . it is best . . . to read in the half-darkness . . . some pleasant and refreshing book, for example the imaginary journeys of M. Jules Verne . . . *The British at the North Pole* and *The Desert of Ice* . . . especially, are excellent today . . . These Arctic books come at the right time. When you hold them they almost give you frostbite: you can see your breath stretching out as fog while an invisible snow falls on your shoulders. Like doctors, M. Jules Verne knows how to make ice at the heart of a white-hot tomb. There exists an extensive collection of imaginary journeys, ancient and modern: from Lucian's *True History* to *Gulliver's Travels*, the human imagination has revelled in wild fantasies where, on the pretext of excursions to unknown lands, authors with more or less talent develop their utopias or exercise their satirical verve. The journeys of M. Jules Verne belong to neither of these categories. If they have not really been carried out—even if they could not yet be done—they present the most rigorous scientific possibilities, and the most daring are only the paradox or exaggeration of a truth soon to come. Here the chimera is written and guided by a mathematical spirit. It is the application to an invention of all those true, real, and precise details that produce the most complete illusion. There is more Edgar

Allan Poe and Daniel Defoe than Swift in M. Jules Verne—or rather he has found his method on his own and at the first attempt taken it to the highest degree of perfection.

The adventures of Captain Hatteras in *The British at the North Pole* exceed the interest of the most absorbing novel. This mysterious departure of the *Forward* for an unknown destination, with a crew recruited so strangely, strikes the imagination immediately, which goes on board, determined to follow the brave explorers to the end. You share the sailors' almost superstitious curiosity about the invisible captain, whose orders on extreme occasions arrive on board in such an unforeseen way, and when he reveals himself, you like him even more. He has an iron will in an iron body, and, to reach his goal, he smashes all the obstacles of nature with that particular obstinacy of the Anglo-Saxon race, more irritated than discouraged by barriers . . .

This short study can only give a slight idea of *The British at the North Pole* and *The Desert of Ice*. M. Jules Verne generates an absolute sensation of reality in his narration, which is as accurate and detailed as a logbook. The maritime, mathematical, and scientific data, soberly employed to good purpose, set such a seal of truth on this fantastic *Forward* that you cannot convince yourself she has not carried out her voyage of discovery. When Hatteras shoots the sun, no naval captain could find the least error, and the same applies to the tiniest details. Only Robinson Crusoe's diary by Defoe reaches this degree of verisimilitude. But in addition, M. Jules Verne, who does not neglect the human and cordial side, ensures his characters are liked, and, above all on days as hot as when this article is written, he creates the desire to go and spend a few hours with those good companions in the snow-house in the desert of ice!

EXPLANATORY NOTES

5 *the brig the 'Forward', captain KZ*: a ship of that name transported emigrants to Baltimore in 1737; MS has 'the *Foreward*' throughout and 'Captain X . . .' here.

the 'Liverpool Herald' of 5 April 1860: the *Herald* was published 1855–66. Liverpool was the first foreign town Verne visited (1859). In *Backwards to Britain* (chs. 15–16), he and his companion go sightseeing in the docks, with a virtuoso description of the ships' movements and port machinery. The two dine in a dock tavern, but leave abruptly following a free-for-all. Chs. 1–5 of *A Floating City* (1871), a semi-fictional account of Verne's 1867 visit to America, are also set in Liverpool docks. MS: '*Nautical Paper* of 6 5 April 1860'; no trace of this newspaper has been found—perhaps the (HM) *Nautical Almanac* or the *Nautical Magazine*, which first published *The Arctic Dispatches* by McClure, who is cited in this same I 1.

of every size and nationality: MS: 'of every size, shape, and nationality'; '120 horsepower', two paragraphs lower, is '80 horsepower'. Franklin's *Erebus* and *Terror* had entire fifteen-ton locomotive engines acquired from London Railways.

the 'Nautilus': the use of the name in *Twenty Thousand Leagues* shows how common it was for vessels of all sorts. The best-known submarine predecessors were Hallet's *Nautilus* (1857) and two *Nautilus*es built by American Robert Fulton at the beginning of the century to launch mines against British ships.

6 *Cornhill*: given that Verne's novels appeared first as serials, perhaps a reference to the *Cornhill Magazine* (1860–1939), a serial fiction pioneer which may have influenced Hetzel's venture. The first issue featured Allen William Young, 'The Search for Sir John Franklin' (pp. 96–121), with a map of McClintock's expedition.

7 *'second only to God'*: Dupanloup and Aubineau's obscurantist attacks on Verne's omission of the word 'God' (see Introduction, above) are ill-founded, for it occurs in fact twenty-seven times in *Hatteras*. Their criticisms were based on a half-truth, though, for Verne rarely mentions Christ and avoids explanations in terms of divine intervention.

8 *this dog-captain*: the idea may easily be drawn from the insignia of the Isle of Man, which depict human 'shoulders carrying the magnificent head of a Great Dane', according to Charles Nodier, 'La Fée aux miettes', in *Contes* (1961), 245.

9 *Scott and Co.*: the screw for Nemo's *Nautilus* (20T I 13) is provided by John Scott, shipbuilders 'of Glasgow' (in fact of Greenock). In 1862, they constructed a huge shipyard in the centre of Verne's home town of Nantes, taking on 1,800 men.

9 *good reasons for his decision*: the ship is built of wood to enable it to be cannibalized or provide fuel, another sign of its polar destiny (stated in any case in the part title).

R. Hawthorn of Newcastle: R. and W. Hawthorn, active until the 1980s, building steam locomotives and engines for ships.

Sir John Franklin: (1786–1847), author of *Narrative of a Journey to the Shores of the Polar Sea* (1823) and *Narrative of a Second Expedition* (1828); in 1845, aged 59, he led an expedition on the *Erebus* and *Terror* to search for the Northwest Passage. From 1848, more than forty expeditions were dispatched to look for his traces. Although the geographical and scientific knowledge gained was immense, no evidence of his fate emerged before Rae, in 1853–4, and McClintock, in 1857–9.

10 *Captain McClintock . . . proof of the loss of the unhappy expedition*: (Verne: 'MacClintock') Sir Leopold McClintock (1819–1907), member of Belcher's 1852–4 expedition, then commander of an expedition (1857–9) sent by Lady Franklin to investigate her husband's fate, and author of *The Voyage of the 'Fox' in the Arctic Seas* (1859, French translation in *Le Tour du Monde* (1860), to which Verne subscribed). A page McClintock and Hobson discovered in a cairn at Point Victory gave information up to 25 April 1848 (see below, note to p. 99), namely that the ships had been trapped in ice between Victoria and King William Islands; and an old Eskimo woman told him that the crew had died in their tracks. The survivors had in fact abandoned ship and set off south over Boothia Peninsula, but all 138 crew died.

Captain McClure . . . Lieutenant Cresswell: Sir Robert McClure (Verne: 'MacCure' or 'McClur' in different editions) (1807–73), author of *The Arctic Dispatches: Containing an Account of the Discovery of the North-West Passage* [1854?]. Lieutenant S. Gurney Cresswell (Verne: 'Creswel') (1827–67), author of *Series of Eight Sketches in Colour (together with a Chart of the Route) during the Discovery of the North-West Passage* (1854). McClure, Cresswell, and their crew were the first to complete the Passage (1850–3), although partly by sledge (the first single ship was Amundsen's in 1906). In *The Fur Country* Verne describes McClure as 'the only man really to have gone from one ocean to the other via the Polar Sea'.

the whaler Weddell . . . Captain James Ross: James Weddell (Verne: 'Weddel' or 'Wedell' in different editions) (1787–1834), discovered the Weddell Sea. 'In 1825 [in reality, 1823] . . . a mere sealer, the Briton Weddell, went as far as . . . 74° 15′ on the thirty-sixth [meridian]' (*20 T* II 15). Admiral Sir James (Clark) Ross (1800–62), nephew of John Ross, located the North Magnetic Pole in 1831 and discovered Victoria Land. His southwards record was 78° 4′ on 2 February 1842 (*20 T* II 15). The opening chapters of *Hatteras* as far as Bellot Strait (I 16) draw much from James Ross's second journey.

11 *lime juice, the lime pastils, or the packets of mustard and sorrel and Cochlearia seeds*: in a footnote Verne translates his own 'lime-juice' as 'Jus

de citron': 'lime' is 'citron vert', but 'citron' can include both lemon and lime, especially given that lemon seems to have been generally used by British mariners, rather than the lime of popular belief. Verne wrote 'des pastilles de chaux' ('(quick)lime pastils'), a mistranslation from English.

a ship's boat of tin-plate covered with gutta-percha, and a number of Halkett boats: this phrase sums up the quirky improvisation of Verne's preferred technology, in contrast with his erroneous reputation for futuristic sophistication. Halkett boats were invented in 1844 by Lieutenant Peter Halkett, author of *Boat-cloak or cloak-boat, constructed of MacIntosh india-rubber cloth, umbrella-sail, bellows, &c* (1848). His circular boats were successfully used on Rae's and Richardson's expeditions, and one survives on Orkney, marked 'James Fitzjames', commander of the *Erebus* on the Franklin expedition. Verne inserts a phallic-inspired footnote in II 1, explaining that the boat 'can expand as much as wished'. In *The Tribulations of a Chinese in China* (1879), the hero sails the China Sea in a Boyton Suit, a similar coat-vessel, but now with a sail and a small stove.

12 *2 August 1859*: the date when Verne's seminal visit to Scotland and England ended, and he resolved only to 'travel in his memories' (*Backwards to Britain*, 48).

Marcuart and Co., bankers of Liverpool: not found—perhaps Marquart or MacCuart?

engineers: Verne inserts a footnote reading 'Ingénieurs-mécaniciens' to explain 'ingénieurs'.

Dr Clawbonny: the surname is taken from that of a slave family, later freed, named after a locality near the Hudson in Fenimore Cooper's *Afloat and Ashore* (1844) and *Miles Wallingford* (1844), and especially from Neb(uchadnezzar) Clawbonny, as confirmed by the use of both first names for the black in *The Mysterious Island*. But 'Clawbonny' also has a Scottish consonance, confirmed by his Glengarry and membership of the Royal Society of Edinburgh. Dr Clawbonny is undoubtedly based on Dr John Richardson.

13 *Those invited to participate in the campaign of the 'Forward' should be British*: Hetzel suggested including a French crew member, but Verne replied: 'impossible; there need to be just *Britons*; I'll have it announced in [the captain's] letter. It'll be a condition for being taken on' (16 September 1863).

14 *the Glacial Sea*: Verne may mean the sea north of Eurasia, as distinct from the Polar Sea, above America.

15 *'Kane had for his famous advance towards the Pole'*: Elisha Kent Kane (1820–57), explorer and doctor. His *Advance* sailed through Baffin Bay and Smith Sound into Kane Basin, reaching 80° 35′ N; abandoning ship when supplies ran low, he returned overland to Uppernawik (1853–5).

Johnson . . . was quartermaster on the 'Phoenix' . . . Bellot, the French lieutenant: *Johnson*: Escaich and Gehu say that Verne's character is the authentic 'William Johnson', but without further information. MS reads ~~Harvey~~ 'Johnson' (probably based on quartermaster Harvey of the *North Star*) up to I 19, then 'Johnson' thereafter. *Bellot*: Joseph-René Bellot (1826–53), accompanied ~~William~~ Kennedy on the *Prince Albert*, financed by Lady Franklin (1851–3), and author of 'Journal of a Voyage to the Polar Seas' (1853). During a second campaign under Belcher and Inglefield, he disappeared into a crevasse, while accompanied by crew from the *North Star* (see below, note to p. 119). In 'Wintering in the Ice' (1855), a note, probably written by Verne, cites La Pérouse, Franklin, Bellot, and McClure as sources.

17 *a helm at each end to . . . ensure rapid service between the banks of the Mersey*: much of the local colour, including the three-legged symbol of the Isle of Man (I 5), is drawn from Verne's 1859 visit to Liverpool (*Backwards to Britain*, 14–17).

18 *'you are a fine sailor!'*: in addition to the homosexual innuendo, this dialogue describes Verne's own long wait for success in his writing career.

19 *to study in the exercise of their functions*: MS: 'to surprise in the exercise of their functions', with lavatorial/sexual humour.

   the Literary and Philosophical Society of Liverpool: published *Proceedings* for several decades.

20 *On 15 March . . . a Great Dane had been sent by railway from Edinburgh to . . . Liverpool*: in I 2 the date was '15 February'; Verne himself delightedly took the Liverpool–Edinburgh train in August 1859.

   Foker . . . Bolton . . . Gripper: the names Foker and Bolton are taken from Thackeray's *History of Pendennis* (1850); Gripper, which is not a normal surname, may come from the *Griper*, used on Parry's 1819–20 expedition.

22 *unlike Socrates, he ended up saying*: | *'My house is small, but may heaven grant that it is never full of friends!'*: Socrates: (469–399 BC), Greek philosopher who profoundly influenced Plato. The quotation may in fact be from Lucian of Samosata's *Onos*: 'You see . . . my house is small, but ready to receive a guest. You will enlarge it by having the goodness to stay.'

25 *the time for the midday collection [levée] had passed*: does Verne mean 'delivery'?

26 *you will enter Davis Strait, and cross Baffin Bay to Melville Bay*: towards both the Northwest Passage and the Pole.

27 *Point of Ayre*: Verne erroneously wrote 'Ayr', on the Scottish mainland.

28 *'On the "Victory" . . . fitted with a steam-engine'*: James Ross set out in May 1829, under his uncle John Ross, and wintered at Felix Harbour. Their paddle-steamer, a strange choice as the boxes got stuck in ice, was the first powered Arctic vessel.

   'Parry, Ross, and Franklin's books and Kennedy, Kane, and McClintock's reports': authors of works of exploration central to *Hatteras*. Sir William

Edward Parry (1790–1855) reached 82° 45′ N in 1827, a record until 1875–6, and published the journals of his Arctic expeditions. Verne (*Travellers*, II 3 2) devotes five pages to his 1819–20 expedition, which 'obtained more results than those of the next thirty years combined'. James Ross, *A Voyage of Discovery and Research in the Southern and Antarctic Regions* (1847). Franklin, *Narrative of a Journey to the Shores of the Polar Sea* (1823). William Kennedy (1813–90), a whaling captain who led the 1850–3 expedition financed by Lady Franklin and discovered Bellot Strait; author of *A Short Narrative of the Second Voyage of the 'Prince Albert'* (1853). Kane, author of *The United States Grinnell Expedition in Search of Sir John Franklin* (1853) and *Arctic Explorations: The Second Grinnell Expedition in Search of Sir John Franklin* (1856). McClintock, *Voyage of the 'Fox' in the Arctic Seas* (1859).

'we get trapped . . . like the "Fox" in 1857 . . . amongst the pack ice': the *Fox* was a 340-foot wooden boat of 170 tons burden; McClintock was pushed southwards into the Davis Strait from September 1857 to April 1858.

29 *55° 57′*: from this point, Malin Head, about fifty-five miles away, would not normally be visible.

31 *They were now at 51° 37′ latitude and 22° 58′ longitude, or 200 miles from the tip of Greenland*: both coordinates must be slips, with this point about a thousand miles from Greenland.

'the whaler Scoresby, who belonged to the Royal Society of Edinburgh': Captain William Scoresby (1789–1857), Scottish Arctic explorer, elected to the RSE in 1819 and author of *An Account of the Arctic Regions and Northern Whale Fishery* (1820) and *Journal of a Voyage to the Northern Whale Fishery* (1823), called 'the best existing authority' on Greenland whales in *Moby-Dick*. In 1816–17 his ship, under his father, William Scoresby (1760–1829), reached 82° 30′ near Greenland, where he discovered an open sea to the east perhaps leading to the Pole (*Travellers*, II 3 2).

32 *'the brig "Ann of Poole", coming from Greenspond, was caught in genuine ice-fields at forty-four degrees north, and because Dyment, its captain, counted hundreds of icebergs!'*: (Verne wrote 'Dayement', but this has been amended to the Newfoundland name 'Dyment') the brig was in fact the *Lady Ann*, from Poole. Icebergs may be seen on occasion at thirty degrees.

'having been a cabin boy on the sloop-of-war the "Fly"': possibly the schooner the *Fly* of Bridport, active in 1809.

33 *warblers*: according to *Littré*, Verne's 'contre-maîtres' occur only in Paraguay.

34 the *'Valkyrien', a Danish corvette*: in *Journey to the Centre of the Earth* the heroes take 'the *Valkyrie*, a little Danish schooner' from Copenhagen to Reykjavik. A Valkyrie, in Norse mythology, was a maiden who took dead heroes to Valhalla; also an allusion to *Die Walküre* (1856) by Wagner, whom Verne discusses in several works.

372   *Explanatory Notes*

34 *'whales wounded in Davis Strait were captured some time later near Tartary
    with European harpoons still in their flanks'*: cf. *Moby-Dick*: 'Scoresby
    [wrote] that some whales have been captured far north in the Pacific,
    in whose bodies have been found the barbs of harpoons darted in the
    Greenland seas.'

36 *at 37° 2' 7" W the coast of Greenland put in a brief appearance*: a slip,
    even if the longitude is that of the coast.

    Snow saw it: W. Parker Snow (1817–95), author of *Voyage of the 'Prince
    Albert' in Search of Sir John Franklin: A Narrative of Every-Day Life in
    the Arctic Seas* (1851).

    for each foot out of the water they have about two under: modern measure-
    ments are much greater, although varying according to the water
    temperature and the salinity of the ice.

    *You passed here, Frobisher, Knight, Berley, Vaughan, Scroggs, Barents,
    Hudson, Blosseville, Franklin, Crozier, and Bellot, never to return home
    again*: explorers lost seeking a passage to Asia, all British except for
    Blosseville, Bellot, and Barents; the list is partly derived from Sir John
    Ross, 'Introduction' to *Narrative of a Second Voyage* (1835), in Verne's
    book collection, from which much of the information in the following
    pages is also borrowed: '1719–1722 | There are voyages recorded . . . by
    Knight, Barlow, Vaughan, and Scroggs . . . no account of them was ever
    received.' *Frobisher*: Sir Martin Frobisher (1535?–94), made three voy-
    ages to the north, with seven pages in Verne's *The First Explorers* (II 3).
    Knight: James Knight (1640–1720/2), left with the *Albany* and *Discovery*
    (1719?), attempted to take refuge on Marble Island in Hudson Bay, but
    was then lost. *Berley*: (Verne: 'Barlow') George Berley (?–1720/2), com-
    mander of the *Albany* on Knight's expedition. *Vaughan*: George Vaughan
    (1676–1720/2), commander of the *Discovery*. *Scroggs*: John Scroggs
    (dates unknown): sent in search of Knight's expedition in 1722, but
    reported back that all had been killed by Eskimos; the odd man out in
    Verne's list of lost men. *Barents*: Willem Barents (1550?–97), Dutch,
    made three voyages in search of a Northeast Passage, although there is no
    record of him passing Cape Farewell; *The First Explorers* (II 3) devotes
    twelve pages to his expedition, the first to over-winter. *Hudson*: Henry
    Hudson (?–1611?), made four voyages of discovery, giving his name to
    Hudson Bay and the Hudson. *Blosseville*: Jules Poret de Blosseville
    (1802–33/4), disappeared off the coast of Greenland, cited in *Journey to
    the Centre of the Earth* (1864) and *An Antarctic Mystery* (1897). *Franklin*:
    see note to p. 9. *Crozier*: Captain Francis (Rawdon) Crozier (1796–
    1848): as Verne says in *Travellers*, he was Parry's companion in 1824;
    died on Franklin's expedition. *Bellot*: see notes to pp. 15, 85, 119.

37 *In 1498 Sebastian Cabot . . . Gaspar and Miguel Corte Real*: *Cabot*:
    Sebastian Cabot (1476?–1557), Italian navigator and cartographer, sailed
    to South and North America, probably only in 1508. *Gaspar and Miguel
    Corte Real*: (Verne: 'Gaspard et Michel Cotréal', but 'Cortereal' in *The*

First Explorers (II 3) and 'Corteréal' in *The Purchase of the North Pole*) (1450?–1501?) and (1450?–1502?), Portuguese navigators to Labrador. When Gaspar did not return, his brother Miguel set out to find him, but also disappeared.

To John Davis the honour of discovering his strait in 1585: (1550?–1605), made three voyages in search of the Northwest Passage (1585–7), with three pages in *The First Explorers* (II 3).

Weymouth in 1602, James Hall in 1605 and 1607 . . . James Poole in 1611: *Weymouth*: George Weymouth (dates unknown), reached the entrance to Hudson Strait, but his crew mutinied, forcing a return to Britain; his journal was published in 1625. *James Hall*: (?–1612), killed by an Eskimo while on a fourth exploration of Greenland in search of the Viking settlements; reached sixty-seven degrees. *James Poole*: (dates unknown), made two voyages (1609–11) and reached seventy-three degrees.

Jens Munk: (Verne: 'James Munk', probably conflating two explorers cited by Chateaubriand, 'James, Munk' (*Voyage en Amérique*, 1827— Gallica), but 'Jean Munk' in *The Purchase of the North Pole*) Danish explorer (1579–1628) of Greenland.

Lieutenant Pickersgill, sent to meet Captain Cook trying to return via Bering Strait, advanced to the sixty-eighth degree; the following year Young reached Woman's Islands: *Pickersgill*: Richard Pickersgill (1749–79), of the *Lion*: late in attempting to meet Cook in the Arctic, he was court-martialled; he drowned in the Thames. *Cook*: James Cook (1728–79), three voyages of exploration to the South Pacific and North America, including the discovery of Hawaii. *Young . . . Woman's Islands*: (Verne: 'l'île des Femmes'), near Holsteinborg, but not identified, although John Ross (*Narrative of a Second Voyage*) writes: '1777: Lieutenant Young, in the same ship [as Pickersgill] . . . reached 72° 40′ (Woman's islands)' and de Bray, '[les] îles Woman' (72).

who first crossed the hundred and seventieth meridian above the seventy-seventh parallel: a slip for 'hundred and tenth'. This was the furthest west ships from the Atlantic got in the nineteenth century.

In 1826 Beechey touched Chamisso Island . . . Prince Regent Inlet: Frederick William Beechey (1796–1856), explored Bering Strait and wrote *A Narrative of a Voyage . . . to the Pacific and Behring's Strait* (1831). Verne uses both 'le détroit du Prince Régent' and 'le passage du Régent'.

Captain Back . . . from 1823 to 1835 . . . explorations . . . completed in 1839 by Messrs Dease and Simpson and Dr Rae: *Back*: Sir George Back (1796–1878), took part in expeditions in 1819–22, 1833–5, and 1836–7 (making Verne's '1823' a slip) and author of *Narrative of the Arctic Land Expedition to the mouth of the Great Fish River, and along the shores of the Arctic Ocean* (1836); his observation of the 'green ray' may be a source of Verne's *The Green Ray* (1882). *Dease*: Peter Warren Dease (1788–1863), member of Franklin's second Arctic expedition and author of *From Barrow to Boothia* (2002). *Simpson*: (Verne: 'Sompson') Thomas Simpson

(1808–40), discovered Victoria Island and wrote *Narrative of the Discoveries on the North Coast of America* (1843). *Rae*: Dr John Rae (1813–93), made Arctic expeditions in 1846–7, 1848–9, 1851–2, and 1853–4, and published *Narrative of the Expedition . . . in 1846 and 1847* (1850).

38 *Davis Strait*: 1866: 'The Entrance of Davis Strait'.

40 *Anxiety Port . . . Cape Eden*: no trace has been found of Verne's 'port Anxiety . . . [le] cap Éden'.

41 *the Chapel of Henry VII*: the medieval Lady Chapel at Westminster, the resting place of fifteen monarchs.

42 *an underwater current at their bases and drifting in the opposite direction*: Scoresby reported a similar phenomenon lasting two days ('Observations sur les courans et les animalcules de la mer du Groënland; par William Scoresby jeune, dans une lettre au professeur Jameson', Gallica).

45 *'I don't think you should do anything like that,' replied Garry*: Garry's behaviour is already different from the other sailors: in addition to asking difficult questions and being exceptionally competent, he is suspiciously loyal.

47 *The other sailors remained silent*: 1866 adds the following passage after 'silent': ' "Well," said Clifton, "*I* tell you that if you pretend not to believe, there are people on board cleverer than you who don't seem very confident." | "You mean the commander?" asked Bolton. | "The commander and the doctor." | "And you claim they think the same as you?" | "I heard them discussing, and I tell you they didn't understand a thing; they made hundreds of guesses which didn't get them any further." | "And they talked about the dog just like you?" asked the carpenter. | "If they didn't talk about the dog," answered Clifton, his back against the wall, "they spoke about the captain, which is the same thing, and they admitted it was all very spooky." | "Well, my friends," said Bell, "do you want to know what I think?" | "Yes!" from everyone. | "There is not, and never will be, any other captain than Richard Shandon." | "And the letter?" asked Clifton. | "The letter exists; it is perfectly true that some unknown person armed the *Forward* for a voyage in the ice; but now the ship's left, nobody else will come on board." '

50 *A New Letter*: the title is 'A Variant' in MS.

alca alle: (Verne: 'alca-alla') little auk or Greenland roach, named by Linnaeus and observed by Scoresby.

showed it to them: MS adds ~~'which he had not even touched'~~.

51 *Smith Sound*: (Verne's map: 'Dét. de Smith ou de Kane', although the latter has not been traced) now called Nares Strait, after the Nares expedition (1875–6).

52 *'But who?'*: why does Shandon not ask for a sample of handwriting from all on board?

53 *to Captain-Dog*: 1867 omits the article, making it a name, unlike 1866: 'au dog-captain'.

54 *Godhavn*: (Verne: 'Godavhn'; 'Godhavm' on his map) Erik visits 'Godhaven' in *The Wreck of the 'Cynthia'*, calling it 'a poor village serv[ing] as entrepôt for traders in oil and furs' (15).

55 *'Eskimo' means 'eater of raw fish'*: in fact 'eater of raw flesh'; Verne's information probably comes from Dubois, *Le Pôle et l'équateur* (1863), 104.

More generally, Dubois's 1863 work is Verne's second most important source, with many borrowings, even if Dubois seems to have read HL and Verne himself, for one of his chapters is called 'Wintering in the Ice', like Verne's 1855 tale. Much of Verne's English vocabulary, and paraphrases, and even one or two mistakes, must come from Dubois, especially icebergs, ice stream, ice-field, pack, hummocks, pemmican, 'grog', snow-blindness, drift, Christmas pudding, fiords, and Devil's Thumb. Other ideas shared with Dubois include polar bears riding icebergs (22), crews repulsing attacks by massed pieces of ice (25), the symbolism of Cape Farewell (29), skin sticking to metal objects (36), Penny's 1851 observation of an open sea (37), the magnetic mountain at the Magnetic Pole (38), trekking across ice using snow shoes, green snow-goggles, and spirits-of-wine (43), Halkett boats (46), the symptoms of frostbite (46), the astonishing transmission of sound (47), putting gloves and socks on chests overnight to dry them out (48), dogs sleeping outside (48), Bellot's remark that nature seems to compensate for polar rigour by its most magnificent phenomena, such as parhelia and paraselenes (49), animals changing colour in spring (55), the exact quotation of Bellot's last words (57), the stripping off of ships' copper sheathing (64), and whales escaping whalers at the Pole and demonstrating the existence of the Northwest Passage (132). On occasion, Verne constructs whole scenes from odd remarks of Dubois, such as the fox taken for a huge polar bear because of the refraction (46), the idea of blowing up blockages by placing large amounts of explosives in the ice (64), or the ship's 'organs' providing fuel for heating (122).

56 *which lets the smoke out but not the smell*: Verne's description of Uppernawik may be based on Kane's, even more critical.

Hans Christian, a skilful dog driver who took part in Captain McClintock's expedition, but this Hans was at that time in southern Greenland: Hans Christian Hendrik (1834–89), Eskimo guide to Kane, Morton, and Hall (1853–76); he may be unavailable for Hatteras because required to work for Hayes's simultaneous, real-life, expedition (1860–1). A very similar Hans becomes the third hero of *Journey to the Centre of the Earth*. This Danish-speaking Icelandic guide is a placid eider-'hunter', with his laconicism similar to Hans's, as reported by Hayes: 'I asked Hans if he would go with us. "Yes!" Would he take his wife and baby. "Yes!" Would he go without them. "Yes!" ' (*The Open Polar Sea* (1867), 6).

57 *mollymawks*: Verne: 'molly-mokes', perhaps derived from 'mollemokes' in John Ross (*Narrative of a Second Voyage*, III 38); in I 15, Verne writes 'molly-nochtes'.

376   *Explanatory Notes*

58 *Crimson Cliffs ... covered with red snow ... to which Dr Kane ascribes a
purely vegetable origin*: modern explanations confirm that the pigments
are due to the cell walls of freshwater algae. Clawbonny's wish to study
the phenomenon is granted in II 19.

    'nipped': the term is probably from 'A "Nip" in Melville Bay, off the
Devil's Thumb' (1853), an engraving by Walter May, showing the *Resolute*
and an iceberg in the distance overshadowing the *Intrepid*.

64 *Devil's Thumb | On this same spot, the 'Prince Albert' in 1851 and the
'Advance' with Kane in 1853 were obstinately held by the ice for several
weeks*: the *Prince Albert*, under Kennedy, was part of an 1850–3 expedition financed by Lady Franklin; *the Advance*, under Kane, was in fact
caught from September 1853 to June 1854.

66 *it appeared to be more than twenty feet tall*: MS adds ~~'and thirty feet long'~~.

67 *'the Beast of Gévaudan'*: a gigantic wolf-like creature that killed people in
Lozère, south-east France (1764–7; cf. the film *Le Pacte des loups*).

    'the Lion of the Apocalypse': Revelations 5: 5–6: 'Then one of the elders
said to me, "Weep not; lo, the Lion of the tribe of Judah, the Root of
David, has conquered, so that he can open the scroll and its seven
seals" .'

70 *'Duke'*: Verne's 'Duk', not a dog's name, has been amended.

71 *'Admiral Nelson's: | "England expects every man to do his duty" '*: quoted
accurately as 'L'Angleterre attend que chacun fasse son devoir', but
incorrectly in English in a footnote as 'England expects every one to
make his duty'. The message was sent at Trafalgar (21 October 1805),
and recorded in a colour engraving by William Marshall Craig (1806).
The victories of Horatio Nelson (1758–1805) on the Nile and at Trafalgar
made him a national hero. He had previously been on Phipps's
expedition, when he was attacked by a polar bear (1773).

    'Captain Hatteras': Cap. Hatteras's name must derive from the expres-
sion 'mad as a hatter', found in Thackeray's *Pendennis* (1850), or from
Cape Hatteras and Hatteras Inlet, N. Carolina, the site of a Civil War
naval battle (1861) and of the loss of Villeroi's submarine *Alligator*
(1863). In a typical Vernian trope, Hatteras will give his name back to the
landscape, as Mount Hatteras. His character seems based on John Ross,
similarly haughty and hermit-like.

72 *think carefully before joining his ventures*: MS adds a paragraph: 'Also,
success had constantly escaped him until now; an invincible fatality
seemed attached to him; the "unlucky!" of the French was written on his
forehead, and he was known as such in every port of the United Kingdom.'
The idea came from the publisher (16 September 1863). Hatteras's
Gallic qualities, especially his lack of luck (together with Clawbonny's
southern exuberance), may compensate for the absence of real Frenchmen
on the expedition.

    'If I were not French, I would want to be British': an adaptation of Victor

Hugo's saying 'If I were not French, I would like to be German' (to Alexandre Weill on 16 May 1840—cited on www.chronologievictor-hugo.com).

Christopher Columbus ... Vasco de Gama ... Fernand d'Andrada ... Magellan ... Jacques Cartier ... Cap Blanc ... Louisiana: early explorers and discoveries. *Christopher Columbus*: (1451–1506), discovered America in 1492; *Vasco de Gama*: (1469?–1524), the first European to reach India by sea (1497–8); *Fernand d'Andrada*: Antonio d'Andrada, Jesuit and author of *Voyages au Thibet, faits en 1625 et 1626*, although not the first European to visit Tibet or China; *Magellan*: (1480?–1521), leader of the first circumnavigation (1519–22); *Jacques Cartier*: (1491–1557), discovered the St Lawrence River; *Cap Blanc*: a cape near Quebec City; *Louisiana*: MS has the preferable 'Louisiade'.

Sturt, McDouall Stuart, Burke, Wills, King, and Gray in Australia, Palliser in America, Cyril Graham, Waddington, and Cunningham in India, and Burton, Speke, Grant, and Livingstone in Africa: contemporary British explorers. *Sturt*: Captain Charles Sturt (1795–1869), reached the Simpson Desert, near the centre of Australia (1844–6). *McDouall Stuart, Burke, Wills, King, and Gray*: John McDouall Stuart (MS: 'Douall Stuart'; 1867: 'Doual Stuart'; 1866: 'Donall Stuart') (1815–66), Robert O'Hara Burke (MS and 1866: 'Burcke') (1820–61), William John Wills (1834–61), John King (?–1872), and Charles Gray (?–1861): the first Europeans to cross Australia from south to north; apart from Stuart and King, all died from exhaustion and starvation. The information may be taken from Vivien de Saint-Martin, 'Explorations des parties centrales de l'Australie' ('L'Année géographique', *Le Tour du monde* 5 (1862), 19), especially since de Saint-Martin reviewed *Hatteras* in the *MÉR* (see Appendix B). *Palliser*: Captain John Palliser (1807–87), surveyed Palliser's Triangle, SE Alberta (1857–60) and explored western Canada. 1866 here inserts 'Haouran in Syria': (le) Haouran is in fact an area in Syria, cited by Verne in *Travellers* (I 1), and seems to have little connection with British explorers. *Cyril Graham, Waddington*: (MS, 1867, and 1866: 'Wadington') not traced. *Cunningham*: (MS, 1867, and 1866: 'Cummingham') probably General Sir Alexander Cunningham (1814–93), engineer and head (1861–5) of the archaeological survey of India. *Burton*: Sir Richard Francis Burton (1821–90), Asian specialist and explorer of Africa. *Speke*: John Hanning Speke (1827–64), identified Lake Victoria as the main source of the Nile (1860–1). *Grant*: James Augustus Grant (1827–92), accompanied Speke. 1866 inserts 'Barth' before 'Burton' (omitted in 1867 presumably because he was not British): Heinrich Barth (1821–65), German explorer of Africa.

73   *Nova Zembla ... 1616*: early British Arctic discoveries. *Willoughby*: Sir Hugh Willoughby (?–1553/4), sighted Nova Zembla, but died searching for the Northeast Passage; although two of his ships were lost, the third, with Richard Chancellor, reached Archangel. The year 1596 for the discovery of Spitzbergen by Willoughby is an error; although

Willoughby did 'sight' it (Dubois, *Le Pôle et l'équateur*, 8), its discovery is often ascribed to the Dutchman Barents. *Hudson*: see note to p. 36. *Waigats*: Verne has 'Waigattet' (apparently a Danish form) on his map, but MS has 'Weigats', and 1867 and 1866, 'Weigatz', probably taken from Ross, 'Introduction' to *Narrative of a Second Voyage* (1835); *The First Explorers* (II 3) has 'Waigatz'. *Borough*: (Verne: 'Barrough'; 'Burrough' in *The First Explorers* (II 3)) Stephen Borough (1525–84), explorer and author. *Davis*: see note to p. 37. *Baffin*: William Baffin (1584–1622), discovered Baffin Island and Baffin Bay, reaching Smith Sound.

73 *Hearne, Mackenzie, John Ross, Parry, Franklin, Richardson, Beechey, James Ross, Back, Dease, Simpson, Rae, Inglefield, Belcher, Austin, Kellett, Moore, McClure, Kennedy, and McClintock*: British explorers, many Scottish, seeking Franklin, the Northwest Passage, or the Pole, a list similar to Dubois's (*Le Pôle et l'équateur*, 43). All are mentioned in earlier chapters except *Hearne*: Samuel Hearne (1745–92), the first to reach Canada's Arctic coast (1769–72), proving that the Northwest Passage had to be sought further north (*The Great Navigators*) and author of *A Journey from Prince of Wales' Fort in Hudson's Bay to the Northern Ocean* (1795). *Mackenzie*: (Verne: 'Mackensie') Sir Alexander Mackenzie (1764?–1820), explored north-west Canada (1789–93) (*The Great Navigators*), the first to cross North America, and author of *Voyages . . . to the Frozen and Pacific Oceans* (1801). *John Ross*: (1777–1856), discovered King William Island and author of *A Voyage of Discovery* (1819) and *Narrative of a Second Voyage* (1835). *Richardson*: Dr John Richardson (1787–1865), from Edinburgh, mapped the Arctic coast from the Mackenzie River to the Coppermine (1826), author of *Arctic Searching Expedition* (1851), friend of Robbie Burns, and undoubted model for Dr Clawbonny. *Inglefield*: John Nicholson Inglefield (1748–1828), sailed on the *Isabella* to Smith Sound and Alexander Cape (1852–3) and author of 'Voyage du capitaine Inglefield . . . à la recherche de sir John Franklin', in which he reports his observation of an open sea at seventy-eight degrees; *Belcher*: Admiral Sir Edward Belcher (1799–1877), Nova Scotian prominent in the acquisition of Hong Kong Island and the capture of Canton (1841), and author of *The Last of the Arctic Voyages* (1855; French trans. 1855). *Austin*: Sir Horatio Austin (1801–65), discovered traces of the Franklin expedition at Cape Riley and Beechey Island (1850) and author of *A Review of the Proceedings of the Arctic Searching Expeditions* (1851). *Kellett*: (Verne: 'Kellet') Sir Henry Kellett (1807–75), discovered Herald (now Wrangell) Land (1849), was with Belcher in 1852–4 as commander of the *Resolute*, and rescued McClure and the crew of the *Investigator*; Mount Kellett on Hong Kong is named after him. *Moore*: Captain Thomas E. L. Moore (dates unknown), author of 'Narrative of the Proceedings . . . of her Majesty's Ship, *Plover* . . .' (House of Commons, *Sessional Papers*, 33 (1851), 97).

the 'Halifax': MS: ~~the *Porpoise*~~ 'the *Halifax*'.

the 'Farewell': (MS: 'the *farevvel*') probably from a ship of that name which discovered Falkland Sound in 1689.

74 *Following the route taken by the 'Neptune' of Aberdeen in 1817, the 'Farewell' sailed north from Spitzbergen, as far as the seventy-sixth parallel*: (MS: '... eightieth') Verne later says the *Neptune* 'reached the eighty-second degree, north of Spitzbergen' (I 13); however, no trace of this voyage has been found, unless it is connected with Scoresby's.

Grinnell: Henry Grinnell (1799–1874), New York shipping merchant who financed Kane's, Wilkes's, and Altamont's expeditions.

Duke, the companion of his expeditions, had been the first to recognize him: why didn't he recognize him before? Also, if the dog took part in the 1846 expedition, that would make him at least 14 now.

76 *In 1852, Captain Inglefield reached 78° 25' N through the entrance of Smith*: Dubois (*Le Pôle et l'équateur*, 75): 'Inglefield penetrated Smith Strait as far as 78° 35' [*sic*]'.

'in 1850 ... his second Morton ... beyond the eighty-second degree': a slip for '1853'; William Morton (dates unknown); his claim was in fact 81° 22', less than Parry in 1827, meaning that 'nearer the Pole than anyone had gone before' in this same chapter cannot be sustained.

'the captains of the "Neptune", "Enterprise", "Isabella", and "Advance"': respectively not known, James Ross then Richard Collinson, Inglefield, and Kane.

'Commander Penny ... Stewart': *Penny*: Captain William Penny (1809–92), brought back to Aberdeen an Eskimo named Eenooloo Apik (1839), and in 1850 found traces of Franklin's 1845–6 winter quarters on Beechey Island. *Stewart*: Alexander Stewart (1794–1865), saw the open sea from Beechey Point on North Cornwall Island, 'at about 76° 20' N on 30 May 1851' (I 22), probably determining Hatteras's own route. Modern maps show merely straits in this area, and *The Fur Country* points out that 'even if this sea exists ... nobody can guarantee ... it reaches as far as the Pole'.

77 *'Brewster, Bergham'*: *Brewster*: Sir David Brewster (1781–1868), Scottish physicist who invented the kaleidoscope and wrote *Letters on Natural Magic* (1832); *Bergham*: possibly Bergman, Swedish, or Heinrich Karl Wilhelm Berghaus (1797–1884), German author of atlases.

'a Cossack called Alexis Markoff covered a distance of 800 miles in twenty-four hours ... using dog sledges': or an average of thirty-two miles per hour! The Cossack has not been traced, unless it is 'Alexis Tschirikof', companion of Vitus Bering cited by Verne in *The Purchase of the North Pole*.

80 *Burney Cape*: no trace has been found of Verne's 'le cap Burney'.

81 *Shooting the sun gave the latitude as 74° 1'; the chronometer, a longitude of 77° 15'. | Catherine and Elisabeth Mountains raised their snowy caps*

above the clouds: John Ross (*Narrative of a Second Voyage*, I 7): 'our latitude, by observation, was 74° 1′, and longitude, according to the chronometer, 77° . . . two remarkable mountains called Catherine and Elisabeth'.

81 *Cape York, identifiable from the almost vertical mountain of great height; the weather had lifted a little and the sun appeared for a moment at midday, allowing quite a good shooting of the sun: 74° 4′ N, 84° 23′ W*: John Ross (*Narrative of a Second Voyage*, I 7): 'while we were rounding Cape York, Commander [James] Ross sighted a steep mountain . . . the weather cleared and allowed us . . . to make a good observation at midday. We were at 73° [*sic*] 4′ N, 84° 23′ W'.

82 *'because their rotation was too slow'*: Clawbonny starts by implying that the southern hemisphere is less broken up than the northern, but apparently concludes that the equator forms an axis of symmetry: is he implying the equator has moved?

83 *'copper collars on their necks . . . Somerset'*: HL (236), citing Ross: 'I attached to their necks copper collars on which were indicated the positions of the ships and the food dumps.' Verne generally uses 'North-Sommerset', probably taken from de Bray (*Journal de bord*, map on 132); modern usage, omitting 'North', is followed here.

84 *'Captain Penny explored Wellington Channel on the "Assistance" and "Resolue"'*: all editions read '*la Résolue*', but '*le Résolute*' two paragraphs below. In I 21, Verne says 'Wellington Channel was explored in 1851 by Captain Penny on the whalers *Lady Franklin* and *Sophia*', but the contradiction may only be apparent.

   'Lady Franklin . . . Captain Haven': *Lady Franklin*: Lady Jane Franklin (1791–1875), Franklin's second wife, who sent many expeditions in search of him (1848–59); *Captain Haven*: Edwin J. De Haven (1819–65) ('Lieutenant De Haven' in I 22, and 'Captain De Haven' (Verne: '. . . de . . .') in I 21) leader of the first US Arctic expedition (1850–1).

   'Collinson': Captain Sir Richard Collinson (1811–83), led an expedition in search of Franklin (1851–4), reaching McClintock Strait.

   '1855': a slip for 1853.

85 *'Bellot['s] . . . memory is honoured in Britain'*: an obelisk to Bellot was built at the Old Royal Naval College, Greenwich, following a subscription by the *Morning Herald* and the Royal Geographical Society.

   'since the "Fox"'s return, not a single ship has tried its luck in these dangerous seas': the interval in question is only about six months, and Hayes's expedition is on its way (1860–1), together with Altamont's (I 30).

87 *eider-ducks . . . pad their nest*: *Journey to the Centre of the Earth* devotes two paragraphs to the nest-making habits of this 'prettified duck' (*JCE* 11).

   a stone engraved with the symbols | [E I] | 1849 | commemorating the passage of the 'Enterprise' and 'Investigator': it was still on the beach at

Port Leopold in 2001, reading '·E·I·', to commemorate Ross and McClintock's wintering.

88 *Adelaide Bay*: no trace has been found of Verne's 'baie Adélaïde'.

Fury and Hecla Strait: Verne seems to have borrowed the form 'le détroit . . . de *la Fury* et de *l'Hécla*' from *Voyage en Amérique*; as Chateaubriand points out, Parry gave his 1821 discovery the names of his ships. On his map Verne writes '. . . du Fury' and in *Travellers* (II 3 2) refers to 'the Fury and Hecla Straits'.

89 *'abandon ship in 1815'*: a slip for 1825, correctly indicated five paragraphs below.

90 *In 1851, when Prince Albert sent out an expedition*: the expedition was Kennedy's on the *Prince Albert* (in fact 1850–3).

his 1828 expedition: a slip for 1829, perhaps influenced by Verne's date of birth.

93 *Thomas Young's ingenious theory about meteors*: Thomas Young (1773–1829), doctor and physicist who studied light. 'Meteors' here means 'transient luminous bodies or phenomena in the atmosphere'.

96 *no way out westwards*: Verne's map shows that there is a way out westwards, via Simpson Strait.

70° 5′ 17″ for the latitude and 96° 46′ 45″ for the longitude: since then the Magnetic Pole has moved: Amundsen situated it at 70° 30′ N, 95° 30′ W (1904); modern maps, at 82° N, 110° W.

the true magnetic point was a minute away: Verne seems to be erroneously equating the horizontal distance with the difference in compass inclination. He is also making phallic jokes, as shown by Clawbonny's 'huge satisfaction of seeing his inclination at ninety degrees'.

97 *'not the slightest mountain capable of attracting vessels, tearing off their iron, anchor by anchor, nail by nail'*: the centrepiece of Verne's *An Antarctic Mystery* (1897) is a mountain capable of doing just that. The idea ultimately comes from Pliny, who describes magnetite, discovered by an Ethiopian shepherd when the nails of his sandals and the tip of his goad stuck to it.

98 *'with Fitzjames as commander, Gore and Le Vesconte as lieutenants, Des Voeux, Sargent, and Couch as mates, and Stanley as surgeon'*: James Fitzjames (died 1847/8, as did all the others in this and the following note), Graham Gore, Henry Thomas Dundas Le(s) Vesconte (born 1813), buried on King William Island, Charles Frederick Des Voeux, Robert (Orme) Sargent, Edward Couch (Verne: 'Conch'), Stephen (Samuel) Stanley. A memorial in Greenwich lists other officers and gives (final) ranks as Fitzjames, captain; Gore, commander; and Des Voeux, Sargent, and Couch, lieutenants.

'Captain Crozier, lieutenants Little, Hodgson, and Irving, mates Hornby and Thomas, surgeon Peddie': (Verne: 'Little Hodgson et Irving') Crozier: see note to p. 36; Edward Little; George (Henry) Hodgson; John Irving,

buried at Irving Bay, King William Island; (Frederick) John Hornby (Verne: 'Horsley'); Robert Thomas; John (Smart) Peddie. Other officers are again omitted, and the Greenwich memorial ascribes the following ranks: Little, commander; Hornby and Thomas, lieutenants.

99 '*a document dated 25 April 1848, found by Lieutenant Hobson of the "Fox"*': William Robert Hobson (1831–80); the document, found in 1859, says that the *Erebus* and *Terror* had navigated Peel Sound and Franklin Strait southwards, but been stopped by ice between Victoria and King William Islands in September 1846.

100 '*a letter by Dr Rae in 1854 stated that in 1850 the Eskimos had encountered a detachment of forty men on this King William Island*': a translation of Rae's letter of 29 July 1854 appears in Lanoye (ed.), *La Mer polaire* (1864), 157–61, and is clearly Verne's source for nearly all of this paragraph, especially the evidence for cannibalism. While Lanoye also reads '1850', it is known that everyone had died by 1848.

while the opposite shore is still unknown: this coast is now called King Haakon 7, explored in 1905.

103 *Melville Sound*: Verne erroneously uses 'la baie Melville' ('Melville Bay', in Baffin Bay).

104 '*the silver sea*': Shakespeare's *Richard II*: 'This precious stone set in the silver sea, this sceptr'd isle', referring to Britain.

108 *whales of more than one hundred and eighty feet*: modern measurements give a maximum of less than a hundred and ten feet.

109 *straight through the wood*: this sentence and the preceding one are taken word for word from Dubois, (*Le Pôle et l'équateur*, 21).

110 *Captain Ommanney*: Sir Erasmus Ommanney (1814–1904), captained the *Assistance* on Austin's 1850 expedition.

Macleod Bay . . . (Bellot) Point: no trace has been found of Verne's 'baie de Mac-Leon' or 'le cap Bellot'.

On 25 June . . . Beechey Island: the four preceding paragraphs are based on Kennedy's *A Short Narrative* (1853) and the Admiralty charts of the region.

111 *There Cresswell, McClure's lieutenant, having covered 470 miles over the ice, re-embarked on the 'Phoenix' and went back to Britain*: MÉR (IV 39–40/II 19) has this information in the prelude to the argument between Hatteras and Altamont, and in a different form: ' "And, on 7 October," continued the doctor, "Cresswell arrived in London, having covered all the space between Bering Strait and Cape Farewell." '

11 August 1855: (cf. eight paragraphs below) the correct year, 1858, was given in I 14.

112 *to Dr Kane in 1855 . . . on Beechey Island*: given that the tablet is dated '1855', but Kane left in 1853, there are two problems with the dates. Both memorials are described in Dubois, *Le Pôle et l'équateur*, 133.

erected in Bellot's memory, thanks to Sir John Barrow: Sir John Barrow (1764–1848), Second Lord of the Admiralty and organizer of the fatal Franklin expedition. The Bellot memorial reads: 'Sacred to the memory of Monsieur Bellot, lieutenant in the French Navy . . . In a heavy gale of wind on the eighteenth August 1853, he was drowned by the disruption of the ice near Cape Grinnell'.

113 *So He brings them into the deserved haven | 1855*: Verne's French translation of the inscription is identical to Lanoye's (*La Mer polaire*, 253). Although the quotation 'C'est ainsi qu'il les conduisit au port suprême où tous reposent' has not been traced, McClintock's memorial in Portsmouth reads 'So He brings them into the deserved haven'.

115 *ptarmites, a sort of grouse, very good to eat*: 'ptarmite' is unattested in any language and is presumably a slip for 'ptarmigan'. Verne's list is probably derived from HL's (254) and Dubois's (*Le Pôle et l'équateur*, 93), which contain many of the same birds.

116 *Wellington Channel*: Verne uses both 'le canal Wellington' and 'le détroit de Wellington'.

Capes Spencer and Innis: both capes are cited in Kane's *The United States Grinnell Expedition*, making it a possible source here.

117 *'Captain Pullen'*: William John Samuel Pullen (1813–87), of the *North Star*.

'in 1850': a slip for 1851.

118 *Harvey, the quartermaster of the 'North Star', and . . . sailors, Madden, David Hook*: no trace has been found.

119 *'our brave officer'*: Johnson's account of the death of Bellot is drawn almost word for word from Inglefield's piece in the *Athenaeum* of 1853. HL seem to have drawn from the same source, since their account (263–4) is near-identical to Verne's, although with fewer details; they confirm that the group contained four men, but say Bellot left on 16, not 12, August; have 'eight o'clock' where Verne has 'quarter past six'; and say that Johnson and Hook remained crippled after their day on the floating ice—meaning Johnson could not serve under Hatteras.

Cape[s] . . . Helpman: no trace has been found of Verne's 'Cape Helpman'.

120 *Queen Channel*: from North Devon to Cornwallis, the *Forward* is following the route of Penny and Stewart, who spotted an open sea north of Cornwall Island.

pull: Verne uses the marine term 'nager' and explains it in a note as 'Ramer' ('to row'); the note is repeated in II 23.

23 June: previously it had been 'the thirtieth'. The chronology is again inconsistent below, with about ten dates indicated as being from early June onwards.

122 *Cape Becher*: Verne uses both 'la pointe Becher' and '[le] cap Becher'.

125 *Prince Albert Land, also known as Grinnell Land*: Prince Albert Land is in fact well to the south; Verne's own map reads 'Î. Grinnell Franklin' (the 'or' being omitted through lack of space), but no trace has been found of a Franklin (Is)land.

128 *'£375 each—six times eight degrees!'*: given that the sum is '£62. 10s. per man and per degree' (I 18) for each of the sixteen officers and men and the number of degrees is six, 'six times eight degrees' makes no sense.

131 *eased*: Verne inserts a note, explaining 'soulagé' as 'Soulevé' ('lifted'). The scene of being pursued by an ice avalanche, like a pack of wild animals, may come from Ross's similar description at Batty Bay in 1833.

132 *no land in view, at 78° 15′ N, 95° 35′ W ... the pole of cold*: these coordinates are on Amund Ringnes Island, discovered in 1901. Verne's map indicates the pole of cold as 79° N, 98° W, and in I 13, he places it at '78° N, 97° W' and in *The Fur Country*, 'on the shores of North Georgia, at 78° N, 95° W'. The discrepancies are minor, given the imprecision and variability of the pole of cold and the existence of Paris and Greenwich meridians.

133 *what desolation at this latitude, what saddening nature, what lamentable contemplations!*: Verne is hamming up vocabulary from Baudelaire's *Spleen de Paris*.

135 *'Hyde Park or the Hanging Gardens of Babylon'*: the first world fair was held in Hyde Park in London in 1851; the Hanging Gardens were one of the Seven Wonders of the World, probably built by Nebuchadnezzar II in about 600 BC. The gardens in fact grew directly on the roofs and terraces of the royal palace.

noted by a French scientist: Verne inserts a footnote reading 'François Arago'. François Arago (1786–1853), the brother of Jacques, mentioned in II 24, was a mathematician, scientist, politician, and associate of Verne's.

corners ... had been eliminated ... the walls were covered with buckskin: the wintering accommodation reproduces Verne's first home environment, in his grandparents' flat at 4 Rue de Clisson on Feydeau Island, Nantes, where the living room similarly lacked corners and the walls were covered with tapestries and a portrait of his great-grandfather, François Guillochet, Arctic mariner.

scrapers: in English in the text; Verne was impressed by the foot-scrapers of Edinburgh's New Town in 1859.

136 *'we'll have to employ substances rich in sugar and fat'*: while Clawbonny's diet seems unhealthy, the vitamin C in animal fat is good for preventing scurvy.

140 *the doctor organized his travel notes—of which this narrative is the faithful reproduction*: Clawbonny must have taken his notes with him when he searched for coal, otherwise they would have been destroyed with the *Forward*.

142 *'a fox caught by James Ross in 1848'*: this incident is cited in *The Fur Country*: '"I remember . . . one of these foxes . . . was caught by Captain Hatteras on his journey of discovery"', assimilating Hatteras to a real-life explorer. However, the systematically ironic *The Purchase of the North Pole* has a footnote: 'In his list of discoverers who have attempted to reach the North Pole, [the character] omits the name of Captain Hatteras, whose flag is reported to have flown at the ninetieth degree. This is easy to understand, since the aforesaid captain was probably just a fictional hero. (*British at the North Pole* and *Desert of Ice*, by the same author)'.

143 *A few Moravian Brothers observed [shooting stars] in Greenland in 1799*: an Eskimo called Kapik was so impressed by fireballs in the sky on 12 November 1799 that he immediately converted to Christianity. Humboldt also observed the shower in Cumaná, Venezuela. In 1833, the same stars came back, and were baptized the Leonids; in 1864 their periodicity was realized to be 33.25 years, meaning that they were due to return in 1866.

145 *the Northern Lights glimpsed in temperate zones do not give the slightest impression*: on 28 August 1859 and in the following weeks, a spectacular Aurora (Borealis) was observed across Europe as far south as Italy. Verne observed it during his visit to Scotland. After 'a luminous circle' in the following paragraph, MS has fourteen crossed-out lines describing Clawbonny's observations of the pole of cold, causing him to burn his eyelids; he goes in to share his ideas with the captain, but receives a brush-off.

On 26 November . . . the water rushed violently up through the fire hole: John Ross (*Narrative of a Second Voyage*) noted in his journal for a similar 26 November that this was the period for high tides and that water flowed up through his fire hole.

146 *defibrinated*: Verne's 'défibrinisée' is not attested (Littré gives 'défibriné'), and may be an Anglicism.

150 *'burn the least useful parts, the gunnels and the rails'*: on the Kane expedition (1853–5), the crew was forced to cannibalize the ship for heating and then construct smaller vessels; Phileas Fogg will later develop the idea to self-fuel his way to Liverpool.

151 *'I will not give consent. Disobey me if you want!'*: an echo of Victor Hugo's 'At bottom, God wants man to disobey. To disobey is to seek' (*Tas de pierres*).

152 *he was reading Sir Edward Belcher's relation of his expedition to the polar seas . . . 'We found coal there'*: Belcher's book is *The Last of the Arctic Voyages* (1855), but Verne is in fact citing HL, for he lifts their passage (266), added *in extremis* to their 1854 volume, inserting only italics for the last sentence. Although Verne does not initially make it clear whether these are natural coal deposits, HL criticizes Belcher for not explaining that the coal and the house meant that previous Europeans had been there.

153 *150 miles further north*: four paragraphs previously, the distance was
     200 miles. This chapter opening also repeats information given at the end
     of the previous one.

     since 1853: Belcher's exploration of southern Cornwall Island marked an
     extreme of discovery, and only in the twentieth century were the islands
     further north visited. This page represents Verne's transition from
     closely adhering to previous accounts to freely inventing.

160 *a vast cemetery . . . in which twenty generations . . . could easily have lain
     down for eternal slumber*: cf. *Journey to the Centre of the Earth* (37): 'It
     looked like an immense cemetery, where the generations of 2,000 years
     mingled their eternal dust.'

161 *15 February, a Sunday*: in fact a Friday ('15 February' in *MÉR* and 1867,
     '15 January' (a Tuesday) in 1866); it is not clear whether the '15 January'
     of the previous paragraph is meant to be the same day.

164 *faster than a horse's gallop*: (cf. 'fast enough on such terrain to overtake the
     quickest horse' (I 12)) the speed of polar bears is at most forty kilometres
     per hour, compared with a horse's seventy.

165 *New Cornwall*: Verne's rare expression 'Nouveau Cornouailles' is used by
     Chateaubriand in *Voyage en Amérique*.

167 *'on condition I do the same for you'*: this scene, with much reciprocal
     rubbing of 'that ornament, inconvenient while travelling, but necessary
     to existence', abounds with innuendo.

169 *'Altam . . . "Porpoise", 13 Dec. . . . 1860, 12 . . . ° long. . . . 8 . . . ° 35′ lat.
     . . .'*: the position can be understood as 12x° W, 8x° N. In II 2, we learn
     that the position is '120° 15′ W, 83° 35′ N'. MS reads '"Altamont, of the
     brig the *Porpoise*, 19 December 1863, 79° 15′ latitude, 91° 37′ longi-
     tude"', with a large editorial '?' in the margin questioning '1863'. (I 27 in
     MS has a similar '. . . that fateful 1863 1860 ended'.) Not only are full
     coordinates provided, breaking the suspense, but the *Porpoise* has not set
     any record northwards. The '91°' perhaps indicates that in the manu-
     script, the *Porpoise* travels via Smith Sound. On 19 December 1863,
     Verne was already working on Part II. But in any case the whole scene is
     redundant, as it has no influence on subsequent events.

     'The "Porpoise"!': the name of the lead ship on Charles Wilkes's
     American expedition to investigate Antarctic magnetism (1838–42)
     (Verne: '[le] *Purpoise*' in *Travellers*, II 3 2). It met Dumont d'Urville's
     ship in the Southern Seas, but arguments broke out between the crews.
     Wilkes was court-martialled on his return, accused of pre-dating his
     documents to imply he had started before Dumont d'Urville.

170 *white sickness*: Verne here adds to the French language the phrase 'le mal
     de la blancheur', modelled on 'space sickness'.

172 *17 January*: previously the date had been '25 January'.

177 *'Altamont'*: 'high mountain'; John Dennis Browne, third Earl of
     Altamont, was a Cambridge whoring companion of Byron's (cited in

Thackeray, *Pendennis*, ch. 62); also a locality near Albany (NY), which Verne visited in 1867.

179 *without resources, lost and alone at the eightieth degree, in the heart of the Arctic!*: Verne asked for his publisher's opinion of the ending (4 September 1863), worried no doubt by its boldness.

187 *lime juice*: MÉR and 1866 have a note translating Verne's 'lime-juice' as 'Jus de citron'; 1867 has a superscript '2' in the text, but the corresponding footnote is missing.

189 *the east coast of Greenland*: a slip for 'west coast', repeating an identical one in I 6; 'closest sea to the west' one page below should be 'east'; there are scores of similar east–west confusions in Verne's works.

195 *an American*: Altamont is based on Wilkes and Kane (he has the same sponsor, Grinnell). The position of the *Porpoise* at 83° 35′ is just beyond Parry's record.

197 *jointly shared*: Verne uses the legal term 'de compte à demi' ('with joint participation').

210 *the bear rolled on the ice*: Parry's 1827 expedition similarly avoided starvation by shooting a bear. From Parry also seem to come: divine service and the avoidance of spirits; the idea of having two ships in case one has problems: leaving carcasses in Arctic water overnight so thousands of small shrimps will remove every fragment of flesh; Cochlearia, sorrel, mustard, and cress as anti-scorbutics; and many of the details of wintering, especially covering the deck with thick snow and gravel and adding a roof made of sails, ensuring water vapour does not accumulate, and having antechambers to leave snow-covered clothes in.

213 *It caught fire a few seconds later*: the source is probably Scoresby's similar use of a lens made of ice.

fall asleep in the delights of Capua: a proverbial expression, 'to have fun when work remains', favoured by Verne's friend Dumas and derived from Livy's description of Hannibal overstaying in Capua (212 BC), allowing the Romans to regroup.

215 *Her Gracious Majesty, or the Royal Family*: Queen Victoria (1819–1901), Prince Albert (1819–61), and their nine children (born 1840–57); Albert died of typhoid nine months after Clawbonny's cogitations.

216 *Palm Sunday*: the Sunday before Easter, when branches are carried to commemorate Jesus's triumphant entry into Jerusalem.

218 *Bunsen battery*: a zinc-carbon battery invented by Robert Wilhelm Bunsen (1811–99), German chemist famous for the Bunsen burner.

220 *between its two windows, stretched a passage*: the passage must be at right angles to the house.

Saxon Gothic: Verne's unconventional expression ('gothique saxon') may be drawn from Antoine d'Abbadie, *Pensées, études et voyages de 1835*; it seems to mean the Gothic style (fourteenth to sixteenth centuries), as interpreted by the 'Anglo-Saxons' in the nineteenth century.

221 *book by Mr Krafft . . . 'A Description . . . 1740'*: (Verne: 'Kraft . . . *Descrip-tion détaillée de la maison de glace construite à Saint-Pétersbourg, en janvier 1740, et de tous les objets qu'elle renfermait'*) Georg Wolfgang Krafft (1701–54), author of *Description et représentation exacte de la maison de glace construite à Saint-Pétersbourg . . .*, trans. from German by Pierre-Louis Le Roy (1741).

the Empress Anne: Anna Ivanovna (1693–1740, reigned 1730–40), Empress of Russia.

222 *Sterne's good Uncle Toby*: Laurence Sterne (1713–68), author of *The Life and Opinions of Tristram Shandy, Gentleman* (1759–67); the construction of Clawbonny's fort borrows from Toby's obsessive recreation of medi-eval defence systems (III 38). Doctor's House itself may be based on Somerset House (1832), built by Ross.

the two ends of the snow parapet followed the shape of the plateau as they left the rock wall and came to join the two sides of the house: it is not clear how, or why, the two ends of the wall join the house—or how the beacon is subsequently built, given that the house has no back door.

223 *the famous Grinnell*: a note in *MÉR* and 1866, absent in 1867, reads 'Rich American ship-owner who paid for Dr Kane's expedition'.

224 *the second Low Sunday*: Verne wrote an unattested 'le second dimanche de la Quasimodo' (Low Sunday is the first Sunday after Easter).

227 *'New America'*: although the name is invented, and may not be a national claim, it points to American expansionism. The acquisition of Alaska in 1867 is central to Verne's *The Fur Country*; and the settlers of *The Mysterious Island* (1874) propose attaching their Pacific colony to the Union.

228 *Johnson Island*: Johnson's Island in Lake Erie was a famous Unionist prison-of-war from 1861.

Washington: George Washington (1732–99), commander-in-chief in the War of Independence and president (1789–97).

Fort Providence: another Fort Providence already existed in the Northwest Territories.

231 *intense light*: contemporary batteries were weak, making this passage implausible.

234 *bread made from birchskin*: an attested food in many northern climes, made by grinding the inner bark of older birches. It forms part of a sustained Vernian equivalence between the bodies of boats and men, wood and flesh, with underlying images of cannibalization and cannibalism.

235 *minus seventy-three (−31 °C)*: minus seventy-three Fahrenheit is −58°C. Similarly 'three hundred (132°C)—eighty-nine above boiling point' below is a slip for 'eighty-eight'.

236 *'where it can't'*: 1867 (but not *MÉR* or 1866) is defective, reading: '. . . celles-ci' ('where *they* can't').

237 *'In 1774 nine of our compatriots . . . stood a temperature of two hundred and ninety-five (128 °C) while eggs and roast beef cooked beside them'*: Verne provides only eight names. *Fordyce*: Dr George Fordyce (1736–1802), doctor, chemist, balloon enthusiast, and friend of Samuel Johnson; *Banks*: Sir Joseph Banks (1743–1820), naturalist who helped establish botany as a science, president of the Royal Society, friend of Scoresby, and promoter of Arctic expeditions; *Solander*: Dr Daniel Solander (1733–82), FRS, Swedish-born botanist; Banks and Solander took part in Cook's circumnavigation; *Blagden*: (Verne: 'Blagdin') Sir Charles Blagden (1748–1820), author of 'Experiments and Observations in a Heated Room' (*Phil. Trans. Roy. Soc. Lond.* 65 (1774), 111–23), about the body's temperature control mechanisms; *Home, Nooth, Lord Seaforth*: not traced; *Captain Phillips*: perhaps Captain Constantine John Phipps, Baron Mulgrave, RN (1744–92), leader of an Arctic expedition, who sailed with Banks. The temperature when the eggs and beef were cooking was in fact about two hundred and forty, according to Sir David Brewster, *Letters on Natural Magic* (1832, 305), who seems to be the source of Verne's information, since he is cited in I 13 and in other works and Brewster and Verne both quote the Rochefoucault [*sic*] case, where a Duhamel and Tillet are reported as observing that the girls endured a temperature of two hundred and seventy degrees.

'the Duke of Raguse and Dr Jung, a Frenchman and an Austrian': Field Marshal Auguste Frédéric Louis Viesse de Marmont, Duke of Raguse (1774–1852), worked in Vienna; Dr Jung has not been identified.

238 *'the temperature of the British is normally a hundred and one (37 °C)'*: in fact between ninety-eight and ninety-nine.

239 *extremes come back periodically, about every forty-one years, a period which coincides with the most frequent appearance of sunspots*: Humboldt, cited in this same chapter, publicized Schwabe's observation of the periodicity of sunspots. Sabine also mentioned in this chapter, confirmed in 1852 that geomagnetic disturbances were strongly correlated with the appearance of sunspots.

'seventy at Fort Reliance': Dease and Simpson recorded −59.5 °C at Fort Confidence in February 1838; in September 1833 Captain Ross wrote to George Elliot, in Baffin Bay: 'the winters of 1830 and 1831 set in with a degree of violence hitherto beyond record, the thermometer sank to 92 below the freezing point' (cited on www.arcticwebsite.com). *The Guinness Book of Records* reports −70 °C frequently occurring in Siberia and a record of −89 °C in Antarctica.

240 *'Fourier . . . on this spot'*: Jean-Baptiste-Joseph Fourier (1768–1830), mathematician and author of the *Analytical Theory of Heat* (1822), about thermal conductivity and the Fourier series. Hatteras seems to be arguing for the existence of an absolute zero, meaning that his 'much more intense' should logically be preceded by 'not'. Absolute zero is now known to be about −273 °C.

240 *Halley*: Sir Edmond Halley (1656–1742), astronomer who first calculated the elliptical orbit of a comet.

241 *'The Weather Book'*: in English in Verne's text, with a footnote reading 'Book on the weather, by Admiral Fitz-Roy [*sic*], which reports all meteorological facts'. The full title was *The Weather Book: A Manual of Practical Meteorology* (1863), by Robert Fitzroy (1805–65), hydrographer and captain of the *Beagle* on Darwin's 1831–6 trip.

242 *to instruct . . . personal arguments*: this paragraph sets out Verne's literary manifesto, sharing a few features with Hetzel's 'Announcement' in the 1867 edition.

243 *an American and a Briton . . . the one full of all the insular arrogance, the other with his nation's speculative, audacious, and brutal mind*: in calling the American insular and the Briton brutal, Verne may be inverting stereotypes and so emphasizing the similarities. A corresponding chiasmus exists in his use of American places to name Clawbonny and Hatteras and a probably British name for Altamont—all names that will be returned to the landscape of British America.

244 *'Captain Sabine, the editor of the "North Georgia Gazette and Winter Chronicle"'*: Sir Edward Sabine (1788–1883), expeditions in 1818, 1819, and 1823 and author of *Remarks on the Account of the Late Voyage of Discovery . . . by Captain J. Ross* (1819); Verne (*Travellers*, II 3 2) says the *Gazette* ran to twenty-one issues and was printed in Britain (1821). It contained articles, songs, verse, letters, and reports on social activities, including a long poem on the Northern Lights by the 19-year-old James Ross (82–3), and was reprinted as vol. iv of Parry's *Voyages* (1821–8). Sabine and Beechey took major roles in most of the plays, with Ross invariably playing women's parts. 'North Georgia' was the name Parry gave to the Parry Islands. Echoes of the *Gazette* in *Hatteras* may include the essence of frozen alcohol virtually disappearing (*Voyages*, 3), the coldest temperature recorded (80), the 'mallemuke' bird (81), and the idea of wolves luring away ships' dogs (96), although Verne omits that the lure is sexual.

the Philosophical Society of Liverpool or the Literary Institution of London: the Literary and Philosophical Society of Liverpool (see note to p. 19) and either the Jewish and General Literary Institution, in Leadenhall Street, or the London Institution, founded in 1806 'for the Advancement of Literature and the Diffusion of Useful Knowledge'.

'Parry's . . . own account': *Voyages for the Discovery of a Northwest Passage, 1819–1825; and, Narrative of an Attempt to Reach the North Pole, 1827* (1821–8).

'a few extracts from the "North Georgia Gazette"': rather than retranslating the French text, the present text directly cites the *Gazette* as republished in Parry's *Voyages*, 1–4, 33 ('Wanted . . . preferred'), and 44 ('GENTLEMEN . . . HANDICRAFT'). The French translation is a reasonable one, although not indicating deletions from the text.

Explanatory Notes

After 'to the editor' MS has an important footnote, the only indication of any of the French sources for *Hatteras*: '*Voyage au Pôle arctique*, d'Hervé et de Lanoye'. This book (HL, 1854) does indeed contain exactly the same four extracts from Parry as Verne, in an identical translation (84–6)—the most extensive case of plagiarism in his works identified to date.

HL is also undoubtedly the most important source for *Hatteras*. Other borrowed episodes include Hatteras as a sole survivor from an earlier expedition and perhaps even his subsequent madness and suicide, from HL's description of Munk; and Hatteras's vain trek in search of coal, from HL's translation of Belcher about a mysterious coal dump (266). Shared ideas include the freezing point of mercury (10), rubbing with snow to treat frostbite (89), instantly freezing water by putting frozen hands in (89, although, in Verne's case, amputation is avoided), the vegetation of 'moss . . . saxifrage, and poppies' (90), details of the musk ox scene (165), the need to cut up game before it freezes (166), ships being bodily moved by ice at speed (240), and trekkers keeping a straight line by spacing out (260). Even HL's mistakes, for instance 'Haswelt . . . Creswell' (285), are reproduced by Verne. Since HL do not indicate the titles they are citing, Verne does not either. Hatteras's affidavit about the discovery of the Pole cites HL's translation of McClure's message of 12 April 1852 (294) almost verbatim; and much of II 15 is a summary of HL's final chapter on McClure.

245 *Serjeant Martin*: a footnote in the *North Georgia Gazette* (omitted from HL and *Hatteras*) reads 'The Serjeant of the Royal Artillery who accompanied Captain Sabine', but this person has not been traced.

246 *a widow, twenty-six years of age*: Verne married a 26-year-old widow two years before, meaning that the ribaldry about the widow's virtue ('keep on their breeches; also, if I may be allowed two or three of the stoutest able-seamen or marines') was guaranteed to upset his wife—if she read his books. However, the choice of citation is HL's, not Verne's.

'*ABIGAIL HANDICRAFT . . . hollands*': in Verne's text, the writer is simply 'A.B.', but a scurrilous 'ABIGAÏL BONNATOUT' ('good for anything') in MS and HL. Although 'hollands' is gin made in Holland, as confirmed later in the *Gazette* (Parry, *Voyages*, 52), the French text reads 'eau-de-vie' ('brandy').

'*steep hole*': a footnote in the *Gazette*, omitted by Verne, reads: 'A hole in the ice for steeping salt meat, etc.'

247 '*Voyage Finished*': HL (87): 'The [fortnightly] repertoire, from just a couple of volumes by chance on board the *Hecla*, was not very varied. Captain Parry . . . composed for Christmas *The North-West Passage; or, The Voyage Finished*, which was very successful.'

248 *Worrying Tracks*: 1866: 'Interesting Tracks'.

their idle solitude, a condition in which even the best of men become embittered: Verne is again alluding to his decades as a not-too-successful author. His descriptions of great fatigue and sadness on finally achieving goals (II 25) must also reflect his own writing experience.

250 *bears . . . are also very intelligent, if not the most intelligent of all animals*: normally apes, dolphins, and elephants are considered the most intelligent.

253 *'But there's an American with us,' said Johnson*: instead of the next paragraphs, *MÉR* (IV 40/II 19) has: '. . . "The launch!" exclaimed Hatteras, who saw an evident intention in these words of Altamont.' Given that MS has '"*To* the launch!"', the implication is that Altamont wants to take physical possession to further his claim.

254 *'But, captain . . .' said Johnson*: virtually the only time Johnson disagrees with anyone, indicating that Hatteras may be wrong to disdain the American wood—and will later change his mind. In 1866, Johnson's 'Never!' five lines above is the more logical 'Never?' Similarly, *MÉR* and 1866 read 'nothing *new*' in 'Altamont had nothing to report' at the end of I 11, and 1866 has 'crust of ice', more expressive than 'layer of ice', in I 12.

256 *The bears stopped . . . to smell the object dropped for their curiosity*: the idea must come from Scoresby, who recounts a similar chase.

261 *the claws; the bears*: Verne's narrator makes statements that are not true, the justification undoubtedly being that they are in free indirect style, representing the characters' thoughts.

269 *pendicles*: Verne's 'pendicules' is not attested in French, although 'pendicle' occurs in Walter Scott.

he almost left it there in the extreme frost: Verne is again making play on similarities between body appendages.

270 *'Saints Mamertus, Pancras, and Servatius, whose feast days fall on the 11th, 12th, and 13th of this month'*: a French proverb runs: 'Mamertus, Pancras, and Servatius are the three saints of ice, but St Urbain controls everything', meaning that planting should be put off until after 25 May. St Mamertus (died shortly after 475) was Bishop of Vienne; St Pancras (290–304) was beheaded during Diocletian's persecution; St Servatius (died *c*.384) was the first bishop of eastern Belgium.

274 *Hatteras could not hide*: from here to the end of the chapter the text was originally different. In the *MÉR* version (1864–5), the preceding section about McClure, the Northwest Passage, and the nationality of the *Porpoise* appears in 'The Northwest Passage' (*MÉR* IV 33–51/II 19), just before the travellers sail towards the Pole (II 21, 'The Open Sea', in 1867). Instead of the next five paragraphs, *MÉR* reads: 'Hatteras could not easily hide his joy at finally finding this famous basin free of ice, and being able to confirm the information of his predecessors, despite so many rebuttals. So, over dinner, the doctor congratulated him on the discovery. | "Your reasoning was correct, but I hope you'll concede, Hatteras, that you always found me a warm supporter of your theory." |

"Certainly, Clawbonny, you also thought that our predecessors had to be right. It's obvious that this liquid basin stretches much further south, and that the sea is now free beyond Victoria Bay, as far as New Cornwall, as far as Queen Channel! Penny and Belcher saw it clearly!" '

'open sea . . . sighted by Morton, Kane's lieutenant, in the strait bearing that bold scientist's name': only Morton (see note to p. 76) spotted open water (with the Eskimo Hans Christian Hendrik), at a claimed 81° 22' on the Greenland coast in July 1854. From a height of 300 feet, he saw a totally ice-free sea stretching more than fifty miles north and eighty-five miles west, with many whales and sea-birds and patches of greenery. But in his official report to the US Navy, Kane exaggeratedly proclaimed the discovery of an 'open and iceless area, abounding with life, and presenting every character of an *open Polar* Sea' and wrote 'Open Sea' in bold letters across his chart of the North Pole. In fact, Morton was mistaken, for the only large stretch of water, Kane Basin, is south of eighty-one degrees.

274 ' *"Kane Sea"* ': Morton named the water 'Kane Sea', followed by Malte-Brun, but 'Kane Basin' was universally adopted. The strait is called 'Kennedy Channel' rather than the unconventional 'Kane Sound' Verne uses.

276 *'you will grant that I can speak of them impartially'*: only pages earlier, Clawbonny was extolling his British virtues; even Verne's narrator seems to sympathize with the British.

277 *'he would find Franklin or the Passage'*: HL (269): 'McClure . . . added . . . "I will find Franklin or the Passage" '.

278 *Haswell . . . Wynniatt*: (Verne: 'Haswelt') Lieutenant William Haswell (dates unknown), Sub-Lieutenant Robert Wynniatt (*MÉR*: 'Wynniat') (dates unknown); although the ultimate source is either de Bray's citing (140) of McClure's note of 18 April 1851 or McClure himself, Verne's immediate source must be HL (285): 'Lieutenant Creswell [*sic*] had as mission to explore Baring Island . . . Lieutenant Haswelt [*sic*] . . . Prince Albert Land . . . Mr Winniat [*sic*] . . . Cape Walker'.

279 *Lieutenant Pim*: Bedford Pim (1826–86). The exact message was: 'I am Lieutenant Pim, late of the *Herald*, and now in the *Resolute*. Captain Kellett is in her at Dealy Island!' (McClure, *Arctic Dispatches*, 290–1).

a sub-lieutenant from a French vessel, M. de Bray: Émile de Bray (1829–79), author of 'Journal de bord de l'enseigne de vaisseau Émile de Bray 1852–1854' (published as *De Bray Pôle Nord*, 1998—*A Frenchman in Search of Franklin: De Bray's Arctic Journal*, 1992), perhaps a source for Verne of a few minor details, such as Bible reading, blowing up ice using a fuse of gutta-percha, the discovery of the Northwest Passage, tots of rum, and parhelia.

'he went on board the "Phoenix" ': all the information in the previous three pages is taken from HL's unreferenced translation (290–2 and 298–301) of McClure, presumably *The Arctic Dispatches*.

280 *'Altamont . . . we must find you in the wrong'*: Clawbonny again seems biased here.

'Yankee Doodle': sung by the British in the War of Independence to taunt the Rebels, who soon adopted it. In *From the Earth to the Moon* Verne compares 'Yankee Doodle' to the Revolutionary 'Marseillaise'.

281 *Soon the whole shrill race . . . a solitary stork: MÉR*: 'With the first warmth, Hatteras and his companions rediscovered the whole flock of birds that they had seen lower, on King William and Beechey Islands, the seagulls, divers, kittywakes, and eider-duck. The seals appeared again, joyously coming out of their holes and on to the rocks of the shore. Hunting of polar hares, foxes, and small game resumed, while waiting for the reindeer and musk oxen to come and offer prey more worthy of being shot'.

a clumsy hand had put too much water: a common Vernian trope, poking fun at explanations of natural phenomena in terms of divine intervention.

282 *Parry found numerous herds on Melville Island*: the head of one of the musk oxen shot on Melville Island is still in the Cork Institution.

285 *they lay down at his feet . . . the relationship between the first man and the first animals when the world was young*: allusions to St Francis of Assisi and Genesis. Verne's polar regions resemble a time machine, providing access to a lost paradise where men and animals are still in their first youth, partly derived from Dubois's description of the friendliness of the first encounters with the herbivores, but not the carnivores, on Melville Island, 'as in the antique days of Eden' (*Le Pôle et l'équateur*, 35).

286 *'Nimrod'*: 'the first potentate on earth', a 'mighty hunter' (Genesis 10: 8–9).

'Orpheus': one of the Argonauts, a mythological musician whose playing enchanted the trees and rocks and tamed the wild beasts.

288 *muzzle . . . nose . . . 'ovibos'*: the vocabulary of *muffle*, *chanfrein*, and *ovibos* (Arctic musk ox) may be taken from a note by Lartet presented by Milne-Edwards (both are praised in *Journey to the Centre of the Earth*), describing the discovery of an ovibos cranium near Paris (*Comptes rendus hebdomadaires des séances de l'Académie des sciences*, 1 (1864), 1198–1201).

half an hour: in the previous paragraph, the run had taken 'an hour and a half'.

289 *'He's done for!' exclaimed the doctor . . . horns and feet*: instead of this passage, *MÉR* (III 325/II 16) has: 'exclaimed the doctor. | "Let's run! Let's run!" said Altamont. | The American ran to the scene of the fight as fast as possible. Hatteras was on his knees, his hatchet in one hand and knife in the other, fending off the blows of the horns and feet as best he could'. Although having Altamont hesitate should make him less likeable and so increase the rivalry with Hatteras, the fact that it is observed in this version is designed to help with the captains' reconciliation, and so please Hetzel.

a terrible axe blow: the corresponding illustration shows Duke also helping attack the ox.

291 *Hatteras was saved ... 'Since I was useless'*: instead of this passage, *MÉR* (III 325–6/II 16) has: 'was saved, although badly bruised. | "Oh, Altamont, Altamont," exclaimed the doctor, "what a good fellow you are!" | "Pshaw, huntsmen return favours!" | Hatteras owed his life to the American; he fully realized it, and, pale from forcing himself, not from the danger undergone, he went up to his rival. | "I thank you," he said. | "What for?" coldly replied Altamont. "You saved my life under the snow, I saved yours today. We're quits!" | "Come on, come on—to work!" said the doctor, regretting this poor response. | "Since I was useless" '.

In his letter to Hetzel (25 April 1864), Verne condemns the idea of a reconciliation directly after the saving of a life as 'diabolically common'; but this is what he does in the 1867 version. As if to compensate, he hams up the whole scene of overt sentimentality, international friendship, and pretence that national differences can be overcome; *MÉR* comes over as more sincere and plausible.

a surgeon practising a delicate autopsy: *MÉR* (III 326): 'a surgeon doing an operation'.

smiling: *MÉR* (III 326): 'without a word'.

set off back for Fort Providence: *MÉR* (III 326) adds a paragraph: 'Fort Providence. | They walked in silence; Hatteras and Altamont were embarrassed, the doctor miserable; this situation, which should have brought the two men together, divided them all the more, and this time Hatteras could not be faulted! | At ten o'clock . . .'

'two brothers': a full-page illustration in the 1867 edition, absent from *MÉR*, shows the five men drinking a toast, with the two captains harmoniously facing each other.

walking in the oblique rays of the sun . . . happy men: instead of this passage, *MÉR* (III 326) omits the chapter break, and reads: 'walking in the powdery rays of the sun, they reached Doctor's House; a good meal was waiting for them and, once supper had been wolfed down, they threw themselves on their bunks, which were sorely needed.'

292 *overcoming the obstacles, easier*: *MÉR* (III 326) has: 'easier. More alarming were the worries inevitably produced by the Briton and American's rivalry. | The doctor had related the episode of the musk oxen, and the old mate had shaken his head. | "I would never have believed that of Altamont," concluded the doctor. | "Oh, those Yankees!" replied Johnson, with a gesture of annoyance.'

excellent nautical qualities: *MÉR* (III 327–8) reads: 'qualities. Altamont was very happy with what Bell had been able to do using the remains of the *Porpoise*; he took visible pleasure in standing in the boat; he considered it his own, and seemed to be doing its honours; he affectedly thanked Bell. The carpenter replied that he had only been working in

everybody's interest. | "Well then," said the American, "I want to thank
you in everybody's name; with such a vessel and good sailors, we can go
to the end of the world!" | Hatteras shuddered at this phrase; the doctor
detected a strange smile on Altamont's lips when he said "to the end of
the world!". Was it just a common expression or did the American give it
a particular meaning? Clawbonny could not guess; but touching
Hatteras's hand, he felt the captain's fingers clenching the deck of the
launch and his nails digging into it. | Perhaps Hatteras was going to
explode and, with right on his side, put the American in his place; but a
glance from the doctor restrained him and he stayed silent.'

293 *fifty pounds of brine and lime juice, five quarters*: it is not clear why they are
carrying brine ('saumure'), unattested in polar expeditions, unless it is to
pickle future kills. In a footnote, Verne explains 'five quarters' as '380
pounds', although a quarter is usually twenty-eight pounds.

295 *attaching great importance to the question of cant*: rather than hypocrisy,
Verne is using the older meaning, 'snobbery'. The sense is vital, since a
surviving fragment of the very first doodles creating *Around the World*
reads 'Fog xxx [cant]': Fogg is initially generated by his snobbery or at
least unfriendliness.

300 *red snow . . . Wollaston, de Candolle, and Bauer . . . de Saussure . . . Ross*:
Wollaston: possibly T. Vernon Wollaston (1822–78); *de Candolle*: probably
Alphonse de Candolle (1806–93); *Bauer*: (Verne: 'Baüer') Francis Bauer
(1758–1840), naturalist and painter, who described the living cells in
snow Ross brought back from Baffin Bay, in 'Microscopical Observations
on the Red Snow' (*Quart. J. Lit. Sci. Arts*, 7 (1819), 222–9). *de Saussure*:
Horace-Bénédict de Saussure (1740–99), describes red snow in *Voyages
dans les Alpes* (1779–96), 2, 44–5 (Gallica). Ross saw 600-foot ridges on
Baffin Bay covered for a distance of eight miles with blood-red snow
many feet in depth (17 August 1819). Some of Verne's information is
drawn from *Comptes rendus hebdomadaires des séances de l'Académie des
sciences* 1/3 (1836), 719–20 (Gallica), which mentions red snow, Bauer,
de Saussure, Wollaston, and Ross.

303 *Daniel Defoe's hero could not have been more surprised when he found a
footprint on the shore of his island*: Daniel Defoe (1660?–1731), author of
Robinson Crusoe (1719). The desert island is closely associated in Verne's
mind with the ideal community; but one of his intentions is often to show
up the facile manipulation of the plot in Defoe's *Robinson Crusoe*. From
the implausibility of Robinson Crusoe's single print, Verne would indeed
invent a whole series of anti-desert-island novels, one of his most characteristic genres, especially *The Mysterious Island*, where nearly every episode is designed to pastiche Defoe's lack of commonsense and abuse of
coincidence. Verne in fact greatly preferred *The Swiss Family Robinson*,
although superficial commentators have often claimed Defoe greatly
influenced him.

304 *'The fact is . . . off again'*: instead of this, *MÉR* (IV 4/II 18) has: ' "a

European!" | "Or an American," said Altamont. | At these words, Hatteras stared at his rival. For a moment the idea came to him that the American might know more about these footprints than he was letting on; but Altamont's annoyance proved sufficiently that his idea was wrong.'

306 *'It's brought joy . . . others'*: instead of this, *MÉR* (IV 7/II 18) has: '"ocean." | "Has it brought joy to your heart to be leaving this island?" the doctor asked the captain. | "I'm happy and sad at the same time, since we'll perhaps need to use that launch we've been dragging with us, but I'll always have the consolation that New America is only an island, separated from the lands of the Pole."'

307 *No objection . . . appropriate*: instead of this, the beginning of II 19 in *MÉR* (IV 33) has: 'Altamont's. | And Hatteras consented without a single objection to Altamont's name being inscribed on the land he had discovered; nothing could be better, provided that he did not later come to claim the same favour for any new lands.'

308 *Did those men . . . this new route?*: instead of this paragraph, *MÉR* has: 'One last night remained to be spent on land, and then these bold mariners were going to expose themselves on a fragile launch to the vagaries of a new ocean. In what port would they find refuge? Where would the winds blow them? These were subjects for serious reflection; nevertheless, each forgot the dangers and thought only of the glory of the endeavour.' *MÉR* then has the two paragraphs where Clawbonny congratulates Hatteras on keeping faith and they agree that Penny and Belcher were right to have recorded observations of the open sea (cited in the endnote to p. 274). Next *MÉR* (IV 33–41/II 19) has the eight pages '"I think as you do . . . without opening his mouth" (in II 15 in the 1867 edition). It then has the following text, which is replaced in 1867 by Clawbonny and Hatteras's discussion, again in II 15, about whether to take Altamont with them: 'Such was this last night spent on the land of New America. | 20: The Open Sea | | The American's obvious intentions had emerged in the discussion the day before; when he thought about it in the morning, Hatteras was beside himself; the doctor could not calm him down; the night had not extinguished his anger; his mind appeared prey to a violent over-excitement; as the Pole got closer, Hatteras seemed less in control of himself; he wanted to leave Altamont, abandon him with food and ammunition on "his New America". | "You can't even think about it," said the doctor. | "I *am* thinking about it, Clawbonny, I am," excitedly replied Hatteras; "that man should stay on the land he discovered!" | "But the poor man will perish!" | "We'll pick him up again on the way back." | "And if we don't come back?" | "Then he will share our fate." | "Hatteras, you shall not act in this way, it would be criminal; you cannot abandon him!" | "Clawbonny, mark my words carefully; sooner or later there will be some act of violence between the two of us! He knows what goal I'm trying to reach. He's ready to take the glory away from us, from Britain and me! I will never tolerate such an affront

from anybody, least of all an American." | "Wait, Hatteras, your rights will be recognized; we will make sure they're respected; but do not dishonour with a crime the honour you are going to win!" | The discussion was a long one; the doctor finally made Hatteras concede that he would give up his plan and that the American would have no inkling of the project against him. But what terrible consequences were building up for the future with the captain's over-excitement, whom already the poor doctor could not restrain!' Finally, from the words 'For the last three days' *MÉR* and 1867 are identical to the end of the novel.

310   *the birds flew in flocks . . . the penguin of the Arctic seas*: the penguin is in fact flightless, and is restricted to the southern hemisphere.

   wingspan . . . twenty feet . . . 'Index Ornithologicus' of London: the greatest recorded wingspan (an albatross) is twelve feet; the *Index Ornithologicus* (Verne: '*Ornithologus*') was a book (1785) by John Latham, listing the 3,000 known birds.

   23,888,000,000,000,000 in an area of two square miles!: (Verne: 'vingt-trois trilliards huit cent quatre-vingt-huit billiards de milliards . . .') Verne's note reads: 'Since this number escapes all imagining, to make it more comprehensible, the British whaler said that to count it, 80,000 individuals would have been busy day and night since the world was created' (an identical statistic appears in John Leslie, *Narrative of Discovery* (1835), 73). Definitions of numbers above million vary considerably. Here Verne's 'milliards' seems to mean thousand billion (10^{12}), 'billiards', 10^{15}, and 'trilliards', 10^{18}. (However, his inconsistency, because of different sources, is shown by his later use of the term 'quadrillions', quoted thirteen notes below, to also mean 10^{18}.) Dividing 23,888,000,000,000,000 seconds by 80,000 gives 2,986,000,000,000 seconds, or 946,850 years. At this time, estimates of the age of the earth ranged widely, with biblical-based calculations of 6,000 years and Kelvin proposing 25 million years (compared with modern estimates of about 4.6 billion).

311   *anarnaks . . . tegusik . . . the Zoological Gardens*: anarnaks (Verne: 'anarnacks'; *MÉR*: 'anarnaks'): 'bottlenose whales' in Greenlandic, a reference to *Histoire naturelle des cétacés* by Lacépède (1804); the phrase 'Greenland anarnak' is directly quoted in Lautréamont's *Les Chants de Maldoror* (Chant IV—1868), a recognition of his debt to Verne. This scene of sea-monsters may derive from Penny. *tegusik*: not found. *the Zoological Gardens*: the London Zoo, opened in Regent's Park in 1826.

316   *unfurling the Union Jack*: beneath the standard late-Romantic dream and space-time association of the four preceding paragraphs are two opposing modes of considering time. The first, characterized as 'thought', is linked to the past, reproduces real events, and is exhaustive. The second, a time of 'dream' and 'imagination', is incalculable and appears under the sign of potentiality, selectivity, liberty, and creativity.

319   *Maelstrom*: Verne wrote 'Maëlstroem', not attested in any language;

Twenty Thousand Leagues culminates in the famous Maelstrom off Norway, probably derived from Poe and Pontoppidan.

320 *a thousand turns a second*: a slip for 'a minute', though sixteen revolutions a second is still implausible.

So close to the goal he had merely glimpsed!: an allusion to Moses's glimpse of the promised land of Canaan.

321 *vomiting . . . trembling . . . ejected matter rose to a great height . . . flanks . . . impetuous torrents*: as well as the digestive imagery, the land is alive with sexuality.

masses of ash thrown out of the crater of the island of St Vincent: Mont Soufrière erupted on 12 March 1812, as vividly described by Humboldt; Barbados was in darkness for four and a half hours as ash fell inches deep.

Hekla: Mount Hekla, 4,892 feet, near Mýrdals-joküll, S. Iceland, the route to the Centre of the Earth; famous as a gateway to hell and for eruptions in 1104, 1766, and 1980.

an angle of about eleven degrees to the horizon: this would mean the radius of the island was more than three miles, although the grotto, near the sea, is later said to be 'three-quarters of a mile' from the centre.

323 *a body wrapped in a Union Jack*: a sign of Hatteras's impending death.

324 *the ninetieth degree was only forty-five seconds away . . . at the summit of the volcano*: Verne was surely aware that locations could not be identified with that degree of precision, but this plot here required suspension of disbelief.

325 *'this discovery would come before those of the centres of Africa and Australia'*: in the mid-1860s Livingstone was still exploring central Africa, with the ultimate source of the Nile unknown. Central Mount Sturt, near the centre of Australia, was named by John McDouall Stuart in 1862, the year after Clawbonny's speech.

327 *'weight of . . . 5,881,000,000,000,000,000,000 tons'*: ('cinq mille huit cent quatre-vingt-un quadrillions de tonneaux') $5,881 \times 10^{18}$ tons. Modern estimates are $5,803 \times 10^{18}$ tons or $5,978 \times 10^{18}$ tonnes, the slight discrepancy being presumably due to refinements in measuring the force of gravity. The word 'mass' would be more accurate than 'weight'.

'seventy-five moons to make the weight of the earth, and 350,000 earths for the weight of the sun': the moon is now calculated to have a mass of 7.35×10^{19} tonnes, or about 1/81 the earth's. The sun is 1.99×10^{27} tonnes, or about 328,900 times the earth.

328 *'In 1771, the body of a rhinoceros was discovered on the edge of the Glacial Sea, and in 1799, an elephant's on the coast of Siberia'*: a hunter named Jakoutzki found the frozen giant rhinoceros, which was publicized by Peter Simon Pallas; 'Adams's Mammoth' was in the Bykovsky Peninsula unearthed by botanist Mikhail Adams.

M. Élie de Beaumont, who later demonstrated that these animals lived at already high latitudes: Beaumont (1798–1874), a geologist, rejected with

scorn the idea that man could have coexisted with the mammoth
(Académie des Sciences, 18 and 23 May 1863).

328 *British America*: Verne uses the dated term 'la Nouvelle-Bretagne',
although he had already used the phrase to mean 'New Britain' in I 12.

330 *'reach the centre of the earth! Has anyone ever thought of undertaking such a
journey?'*: a reference to *Journey to the Centre of the Earth*, published the
same year as *Hatteras*.

331 *the Garden of Hesperides*: it had nymphs and a tree with golden apples, in
the Arcadian Mountains of Greece or near Mount Atlas.

*a French astronomer, Bailly, who maintained that the Atlanteans, that civil-
ized lost race of which Plato speaks, lived on this very spot*: Jean-Sylvain
Bailly (1736–93), author of *Lettres sur l'Atlantide de Platon* (1779–
Gallica), especially Letter 21, 'Of the Languages of the North and the
Garden of Hesperides'; president of the States-General (1789) and
mayor of Paris (1790); guillotined. Plato uses Atlantis to present human
history as a cyclical rise and fall. His *Timaeus* describes a large island
containing a utopia, in 'the western sea' beyond the Pillars of Hercules:
'There occurred violent earthquakes and floods; and in a single day and
night of misfortune all your warlike men in a body sank into the earth,
and the island of Atlantis in like manner disappeared into the depths of
the sea'.

*two planets, Pluto and Proserpina, and air that is luminous, because of the
high pressure it is at*: the idea of a hollow earth accessible through the Poles
closely links *Hatteras* with *Journey to the Centre of the Earth*, which
similarly quotes that 'theory of a British captain's which compared the
earth to a vast hollow sphere, inside which . . . two heavenly bodies, Pluto
and Proserpina, traced their mysterious orbits' (*JCE* 30). The notion had
scientific backing from Halley and Euler, who used it to explain why the
Magnetic Pole moved. Critics have often deduced that the 'British captain' is Captain John Cleves Symmes (1780–1829), the probable author of
Symzonia (1820). But Symmes was American and in fact postulated five
concentric spheres; in reality the idea of Pluto and Proserpina was due to
the Edinburgh physicist Sir John Leslie (1766–1832) (anthologized in
Subterranean Worlds, ed. Walter Kafton-Minkel (1989), 55). Verne's
immediate source is probably his friend and collaborator Dumas's 'At the
centre of the earth, where the compressed air has, under the pressure of
the upper strata, acquired a density greater than mercury, there exists a
cavern of spherical form, without exit, illuminated by two astral bodies
emitting a pale light, one called Pluto and the other Proserpina.' (*Isaac
Laquedem* (1855), ch. 41, which begins with a mention of the *'facilis
descensus Averni* de Virgile', also cited by Verne (*JCE* 18)). But Verne
may also have taken the idea from the French translation of Humboldt's
Cosmos (1846), which sarcastically cites Leslie as having conceived of 'the
interior of the terrestrial globe as a spherical cavern . . . endowed with
animals and . . . two astral bodies, Pluto and Proserpina' (I 192–3).

'*Captain Symmes, one of our compatriots, even suggested to Humphry Davy, Humboldt, and Arago*': *Captain Symmes* (Verne: 'Synness'): see previous note. *Davy*: Sir Humphry Davy (1778–1829), chemist who discovered laughing gas, invented the miners' safety-lamp, proved that diamond was a form of carbon, befriended Parry, and visited Professor Lidenbrock in 1825 (*JCE* 1). *Humboldt*: Baron Alexander von Humboldt (1769–1859), German naturalist and traveller who worked in Paris and wrote *Cosmos* (1845; French trans. 1846–59), on the physical constitution of the globe, one of Verne's sources here: 'Sir Humphrey [sic] Davy and I were summarily and publicly invited by Captain Symmes to undertake this underground expedition'. *Arago*: Jacques Arago (1790–1855), a friend of Verne's, brother of François (mentioned in the footnote to I 24), and author of *Voyage autour du monde* (1844).

332 *that sadness which always follows satisfied desires*: a paraphrase of 'post coitum, animal triste' ('after sex animals are sad').

did he find the world too small because he had been everywhere on it?: an expression of the tension governing the series of Extraordinary Voyages, which depend on the existence of virgin territory.

333 *'may my heart blow its top in your hands!'*: more sexual innuendo, stronger in French due to the homonymy between 'cœur' ('heart') and 'queue' ('tail' or 'prick').

335 *Mount Nuovo, near Naples, generated by scoria in the short space of forty-eight hours*: the eruption, within Lake Lucrino, started on 29 September 1538 and built up a 400-foot cone. Jules Michelet (*Roman History* (1831), 2—Gallica) points out that 'on the other side of Monte Nuovo is Avernus', the lake in a crater associated with Hades and the Styx, cited in *Journey to the Centre of the Earth* (4); Chateaubriand (*Journey to Italy*, 9 January 1804—Gallica) also remarks that 'Avernus communicated with Lake Lucrino.'

338 *the Union Jack*: in February 1872, Verne planned an adaptation of his novel with the playwright Édouard Cadol: 'The idea came to me that there is a grand drama, completely new, a panoramic drama to be got from *Hatteras*, a drama where there would be Northern Lights, whales, shipwrecked men, in a word things that have never been seen in the theatre. I'd replace the American found buried under the ice with a Frenchman so as to wave the tricolour at the Pole! . . .' The six-page scenario was entitled *The North Pole*, with six acts, one prologue, and a list of characters and plot similar to the book (volume 1 of manuscripts at Nantes, 45–50). Tabarin (*L'Événement*, 13 December 1875) wrote that Cadol and Verne co-wrote a complete manuscript entitled *Voyage aux deux pôles*. But the idea was not accepted, and on 24 November 1872 Verne claimed he had told Hetzel that *Around the World* would make a better play. Perhaps to compensate, in Verne's play *Journey through the Impossible* (1882), John Hatteras is revived, although in unrecognizable form.

339   *Hatteras was shaking the standard with one hand*: the final illustration of
      the captain, as late-Romantic hero with a curl of hair, slightly resembles
      Napoleon.

      But Altamont was there: Altamont takes only a few minutes to cover what
      took Hatteras 'more than an hour'.

      saved against his will: Tolkien's *Lord of the Rings* contains troubling simi-
      larities with *Hatteras*: a multi-volume epic steeped in Nordic mythology
      and British tradition, in a fictional world based on authentic history,
      geography, language, and culture, with an erupting volcano the geo-
      graphical and spiritual focus, meaning one deus ex machina is required to
      stop the hero from diving in and another to get him home again.

340   *'JOHN HATTERAS | 1861'*: both the duel and Hatteras's suicide had been
      deleted by the time of the *MÉR* edition; but the inscription on the cairn
      continues to resemble that on a gravestone.

341   *Monday, 23 July*: in fact a Tuesday.

344   *the Trauter Mountains*: Verne's 'monts Trauter' have not been traced.
      However, given that the travellers are near Jones Sound, they may be the
      'Croker Mountains' which John Ross identified in 1818 as blocking any
      way out of Baffin Bay westwards, but were proved to be a mirage.

346   *under the snows of the Pole for ever*: the fate of Hatteras's crew is similar to
      Franklin's, who, after the death of their leader, abandoned ship and
      trekked southwards, finally resorting to cannibalism.

      Johnson felt he was dying: Hatteras's existence has not been mentioned for
      several weeks, because in the manuscript version he died at the Pole and
      Verne is still reluctant to bring him back.

347   *this fragile raft*: the idea comes from Johnson's previous description,
      simultaneously real-life and fictional, of the 'floe that could carry us and
      manoeuvre like a raft' after Bellot's death (I 21), meaning that he should
      not be surprised at the idea.

      on the thirteenth of the same month: a slip, since the previous dates were '9
      September', then 'ten days later'. Similarly 'the session of 15 July' in the
      following sentence is illogical.

348   *the doctor, Bell, and Johnson*: we are unaware what has happened to
      Hatteras—another sign of the manuscript and of the captain's mental
      absence.

      Sten Cottage Nursing Home: no trace has been found—possibly a variant
      on Stenhouse, Edinburgh, or the Christian name of a Scandinavian
      explorer.

349   *under the influence . . . of a magnetic force*: Verne was influenced by Franz
      Friedrich Anton Mesmer (1734–1815), a Viennese doctor who used
      magnets to explore human sensitivity to the 'magnetic fluid', an idea not
      totally discredited today, and one which led to Charcot's work on hysteria
      and to Freud.